NEW YORK TIMES BESTSEL

DEBBIE MACOMBER

with

SHEILA ROBERTS

SHERRYL WOODS

RAEANNE THAYNE

A *Christmas* WISH

MILLS & BOON

Published by
Mills & Boon
An imprint of Harlequin Enterprises (Australia) Pty Limited
(ABN 47 001 180 918), a subsidiary of HarperCollins
Publishers Australia Pty Limited (ABN 36 009 913 517)
Level 13, 201 Elizabeth Street
SYDNEY NSW 2000
AUSTRALIA

Printed and bound in Australia by McPherson's Printing Group

CONTENTS

THE FORGETFUL BRIDE   5
Debbie Macomber

A LITTLE CHRISTMAS SPIRIT   127
Sheila Roberts

A CHRISTMAS BLESSING   347
Sherryl Woods

CHRISTMAS IN SNOWFLAKE CANYON   499
RaeAnne Thayne

The Forgetful Bride

Debbie Macomber

Also available from
Debbie Macomber

Blossom Street

The Shop on Blossom Street
A Good Yarn
Susannah's Garden
Back on Blossom Street
Twenty Wishes
Summer on Blossom Street
Hannah's List
"The Twenty-First Wish"
    (in *The Knitting Diaries*)
A Turn in the Road

Cedar Cove

16 Lighthouse Road
204 Rosewood Lane
311 Pelican Court
44 Cranberry Point
50 Harbor Street
6 Rainier Drive
74 Seaside Avenue
8 Sandpiper Way
92 Pacific Boulevard
1022 Evergreen Place
Christmas in Cedar Cove
    (*5-B Poppy Lane* and
    A Cedar Cove Christmas)
1105 Yakima Street
1225 Christmas Tree Lane

The Dakota Series

Dakota Born
Dakota Home
Always Dakota
Buffalo Valley

The Manning Family

The Manning Sisters
    (*The Cowboy's Lady* and
    The Sheriff Takes a Wife)
The Manning Brides
    (*Marriage of Inconvenience*
    and *Stand-In Wife*)

The Manning Grooms
    (*Bride on the Loose* and
    Same Time, Next Year)

Christmas Books

A Gift to Last
On a Snowy Night
Home for the Holidays
Glad Tidings
Christmas Wishes
Small Town Christmas
When Christmas Comes
    (now retitled *Trading Christmas*)
There's Something About Christmas
Christmas Letters
The Perfect Christmas
Choir of Angels
    (*Shirley, Goodness and Mercy,*
    Those Christmas Angels, and
    Where Angels Go)
Call Me Mrs. Miracle

Heart of Texas

Texas Skies
    (*Lonesome Cowboy*
    and *Texas Two-Step*)
Texas Nights
    (*Caroline's Child* and *Dr. Texas*)
Texas Home
    (*Nell's Cowboy* and *Lone Star Baby*)
Promise, Texas
Return to Promise

Midnight Sons

Alaska Skies
    (*Brides for Brothers* and
    The Marriage Risk)
Alaska Nights
    (*Daddy's Little Helper* and
    Because of the Baby)
Alaska Home
    (*Falling for Him, Ending in
    Marriage,* and *Midnight Sons
    and Daughters*)

This Matter of Marriage
Montana
Thursdays at Eight
Between Friends
Changing Habits
Married in Seattle
  (*First Comes Marriage* and
  Wanted: Perfect Partner)
Right Next Door
  (*Father's Day* and *The Courtship*
  of Carol Sommars)
Wyoming Brides
  (*Denim and Diamonds* and
  The Wyoming Kid)
Fairy Tale Weddings
  (*Cindy and the Prince* and
  Some Kind of Wonderful)
The Man You'll Marry
  (*The First Man You Meet* and
  The Man You'll Marry)
Orchard Valley Grooms
  (*Valerie* and *Stephanie*)
Orchard Valley Brides
  (*Norah* and *Lone Star Lovin'*)
The Sooner the Better
An Engagement in Seattle
  (*Groom Wanted* and *Bride Wanted*)
Out of the Rain
  (*Marriage Wanted* and
  Laughter in the Rain)
Learning to Love
  (*Sugar and Spice* and *Love by Degree*)
You…Again
  (*Baby Blessed* and *Yesterday Once More*)
The Unexpected Husband
  (*Jury of His Peers* and *Any Sunday*)
Three Brides, No Groom
Love in Plain Sight
  (*Love 'n' Marriage* and *Almost an Angel*)
I Left My Heart
  (*A Friend or Two* and *No Competition*)

Marriage Between Friends
  (*White Lace and Promises* and
  Friends—and Then Some)
A Man's Heart
  (*The Way to a Man's Heart*
  and *Hasty Wedding*)
North to Alaska
  (*That Wintry Feeling* and
  Borrowed Dreams)
On a Clear Day
  (*Starlight* and
  Promise Me Forever)
To Love and Protect
  (*Shadow Chasing* and
  For All My Tomorrows)
Home in Seattle
  (*The Playboy and the Widow*
  and *Fallen Angel*)
Together Again
  (*The Trouble with Caasi* and
  Reflections of Yesterday)
The Reluctant Groom
  (*All Things Considered* and
  Almost Paradise)
A Real Prince
  (*The Bachelor Prince* and
  Yesterday's Hero)
Private Paradise
  (in *That Summer Place*)

Debbie Macomber's
  Cedar Cove Cookbook
Debbie Macomber's
  Christmas Cookbook

For Karen Young and Rachel Hauck,
plotting partners and treasured friends.

PROLOGUE

"NOT UNLESS WE'RE married."

Ten-year-old Martin Marshall slapped his hands against his thighs in disgust. "I told you she was going to be unreasonable about this."

Caitlin watched as her brother's best friend withdrew a second baseball card from his shirt pocket. If Joseph Rockwell wanted to kiss her, then he was going to have to do it the right way. She might be only eight, but Caitlin knew about these things. Glancing down at the doll held tightly in her arms, she realized instinctively that Barbie wouldn't approve of kissing a boy unless he married you first.

Martin approached her again. "Joe says he'll throw in his Don Drysdale baseball card."

"Not unless we're married," she repeated, smoothing the front of her sundress with a haughty air.

"All right, all right, I'll marry her," Joe muttered as he stalked across the backyard.

"How you gonna do that?" Martin demanded.

"Get your Bible."

For someone who wanted to kiss her so badly, Joseph didn't look very pleased. Caitlin decided to press her luck. "In the fort."

"The fort?" Joe exploded. "No girls are allowed in there!"

"I refuse to marry a boy who won't even let me into his fort."

"Call it off," Martin demanded. "She's asking too much."

"You don't have to give me the second baseball card," she said. The idea of being the first girl ever to view their precious fort had a certain appeal. And it meant she'd probably get invited to Betsy McDonald's birthday party.

The boys exchanged glances and started whispering to each other, but Caitlin heard only snatches of their conversation. Martin clearly wasn't thrilled with Joseph's concessions, and he kept shaking his head as though he couldn't believe his friend might actually go through with this. For her part, Caitlin didn't know whether to trust Joseph. He liked playing practical jokes and everyone in the neighborhood knew it.

"It's time to feed my baby," she announced, preparing to leave.

"All right, all right," Joseph said with obvious reluctance. "I'll marry you in the fort. Martin'll say the words, only you can't tell anyone about going inside, understand?"

"If you do," Martin threatened, glaring at his sister, "you'll be sorry."

"I won't tell," Caitlin promised. It would have to be a secret, but that was fine because she liked keeping secrets.

"You ready?" Joseph demanded. Now that the terms were set, he seemed to be in a rush, which rather annoyed Caitlin. The frown on his face didn't please her, either. A bridegroom should at least *look* happy. She was about to say so, but decided not to.

"You'll have to change clothes, of course. Maybe the suit you wore on Easter Sunday…"

"What?" Joseph shrieked. "I'm not wearing any suit. Listen, Caitlin, you've gone about as far as you can with this. I get married exactly the way I am or we call it off."

She sighed, rolling her eyes expressively. "Oh, all right, but I'll need to get a few things first."

"Just hurry up, would you?"

Martin followed her into the house, letting the screen door slam behind him. He took his Bible off the hallway table and rushed back outside.

Caitlin hurried up to her room, where she grabbed a brush to run through her hair and straightened the two pink ribbons tied around her pigtails. She always wore pink ribbons because pink was a color for girls. Boys were supposed to wear blue and brown and boring colors like that. Boys were okay sometimes, but mostly they did disgusting things.

Her four dolls accompanied her across the backyard and into the wooded acre behind. She hated getting her Mary Janes dusty, but that couldn't be avoided.

With a good deal of ceremony, she opened the rickety door and then slowly, the way she'd seen it done at her older cousin's wedding, Caitlin marched into the boys' packing-crate-and-cardboard fort.

Pausing inside the narrow entry, she glanced around. It wasn't anything to brag about. Martin had made it sound like a palace with marble floors and crystal chandeliers. She couldn't help feeling disillusioned. If she hadn't been so eager to see the fort, she would've insisted they do this properly, in church.

Her brother stood tall and proud on an upturned apple crate, the Bible clutched to his chest. His face was dutifully somber. Caitlin smiled approvingly. He, at least, was taking this seriously.

"You can't bring those dolls in here," Joseph said loudly.

"I most certainly can. Barbie and Ken and Paula and Jane are our children."

"Our children?"

"Naturally they haven't been born yet, so they're really just a glint in your eye." She'd heard her father say that once and it sounded special. "They're angels for now, but I thought they should be here so you could meet them." She was busily arranging her dolls in a tidy row behind Martin on another apple crate.

Joseph covered his face with his hands and it looked for a moment like he might change his mind.

"Are we going to get married or not?" she asked.

"All right, all right." Joseph sighed heavily and pulled her forward, a little more roughly than necessary, in Caitlin's opinion.

The two of them stood in front of Martin, who randomly opened his Bible. He gazed down at the leather-bound book and then at Caitlin and his best friend. "Do you, Joseph James Rockwell, take Caitlin Rose Marshall for your wife?"

"Lawfully wedded," Caitlin corrected. She remembered this part from a television show.

"Lawfully wedded wife," Martin amended grudgingly.

"I do." Caitlin noticed that he didn't say it with any real enthusiasm. "I think there's supposed to be something about richer or poorer and sickness and health," Joseph said, smirking at Caitlin as if to say she wasn't the only one who knew the proper words.

Martin nodded and continued. "Do you, Caitlin Rose Marshall, hereby take Joseph James Rockwell in sickness and health and in riches and in poorness?"

"I'm only going to marry a man who's healthy and rich."

"You can't go putting conditions on this now," Joseph argued. "We already agreed."

"Just say 'I do,'" Martin urged, his voice tight with annoyance. Caitlin suspected that only the seriousness of the occasion prevented him from adding, "You pest."

She wasn't sure if she should go through with this or not. She was old enough to know that she liked pretty things and when she married, her husband would build her a castle at the edge of the forest. He would love her so much, he'd bring home silk ribbons for her hair, and bottles and bottles of expensive perfume. So many that there wouldn't be room for all of them on her makeup table.

"Caitlin," Martin said through clenched teeth.

"I do," she finally answered.

"I hereby pronounce you married," Martin proclaimed, closing the Bible with a resounding thud. "You may kiss the bride."

Joseph turned to face Caitlin. He was several inches taller than she was. His eyes were a pretty shade of blue that reminded her of the way the sky looked the morning after a bad rainstorm. She liked Joseph's eyes.

"You ready?" he asked.

She nodded, closed her eyes and pressed her lips tightly together as she angled her head to the left. If the truth be known, she wasn't all that opposed to having Joseph kiss her, but she'd never let him know that because... well, because kissing wasn't something ladies talked about.

A long time passed before she felt his mouth touch hers. Actually his lips sort of bounced against hers. Gee, she thought. What a big fuss over nothing.

"Well?" Martin demanded of his friend.

Caitlin opened her eyes to discover Joseph frowning down at her. "It wasn't anything like Pete said it would be," he grumbled.

"Caitlin might be doing it wrong," Martin offered, frowning accusingly at his sister.

"If anyone did anything wrong, it's Joseph." They were making it sound like she'd purposely cheated them. If anyone was being cheated, it was Caitlin, because she couldn't tell Betsy McDonald about going inside their precious fort.

Joseph didn't say anything for a long moment. Then he slowly withdrew his prized baseball cards from his shirt pocket. He gazed at them lovingly before he reluctantly held them out to her. "Here," he said, "these are yours now."

"You aren't going to *give* 'em to her, are you? Not when she messed up!" Martin cried. "Kissing a girl wasn't like Pete said, and that's got to be Caitlin's fault. I told you she's not really a girl, anyway. She's a pest."

"A deal's a deal," Joseph said sadly.

"You can keep your silly old baseball cards." Head held high, Caitlin gathered up her dolls in a huff, prepared to make a dignified exit.

"You won't tell anyone about us letting you into the fort, will you?" Martin shouted after her.

"No." She'd keep that promise.

But neither of them had said a word about telling everyone in school that she and Joseph Rockwell had gotten married.

CHAPTER ONE

FOR THE THIRD time that afternoon, Cait indignantly wiped sawdust from the top of her desk. If this remodeling mess got much worse, the particles were going to get into her computer, destroying her vital link with the New York Stock Exchange.

"We'll have to move her out," a gruff male voice said from behind her.

"I beg your pardon," Cait demanded, rising abruptly and whirling toward the doorway. She clapped the dust from her hands, preparing to do battle. So much for this being the season of peace and goodwill. All these men in hard hats strolling through the office, moving things around, was inconvenient enough. But at least she'd been able to close her door to reduce the noise. Now, it seemed, even that would be impossible.

"We're going to have to pull some electrical wires through there," the same brusque voice explained. She couldn't see the man's face, since he stood just outside her doorway, but she had an impression of broad-shouldered height. "We'll have everything back to normal within a week."

"A week!" She wouldn't be able to service her customers, let alone function, without her desk and phone. And exactly where did they intend to put her? Certainly not in a hallway! She wouldn't stand for it.

The mess this simple remodeling project had created was one thing, but transplanting her entire office as if she were nothing more than a...a tulip bulb was something else again.

"I'm sorry about this, Cait," Paul Jamison said, slipping past the crew foreman to her side.

The wind went out of her argument at the merest hint of his devastating smile. "Don't worry about it," she said, the picture of meekness and tolerance. "Things like this happen when a company grows as quickly as ours."

She glanced across the hallway to her best friend's office, shrugging as if to ask, *Is Paul ever going to notice me?* Lindy shot her a crooked grin and a quick nod that suggested Cait stop being so negative. Her friend's confidence didn't help. Paul was a wonderful district manager and she was fortunate to have the opportunity to work with him. He was both talented and resourceful. The brokerage firm of Webster, Rodale and Missen was an affiliate of the fastest-growing firm in the country. This branch had been open for less than two years and already they were breaking national sales records. Due mainly, Cait believed, to Paul's administrative skills.

Paul was slender, dark-haired and handsome in an urbane, sophisticated way—every woman's dream man. Certainly Cait's. But as far as she could determine, he didn't see her in a similar romantic light. He thought of her as an important team member. One of the staff. At most, a friend.

Cait knew that friendship was often fertile ground for romance, and she hoped for an opportunity to cultivate it. Willingly surrendering her office to an irritating crew of carpenters and electricians was sure to gain her a few points with her boss.

"Where would you like me to set up my desk in the meantime?" she asked, smiling warmly at Paul. From habit, she lifted her hand to push back a stray lock of hair, forgetting she'd recently had it cut. That had been another futile attempt to attract Paul's affections—or at least his attention. Her shoulder-length chestnut-brown hair had been trimmed and permed into a pixie style with a halo of soft curls.

The difference from the tightly styled chignon she'd always worn to work was striking, or so everyone said. Everyone except Paul. The hairdresser had claimed it changed Cait's cooly polished look into one of warmth and enthusiasm. It was exactly the image Cait wanted Paul to have of her.

Unfortunately he didn't seem to detect the slightest difference in her appearance. At least not until Lindy had pointedly commented on the change within earshot of their absentminded employer. Then, and only then, had Paul made a remark about noticing something different; he just hadn't been sure what it was, he'd said.

"I suppose we could move you...." Paul hesitated.

"Your office seems to be the best choice," the foreman said.

Cait resisted the urge to hug the man. He was tall, easily six three, and as solid as Mount Rainier, the majestic mountain she could see from her office window. She hadn't paid much attention to him until this moment and was surprised to note something vaguely familiar about him. She'd assumed he was the foreman, but she wasn't certain. He seemed to be around the office fairly often, although not on a predictable schedule. Every time he did show up, the level of activity rose dramatically.

"Ah... I suppose Cait could move in with me for the time being," Paul agreed. In her daydreams, Cait would play back this moment; her version had Paul looking at her with surprise and wonder, his mouth moving toward hers and—

"Miss?"

Cait broke out of her reverie and glanced at the foreman—the man who'd suggested she share Paul's office. "Yes?"

"Would you show us what you need moved?"

"Of course," she returned crisply. This romantic heart of hers was always getting her into trouble. She'd look at Paul and her head would start to spin with hopes and fantasies and then she'd be lost....

Cait's arms were loaded with files as she followed the carpenters, who hauled her desk into a corner of Paul's much larger office. Her computer and phone came next, and within fifteen minutes she was back in business.

She was on the phone, talking with one of her most important clients, when the same man walked back, unannounced, into the room. At first Caitlin assumed he was looking for Paul, who'd stepped out of the office. The foreman—or whatever he was—hesitated for a few seconds. Then, scooping up her nameplate, he grinned at her as if he found something highly entertaining. Cait did her best to ignore him, flipping needlessly through the pages of the file.

Not taking the hint, he stepped forward and plunked the nameplate on the edge of her desk. As she looked up in annoyance, he boldly winked at her.

Cait was not amused. How dare this...this...redneck flirt with her!

She glared at him, hoping he'd have the good manners and good sense to leave—which, of course, he didn't. In fact, he seemed downright stubborn about staying and making her as uncomfortable as possible. Her phone conversation ran its natural course and after making several notations, she replaced the receiver.

"You wanted something?" she demanded, her eyes meeting his. Once more she noted his apparent amusement. She didn't understand it.

"No," he answered, grinning again. "Sorry to have bothered you."

For the second time, Cait was struck by a twinge of the familiar. He strolled out of her makeshift office as if he owned the building.

Cait waited a few minutes, then approached Lindy. "Did you happen to catch his name?"

"Whose name?"

"The...man who insisted I vacate my office. I don't know who he is. I thought he was the foreman, but..." She crossed her arms and furrowed her brow, trying to remember if she'd heard anyone say his name.

"I have no idea." Lindy pushed back her chair and rolled a pencil between her palms. "He is kinda cute, though, don't you think?"

A smile softened Cait's lips. "There's only one man for me and you know it."

"Then why are you asking questions about the construction crew?"

"I...don't know. That guy seems familiar for some reason, and he keeps grinning at me as if he knows something I don't. I hate it when men do that."

"Then ask one of the others what his name is. They'll tell you."

"I can't do that."

"Why not?"

"He might think I'm interested in him."

"And we both know how impossible that would be," Lindy said with mild sarcasm.

"Exactly." Lindy and probably everyone else in the office complex knew how Cait felt about Paul. The district manager himself, however, seemed to be completely oblivious. Other than throwing herself at him, which she'd seriously considered more than once, there was little she could do but be patient. One of these days Cupid was going to let fly an arrow and hit her lovable boss directly between the eyes.

When it happened—and it would!—Cait planned to be ready.

"You want to go for lunch now?" Lindy asked.

Cait nodded. It was nearly two and she hadn't eaten since breakfast, which had consisted of a banana and a cup of coffee. A West Coast stockbroker's day started before dawn. Cait was generally in the office by six and didn't stop work until the market closed at one-thirty, Seattle time. Only then did she break for something to eat.

Somewhere in the middle of her turkey on whole wheat, Cait convinced herself she was imagining things when it came to that construction worker. He'd probably been waiting around to ask her where Paul was and then changed his mind. He did say he was sorry for bothering her.

If only he hadn't winked.

HE WAS BACK the following day, a tool pouch riding on his hip like a six-shooter, hard hat in place. He was issuing orders like a drill sergeant, and Cait found herself gazing after him with reluctant fascination. She'd heard he owned the construction company, and she wasn't surprised.

As she studied him, she realized once again how striking he was. Not because he was extraordinarily handsome, but because he was somehow commanding. He possessed an authority, a presence, that attracted attention wherever he went. Cait was as drawn to it as those around her. She observed how the crew instinctively turned to him for directions and approval.

The more she observed him, the more she recognized that he was a man who had an appetite for life. Which meant excitement, adventure and probably women, and that confused her even more because she couldn't recall ever knowing anyone quite like him. Then why did she find him so...familiar?

Cait herself had a quiet nature. She rarely ventured out of the comfortable, compact world she'd built. She had her job, a nice apartment in Seattle's university district, and a few close friends. Excitement to her was growing herbs and participating in nature walks.

The following day while she was studying the construction worker, he'd unexpectedly turned and smiled at something one of his men had said. His smile, she decided, intrigued her most. It was slightly off center and seemed to tease the corners of his mouth. He looked her way more than once and each time she thought she detected a touch of humor, an amused knowledge that lurked just beneath the surface.

"It's driving me crazy," Cait confessed to Lindy over lunch.

"What is?"

"That I can't place him."

Lindy set her elbows on the table, holding her sandwich poised in front of her mouth. She nodded slowly, her eyes distant. "When you figure it out, introduce me, will you? I could go for a guy this sexy."

So Lindy had noticed that earthy sensuality about him, too. Well, of course she had—any woman would.

After lunch, Cait returned to the office to make a few calls. He was there again.

No matter how hard she tried, she couldn't place him. Work became a pretense as she continued to scrutinize him, racking her brain. Then, when she least expected it, he strolled past her and brazenly winked a second time.

As the color clawed up her neck, Cait flashed her attention back to her computer screen.

"His name is Joe," Lindy rushed in to tell her ten minutes later. "I heard one of the men call him that."

"Joe," Cait repeated slowly. She couldn't remember ever knowing anyone named Joe.

"Does that help?"

"No," Cait said, shaking her head regretfully. If she'd ever met this man, she wasn't likely to have overlooked the experience. He wasn't someone a woman easily forgot.

"Ask him," Lindy said. "It's ridiculous not to. It's driving you insane. Then," she added with infuriating logic, "when you find out, you can nonchalantly introduce me."

"I can't just waltz up and start quizzing him," Cait argued. The idea was preposterous. "He'll think I'm trying to pick him up."

"You'll go crazy if you don't."

Cait sighed. "You're right. I'm not going to sleep tonight if I don't settle this."

With Lindy waiting expectantly in her office, Cait approached him. He was talking to another member of the crew and once he'd finished, he turned to her with one of his devastating lazy smiles.

"Hello," she said, and her voice shook slightly. "Do I know you?"

"You mean you've forgotten?" he asked, sounding shocked and insulted.

"Apparently. Though I'll admit you look somewhat familiar."

"I should certainly hope so. We shared something very special a few years back."

"We did?" Cait was more confused than ever.

"Hey, Joe, there's a problem over here," a male voice shouted. "Could you come look at this?"

"I'll be with you in a minute," he answered brusquely over his shoulder. "Sorry, we'll have to talk later."

"But—"

"Say hello to Martin for me, would you?" he asked as he stalked past her and into the room that had once been Cait's office.

Martin, her brother. Cait hadn't a clue what her brother could possibly have to do with this. Mentally she ran through a list of his teenage friends and came up blank.

Then it hit her. Bull's-eye. Her heart started to pound until it roared like a tropical storm in her ears. Mechanically Cait made her way back to Lindy's office. She sank into a chair beside the desk and stared into space.

"Well?" Lindy pressed. "Don't keep me in suspense."

"Um, it's not that easy to explain."

"You remember him, then?"

She nodded. Oh, Lord, did she ever.

"Good grief, what's wrong? You've gone so pale!"

Cait tried to come up with an explanation that wouldn't sound... ridiculous.

"Tell me," Lindy said. "Don't just sit there wearing a foolish grin and looking like you're about to faint."

"Um, it goes back a few years."

"All right. Start there."

"Remember how kids sometimes do silly things? Like when you're young and foolish and don't know any better?"

"Me, yes, but not you," Lindy said calmly. "You're perfect. In all the time we've been friends, I haven't seen you do one impulsive thing. Not one. You analyze everything before you act. I can't imagine you ever doing anything silly."

"I did once," Cait told her, "but I was only eight."

"What could you have possibly done at age eight?"

"I... I got married."

"Married?" Lindy half rose from her chair. "You've got to be kidding."

"I wish I was."

"I'll bet a week's commissions that your husband's name is Joe." Lindy was smiling now, smiling widely.

Cait nodded and tried to smile in return.

"What's there to worry about? Good grief, kids do that sort of thing all the time! It doesn't mean anything."

"But I was a real brat about it. Joe and my brother, Martin, were best friends. Joe wanted to know what it felt like to kiss a girl, and I insisted he marry me first. If that wasn't bad enough, I pressured them into performing the ceremony inside their boys-only fort."

"So, you were a bit of pain—most eight-year-old girls are when it comes to dealing with their brothers. He got what he wanted, didn't he?"

Cait took a deep breath and nodded again.

"What was kissing him like?" Lindy asked in a curiously throaty voice.

"Good heavens, I don't remember," Cait answered shortly, then reconsidered. "I take that back. As I recall, it wasn't so bad, though obviously neither one of us had any idea what we were doing."

"Lindy, you're still here," Paul said as he strolled into the office. He inclined his head briefly in Cait's direction, but she had the impression he barely saw her. He'd hardly been around in the past couple of days—almost as if he was purposely avoiding her, she mused, but that thought was too painful to contemplate.

"I was just finishing up," Lindy said, glancing guiltily toward Cait. "We both were."

"Fine, fine, I didn't mean to disturb you. I'll see you two in the morning." A second later, he was gone.

Cait gazed after him with thinly disguised emotion. She waited until Paul was well out of range before she spoke. "He's so blind. What do I have to do, hit him over the head?"

"Quit being so negative," Lindy admonished. "You're going to be sharing an office with him for another five days. Do whatever you need to make darn sure he notices you."

"I've tried," Cait murmured, discouraged. And she had. She'd tried every trick known to woman, with little success.

Lindy left the office before her. Cait gathered up some stock reports to read that evening and stacked them neatly inside her leather briefcase. What Lindy had said about her being methodical and careful was true. It was also a source of pride; those traits had served her clients well.

To Cait's dismay, Joe followed her. "So," he said, smiling down at her, apparently oblivious to the other people clustering around the elevator. "Who have you been kissing these days?"

Hot color rose instantly to her face. Did he have to humiliate her in public?

"I could find myself jealous, you know."

"Would you kindly stop," she whispered furiously, scowling at him. Her hand tightened around the handle of her briefcase so hard her fingers ached.

"You figured it out?"

She nodded, her eyes darting to the lighted numbers above the elevator door, praying it would make its descent in record time instead of pausing on each floor.

"The years have been good to you."

"Thank you." *Please hurry,* she urged the elevator.

"I never would've believed Martin's little sister would turn out to be such a beauty."

If he was making fun of her, she didn't appreciate it. She was attractive, she knew that, but she certainly wasn't waiting for anyone to place a tiara on her head. "Thank you," she repeated grudgingly.

He gave an exaggerated sigh. "How are our children doing? What were their names again?" When she didn't answer right away, he added, "Don't tell me you've forgotten."

"Barbie and Ken," she muttered under her breath.

"That's right. I remember now."

If Joe hadn't drawn the attention of her co-workers before, he had now. Cait could have sworn every single person standing by the elevator turned to stare at her. The hope that no one was interested in their conversation was forever lost.

"Just how long do you intend to tease me about this?" she snapped.

"That depends," Joe responded with a chuckle Cait could only describe as sadistic. She gritted her teeth. He might have found the situation amusing, but she derived little enjoyment from being the office laughingstock.

Just then the elevator arrived, and not a moment too soon to suit Cait. The instant the doors slid open, she stepped toward it, determined to get as far away from this irritating man as possible.

He quickly caught up with her and she swung around to face him, her back ramrod stiff. "Is this really necessary?" she hissed, painfully conscious of the other people crowding into the elevator ahead of her.

He grinned. "I suppose not. I just wanted to see if I could get a rise out of you. It never worked when we were kids, you know. You were always so prim and proper."

"Look, you didn't like me then and I see no reason for you to—"

"Not *like* you?" he countered loudly enough for everyone in the building to hear. "I married you, didn't I?"

CHAPTER TWO

CAIT'S HEART SEEMED to stop. She realized that not only the people on the elevator but everyone left in the office was staring at her with unconcealed interest. The elevator was about to close and she quickly stepped forward, stretching out her arms to hold the doors open. She felt like Samson balanced between two marble columns.

"It's not the way it sounds," she felt obliged to explain in a loud voice, her gaze pleading.

No one made eye contact with her and, desperate, she turned to Joe, sending him a silent challenge to retract his words. His eyes were sparkling with mischief. If he did say anything, Cait thought in sudden horror, it was bound to make things even worse.

There didn't seem to be anything to do but tell the truth. "In case anyone has the wrong impression, this man and I are not married," she shouted. "Good grief, I was only eight!"

There was no reaction. It was as if she'd vanished into thin air. Defeated, she dropped her arms and stepped back, freeing the doors, which promptly closed.

Ignoring the other people on the elevator—who were carefully ignoring her—Cait clenched her hands into hard fists and glared up at Joe. Her face tightened with anger. "That was a rotten thing to do," she whispered hoarsely.

"What? It's true, isn't it?" he whispered back.

"You're being ridiculous to talk as though we're married!"

"We were once. It wounds me that you treat our marriage so lightly."

"I...it wasn't legal." The fact that they were even discussing this was preposterous. "You can't possibly hold me responsible for something that happened so long ago. To play this game now is...is infantile, and I refuse to be part of it."

The elevator finally came to a halt on the ground floor and, eager to make her escape, Cait rushed out. Straightening to keep her dignity intact, she headed through the crowded foyer toward the front doors. Although it was midafternoon, dusk was already setting in, casting dark shadows between the towering office buildings.

Cait reached the first intersection and sighed in relief as she glanced around her. Good. No sign of Joseph Rockwell. The light was red and she paused, although others hurried across the street after checking for traffic; Cait always felt obliged to obey the signal.

"What do you think Paul's going to say when he hears about this?" Joe asked from behind her.

Cait gave a start, then turned to look at her tormenter. She hadn't thought about Paul's reaction. Her throat seemed to constrict, rendering her speechless, otherwise she would have demanded Joe leave her alone. But he'd raised a question she dared not ignore. Paul might hear about her so-called former relationship with Joe and might even think there was something between them.

"You're in love with him, aren't you?"

She nodded. At the very mention of Paul's name, her knees went weak. He was everything she wanted in a man and more. She'd been crazy about him for months and now it was all about to be ruined by this irritating, unreasonable ghost from her past.

"Who told you?" Cait snapped. She couldn't imagine Lindy betraying her confidence, but Cait hadn't told anyone else.

"No one had to tell me," Joe said. "It's written all over you."

Shocked, Cait stared at Joe, her heart sinking. "Do...do you think Paul knows how I feel?"

Joe shrugged. "Maybe."

"But Lindy said..."

The light changed and, clasping her elbow, Joe urged her into the street. "What was it Lindy said?" he prompted when they'd crossed.

Cait looked up, about to tell him, when she realized exactly what she was doing—conversing with her antagonist. This was the very man who'd gone out of his way to embarrass and humiliate her in front of the entire office staff. Not to mention assorted clients and carpenters.

She stiffened. "Never mind what Lindy said. Now if you'll kindly excuse me..." With her head high, she marched down the sidewalk. She hadn't gone more than a few feet when the hearty sound of Joe's laughter caught up with her.

"You haven't changed in twenty years, Caitlin Marshall. Not a single bit."

Gritting her teeth, she marched on.

"DO YOU THINK Paul's heard?" Cait asked Lindy the instant she had a free moment the following afternoon. The New York Stock Exchange had closed for the day and Cait hadn't seen Paul since morning. It looked like he really *was* avoiding her.

"I wouldn't know," Lindy said as she typed some figures into her computer. "But the word about your childhood marriage has spread like wildfire everywhere else. It's the joke of the day. What did you and Joe do? Make a public announcement before you left the office yesterday afternoon?"

It was so nearly the truth that Cait guiltily lowered her eyes. "I didn't say a word," she defended herself. "Joe was the one."

"He told everyone you were married?" A suspicious tilt at the corner of her mouth betrayed Lindy's amusement.

"Not exactly. He started asking about our children in front of everyone."

"There were children?"

Cait resisted the urge to close her eyes and count to ten. "No. I brought my dolls to the wedding. Listen, I don't want to rehash a silly incident that happened years ago. I'm more afraid Paul's going to hear about it and put the wrong connotation on the whole thing. There's absolutely nothing between me and Joseph Rockwell. More than likely Paul won't give it a second thought, but I don't want there to be any...doubts between us, if you know what I mean."

"If you're so worried about it, talk to him," Lindy advised without lifting her eyes from the screen. "Honesty is the best policy, you know that."

"Yes, but it could prove to be a bit embarrassing, don't you think?"

"Paul will respect you for telling him the truth before he hears the rumors from someone else. Frankly, Cait, I think you're making a fuss over nothing. It isn't like you've committed a felony, you know."

"I realize that."

"Paul will probably be amused, like everyone else. He's not going to say anything." She looked up quickly, as though she expected Cait to try yet another argument.

Cait didn't. Instead she mulled over her friend's advice, gnawing on her lower lip. "You might be right. Paul will respect me for explaining the situation myself, instead of ignoring everything." Telling him the truth could be helpful in other respects, too, now that she thought about it.

If Paul had any feeling for her whatsoever, and oh, how she prayed he did, then he might become just a little jealous of her relationship with Joseph Rockwell. After all, Joe was an attractive man in a rugged outdoor sort of way. He was tall and muscular and, well, good-looking. The kind of good-looking that appealed to women—not Cait, of course, but other women. Hadn't Lindy commented almost immediately on how attractive he was?

"You're right," Cait said, walking resolutely toward the office she was temporarily sharing with Paul. Although she'd felt annoyed at first about being shuffled out of her own space, she'd come to think of this inconvenience as a blessing in disguise. However, she had to admit she'd been disappointed thus far. She had assumed she'd be spending a lot of time alone with him. That hadn't happened yet.

The more Cait considered the idea of a heart-to-heart talk with her boss, the more appealing it became. As was her habit, she mentally rehearsed what she wanted to say to him, then gave herself a small pep talk.

"I don't remember that you talked to yourself." The male voice booming behind her startled Cait. "But then there's a great deal I've missed over the years, isn't there, Caitlin?"

Cait was so rattled she nearly stumbled. "What are you doing here?" she demanded. "Why are you following me around? Can't you see I'm busy?" He was the last person she wanted to confront just now.

"Sorry." He raised both hands in a gesture of apology contradicted by his twinkling blue eyes. "How about lunch later?"

He was teasing. He had to be. Besides, it would be insane for her to have anything to do with Joseph Rockwell. Heaven only knew what would happen if she gave him the least bit of encouragement. He'd probably hire a skywriter and announce to the entire city that they'd married as children.

"It shouldn't be that difficult to agree to a luncheon date," he informed her coolly.

"You're serious about this?"

"Of course I'm serious. We have a lot of years to catch up on." His hand rested on his leather pouch, giving him a rakish air of indifference.

"I've got an appointment this afternoon..." She offered the first plausible excuse she could think of; it might be uninspired but it also happened to be true. She'd made plans to have lunch with Lindy.

"Dinner then. I'm anxious to hear what Martin's been up to."

"Martin," she repeated, stalling for time while she invented another excuse. This wasn't a situation she had much experience with. She did date, but infrequently.

"Listen, bright eyes, no need to look so ⸻ tion to the senior prom. It's one friend to ⸻

"You won't mention…our wedding to the ⸻

"I promise." As if to offer proof of his intent, ⸻ index finger and crossed his heart. "That was Martin's ⸻ sign. If either of us broke our word, the other was entitled ⸻ a punishment. We both understood it would be a fate worse th⸻

"I don't need any broken pledge in order to torture you, Joseph⸻ well. In two days you've managed to turn my life into—" She paused m⸻ sentence as Paul Jamison casually strolled past. He waved in Cait's direction and smiled benignly.

"Hello, Paul," she called out, weakly raising her right hand. He looked exceptionally handsome this morning in a three-piece dark blue suit. The contrast between him and Joe, who was wearing dust-covered jeans, heavy boots and a tool pouch, was so striking that Cait had to force herself not to stare at her boss. If only Paul had been the one to invite her to dinner…

"If you'll excuse me," she said politely, edging her way around Joe and toward Paul, who'd gone into his office. Their office. The need to talk to him burned within her. Words of explanation began to form themselves in her mind.

Joe caught her by the shoulders, bringing her up short. Cait gasped and raised shocked eyes to his.

"Dinner," he reminded her.

She blinked, hardly knowing what to say. "All right," she mumbled distractedly and recited her address, eager to have him gone.

"Good. I'll pick you up tonight at six." With that he released her and stalked away.

After taking a couple of moments to compose herself, Cait headed toward the office. "Hello, Paul," she said, standing just inside the doorway. "Do you have a moment to talk?"

He glanced up from a file on his desk. "Of course, Cait. Sit down and make yourself comfortable."

She moved into the room, closing the door behind her. When she looked back at Paul, he'd cocked his eyebrows in surprise. "Problems?" he asked.

"Not exactly." She pulled out the chair opposite his desk and slowly sat down. Now that she had his full attention, she was at a loss. All her prepared explanations and witticisms had flown out of her head. "The rate on municipal bonds has been extremely high lately," she said nervously.

Paul agreed with a quick nod. "They have been for several months now."

s, I know. That's what makes them such excellent value." Cait had
selling bonds heavily in the past few weeks.

You didn't close the door to talk to me about bonds," Paul said softly.
What's troubling you, Cait?"

She laughed uncomfortably, wondering how a man could be so astute in
one area and so blind in another. If only he'd reveal some emotion toward
her. Anything. All he did was sit across from her and wait. He was cordial
enough, gracious even, but there was no hint of anything more. Nothing to
give Cait any hope that he was starting to care for her.

"It's about Joseph Rockwell."

"The contractor who's handling the remodeling?"

Cait nodded. "I knew him years ago when we were just children." She
glanced at Paul, whose face remained blank. "We were neighbors. In fact
Joe and my brother, Martin, were best friends. Joe moved out to the suburbs when he and Martin were in the sixth grade and I hadn't heard anything from him since."

"It's a small world, isn't it?" Paul remarked affably.

"Joe and Martin were typical young boys," she said, rushing her words
a little in her eagerness to have this out in the open. "Full of tomfoolery
and pranks."

"Boys will be boys," Paul said without any real enthusiasm.

"Yes, I know. Once—" she forced a light laugh "—they actually involved
me in one of their crazy schemes."

"What did they put you up to? Robbing a bank?"

She somehow managed a smile. "Not exactly. Joe—I always called him
Joseph back then, because it irritated him. Anyway, Joe and Martin had this
friend named Pete who was a year older and he'd spent part of his summer
vacation visiting his aunt in Peoria. I think it was Peoria.... Anyway he came
back bragging about having kissed a girl. Naturally Martin and Joe were
jealous and as you said, boys will be boys, so they decided that one of them
should test it out and see if kissing a girl was everything Pete claimed it was."

"I take it they decided to make you their guinea pig."

"Exactly." Cait slid to the edge of the chair, pleased that Paul was following this rather convoluted explanation. "I was eight and considered something
of a...pest." She paused, hoping Paul would make some comment about how
impossible that was. When he didn't, she continued, a little let down at his
restraint. "Apparently I was more of one than I remembered," she said, with
another forced laugh. "At eight, I didn't think kissing was something nice
girls did, at least not without a wedding band on their finger."

"So you kissed Joseph Rockwell," Paul said absently.

"Yes, but there was a tiny bit more than that. I made him marry me."

Paul's eyebrows shot to the ceiling.

"Now, almost twenty years later, he's getting his revenge by going around telling everyone that we're actually married. Which of course is ridiculous."

A couple of strained seconds followed her announcement.

"I'm not sure what to say," Paul murmured.

"Oh, I wasn't expecting you to say anything. I thought it was important to clear the air, that's all."

"I see."

"He's only doing it because...well, because that's Joe. Even when we were kids he enjoyed playing these little games. No one really minded, though, especially not the girls, because he was so cute." She certainly had Paul's attention now.

"I thought you should know," she added, "in case you happened to hear a rumor or something. I didn't want you thinking Joe and I were involved, or even considering a relationship. I was fairly certain you wouldn't, but one never knows and I'm a firm believer in being forthright and honest."

Paul blinked. Wanting to fill the awkward silence, Cait chattered on. "Apparently Joe recognized my name when he and his men moved my office in here with yours. He was delighted when I didn't recognize him. In fact, he caused a commotion by asking me about our children in front of everyone."

"Children?"

"My dolls," Cait was quick to explain.

"Joe Rockwell's an excellent man. I couldn't fault your taste, Cait."

"The two of us *aren't* involved," she protested. "Good grief, I haven't seen him in nearly twenty years."

"I see," Paul said slowly. He sounded...disappointed, Cait thought. But she must have misread his tone because there wasn't a single, solitary reason for him to be disappointed. Cait felt foolish now for even trying to explain this fiasco. Paul was so oblivious about her feelings that there was nothing she could say or do to make him understand.

"I just wanted you to know," she repeated, "in case you heard the rumors and were wondering if there was anything between me and Joseph Rockwell. I wanted to assure you there isn't."

"I see," he said again. "Don't worry about it, Cait. What happened between you and Rockwell isn't going to affect your job."

She stood up to leave, praying she'd detect a suggestion of jealousy. A hint of rivalry. Anything to show he cared. There was nothing, so she tried again. "I agreed to have dinner with him, though."

Paul had returned his attention to the papers he'd been reading when she'd interrupted him.

"For old times' sake," she said in a reassuring voice—to fend off any violent display of resentment, she told herself. "I certainly don't have any intention of dating him on a regular basis."

Paul grinned. "Have a good time."

"Yes, I will, thanks." Her heart felt as heavy as a sinking battleship. Without knowing where she was headed or who she'd talk to, Cait wandered out of Paul's office, forgetting for a second that she had no office of her own. The area where her desk once sat was cluttered with wire reels, ladders and men. Joe must have left, a fact for which Cait was grateful.

She walked into Lindy's small office across the hall. Her friend glanced up. "So?" she murmured. "Did you talk to Paul?"

Cait nodded.

"How'd it go?"

"Fine, I guess." She perched on the corner of Lindy's desk, crossing her arms around her waist as her left leg swung rhythmically, keeping time with her discouraged heart. She should be accustomed to disappointment when it came to Paul, but somehow each rejection inflicted a fresh wound on her already battered ego. "I was hoping Paul might be jealous."

"And he wasn't?"

"Not that I could tell."

"It isn't as though you and Joe have anything to do with each other now," Lindy sensibly pointed out. "Marrying him was a childhood prank. It isn't likely to concern Paul."

"I even mentioned that I was going out to dinner with Joe," Cait said morosely.

"You are? When?" Lindy asked, her eyes lighting up. "Where?"

If only Paul had revealed half as much interest. "Tonight. And I don't know where."

"You are going, aren't you?"

"I guess. I can't see any way of avoiding it. Otherwise he'd pester me until I gave in. If I ever marry and have daughters, Lindy, I'm going to warn them about boys from the time they're old enough to understand."

"Don't you think you should follow your own advice?" Lindy asked, glancing pointedly in the direction of Paul's office.

"Not if I were to have Paul's children," Cait said, eager to defend her boss. "Our daughter would be so intelligent and perceptive she wouldn't need to be warned."

Lindy's smile was distracted. "Listen, I've got a few things to finish up here. Why don't you go over to the deli and grab us a table. I'll meet you there in fifteen minutes."

"Sure," Cait said. "Do you want me to order for you?"

"No. I don't know what I want yet."

"Okay, I'll see you in a few minutes."

They often ate at the deli across the street from their office complex. The food was good, the service fast, and generally by three in the afternoon, Cait was famished.

She was so wrapped up in her thoughts, which were muddled and gloomy after her talk with Paul, that she didn't notice how late Lindy was. Her friend rushed into the restaurant more than half an hour after Cait had arrived.

"I'm sorry," she said, sounding flustered and oddly shaken. "I had no idea those last few chores would take me so long. Oh, you must be starved. I hope you've ordered." Lindy removed her coat and stuffed it into the booth before sliding onto the red upholstered seat herself.

"Actually, no, I didn't." Cait sighed. "Just tea." Her spirits were at an all-time low. It was becoming painfully clear that Paul didn't harbor a single romantic feeling toward her. She was wasting her time and her emotional energy on him. If only she'd had more experience with the opposite sex. It seemed her whole love life had gone into neutral the moment she'd graduated from college. At the rate things were developing, she'd still be single by the time she turned thirty—a possibility too dismal to contemplate. She hadn't given much thought to marriage and children, always assuming they'd naturally become part of her life; now she wasn't so sure. Even as a child, she'd pictured her grown-up self with a career *and* a family. Behind the business exterior was a woman traditional enough to hunger for that most special of relationships.

She had to face the fact that marriage would never happen if she continued to love a man who didn't return her feelings. She gave a low groan, then noticed that Lindy was gazing at her in concern.

"Let's order something," Lindy said quickly, reaching for the menu tucked behind the napkin holder. "I'm starved."

"I was thinking I'd skip lunch today," Cait mumbled. She sipped her lukewarm tea and frowned. "Joe will be taking me out to dinner soon. And frankly, I don't have much of an appetite."

"This is all my fault, isn't it?" Lindy asked, looking guilty.

"Of course not. I'm just being practical." If Cait was anything, it was practical—except about Paul. "Go ahead and order."

"You're sure you don't mind?"

Cait gestured nonchalantly. "Heavens, no."

"If you're sure, then I'll have the turkey on whole wheat," Lindy said after a moment. "You know how much I like turkey, though you'd think I'd have gotten enough over Thanksgiving."

"I'll just have a refill on my tea," Cait said.

"You're still flying to Minnesota for the holidays, aren't you?" Lindy asked, fidgeting with the menu.

"Mmm-hmm." Cait had purchased her ticket several months earlier. Martin and his family lived near Minneapolis. When their father had died several years earlier, Cait's mother moved to Minnesota, settling down in a new subdivision not far from Martin, his wife and their four children. Cait tried to visit at least once a year. However, she'd been there in August, stopping off on her way home from a business trip. Usually she made a point of visiting her brother and his family over the Christmas holidays. It was generally a slow week on the stock market, anyway. And if she was going to travel halfway across the country, she wanted to make it worth her while.

"When will you be leaving?" Lindy asked, although Cait was sure she'd already told her friend more than once.

"The twenty-third." For the past few years, Cait had used one week of her vacation at Christmas time, usually starting the weekend before.

But this year Paul was having a Christmas party and Cait didn't want to miss that, so she'd booked her flight closer to the holiday.

The waitress came to take Lindy's order and replenish the hot water for Cait's tea. The instant she moved away from their booth, Lindy launched into a lengthy tirade about how she hated Christmas shopping and how busy the malls were this time of year. Cait stared at her, bewildered. It wasn't like her friend to chat nonstop.

"Lindy," she interrupted, "is something wrong?"

"Wrong? What could possibly be wrong?"

"I don't know. You haven't stopped talking for the last ten minutes."

"I haven't?" There was an abrupt, uncomfortable silence.

Cait decided it was her turn to say something. "I think I'll wear my red velvet dress," she mused.

"To dinner with Joe?"

"No," she said, shaking her head. "To Paul's Christmas party."

Lindy sighed. "But what are you wearing tonight?"

The question took Cait by surprise. She didn't consider this dinner with Joe a real date. He just wanted to talk over old times, which was fine with Cait as long as he behaved himself. Suddenly she frowned, then closed her eyes. "Martin's a Methodist minister," she said softly.

"Yes, I know," Lindy reminded her. "I've known that since I first met you, which was what? Three years ago now."

"Four last month."

"So what does Martin's occupation have to do with anything?" Lindy asked.

"Joe Rockwell can't find out," Cait whispered.

"I didn't plan on telling him," Lindy whispered back.

"I've got to make up some other occupation like…"

"Counselor," Lindy suggested. "I'm curious, though. Why can't you tell Joe about Martin?"

"Think about it!"

"I am thinking. I really doubt Joe would care one way or the other."

"He might try to make something of it. You don't know Joe like I do. He'd razz me about it all evening, claiming the marriage was valid. You know, because Martin really *is* a minister, and since Martin performed the ceremony, we must really be married—that kind of nonsense."

"I didn't think about that."

But then, Lindy didn't seem to be thinking much about anything lately. It was as if she was walking around in a perpetual daydream. Cait couldn't remember Lindy's ever being so scatterbrained. If she didn't know better, she'd guess there was a man involved.

CHAPTER THREE

AT TEN TO SIX, Cait was blow-drying her hair in a haphazard fashion, regretting that she'd ever had it cut. She was looking forward to this dinner date about as much as a trip to the dentist. All she wanted was to get it over with, come home and bury her head under a pillow while she sorted out how she was going to get Paul to notice her.

Restyling her hair hadn't done the trick. Putting in extra hours at the office hadn't impressed him, either. Cait was beginning to think she could stand on top of his desk naked and not attract his attention.

She walked into her compact living room and smoothed the bulky-knit sweater over her slim hips. She hadn't dressed for the occasion, although the sweater was new and expensive. Gray wool slacks and a powder-blue turtleneck with a silver heart-shaped necklace dangling from her neck were about as dressy as she cared to get with someone like Joe. He'd probably be wearing cowboy boots and jeans, if not his hard hat and tool pouch.

Oh, yes, Cait had recognized his type when she'd first seen him. Joe Rockwell was a man's man. He walked and talked macho. No doubt he drove a truck with tires so high off the ground she'd need a stepladder to climb inside. He was tough and gruff and liked his women meek and submissive. In that case, of course, she had nothing to worry about; he'd lose interest immediately.

He arrived right on time, which surprised Cait. Being prompt didn't fit the image she had of Joe Rockwell, redneck contractor. She sighed and painted on a smile, then walked slowly to the door.

The smile faded. Joe stood before her, tall and debonair, dressed in a dark gray pin-striped suit. His gray silk tie had *pink* stripes. He was the picture of smooth sophistication. She knew that Joe was the same man she'd seen earlier in dusty work clothes—yet he was different. He was nothing like Paul, of course. But Joseph Rockwell was a devastatingly handsome man.

With a devastating charm. Rarely had she seen a man smile the way he did. His eyes twinkled with warmth and life and mischief. It wasn't difficult to imagine Joe with a little boy whose eyes mirrored his. Cait didn't know where that thought came from, but she pushed it aside before it could linger and take root.

"Hello," he said, flashing her that smile.

"Hi." She couldn't stop looking at him.

"May I come in?"

"Oh...of course. I'm sorry," she faltered, stumbling in her haste to step aside. He'd caught her completely off guard. "I was about to change clothes," she said quickly.

"You look fine."

"These old things?" She feigned a laugh. "If you'll excuse me, I'll only be a minute." She poured him a cup of coffee, then dashed into her bedroom, ripping the sweater over her head and closing the door with one foot. Her shoes went flying as she ran to her closet. Jerking aside the orderly row of business jackets and skirts, she pulled clothes off their hangers, considered them, then tossed them on the bed. Nearly everything she owned was more suitable for the office than a dinner date.

The only really special dress she owned was the red velvet one she'd purchased for Paul's Christmas party. The temptation to slip into that was strong but she resisted, wanting to save it for her boss, though heaven knew he probably wouldn't notice.

Deciding on a skirt and blazer, she hopped frantically around her bedroom as she pulled on her panty hose. Next she threw on a rose-colored silk blouse and managed to button it while stepping into her skirt. She tucked the blouse into the waistband and her feet into a pair of medium-heeled pumps. Finally, her velvet blazer and she was ready. Taking a deep breath, she returned to the living room in three minutes flat.

"That was fast," Joe commented, standing by the fireplace, hands clasped behind his back. He was examining a framed photograph that sat on the mantel. "Is this Martin's family?"

"Martin...why, yes, that's Martin, his wife and their children." She hoped he didn't detect the breathless catch in her voice.

"Four children."

"Yes, he and Rebecca wanted a large family." Her heartbeat was slowly returning to normal though Cait still felt light-headed. She had a sneaking suspicion that she was suffering from the effects of unleashed male charm.

She realized with surprise that Joe hadn't said or done anything to embarrass or fluster her. She'd expected him to arrive with a whole series of remarks designed to disconcert her.

"Timmy's ten, Kurt's eight, Jenny's six and Clay's four." She introduced the freckle-faced youngsters, pointing each one out.

"They're handsome children."

"They are, aren't they?"

Cait experienced a twinge of pride. The main reason she went to Minneapolis every year was Martin's children. They adored her and she was crazy about them. Christmas wouldn't be Christmas without Jenny and Clay snuggling on her lap while their father read the Nativity story. Christmas was singing carols in front of a crackling wood fire, accompanied by Martin's guitar. It meant stringing popcorn and cranberries for the seven-foot-tall tree that always adorned the living room. It was having the children take turns scraping fudge from the sides of the copper kettle, and supervising the decorating of sugar cookies with all four crowded around the kitchen table. Caitlin Marshall might be a dedicated stockbroker with an impressive clientele, but when it came to Martin's children, she was Auntie Cait.

"It's difficult to think of Martin with kids," Joe said, carefully placing the family photo back on the mantel.

"He met Rebecca his first year of college and the rest, as they say, is history."

"What about you?" Joe asked, turning unexpectedly to face her.

"What about me?"

"Why haven't you married?"

"Uh…" Cait wasn't sure how to answer him. She had a glib reply she usually gave when anyone asked, but somehow she knew Joe wouldn't accept that. "I… I've never really fallen in love."

"What about Paul?"

"Until Paul," she corrected, stunned that she'd forgotten the strong feelings she held for her employer. She'd been so concerned with being honest that she'd overlooked the obvious. "I am deeply in love with Paul," she said defiantly, wanting there to be no misunderstanding.

"There's no need to convince me, Caitlin."

"I'm not trying to convince you of anything. I've been in love with Paul for nearly a year. Once he realizes he loves me, too, we'll be married."

Joe's mouth slanted in a wry line and he seemed about to argue with her. Cait waylaid any attempt by glancing pointedly at her watch. "Shouldn't we be leaving?"

After a long moment, Joe said, "Yes, I suppose we should," in a mild, neutral voice.

Cait went to the hall closet for her coat, aware with every step she took that Joe was watching her. She turned back to smile at him, but somehow the smile didn't materialize. His blue eyes met hers, and she found his look disturbing—caressing, somehow, and intimate.

Joe helped her on with her coat and led her to the parking lot, where he'd left his car. Another surprise awaited her. It wasn't a four-wheel-drive truck, but a late sixties black convertible in mint condition.

The restaurant was one of the most respected in Seattle, with a noted chef and a reputation for excellent seafood. Cait chose grilled salmon and Joe ordered Cajun shrimp.

"Do you remember the time Martin and I decided to open our own business?" Joe asked, as they sipped a predinner glass of wine.

Cait did indeed recall that summer. "You might have been a bit more ingenious. A lemonade stand wasn't the world's most creative enterprise."

"Perhaps not, but we were doing a brisk business until an annoying eight-year-old girl ruined everything."

Cait wasn't about to let that comment pass. "You were using moldy lemons and covering the taste with too much sugar. Besides, it's unhealthy to share paper cups."

Joe chuckled, the sound deep and rich. "I should've known then that you were nothing but trouble."

"It seems to me the whole mess was your own fault. You boys wouldn't listen to me. I had to do something before someone got sick on those lemons."

"Carrying a picket sign that read 'Talk to me before you buy this lemonade' was a bit drastic even for you, don't you think?"

"If anything, it brought you more business," Cait said dryly, recalling how her plan had backfired. "All the boys in the neighborhood wanted to see what contaminated lemonade tasted like."

"You were a damn nuisance, Cait. Own up to it." He smiled and Cait sincerely doubted that any woman could argue with him when he smiled full-force.

"I most certainly was not! If anything you two were—"

"Disgusting, I believe, was your favorite word for Martin and me."

"And you did your level best to live up to it," she said, struggling to hold back a smile. She reached for a breadstick and bit into it to disguise her amusement. She'd always enjoyed rankling Martin and Joe, though she'd never have admitted it, especially at the age of eight.

"Picketing our lemonade stand wasn't the worst trick you ever pulled, either," Joe said mischievously.

Cait had trouble swallowing. She should have been prepared for this. If he remembered her complaints about the lemonade stand, he was sure to remember what had happened once Betsy McDonald found out about the kissing incident.

"It wasn't a trick," Cait protested.

"But you told everyone at school that I'd kissed you—even though you'd promised not to."

"Not exactly." There was a small discrepancy that needed clarification. "If you think back you'll remember you said I couldn't tell anyone I'd been inside the fort. You didn't say anything about the kiss."

Joe frowned darkly as if attempting to jog his memory. "How can you remember details like that? All of this happened years ago."

"I remember everything," Cait said grandly—a gross exaggeration. She hadn't recognized Joe, after all. But on this one point she was absolutely clear. "You and Martin were far more concerned that I not tell anyone about going inside the fort. You didn't say a word about keeping the kiss a secret."

"But did you have to tell Betsy McDonald? That girl had been making eyes at me for weeks. As soon as she learned I'd kissed you instead of her, she was furious."

"Betsy was the most popular girl in school. I wanted her for my friend, so I told."

"And sold me down the river."

"Would an apology help?" Confident he was teasing her once again, Cait gave him her most charming smile.

"An apology just might do it." Joe grinned back, a grin that brightened his eyes to a deeper, more tantalizing shade of blue. It was with some difficulty that Cait pulled her gaze away from his.

"If Betsy liked you," she asked, smoothing the linen napkin across her lap, "then why didn't you kiss her? She'd probably have let you. You wouldn't have had to bribe her with your precious baseball cards, either."

"You're kidding. If I kissed Betsy McDonald I might as well have signed over my soul," Joe said, continuing the joke.

"Even as mere children, men are afraid of commitment," Cait said solemnly.

Joe ignored her remark.

"Your memory's not as sharp as you think," Cait felt obliged to tell him, enjoying herself more than she'd thought possible.

Once again, Joe overlooked her comment. "I can remember Martin com-plaining about how you'd line up your dolls in a row and teach them school. Once you even got him to come in as a guest lecturer. Heaven knew what you had to do to get him to play professor to a bunch of dolls."

"I found a pair of dirty jeans stuffed under the sofa with something dead in the pocket. Mom would have tanned his hide if she'd found them, so Martin owed me a favor. Then he got all bent out of shape when I collected it. He didn't seem the least bit appreciative that I'd saved him."

"Good old Martin," Joe said, shaking his head. "I swear he was as big on ceremony as you were. Marrying us was a turning point in his life. From that point on, he started carting a Bible around with him the way some kids do a slingshot. Right in his hip pocket. If he wasn't burying something, he was holding revival meetings. Remember how he got in a pack of trouble at school for writing 'God loves you, ask Martin' on the back wall of the school?"

"I remember."

"I sort of figured he might become a missionary."

"Martin?" She gave an abrupt laugh. "Never. He likes his conveniences. He doesn't even go camping. Martin's idea of roughing it is doing without valet service."

She expected Joe to chuckle. He did smile at her attempted joke, but that was all. He seemed to be studying her the same way she'd been studying him.

"You surprise me," Joe announced suddenly.

"I do? Am I a disappointment to you?"

"Not at all. I always thought you'd grow up and have a house full of chil-dren yourself. You used to haul those dolls of yours around with you every-where. If Martin and I were too noisy, you'd shush us, saying the babies were asleep. If we wanted to play in the backyard, we couldn't because you were having a tea party with your dolls. It was enough to drive a ten-year-old boy crazy. But if we ever dared complain, you'd look at us serenely and with the sweetest smile tell us we had to be patient because it was for the children."

"I did get carried away with all that motherhood business, didn't I?" Joe's words stirred up uncomfortable memories, the same ones she'd entertained earlier that afternoon. She really did love children. Yet, somehow, without her quite knowing how, the years had passed and she'd buried the dream. Nowadays she didn't like to think too much about a husband and family— the life that hadn't happened. It haunted her at odd moments.

"I should have known you'd end up in construction," she said, switching the subject away from herself.

"How's that?" Joe asked.

"Wasn't it you who built the fort?"

"Martin helped."

"Sure, by staying out of the way." She grinned. "I know my brother. He's a marvel with people, but please don't ever give him a hammer."

Their dinner arrived, and it was as delicious as Cait had expected, although by then she was enjoying herself so much that even a plateful of dry toast would have tasted good. They drank two cups of cappuccino after their meal, and talked and laughed as the hours melted away. Cait couldn't remember the last time she'd laughed so much.

When at last she glanced at her watch, she was shocked to realize it was well past ten. "I had no idea it was so late!" she said. "I should get home." She had to be up by five.

Joe took care of the bill and collected her coat. When they walked outside, the December night was clear and chilly, with a multitude of stars twinkling brightly above.

"Are you cold?" he asked as they waited for the valet to deliver the car.

"Not at all." Nevertheless, he placed his arm around her shoulders, drawing her close.

Cait didn't protest. It felt natural for this man to hold her close.

His car arrived and they drove back to her apartment building in silence. When he pulled into the parking lot, she considered inviting him in for coffee, then decided against it. They'd already drunk enough coffee, and besides, they both had to work the following morning. But more important, Joe might read something else into the invitation. He was an old friend. Nothing more. And she wanted to keep it that way.

She turned to him and smiled softly. "I had a lovely time. Thank you so much."

"You're welcome, Cait. We'll do it again."

Cait was astonished to realize how appealing another evening with Joseph Rockwell was. She'd underestimated him.

Or had she?

"There's something else I'd like to try again," he was saying, his eyes filled with devilry.

"Try again?" she repeated. "What?"

He slid his arm behind her and for a breathless moment they looked at each other. "I don't know if I've got a chance without trading a few baseball cards, though."

Cait swallowed. "You want to kiss me?"

He nodded. His eyes seemed to grow darker, more intense. "For old times' sake." His hand caressed the curve of her neck, his thumb moving slowly toward the scented hollow of her throat.

"Well, sure. For old times' sake." She was astonished at the way her heart was reacting to the thought of Joe holding her...kissing her.

His mouth began a slow descent toward hers, his warm breath nuzzling her skin.

"Just remember," she whispered when his mouth was about to settle over hers. Her hands gripped his lapels. "Old times'..."

"I'll remember," he said as his lips came down on hers.

She sighed and slid her hands up his solid chest to link her fingers at the base of his neck. The kiss was slow and thorough. When it was over, Cait's hands were clutching his collar.

Joe's fingers were in her hair, tangled in the short, soft curls, cradling the back of her head.

A sweet rush of joy coursed through her veins. Cait felt a bubbling excitement, a burst of warmth, unlike anything she'd ever known before.

Then he kissed her a second time...

"Just remember..." she repeated when he pulled his mouth from hers and buried it in the delicate curve of her neck.

He drew in several ragged breaths before asking, "What is it I'm supposed to remember?"

"Yes, oh, please, remember."

He lifted his head and rested his hands lightly on her shoulders, his face only inches from hers. "What's so important you don't want me to forget?" he whispered.

It wasn't Joe who was supposed to remember; it was Cait. She didn't realize she'd spoken out loud. She blinked, uncertain, then tilted her head to gaze down at her hands, anywhere but at him. "Oh...that I'm in love with Paul."

There was a moment of silence. An awkward moment. "Right," he answered shortly. "You're in love with Paul." His arms fell away and he released her.

Cait hesitated, uneasy. "Thanks again for a wonderful dinner." Her hand closed around the door handle. She was eager now to make her escape.

"Any time," he said flippantly. His own hands gripped the steering wheel. "I'll see you soon."

"Soon," he echoed. She climbed out of the car, not giving Joe a chance to come around and open the door for her. She was aware of him sitting in the car, waiting until she'd unlocked the lobby door and stepped inside. She hurried down the first-floor hall and into her apartment, turning on the lights so he'd know she'd made it safely home.

Then she removed her coat and carefully hung it in the closet. When she peeked out the window, she saw that Joe had already left.

LINDY WAS AT her desk working when Cait arrived the next morning. Cait smiled at her as she hurried past, but didn't stop to indulge in conversation.

Cait could feel Lindy's gaze trailing after her and she knew her friend was disappointed that she hadn't told her about the dinner date with Joe Rockwell.

Cait didn't want to talk about it. She was afraid that if she said anything to Lindy, she wouldn't be able to avoid mentioning the kiss, which was a subject she wanted to avoid at all costs. She wouldn't be able to delay her friend's questions forever, but Cait wanted to put them off until at least the end of the day. Longer, if possible.

What a fool she'd been to let Joe kiss her. It had seemed so right at the time, a natural conclusion to a delightful evening.

The fact that she'd let him do it without even making a token protest still confused her. If Paul happened to hear about it, he might think she really *was* interested in Joe. Which, of course, she wasn't.

Her boss was a man of principle and integrity—and altogether a frustrating person to fall in love with. Judging by his reaction to her dinner with Joe, he seemed immune to jealousy. Now if only she could discover a way of letting him know how she felt…and spark his interest in the process!

The morning was hectic. Out of the corner of her eye, Cait saw Joe arrive. Although she was speaking to an important client on the phone, she stared after him as he approached the burly foreman. She watched Joe remove a blueprint from a long, narrow tube and roll it open so two other men could study it. There seemed to be some discussion, then the foreman nodded and Joe left, without so much as glancing in Cait's direction.

That stung.

At least he could have waved hello. But if he wanted to ignore her, well, fine. She'd do the same.

The market closed on the up side, the Dow Jones industrial average at 2600 points after brisk trading. The day's work was over.

As Cait had predicted, Lindy sought her out almost immediately.

"So how'd your dinner date go?"

"It was fun."

"Where'd he take you? Sam's Bar and Grill as you thought?"

"Actually, no," she said, clearing her throat, feeling more than a little foolish for having suggested such a thing. "He took me to Henry's." She announced it louder than necessary, since Paul was strolling into the office just then. But for all the notice he gave her, she might as well have been fresh paint drying on the office wall.

"Henry's," Lindy echoed. "He took you to Henry's? Why, that's one of the best restaurants in town. It must have cost him a small fortune."

"I wouldn't know. My menu didn't list any prices."

"You're joking. No one's ever taken me anyplace so fancy. What did you order?"

"Grilled salmon." She continued to study Paul for some clue that he was listening in on her and Lindy's conversation. He was seated at his desk, reading a report on short-term partnerships as a tax advantage. Cait had read it earlier in the week and had recommended it to him.

"Was it wonderful?" Lindy pressed.

It took Cait a moment to realize her friend was quizzing her about the dinner. "Excellent. The best fish I've had in years."

"What did you do afterward?"

Cait looked back at her friend. "What makes you think we did anything? We had dinner, talked, and then he drove me home. Nothing more happened. Understand? Nothing."

"If you say so," Lindy said, eyeing her suspiciously. "But you're certainly defensive about it."

"I just want you to know that nothing happened. Joseph Rockwell is an old friend. That's all."

Paul glanced up from the report, but his gaze connected with Lindy's before slowly progressing to Cait.

"Hello, Paul," Cait greeted him cheerfully. "Are Lindy and I disturbing you? We'd be happy to go into the hallway if you'd like."

"No, no, you're fine. Don't worry about it." He looked past them to the doorway and got to his feet. "Hello, Rockwell."

"Am I interrupting a meeting?" Joe asked, stepping into the office as if it didn't really matter whether he was or not. His hard hat was back in place, along with the dusty jeans and the tool pouch. And yet Cait had no difficulty remembering last night's sophisticated dinner companion when she looked at him.

"No, no," Paul answered, "we were just chatting. Come on in. Problems?"

"Not really. But there's something I'd like you to take a look at in the other room."

"I'll be right there."

Joe threw Cait a cool smile as he strolled past. "Hello, Cait."

"Joe." Her heart was pounding hard, and that was ridiculous. It must have been due to embarrassment, she told herself. Joe was a friend, a boy from the old neighborhood; just because she'd allowed him to kiss her didn't mean there was—or ever would be—anything romantic between them. The sooner she made him understand this, the better.

"Joe and Cait went out to dinner last night," Lindy said pointedly to Paul. "He took her to Henry's."

"How nice," Paul commented, clearly more interested in troubleshooting with Joe than discussing Cait's dating history.

"We had a good time, didn't we?" Joe asked Cait.

"Yes, very nice," she responded stiffly.

Joe waited until Paul was out of the room before he stepped back and dropped a kiss on her cheek. Then he announced loudly enough for everyone in the vicinity to hear, "You were incredible last night."

CHAPTER FOUR

"I THOUGHT YOU said nothing happened," Lindy said, looking intently at a red-faced Cait.

"Nothing did happen." Cait was furious enough to kick Joe Rockwell in the shins the way he deserved. How dared he say something so...so embarrassing in front of Lindy! And probably within earshot of Paul!

"But then why would he say something like that?"

"How should I know?" Cait snapped. "One little kiss and he makes it sound like—"

"He kissed you?" Lindy asked sharply, her eyes narrowing. "You just got done telling me there's nothing between the two of you."

"Good grief, the kiss didn't mean anything. It was for old times' sake. Just a platonic little kiss." All right, she was exaggerating a bit, but it couldn't be helped.

While she was speaking, Cait gathered her things and shoved them in her briefcase. Then she slammed the lid closed and reached for her coat, thrusting her arms into the sleeves, her movements abrupt and ungraceful.

"Have a nice weekend," she said tightly, not completely understanding why she felt so annoyed with Lindy. "I'll see you Monday." She marched through the office, but paused in front of Joe.

"You wanted something, sweetheart?" he asked in a cajoling voice.

"You're despicable!"

Joe looked downright disappointed. "Not low and disgusting?"

"That, too."

He grinned from ear to ear just the way she knew he would. "I'm glad to hear it."

Cait bit back an angry retort. It wouldn't do any good to engage in a verbal battle with Joe Rockwell. He'd have a comeback for any insult she could hurl. Seething, Cait marched to the elevator and jabbed the button impatiently.

"I'll be by later tonight, darling," Joe called to her just as the doors were closing, effectively cutting off any protest.

He was joking. He had to be joking. No man in his right mind could possibly expect her to invite him into her home after this latest stunt. Not even the impertinent Joe Rockwell.

Once home, Cait took a long, soothing shower, dried her hair and changed into jeans and a sweater. Friday nights were generally quiet ones for her. She was munching on pretzels and surveying the bleak contents of her refrigerator when there was a knock on the door.

It couldn't possibly be Joe, she told herself.

It *was* Joe, balancing a large pizza on the palm of one hand and clutching a bottle of red wine in the other.

Cait stared at him, too dumbfounded at his audacity to speak.

"I come bearing gifts," he said, presenting the pizza to her with more than a little ceremony.

"Listen here, you...you fool, it's going to take a whole lot more than pizza to make up for that stunt you pulled this afternoon."

"Come on, Cait, lighten up a little."

"Lighten up! You...you..."

"I believe the word you're looking for is fool."

"You have your nerve." She dug her fists into her hips, knowing she should slam the door in his face. She would have, too, but the pizza smelled *so* good it was difficult to maintain her indignation.

"Okay, I'll admit it," Joe said, his deep blue eyes revealing genuine contrition. "I got carried away. You're right, I am an idiot. All I can do is ask your forgiveness." He lifted the lid of the pizza box and Cait was confronted by the thickest, most mouthwatering masterpiece she'd ever seen. The top was crowded with no less than ten tempting toppings, all covered with a thick layer of hot melted cheese.

"Do you accept my humble apology?" Joe pressed, waving the pizza under her nose.

"Are there any anchovies on that thing?"

"Only on half."

"You're forgiven." She took him by the elbow and dragged him inside her apartment.

Cait led the way into the kitchen. She got two plates from the cupboard and collected knives, forks and napkins as she mentally reviewed his crimes.

"I couldn't believe you actually said that," she mumbled, shaking her head. She set the kitchen table, neatly positioning the napkins after shoving the day's mail to one side. "The least you can do is tell me why you found it necessary to say that in front of Paul. Lindy had already started grilling me. Can you imagine what she and Paul must think now?" She retrieved two wineglasses from the cupboard and set them by the plates. "I've never been more embarrassed in my life."

"Never?" he prompted, opening and closing her kitchen drawers until he located a corkscrew.

"Never," she repeated. "And don't think a pizza's going to ensure lasting peace."

"I wouldn't dream of it."

"It's a start, but you're going to owe me a long time for this prank, Joseph Rockwell."

"I'll be good," he promised, his eyes twinkling. He agilely removed the cork, tested the wine and then filled both glasses.

Cait jerked out a wicker-back chair and threw herself down. "Did Paul say anything after I left?"

"About what?" Joe slid out a chair and joined her.

Cait had already dished up a large slice for each of them, fastidiously using a knife to disconnect the strings of melted cheese that stretched from the box to their plates.

"About me, of course," she growled.

Joe handed her a glass of wine. "Not really."

Cait paused and lifted her eyes to his. "Not really? What does that mean?"

"Only that he didn't say much about you."

Joe was taunting her, dangling bits and pieces of information, waiting for her reaction. She should have known better than to trust him, but she was so anxious to find out what Paul had said that she ignored her pride. "Tell me everything he said," she demanded, "word for word."

Joe had a mouthful of pizza and Cait was left to wait several moments until he swallowed. "I seem to recall he said you explained that the two of us go a long way back."

Cait straightened, too curious to hide her interest. "Did he look concerned? Jealous?"

"Paul? No, if anything, he looked bored."

"Bored," Cait repeated. Her shoulders sagged with defeat. "I swear that man wouldn't notice me if I pranced around his office naked."

"That's a clever idea, and one that just might work. Maybe you should practice around the house first, get the hang of it. I'd be willing to help you out if you're serious about this." He sounded utterly nonchalant, as though she'd suggested subscribing to cable television. "This is what friends are for. Do you need help undressing?"

Cait took a sip of her wine to hide a smile. Joe hadn't changed in twenty years. He was still witty and fun-loving and a terrible tease. "Very funny."

"Hey, I wasn't kidding. I'll pretend I'm Paul and—"

"You promised you were going to be good."

He wiggled his eyebrows suggestively. "I will be. Just you wait."

Cait could feel the tide of color flow into her cheeks. She quickly lowered her eyes to her plate. "Joe, cut it out. You're making me blush and I hate to blush. It makes my face look like a ripe tomato." She lifted her slice of pizza and bit into it, chewing thoughtfully. "I don't understand you. Every time I think I have you figured out you do something to surprise me."

"Like what?"

"Like yesterday. You invited me to dinner, but I never dreamed you'd take me someplace as elegant as Henry's. You were the perfect gentleman all evening and then today, you were so…"

"Low and disgusting."

"Exactly." She nodded righteously. "One minute you're the picture of charm and culture and the next you're badgering me with your wisecracks."

"I'm a tease, remember?"

"The problem is I can't deal with you when I don't know what to expect."

"That's my charm." He reached for a second piece of pizza. "Women are said to adore the unexpected in a man."

"Not this woman," she informed him promptly. "I need to know where I stand with you."

"A little to the left."

"Joe, please, I'm not joking. I can't have you pulling stunts like you did today. I've lived a good, clean life for the past twenty-eight years. Two days with you has ruined my reputation with the company. I can't walk into the office and hold my head up any longer. I hear people whispering and I know they're talking about me."

"Us," he corrected. "They're talking about us."

"That's even worse. If they want to talk about me and a man, I'd rather it was Paul. Just how much longer is this remodeling project going to take, anyway?" As far as Cait was concerned, the sooner Joe and his renegade crew were out of her office, the sooner her life would return to normal.

"Not too much longer."

"At the rate you're progressing, Webster, Rodale and Missen will have offices on the moon."

"Before the end of the year, I promise."

"Yes, but just how reliable are your promises?"

"I'm being good, aren't I?"

"I suppose," she conceded ungraciously, jerking a stack of mail away from Joe as he started to sort through it.

"What's this?" Joe asked, rescuing a single piece of paper before it fluttered to the floor.

"A Christmas list. I'm going shopping tomorrow."

"I should've known you'd be organized about that, too." He sounded vaguely insulting.

"I've been organized all my life. It isn't likely to change now."

"That's why I want you to lighten up a little." He continued studying her list. "What time are you going?"

"The stores open at eight and I plan to be there then."

"I suppose you've written down everything you need to buy so you won't forget anything."

"Of course."

"Sounds sensible." His remark surprised her. He scanned her list, then yelped, "Hey, I'm not on here!" He withdrew a pen from his shirt pocket and added his own name. "Do you want me to give you a few suggestions about what I'd like?"

"I already know what I'm getting you."

Joe arched his brows. "You do? And please don't say 'nothing.'"

"No, but it'll be something appropriate—like a muzzle."

"Oh, Caitlin, darling, you injure me." He gave her one of his devilish smiles, and Cait could feel herself weakening. Just what she didn't want! She had every right to be angry with Joe. If he hadn't brought that pizza, she'd have slammed the door in his face. Wouldn't she? Sure, she would! But she'd always been susceptible to Italian food. Her only other fault was Paul. She did love him. No one seemed to believe that, but she'd known almost from the moment they'd met that she was destined to spend the rest of her life loving Paul Jamison. Only she'd rather do it as his wife than his employee....

"Have you finished your shopping?" she asked idly, making small talk with Joe since he seemed determined to hang around.

"I haven't started. I have good intentions every year, you know, like I'll get a head start on finding the perfect gifts for my nieces and nephews, but they never work out. Usually panic sets in Christmas Eve and I tear around the stores like mad and buy everything in sight. Last year I forgot wrapping paper. My mother saved the day."

"I doubt it'd do any good to suggest you get organized."

"I haven't got the time."

"What are you doing right now? Write out your list, stick to it and make the time to go shopping."

"My darling Cait, is this an invitation for me to join you tomorrow?"

"Uh…" Cait hadn't intended it to be, but she supposed she couldn't object as long as he behaved himself. "You're welcome on one condition."

"Name it."

"No jokes, no stunts like you pulled today and absolutely no teasing. If you announce to even one person that we're married, I'm walking away from you and that's a promise."

"You've got it." He raised his hand, then ceremoniously crossed his heart.

"Lick your fingertips first," Cait demanded. The instant the words were out of her mouth, she realized how ridiculous she sounded, as if they were eight and ten all over again. "Forget I said that."

His eyes were twinkling as he stood to bring his plate to the sink. "I swear it's a shame you're so in love with Paul," he told her. "If I'm not careful, I could fall for you myself." With that, he kissed her on the cheek and let himself out the door.

Pressing her fingers to her cheek, Cait drew in a deep, shuddering breath and held it until she heard the door close. Then and only then did it seep out in ragged bursts, as if she'd forgotten how to breathe normally.

"Oh, Joe," she whispered. The last thing she wanted was for Joe to fall in love with her. Not that he wasn't handsome and sweet and wonderful. He was. He always had been. He just wasn't for her. Their personalities were poles apart. Joe was unpredictable, always doing the unexpected, whereas Cait's life ran like clockwork.

She liked Joe. She almost wished she didn't, but she couldn't help herself. However, a steady diet of his pranks would soon drive her into the nearest asylum.

Standing, Cait closed the pizza box and tucked the uneaten portion onto the top shelf of her refrigerator. She was putting the dirty plates in her dishwasher when the phone rang. She quickly washed her hands and reached for it.

"Hello."

"Cait, it's Paul."

Cait was so startled that the receiver slipped out of her hand. Grabbing for it, she nearly stumbled over the open dishwasher door, knocking her shin against the sharp edge. She yelped and swallowed a cry as she jerked the dangling phone cord toward her.

"Sorry, sorry," she cried, once she'd rescued the telephone receiver. "Paul? Are you still there?"

"Yes, I'm here. Is this a bad time? I could call back later if this is inconvenient. You don't have company, do you? I wouldn't want to interrupt a party or anything."

"Oh, no, now is perfect. I didn't realize you had my home number...but obviously you do. After all, we've been working together for nearly a year now." Eleven months and four days, not that she was counting or anything. "Naturally my number would be in the Human Resources file."

He hesitated and Cait bent over to rub her shin where it had collided with the dishwasher door. She was sure to have an ugly bruise, but a bruised leg was a small price to pay. Paul had phoned her!

"The reason I'm calling..."

"Yes, Paul," she prompted when he didn't immediately continue.

The silence lengthened before he blurted out, "I just wanted to thank you for passing on that article on the tax advantages of limited partnerships. It was thoughtful of you and I appreciate it."

"I've read quite a lot in that area, you know. There are several recent articles on the same subject. If you'd like, I could bring them in next week."

"Sure. That would be fine. Thanks again, Cait. Goodbye."

The line was disconnected before Cait could say anything else and she was left holding the receiver. A smile came, slow and confident, and with a small cry of triumph, she tossed the telephone receiver into the air, caught it behind her back and replaced it with a flourish.

CAIT WAS DRESSED and waiting for Joe early the next morning. "Joe," she cried, throwing open her apartment door, "I could just kiss you."

He was dressed in faded jeans and a hip-length bronze-colored leather jacket. "Hey, I'm not stopping you," he said, opening his arms.

Cait ignored the invitation. "Paul phoned me last night." She didn't even try to contain her excitement; she felt like leaping and skipping and singing out loud.

"Paul did?" Joe sounded surprised.

"Yes. It was shortly after you left. He thanked me for giving him an interesting article I found in one of the business journals and—this is the good part—he asked if I was alone…as if it really mattered to him."

"If you were alone?" Joe repeated, and frowned. "What's that got to do with anything?"

"Don't you understand?" For all his intelligence Joe could be pretty obtuse sometimes. "He wanted to know if *you* were here with me. It makes sense, doesn't it? Paul's jealous, only he doesn't realize it yet. Oh, Joe, I can't remember ever being this happy. Not in years and years and years."

"Because Paul Jamison phoned?"

"Don't sound so skeptical. It's exactly the break I've been waiting for all these months. Paul's finally noticed me, and it's thanks to you."

"At least you're willing to give credit where credit is due." But he still didn't seem particularly thrilled.

"It's just so incredible," she continued. "I don't think I slept a wink last night. There was something in his voice that I've never heard before. Something…deep and personal. I don't know how to explain it. For the first time in a whole year, Paul knows I'm alive!"

"Are we going Christmas shopping or not?" Joe demanded brusquely. "Damn it all, Cait, I never expected you to go soft over a stupid phone call."

"But this wasn't just any call," she reminded him. She reached for her purse and her coat in one sweeping motion. "It was was from *Paul.*"

"You sound like a silly schoolgirl." Joe frowned, but Cait wasn't about to let his short temper destroy her mood. Paul had phoned her at home and she was sure that this was the beginning of a *real* relationship. Next he'd ask her out for lunch, and then…

They left her apartment and walked down the hall, Cait grinning all the way. Standing just outside the front doors was a huge truck with gigantic wheels. Just the type of vehicle she'd expected him to drive the night he'd taken her to Henry's.

"This is your truck?" she asked when they were outside. She couldn't keep the laughter out of her voice.

"Something wrong with it?"

"Not a single thing, but Joe, honestly, you are so predictable."

"That's not what you said yesterday."

She grinned again as he opened the truck door, set down a stool for her and helped her climb into the cab. The seat was cluttered, but so wide she was able to shove everything to one side. When she'd made room for herself, she fastened the seat belt, snapping it jauntily in place. She was so happy, the whole world seemed delightful this morning.

"Will you quit smiling before someone suggests you've been overdosing on vitamins?" Joe grumbled.

"My, aren't we testy this morning."

"Where to?" he asked, starting the engine.

"Any of the big malls will do. You decide. Do you have your list all made out?"

Joe patted his heart. "It's in my shirt pocket."

"Good."

"Have you decided what you're going to buy for whom?"

His smile was slightly off-kilter. "Not exactly. I thought I'd follow you around and buy whatever you did. Do you know what you're getting your mother? Mine's damn difficult to buy for. Last year I ended up getting her a dozen bags of cat food. She's got five cats of her own and God only knows how many strays she's feeding."

"At least your idea was practical."

"Well, there's that, and the fact that by the time I started my Christmas shopping the only store open was a supermarket."

Cait laughed. "Honestly, Joe!"

"Hey, I was desperate and before you get all righteous on me, Mom thought the cat food and the two rib roasts were great gifts."

"I'm sure she did," Cait returned, grinning. She found herself doing a lot of that when she was with Joe. Imagine buying his mother rib roasts for Christmas!

"Give me some ideas, would you? Mom's a hard case."

"To be honest, I'm not all that imaginative myself. I buy my mother the same thing every year."

"What is it?"

"Long-distance phone cards. That way she can phone her sister in Dubuque and her high-school friend in Kansas. Of course she calls me every now and then, too."

"Okay, that takes care of Mom. What about Martin? What are you buying him?"

"A bronze eagle." She'd decided on that gift last summer when she'd attended Sunday services at Martin's church. In the opening part of his sermon, Martin had used eagles to illustrate a point of faith.

"An eagle," Joe repeated. "Any special reason?"

"Y-yes," she said, not wanting to explain. "It's a long story, but I happen to be partial to eagles myself."

"Any other hints you'd care to pass on?"

"Buy wrapping paper in the after-Christmas sales. It's about half the price and it stores easily under the bed."

"Great idea. I'll have to remember that for next year."

Joe chose Northgate, the shopping mall closest to Cait's apartment. The parking lot was already beginning to fill up and it was only a few minutes after eight.

Joe managed to park fairly close to the entrance and came around to help Cait out of the truck. This time he didn't bother with the step stool, but clasped her around the waist to lift her down. "What did you mean when you said I was so predictable?" he asked, giving her a reproachful look.

With her hands resting on his shoulders and her feet dangling in mid-air, she felt vulnerable and small. "Nothing. It was just that I assumed you drove one of these Sherman-tank trucks, and I was right. I just hadn't seen it before."

"The kind of truck I drive bothers you?" His brow furrowed in a scowl.

"Not at all. What's the matter with you today, Joe? You're so touchy."

"I am not touchy," he snapped.

"Fine. Would you mind putting me down then?" His large hands were squeezing her waist almost painfully, though she doubted he was aware of it. She couldn't imagine what had angered him. Unless it was the fact that Paul had called her—which didn't make sense. Maybe, like most men, he just hated shopping.

He lowered her slowly to the asphalt and released her with seeming reluctance. "I need a coffee break," he announced grimly.

"But we just arrived."

Joe forcefully expelled his breath. "It doesn't matter. I need something to calm my nerves."

If he needed a caffeine fix so early in the day, Cait wondered how he'd manage during the next few hours. The stores quickly became crowded this time of year, especially on a Saturday. By ten it would be nearly impossible to get from one aisle to the next.

By twelve, she knew: Joe disliked Christmas shopping every bit as much as she'd expected.

"I've had it," Joe complained after making three separate trips back to the truck to deposit their spoils.

"Me, too," Cait agreed laughingly. "This place is turning into a madhouse."

"How about some lunch?" Joe suggested. "Someplace far away from here. Like Tibet."

Cait laughed again and tucked her arm in his. "That sounds like a great idea."

Outside, they noticed several cars circling the lot looking for a parking space and three of them rushed to fill the one Joe vacated. Two cars nearly collided in their eagerness. One man leapt out of his and shook an angry fist at the other driver.

"So much for peace and goodwill," Joe commented. "I swear Christmas brings out the worst in everyone."

"And the best," Cait reminded him.

"To be honest, I don't know what crammed shopping malls and fighting the crowds and all this commercialism have to do with Christmas in the first place," he grumbled. A car cut in front of him, and Joe blared his horn.

"Quite a lot when you think about it," Cait said softly. "Imagine the streets of Bethlehem, the crowds and the noise…" The Christmas before, fresh from a shopping expedition, Cait had asked herself the same question. Christmas seemed so commercial. The crowds had been unbearable. First at Northgate, where she did most of her shopping and then at the airport. Sea-Tac had been filled with activity and noise, everyone in a hurry to get someplace else. There seemed to be little peace or good cheer and a whole lot of selfish concern and rudeness. Then, in the tranquility of church on Christmas Eve, everything had come into perspective for Cait. There had been crowds and rudeness that first Christmas, too, she reasoned. Yet in the midst of that confusion had come joy and peace and love. For most people, it was still the same. Christmas gifts and decorations and dinners were, after all, expressions of the love you felt for your family and friends. And if the preparations sometimes got a bit chaotic, well, that no longer bothered Cait.

"Where should we go to eat?" Joe asked, breaking into her thoughts. They were barely moving, stuck in heavy traffic.

She looked over at him and smiled serenely. "Any place will do. There're several excellent restaurants close by. You choose, only let it be my treat this time."

"We'll talk about who pays later. Right now, I'm more concerned with getting out of this traffic sometime within my life span."

Still smiling, Cait said, "I don't think it'll take much longer."

He returned her smile. "I don't, either." His eyes held hers for what seemed an eternity—until someone behind them honked irritably. Joe glanced up and saw that traffic ahead of them had started to move. He immediately stepped on the gas.

Cait didn't know what Joe had found so fascinating about her unless it was her unruly hair. She hadn't combed it since leaving the house; it was probably a mass of tight, disorderly curls. She'd been so concerned with finding the right gift for her nephews and niece that she hadn't given it a thought.

"What's wrong?" she asked, feeling self-conscious.

"What makes you think anything's wrong?"

"The way you were looking at me a few minutes ago."

"Oh, that," he said, easing into a restaurant parking lot. "I don't think I've ever fully appreciated how lovely you are," he answered in a calm, matter-of-fact voice.

Cait blushed and glanced away. "I'm sure you're mistaken. I'm really not all that pretty. I sometimes wondered if Paul would have noticed me sooner if I was a little more attractive."

"Trust me, Bright Eyes," he said, turning off the engine. "You're pretty enough."

"For what?"

"For this." And he leaned across the seat and captured her mouth with his.

CHAPTER FIVE

"I...WISH YOU hadn't done that," Cait whispered, slowly opening her eyes in an effort to pull herself back to reality.

As far as kisses went, Joe's were good. Very good. He kissed better than just about anyone she'd ever kissed before—but that didn't alter the fact that she was in love with Paul.

"You're right," he muttered, opening the door and climbing out of the cab. "I shouldn't have done that." He walked around to her side and yanked the door open with more force than necessary.

Cait frowned, wondering at his strange mood. One minute he was holding her in his arms, kissing her tenderly; the next he was short-tempered and irritable.

"I'm hungry," he barked, lifting her abruptly down to the pavement. "I sometimes do irrational things when I haven't eaten."

"I see." The next time she went anywhere with Joseph Rockwell, she'd have to make sure he ate a good meal first.

The restaurant was crowded and Joe gave the hostess their names to add to the growing waiting list. Sitting on the last empty chair in the foyer, Cait set her large black leather purse on her lap and started rooting through it.

"What are you searching for? Uranium?" Joe teased, watching her.

"Crackers," she answered, shifting the bulky bag and handing him several items to hold while she continued digging.

"You're searching for crackers? Whatever for?"

She glanced up long enough to give him a look that questioned his intelligence. "For obvious reasons. If you're irrational when you're hungry, you might do something stupid while we're here. Frankly, I don't want you to embarrass me." She returned to the task with renewed vigor. "I can just see you standing on top of the table dancing."

"That's one way to get the waiter's attention. Thanks for suggesting it."

"Aha!" Triumphantly Cait pulled two miniature bread sticks wrapped in cellophane from the bottom of her purse. "Eat," she instructed. "Before you're overcome by some other craziness."

"You mean before I kiss you again," he said in a low voice, bending his head toward hers.

She leaned back quickly, not giving him any chance of following through on that. "Exactly. Or waltz with the waitress or any of the other loony things you do."

"You have to admit I've been good all morning."

"With one minor slip," she reminded him, pressing the bread sticks into his hand. "Now eat."

Before Joe had a chance to open the package, the hostess approached them with two menus tucked under her arm. "Mr. and Mrs. Rockwell. Your table is ready."

"Mr. and Mrs. Rockwell," Cait muttered under her breath, glaring at Joe. She should've known she couldn't trust him.

"Excuse me," Cait said, standing abruptly and raising her index finger. "His name is Rockwell, mine is Marshall," she explained patiently. She was not about to let Joe continue his silly games. "We're just friends here for lunch." Her narrowed eyes caught Joe's, which looked as innocent as freshly fallen snow. He shrugged as though to say any misunderstanding hadn't been *his* fault.

"I see," the hostess replied. "I'm sorry for the confusion."

"No problem." Cait hadn't wanted to make a big issue of this, but on the other hand she didn't want Joe to think he was going to get away with it, either.

The woman led them to a linen-covered table in the middle of the room. Joe held out Cait's chair for her, then whispered something to the hostess who immediately cast Cait a sympathetic glance. Joe's own gaze rested momentarily on Cait before he pulled out his chair and sat across from her.

"All right, what did you say to her?" she hissed.

The menu seemed to command his complete interest for a couple of minutes. "What makes you think I said anything?"

"I heard you whispering and then she gave me this pathetic look like she wanted to hug me and tell me everything was going to be all right."

"Then you know."

"Joe, don't play games with me," Cait warned.

"All right, if you must know, I explained that you'd suffered a head injury and developed amnesia."

"Amnesia," she repeated loudly enough to attract the attention of the diners at the next table. Gritting her teeth, Cait snatched up her menu, gripping it so tightly the edges curled. It didn't do any good to argue with Joe. The man was impossible. Every time she tried to reason with him, he did something to make her regret it.

"How else was I supposed to explain the fact that you'd forgotten our marriage?" he asked reasonably.

"I did not forget our marriage," she informed him from between clenched teeth, reviewing the menu and quickly making her selection. "Good grief, it wasn't even legal."

She realized that the waitress was standing by their table, pen and pad in hand. The woman's ready smile faded as she looked from Cait to Joe and back again. Her mouth tightened as if she suspected they really were involved in something illegal.

"Uh…" Cait hedged, feeling like even more of an idiot. The urge to explain was overwhelming, but every time she tried, she only made matters worse. "I'll have the club sandwich," she said, glaring across the table at Joe.

"That sounds good. I'll have the same," he said, closing his menu.

The woman scribbled down their order, then hurried away, pausing to glance over her shoulder as if she wanted to be able to identify them later in a police lineup.

"Now look what you've done," Cait whispered heatedly once the waitress was far enough away from their table not to overhear.

"Me?"

Maybe she was being unreasonable, but Joe was the one who'd started this nonsense in the first place. No one could rattle her as effectively as Joe did. And worse, she let him.

This shopping trip was a good example, and so was the pizza that led up to it. No woman in her right mind should've allowed Joe into her apartment after what he'd said to her in front of Lindy. Not only had she invited him inside her home, she'd agreed to let him accompany her Christmas shopping. She ought to have her head examined!

"What's wrong?" Joe asked, tearing open the package of bread sticks. Rather pointless in Cait's opinion, since their lunch would be served any minute.

"What's wrong?" she cried, dumbfounded that he had to ask. "You mean other than the hostess believing I've suffered a head injury and the waitress thinking we're drug dealers or something equally disgusting?"

"Here." He handed her one of the miniature bread sticks. "Eat this and you'll feel better."

Cait sincerely doubted that, but she took it, anyway, muttering under her breath.

"Relax," he urged.

"Relax," she mocked. "How can I possibly relax when you're doing and saying things I find excruciatingly embarrassing?"

"I'm sorry, Cait. Really, I am." To his credit, he did look contrite. "But you're so easy to fluster and I can't seem to stop myself."

Their sandwiches arrived, thick with slices of turkey, ham and a variety of cheeses. Cait was reluctant to admit how much better she felt after she'd eaten. Joe's spirits had apparently improved, as well.

"So," he said, his hands resting on his stomach. "What do you have planned for the rest of the afternoon?"

Cait hadn't given it much thought. "I suppose I should wrap the gifts I bought this morning." But that prospect didn't particularly excite her. Good grief, after the adventures she'd had with Joe, it wasn't any wonder.

"You mean you actually wrap gifts before Christmas Eve?" Joe asked. "Doesn't that take all the fun out of it? I mean, for me it's a game just to see if I can get the presents bought."

She grinned, trying to imagine herself in such a disorganized race to the deadline. Definitely not her style.

"How about a movie?" he suggested out of the blue. "I have the feeling you don't get out enough."

"A movie?" Cait ignored the comment about her social life, mainly because he was right. She rarely took the time to go to a show.

"We're both exhausted from fighting the crowds," Joe added. "There's a six-cinema theater next to the restaurant. I'll even let you choose."

"I suppose you'd object to a love story?"

"We can see one if you insist, only…"

"Only what?"

"Only promise me you won't ever expect a man to say the kinds of things those guys on the screen do."

"I beg your pardon?"

"You heard me. Women hear actors say this incredible drivel and then they're disappointed when real men don't."

"Real men like you, I suppose?"

"Right." He looked smug, then suddenly he frowned. "Does Paul like romances?"

Cait had no idea, since she'd never gone on a date with Paul and the subject wasn't one they'd ever discussed at the office. "I imagine he does," she said, dabbing her mouth with her napkin. "He isn't the type of man to be intimidated by such things."

Joe's deep blue eyes widened with surprise and a touch of respect. "Ouch. So Martin's little sister reveals her claws."

"I don't have claws. I just happen to have strong opinions on certain subjects." She reached for her purse while she was speaking and removed her wallet.

"What are you doing now?" Joe demanded.

"Paying for lunch." She sorted through the bills and withdrew a twenty. "It's my turn and I insist on paying…" She hesitated when she saw Joe's deepening frown. "Or don't real men allow women friends to buy their lunch?"

"Sure, go ahead," he returned flippantly.

It was all Cait could do to hide a smile. She guessed that her gesture in paying for their sandwiches would somehow be seen as compromising his male pride.

Apparently she was right. As they were walking toward the cashier, Joe stepped up his pace, grabbed the check from her hand and slapped some money on the counter. He glared at her as if he expected a drawn-out public argument. After the fuss they'd already caused in the restaurant, Cait was darned if she was going to let that happen.

"Joe," she argued the minute they were out the door. "What was *that* all about?"

"Fine, you win. Tell me my views are outdated, but when a woman goes out with me, I pick up the tab, no matter how liberated she is."

"But this isn't a real date. We're only friends, and even that's—"

"I don't give a damn. Consider it an apology for the embarrassment I caused you earlier."

"Isn't that kind of sexist?"

"No! I just have certain…standards."

"So I see." His attitude shouldn't have come as any big surprise. Just as Cait had told him earlier, he was shockingly predictable.

Hand at her elbow, Joe led the way across the car-filled lot toward the sprawling theater complex. The movies were geared toward a wide audience. There was a Disney classic, along with a horror flick and a couple of adventure movies and last but not least, a well-publicized love story.

As they stood in line, Cait caught Joe's gaze lingering on the poster for one of the adventure films—yet another story about a law-and-order cop with renegade ideas.

"I suppose you're more interested in seeing that than the romance."

"I already promised you could choose the show, and I'm a man of my word. If, however, you were to pick another movie—" he buried his hands in his pockets as he grinned at her appealingly "—I wouldn't complain."

"I'm willing to pick another movie, but on one condition."

"Name it." His eyes lit up.

"I pay."

"Those claws of yours are out again."

She raised her hands and flexed her fingers in a catlike motion. "It's your decision."

"What about popcorn?"

"You can buy that if you insist."

"All right," he said, "you've got yourself a deal."

When it was Cait's turn at the ticket window, she purchased two for the Disney classic.

"Disney?" Joe yelped, shocked when Cait handed him his ticket.

"It seemed like a good compromise," she answered.

For a moment it looked as if he was going to argue with her, then a slow grin spread across his face. "Disney," he said again. "You're right, it does sound like fun. Only I hope we're not the only people there over the age of ten."

They sat toward the back of the theater, sharing a large bucket of buttered popcorn. The theater was crowded and several kids seemed to be taking turns running up and down the aisles. Joe needn't have worried; there were plenty of adults in attendance, but of course most of them were accompanying children.

The lights dimmed and Cait reached for a handful of popcorn, relaxing in her seat. "I love this movie."

"How many times have you seen it?"

"Five or six. But it's been a few years."

"Me, too." Joe relaxed beside her, crossing his long legs and leaning back.

The credits started to roll, but the noise level hadn't decreased much. "Will the kids bother you?" Joe wanted to know.

"Heavens, no. I love kids."

"You do?" The fact that he was so surprised seemed vaguely insulting and Cait frowned.

"We've already had this discussion," she responded, licking the salt from her fingertips.

"We did? When?"

"The other day. You commented on how much I used to enjoy playing with my dolls and how you'd expected me to be married with a house full of children." His words had troubled her then, because "a house full of children" was exactly what Cait would have liked, and she seemed a long way from realizing her dream.

"Ah, yes, I remember our conversation about that now." He scooped up a large handful of popcorn. "You'd be a very good mother, you know."

That Joe would say this was enough to bring an unexpected rush of tears to her eyes. She blinked them back, annoyed that she'd get weepy over something so silly.

The previews were over and the audience settled down as the movie started. Cait focused her attention on the screen, munching popcorn every now and then, reaching blindly for the bucket. Their hands collided more than once and almost before she was aware of it, their fingers were entwined. It was a peaceful sort of feeling, being linked to Joe in this way. There was a *rightness* about it that she didn't want to explore just yet. He hadn't really changed; he was still lovable and funny and fun. For that matter, she hadn't changed very much, either. . . .

The movie was as good as Cait remembered, better, even—perhaps because Joe was there to share it with her. She half expected him to make the occasional wisecrack, but he seemed to respect the artistic value of the classic animation and, judging by his wholehearted laughter, he enjoyed the story.

When the show was over, he released Cait's hand. Hurriedly she gathered her purse and coat. As they walked out of the noisy, crowded theater, it seemed only natural to hold hands again.

Joe opened the truck, lifted down the step stool and helped her inside. Dusk came early these days, and bright, cheery lights were ablaze on every street. A vacant lot across the street was now filled with Christmas trees. A row of red lights was strung between two posts, sagging in the middle, and a portable CD player sent forth saccharine versions of better-known Christmas carols.

"Have you bought your tree yet?" Joe asked, nodding in the direction of the lot after he'd climbed into the driver's seat and started the engine.

"No. I don't usually put one up since I spend the holidays with Martin and his family."

"Ah."

"What about you? Or is that something else you save for Christmas Eve?" she joked. It warmed her a little to imagine Joe staying up past midnight to decorate a Christmas tree for his nieces and nephews.

"Finding time to do the shopping is bad enough," he said, not really answering her question.

"Your construction projects keep you that busy?" She hadn't given much thought to Joe's business. She knew from remarks Paul had made that Joe was very successful. It wasn't logical that she should feel pride in his accomplishments, but she did.

"Owning a business isn't like being in a nine-to-five job. I'm on call twenty-four hours a day, but I wouldn't have it any other way. I love what I do."

"I'm happy for you, Joe. I really am."

"Happy enough to decorate my Christmas tree with me?"

"When?"

"Next weekend."

"I'd like to," she told him, touched by the invitation, "but I'll have left for Minnesota by then."

"That's all right," Joe said, grinning at her. "Maybe next time."

She turned, frowning, to hide her blush.

They remained silent as he concentrated on easing the truck into the heavy late-afternoon traffic.

"I enjoyed the movie," she said some time later, resisting the urge to rest her head on his shoulder. The impulse to do that arose from her exhaustion, she told herself. Nothing else!

"So did I," he said softly. "Only next time, I'll be the one to pay. Understand?"

Next time. There it was again. She suspected Joe was beginning to take their relationship, such as it was, far too seriously. Already he was suggesting they'd be seeing each other soon, matter-of-factly discussing dates and plans as if they were longtime companions. Almost as if they were married...

She was mulling over this realization when Joe pulled into the parking area in front of her building. He climbed out and began to gather her packages, bundling them in his arms. She managed to scramble down by herself, not giving him a chance to help her, then she led the way into the building and unlocked her door.

Cait stood just inside the doorway and turned slightly to take a couple of the larger packages from Joe's arms.

"I had a great time," she told him briskly.

"Me, too." He nudged her, forcing her to enter the living room. He followed close behind and unloaded her remaining things onto the sofa. His presence seemed to reach out and fill every corner of the room.

Neither of them spoke for several minutes, but Cait sensed Joe wanted her to invite him to stay for coffee. The idea was tempting but dangerous. She mustn't let him think there might ever be anything romantic between them. Not when she was in love with Paul. For the first time in nearly a year, Paul was actually beginning to notice her. She refused to ruin everything now by becoming involved with Joe.

"Thank you for…today," she said, returning to the door, intending to open it for him. Instead, Joe caught her by the wrist and pulled her against him. She was in his arms before she could voice a protest.

"I'm going to kiss you," he told her, his voice rough yet strangely tender.

"You are?" She'd never been more aware of a man, of his hard, muscular body against hers, his clean, masculine scent. Her own body reacted in a chaotic scramble of mixed sensations. Above all, though, it felt *good* to be in his arms. She wasn't sure why and dared not examine the feeling.

Slowly, leisurely, he lowered his head. She made a soft weak sound as his mouth touched hers.

Cait sighed, forgetting for a moment that she meant to free herself before his kiss deepened. Before things went any further…

Joe must have sensed her resolve because his hands slid down her spine in a gentle caress, drawing her even closer. His mouth began a sensuous journey along her jaw, and down her throat—

"Joe!" She moaned his name, uncertain of what she wanted to say.

"Hmm?"

"Are you hungry again?" She wondered desperately if there were any more bread sticks in the bottom of her purse. Maybe that would convince him to stop.

"Very hungry," he told her, his voice low and solemn. "I've never been hungrier."

"But you had lunch and then you ate nearly all the popcorn."

He slowly raised his head. "Cait, are we talking about the same things here? Oh, hell, what does it matter? The only thing that matters is this." He covered her parted lips with his.

Cait felt her knees go weak and sagged against him, her fingers gripping his jacket as though she expected to collapse any moment. Which was becoming a distinct possibility as he continued to kiss her….

"Joe, no more, please." But she was the one clinging to him. She had to do something, and fast, before her ability to reason was lost entirely.

He drew an unsteady breath and muttered something she couldn't decipher as his lips grazed the delicate line of her jaw.

"We...need to talk," she announced, keeping her eyes tightly closed. If she didn't look at Joe, then she could concentrate on what she had to do.

"All right," he agreed.

"I'll make a pot of coffee."

With a heavy sigh, Joe abruptly released her. Cait half fell against the sofa arm, requiring its support while she collected herself enough to walk into the kitchen. She unconsciously reached up and brushed her lips, as if she wasn't completely sure even now that he'd taken her in his arms and kissed her.

He hadn't been joking this time, or teasing. The kisses they'd shared were serious kisses. The type a man gives a woman he's strongly attracted to. A woman he's interested in developing a relationship with. Cait found herself shaking, unable to move.

"You want me to make that coffee?" he suggested.

She nodded and sank down on the couch. She could scarcely stand, let alone prepare a pot of coffee.

Joe returned a few minutes later, carrying two steaming mugs. Carefully he handed her one, then sat across from her on the blue velvet ottoman.

"You wanted to talk?"

Cait nodded. "Yes." Her throat felt thick, clogged with confused emotion, and forming coherent words suddenly seemed beyond her. She tried gesturing with her free hand, but that only served to frustrate Joe.

"Cait," he asked, "what's wrong?"

"Paul." The name came out in an eerie squeak.

"What about him?"

"He phoned me."

"Yes, I know. You already told me that."

"Don't you understand?" she cried, her throat unexpectedly clearing. "Paul is finally showing some interest in me and now you're kissing me and telling anyone who'll listen that the two of us are married and you're doing ridiculous things like..." She paused to draw in a deep breath. "Joe, oh, please, Joe, don't fall in love with me."

"Fall in love with you?" he echoed incredulously. "Caitlin, you can't be serious. It won't happen. No chance."

CHAPTER SIX

"NO CHANCE?" Cait repeated, convinced she'd misunderstood him. She blinked a couple of times as if that would correct her hearing. Either Joe was underestimating her intelligence, or he was more of a...a cad than she'd realized.

"You have nothing to worry about." He sipped coffee, his gaze steady and emotionless. "I'm not falling in love with you."

"In other words you make a habit of kissing unsuspecting women."

"It isn't a habit," he answered thoughtfully. "It's more of a pastime."

"You certainly seem to be making a habit of it with me." Her anger was quickly gaining momentum and she was at odds to understand why she found his casual attitude so offensive. He was telling her exactly what she wanted to hear. But she hadn't expected her ego to take such a beating in the process. The fact that he wasn't the least bit tempted to fall in love with her should have pleased her.

It didn't.

It was as if their brief kisses were little more than a pleasant interlude for him. Something to occupy his time and keep him from growing bored with her company.

"This may come as a shock to you," Joe continued indifferently, "but a man doesn't have to be in love with a woman to kiss her."

"I know that," Cait snapped, fighting to hold back her temper, which was threatening to break free at any moment. "But you don't have to be so... so casual about it, either. If I wasn't involved with Paul, I might have taken you seriously."

"I didn't know you were involved with Paul," he returned with mild sarcasm. He leaned forward and rested his elbows on his knees, his pose infuriatingly relaxed. "If that was true I'd never have taken you out. The way I see it, the involvement is all on your part. Am I wrong?"

"No," she admitted reluctantly. How like a man to bring up semantics in the middle of an argument!

"So," he said, leaning back again and crossing his legs. "Are you enjoying my kisses? I take it I've improved from the first go-around."

"You honestly want me to rate you?" she sputtered.

"Obviously I'm much better than I was as a kid, otherwise you wouldn't be so worried." He took another drink of his coffee, smiling pleasantly all the while.

"Believe me, I'm not worried."

He arched his brows. "Really?"

"I'm sure you expect me to fall at your feet, overcome by your masculine charm. Well, if that's what you're waiting for, you'll have one hell of a long wait!"

His grin was slightly off center, as if he was picturing her arrayed at his feet—and enjoying the sight. "I think the problem here is that *you* might be falling in love with *me* and just don't know it."

"Falling in love with you and not know it?" she repeated with a loud disbelieving snort. "You've gone completely out of your mind. There's no chance of that."

"Why not? Plenty of women have told me I'm a handsome son of a gun. Plus, I'm said to possess a certain charm. Heaven knows, I'm generous enough and rather—"

"Who told you that? Your mother?" She made it sound like the most ludicrous thing she'd heard in years.

"You might be surprised to learn that I do have admirers."

Why this news should add fuel to the fire of her temper was beyond Cait, but she was so furious with him she could barely sit still. "I don't doubt it, but if I fall in love with a man you can believe it won't be just because he's 'a handsome son of a gun,'" she quoted sarcastically. "Look at Paul—he's the type of man I'm attracted to. What's on the inside matters more than outward appearances."

"Then why are you so worried about falling in love with me?"

"I'm not worried! You've got it the wrong way around. The only reason I mentioned anything was because I thought *you* were beginning to take our times together too seriously."

"I already explained that wasn't a problem."

"So I heard." Cait set her coffee aside. Joe was upsetting her so much that her hand was shaking hard enough to spill it.

"Well," Joe murmured, glancing at her. "You never did answer my question."

"Which one?" she asked irritably.

"About how I rated as a kisser."

"You weren't serious!"

"On the contrary." He set his own coffee down and raised himself off the ottoman far enough to clasp her by the waist and pull her into his lap.

Caught off balance, Cait fell onto his thighs, too astonished to struggle.

"Let's try it again," he whispered in a rough undertone.

"Ah…" A frightening excitement took hold of Cait. Her mind commanded her to leap away from this man, but some emotion, far stronger than common sense or prudence, urged the opposite.

Before she could form a protest, Joe bent toward her and covered her mouth with his. She'd hold herself stiff in his arms, that was what she'd do, teach him the lesson he deserved. How dared he assume she'd automatically fall in love with him. How dared he insinuate he was some…some Greek god all women adored. But the instant his lips met hers, Cait trembled with a mixture of shock and profound pleasure.

Everything within her longed to cry out at the unfairness of it all. It shouldn't be this good with Joe. They were friends, nothing more. This was the kind of response she expected when Paul kissed her. If he ever did.

She meant to pull away, but instead, Cait moaned softly. It felt so incredibly wonderful. So incredibly right. At that moment, there didn't seem to be anything to worry about—except the likelihood of dissolving in his arms then and there.

Suddenly Joe broke the contact. Her instinctive disappointment, even more than the unexpectedness of the action, sent her eyes flying open. Her own dark eyes met his blue ones, which now seemed almost aquamarine.

"So, how do I rate?" he murmured thickly, as though he was having trouble speaking.

"Good." A one-word reply was all she could manage, although she was furious with him for asking.

"Just good?"

She nodded forcefully.

"I thought we were better than that."

"We?"

"Naturally I'm only as good as my partner."

"Th-then how do you rate me?" She had to ask. Like a fool she handed him the ax and laid her neck on the chopping board. Joe was sure to use the opportunity to trample all over her ego, to turn the whole bewildering experience into a joke. She couldn't take that right now. She dropped her gaze, waiting for him to devastate her.

"Much improved."

She cocked one eyebrow in surprise. She had no idea what to say next.

They were both silent. Then he said softly, "You know, Cait, we're getting better at this. Much, much better." He pressed his forehead to hers. "If we're not careful, you just might fall in love with me, after all."

"WHERE WERE YOU all day Saturday?" Lindy asked early Monday morning, walking into Cait's office. The renovations to it had been completed late Friday and Cait had moved everything back into her office first thing this morning. "I must have tried calling you ten times."

"I told you I was going Christmas shopping. In fact, I bought some decorations for my office."

Lindy nodded. "But all day?" Her eyes narrowed suspiciously as she set down her briefcase and leaned against Cait's desk, crossing her arms. "You didn't happen to be with Joe Rockwell, did you?"

Cait could feel a telltale shade of pink creeping up her neck. She lowered her gaze to the list of current Dow Jones stock prices and took a moment to compose herself. She couldn't admit the truth. "I told you I was shopping," she said somewhat defensively. Then, in an effort to change the topic, she reached for a thick folder with Paul's name inked across the top and muttered, "You wouldn't happen to know Paul's schedule for the day, would you?"

"N-no, I haven't seen him yet. Why do you ask?"

Cait flashed her friend a bright smile. "He phoned me Friday night. Oh, Lindy, I was so excited I nearly fell all over myself." She dropped her voice as she glanced around to make sure none of the others could hear her. "I honestly think he intends to ask me out."

"Did he say so?"

"Not exactly." Cait frowned. Lindy wasn't revealing any of the enthusiasm she expected.

"Then why did he phone?"

Cait rolled her chair away from the desk and glanced around once again. "I think he might be jealous," she whispered.

"Really?" Lindy's eyes widened.

"Don't look so surprised." Cait, however, was much too excited recounting Paul's phone call to be offended by Lindy's attitude.

"What makes you think Paul would be jealous?" Lindy asked next.

"Maybe I'm magnifying everything in my own mind because it's what I so badly want to believe. But he did phone..."

"What did he say?" Lindy pressed, sounding more curious now. "It seems to me he must have had a reason."

"Oh, he did. He mentioned something about appreciating an article I'd given him, but we both know that was just an excuse. What clued me in to his jealousy was the way he kept asking if I was alone."

"But that could've been for several different reasons, don't you think?" Lindy suggested.

"Yes, but it made sense that he'd want to know if Joe was at the apartment or not."

"And was he?"

"Of course not," Cait said righteously. She didn't feel guilty about hiding the fact that he'd been there earlier, or that they'd spent nearly all of Saturday together. "I'm sure Joe's ridiculous remark when I left the office on Friday is what convinced Paul to phone me. If I wasn't so furious with Joe, I might even be grateful."

"What's that?" Lindy asked abruptly, pointing to the folder in front of Cait. Her lips had thinned slightly as if she was confused or annoyed—about what, Cait couldn't figure out.

"This, my friend," she began, holding up the folder, "is the key to my future with our dedicated manager."

Lindy didn't immediately respond and looked more puzzled than before. "How do you mean?"

Cait couldn't get over the feeling that things weren't quite right with her best friend; she seemed to be holding something back. But Cait realized Lindy would tell her when she was ready. Lindy always hated being pushed or prodded.

"The folder?" Lindy prompted when Cait didn't answer.

Cait flipped it open. "I spent all day Sunday reading through old business journals looking for articles that might interest Paul. I must've gone back five years. I copied the articles I consider the most valuable and included a brief analysis of my own. I was hoping to give it to him sometime today. That's why I was asking if you knew his schedule."

"Unfortunately I don't," Lindy murmured. She straightened, picked up her briefcase and made a show of checking her watch. Then she looked up to smile reassuringly at Cait. "I'd better get to work. I'll come by later to help you put up your decorations, okay?"

"Thanks," Cait said, then added, "Wish me luck with Paul."

"You know I do," Lindy mumbled on her way out the door.

Mondays were generally slow for the stock market—unless there was a crisis. World events and financial reports had a significant impact on the market. However, as the day progressed, everything ran smoothly.

Cait looked up every now and then, half expecting to see Joe lounging in her doorway. His men had started early that morning, but by noon, Joe still hadn't arrived.

Not until much later did she realize it was Paul she should be anticipating, not Joe. Paul was the romantic interest of her life and it annoyed her that Joe seemed to occupy her thoughts.

As it happened, Paul did stroll past her office shortly after the New York market closed. Grabbing the folder, Cait raced toward his office, not hesitating for an instant. This was her golden opportunity and she was taking hold of it with both hands.

"Good afternoon, Paul," she said cordially as she stood in his doorway, clutching the folder. "Do you have a moment or would you rather I came back later?"

He looked tired, as if the day had already been a grueling one. It was all Cait could do not to offer to massage away the stress and worry that complicated his life. Her heart swelled with a renewed wave of love. For a wild, impetuous moment, it was true, she'd suffered her doubts. Any woman would have when a man like Joe took her in his arms. He might be arrogant in the extreme and one of the worst pranksters she'd ever met; despite all that, he had a certain charm. But now that she was with Paul, Cait remembered sharply who it was she really loved.

"I don't want to be a bother," she told him softly.

He give her a listless smile. "Come in, Cait. Now is fine." He gestured toward a chair.

She hurried into the office, trying to keep the bounce out of her step. Knowing she'd be spending a few extra minutes alone with Paul, Cait had taken special care with her appearance that morning.

He glanced up and smiled at her again, but this time Cait thought she could see a glimmer of appreciation in his eyes. "What can I do for you? I hope you're pleased with your office." He frowned slightly.

For a second, she forgot what she was doing in Paul's office and stared at him blankly until his own gaze fell to the folder. "The office looks great," she said quickly. "Um, the reason I'm here…" She faltered, then gulped in a quick breath and continued, "I went through some of the business journals I have at home and found several articles I felt would interest you." She extended the folder to him, like a ceremonial offering.

He took it from her and opened it gingerly. "Gracious," he said, flipping through the pages and scanning her written comments, "you must've spent hours on this."

"It was…nothing." She'd willingly have done a good deal more to gain his appreciation and eventually his love.

"I won't have a chance to look at this for a few days," he said.

"Oh, please, there's no rush. You happened to mention you got some useful insights from the previous article I gave you. So I thought I'd share a few others that seem relevant to what's going on with the market now."

"It's very thoughtful of you."

"I was happy to do it. More than happy," she amended with her most brilliant smile. When he didn't say anything more, Cait rose reluctantly to her feet. "You must be swamped after being in meetings for most of the day, so I'll leave you now."

She was almost at the door when he spoke. "Actually I only dropped in to the office to collect a few things before heading out again. I've got an important date this evening."

Cait felt as if the floor had suddenly disappeared and she was plummeting through empty space. "Date?" she repeated before she could stop herself. It was a struggle to keep smiling.

Paul's grin was downright boyish. "Yes, I'm meeting her for dinner."

"In that case, have a good time."

"Thanks, I will," he returned confidently, his eyes alight with excitement. "Oh, and by the way," he added, indicating the folder she'd worked so hard on, "thanks for all the effort you put into this."

"You're…welcome."

By the time Cait got back to her office she felt numb. Paul had an important date. It wasn't as though she'd expected him to live the life of a hermit, but before today, he'd never mentioned going out with anyone. She might have suspected he'd thrown out the information hoping to make her jealous if it hadn't been for one thing. He seemed genuinely thrilled about this date. Besides, Paul wasn't the kind of man to resort to pretense.

"Cait, my goodness," Lindy said, strolling into her office a while later, "what's wrong? You look dreadful."

Cait tried to swallow the lump in her throat and managed a shaky smile. "I talked to Paul and gave him the research I'd done."

"He didn't appreciate it?" Lindy picked up the Christmas wreath that lay on Cait's desk and pinned it to the door.

"I'm sure he did," she replied. "What he doesn't appreciate is me. I might as well be invisible to that man." She pushed the hair away from her forehead and braced both elbows on her desk, feeling totally disheartened. Unless she acted quickly, she was going to lose Paul to some faceless, nameless woman.

"You've been invisible to him before. What's different about this time?" Lindy fastened a silver bell to the window as Cait abstractedly fingered her three ceramic wise men.

"Paul's got a date, and from the way he talked about it, this isn't with just any woman, either. Whoever she is must be important, otherwise he wouldn't have said anything. He looked like a little kid who's been given the keys to a candy store."

The information seemed to surprise Lindy as much as it had Cait. She was quiet for a few minutes before she asked, "What are you going to do about it?"

"I don't know," Cait cried, hiding her face in her hands. She'd once jokingly suggested to Joe that she parade around naked in an effort to gain Paul's attention. Of course she'd been exaggerating, but some form of drastic action was obviously needed. If only she knew what.

Lindy mumbled an excuse and left. It wasn't until Cait looked up that she realized her friend was gone. She sighed wearily. She'd arrived at work this morning with such bright expectations, and now everything had gone wrong. She felt more depressed than she'd been in a long time. She knew the best remedy would be to force herself into some physical activity. Anything. The worst possible thing she could do was sit home alone and mope. Maybe she should plan to buy herself a Christmas tree and some ornaments. Her spirits couldn't help being at least a little improved by that; it would get her out of the house, if nothing else. And then she'd have something to entertain herself with, instead of brooding about this unexpected turn of events. Getting out of the house had an added advantage. If Joe phoned, she wouldn't be there to answer.

No sooner had that thought passed through her mind when a large form filled her doorway.

Joe.

A bright orange hard hat was pushed back on his head, the way movie cowboys wore their Stetsons. His boots were dusty and his tool pouch rode low on his hip, completing the gunslinger image. Even the way he stood with his thumbs tucked in his belt suggested he was waiting for a showdown.

"Hi, beautiful," he drawled, giving her that lazy, intimate smile of his.

The one designed, Cait swore, just to unnerve her. But it wasn't going to work, not in her present state of mind.

"Don't you have anyone else to pester?" she asked coldly.

"My, my," Joe said, shaking his head in mock chagrin. Disregarding her lack of welcome, he strode into the office and threw himself down in the chair beside her desk. "You're in a rare mood."

"You would be too after the day I've had. Listen, Joe. As you can see, I'm poor company. Go flirt with the receptionist if you're trying to make someone miserable."

"Those claws are certainly sharp this afternoon." He ran his hands down the front of his shirt, pretending to inspect the damage she'd inflicted. "What's wrong?" Some of the teasing light faded from his eyes as he studied her.

She sent him a look meant to blister his ego, but as always Joe seemed invincible against her practiced glares.

"How do you know I'm not here to invest fifty thousand dollars?" he demanded, making himself at home by reaching across her desk for a pen. He rolled it casually between his palms.

Cait wasn't about to fall for this little game. "Are you here to invest money?"

"Not exactly. I wanted to ask you to—"

"Then come back when you are." She grabbed a stack of papers and slapped them down on her desk. But being rude, even to Joe, went against her nature. She was battling tears and the growing need to explain her behavior, apologize for it, when he rose to his feet. He tossed the pen carelessly onto her desk.

"Have it your way. If asking you to join me to look for a Christmas tree is such a terrible crime, then—"

"You're going to buy a Christmas tree?"

"That's what I just said." He flung the words over his shoulder as he strode out the door.

In that moment, Cait felt as though the whole world was tumbling down around her shoulders. She felt like such a shrew. He'd come here wanting to include her in his Christmas preparations and she'd driven him away with a spiteful tongue and a haughty attitude.

Cait wasn't a woman easily given to tears, but she struggled with them now. Her lower lip started to quiver. She might have been eight years old all over again—this was like the day she'd found out she wasn't invited to Betsy McDonald's birthday party. Only now it was Paul doing the excluding. He and this important woman of his were going out to have the time of their lives while she stayed home in her lonely apartment, suffering from a serious case of self-pity.

Gathering up her things, Cait thrust the papers into her briefcase with uncharacteristic negligence. She put on her coat, buttoned it quickly and wrapped the scarf around her neck as though it were a hangman's noose.

Joe was talking to his foreman, who'd been unobtrusively working around the office all day. He hesitated when he saw her, halting the conversation. Cait's eyes briefly met his and although she tried to disguise how regretful she felt, she obviously did a poor job of it. He took a step toward her, but she raised her chin a notch, too proud to admit her feelings.

She had to walk directly past Joe on her way to the elevator and forced herself to look anywhere but at him.

The stocky foreman clearly wanted to resume the discussion, but Joe ignored him and stared at Cait instead, with narrowed, assessing eyes. She could feel his questioning concern as profoundly as if he'd touched her. When she could bear it no longer, she turned to face him, her lower lip quivering uncontrollably.

"Cait," he called out.

She raced for the elevator, fearing she'd burst into tears before she could make her grand exit. She didn't bother to respond, knowing that if she said anything she'd make a greater fool of herself than usual. She wasn't even sure what had prompted her to say the atrocious things to Joe that she had. He wasn't the one who'd upset her, yet she'd unfairly taken her frustrations out on him.

She should've known it would be impossible to make a clean getaway. She almost ran through the office, past the reception desk, toward the elevator.

"Aren't you going to answer me?" Joe demanded, following on her heels.

"No." She concentrated on the lighted numbers above the elevator, which moved with painstaking slowness. Three more floors and she could make her escape.

"What's so insulting about inviting you to go Christmas-tree shopping?" he asked.

Close to weeping, she waved her free hand, hoping he'd understand that she was incapable of explaining just then. Her throat was clogged and it hurt to breathe, let alone talk. Her eyes filled with tears, and everything started to blur.

"Tell me," he commanded a second time.

Cait gulped at the tightness in her throat. "Y-you wouldn't understand." Why, oh, why, wouldn't that elevator hurry?

"Try me."

It was either give in and explain, or stand there and argue. The first choice was easier; frankly, Cait didn't have the energy to fight with him. Sighing deeply, she began, "It—it all started when I made up this folder of business articles for Paul..."

"I might've known Paul had something to do with this," Joe muttered under his breath.

"I spent hours putting it together, adding little comments, and...and... I don't know what I expected but it wasn't..."

"What happened? What did Paul do?"

Cait rubbed her eyes with the back of her hand. "If you're going to interrupt me, then I can't see any reason to explain."

"Boss?" the foreman called out, sounding impatient.

Just then the elevator arrived and the doors opened, revealing half a dozen men and women. They stared out at Cait and Joe as he blocked the entrance, gripping her by the elbow.

"Joseph," she hissed, "let me go!" Recognizing her advantage, she called out, "This man refuses to release my arm." If she expected a knight in shining armor to leap to her rescue, Cait was to be sorely disappointed. It was as if no one had heard her.

"Don't worry, folks, we're married." Joe charmed them with another of his lazy, lopsided grins.

"Boss?" the foreman pleaded again.

"Take the rest of the day off," Joe shouted. "Tell the crew to go out and buy Christmas gifts for their wives."

"You want me to do *what?*" the foreman shouted back. Joe moved into the elevator with Cait.

"You heard me."

"Let me make sure I understand you. You want the men to go Christmas shopping for their wives? I thought you just said we're on a tight schedule?"

"That's right," Joe said loudly as the elevator doors closed.

Cait had never felt more conspicuous in her life. Every eye was focused on her and Joe, and it was all she could do to keep her head high.

When the tension became intolerable, Cait turned to face her fellow passengers. "We are not married," she announced.

"Yes, we are," Joe insisted. "She's simply forgotten."

"I did not forget our marriage and don't you dare tell them that cock-and-bull story about amnesia."

"But, darling—"

"Stop it right now, Joseph Rockwell! No one believes you. I'm sure these people can figure out that I'm the one who's telling the truth."

The elevator finally stopped on the ground floor, a fact for which Cait was deeply grateful. The doors glided open and two women stepped out first, but not before pausing to get a good appreciative look at Joe.

"Does she do this often?" one of the men asked, directing his question to Joe, his amusement obvious.

"Unfortunately, yes," he answered, chuckling as he tucked his hand under Cait's elbow and led her into the foyer. She tried to jerk her arm away, but he wouldn't allow it. "You see, I married a forgetful bride."

CHAPTER SEVEN

PACING THE CARPET in the living room, Cait nervously smoothed the front of her red satin dress, her heart pumping furiously while she waited for Joe to arrive. She'd spent hours preparing for this Christmas party, which was being held in Paul's home. Her stomach was in knots.

She, the mysterious woman Paul was dating, would surely be there. Cait would have her first opportunity to size up the competition. Cait had studied her reflection countless times, trying to be objective about her chances with Paul based on looks alone. The dress was gorgeous. Her hair flawless. Everything else was as perfect as she could make it.

The doorbell sounded and Cait hurried across the room, throwing open the door. "You know what you are, Joseph Rockwell?"

"Late?" he suggested.

Cait pretended not to hear him. "A bully," she said. "A badgering bully, no less. I'm sorry I ever agreed to let you take me to Paul's party. I don't know what I was thinking."

"You were probably hoping to corner me under the mistletoe," he remarked with a wink that implied he wouldn't be difficult to persuade.

"First you practically kidnap me into going Christmas-tree shopping with you," she raged. "Then—"

"Come on, Cait, admit it, you had fun." He lounged indolently on her sofa while she got her coat and purse.

She hesitated, her mouth twitching with a smile. "Who'd ever believe that a man who bought his mother a rib roast and a case of cat food for Christmas last year would be so particular about a silly tree?" Joe had dragged her to no fewer than four lots yesterday, searching for the perfect tree.

"I took you to dinner afterward, didn't I?" he reminded her.

Cait nodded. She had to admit it: Joe had gone out of his way to help her forget her troubles. Although she'd made the tree-shopping expedition sound like a chore, he'd turned the evening into an enjoyable and, yes, memorable one.

His good mood had been infectious and after a while she'd completely forgotten Paul was out with another woman—someone so special that his enthusiasm about her had overcome his normal restraint.

"I've changed my mind," Cait decided suddenly, clasping her hands over her stomach, which was in turmoil. "I don't want to go to this Christmas party, after all." The evening was already doomed. She couldn't possibly have a good time watching the man she loved entertain the woman *he* loved. Cait couldn't think of a single reason to expose herself to that kind of misery.

"Not go to the party?" Joe repeated. "But I thought you'd arranged your flight schedule just so you could."

"I did, but that was before." Cait stubbornly squared her shoulders and elevated her chin just enough to convince Joe she meant business. He might be able to bully her into going shopping with him for a Christmas tree, but this was entirely different. "*She'll* be there," Cait added as an explanation.

"She?" Joe repeated slowly, burying his hands in his suit pockets. He was exceptionally handsome in his dark blue suit and no doubt knew it. He was as comfortable in tailored slacks as he was in dirty jeans.

A lock of thick hair slanted across his forehead; Cait managed—it was an effort—to resist brushing it back. An effort not because it disrupted his polished appearance, but because she had the strangest desire to run her fingers through his hair. Why she'd think such a thing now was beyond her. She'd long since stopped trying to figure out her feelings for Joe. He was a friend and a confidant even if, at odd moments, he behaved like a luna-tic. Just remembering some of the comments he'd made to embarrass her brought color to her cheeks.

"I'd imagine you'd want to meet her," Joe challenged. "That way you can size her up."

"I don't even want to know what she looks like," Cait countered sharply. She didn't need to. Cait already knew everything she cared to about Paul's hot date. "She's beautiful."

"So are you."

Cait gave a short, derisive laugh. She wasn't discounting her own home-spun appeal. She was reasonably attractive, and never more so than this evening. Catching a glimpse of herself in the mirror, she was pleased to see how nice her hair looked, with the froth of curls circling her head. But she wasn't going to kid herself, either. Her allure wasn't extraordinary by any stretch of the imagination. Her eyes were a warm shade of brown, though, and her nose was kind of cute. Perky, Lindy had once called it. But none of that mattered. Measuring herself against Paul's sure-to-be-gorgeous, nameless date was like comparing bulky sweat socks with a silk stocking. She'd already spent hours picturing her as a classic beauty...tall...sophisticated.

"I've never taken you for a coward," Joe said in a flat tone as he headed toward the door.

Apparently he wasn't even going to argue with her. Cait almost wished he would, just so she could show him how strong her will was. Nothing he could say or do would convince her to attend this party. Besides, her feet hurt. She was wearing new heels and hadn't broken them in yet, and if she did go, she'd be limping for days afterward.

"I'm not a coward," she told him, schooling her face to remain as emotionless as possible. "All I'm doing is exercising a little common sense. Why depress myself over the holidays? This is the last time I'll see Paul before Christmas. I leave for Minnesota in the morning."

"Yes, I know." Joe frowned as he said it, hesitating before he opened her door. "You're sure about this?"

"Positive." She was mildly surprised Joe wasn't making more of a fuss. From past experience, she'd expected a full-scale verbal battle.

"The choice is yours of course," he granted, shrugging. "But if it was me, I know I'd spend the whole evening regretting it." He studied her when he'd finished, then gave her a smile Cait could only describe as crafty.

She groaned inwardly. If there was one thing that drove her crazy about Joe it was the way he made the most outrageous statements. Then every once in a while he'd say something so wise it caused her to doubt her own conclusions and beliefs. This was one of those times. He was right: if she didn't go to Paul's, she'd regret it. Since she was leaving for Minnesota the following day, she wouldn't be able to ask anyone about the party, either.

"Are you coming or not?" he demanded.

Grumbling under her breath, Cait let him help her on with her coat. "I'm coming, but I don't like it. Not one darn bit."

"You're going to do just fine."

"They probably said that to Joan of Arc, too."

CAIT CLUTCHED THE punch glass in both hands, as though terrified someone might try to take it back. Standing next to the fireplace, with its garlanded mantel and cheerful blaze, she hadn't moved since they'd arrived a half hour earlier.

"Is *she* here yet?" she whispered to Lindy when her friend walked past carrying a tray of canapés.

"Who?"

"Paul's woman friend," Cait said pointedly. Both Joe and Lindy were beginning to exasperate her. "I've been standing here for the past thirty minutes hoping to catch a glimpse of her."

Lindy looked away. "I... I don't know if she's here or not."

"Stay with me, for heaven's sake," Cait requested, feeling shaky inside and out. Joe had deserted her almost as soon as they got there. Oh, he'd stuck around long enough to bring her a cup of punch, but then he'd drifted away, leaving Cait to deal with the situation on her own. This was the very man who'd insisted she attend this Christmas party, claiming he'd be right by her side the entire evening in case she needed him.

"I'm helping Paul with the hors d'oeuvres," Lindy explained, "otherwise I'd be happy to stay and chat."

"See if you can find Joe for me, would you?" She'd do it herself, but her feet were killing her.

"Sure."

Once Lindy was gone, Cait scanned the crowded living room. Many of the guests were business associates and clients Paul had worked with over the years. Naturally everyone from the office was there, as well.

"You wanted to see me?" Joe asked, reaching her side.

"Thank you very much," she muttered, doing her best to sound sarcastic and keep a smile on her face at the same time.

"You're welcome." He leaned one elbow on the fireplace mantel and grinned at her boyishly. "Might I ask what you're thanking me for?"

"Don't play games with me, Joe. Not now, please." She shifted her weight from one foot to the other, drawing his attention to her shoes.

"Your feet hurt?" he asked, frowning.

"Walking across hot coals would be less painful than these stupid high heels."

"Then why did you wear them?"

"Because they go with the dress. Listen, would you mind very much if we got off the subject of my shoes and discussed the matter at hand?"

"Which is?"

Joe was being as obtuse as Lindy had been. She assumed he was doing it deliberately, just to get a rise out of her. Well, it was working.

"Did you see her?" she asked with exaggerated patience.

"Not yet," he whispered back as though they were exchanging top-secret information. "She doesn't seem to have arrived."

"Have you talked to Paul?"

"No. Have you?"

"Not really." Paul had greeted them at the door, but other than that, Cait hadn't had a chance to do anything but watch him mingle with his guests. The day at the office hadn't been any help, either. Paul had breezed in and out without giving Cait more than a friendly wave. Since they hadn't exchanged a single word, it was impossible for her to determine how his date had gone.

It must have been a busy day for Lindy, as well, because Cait hadn't had a chance to talk to her, either. They'd met on their way out the door late that afternoon and Lindy had hurried past, saying she'd see Cait at Paul's party.

"I think I'll go help Lindy with the hors d'oeuvres," Cait said now. "Do you want me to get you anything?"

"Nothing, thanks." He was grinning as he strolled away, leaving Cait to wonder what he found so amusing.

Cait limped into the kitchen, leaving the polished wooden door swinging in her wake. She stopped abruptly when she encountered Paul and Lindy in the middle of a heated discussion.

"Oh, sorry," Cait apologized automatically.

Paul's gaze darted to Cait's. "No problem," he said quickly. "I was just leaving." He stalked past her, shoving the door open with the palm of his hand. Once again the door swung back and forth.

"What was that all about?" Cait wanted to know.

Lindy continued transferring the small cheese-dotted crackers from the cookie sheet onto the serving platter. "Nothing."

"It sounded as if you and Paul were arguing."

Lindy straightened and bit her lip. She avoided looking at Cait, concentrating on her task as if it was of vital importance to properly arrange the crackers on the plate.

"You were arguing, weren't you?" Cait pressed.

"Yes."

As far as she knew, Lindy and Paul had always gotten along. The fact that they were at odds surprised her. "About what?"

"I—I gave Paul my two-week notice this afternoon."

Cait was so shocked, she pulled out a kitchen chair and sank down on it. "You did *what?*" Removing her high heels, she massaged her pinched toes.

"You heard me."

"But why? Good grief, Lindy, you never said a word to anyone. Not even me. The least you could've done was talk to me about it first." No wonder Paul was angry. If Lindy left, it would mean bringing in someone new when the office was already short-staffed. With Cait and a number of other people away for the holidays, the place would be a madhouse.

"Did you receive an offer you couldn't refuse?" Cait hadn't had any idea her friend was unhappy at Webster, Rodale and Missen. Still, that didn't shock her nearly as much as Lindy's remaining tight-lipped about it all.

"It wasn't exactly an offer—but it was something like that," Lindy replied vaguely. She set aside the cookie sheet, smiled at Cait and then carried the platter into the living room.

For the past couple of weeks Cait had noticed that something was troubling her friend. It hadn't been anything she could readily name. Just that Lindy hadn't been her usual high-spirited self. Cait had meant to ask her about it, but she'd been so busy herself, so involved with her own problems, that she'd never brought it up.

She was still sitting there rubbing her feet when Joe sauntered into the kitchen, nibbling on a cheese cracker. "I thought I'd find you in here." He pulled out the chair across from her and sat down.

"Has she arrived yet?"

"Apparently so."

Cait dropped her foot and frantically worked the shoe back and forth until she'd managed to squeeze her toes inside. Then she forced her other foot into its shoe. "Well, for heaven's sake, why didn't you say something sooner?" she chastised. She stood up, ran her hands down the satin skirt and drew a shaky breath. "How do I look?"

"Like your feet hurt."

She sent him a scalding frown. "Thank you very much," she said sarcastically for the second time in under ten minutes. Hobbling to the door, she opened it a crack and peeked out, hoping to catch sight of the mystery woman. From what she could see, there weren't any new arrivals.

"What does she look like?" Cait demanded and whirled around to discover Joe standing directly behind her. She nearly collided with him and gave a small cry of surprise. Joe caught her by the shoulders to keep her from stumbling. Eager to question him about Paul's date, she didn't take the time to analyze why her heartrate soared when his hands made contact with her bare skin.

"What does she look like?" Cait asked again.

"I don't know," Joe returned flippantly.

"What do you mean you don't know? You just said she'd arrived."

"Unfortunately she doesn't have a tattoo across her forehead announcing that she's the woman Paul's dating."

"Then how do you know she's here?" If Joe was playing games with her, she'd make damn sure he'd regret it. Her love for Paul was no joking matter.

"It's more a feeling I have."

"You had me stuff my feet back into these shoes for a stupid feeling?" It was all she could do not to slap him silly. "You are no friend of mine, Joseph Rockwell. No friend whatsoever." Having said that, she limped back into the living room.

Obviously unscathed by her remark, Joe wandered out of the kitchen behind her. He walked over to the tray of canapés and helped himself to three or four while Cait did her best to ignore him.

Since the punch bowl was close by, she poured herself a second glass. The taste was sweet and cold, but Cait noticed that she felt a bit light-headed afterward. Potent drinks didn't sit well on an empty stomach, so she scooped up a handful of mixed nuts.

"I remember a time when you used to line up all the Spanish peanuts and eat those first," Joe said from behind her. "Then it was the hazelnuts, followed by the—"

"Almonds." Leave it to him to bring up her foolish past. "I haven't done that since I was—"

"Twenty," he guessed.

"Twenty-five," she corrected.

Joe laughed, and despite her aching feet and the certainty that she should never have come to this party, Cait laughed, too.

Refilling her punch glass, she downed it all in a single drink. Once more, it tasted cool and refreshing.

"Cait," Joe warned, "how much punch have you had?"

"Not enough." She filled the crystal cup a third time—or was it the fourth?—squared her shoulders and gulped it down. When she'd finished, she wiped the back of her hand across her mouth and smiled bravely.

"Are you purposely trying to get drunk?" he demanded.

"No." She reached for another handful of nuts. "All I'm looking for is a little courage."

"Courage?"

"Yes," she said with a sigh. "The way I figure it..." She paused, smiling giddily, then whirled around in a full circle. "There *is* some mistletoe here, isn't there?"

"I think so," Joe said, frowning. "What makes you ask?"

"I'm going to kiss Paul," she said proudly. "All I have to do is wait until he walks past. Then I'll grab him by the hand, wish him a merry Christmas and give him a kiss he won't soon forget." If the fantasy fulfilled itself, Paul would immediately realize he'd met the woman of his dreams, and propose marriage on the spot....

"What is kissing Paul supposed to prove?"

She returned to reality. "Well, this is where you come in. I want you to look around and watch the faces of the other women. If one of them shows signs of jealousy, then we'll know who it is."

"I'm not sure this plan of yours is going to work."

"It's better than trusting those feelings of yours," she countered.

She saw the mistletoe hanging from the archway between the formal dining room and the living room. Slouched against the wall, hands tucked behind her back, Cait waited patiently for Paul to stroll past.

Ten minutes passed or maybe it was fifteen—Cait couldn't tell. Yawning, she covered her mouth. "I think we should leave," Joe suggested as he casually walked by. "You're ready to fall asleep on your feet."

"I haven't kissed Paul yet," she reminded him.

"He seems to be involved in a lengthy discussion. This could take a while."

"I'm in no hurry." Her throat felt unusually dry. She would have preferred something nonalcoholic, but the only drink nearby was the punch.

"Cait," Joe warned when he saw her helping herself to yet another glass.

"Don't worry, I know what I'm doing."

"So did the captain of the *Titanic*."

"Don't get cute with me, Joseph Rockwell. I'm in no mood to deal with someone amusing." Finding herself hilariously funny, she smothered a round of giggles.

"Oh, no," Joe groaned. "I was afraid of this."

"Afraid of what?"

"You're drunk!"

She gave him a sour look. "That's ridiculous. All I had is four little, bitty glasses of punch." To prove she knew exactly what she was doing, she held up three fingers, recognized her mistake and promptly corrected herself. At least she tried to do it promptly, but figuring out how many fingers equaled four seemed to take an inordinate amount of time. She finally held up two from each hand.

Expelling her breath, she leaned back against the wall and closed her eyes. That was her second mistake. The world took a sharp and unexpected nosedive. Snapping open her eyes, Cait looked to Joe as the anchor that would keep her afloat. He must have read the panic in her expression because he moved toward her and slowly shook his head.

"That does it, Ms. Singapore Sling. I'm getting you out of here."

"But I haven't been under the mistletoe yet."

"If you want anyone to kiss you, it'll be me."

The offer sounded tempting, but it was her stubborn boss Cait wanted to kiss, not Joe. "I'd rather dance with you."

"Unfortunately there isn't any music at the moment."

"You need music to dance?" It sounded like the saddest thing she'd ever heard, and her bottom lip began to tremble at the tragedy of it all. "Oh, dear, Joe," she whispered, clasping both hands to the sides of her head. "I think you might be right. The punch seems to be affecting me...."

"It's that bad, is it?"

"Uh, yes... The whole room's just started to pitch and heave. We're not having an earthquake, are we?"

"No." His hand was on her forearm, guiding her toward the front door.

"Wait," she said dramatically, raising her index finger. "I have a coat."

"I know. Stay here and I'll get it for you." He seemed worried about leaving her. Cait smiled at him, trying to reassure him she'd be perfectly fine, but she seemed unable to keep her balance. He urged her against the wall, stepped back a couple of paces as though he expected her to slip sideways, then hurriedly located her coat.

"What's wrong?" he asked when he returned.

"What makes you think anything's wrong?"

"Other than the fact that you're crying?"

"My feet hurt."

Joe rolled his eyes. "Why did you wear those stupid shoes in the first place?"

"I already told you," she whimpered. "Don't be mad at me." She held out her arms to him, needing his comfort. "Would you carry me to the car?"

Joe hesitated. "You want me to carry you?" He sounded as though it was a task of Herculean proportions.

"I can't walk." She'd taken the shoes off, and it would take God's own army to get them back on. She couldn't very well traipse outside in her stocking feet.

"If I carry you, we'd better find another way out of the house."

"All right." She agreed just to prove what an amicable person she actually was. When she was a child, she'd been a pest, but she wasn't anymore and she wanted to be sure Joe understood that.

Grasping Cait's hand, he led her into the kitchen.

"Don't you think we should make our farewells?" she asked. It seemed the polite thing to do.

"No," he answered sharply. "With the mood you're in you're likely to throw yourself into Paul's arms and demand that he make mad passionate love to you right then and there."

Cait's face went fire-engine red. "That's ridiculous."

Joe mumbled something she couldn't hear while he lifted her hand and slipped one arm, then the other, into the satin-lined sleeves of her full-length coat.

When he'd finished, Cait climbed on top of the kitchen chair, stretching out her arms to him. Joe stared at her as though she'd suddenly turned into a werewolf.

"What are you doing now?" he asked in an exasperated voice.

"You're going to carry me, aren't you?"

"I was considering it."

"I want a piggyback ride. You gave Betsy McDonald a piggyback ride once and not me."

"Cait," Joe groaned. He jerked his fingers through his hair, and offered her his hand, wanting her to climb down from the chair. "Get down before you fall. Good Lord, I swear you'd try the patience of a saint."

"I want you to carry me piggyback," she insisted. "Oh, please, Joe. My toes hurt so bad."

Once again her hero grumbled under his breath. She couldn't make out everything he said, but what she did hear was enough to curl her hair. With obvious reluctance, he walked to the chair, and giving a sigh of pure bliss, Cait wrapped her arms around his neck and hugged his lean hips with her legs. She laid her head on his shoulder and sighed again.

Still grumbling, Joe moved toward the back door.

Just then the kitchen door opened and Paul and Lindy walked in. Lindy gasped. Paul just stared.

"It's all right," Cait was quick to assure them. "Really it is. I was waiting under the mistletoe and you—"

"She downed four glasses of punch nonstop," Joe inserted before Cait could admit she'd been waiting there for Paul.

"Do you need any help?" Paul asked.

"None, thanks," Joe returned. "There's nothing to worry about."

"But..." Lindy looked concerned.

"She ain't heavy," Joe teased. "She's my wife."

THE PHONE RANG, waking Cait from a sound sleep. Her head began throbbing in time to the painful noise and she groped for the telephone receiver.

"Hello," she barked, instantly regretting that she'd spoken loudly.

"How are you feeling?" Joe asked.

"About like you'd expect," she whispered, keeping her eyes closed and gently massaging one temple. It felt as though tiny men with hammers had taken up residence in her head and were pounding away, hoping to attract her attention.

"What time does your flight leave?" he asked.

"It's okay. I'm not scheduled to leave until this afternoon."

"It is afternoon."

Her eyes flew open. "What?"

"Do you still need me to take you to the airport?"

"Yes...please." She tossed aside the covers and reached for her clock, stunned to realize Joe was right. "I'm already packed. I'll be dressed by the time you get here. Oh, thank goodness you phoned."

Cait didn't have time to listen to the pounding of the tiny men in her head. She showered and dressed as quickly as possible, swallowed a cup of coffee and a couple of aspirin, and was just shrugging into her coat when Joe arrived at the door.

She let him in, despite the suspiciously wide grin he wore.

"What's so amusing?"

"What makes you think I'm amused?" He strolled into the room, hands behind his back, as if he owned the place.

"Joe, we don't have time for your little games. Come on, or I'm going to miss my plane. What's with you, anyway?"

"Nothing." He circled her living room, still wearing that silly grin. "I don't suppose you realize it, but liquor has a peculiar effect on you."

Cait stiffened. "It does?" She remembered most of the party with great clarity. Good thing Joe had taken her home when he had.

"Liquor loosens your tongue."

"So?" She picked up two shopping bags filled with wrapped packages, leaving the lone suitcase for him. "Did I say anything of interest?"

"Oh, my, yes."

"Joe!" She glanced quickly at her watch. They needed to get moving if she was to catch her flight. "Discount whatever I said—I'm sure I didn't mean it. If I insulted you, I apologize. If I told any family secrets, kindly forget I mentioned them."

He strolled to her side and tucked his finger under her chin. "This was a secret, all right," he informed her in a lazy drawl. "It was something you told me on the drive home."

"Are you sure it's true?"

"Relatively sure."

"What did I say? Did I declare my undying love for you? Because if I—"

"No, no, nothing like that."

"Just how long do you intend to torment me with this?" She was rapidly losing interest in his little guessing game.

"Not much longer." He looked exceptionally pleased with himself. "So Martin's a minister now. Funny you never thought to mention that before."

"Ah…" Cait set aside the two bags and lowered herself to the sofa. So he'd found out. Worse, she'd been the one to tell him.

"That may well have some interesting ramifications, my dear. Have you ever stopped to think about them?"

CHAPTER EIGHT

"THIS IS EXACTLY why I didn't tell you about Martin," Cait informed Joe as he tossed her suitcase into the back seat of his car. She checked her watch again and groaned. They had barely an hour and a half before her flight was scheduled to leave. Cait was never late. Never—at least not when it was her own fault.

"It seems to me," Joe continued, his face deadpan, "that there could very well be some legal grounds to our marriage."

Joe was saying that just to annoy her, and unfortunately it was working. "I've never heard anything more ludicrous in my life."

"Think about it, Cait," he said, ignoring her protest. "We could be celebrating our anniversary this spring. How many years is it now? Eighteen? How the years fly."

"Listen, Joe, I don't find this amusing." She glanced at her watch. If only she hadn't slept so late. Never again would she have any Christmas punch. Briefly she wondered what else she'd said to Joe, then decided it was better not to know.

"I heard a news report of a three-car pileup on the freeway, so we'll take the side streets."

"Just hurry," Cait urged in an anxious voice.

"I'll do the best I can," Joe said, "but worrying about it isn't going to get us there any faster."

She glared at him. She couldn't help it. He wasn't the one who'd been planning this trip for months. If she missed the flight, her nephews and niece wouldn't have their Christmas presents from their Auntie Cait. Nor would she share in the family traditions that were so much a part of her Christmas. She *had* to get to the airport on time.

Everyone else had apparently heard about the accident on the freeway, too, and the downtown area was crowded with the overflow. Cait and Joe were delayed at every intersection and twice were forced to sit through two changes of the traffic signal.

Cait was growing more panicky by the minute. She just had to make this flight. But it almost seemed that she'd get to the airport faster if she simply jumped out of the car and ran there.

Joe stopped for another red light, but when the signal turned green, they still couldn't move—a delivery truck in front of them had stalled. Furious, Cait rolled down the window and stuck out her head. "Listen here, buster, let's get this show on the road," she shouted at the top of her lungs.

Her head was pounding and she prayed the aspirin would soon take effect.

"Quite the Christmas spirit," Joe muttered dryly under his breath.

"I can't help it. I have to catch this plane."

"You'll be there in plenty of time."

"At this rate we won't make it to Sea-Tac before Easter!"

"Relax, will you?" Joe suggested gently. He turned on the radio and a medley of Christmas carols filled the air. Normally the music would have calmed her, but she was suffering from a hangover, depression and severe anxiety, all at the same time. Her fingernails found their way into her mouth.

Suddenly she straightened. "Darn! I forgot to give you your Christmas gift. I left it at home."

"Don't worry about it."

"I didn't get you a gag gift the way I said." Actually she was pleased with the book she'd managed to find—an attractive coffee-table volume about the history of baseball.

Cait waited for Joe to mention *her* gift. Surely he'd bought her one. At least she fervently hoped he had, otherwise she'd feel like a fool. Though, admittedly, that was a feeling she'd grown accustomed to in the past few weeks.

"I think we might be able to get back on the freeway here," Joe said, as he made a sharp left-hand turn. They crossed the overpass, and from their vantage point, Cait could see that the freeway was unclogged and running smoothly.

"Thank God," she whispered, relaxing against the back of the seat as Joe drove quickly ahead.

Her chauffeur chuckled. "I seem to remember you lecturing me—"

"I never lecture," she said testily. "I may have a strong opinion on certain subjects, but let me assure you, I never lecture."

"You were right, though. The streets of Bethlehem must have been crowded and bustling with activity at the time of that first Christmas. I can see it all now, can't you? A rug dealer is held up by a shepherd driving his flock through the middle of town."

Cait smiled for the first time that morning, because she could easily picture the scene Joe was describing.

"Then some furious woman, impatient to make it to the local camel merchant before closing, sticks her nose in the middle of everything and shouts at the rug dealer to get his show on the road." He paused to chuckle at his own wit. "I'm convinced she wouldn't have been so testy except that she was suffering from one heck of a hangover."

"Very funny," Cait grumbled, smiling despite herself.

He took the exit for the airport and Cait was gratified to note that her flight wasn't scheduled to leave for another thirty minutes. She was cutting it close, closer than she ever had before, but she'd confirmed her ticket two days earlier and had already been assigned her seat.

Joe pulled up at the drop-off point for her airline and gave Cait's suitcase to a skycap while she rummaged around in her purse for her ticket.

"I suppose this is goodbye for now," he said with an endearingly crooked grin that sent her pulses racing.

"I'll be back in less than two weeks," she reminded him, trying to keep her tone light and casual.

"You'll phone once you arrive?"

She nodded. For all her earlier panic, Cait now felt oddly unwilling to leave Joe. She should be rushing through the airport to her airline's check-in counter to get her boarding pass, but she lingered, her heart overflowing with emotions she couldn't identify.

"Have a safe trip," he said quietly.

"I will. Thanks so much…for everything."

"You're welcome." His expression sobered and the ever-ready mirth fled from his eyes. Cait wasn't sure who moved first. All she knew was that she was in Joe's arms, his thumb caressing the softness of her cheek as they gazed hungrily into each other's eyes.

He leaned forward to kiss her. Cait's eyes drifted shut as his mouth met hers.

At first Joe's kiss was tender but it quickly grew in fervor. The noise and activity around them seemed to fade into the distance. Cait could feel herself dissolving. She moaned and arched closer, not wanting to leave the protective haven of his arms. Joe shuddered and hugged her tight, as if he, too, found it difficult to part.

"Merry Christmas, love," he whispered, releasing her with a reluctance that made her feel...giddy. Confused. *Happy.*

"Merry Christmas," she echoed, but she didn't move.

Joe gave her the gentlest of nudges. "You'd better hurry, Cait."

"Oh, right," she said, momentarily forgetting why she was at the airport. Reaching for the bags filled with gaily wrapped Christmas packages, she took two steps backward. "I'll phone when I get there."

"Do. I'll be waiting to hear from you." He thrust his hands into his pockets and Cait had the distinct impression he did it to stop himself from reaching for her again. The thought was a romantic one, a certainty straight from her heart.

Her heart... Her heart was full of feeling for Joe. More than she'd ever realized. He'd dominated her life these past few weeks—taking her to dinner, bribing his way back into her good graces with pizza, taking her on a Christmas shopping expedition, escorting her to Paul's party. Joe had become her whole world. Joe, not Paul. Joe.

Given no other choice, Cait abruptly turned and hurried into the airport, where she checked in, then went through security and down the concourse to the proper gate.

The flight had already been called and only a handful of passengers had yet to board.

Cait dashed to the counter with her boarding pass. A young soldier stood just ahead of her. "But you don't understand," the tall marine was saying to the airline employee. "I booked this flight over a month ago. I've got to be on that plane!"

"I'm so sorry," the woman apologized, her dark eyes regretful. "This sort of thing happens, especially during holidays, but your ticket's for standby. I wish I could do something for you, but there isn't a single seat available."

"But I haven't seen my family in over a year. My uncle Harvey's driving from Duluth to visit. He was in the marines, too. My mom's been baking for three weeks. Don't you see? I can't disappoint them now!"

Cait watched as the agent rechecked her computer. "If I could magically create a seat for you, I would," she said sympathetically. "But there just isn't one."

"But when I bought the ticket, the woman told me I wouldn't have a problem getting on the flight. She said there're always no-shows."

"I'm so sorry," the agent repeated, looking past the young marine to Cait.

"All right," he said, forcefully expelling his breath. "When's the next flight with available space? Any flight within a hundred miles of Minneapolis. I'll walk the rest of the way if I have to."

Once again, the woman consulted her computer. "We have space available the evening of the twenty-sixth."

"The twenty-sixth!" the young man shouted. "But that's after Christmas and eats up nearly all my leave. I'd be home for less than a week."

"May I help you?" the airline employee said to Cait. She looked almost as unhappy as the marine, but apparently there wasn't anything she could do to help him.

Cait stepped forward and handed the woman her boarding pass. The soldier gazed at it longingly, then moved dejectedly from the counter and lowered himself into one of the molded plastic chairs.

Cait hesitated, remembering how she'd stuck her head out the window of Joe's truck on their drive to the airport and shouted impatiently at the truck driver who was holding up traffic. A conversation she'd had with Joe earlier returned to haunt her. She'd argued that Christmas was a time filled with love and good cheer, the one holiday that brought out the very best in everyone. And sometimes, Joe had insisted, the very worst.

"Since you already have your seat assignment, you may board the flight now."

The urge to hurry nearly overwhelmed Cait, yet she hesitated once again.

"Excuse me," Cait said, drawing a deep breath and making her decision. She approached the soldier. He seemed impossibly young now that she had a good look at him. No more than eighteen, maybe nineteen. He'd probably joined the service right out of high school. His hair was cropped close to his head and his combat boots were so shiny Cait could see her reflection in them.

The marine glanced up at her, his face heavy with defeat. "Yes?"

"Did I hear you say you needed to be on this flight?"

"I have a ticket, ma'am. But it's standby and there aren't any seats."

"Listen," she said. "You can have mine."

The way his face lit up was enough to blot out her own disappointment at missing Christmas with Martin and her sister-in-law. The kids. Her mother... "My family's in Minneapolis, too, but I was there this summer."

"Ma'am, I can't let you do this."

"Don't cheat me out of the pleasure."

They approached the counter to effect the exchange. The marine stood, his eyes wide with disbelief. "I insist," Cait said. "Here." She handed him the two bags full of gifts for her nephews and nieces. "There'll be a man waiting at the other end. A tall minister—he'll have a collar on. Give him these. I'll phone so he'll know to look for you."

"Thank you for everything... I can't believe you're doing this."

Cait smiled. Impulsively the marine hugged her, then swinging his duffel bag over his shoulder, he picked up the two bags of gifts and jogged over to Security.

Cait waited for a couple of minutes, then wiped the tears from her eyes. She wasn't completely sure why she was crying. She'd never felt better in her life.

IT WAS AROUND six when she awoke. The apartment was dark and silent. Sighing, she picked up the phone, dragged it onto the bed with her and punched out Joe's number.

He answered on the first ring, as if he'd been waiting for her call. "How was the flight?" he asked immediately.

"I wouldn't know. I wasn't on it."

"You missed the plane!" he shouted incredulously. "But you were there in plenty of time."

"I know. It's a long story, but basically, I gave my seat to someone who needed it more than I did." She smiled dreamily, remembering how the young marine's face had lit up. "I'll tell you about it later."

"Where are you now?"

"Home."

He exhaled sharply, then said, "I'll be over in fifteen minutes."

Actually it took him twelve. By then Cait had brewed a pot of coffee and made herself a peanut-butter-and-jelly sandwich. She hadn't eaten all day and was starved. She'd just finished the sandwich when Joe arrived.

"What about your luggage?" Joe asked, looking concerned. He didn't give her a chance to respond. "Exactly what do you mean, you gave your seat away?"

Cait explained as best she could. Even now she found herself surprised by her actions. Cait rarely behaved spontaneously. But something about that young soldier had reached deep within her heart and she'd reacted instinctively.

"The airline is sending my suitcase back to Seattle on the next available flight, so there's no need to worry," Cait said. "I talked to Martin, who was quick to tell me the Lord would reward my generosity."

"Are you going to catch a later flight, then?" Joe asked. He helped himself to a cup of coffee and pulled out the chair across from hers.

"There aren't any seats," Cait said. She leaned back, yawning, and covered her mouth. Why she should be so tired after sleeping away most of the afternoon was beyond her. "Besides, the office is short-staffed. Lindy gave Paul her notice and a trainee is coming in, which makes everything even more difficult. They can use me."

Joe frowned. "Giving up your vacation is one way to impress Paul."

Words of explanation crowded her tongue. She realized Joe wasn't insulting her; he was only stating a fact. What he didn't understand was that Cait hadn't thought of Paul once the entire day. Her staying or leaving had absolutely nothing to do with him.

If she'd been thinking of anyone, it was Joe. She knew now that giving up her seat to the marine hadn't been entirely unselfish. When Joe kissed her goodbye, her heart had started telegraphing messages she had yet to fully decode. The plain and honest truth was that she hadn't wanted to leave him. It was as if she really did belong with him....

That perception had been with her from the moment they'd parted at the airport. It had followed her in the taxi on the ride back to the apartment. Joe was the last person she'd thought of when she'd fallen asleep, and the first person she'd remembered when she awoke.

It was the most unbelievable thing.

"What are you going to do for Christmas?" Joe asked, still frowning into his coffee cup. For someone who'd seemed downright regretful that she was flying halfway across the country, he didn't seem all that pleased to be sharing her company now.

"I...haven't decided yet. I suppose I'll spend a quiet day by myself." She'd wake up late, indulge in a lazy scented bath, find something sinful for breakfast. Ice cream, maybe. Then she'd paint her toenails and settle down with a good book. The day would be lonely, true, but certainly not wasted.

"It'll be anything but quiet," Joe challenged.

"Oh?"

"You'll be spending it with me and my family."

"THIS IS THE first time Joe has ever brought a girl to join us for Christmas," Virginia Rockwell said as she set a large tray of freshly baked cinnamon rolls in the center of the huge kitchen table. She wiped her hands clean on the apron that was secured around her thick waist.

Cait felt she should explain. She was a little uncomfortable arriving unannounced with Joe like this. "Joe and I are just friends."

Mrs. Rockwell shook her head, which set the white curls bobbing. "I saw my son's eyes when he brought you into the house." She grinned knowingly. "I remember you from the old neighborhood, with your starched dresses and the pigtails with those bright pink ribbons. You were a pretty girl then and you're even prettier now."

"The starched dresses were me, all right," Cait confirmed. She'd been the only girl for blocks around who always wore dresses to school.

Joe's mother chuckled again. "I remember the sensation you caused in the neighborhood when you said Joe had kissed you." She chuckled, her eyes shining. "His father and I got quite a kick out of that. I still remember how furious Joe was when he learned his secret was out."

"I only told one person," Cait protested. But Betsy had told plenty of others, and the news had spread with alarming speed. However, Cait figured she'd since paid for her sins tenfold. Joe had made sure of that in the past few weeks.

"It's so good to see you again, Caitlin. When we've got a minute I want you to sit down and tell me all about your mother. We lost contact years ago, but I always thought she was a darling."

"I think so, too," Cait agreed, carrying a platter of scrambled eggs to the table. She did miss being with her family, but Joe's mother made it almost as good as being home. "I know that's how Mom feels about you, too. She'll want to thank you for being kind enough to invite me into your home for Christmas."

"I wouldn't have it any other way."

"I know." She glanced into the other room where Joe was sitting with his brother and sister-in-law. Her heart throbbed at the sight of him with his family. But these newfound feelings for Joe left her at a complete loss. What she'd told Mrs. Rockwell was true. Joe was her friend. The very best friend she'd ever had. She was grateful for everything he'd done for her since they'd chanced upon each other, just weeks ago, really. But their friendship was developing into something much stronger. If only she didn't feel so... so ardent about Paul. If only she didn't feel so confused!

Joe laughed at something one of his nephews said and Cait couldn't help smiling. She loved the sound of his laughter. It was vigorous and robust and lively—just like his personality.

"Joe says you're working as a stockbroker right here in Seattle."

"Yes. I've been with Webster, Rodale and Missen for over a year now. My degree was in accounting but—"

"Accounting?" Mrs. Rockwell nodded approvingly. "My Joe has his own accountant now. Good thing, too. His books were in a terrible mess. He's a builder, not a pencil pusher, that boy."

"Are you telling tales on me, Mom?" Joe asked as he sauntered into the kitchen. He picked up a piece of bacon and bit off the end. "When are we going to open the gifts? The kids are getting restless."

"The kids, nothing. You're the one who's eager to tear into those packages," his mother admonished. "We'll open them after breakfast, the way we do every Christmas."

Joe winked at Cait and disappeared into the living room once more.

Mrs. Rockwell watched her son affectionately. "Last year he shows up on my doorstep bright and early Christmas morning needing gift wrap. Then, once he's got all his presents wrapped, he walks into my kitchen—" her face crinkled in a wide grin "—and he sticks all those presents in my refrigerator." She smiled at the memory. "For his brother, he bought two canned hams and three gallons of ice cream. For me it was cat food and a couple of rib roasts."

Breakfast was a bustling affair, with Joe's younger brother, his wife and their children gathered around the table. Joe sat next to Cait and held her hand while his mother offered the blessing. Although she wasn't home with her own family, Cait felt she had a good deal for which to be thankful.

Conversation was pleasant and relaxed, but foremost on the children's minds was opening the gifts. The table was cleared and plates and bowls arranged inside the dishwasher in record time.

Cait sat beside Joe, holding a cup of coffee, as the oldest grandchild handed out the presents. While Christmas music played softly in the background, the children tore into their packages. The youngest, a two-year-old girl, was more interested in the box than in the gift itself.

When Joe came to the square package Cait had given him, he shook it enthusiastically.

"Be careful, it might break," she warned, knowing there was no chance of that happening.

Carefully he removed the bows, then unwrapped his gift. Cait watched expectantly as he lifted the book from the layers of bright paper. "A book on baseball?"

Cait nodded, smiling. "As I recall, you used to collect baseball cards."

"I ended up trading away my two favorites."

"I'm sure it was for a very good reason."

"Of course."

Their eyes held until it became apparent that everyone in the room was watching them. Cait glanced self-consciously away.

Joe cleared his throat. "This is a great gift, Cait. Thank you very much."

"You're welcome very much."

He leaned over and kissed her as if it was the most natural thing in the world. It felt right, their kiss. If anything, Cait was sorry to stop at one.

"Surely you have something for Cait," Virginia Rockwell prompted her son.

"You bet I do."

"He's probably keeping it in the refrigerator," Cait suggested, to the delight of Joe's family.

"Oh, ye of little faith," he said, removing a box from his shirt pocket.

"I recognize that paper," Sally, Joe's sister-in-law, murmured to Cait. "It's from Stanley's."

Cait's eyes widened at the name of an expensive local jewelry store. "Joe?"

"Go ahead and open it," he urged.

Cait did, hands fumbling in her eagerness. She slipped off the ribbon and peeled away the gold textured wrap to reveal a white jeweler's box. It contained a second box, a small black velvet one, which she opened very slowly. She gasped at the lovely cameo brooch inside.

"Oh, Joe," she whispered. It was a lovely piece carved in onyx and overlaid with ivory. She'd longed for a cameo, a really nice one, for years and wondered how Joe could possibly have known.

"You gonna kiss Uncle Joe?" his nephew, Charlie, asked, "'Cause if you are, I'm not looking."

"Of course she's going to kiss me," Joe answered for her. "Only she can do it later when there aren't so many curious people around." He glanced swiftly at his mother. "Just the way Mom used to thank Dad for her Christmas gift. Isn't that right, Mom?"

"I'm sure Cait…will," Virginia answered, clearly flustered. She patted her hand against the side of her head as though she feared the pins had fallen from her hair, her eyes downcast.

Cait didn't blame the older woman for being embarrassed, but one look at the cameo and she was willing to forgive Joe anything.

The day flew past. After the gifts were opened—with everyone exclaiming in surprised delight over the gifts Joe had bought, with Cait's help—the family gathered around the piano. Mrs. Rockwell played as they sang a variety of Christmas carols, their voices loud and cheerful. Joe's father had died several years earlier, but he was mentioned often throughout the day, with

affection and love. Cait hadn't known him well, but the family obviously felt
Andrew Rockwell's presence far more than his absence on this festive day.

Joe drove Cait back to her apartment late that night. Mrs. Rockwell had
insisted on sending a plate of cookies home with her, and Cait swore it was
enough goodies to last her a month of Sundays. Now she felt sleepy and
warm; leaning her head against the seat, she closed her eyes.

"We're here," Joe whispered close to her ear.

Reluctantly Cait opened her eyes and sighed. "I had such a wonderful
day. Thank you, Joe." She couldn't quite stifle a yawn as she reached for the
door handle, thinking longingly of bed.

"That's it?" He sounded disappointed.

"What do you mean, that's it?"

"I seem to remember a certain promise you made this morning."

Cait frowned, not sure she understood what he meant. "When?"

"When we were opening the gifts," he reminded her.

"Oh," Cait said, straightening. "You mean when I opened your gift to me
and saw the brooch."

Joe nodded with exaggerated emphasis. "Right. *Now* do you remember?"

"Of course." The kiss. He planned to claim the kiss she'd promised him.
She brushed her mouth quickly over his and grinned. "There."

"If that's the best you can do, you should've kissed me in front of Charlie."

"You're faulting my kissing ability?"

"Charlie's dog gives better kisses than that."

Cait felt more than a little insulted. "Is this a challenge, Joseph Rockwell?"

"Yes," he returned archly. "You're darn right it is."

"All right, then you're on." She set the plate of cookies aside, slid closer
and slipped her arms around Joe's neck. Next she wove her fingers into his
thick hair.

"This is more like it," Joe murmured contentedly.

Cait paused. She wasn't sure why. Perhaps because she'd suddenly lost
all interest in making fun out of something that had always been so wonderful between them.

Joe's eyes met hers, and the laughter and fun in them seemed to disappear. Slowly he expelled his breath and brushed his lips along her jaw. The
warmth of his breath was exciting as his mouth skimmed toward her temple. His arms closed around her waist and he pulled her tight against him.

Impatiently he began to kiss her, introducing her to a world of warm,
thrilling sensations. His mouth then explored the curve of her neck. It felt

so good that Cait closed her eyes and experienced a curious weightlessness she'd never known—a heightened awareness of physical longing.

"Oh, Cait…" He broke away from her, his breathing labored and heavy. She knew instinctively that he wanted to say more, but he changed his mind and buried his face in her hair, exhaling sharply.

"How am I doing?" she whispered once she found her voice.

"Just fine."

"Are you ready to retract your statement?"

He hesitated. "I don't know. Convince me again." So she did, her kiss moist and gentle, her heart fluttering against her ribs.

"Is that good enough?" she asked when she'd recovered her breath.

Joe nodded, as though he didn't quite trust his own voice. "Excellent."

"I had a wonderful day," she whispered. "I can't thank you enough for including me."

Joe shook his head lightly. There seemed to be so much more he wanted to say to her and couldn't. Cait slipped out of the car and walked into her building, turning on the lights when she entered her apartment. She slowly put away her things, wanting to wrap this feeling around her like a warm quilt. Minutes later, she glanced out her window to see Joe still sitting in his car, his hands gripping the steering wheel, his head bent. It looked to Cait as though he was battling with himself to keep from following her inside. She would have welcomed him if he had.

CHAPTER NINE

CAIT STARED AT the computer screen for several minutes, blind to the information in front of her. Deep in thought, she released a long, slow breath.

Paul had been grateful to see her when she'd shown up at the office that morning. The week between Christmas and New Year's could be a harried one. Lindy had looked surprised, then quickly retreated into her own office after exchanging a brief good-morning and little else. Her friend's behavior continued to baffle Cait, but she couldn't concentrate on Lindy's problems just now, or even on her work.

No matter what she did, Cait couldn't stop thinking about Joe and the kisses they'd exchanged Christmas evening. Nor could she forget his tortured look as he'd sat in his car after she'd gone into her apartment. Even now she wasn't certain why she hadn't immediately run back outside. And by the time she'd decided to do that, he was gone.

Cait was so absorbed in her musings that she barely heard the knock at her office door. Guiltily she glanced up to find Paul standing just inside her doorway, his hands in his pockets, his eyes weary.

"Paul!" Cait waited for her heart to trip into double time the way it usually did whenever she was anywhere near him. It didn't, which was a relief but no longer much of a surprise.

"Hello, Cait." His smile was uneven, his face tight. He seemed ill at ease and struggling to disguise it. "Have you got a moment?"

"Sure. Come on in." She stood and motioned toward her client chair. "What can I do for you?"

"Nothing much," he said vaguely, sitting down. "Uh, I just wanted you to know how pleased I am that you're here. I'm sorry you canceled your vacation, but I appreciate your coming in today. Especially in light of the fact that Lindy will be leaving." His mouth thinned briefly.

No one, other than Joe and Martin, was aware of the real reason Cait wasn't in Minnesota the way she'd planned. Nor had she suggested to Paul that she'd changed her plans to help him out because they'd be short-staffed; obviously he'd drawn his own conclusions.

"So Lindy's decided to follow through with her resignation?"

Paul nodded, then frowned anew. "Nothing I say will change her mind. That woman's got a stubborn streak as wide as a..." He shrugged, apparently unable to come up with an appropriate comparison.

"The construction project's nearly finished," Cait offered, making small talk rather than joining in his criticism of Lindy. Absently she stood up and wandered around her office, stopping to straighten the large Christmas wreath on her door, the one she and Lindy had put up earlier in the month. Lindy was her friend and she wasn't about to agree with Paul, or argue with him, for that matter. Actually she should've been pleased that Paul had sought her out, but she felt curiously indifferent. And she did have work she needed to do.

"Yes, I'm delighted with the way everything's turned out," Paul said, "Joe Rockwell's done a fine job. His reputation is excellent and I imagine he'll be one of the big-time contractors in the area within the next few years."

Cait nodded casually, hoping she'd concealed the thrill of excitement that had surged through her at the mention of Joe's name. She didn't need Paul to tell her Joe's future was bright; she could see that for herself. At Christmas, his mother had boasted freely about his success. Joe had recently received a contract for a large government project—his most important to date—and she was extremely proud of him. He might have trouble keeping his books straight, but he left his customers satisfied. If he worked as hard at satisfying them as he did at finding the right Christmas tree, Cait could well believe he was gaining a reputation for excellence.

"Well, listen," Paul said, drawing in a deep breath, "I won't keep you." His eyes were clouded as he stood and headed toward the door. He hesitated, turning back to face her. "I don't suppose you'd be free for dinner tonight, would you?"

"Dinner," Cait repeated as though she'd never heard the word before. Paul was inviting her to dinner? After all these months? Now, when she least expected it? Now, when it no longer mattered? After all the times she'd ached to the bottom of her heart for some attention from him, he was finally asking her out on a date? Now?

"That is, if you're free."

"Uh...yes, sure...that would be nice."

"Great. How about if I pick you up around five-thirty? Unless that's too early for you?"

"Five-thirty will be fine."

"I'll see you then."

"Thanks, Paul." Cait felt numb. There wasn't any other way to describe it. It was as if her dreams were finally beginning to play themselves out—too late. Paul, whom she'd loved from afar for so long, wanted to take her to dinner. She should be dancing around the office with glee, or at least feeling something other than this peculiar dull sensation in the pit of her stomach. If this was such a significant, exciting, hoped-for event, why didn't she feel any of the exhilaration she'd expected?

After taking a moment to collect her thoughts, Cait walked down the hallway to Lindy's office and found her friend on the phone. Lindy glanced up, smiled feebly in Cait's direction, then abruptly dropped her gaze as if the call demanded her full concentration.

Cait waited a couple of minutes, then decided to return later when Lindy wasn't so busy. She needed to talk to her friend, needed her counsel. Lindy had always encouraged Cait in her dreams of a relationship with Paul. When she was discouraged, it was Lindy who bolstered her sagging spirits. Yes, it was definitely time for a talk. She'd try to get Lindy to confide in her, too. Cait valued Lindy's friendship; true, she couldn't help being hurt that the person she considered one of her best friends would give notice to leave the firm without even discussing it with her. But Lindy must've had her reasons. And maybe she, too, needed some support right about now.

Hearing her own phone ring, Cait hurried back to her office. She was consistantly busy from then on. The New York Stock Exchange was due to close in a matter of minutes when Joe happened by.

"Hi," Cait greeted him, her smile wide and welcoming. Her gaze connected with Joe's and he returned her smile. Her heart reacted automatically, leaping with sheer happiness.

"Hi, yourself." He sauntered into her office and threw himself down in the same chair Paul had taken earlier, stretching his long legs in front of him and folding his hands over his stomach. "So how's the world of finance doing this fine day?"

"About as well as usual."

"Then we're in deep trouble," he joked.

His smile was infectious. It always had been, but Cait had initially resisted him. Her defenses had weakened, though, and she responded readily with a smile of her own.

"You done for the day?"

"Just about." She checked the time. In another five minutes, New York would be closing down. There were several items she needed to clear from her desk, but nothing pressing. "Why?"

"Why?" It was little short of astonishing how far Joe's eyebrows could reach, Cait noted, all but disappearing into his hairline.

"Can't a man ask a simple question?" Joe asked.

"Of course." The banter between them was like a well-rehearsed play. Never had Cait been more at ease with a man—or had more fun with a man. Or with anyone, really. "What I want to know is whether 'simple' refers to the question or to the man asking it."

"Ouch," Joe said, grinning broadly. "Those claws are sharp this afternoon."

"Actually today's been good." Or at least it had since he'd arrived.

"I'm glad to hear it. How about dinner?" He jumped to his feet and pretended to waltz around her office, playing a violin. "You and me. Wine and moonlight and music. Romance and roses." He wiggled his eyebrows at her suggestively. "You work too hard. You always have. I want you to enjoy life a little more. It would be good for both of us."

Joe didn't need to give her an incentive to go out with him. Cait was thrilled at the mere idea. Joe made her laugh, made her feel good about herself and the world. Of course, he possessed a remarkable talent for driving her crazy, too. But she supposed a little craziness was good for the spirit.

"Only promise me you won't wear those high heels of yours," he chided, pressing his hand to the small of his back. "I've suffered excruciating back pains ever since Paul's Christmas party."

Paul's name seemed to leap out and grab Cait by the throat. "Paul," she repeated, sagging against the back of her chair. "Oh, dear."

"I know you consider him a dear," Joe teased. "What has your stalwart employer done this time?"

"He asked me out to dinner," Cait admitted, frowning. "Out of the blue this morning he popped into my office and invited me to dinner as if we'd been dating for months. I was so stunned, I didn't know what to think."

"What did you tell him?" Joe seemed to consider the whole thing a huge joke. "Wait—" he held up his hand "—you don't need to answer that. I already know. You sprang at the offer."

"I didn't exactly spring," she said, somewhat offended by Joe's attitude. The least he could do was show a little concern. She'd spent Christmas with him, and according to his own mother this was the first time he'd ever brought a woman home for the holiday. Furthermore, despite his insisting to all and sundry that they were married, he certainly didn't seem to mind her seeing another man.

"I'll bet you nearly went into shock." A smile trembled at the edges of his mouth as if he was picturing her reaction to Paul's invitation and finding it all terribly entertaining.

"I did not go into shock." She defended herself heatedly. She'd been taken by surprise, that was all.

"Listen," he said, walking toward the door, "have a great time. I'll catch you later." With that he was gone.

Cait couldn't believe it. Her mouth dropped open and she paced frantically, clenching and unclenching her fists. It took her a full minute to recover enough to run after him.

Joe was talking to his foreman, the same stocky man he'd been with the day he followed Cait into the elevator.

"Excuse me," she said, interrupting their conversation, "but when you're finished I'd like a few words with you, Joe." Her back was ramrod stiff and she kept flexing her hands as though preparing for a fight.

Joe glanced at his watch. "It might be a while."

"Then might I have a few minutes of your time now?"

The foreman stepped away, his step cocky. "You want me to dismiss the crew again, boss? I can tell them to go out and buy New Year's presents for their wives, if you like."

The man was rewarded with a look that was hot enough to barbecue spareribs. "That won't be necessary, thanks, anyway, Harry."

"You're welcome, boss. We serve to please."

"Then please me by kindly shutting up."

Harry chuckled and returned to another section of the office.

"You wanted something?" Joe asked.

Boy, did she. "Is that all you're going to say?"

"About what?"

"About my going to dinner with Paul? I expected you to be... I don't know, upset."

"Why should I be upset? Is he going to have his way with you? I sincerely doubt it, but if you're worried, invite me along and I'll be more than happy to protect your honor."

"What's the matter with you?" she demanded, not bothering to disguise her fury and disappointment. She stared at Joe, waiting for him to mock her again, but once more he surprised her. His gaze sobered.

"You honestly expect me to be jealous?"

"Not jealous exactly," she said, although he wasn't far from the truth. "Concerned."

"I'm not. Paul's a good man."

"I know, but—"

"You've been in love with him for months—"

"I think it was more of an infatuation."

"True. But he's finally asked you out, and you've accepted."

"Yes, but—"

"We know each other well, Cait. We were married, remember?"

"I'm not likely to forget it." Especially when Joe took pains to point it out at every opportunity. "Shouldn't that mean...something?" Cait was embarrassed she'd said that. For weeks she'd suffered acute mortification every time Joe mentioned the childhood stunt. Now she was using it to suit her own purposes.

Joe took hold of her shoulders. "As a matter of fact, our marriage means a lot to me. Because I care about you, Cait."

Hearing Joe admit as much was gratifying.

"I want only the best for you," he continued. "It's what you deserve. All I can say is that I'd be more than pleased if everything worked out between you and Paul. Now if you'll excuse me, I need to talk something over with Harry."

"Oh, right, sure, go ahead." She couldn't seem to get the words out fast enough. When she'd called Martin to explain why she wouldn't be in Minnesota for Christmas, he'd claimed that God would reward her sacrifice. If Paul's invitation to dinner was God's reward, she wanted her airline ticket back.

The numb feeling returned as Cait returned to her office. She didn't know what to think. She'd believed...she'd hoped that she and Joe shared a very special feeling. Clearly their times together meant something entirely different to him than they had to her. Otherwise he wouldn't behave so casually about her going out with Paul. And he certainly wouldn't seem so pleased about it!

That was what hurt Cait the most, and yes, she was hurt. It had taken her several minutes to identify her feelings, but now she knew...

More by accident than design, Cait walked into Lindy's office. Her friend had already put on her coat and was closing her briefcase, ready to leave the office.

"Paul asked me to dinner," Cait blurted out.

"He did?" Lindy's eyes widened with astonishment. But she didn't turn it into a joke, the way Joe had.

Cait nodded. "He just strolled in as if it was nothing out of the ordinary and asked me to have dinner with him."

"Are you happy about it?"

"I don't know," Cait answered honestly. "I suppose I should be pleased. It's what I'd prayed would happen for months."

"Then what's the problem?" Lindy asked.

"Joe doesn't seem to care. He said he hopes everything works out the way I want it to."

"Which is?" Lindy pressed.

Cait had to think about that a moment, her heart in her throat. "Honest to heaven, Lindy, I don't know anymore."

"I UNDERSTAND THE salmon here is superb," Paul was saying, reading over the Boathouse menu. It was a well-known restaurant on Lake Union.

Cait scanned the list of entrées, which featured fresh seafood, then chose the grilled salmon—the same dish she'd ordered that night with Joe. Tonight, though, she wasn't sure why she was even bothering. She wasn't hungry, and Paul was going to be wasting good money while she made a pretense of enjoying her meal.

"I understand you've been seeing a lot of Joe Rockwell," he said conversationally.

That Paul should mention Joe's name right now was ironic. Cait hadn't stopped thinking about him from the moment he'd dropped into her office earlier that afternoon. Their conversation had left a bitter taste in her mouth. She'd sincerely believed their relationship was developing into something... special. Yet Joe had gone out of his way to give her the opposite impression.

"Cait?" Paul stared at her.

"I'm sorry, what were you saying?"

"Simply that you and Joe Rockwell have been seeing a lot of each other recently."

"Uh, yes. As you know, we were childhood friends," she murmured. "Actually Joe and my older brother were best friends. Then Joe's family moved to the suburbs and our families lost contact."

"Yes, I remember you mentioned that."

The waitress came for their order, and Paul requested a bottle of white wine. Then he chatted amicably for several minutes, bringing up subjects of shared interest from the office.

Cait listened attentively, nodding from time to time or adding the occasional comment. Now that she had his undivided attention, Cait wondered what it was about Paul that she'd found so extraordinary. He was attractive, but not nearly as dynamic or exciting as she found Joe. True, Paul possessed a certain charm, but compared to Joe, he was subdued and perhaps even a little dull. Cait couldn't imagine her stalwart boss carrying her piggyback out the back door because her high heels were too tight. Nor could she see Paul bantering with her the way Joe did.

The waitress delivered the wine, opened the bottle and poured them each a glass, once Paul had given his approval. Their dinners followed shortly afterward. After taking a bite or two of her delicious salmon, Cait noticed that Paul hadn't touched his meal. If anything, he seemed restless.

He rolled the stem of the wineglass between his fingers, watching the wine swirl inside. Then he suddenly blurted out, "What do you think of Lindy's leaving the firm?"

Cait was taken aback by the fervor in his voice when he mentioned Lindy's name. "Frankly I was shocked," Cait said. "Lindy and I have been good friends for a couple of years now." There'd been a time when the two had done nearly everything together. The summer before, they'd vacationed in Mexico and returned to Seattle with enough handwoven baskets and bulky blankets to set up shop themselves.

"Lindy's resigning came as a surprise to you, then?"

"Yes, this whole thing caught me completely unawares. Lindy didn't even mention the other job offer to me. I always thought we were good friends."

"Lindy *is* your friend," Paul said with enough conviction to persuade the patrons at the nearby tables. "You wouldn't believe what a good friend she is."

"I...know that." But friends sometimes had surprises up their sleeves. Lindy was a good example of that, and apparently so was Joe.

"I find Lindy an exceptional woman," Paul commented, watching Cait closely.

"She's probably one of the best stockbrokers in the business," Cait said, taking a sip of her wine.

"My...admiration for her goes beyond her keen business mind."

"Oh, mine, too," Cait was quick to agree. Lindy was the kind of friend who would trudge through the blazing sun of Mexico looking for a conch shell because she knew Cait really wanted to take one home. And Lindy had listened to countless hours of Cait's bemoaning her sorry fate of unrequited love for Paul.

"She's a wonderful woman."

Joe was wonderful, too, Cait thought. So wonderful her heart ached at his indifference when she'd announced she would be dining with Paul.

"Lindy's the kind of woman a man could treasure all his life," Paul went on.

"I couldn't agree with you more," Cait said. Now, if only Joe would realize what a treasure *she* was. He'd married her once—well, sort of—and surely the possibility of spending their lives together had crossed his mind in the past few weeks.

Paul hesitated as though at a loss for words. "I don't suppose you've given any thought to the reason Lindy made this unexpected decision to resign?"

Frankly Cait hadn't. Her mind and her heart had been so full of Joe that deciphering her friend's actions had somehow escaped her. "She received a better offer, didn't she?" Which was understandable. Lindy would be an asset to any firm.

It was then that Cait understood. Paul hadn't asked her to dinner out of any desire to develop a romantic relationship with her. He saw her as a means of discovering what had prompted Lindy to resign. This new awareness came as a relief, a burden lifted from her shoulders. Paul wasn't interested in her. He never had been and probably never would be. A few weeks ago, that realization would have been a crushing defeat, but all Cait experienced now was an overwhelming sense of gratitude.

"I'm sure if you talk to Lindy, she might reconsider," Cait suggested.

"I've tried, trust me. But there's a problem."

"Oh?" Now that Cait had sampled the salmon, she discovered it to be truly delicious. She hadn't realized how hungry she was.

"Cait, look at me," Paul said, raising his voice slightly. His face was pinched, his eyes intense. "Damn, but you've made this nearly impossible."

She looked up at him, her face puzzled. "What is it, Paul?"

"You have no idea, do you? I swear you've got to be the most obtuse woman in the world." He pushed aside his plate and briefly closed his eyes, shaking his head. "I'm in love with Lindy. I have been for weeks...months. But for the life of me I couldn't get her to notice me. I swear I did everything but turn cartwheels in her office. It finally dawned on me why she wasn't responding."

"Me?" Cait asked in a feeble, mouselike squeak.

"Exactly. She didn't want to betray your friendship. Then one afternoon—I think it was the day you first recognized Joe—we, Lindy and I, were in my office and— Oh, hell, I don't know how it happened, but Lindy was looking something up for me and she stumbled over one of the cords the construction crew was using. Fortunately I was able to catch her before she fell to the floor. I know it wasn't her fault, but I was so angry, afraid she might have been hurt. Lindy was just as angry with me for being angry with her, and it seemed the only way to shut her up was to kiss her. That was the beginning and I swear to you everything exploded in our faces at that moment."

Cait swallowed, fascinated by the story. "Go on."

"I tried for days to get her to agree to go out with me. But she kept refusing until I demanded to know why."

"She told you...how I felt about you?" The thought was mortifying.

"Of course not. Lindy's too good a friend to divulge your confidence. Besides, she didn't need to tell me. I've known all along. Good grief, Cait, what did I have to do to discourage you? Hire a skywriter?"

"I don't think anything that drastic was necessary," she muttered, humiliated to her very bones.

"I repeatedly told Lindy I wasn't attracted to you, but she wouldn't listen. Finally she told me if I'd talk to you, explain everything myself, she'd agree to go out with me."

"The phone call," Cait said with sudden comprehension. "That was the reason you called me, wasn't it? You wanted to talk about Lindy, not that business article."

"Yes." He looked deeply grateful for her insight, late though it was.

"Well, for heaven's sake, why didn't you?"

"Believe me, I've kicked myself a dozen times since. I wish I knew. I suppose it seemed heartless to have such a frank discussion over the phone. Again and again, I promised myself I'd say something. Lord knows I dropped enough hints, but you weren't exactly receptive."

She winced. "But why is Lindy resigning?"

"Isn't it obvious?" Paul asked. "It was becoming increasingly difficult for us to work together. She didn't want to betray her best friend, but at the same time..."

"But at the same time you two were falling in love."

"Exactly. I can't lose her, Cait. I don't want to hurt your feelings, and believe me, it's nothing personal—you're a trustworthy employee and a decent person—but I'm simply not attracted to you."

Paul didn't seem to be the only one. Other than treating their relationship like one big joke, Joe hadn't ever claimed any romantic feelings for her, either.

"I had to do something before I lost Lindy."

"I agree completely."

"You're not angry with her, are you?"

"Good heavens, no," Cait said, offering him a brave smile.

"We both thought something was developing between you and Joe Rockwell. Like I said, you seemed to be seeing quite a bit of each other, and then at the Christmas party—"

"Don't remind me," Cait said with a low groan.

Paul's face creased in a spontaneous smile. "Joe certainly has a wit about him, doesn't he?"

Cait gave a resigned nod.

Now that Paul had cleared the air, he seemed to develop an appetite. He reached for his dinner and ate heartily. By contrast, Cait's salmon had lost its appeal. She stared down at her plate, wondering how she could possibly make it through the rest of the evening.

She did, though, quite nicely. Paul didn't even seem to notice that anything was amiss. It wasn't that Cait was distressed by his confession. If anything, she was relieved at this turn of events and delighted that Lindy had fallen in love. Paul was obviously crazy about her; she'd never seen him more animated than when he was discussing Lindy. It still shocked Cait that she'd been so unperceptive about Lindy's real feelings. Not to mention Paul's...

Paul dropped her off at her building and saw her to the front door. "I can't thank you enough for understanding," he said, his voice warm. Impulsively he hugged her, then hurried back to his sports car.

Although she was certainly guilty of being obtuse, Cait knew exactly where Paul was headed. No doubt Lindy would be waiting for him, eager to hear the details of their conversation. Cait planned to talk to her friend herself, first thing in the morning.

Cait's apartment was dark and lonely. So lonely the silence seemed to echo off the walls. She hung up her coat before turning on the lights, her thoughts as dark as the room had been.

She made herself a cup of tea. Then she sat on the sofa, tucking her feet beneath her as she stared unseeing at the walls, assessing her options. They seemed terribly limited.

Paul was in love with Lindy. And Joe... Cait had no idea where she stood with him. For all she knew—

Her thoughts were interrupted by the phone. She answered on the second ring.

"Cait?" It was Joe and he seemed surprised to find her back so early. "When did you get in?"

"A few minutes ago."

"You don't sound like yourself. Is anything wrong?"

"No," she said, breaking into sobs. "What could possibly be wrong?"

CHAPTER TEN

THE FLOW OF emotion took Cait by storm. She'd had no intention of crying; in fact, the thought hadn't even entered her mind. One moment she was sitting there, contemplating the evening's revelations, and the next she was sobbing hysterically into the phone.

"Cait?"

"Oh," she wailed. "This is all your fault in the first place." Cait didn't know what made her say that. The words had slipped out before she'd realized it.

"What happened?"

"Nothing. I... I can't talk to you now. I'm going to bed." With that, she gently replaced the receiver. Part of her hoped Joe would call back, but the telephone remained stubbornly silent. She stared at it for several minutes. Apparently Joe didn't care if he talked to her or not.

The tears continued to flow. They remained a mystery to Cait. She wasn't a woman given to bouts of crying, but now that she'd started she couldn't seem to stop.

She changed out of her dress and into a pair of sweats, pausing halfway through to wash her face.

Sniffling and hiccuping, she sat on the end of her bed and dragged a shuddering breath through her lungs. Crying like this made no sense whatsoever.

Paul was in love with Lindy. At one time, the news would have devastated her, but not now. Cait felt a tingling happiness that her best friend had found a man to love. And the infatuation she'd held for Paul couldn't compare with the strength of her love for Joe.

Love.

There, she'd admitted it. She was in love with Joe. The man who told restaurant employees that she was suffering from amnesia. The man who walked into elevators and announced to total strangers that they were married. Yet this was the same man who hadn't revealed a minute's concern about her dating Paul Jamison.

Joe was also the man who'd gently held her hand through a children's movie. The man who made a practice of kissing her senseless. The man who'd held her in his arms Christmas night as though he never intended to let her go.

Joseph Rockwell was a fun-loving jokester who took delight in teasing her. He was also tender and thoughtful and loving—the man who'd captured her heart only to drop it so carelessly.

Her doorbell chimed and she didn't need to look in the peephole to know it was Joe. But she felt panicky all of a sudden, too confused and vulnerable to see him now.

She walked slowly to the door and opened it a crack.

"What the hell is going on?" Joe demanded, not waiting for an invitation to march inside.

Cait wiped her eyes on her sleeve and shut the door. "Nothing."

"Did Paul try anything?"

She rolled her eyes. "Of course not."

"Then why are you crying?" He stood in the middle of her living room, fists planted on his hips as if he'd welcome the opportunity to punch out her boss.

If Cait knew why she was crying nonstop like this, she would have answered him. She opened her mouth, hoping some intelligent reason would emerge, but the only thing that came out was a low-pitched moan. Joe was gazing at her in complete confusion. "I... Paul's in love."

"With *you?*" His voice rose half an octave with disbelief.

"Don't make it sound like such an impossibility," she said crossly. "I'm reasonably attractive, you know." If she was expecting Joe to list her myriad charms, Cait was disappointed.

Instead, his frown darkened. "So what's Paul being in love got to do with anything?"

"Absolutely nothing. I wished him and Lindy the very best."

"So it is Lindy?" Joe murmured as though he'd known it all along.

"You didn't honestly think it was me, did you?"

"Hell, how was I supposed to know? I *thought* it was Lindy, but it was you he was taking to dinner. Frankly it didn't make a whole lot of sense to me."

"Which is something else," Cait grumbled, standing so close to him, their faces were only inches apart. Her hands were on her hips, her pose mirroring his. It occurred to Cait that they resembled a pair of gunslingers ready for a shootout. "I want to know one thing. Every time I turn around, you're telling anyone and everyone who'll listen that we're married. But when it really matters you—"

"When did it really matter?"

Cait ignored the question, thinking the answer was obvious. "You casually turn me over to Paul as if you can't wait to be rid of me. Obviously you couldn't have cared less."

"I cared," he shouted.

"Oh, right," she shouted back, "but if that was the case, you certainly didn't bother to show it!"

"What was I supposed to do, challenge him to a duel?"

He was being ridiculous, Cait decided, and she refused to take the bait. The more they talked, the more unreasonable they were both becoming.

"I thought dating Paul was what you wanted," he complained. "You talked about it long enough. Paul this and Paul that. He'd walk past and you'd all but swoon."

"That's not the least bit true." Maybe it had been at one time, but not now and not for weeks. "If you'd taken the trouble to ask me, you might have learned the truth."

"You mean you don't love Paul?"

Cait rolled her eyes again. "Bingo."

"It isn't like you to be so sarcastic."

"It isn't like you to be so...awful."

He seemed to mull that over for a moment. "If we're going to be throwing out accusations," he said tightly, "then maybe you should take a look at yourself."

"What exactly do you mean by that?" As usual, no one could get a reaction out of Cait more effectively than Joe. "Never mind," she answered, walking to the door. "This discussion isn't getting us anywhere. All we seem capable of doing is hurling insults at each other."

"I disagree," Joe answered calmly. "I think it's time we cleared the air."

She took a deep breath, feeling physically and emotionally deflated.

"Joe, it'll have to wait. I'm in no condition to be rational right now and I don't want either of us saying things we'll regret." She held open her door for him. "Please?"

He seemed about to argue with her, then he sighed and dropped a quick kiss on her mouth. Wide-eyed, she watched him leave.

LINDY WAS WAITING in Cait's office early the next morning, holding two cups of freshly brewed coffee. Her eyes were vulnerable as Cait entered the office. They stared at each other for a long moment.

"Are you angry with me?" Lindy whispered. She handed Cait one of the cups as an apparent peace offering.

"Of course not," Cait murmured. She put down her briefcase and accepted the cup, which she placed carefully on her desk. Then she gave Lindy a reassuring hug, and the two of them sat down for their much-postponed talk.

"Why didn't you tell me?" Cait burst out.

"I wanted to," Lindy said earnestly. "I had to stop myself a hundred times. The worst part of it was the guilt—knowing you were in love with Paul, and loving him myself."

Cait wasn't sure how she would have reacted to the truth, but she preferred to think she would've understood, and wished Lindy well. It wasn't as though Lindy had stolen Paul away from her.

"I don't think I realized how I felt," Lindy continued, "until one afternoon when I tripped over a stupid cord and fell into Paul's arms. From there, everything sort of snowballed."

"Paul told me."

"He…told you about that afternoon?"

Cait grinned and nodded. "I found the story wildly romantic."

"You don't mind?" Lindy watched her closely as if half-afraid of Cait's reaction even now.

"I think it's wonderful."

Lindy's smile was filled with warmth and excitement. "I never knew being in love could be so exciting, but at the same time cause so much pain."

"Amen to that," Cait stated emphatically.

Her words shot like live bullets into the room. If Cait could have reached out and pulled them back, she would have.

"Is it Joe Rockwell?" Lindy asked softly.

Cait nodded, then shook her head. "See how much he's confused me?" She made a sound that was half sob, half giggle. "Sometimes that man infuriates me so much I want to scream. Or cry." Cait had always thought of herself as a sane and sensible person. She lived a quiet life, worked hard at her job, enjoyed traveling and crossword puzzles. Then she'd bumped into Joe. Suddenly she found herself demanding piggyback rides, talking to strangers in elevators and seeking out phantom women at Christmas parties while downing spiked punch like it was soda pop.

"But then at other times?" Lindy prompted.

"At other times I love him so much I hurt all the way through. I love everything about him. Even those loony stunts of his. In fact, I usually laugh as hard as everyone else. Even if I don't always want him to know it."

"So what's going to happen with you two?" Lindy asked. She took a sip of coffee and as she did, Cait caught a flash of diamond.

"Lindy?" Cait demanded, jumping out of her seat. "What's that on your finger?"

Lindy's face broke into a smile so bright Cait was nearly blinded. "You noticed."

"Of course I did."

"It's from Paul. After he had dinner with you, he came over to my apartment. We talked for hours and then...he asked me to marry him. At first I didn't know what to say. It seems so soon. We...we hardly know each other."

"Good grief, you've worked together for ages."

"I know," Lindy said with a shy smile. "That's what Paul told me. It didn't take him long to convince me. He had the ring all picked out. Isn't it beautiful?"

"Oh, Lindy." The diamond was a lovely solitaire set in a wide band of gold. The style and shape were perfect for Lindy's long, elegant finger.

"I didn't know if I should wear it until you and I had talked, but I couldn't make myself take it off this morning."

"Of course you should wear it!" The fact that Paul had been carrying it around when he'd had dinner with her didn't exactly flatter Cait's ego, but she was so thrilled for Lindy that seemed a minor concern.

Lindy splayed her fingers out in front of her to better show off the ring. "When he slipped it on my finger, I swear it was the most romantic moment of my life. Before I knew it, tears were streaming down my face. I still don't understand why I started crying. I think Paul was as surprised as I was."

There must have been something in the air that reduced susceptible females to tears, Cait decided. Whatever it was had certainly affected her.

"Now you've sidetracked me," Lindy said, looking up from her diamond, her gaze dreamy. "You were telling me about you and Joe."

"I was?"

"Yes, you were," Lindy insisted.

"There's nothing to tell. If there was, you'd be the first person to hear. I know," she admitted before her friend could bring up the point, "we have seen a lot of each other recently, but I don't think it meant anything to Joe. When he found out Paul had invited me to dinner, he seemed downright delighted."

"I'm sure it was all an act."

Cait shrugged. She wished she could believe that. Oh, how she wished it.

"You're sure you're in love with him?" Lindy asked hesitantly.

Cait nodded and lowered her eyes. It hurt to think about Joe. Everything was a game to him——a big joke. Lindy had been right about one thing, though. Love was the most wonderful experience of her life. And the most painful.

THE NEW YORK Stock Exchange had closed and Cait was punching some figures into her computer when Joe strode into her office and closed the door.

"Feel free to come in," she muttered, continuing her work. Her heart was pounding but she dared not let him know the effect he had on her.

"I will make myself at home, thank you," he answered cheerfully, ignoring her sarcasm. He pulled out a chair and sat down expansively, resting one ankle on the opposite knee and relaxing as if he was in a movie theater, waiting for the main feature to begin.

"If you're here to discuss business, might I suggest investing in blue-chip stocks? They're always a safe bet." Cait went on typing, doing her best to ignore Joe——which was nearly impossible, although she gave an Oscar-winning performance, if she did say so herself.

"I'm here to talk business, all right," Joe said, "but it has nothing to do with the stock market."

"What business could the two of us possibly have?" she asked, her voice deliberately ironic.

"I want to resume the discussion we were having last night."

"Perhaps you do, but unfortunately that was last night and this is now." How confident she sounded, Cait thought, mildly pleased with herself. "I can do without hearing you list my no doubt numerous flaws."

"Your being my wife is what I want to talk about."

"Your wife?" She wished he'd quit throwing the subject at her as if it meant something to him. Something other than a joke.

"Yes, my wife." He gave a short laugh. "Believe me, it isn't your flaws I'm here to discuss."

Despite everything, Cait's heart raced. She reached for a stack of papers and switched them from one basket to another. Her entire filing system was probably in jeopardy, but she needed some activity to occupy her hands before she stood up and reached out to Joe. She did stand then, but it was to remove a large silver bell strung from a red velvet ribbon hanging in her office window.

"Paul and Lindy are getting married," he said next.

"Yes, I know. Lindy and I had a long talk this morning." She took the wreath off her door next.

"I take it the two of you are friends again?"

"We were never not friends," Cait answered stiffly, stuffing the wreath, the bell and the three ceramic wise men into the bottom drawer of her filing cabinet. Hard as she tried to prevent it, she could feel her defenses crumbling. "Lindy's asked me to be her maid of honor and I've agreed."

"Will you return the favor?"

It took a moment for the implication to sink in, and even then Cait wasn't sure she should follow the trail Joe seemed to be forging through this conversation. She leaned forward and rested her hands on the edge of the desk.

"I'm destined to be an old maid," she said flippantly, although she couldn't help feeling a sliver of real hope.

"You'll never be that."

Cait was hoping he'd say her beauty would make her irresistible, or that her warmth and wit and intelligence were sure to attract a dozen suitors. Instead he said the very thing she could have predicted. "We're already married, so you don't need to worry about being a spinster."

Cait released a sigh of impatience. "I wish you'd give up on that, Joe. It's growing increasingly old."

"As I recall, we celebrated our eighteenth anniversary not long ago."

"Don't be ridiculous. All right," she said, straightening abruptly. If he wanted to play games, then she'd respond in kind. "Since we're married, I want a family."

"Hey, sweetheart," he cried, throwing his arms in the air, "that's music to my ears. I'm willing."

Cait prepared to leave the office, if not the building. "Somehow I knew you would be."

"Two or three," he interjected, then chuckled and added, "I suppose we should name the first two Ken and Barbie."

Cait's scowl made him chuckle even louder.

"If you prefer, we'll leave the names open to negotiation," he said.

"Of all the colossal nerve..." Cait muttered, moving to the window and gazing out.

"If you want daughters, I've got no objection, but from what I understand that's not really up to us."

Cait turned around, crossing her arms. "Correct me if I'm wrong," she said coldly, certain he'd delight in doing so. "But you did just ask me to marry you. Could you confirm that?"

"All I want is to make legal what's already been done."

Cait sighed in exasperation. Was he serious, or wasn't he? He was talking about marriage, about joining their lives, as if he were planning a bid on a construction project.

"When Paul asked Lindy to marry him, he had a diamond ring."

"I was going to buy you a ring," Joe said emphatically. "I still am. But I thought you'd want to pick it out yourself. If you wanted a diamond, why didn't you say so? I'll buy you the whole store if that'll make you happy."

"One ring will suffice, thank you."

"Pick out two or three. I understand diamonds are an excellent investment."

"Not so fast," she said, holding out her arm. It was vital she maintain some distance between them. If Joe kissed her or started talking about having children again, they might never get the facts clear.

"Not so fast?" he repeated incredulously. "Honey, I've been waiting eighteen years to discuss this. You're not going to ruin everything now, are you?" He advanced a couple of steps toward her.

"I'm not agreeing to anything until you explain yourself." For every step he took toward her, Cait retreated two.

"About what?" Joe was frowning, which wasn't a good sign.

"Paul."

His eyelids slammed shut, then slowly rose. "I don't understand why that man's name has to come into every conversation you and I have."

Cait decided it was better to ignore that comment. "You haven't even told me you love me."

"I love you." He actually sounded annoyed, as if she'd insisted on having the obvious reiterated.

"You might say it with a little more feeling," Cait suggested.

"If you want feeling, come here and let me kiss you."

"No."

"Why not?" By now they'd completely circled her desk. "We're talking serious things here. Trust me, sweetheart, a man doesn't bring up marriage and babies with just any woman. I love you. I've loved you for years, only I didn't know it."

"Then why did you let Paul take me out to dinner?"

"You mean I could've stopped you?"

"Of course. I didn't want to go out with him! I was sick about having to turn you down for dinner. Not only that, you didn't even seem to care that I was going out with another man. And as far as you were concerned, he was your main competition."

"I wasn't worried."

"That wasn't the impression I got later."

"All right, all right," Joe said, drawing his fingers through his hair. "I didn't think Paul was interested in you. I saw him and Lindy together one night at the office and the electricity between them was so thick it could've lit up Seattle."

"You knew about Lindy and Paul?"

Joe shrugged. "Let me put it this way. I had a sneaking suspicion. But when you started talking about Paul as though you were in love with him, I got worried."

"You should have been." Which was a bold-faced lie.

Somehow, without her being quite sure how it happened, Joe maneuvered himself so only a few inches separated them.

"Are you ever going to kiss me?" he demanded.

Meekly Cait nodded and stepped into his arms like a child opening the gate and skipping up the walkway to home. This was the place she belonged. With Joe. This was home and she need never doubt his love again.

With a sigh that seemed to come from the deepest part of him, Joe swept her close. For a breathless moment they looked into each other's eyes. He was about to kiss her when there was a knock at the door.

Harry, Joe's foreman, walked in without waiting for a response. "I don't suppose you've seen Joe—" He stopped abruptly. "Oh, sorry," he said, flustered and eager to make his escape.

"No problem," Cait assured him. "We're married. We have been for years and years."

Joe was chuckling as his mouth settled over hers, and in a single kiss he wiped out all the doubts and misgivings, replacing them with promises and thrills.

EPILOGUE

THE ROBUST SOUND of organ music surged through the Seattle church as Cait walked slowly down the center aisle, her feet moving in time to the traditional music. As the maid of honor, Lindy stood to one side of the altar while Joe and his brother, who was serving as best man, waited on the other. The church was decorated with poinsettias and Christmas greenery, accented by white roses.

Cait's brother, Martin, stood directly ahead of her. He smiled at Cait as the assembly rose and she came down the aisle, her heart overflowing with happiness.

Cait and Joe had planned this day, their Christmas wedding, for months. If there'd been any lingering doubts that Joe really loved her, they were long gone. He wasn't the type of man who expressed his love with flowery words and gifts. But Cait had known that from the first. He'd insisted on building their home before the wedding and they'd spent countless hours going over the architect's plans. Cait was helping Joe with his accounting and would be taking over the task full-time when they started their family. Which would be soon. The way Cait figured it, she'd be pregnant by next Christmas.

But before they began their real life together, they'd enjoy a perfect honeymoon in New Zealand. He'd wanted to surprise her with the trip, but Cait had needed a passport. They'd only be gone two weeks, which was all the time Joe could afford to take, since he had several large projects coming up.

As the organ concluded the "Wedding March," Cait handed her bouquet to Lindy and placed her hands in Joe's. He smiled down on her as if he'd never seen a more beautiful woman in his life. Judging by the look on his face, Cait knew he could hardly keep from kissing her right then and there.

"Dearly beloved," Martin said, stepping forward, "we are gathered here today in the sight of God and man to celebrate the love of Joseph James Rockwell and Caitlin Rose Marshall."

Cait's eyes locked with Joe's. She did love him, so much that her heart felt close to bursting. After all these months of waiting for this moment, Cait was sure she'd be so nervous her voice would falter. That didn't happen. She'd never felt more confident of anything than her feelings for Joe and his for her. Cait's voice rang out strong and clear, as did Joe's.

As they exchanged the rings, Cait could hear her mother and Joe's weeping softly in the background. But these were tears of shared happiness. The two women had renewed their friendship and were excited about the prospect of grandchildren.

Cait waited for the moment when Martin would tell Joe he could kiss his bride. Instead he closed his Bible, reverently set it aside, and said, "Joseph James Rockwell, do you have the baseball cards with you?"

"I do."

Cait looked at the two men as if they'd both lost their minds. Joe reached inside his tuxedo jacket and produced two flashy baseball cards.

"You may give them to your bride."

With a dramatic flourish, Joe did as Martin instructed. Cait stared down at the two cards and grinned broadly.

"You may now kiss the bride," Martin declared.

Joe was more than happy to comply.

* * * * *

A Little Christmas Spirit
Sheila Roberts

Praise for the novels of Sheila Roberts

"Christmas wouldn't be Christmas without a Sheila Roberts story. This can't-miss author has a singular talent for touching the heart *and* the funny bone.... Once again, Sheila Roberts gifts us with a heartwarming confection that's as sweet as a sugarplum, and as deeply moving as snowfall."

—Susan Wiggs

"A tender story guaranteed to warm your heart this holiday season. When I read anything from Sheila Roberts, I know I will laugh, cry and close the book with a happy sigh."

—RaeAnne Thayne

"No one is better at expertly fusing small-town charm and holiday cheer than Roberts...[and this book is] the literary equivalent of watching *It's a Wonderful Life* with a mug of hot chocolate and a plate of cookies."
—*Booklist Reader* on *Christmas from the Heart*

"[This is] a warmhearted story filled with holiday cheer and charm, [and] readers will love this romantic twist on a Christmas classic."
—Debbie Mason on *Christmas from the Heart*

"A deftly crafted and delightfully entertaining novel from the pen of an author with a genuine flair for originality and the creation of memorable characters."
—Midwest Book Review on *Christmas from the Heart*

"I can always count on Sheila Roberts for humorous, heartwarming, holiday romance... I turned the final page with a smile on my face, joy in my heart, and the conviction that, once again, two deserving characters have found the person they're meant to share life with."
—*Romance Dish* on *Christmas from the Heart*

"Sheila Roberts makes me laugh...and come away inspired, hopeful and happy."
—Debbie Macomber, #1 *New York Times* bestselling author

"A lovely blend of romance and women's fiction, this insightful holiday treat hits all the right notes."
—*Library Journal* on *Christmas in Icicle Falls*

For Sammy, with love.

CHAPTER ONE

IT WAS THE sixth call in two days, all from the same person. Wouldn't you think, if a man didn't answer his phone the first five times, that the pest would get the message and quit bugging him?

But no, and now Stanley Mann was irritated enough to pick up and say a gruff "Hello." Translation: Why are you bugging me?

"It's about time you answered," said his sister-in-law, Amy. "I was beginning to wonder if you were okay."

Of course, he wasn't okay. He hadn't been okay since Carol had died.

"I'm fine. Thanks for checking."

The words didn't come out with any sense of warmth or appreciation for her concern to encourage conversation, but Amy soldiered on. "Stan, we all want you to come down for Thanksgiving. You haven't seen the family in ages."

Not since the memorial service, and he hadn't really missed them. He liked his brother-in-law well enough, but his wife's younger sister was a ding-dong, her daughters were drama queens and their husbands were idiots. The younger generation were all into their selfies and their jobs and their crazy vacations where they swam with sharks. Who in their right mind swam with sharks? He had better things to do than subject himself to spending an entire day with them.

He did have enough manners left to thank Amy for the invite before turning her down.

"You really should come," she persisted.

No, he shouldn't.

"Don't you want to see the new great-niece?"

No, he didn't. "I've got plans."

"What? To hole up in the house with a turkey frozen dinner?"

"No." Not turkey. He hated turkey. It made him sleepy.

"You know Carol would want you to be with us."

He'd been with them pretty much every Thanksgiving of his married life. He'd paid his dues.

"You don't have any family of your own."

Thanks for rubbing it in. He'd lost his brother ten years earlier to a heart attack, and both his parents were gone now as well. He and Carol had never had any kids of their own.

But he was fine. He was perfectly happy in his own company.

"I'm good, Amy. Don't worry about me."

"I can't help it. You know, Carol was always afraid that if something happened to her you'd become a hermit."

Hermits were scruffy old buzzards with bad teeth and long beards who hated people. Stanley didn't hate people. He just didn't need to be around them all the time. There was a difference. And he wasn't scruffy. He brushed his teeth. And he shaved…every once in a while.

"Amy, I'm fine. Don't worry. Happy Thanksgiving, and tell Jimmy he can have my share of the turkey," Stanley said, then ended the call before she could grill him further regarding those plans he'd said he had.

They were perfectly good plans. He was going to pick up a frozen pizza and watch something on TV. That sure beat driving all the way from Fairwood, Washington, to Gresham, Oregon, to be alternately bored and irritated by his in-laws. If Amy really wanted to do something good for him, she could leave him alone.

At first everyone had. He was a man in mourning. Then came COVID-19, and he was a senior self-quarantining. Now, however, it appeared he was supposed to be ready to party on. Well, he wasn't.

Two days before Thanksgiving he made the one-mile journey to the grocery store, figuring he'd dodge the crowd. He'd figured wrong, and the store was packed with people finishing up the shopping for their holiday meal. The turkey supply in the meat freezer was running dangerously low, and half a dozen women and a lone man crowded around it like miners at the river's edge, searching for gold, each trying to snag the best bird from the selection that remained. A woman rolled past him with a mini-mountain of food in her cart, a wailing toddler in the seat and two kids dragging along behind her, one of them pointing to the chips aisle and whining.

"I said no," she snapped. "We don't need chips."

Nope. That woman needed a stiff drink.

Stanley grabbed his pizza and some pumpkin ice cream and got in the checkout line.

Two men around his age stood in front of him, talking. "They're out of black olives," said the first one. "I got green instead."

The second man shook his head. "Your wife ain't gonna like that. Everyone knows you got to have black olives at Thanksgiving."

"I can't help it if there's none left on the shelves. Anyway, the only one who eats 'em is her brother, and the loser can suck it up and do without."

Yep, family togetherness. Stanley wasn't going to miss that.

He'd miss being with Carol, though. He missed her every day. Her absence was an ache that never left him, and resentment kept it ever fresh.

They'd reached what was often referred to as the *Golden Circle*, that time in life when you had enough money to travel and enjoy yourself, when your health was still good and you could carry your own luggage. They'd enjoyed traveling and had planned on doing so much more together—taking a world cruise, renting a beach house in California for a summer, even going deep-sea fishing in Mexico. Their golden years were going to be great.

Those golden years turned to brass the day she died. She didn't even die of cancer or a stroke or something he could have accepted. She was killed in a car accident. A drunk driver in a truck had done her in and walked away with nothing more than some bruises from his airbag. It wasn't right, and it wasn't fair. And Stanley didn't really have anything to be thankful about. He didn't like Thanksgiving.

There would be worse to follow. After Thanksgiving it would be *Merry Christmas!*, *Happy Hanukkah!*, *Happy Kwanzaa!*, you name it. All that *happy* would finally get tied up in a big *Happy New Year!* bow. As if buying a new calendar magically made everything better. Well, it didn't.

Stanley spent his Thanksgiving Day in lonely splendor, watching football on TV and eating his pizza. *It's not delivery. It's DiGiorno.* Worked for him. He ate two-thirds of it before deciding he should pace himself. Got to save room for dessert. Pumpkin ice cream—just as good as the traditional pie and whipped cream, and it didn't come with any irritating in-laws. Ice cream was the food of the gods. After his pizza, he pulled out a large bowl, filled it and dug in.

When they got older, Carol had turned into the ice cream police, limiting his consumption. She'd pat his belly and say, "Now, Manly Stanley, too much of that and you'll ending up looking like a big, fat snowman. Plus you'll clog your arteries, and that's not good. I don't want to risk losing you."

Ironic. He'd wound up losing her instead.

Between all the ice cream and the beer he'd been consuming with no one to police him, he was starting to look a little like Frosty the Snowman.

(Before he melted.) But who cared? He got himself a second bowl of ice cream.

He topped it off with a couple of beers and a movie along with some store-bought cookies. *There you go. Happy Thanksgiving.*

For a while, anyway. Until everything got together in his stomach and began to misbehave. He shouldn't have eaten so much. Especially the pizza. He really couldn't do spicy now that he was older. Telling everyone down there that all would soon be well, he took a couple of antacids.

No one down there was listening, and all that food had its own Turkey Day football game still going in his gut when he went to bed. He tossed and turned and groaned until, finally, he fell into an uneasy sleep.

"Pepperoni and sausage?" scolded a voice in his ear. "You know better than to eat that spicy food, Stanley."

"I know, I know," he muttered. "You're right, Carol."

Carol! Stanley rolled over and saw his wife standing by the side of his bed. She was wearing the black nightie he always loved to see her in. And then out of. Her eyes were as blue as ever. How he'd missed that sweet face!

But what was she doing here?

He blinked. "Is it really you?" He thought he'd never see her again in this lifetime, but there she was. His heart turned over.

"Yes, it's really me," she said.

She looked radiant and so kissable, but that quickly changed. Suddenly, her body language wasn't very lovey-dovey. She frowned and put her hands on her hips, a sure sign she was about to let him have it.

"What were you thinking?" she demanded.

He didn't have to ask what she was referring to. He knew.

"It's Thanksgiving. I was celebrating," he said.

She frowned. "All by yourself."

"I happen to like my own company. You know that."

"There's liking your own company, and there's hiding."

"I am not hiding," he insisted.

"Yes, you are. I gave you time to mourn, time to adjust, but enough is enough. Life is short, Stanley. It's like living off your savings. Each day you take another withdrawal, and pretty soon there's nothing left. You have to spend those days wisely. You're wasting yours, dribbling away the last of your savings."

"That's fine with me," he insisted. "I hate my life."

He hated waking up to find her side of the bed empty and ached for her smile. Without her the house felt deserted. He felt deserted.

"You still like ice cream, don't you?" she argued.

Except for when he paired it with pizza.

"Stanley, you need to get out there and...live."

"What do you think I'm doing?" he grumped.

"Going through the motions, hanging in limbo."

What else could she expect? "It's not the same without you," he protested.

"Of course it's not. But you're still here, and you're here for a reason. Don't make what happened to me a double waste. Somebody snatched my life from me, and I wasn't done with it. I want you to go on living for the both of us."

"How can I do that? This isn't a life, not without you sharing it."

"It's a different kind of life, that's all."

It was a subpar, meager existence. "I miss you, Carol. I miss you sitting across from me at the breakfast table. I miss us doing things together and sitting together at night, watching TV. I miss...your touch." He finished on a sob.

"I know." She sat down on the bed next to him, and he couldn't help noticing how the blankets didn't shift under her. "But you have to start filling those empty places, Stanley."

"I don't want to," he cried. "I don't want to."

He was still muttering "I don't want to" when he woke up.

Alone. For a moment there, her presence had felt so real.

"She wasn't there at all, you dope," he muttered.

Except why was there a faint scent of peppermint in the bedroom? It made him think of the chocolate Christmas cookies she used to make with the mint-candy frosting and sprinkles on them. After a few big sniffs, he couldn't detect so much as a whiff of peppermint and shook his head in disgust. Indigestion and memory. That was all she was.

CHAPTER TWO

STANLEY FIRST SAW Carol Barrett at a car show, eating a corn dog and checking out a 1954 Thunderbird. He was a gawky nineteen-year-old, and she was a vision in a red top and white hot pants that showed off the most gorgeous pair of tanned legs on the planet. She had full lips and blond hair that fell straight to her shoulders. She wore sunglasses so he couldn't see her eyes, but he was willing to bet they were as gorgeous as her lips.

Those lips were smiling, giving away a hint of dimples. He bet she smiled a lot.

She was with another girl and a guy. The girl's hair was almost the same blond as hers. Similar round face and slender body. Sisters? The guy was dark-haired and looked like a water heater with a head. Probably not related. A boyfriend, then? *Say it ain't so.*

Stanley's friend Walt elbowed him. "Check that out."

From the expression on Walt's face, Stanley knew he wasn't talking about the Thunderbird. Cars were cool. Who didn't love cars, especially muscle cars? But girls beat cars by a mile. And this woman beat cars by about a million.

Was she stuck-up? In Stanley's experience most cute girls were. They didn't bother with average guys. They went for the class president or the captain of the football team or valedictorian.

Stanley had been neither. He'd done okay in high school, especially in shop. And math. But history? It was all about memorizing dates. Who did what and when. He hadn't cared. And English? He hadn't been interested in reading most of those books his teachers assigned. *Lord of the Flies* had been pretty okay, but he'd much preferred novels by Ian Fleming and Dean Koontz to those other long-winded books full of flowery words his teachers had wanted him to try to digest. Anyway, reading was for camping trips, when you read in the tent by flashlight. As for grammar, what did he care about diagramming sentences, about verbs and adverbs and adjectives?

Except now. Adjectives. How to describe this girl? *Eye-popping, heart-stopping.* Then another adjective came to mind: *unattainable.*

He knew that word because for him it had applied to just about every girl he'd liked all through high school. He'd never mastered the easy charm so many other guys seemed to have. Walt was always giving him pointers on what to say to girls. Good stuff, but the words usually got stuck at the back of Stanley's mouth. He was much more comfortable hanging out with his pals, working on cars or shooting some hoops, or racing on the viaduct on a Friday night than trying to impress a girl.

This girl was different. He already wanted to impress her in the worst kind of way.

"Man, oh, man, wouldn't you like to have that girl riding shotgun with you?" Walt said.

Like to? No, he had to.

She looked his way and shared that smile with him. It was a friendly one. It said *Come on, take a chance.* Maybe she wasn't so stuck-up. Maybe there was hope.

"I'm gonna go talk to her," Stanley said.

"Whoa, man, slow down. You know you're not that good with women, and that one's not just a woman, she's a goddess."

Yes, a mere mortal working as a gopher at a construction company was not even close to her league. Suddenly, like a gift from Cupid, a quote popped into his mind. Something from a poem he'd had to read in English class. *...a man's reach should exceed his grasp, or what's a heaven for?* He'd never understood that poem before, wasn't sure he fully understood it now, but one thing he was sure of. It was a sign.

"I know, but I've gotta meet her."

"I'd better go with you so you don't mess this up," Walt said.

She was way out of Walt's league, too. Walt was short and no better-looking than Stanley. At least he had the gift of gab and a reputation for being able to charm the ladies. If they could get close enough for him to use it.

Stanley was medium height, still filling out. He had brownish hair and an okay face—nice brown eyes (or so his mother always said)—but he was no Steve McQueen or Clint Eastwood. He was never going to get this girl. What was he thinking?

That he wanted her more than air. He tried to put on a cool, casual front to hide his terror.

Once they got close enough he let Walt start things out. "Hey, there," Walt said with a big grin to the goddess. "That your dream car?"

"It's pretty cool," she said and smiled at Stanley.

"It's okay," said the other guy, stepping into the conversation. "I got a Chevy."

Walt nodded. "Yeah? What model?"

His friend was distracting the competition. Here was Stanley's chance. "Hi," he said. "I'm Stanley."

The goddess's smile widened. "I'm Carol. This is my sister, Amy. That's her boyfriend, Jimmy."

She wasn't taken. Was it truly possible? *Ask.* The words turned into cement and lodged in his mouth.

He cleared his throat. "You into cars?" *You dumb shit. Of course she's into cars. Otherwise she wouldn't be here.* He started to sweat, and it had nothing to do with the July heat.

"I think they're fun to look at. I like cute little sports cars, and I love red ones." She moved a little away from the others, took a nibble of her corn dog. Stanley followed her like a hungry puppy. "One of my friends at Lincoln— that's where I went to school—had a red Mustang. It was so cool. I think she was rich." Carol finished with a shrug. "I'll probably never have one."

If he had the money, he'd have promised right then and there to buy her one. "'Stangs are cool," he said. "I've got a red car. A GTO. That thing can move." Yes, when it came to cars, he could talk up a storm. But this wasn't getting to the heart of the matter.

"I bet it can." She took another bite of her corn dog, waiting for him to say something else.

"You still in school?" he asked. Another dumb question. *Went to school. That means she's done.* So far he was not making a good impression.

"I graduated this year. How about you?"

"Last year."

"Where'd you go?"

"Queen Anne."

"Queen Anne High School, on the hilltop," she began to sing, and he chuckled.

"You went to Lincoln, and you know our fight song."

"I went out with a guy from Queen Anne a couple of times. I always thought your school song was catchy."

She had to be going out with somebody. She was too perfect not to have a boyfriend. He couldn't stand the suspense any longer. "Are you with some-one now?"

"My sister and her boyfriend," she said, her smile teasing.

He frowned. "You know what I mean."

"I'm not with anyone right now. It's just as well, I suppose. I don't want to get distracted. I'm going to U-Dub this fall."

The University of Washington. A college girl. Yep, totally out of his league. He'd have had better success trying to reach the moon in a paper airplane than getting this girl to go out with him. So much for poetry.

"Guess that counts me out," he mumbled.

She cocked her head. "You sure give up easy."

"Look, I'm not going to college. I did okay in school, but another four years, that's not for me. I don't want to sit in a classroom and then end up sitting in an office all day. I like to build things. I like to work on cars. And I like to be outside, hiking or fishing in a stream. I'm no football hero," he added. "I wasn't even that good at track. I bowl."

Good grief. When did he catch diarrhea of the mouth? He could feel his cheeks burning, and he clamped his lips shut.

She smiled. "I can't bowl very well, but I think it's fun."

He blinked in surprise. "You do?"

"Sure. And I like to hike."

"Really?"

"I also happen to like classrooms," she said, raising an eyebrow. "I want to be teacher."

"Yep, you're a brain," he said. It was hopeless.

"Everybody's a brain, Stanley. There are all kinds of ways to be smart." She paused, smiled again. "Did I mention that I like to ride in fast cars?"

Was that a hint? Did he dare ask her out? "Umm."

"And I could use some pointers when it comes to bowling."

That was definitely a hint. He hoped.

"Would you like to go bowling?" he ventured.

Her smile lit him up inside. "I would."

She fished in her purse and pulled out a pen. Then she took his hand. He felt the zing all the way up his arm and clear into his chest. She clicked the pen, turned his hand palm up and wrote her phone number on it. Wow. He swallowed hard.

"Call me," she said.

Her sister and the boyfriend had moved on. Walt had let them go and was pretending to look under the T-Bird's open hood. Stanley and Carol were in the middle of a crowd of old guys, teenagers and kids running every which way, but all those people seemed to disappear, leaving just the two of them. They could have been Adam and Eve.

He could barely think, barely speak, but he managed to say, "I will."

"I'll see you around," she said, then turned and ran off to catch up with her sister, her hair swaying as she went.

Wow again.

Walt came around the car and stood next to him, watching the vision run off. "So?"

Stanley held up his hand, showing off the number.

"Lucky dog," Walt said teasingly. "I should have cut you out."

"Don't even think about it," Stanley said and was only half kidding.

"Hey, she's all yours, buddy. If you can manage not to blow it."

"I can," Stanley said, determined.

STANLEY CALLED HER that very night. A girl's voice answered.

"Uh, Carol?"

"No, this is Amy. Is this that guy she met?" She sounded completely unimpressed.

"Yeah."

"She told me about you."

Yes, she was unimpressed. He could tell by her tone of voice. Stanley had no idea what to say to that, so he said nothing.

"Carol," she called. "It's him."

A moment later Carol was on the phone. "Him who?" she teased.

"Him who wants to take you bowling. Will you come?"

"Sure. Why not? I'm busy tonight. How about next Friday?"

"Great." He had a date with Carol. He wanted to throw back his head and howl with delight, but he managed to contain himself enough to set a time and get her address. Then he hung up the phone and let out a whoop.

"Did you win a million bucks?" teased his brother Curtis, who was walking through the front hall on his way upstairs.

"Better. Got a date."

"Huh. No kidding. Don't blow it."

Yep, nothing like a little brotherly encouragement. "I won't," Stanley said and hoped he was right.

STANLEY FINALLY GOT to see Carol's eyes when he picked her up on Friday night. They were as blue as a cloudless sky. Those crazy platform shoes she was wearing made her look even more like a model, but he could tell that once she exchanged them for bowling shoes she'd be just the right height to kiss.

If he could ever get up the nerve.

"You have your own bowling ball?" she asked as they walked into Sunset Bowl in the Ballard neighborhood. "You must be really good."

He was. "I'm not bad," he said modestly.

"Hey, Stan," the man working the shoe-rental counter greeted him. "How's it goin'?"

"Good," Stanley replied, trying not to grin so much that he looked like a dope.

So far he didn't think he'd blown it. He hoped he was doing okay with Carol. Lucky for him, she was easy to talk to, and she carried most of the conversation for him.

"I like your car," she'd said as he opened the door for her.

From there it was on to talk of the church youth-group bowling party she'd been to earlier in the year. "I love parties," she'd said.

Stanley wasn't exactly a party animal. He had his close friends, and they hung out, worked on their cars, played Ping-Pong at Walt's house and, of course, went bowling. He'd been to some bigger parties, always in somebody's basement. There was often dancing, which made him feel self-conscious, noisy talk and teasing, where he never seemed to be able to come up with a cool thing to say, or a game of Twister that could get awkward when you had to bend over a girl in an effort to put your hand on a certain colored circle. He did better with just one or two people.

"How about you?" she'd asked.

"I guess parties are okay," he'd managed. "But I'd rather do things with just a couple of people." *Maybe even just with you.*

"But you do go to parties, don't you?" she persisted.

"Oh, sure." He hadn't wanted her to think he was a social reject. Still, he'd been glad when they arrived at the bowling alley and left that subject behind.

After getting her shoes and getting set up on a lane, it was time to find a ball. "I can never find a ball I like. They're all so heavy," she said, picking one up and frowning.

He found a lighter one. "Here, try this twelve-pounder," he said, handing it to her.

She took it and wrinkled her nose. "It still weighs a ton."

"I bet you can handle it," he said.

"I'm sure going to try."

And try she did. She couldn't get the ball to go straight down the lane, but he had to give her credit for enthusiasm. After rolling gutter balls her first two times, she jumped up and down, squealed and clapped like she'd gotten a strike when she'd actually knocked over three pins.

"I've got potential, don't I?" she crowed.

"Oh, yeah," he agreed. Everybody had potential. He came and stood next to her. "Just try and keep your arm straight when you throw the ball. Follow through. Like you're on the pitcher's mound." He demonstrated, and she nodded.

"Follow through," she repeated. She tried again, and her arm went crooked, and off the ball skittered, edging toward the gutter. Which it hit right before the pins.

"Better luck next time," he said and rolled a strike.

"You make that look so easy," she told him, and he puffed up like a rooster.

"Here, let me help you," he offered as she got ready to take her turn. He pointed to the line of dots on the floor in front of them. "See all these spots? If you use them to line up, you'll have a better chance of the ball going where you want it."

"Really? Where should I stand?"

It was the perfect excuse to make contact. He took her arms, stood behind her and gently moved her to a spot he thought would help. Suddenly he wished they weren't in a bowling alley. He wished they were somewhere quiet, maybe by a mountain stream or on a moonlit beach.

"So here?" she asked, yanking his thoughts back to the game.

"Uh, yeah. That's great. Now, remember, keep your arm straight. Four steps up, and then let the ball go."

"Four steps up, and let the ball go," she repeated.

"Start swinging the ball back as you approach."

He stepped back and watched her, trying to stay objective as he observed her form, and not fully succeeding.

She managed to take down four pins and on her next throw got two more down. "See? Potential," she said happily.

"Yep," he agreed. "Potential." But he wasn't just thinking about bowling. Did they have potential?

He longed to kiss her when they stood on her front porch saying goodnight, but he didn't want her to think he was a wolf.

"I had fun, Stanley," she said. "You're the sweetest guy I've met in a long time."

Her words wrapped around him like a hug. It was almost as good as a kiss. Almost.

"Will you go out with me again?" he asked.

"I will. Call me," she said as she walked inside.

Call me. Best words in the English language. He practically floated back to his car.

Their next date was to a movie. Sitting there in the dark theater, he longed to hold her hand, but he couldn't get up the nerve. Instead, he kept his hands busy digging into the popcorn.

After the movie it was off to Zesto's for a burger and shake. "How did they ever get that car up there?" she wondered, looking at the 1957 Chevy on the roof of the hamburger joint.

"I don't know," he said, "but I think it's cool."

"Yes, it is," she agreed. She moved her straw around to suck up the last of her chocolate shake.

He watched her, wishing he could kiss those pretty lips. What was she doing out with the likes of him?

"I bet you were a cheerleader in high school," he said.

"How'd you guess?"

He shrugged. "You're...bubbly. Were you on the honor roll?"

"I was."

"I wasn't."

"I told you before, there are lots of ways to be smart, Stanley."

"Hey, I never flunked any classes," he quickly clarified.

"I'm sure you didn't."

"It's just that some subjects didn't interest me."

"What does interest you?"

He shrugged. "I like math. I like putting things together. Working with my hands." *I like you.*

By their third date he actually felt comfortable talking with her. Words were coming out more easily instead of stubbornly lodging at the back of his mouth and having to be yanked out.

Once more they found themselves fueling up on burgers and shakes, and he was able to find the nerve to ask, "So how come you're not with anyone? I can't believe you don't have a boyfriend."

"I did."

"I bet he was a football star."

Even though the boyfriend was no longer in the picture, Stanley couldn't help feeling a little jealous. He should have gone out for football. Girls loved football players. Except Stanley had never liked the idea of getting tackled and crushed. *No guts, no glory*, as the saying went. So now here he was, perfectly intact but with nothing to brag about.

Carol made a face. "He was a selfish jerk. Everywhere we went, everything we did, it was all about him and what he wanted. Not that I minded doing things he wanted to do," she hurried on, "but after a while I began to wonder why he never asked me what movie I'd like to see or where I'd like to go eat, why he never asked me what I thought about anything. He did all the talking, and I did all the listening. After a while it didn't feel like we were together. I was just…"

"Fuzzy dice," Stanley supplied, looking at the ones dangling from his rearview mirror.

She smiled at the metaphor, gave them a flick with her finger. "Exactly. He didn't really care about me. I was just decoration, something to make him look cool."

Stanley nodded, taking that in. The ex-boyfriend was obviously a dope who didn't know what he'd had.

"You know, Stanley, I'm not looking for someone who's a hotshot or Mr. Cool. I'm looking for someone who's kind, someone who wants to have fun together. Most important, I'm also looking for someone who thinks about more than himself, someone who wants to be a team. Are you that kind of guy?"

"I am," Stanley said, determined to be.

"Good," she said with a nod. "I'm glad to hear it."

After that conversation he didn't dare try to kiss her. He didn't want to come across as a selfish jerk, out to get what he could as soon as he could.

But he didn't have to. When he brought her home she closed the distance between them there on the front porch.

"Stanley, you really are sweet," she said and kissed him.

It wasn't a long kiss, but it was a perfect one. Her perfume, her soft lips, that beautiful body up close to his was a heady mixture, and for a moment there he was sure he'd died and gone to heaven.

She pulled away and smiled at him.

"Wow," he breathed.

Her smile got bigger. "Yeah, wow. You know what made that so special just now?"

"You."

She chuckled and shook her head. "Knowing that you really care about me."

"I do." *I want to spend the rest of my life with you.*

He didn't say it, but he knew. And he hoped she felt the same, because as far as he was concerned the kiss said it all. They would be together for the rest of their lives.

CHAPTER THREE

LEXIE BELL AWOKE on Black Friday before her six-year-old son and went downstairs to the kitchen, where she pulled out the leftover pumpkin pie she'd brought home from the so-called Orphans Thanksgiving dinner she'd attended.

She didn't know very many people in the town of Fairwood yet, and she'd appreciated the invite from one of the older teachers at Fairwood Elementary who had wanted to make sure everyone, especially a newcomer like Lexie, had a place to go. She'd met some nice people at that party, and it gave her hope that she'd find her tribe and be able to settle into her new town as well as she was settling into her new job. She'd already made one good friend, Shannon, another single teacher at school, and she was looking forward to making more.

As for settling into the job, that had been easy. What was not to like about being a kindergarten teacher? She enjoyed working with children, especially the little ones. She looked forward to going to work every day and seeing all those smiling, innocent faces, looking up at her, eager to learn.

And she was always eager to teach. She loved children, would have liked to have more than one herself. But so far one was all that was in the cards. She'd just discovered she was pregnant when her fiancé confessed that he'd been cheating. She'd ended things right then and there, and there had gone the plans for the big destination wedding they'd been saving for, not to mention the big, happy family she'd dreamed of having.

"That's what comes of putting the cart before the horse," her grandma had said.

Thankfully, she'd only said it once. The last thing Lexie wanted Brock hearing about was horses and carts and how foolish his mother had been and what a loser the man she'd fallen for had turned out to be. She supposed there would come a time when she'd have to address that but not yet.

The cheater had signed over his parental rights and moved to San Diego, so it had always been just Lexie and Brock. A sweeter, more precocious boy you would never find, and while she may have made a mistake in the man she picked, she didn't regret the child she'd gotten out of the deal.

She wished her grandma was still alive so she could see what a great kid Brock was. She hoped Granny would be proud of how Lexie was raising her son. She felt she was doing okay. They both were.

She cut the big slice of pie in two, leaving the slightly smaller half for Brock, then squirted a pile of canned whipped cream on top of her piece. Nourishment for the quest that lay ahead: shopping Black Friday specials online for the perfect presents for her aunt and uncle and cousins back in California, and her mom and, of course, Brock.

She loved holiday sales. They were the only time she could actually afford all the expensive gifts that were usually out of reach for a single mom on a teacher's salary. She settled on the couch with her pie on the coffee table and her laptop in her lap, started some Taylor Swift playing, cracked her knuckles, limbering up. Then she brought her computer to life. Let the adventure begin.

She'd already purchased a plane ticket for her mom so she could fly up from sunny California and join them for the holidays, but Lexie wanted something to put under the tree as well.

What to get? Perfume? No. Mom would say "Your father's gone. What's the point?"

It was what she said about everything, from getting her nails done to whipping up the gourmet meals she used to love cooking. For years Lexie had gotten her a can of tennis balls as a stocking stuffer because Mom loved to play tennis, but that wasn't an option. She'd stopped playing. She'd also given up her book club, claiming that since Daddy's death, it was hard to concentrate on the words on the page, so there was no point in getting her a book. Something for the house? Her mother had enough stuff.

Chocolate! Even the most miserable of women could be helped by chocolate. Lexie knew that from experience.

She ordered a box of Godiva truffles.

She found a deal on body butter and ordered some for the cousins, then started the search for the perfect present for her aunt.

"I'm awake, Mommy."

She looked up to see her son entering the living room, looking adorable in his superhero pj's. His brown curls (a gift from the father fail) were tousled, and he rubbed his eyes (brown, also from the father fail) as he joined her on the couch, snuggling up next to her.

"What are you doing?" he asked.

"I'm checking out the sales. I have to get my holiday shopping done."

"And we have to see Santa," Brock reminded her.

"Don't worry. We have plenty of time to see Santa," she assured him.

"Does he know I want a puppy?"

"I think he does, but I think he also knows that Mommy said no puppy yet. You have to wait until you're older."

Brock's lips dipped downward. "I just want a puppy."

"You'll get one eventually, but not this Christmas. Start thinking about something else to ask Santa for."

The lower lip jutted out.

"Oh, my, what a sad, pitiful mouth," she teased. She leaned over and picked up her pie from the coffee table. "I think it needs something to make it happy," she said, forking off a bite.

Brock squirmed in delight and opened his mouth.

"There. Did that make your mouth happier?" she asked once it was in.

He nodded, chewed and swallowed. "My mouth wants some more."

"It's a good thing I have a piece saved for you in the refrigerator, then. Want to go get it?"

He nodded again, this time even more eagerly, and followed her to the kitchen.

Not the most nutritious breakfast in the world, she thought as she dished it up. But not the worst, either. After all, it did have pumpkin and eggs. Anyway, it was Thanksgiving weekend. Everyone deserved to party a little on a holiday weekend.

She'd hoped to find some people to party with right here in her cul-de-sac when she'd first moved in. She'd fallen in love with the house, with its simple lines and big front porch, and had assumed that there'd be another family living in one of the neighboring houses.

But she hadn't found a family when she moved in. Instead, she'd found workaholics who were rarely around and a divorcing couple whose quarrels she'd heard clear over on her front porch. They'd soon moved out and taken their sulky teenager with them, leaving the house standing empty. The Sold sign now posted in the front yard gave her hope, but it was about her only hope. The little old lady who occupied the house two doors down didn't come out much, and there was a reclusive older couple next door.

At least she assumed it was a couple. So far she'd only seen the husband, and he wasn't inclined to chat.

Once, she'd caught sight of him driving toward his house when she was outside, raking the leaves from the big maple tree in her front yard—a hefty man with thinning gray hair and bushy eyebrows. She'd given him a friendly wave and a smile, and he'd nodded and managed to lift his fingers off the steering wheel, then he'd turned into his garage, and it had swallowed him up. She'd seen him one other time and gotten the same half-hearted acknowledgment. She'd taken over some cookies once when she'd thought she caught sight of someone in their dining-room window, but the only welcome she'd gotten had been from a couple of garden gnomes sitting on the front porch. When no one had answered the door, she'd wound up leaving them on the doorstep.

Did he have a wife? If he did, she had to be bedridden or as reclusive as him. It was like living next door to Boo Radley.

Well, she'd find her peeps. She was working that direction with Mrs. Davidson of the Orphans Thanksgiving dinner and Shannon, who was also nearing the big three-oh and who taught fourth grade. Her social life would sort itself out. Maybe, if she was lucky, her love life would also.

She settled Brock at the kitchen counter with his pie, promising him a trip to town for hamburgers for lunch—let the fun continue—then returned to her computer. There was a lot of Black Friday left, and she had shopping to do.

STANLEY SAT DOWN at his computer to check the stock market and then his email. Not many emails came for him anymore. Still, out of habit, he checked. The inbox was filled with Black Friday offers. Fifty percent off this. Get that now before it's gone. BOGO. Enter this coupon code.

He deleted them all. No need for shopping bargains when he wasn't going to shop. That had been Carol's department, not his. She'd spent a fortune on her sister's family and all her girlfriends, buying stuff that would probably end up in a garage sale or a landfill.

"It's a way to show people you care," she'd tell him.

She had a point there. He still fondly remembered the year she'd gotten him a slick, new bowling ball. She'd wrapped it and put it inside a huge packing crate with a bow on it so he couldn't guess what it was.

"Do you like it?" she'd asked when he took it out of its box.

He had and, more than the gift itself, he'd liked that loving expression on her face.

Even though he never bought gifts for anyone else, he'd always gotten something nice for her: bubble bath, chocolates, jewelry. One year he'd bought season tickets to the local theater because the season included several musicals. Carol loved musicals. (Stopping in the middle of what you're doing to sing a song never made sense to him. But then, he'd been an electrician, not a poet, so what did he know?)

There was no one he needed to lavish presents on now, no one he needed to show that he cared. "Waste of time and money," he muttered. *No holiday shopping this year. Or ever. No presents for anyone. Did you hear that, Carol?*

People shouldn't waste so much time buying crap. When you weren't wandering in and out of stores, you had more time for other things.

Stanley gave his nose a scratch. Other things. Like checking the stock market, doing your sudoku puzzle... He scratched his nose again. Watching TV. Yeah, he had a busy life.

But don't forget keeping the house maintained, emptying the garbage.

Shaking his fist at heaven.

How he'd looked forward to retiring and enjoying himself, spending more time with Carol, doing things together! There was no together. Only the solitary doing of routine.

He sighed and turned off the computer. It was almost time for lunch. A slice of toast with some peanut butter. A glass of milk. A couple of cookies. Hardly gourmet fare, but who cared? He'd never been much of a cook. He wasn't going to start now.

After his busy day of sudoku and TV, he made dinner. This time a ham sandwich. No more spicy food before bed. He topped his meal off with some more ice cream and called it good.

Now, what to watch on TV tonight? He flipped it on and checked his options. Hulu, Netflix, Amazon, Home Movies.

Home Movies! He didn't have a Home Movies option, and he'd never seen that old-fashioned movie-projector icon before. He blinked and leaned forward, squinting at the TV screen. There were his options. Hulu, Netflix, Amazon.

Okay, take a deep breath. That was just a weird...something.

He went to Netflix and opted for one of his favorite police series. There you go. Cops called to a murder scene, people standing behind the yellow tape, gawking. There, toward the back of the crowd was... He let out a yelp and pushed back against his recliner. It was Carol, middle-aged and with that short haircut he'd told her he liked even though he hadn't. She waved at him.

Oh, man. What was wrong with him? He took a deep breath, leaned forward and stared at the screen. She was gone. He kept looking for her throughout the rest of the show, but she never returned.

Both frustrated and unnerved, he shut off the TV and opted for a book. That would do him just fine.

He read until he was sleepy, then went to bed, torn between hoping Carol would make another appearance and dreading another scold. Being nagged from beyond the grave was unsettling.

SHE DID RETURN late that night, and where her first visit had been unsettling, this one was downright scary. She wasn't cute like she'd been the night before. The nightie was gone, and she was in jeans and a red sweater, topping off the outfit with a Santa hat.

That part was okay, but the face under the Santa hat was a different story. Her pretty blue eyes had been replaced with what looked like red-hot coals. *Aaah!*

He bolted upright, his heart pounding. "Carol?" he whimpered, pulling the covers up to his chin like a shield.

Some shield. What he needed to do was dive under the bed.

"Don't be silly. I'd find you there," she said, reading his mind. "I wanted to watch home movies, Stanley. Obviously, you didn't get the message. I don't think you're taking me seriously."

"I am," he whispered, averting his gaze.

Averting didn't work. She whooshed right in his face, forcing him back against the headboard. "I heard what you said about not shopping."

He squeezed his eyes shut tightly. "That was your thing, not mine." Arguing. He was arguing with a ghost. What was he thinking?

"All right, I'll give you that. But you're going to have to find some way to get involved with life. Take an interest. There are people all around who need you."

"Nobody needs me," he grumbled. Not anymore, not with her gone.

"That's not true. There are always people who need you. Open your eyes, and you'll see them."

He didn't want to open his eyes. He might see her.

"If you'd watched those movies like I wanted, you'd have realized how good life is when you're out there doing things."

He'd gotten all their home movies digitized, and they'd barely made a dent in watching them before she was gone.

"There's no point, because I was doing things with you. Life's not good now, and watching them will just piss me off."

"Stanley, stop feeling so sorry for yourself. Start looking out and focusing on others instead of in and only on yourself. It's the season of peace on earth, goodwill toward men. Get out there and show some goodwill. And, while you're at it, decorate this place. It's so...un-Christmassy."

Decorate? "Oh, come on, that was your thing, too," he protested, eyes still squeezed shut.

"Not hanging lights. That was always your job."

"There's no reason to hang the lights. You're not here to appreciate them."

"I'm here now."

He cracked one eye open, only to see those fiery eyes boring into him. Yes, she was.

"I know," he said, "and, no offense, but you don't look so good, babe," he added and shut that eyelid back down.

"It's because I'm not happy. You're killing me, Manly Stanley."

It would probably come across as callous to point out that she was already dead.

"You'd better start taking me seriously."

"I always took you seriously."

"Then, get with the program. I'm going to haunt you till you do."

"Please, no. Don't do that," he begged. "I can't handle seeing you like this." Those glowing eyes really were creepy.

"Then, I suggest you start thinking about making me happy."

"I will, I will," he promised.

"Good. I'll be watching," she said and left in a swirl of cold wind.

Stanley's eyes popped open, and he saw his covers had fallen off. No wonder he'd felt a breeze. It was his subconscious telling him he was cold, that was all. Like those times he'd dream he was looking for a bathroom and would wake up to realize he needed to take a whiz.

But why was he seeing Carol? Why was she choosing now, of all times, to haunt his subconscious?

Because she'd loved Christmas, of course. That was it. That was all.

He could swear he smelled peppermint again. Was there such a thing as olfactory hallucination? That had to be what he was suffering from. Had to be.

He abandoned the idea of trying to go back to sleep. It was four thirty in the morning. He'd conked out around eleven. Five and a half hours was enough. Anyway, he'd rather walk around gritty-eyed than take a chance on meeting Burning-Coals Carol again.

He showered, he shaved. He got dressed. Proof that he was, indeed, taking an interest in life.

"That ought to make her happy," he muttered.

Make her happy. He'd have liked nothing better. If she was still alive. But she wasn't. And he was laying off the ice cream. Ice cream was the culprit.

Or else he was going insane.

No, that couldn't be. Surely if he was going to lose his mind he'd have done so long before this. Of course, it was never too late to go around the bend.

He drank his morning coffee and ate a bowl of cereal. Then he watched the morning news and went online and checked the stock market. His stocks were still holding strong. All was well. Not that his stocks mattered much, these days. He had what he needed to live on stashed away in a retirement account that was intended for two, and no one to leave any money to. Still, it was good to have something to check.

Come ten o'clock, he fetched his coat and hat and gloves and went to the garage. Time to take the SUV to the shop and have snow tires put on. There was no snow in the forecast yet, maybe wouldn't be any at all this winter, but Stanley liked to be prepared.

Stanley also liked to be organized, which was why he always kept the garage immaculate—a sheet of cardboard under the SUV to catch oil drips, his tools neatly hung on a pegboard or stored under his workbench, bins of seasonal decorations that he'd hauled in every year for Carol that belonged on the shelves.

But now one was sitting in the middle of the floor, tipped sideways.

On the floor! What the heck?

CHAPTER FOUR

"LET'S PUT UP Christmas lights," Carol said as they drove home from her parents' late Thanksgiving Day. "Lots of lights with lots of colors."

Stanley sighed inwardly. After eight years of marriage he knew what *let's* meant in a case like this. It meant she had an idea for a project, and he'd be the one doing it.

He also knew how much hassle this would involve. "Do we really need Christmas lights?"

"Yes. Last year our house was the only naked one on the block, and that was just plain sad. The house will look so pretty trimmed with all those colors. Anyway, Christmas lights are to the holidays what frosting is to a cookie. They make something special even better."

He shot a look over at her. "So if I put up lights, does that mean you'll bake those frosted cookies?"

"I will," she promised. "It'll be your reward."

"Okay, deal," he said.

The next day they went shopping for lights. Carol gathered enough to light up the whole street. Plus a string of red plastic letters that spelled out *Season's Greetings*.

"We can hang it across the outside of the living-room window," she said.

Yep, the infamous *we* again.

"Think we might have gotten carried away?" he suggested. *Think I'll be done hanging these before January first?*

"Well, maybe a little," she said. "But better to have too many than not enough. Anyway, we don't have to do only the house. We can do the bushes, too."

It was going to be a Christmas-light marathon.

He got busy outside, and she got busy inside, making cookies. As Stanley was working, Edgar Gimble from next door came by to offer sage advice.

"Better make sure they're nice and secure. Got a windstorm predicted for later this week."

"I will," Stanley assured him. He was an electrician. He knew all about lights.

It took forever plus an eternity to hang the things and another millennium to decorate the bushes and put up the *Season's Greetings* sign, but at last he was done. First ones on the block to have their decorations up that year. He grinned smugly as he put away the ladder.

The house smelled like sugar and vanilla, and Carol was frosting cookies shaped like trees when he came into the kitchen. Their dog Goober, the mutt they'd rescued from the pound, lay nearby, his head on his paws, watching mournfully, knowing he wouldn't get so much as a crumb.

Stanley gave him a dog treat, then snagged a cookie frosted with green frosting and sprinkles. Someone had to sample them.

"This is good," he said. "Thanks for making these."

She danced over and kissed him. "You deserve a reward after all your hard work. And maybe I do, too," she said with a flirty grin. "Think I might get a reward tonight?"

"I think you might," he said, grinning right back.

As soon as it was dark she insisted on turning on the lights and going outside and admiring them. She'd been right, as usual. The lights did make their house look special.

"It's so pretty," she said with a sigh. "It makes my heart happy."

Then, it was worth every moment he'd spent out there freezing his ass off. "I'm glad," he said.

A cold wind was stirring, and she shivered.

"Come on, let's get back in before you freeze," he said, wrapping his arms around her.

"Good idea," she said, squeezing him back. "Let's get inside and warm up."

"It's nice to be inside and cozy," she said later, as they snuggled together.

"It is," he agreed.

Actually, it was more than nice. Being with Carol like this filled him with contentment.

The contentment wasn't quite so deep when he heard her on the phone with her sister the next morning.

"I think that's a great idea," she said.

Uh-oh. What kind of great idea were they talking about?

"I'll check with Stanley. I'm sure he won't mind."

Whatever those two were concocting, he bet he would.

"What won't I mind?" he asked after she hung up the phone.

"Having a little party to kick off the holidays," she said airily.

"A little party," he repeated. He knew Carol and Amy's idea of a little party did not and never would match his. "Define *little*."

"Just the families. Well, and the Gimbles. They're such good neighbors."

That meant both sets of parents, his brother, Amy and her husband and two bratty kids, and probably all the grandparents. Plus Carol would be bound to slip in an extra neighbor or two.

He groaned. "It'll be a zoo."

"Zoos are always fun. You never know what you're going to see."

"I know what I'll see at this one. Your Grandpa Howard will doctor his punch with gin when nobody's looking and get snockered. Amy's girls will break God knows what, and your mom will bring something nobody wants to eat but we'll all have to. Where did you ever learn to cook? Not from her."

"You have a very bad attitude, Manly Stanley. Now, can I tell you what will really happen?"

He leaned against the door frame. "Sure. Go ahead."

"Grandma Bartlett will make that pound cake you love, and I'll make those frosted brownies. You'll gorge yourself, and then you and Curtis and Jimmy and my dad will set up the Ping-Pong table in the garage, and we won't see any of you after that."

"You sure won't," he assured her. Her sister and the girls were enough to make any man want to hide. Some kind of drama was a given anytime they were around.

"Then, it's settled?"

"It looks that way," he grumped.

They'd wind up doing this sooner or later, so there was no point in postponing the inevitable.

"You know you'll have a good time. You always do once these things get going."

"I guess," he said, reluctant to admit that there was a measure of truth in what she said. "When is this big bash supposed to happen?"

"Next Saturday. We'll kick the month off with a bang."

"That's what I'm afraid of," he muttered.

As HE'D PREDICTED, Carol did sneak in some extra names to the guest list, but since they were a couple of buddies from his bowling league and their wives, he could hardly complain. The week before she went into party-prep mode, cleaning and baking, and the whole house smelled like a bakery.

Stanley was put in charge of vacuuming and pulling down the punch bowl from the top cupboard where she kept it and borrowing folding chairs for extra seating from his parents. There were many evening phone conversations with her sister as they came up with games to play and debated over what kind of punch to serve.

Reluctant as he was to have to entertain a crowd of people in his house, Stanley tried to look on the bright side. He would be with friends and family (some of whom were irritating, but oh, well). He didn't have to worry about impressing anyone. And he would for sure be setting up the Ping-Pong table. There would be lots of good food and lots of smiles, especially on his wife's face. And seeing her happy was what mattered most.

The afternoon before the party, a windstorm swept into town, blowing over garbage cans and making tall fir trees sway.

"It's crazy out there," Stanley said when he came in the door from work. "I wouldn't be surprised if we lose power."

"Don't say that. I don't want to cancel our party," Carol said.

"You might have to. Plus I heard on the radio that they're expecting snow." If it snowed, their party size would definitely shrink. People in the Pacific Northwest could handle days of rain on end, but let one snowflake fall and everyone panicked. Their families, all presently located in Seattle, wouldn't so much as poke their noses outdoors, let alone drive twenty-five miles to Fairwood.

Stanley almost smiled. No crowd; small gathering; more cookies for the few who made it: it worked for him.

Carol made a face. "It better not snow until after the party."

They were just sitting down to dinner when the power went out.

"Oh, no," she moaned.

"I'll get the candles and the flashlight," he said.

"What if it doesn't come on before tomorrow?" she fretted.

"More cookies for me," he said jokingly.

Carol was not amused.

But by early Saturday afternoon whatever power line had been taken out had been fixed. The lights were on, the fridge was humming, and the party was a go.

Amy and her family were the first to arrive, her girls excited and dashing through the front door, winding up Goober and making him bark. She carried a bag filled with wrapped boxes for the white-elephant game the sisters had planned and a large foil-covered plate.

"We're here," she announced. "Let the games begin." Then she turned to Stanley. "What's with the *Season's eetings?*"

"Season's eetings?" he repeated, confused.

"Look at your window," she said. "Good job, Stanley."

He stepped outside and saw the string of letters he'd hung across the living-room window were dangling perilously. The *G* and *R* had dropped from *Greetings*. Yep, *Season's eetings*. It looked stupid. He frowned.

"Leave it up," Amy said as he went to fetch the ladder to take down the ruined decoration. "It's funny."

Yeah, anything for a laugh. Some people could laugh at themselves, he supposed, but he had his pride. The sign was coming down.

The sign turned out to be...a sign.

Goober got excited chasing Amy's girls around, and his wagging tail sent several plates of seven-layer dip and chips flying from the living-room coffee table onto the carpet. Mrs. Gimble leaned too near the candles on the dining table when reaching for a piece of pound cake and came close to setting her hair on fire. One of the girls tried to feed Goober a brownie, causing total panic.

Stanley and his fellow Ping-Pongers escaped to the garage for a brief respite. Stanley was good at table tennis, and he and Jimmy were well-matched. It was nice not having to worry about anything but that little white ball bouncing back and forth across the table. But eventually they had to rejoin the chaos of the party.

The capper came later when everyone assembled in the living room to play the Bartlett family's favorite white-elephant game and steal presents back and forth. Grandpa Howard, as Stanley had predicted, had spiked his punch and gotten tipsy. They were halfway through the gift game when he laughed so hard that he lost his balance and fell into the tree, knocking it over and trampling several of the remaining presents still under it. No harm was done to most of the ornaments, but the same couldn't be said for Amy's carefully coiffed hair when the top boughs landed on her, making her shriek.

Both her husband and Stanley had rushed to try and stop it toppling but failed. Jimmy tramped two more presents in the process. One of them, obviously an inflated whoopee cushion, made a noisy protest that sounded like a fart. That about summed up the situation.

"Oh, my gosh, I have sap in my hair," Amy cried, frantically trying to undo the damage and sending fir needles flying.

What comes around goes around. Leave it there, it's funny, Stanley thought, remembering her comment about the *Season's Greetings* letters. But he was smart enough to keep his mouth shut.

"Well, will you look at that," said Grandpa Howard with a grin and a hiccup.

"You should have secured that better," Amy informed Stanley, frowning at him.

"Or else secure Grandpa," he retorted.

The tree was righted and the mess cleaned up, and the game went on. Stanley held his breath, hoping they could get through the rest of the evening without any more disasters. They did. After some major hair repair Amy's sense of humor revived.

Finally, all the food was consumed and the punch bowl drained, the fun and games were over, and the children were exhausted. Someone looked out the window and discovered it had started snowing, and that put a period to the party. Coats were hastily donned, empty serving platters and white-elephant presents gathered, and the guests departed. Stanley breathed a sigh of relief as the last car pulled away from the curb.

"That was fun," Carol said happily.

"Is that what you call it?"

She shook her head at him. "You know you had a good time."

"Yeah, putting the tree back together was a really good time."

"Everyone helped. And that's what it's all about."

"Putting messes back together?" he responded, determined to be obtuse.

"Being together. We need each other. It's important to stay connected."

He wouldn't have minded disconnecting from some members of her family.

"And really, no harm done with the tree."

Stanley thought of Amy, sputtering and buried under boughs of fir, and snickered. Then sobered. "Harm could have been done if I hadn't seen Mellie trying to feed chocolate to Goober. He'd have been one sick pup."

"But we caught her, and now she knows."

Stanley just shook his head. "What a night. Your family is something else."

She smiled. "Yes, they are, and I love them. And I love you," she added, hugging him. "Thanks for helping me get the season off to a wonderful start."

"Anything for you," he said and kissed the top of her head. "I'm glad you had a good time. That's what matters most to me."

"You are a good sport," she said. "Let's enjoy a quick walk in the snow. I bet our lights look beautiful."

They did, indeed. Some of their neighbors had decorated their houses that day and with the snow and the gaily lit homes, it felt a little like being inside a snow globe. As he and Carol stood on the sidewalk, bundled in their winter coats, taking it all in, their arms around each other, he couldn't help but think what a perfect moment it was.

I am one lucky man, he thought. "I wish you could bottle times like right now," he said.

"I guess in a way we do," she mused. "That's what memories are. Let's make sure we bottle up a whole bunch."

Of course, after that year, hanging Christmas lights became a tradition. Much as Stanley hated being out in the cold messing around with them, he always enjoyed seeing how nice the house looked once they were up. Even more, it made him happy to know that he was making Carol happy.

CHAPTER FIVE

STANLEY'S HEART RATE went from a stroll to an uneasy trot as he walked around the front of his vehicle and saw the overturned red bin. Its lid was off, and the carefully wound Christmas lights were escaping.

The trot went to a gallop. How could that bin have fallen? It had been securely stowed on the shelf for nearly three years, right above the one containing the tree ornaments and the one with the nativity set, the Santa teapot Carol had found at a garage sale one year ("Look, Stanley, it's Fitz and Floyd!"), and the ceramic gingerbread house that had been her mother's, along with the myriad scented candles she'd loved to scatter around on every possible surface.

Maybe there'd been an earthquake in the night that he hadn't felt. He could easily believe that. He'd been preoccupied with other things.

Carol.

He frowned. This was not some supernatural message. There was a logical explanation for it. He wished he knew what it was.

He decided to stick with the earthquake theory. It was, after all, the Pacific Northwest, and once in a while they did get a shaking. Hadn't had an earthquake in years. Not even a tremor. It was time. So that was it.

He put the lights back in the bin, set it on the shelf, got in his car and drove to the tire shop.

When he came home he aimed the remote at the garage door.

As it creaked its way up he saw the bin was back on the garage floor again. Once more the lid was off, and the lights were spilling out.

Okay, he was cracking up.

"You're not cracking up," whispered a voice as he got out of the car.

He whirled around, looking for the source. No one was there. A gust of wind swept into the garage, playing with his pant legs. Wind in the trees. That was what he'd heard.

"I won't stop till you get with it."

The voice again. He shivered in spite of the fact that he was wearing a warm, wool coat and the red scarf she'd knitted for him several Christmases ago.

Okay, he'd put up the lights. To honor Carol's memory, not because he thought she'd tipped that box over. He was not being haunted. He didn't believe in ghosts. Anyway, this was Christmas not Halloween. There were not ghosts at Christmas.

Unless you counted the ones that visited Ebenezer Scrooge. An invisible, icy finger tickled its way up his spine, making him shiver harder.

"I *am* finally cracking up," he told himself.

He wished he could talk to someone about what was happening to him, but there was no one. Without Carol to nudge him into what she called his *nice clothes*, he'd stopped going to church. All those concerned faces and big noses anxious to poke into his business, not to mention a predatory widow or two, laying out casseroles like bear traps. No, thanks. He and God could hang out here at home just fine.

He'd given up on his bowling league, too. He'd gone once, a few months after losing her, but it hadn't been fun, and he'd dropped out.

At first his buddies had called to see how he was doing, leaving him voice mails encouraging him to come back. "Come on, Strike King, we need you."

"Hey, Hambone, where are you?"

Who cared how many strikes you bowled? He never called any of the guys back, and after a while they gave up.

Which had been fine with him. He'd never needed a lot of people around to make him happy. All he'd needed was Carol.

The day he lost her it was as if he'd gotten sawed in half. He still was only half of what he'd been when he'd had her, and that wasn't going to change. He could dream about her all he liked, but she wasn't coming back. Life was gray, and it would stay that way no matter how many Christmas lights he put up. Still, to appease…whatever, he'd do it. After lunch.

After lunch, though, he needed a nap. He settled in his recliner. He'd just shut his eyes for a few minutes. Just a few…

"You haven't hung those lights yet," Carol whispered in his ear.

He brushed her away like a pesky fly. "I'll get to it. I'm trying to rest."

"You've had three years to rest. You need to get off your rear, Stanley. I'm losing patience. Stanley! Will you please look at me when I'm talking to you?"

He didn't want to, not after what he'd seen the night before. He took a leery peek, raising one eyelid, then shut it again quickly. The scary, red eyes were still there. What was she doing hanging around here? Shouldn't she be off in heaven, where she belonged?

"I will be soon enough," she said.

"There you go, reading my mind again," he complained. She'd always been good at that. Irritatingly good, as a matter of fact, often finishing his sentences before he even could. That had bugged him, even when what she said had been exactly what he was going to say.

What had bugged her was how he didn't always pay attention when she was talking to him. But honestly, a man couldn't pay attention to everything.

"Stanley!"

"What?" He jerked awake, looking around. Of course, there was no one in the living room but him. Sunlight was filtering in through the sheers at the window, beaming on the fake brown-leather couch they'd picked out together, spreading over the coffee table where she used to set her coffee mug when she was reading.

"*Staaanley.*" He heard his name, soft as a whisper.

"Okay, okay," he said and pushed up from his chair.

This was how they'd often operated. He'd promise to do something and then put it on hold, and she'd keep after him until he did it. He liked to do things on his own timetable. Why couldn't she understand that?

"Because certain things never get on your timetable," she'd once explained. "You say you'll do something just to shut me up."

"I do not," he'd argued. But, truthfully, sometimes he did. He wished she was still there to keep after him.

"*I am here.*"

Being nagged by his flesh-and-blood wife was one thing. Being nagged by…this red-eyed apparition was quite another and not something he wanted to encourage. But there was only one way to make it stop. He fetched the lights and the ladder and got to work.

LEXIE LIKED TO spend Thanksgiving weekend setting out her decorations. It always put her in a holiday mood. Plus it was fun for Brock, who enjoyed helping. As he was getting older she was allowing him to handle more of her treasures.

She started some holiday music streaming and hauled in the box with their decorations, Brock bouncing along beside her.

"I get to help," he reminded her.

"Yes, you do," she said.

She opened the cardboard box, and it was like opening a treasure chest of memories. There was the faux mistletoe she'd bought when she and he-who-would-not-be-named first got together. She'd kept it even after they'd split, thinking she'd make good use of it again. She hung it every year as a kind of positive affirmation. Someday she would find someone wonderful.

So far no one worth kissing under that mistletoe had come along, though. Being a kindergarten teacher didn't exactly throw a lot of single men her way. But you never knew. And you couldn't decorate for the holidays and not hang mistletoe.

One by one, she unwrapped and handed over the vintage wax candles shaped like choirboys and angels that had been her grandma's. Brock lined them up along the coffee table, which he proclaimed to be the perfect place for them. Of course it was. That way he could play with them on a regular basis.

He set the snow globe she'd handcrafted from a jelly jar several Christmases ago right in the middle of the coffee table. It had turned out quite well for a first attempt, if she did say so herself.

Next she let him put the green, pine-scented soy candle in the guest bathroom. She wouldn't light it unless she had company, but even unlit it provided a lovely, fresh fragrance.

As he did that she pulled the ceramic Christmas tree her mother had made back when she was first married out of its box. It had miniature lights on it and cast a gentle glow once it was plugged it in. She set it on the kitchen counter near an electrical outlet.

"There," she said, plugging it in so Brock could see. "Our guests will be able to enjoy it from the living room and the kitchen."

"When are we going to get a big tree?" he asked.

"Closer to Christmas. We're going to get a real, live tree, and we don't want to put it up too early and have it dry out."

Her family had always had an artificial tree. Now that she was in Washington, she wanted a real one for Christmas.

She let Brock settle her cloth elf on the back of the sofa, but her Santa collection she would set out herself. She had china ones and ceramic ones, antique collectibles and newer whimsical ones. They'd look cute on the mantel.

She'd never before had a fireplace and had been thrilled when the Realtor assured her that the insert in this one worked great. She was looking forward to hanging their Christmas stockings from the mantel, enjoying cozy fires and drinking hot chocolate.

There. The house looked so festive. All she had left to do was to set out her Santas, string the garland along the mantel and find a spot to hang the mistletoe. Maybe from that beam that hung between the kitchen and the living area, so accessible from all directions. Then the place would be all dressed up and ready for Christmas.

Funny, she'd never considered owning a house. It had always seemed like such a big step. But when she'd come up here it somehow felt like the thing to do. "A house is a good investment," her dad used to say.

Yes, it was. Buying this one was also a testament to her confidence in her future, that new job was secure and this life she was starting wasn't simply temporary. No more substitute teaching, no more part-time day-care jobs. She was a real teacher now.

Brock, being six and full of energy, had no desire to sit and watch her string a garland along the mantel. "Can I go play?"

"*May I go play?*" she corrected.

"May I go play?"

"Yes, for a little while. Let's get you bundled up." The famous Pacific Northwest drizzle had stayed away so far, but the sky was gray, and it was still nippy outside.

Once she had him in his red parka and his red knit cap and mittens, she started for the back door to usher him out into the back yard.

"I want to play in the front yard," he said.

The back yard was fenced, a big patch of lawn, surrounded by flower beds full of shrubs and flowers and beauty bark. It was great for games of Mother, May I? and bocce ball and two-person tag with Mom. But Brock was in love with the front yard. It offered both the potential for a rare neighbor-sighting as well as that big maple tree with a thick trunk and twisted boughs low enough to reach. He loved scrambling around in it when she was working out there, weeding the flower beds or raking leaves.

Still, the front yard wasn't fenced, and though they were in a cul-de-sac, she didn't like the idea of Brock being out there without her. Any crazy person passing by could grab her little boy and abscond with him.

"No, I think the back yard, Brockie," she said.

"I want to climb the tree," he protested.

It would be hard for a kidnapper to pull her boy out of a tree, she supposed. And on a cold, gray day, how many kidnappers were wandering their quiet suburban neighborhood? It wasn't like Brock had asked to cross the street. Still...

"Please," he begged, both hands steepled in little-boy prayer.

Lexie caved. "All right," she said, doing an about-face. She'd keep an eye on him from the window while she finished up. "Stay in the yard," she commanded as she opened the front door for him. "And don't climb too high in that tree. No more than three boughs up, remember?"

"I remember," he said and dashed across the porch and down the steps.

She watched as he hurled himself across the lawn to the tree, grabbed a thick bough and started clambering up his own personal jungle gym. He got his feet anchored in the Y between those bottom branches and stood there, surveying his domain.

A rather lonely domain. So far, he hadn't quite found his feet socially, and she hadn't managed to score any playdates for him, but she planned to change all that in the New Year. Little boys, like their mamas, needed friends.

She went to the kitchen and made herself some tea and poured it into the Best Teacher Ever mug her aunt had given her when she got her job. "Because you will be," she'd said.

Then she returned to the living room to decorate the mantel and keep a watchful eye out the living-room window.

The maple tree was bare. No leaves. No little boy. He wasn't in the yard, either.

Lexie's heart stopped, and the blood drained from her face. She dropped her mug and raced for the front door.

STANLEY WAS AT the top of the ladder, stringing multicolored lights along the roofline when a new voice invaded the silence. "What are you doing?" it asked.

It sure wasn't Carol. She knew exactly what he was doing.

He looked over his shoulder and saw a little boy looking up at him. He had a round face and brown eyes and a stray brown curl stuck out from under the red knit cap on his head. He was stuffed inside a bulky parka and had red mittens on his hands.

"Where'd you come from?" Stanley asked. It would be nice if the kid said "Far away," but a feeling of foreboding told Stanley that wasn't the answer he was going to get.

The kid pointed to the tan two-story Craftsman next door. "There."

The friendly neighbor who tried to flag him down whenever he drove by, who'd used cookies like a Trojan horse in an attempt to gain access inside his house. Of course it would be her kid.

Stanley grunted and got back to work. "You should go home."

"There's nobody to play with."

Not Stanley's problem. "Go play with your mom."

"She's putting up Santas. I don't get to touch them."

"I'm busy here." Stanley said it brusquely, hoping his tone would shoo the boy away.

Little kids obviously didn't understand the subtlety of brusqueness.

"You're hanging Christmas lights. I like Christmas lights."

"Yeah, a lot of people do." Including Carol.

"I'm going to ask my mommy if we can have Christmas lights," the boy volunteered.

"Good idea. Go do that."

The kid didn't go. "My name's Brock. What's yours?"

"Stanley."

"That's a nice name."

Oh, brother. Stanley shook his head, climbed down the ladder, moved it and went back up to secure more lights.

"Do you have kids?"

"No."

"How come? Don't you like kids?"

"I can take 'em or leave 'em."

"I'm a kid."

"Thanks for sharing."

At that moment the boy's mother appeared on their front porch, calling him, her voice frantic.

The kid waved at her and called, "I'm over here, Mommy."

Bugging the neighbors.

"You come home this minute!" she called.

Stanley knew what that tone of voice meant. He'd heard it enough when his own mother had gotten after him. It said *You're in deep shit.*

"I gotta go now. Bye!"

Yeah, bye. Good riddance.

Kids were pests.

CHAPTER SIX

"I WANT TO have at least three children," Carol said one summer evening when they were strolling the beach at Golden Gardens. They'd been together for a year and were talking more and more of a future together.

Stanley wasn't into kids all that much, but he knew he'd be fine with any kid who was part Carol.

"You'll be teaching them once you get your degree," he'd said. "Maybe after working with them you'll change your mind about wanting any."

"Oh, no. I love children. Don't you?"

His cousin Belinda had just had a baby. Holding it had terrified him. "Don't know much about them."

"Nobody does when they first start out. You learn as you go."

"You'll already be an expert," he said. He'd depend on her to help him figure out the whole parenting thing.

There were more conversations as things continued to get serious between them, and one of them had been with her dad, who summoned him into the living room one evening for a chat.

The family did all their true living in the family room. The living room had cream-colored carpet and fancy furniture and was reserved for important company. And important conversations.

An important conversation with Mr. Bartlett. Stanley began to sweat. Mr. Bartlett had been an army lieutenant during World War II. He'd gone to school on the GI Bill and gotten a teaching degree. Teachers didn't earn much at all back in the fifties, but he'd kept with it and finally become a high-school principal. He was a deacon at his church and a member of the local Lions Club. A cultured, educated man, a mover and shaker. He was everything Stanley wasn't, everything Stanley would probably never be. Stanley stood four inches taller than him, but as they settled in the living room, Mr. Bartlett on the cream-colored sofa and Stanley on the edge of a matching chair, he felt about three feet tall.

"You and my daughter appear to be very fond of each other," Mr. Bartlett began.

"I love her," Stanley blurted.

Oh, boy. That was going to go over like a lead balloon. Every sweat gland in his body went into production, and he felt like his whole face was going up in flames.

Mr. Bartlett nodded solemnly. "Of course you do. What's not to love?"

Did that mean he had the old man's approval? Or...? Stanley's shirt collar was suddenly way too tight.

"Carol is a very special young woman."

"She's the best," Stanley agreed. "I know I don't deserve her." But he wanted her, anyway. Needed her. Couldn't imagine his life without her.

"So what are you going to do to deserve her?"

"Work hard?"

"At what?"

What? What? Stanley frantically searched his mind for the right answer.

Mr. Bartlett didn't wait for it. "You need a skill, Stanley. Something you can depend on." Here he looked meaningfully at Stanley. "Have you thought of going to college?"

"No, sir." Boy, did that make him sound unworthy. He needed to re-think his future.

Mr. Bartlett frowned. "Well, you need to do something more than working as an unskilled laborer. Find out what it takes to move up the ladder or pick a new skill to learn. You can't drift along through life without a purpose, not if you're serious about having a future with my daughter," he added, lowering his brows.

"Yes, sir."

"Carol wants to be a teacher, and she'll be a wonderful one. She's got plans. Goals. She's going places. Where are you going, young man?"

To school. Stanley enrolled in an electrical technology certification program the very next day.

Both families celebrated their accomplishments, but when Carol finally got her teaching degree, her family did so with twice as much fanfare: a big garden party with family and friends, cake, balloons, speeches and plenty of congratulatory cards, most of them filled with money.

Stanley had made his best effort, getting her a card and a book he'd found on child psychology.

"Thought it might come in handy on the job," he said when she opened it.

"That was a very clever gift, Stanley," her mother approved. "Now that you've got your teaching credentials, you can start thinking about other things," she said to Carol and smiled encouragingly at him.

Yes, other things. It was time to propose. But it had to be special. Romantic. Stanley had no idea how to be romantic.

"Give her a long-stemmed red rose," his pal Walt advised. "Women love that. And take her someplace really nice for dinner. With a view."

Dinner and a rose. He could do that. He made reservations at the Windjammer on Shilshole Bay Marina, requesting a window table so they could enjoy the view of the boats. He made a seven-thirty reservation so they'd still be there to catch the summer sunset. That would be romantic. He picked up the rose after work and put it in the trunk so she wouldn't see it. Then he went home and showered and shaved and got dressed in his stylin' flared slacks and sports jacket.

"So this is it," Curtis said, checking out the look.

"Yep."

"She's great," his brother said in approval. "Wish I could find one just like her."

"You're not looking that hard," Stanley pointed out.

"You're right. I'm not ready to settle down."

Stanley was. He could hardly wait to start living with Carol. That was when his life would really begin.

She looked picture-perfect, all dressed up for the big night out he'd promised her in a white granny dress printed with little pink roses. It made him think of wedding dresses. He hoped she'd say yes.

Of course she would. They were in love. He was still nervous.

They got to the restaurant, and he hurried around to the trunk to get the rose. He'd hide it inside his jacket then present it to her when their dessert came and pop the question. Carol had already hopped out of her side, and she came around the car just in time to see him staring aghast at the wilted red thing.

"What's this?" she asked.

"Nothing," he said and started to shut the trunk.

She stopped him. "It looks like something to me." She reached inside and picked it up. It bent its head in shame. "Oh, Stanley," she said softly. "Was this for me?"

"It looked a lot better in the flower shop," he said miserably. "So much for the romantic gesture."

"Dinner at a nice restaurant, a romantic gesture… Hmm," she mused and cocked her head at him.

"I was going to ask you to marry me." Oh, good grief. Just what every woman dreamed about: a proposal in a parking lot with a dead rose.

"Oh, Stanley," she cried and threw her arms around him, apparently unbothered by their surroundings. "You know I will."

"Really?"

"Of course really."

"Wow." Carol Bartlett, the sweetest, most beautiful girl in the world had just said yes. He grabbed her and twirled her around, both of them laughing for joy.

"Everything's turning out beautifully," she said later as they sat at their table, the wilted rose lying next to her plate.

"Yes, it is," he agreed. It didn't get better than this.

BUT IT DID get better. He survived the big church wedding and managed to come up with enough groomsmen to match the six bridesmaids she had. Her cousin, who fancied herself a singer, sang Paul Stookey's "Wedding Song." She didn't murder it, only maimed it severely. Stanley didn't care. All he cared about was seeing Carol in that wedding dress, smiling at him, just as eager to begin their life together as he was.

The reception was in the church basement—punch, nuts and mints, and a three-tiered wedding cake. He didn't care about any of it. All he wanted to do was get to the motel where they were going to have their wedding night.

That, it turned out, was well worth waiting for.

They honeymooned in Victoria, barely leaving the room except to take a romantic, evening carriage ride and do some souvenir shopping. When they returned they moved to the town of Fairwood, north of Seattle, where her first teaching job was waiting. Stanley found employment as well, and they rented an apartment which they furnished with furniture their parents had given them and a few garage-sale bargains. Life was perfect.

After two years they decided it was time to start a family, and Carol began to talk about buying a house.

"It should have at least three bedrooms," she said. "One for us and two for two kids."

"You said you wanted three," he reminded her.

"Two can share a bedroom until we can afford a bigger house."

He laughed. "You aren't even pregnant yet, and we're already talking about doubling kids up in a room and looking for bigger houses."

"You have to plan ahead," she said, that trademark smile beaming at him.

Planning ahead. Kids. The idea of parenthood made him nervous. It was a big responsibility.

"You'll make a wonderful father," Carol assured him when he expressed doubts.

He supposed he'd cross the fatherhood bridge when he came to it. Meanwhile, they bought that three-bedroom house on a cul-de-sac in a nice neighborhood. The woman next door befriended Carol instantly, and the couple across the street who were about their age became friends. Everything was going according to plan, and they were having a lot of fun working on making a baby.

But where were the results? Disappointment became a monthly occurrence, and the pressure to produce began to leech some of the fun out of the procreation process. After three years of failure and enough tears to form a lake, they consulted a specialist. That consultation turned out to be the seal of doom.

"It's all right," Stanley said as they drove home, Carol crying next to him in the front seat. He reached over and laid a hand on her leg. "We still have each other."

That wasn't the comfort he'd hoped it would be. She continued to cry.

Once they got home, he settled with her on the couch, his arms around her, as she sobbed against his shoulder. "I'm sorry, babe," he kept saying. *Sorry* was small comfort for such a huge disappointment. He'd never felt so helpless in his whole life.

The next few weeks felt robotic. They ate breakfast together, they went to work, they came home. She graded papers, he grilled burgers. She talked on the phone with her sister and her mom. They watched TV. They even went bowling a couple of times, but Carol's smiles were weak, and she didn't care what spot she stood on.

"I don't think I was meant to be a bowler," she finally said, and he knew that was one activity they wouldn't be doing together anymore.

There was another activity they weren't doing very much anymore. Carol was always conveniently asleep by the time he came to bed, even if it was only five minutes after her. Or she didn't feel up for it. One time they made love, and he felt so connected, as if they were finally healing...until he saw her tears.

"What's the point?" she said miserably.

"The point is we love each other," he said.

"I do love you, Stanley, you know I do. I'm just so unhappy."

How long was she going to be unhappy? Would he ever hear her laugh
again? If only he could think of some way to bring back those genuine smiles
and her love of life.

"What about adopting?" she suggested one evening as they waited for the
pizza they'd ordered to be delivered.

"Adopting?" he repeated. "Somebody else's kid? I don't know."

"It wouldn't be someone else's. Once you bring a baby home, it's yours."

She had a valid point. But it was still a big leap for him mentally.

"Well..." he said, stalling.

"We have a lot of love to give."

Yeah, to each other.

She was looking at him so hopefully. How could he say no? What kind
of selfish jerk would that make him? *Selfish jerk.* He suddenly remembered
when she told him about the boyfriend she'd broken up with. He didn't
want to be that man. He wasn't that man.

"All right," he said. "Let's go for it."

It was like he'd turned on the sun. The old Carol came back, so bub-
bly and happy, so energetic and full of plans. Yes, this could work. She was
right. They had a lot of love to give.

After a long search, everything started coming together. They met the
birth mother. She gave them a thumbs-up as parents for her baby. They
painted the nursery and got a crib and changing table and clothes. Stanley
sold his GTO, and they bought a station wagon. They were ready.

The baby came. It was a boy. They called all the family and shared the
news.

Then the birth mother changed her mind. She decided to keep the child.

The crib in the nursery mocked them, and there were more tears.

"That's not the only baby in the world," Stanley said that evening as they
sat at the kitchen table, their dinner untouched. "We can start again."

He'd hoped to lift her spirits, but he failed.

She shook her head. "I'm done. I can't go through this kind of disappointment another time." She sighed heavily. "I think it's a sign to quit. Maybe
we're not supposed to have children."

Maybe they weren't. He was fine with it being just the two of them. But
was she?

"Are you okay with that?" he asked.

"I guess I'll have to be, unless a miracle happens and I get pregnant."

"You never know," he said and tried to smile encouragingly. She didn't reflect it back to him. "And don't forget, you already have a whole class-room of kids."

"They're not ours," she snapped.

Carol never snapped, and he blinked in surprise. He wasn't sure what to say next.

He thought a moment, then tried again, hoping to help her look on the bright side. "They're yours every day when you have them in class. That's kind of important, isn't it?"

She bit her lip and looked down at her hands. "I suppose so."

"And Amy's got two daughters now. She'll share."

The look on Carol's face told him what she thought of sharing.

"You'll be their favorite aunt."

"I'll be their only aunt."

"Guaranteed favorite, then. And we still have each other." If he said it enough, maybe it would be enough.

She nodded. "Yes, we do," she said, but she didn't sound all that enthu-siastic.

"We can still have a good life."

"You're right, we can."

Just not the one she'd dreamed about.

He never said anything, but he mourned their loss nearly as deeply as she did. Not so much because of the baby. Even though he'd gotten excited over the prospect, it had never seemed real to him. What had been real was his wife's misery and the knowledge that, while he could comfort her, there was nothing he could do to make up for what they'd lost.

Like she'd said, it was probably a sign. Kids were not supposed to be a part of their life together.

CAROL MANAGED TO make the best of things. She stayed heavily involved with her nieces, and over the years she kept in touch with many of her stu-dents as well.

She and Stanley went hiking, attended church potlucks, watched as friends and family had children. Sometimes he wondered what his life would have been like if he'd had a son to hang out with or a daughter to walk down the aisle. What it would have been like to sit proudly at a kid's high-school graduation or hold a grandbaby in his arms.

But he didn't bother with wondering for long. What was the point? Any-way, Carol had been enough for him. And they'd had a couple of dogs along the way. Carol called them their fur babies. Unlike kids, dogs never gave you any lip, never had you up late at night worried because they'd missed their curfew. Never fell in with the wrong crowd or did drugs. They'd dodged a lot of heartache. And that wasn't such a bad thing, was it?

CHAPTER SEVEN

STANLEY FINISHED HANGING the lights and set the outdoor socket timer. Then he put away the ladder, set the empty bin back on the shelf and went inside where it was warm.

Okay, he thought. He'd done his Christmas chore. The house was decorated, and he'd proved he had Christmas spirit. Now, maybe he could enjoy some peace and quiet.

He'd just gotten a beer out of the fridge when the quiet was shattered. Not by Carol. This time some neighborhood mutt was on his front step, making a ruckus. Good grief. Couldn't a man get a quiet moment to himself?

"Shut up!" he hollered and plopped in his recliner, his remote in hand.

The stupid thing refused to shut up. It kept barking.

And barking, and barking. After half an hour Stanley had had all he could take.

Okay, no more Mr. Nice Guy. He unreclined himself and marched to the front door and threw it open to give Fido the boot.

Before he could say "Scram," the dirty thing rushed past him and into the front hall.

"Hey!" Stanley protested.

Arf! the dog replied happily, prancing around him, tail wagging.

It wasn't a big dog, didn't even come up to his knees. With its pointed ears and doggy snub nose and those bright eyes, it looked like a West Highland terrier, the same breed Carol had been wanting to get before she died. Only this one was so dirty its fur was gray instead of white.

Dirty as the animal was, Carol would have pronounced it adorable. But that was Carol. She'd loved kids and dogs. After their German shepherd, Max, died, Stanley had been done. Carol had lobbied for getting another and really wanted a Westie, but he'd kept resisting. You got too attached to pets, and then they croaked.

His attitude hadn't changed.

"You don't belong here," he informed the intruder. "Out."

The dog sat on its haunches, tail sweeping the carpet, and cocked its head at him as if to ask *What is your problem?* It was a girl. That explained the stubbornness.

"Out!" he commanded more firmly. To make sure she got the message, he moved a foot to her rear and gave her a nudge toward the open door.

The dog let him push her only so far before dodging to the side, backing up and barking, tail wagging.

"This is not a game," he informed the beast.

He'd have grabbed her by the collar and hauled her out the door, but there was no collar, not even a flea collar. What kind of irresponsible loser didn't even get his dog a flea collar?

Maybe the dog had been treated and didn't need a flea collar. Maybe she'd slipped her regular collar and gotten away. Maybe she was chipped. Yes, that was it.

There was one way to find out. "Okay, Dog, we're going to take a ride."

He shut the front door and started for the garage. His visitor trotted along happily after him, probably thinking they were on their way to the kitchen for food. Nope, they were on their way to the garage door. And the SUV. And the vet.

"We're going to find out who owns you," he said to the animal. "I can tell you right now, that's not me, and you're not staying."

The dog was happy enough to hop into the car and sit its muddy butt on the front seat. "You smell," Stanley informed her.

She didn't care. She sat there with her tongue lolling, looking at him like they were buddies. He shook his head and pressed the garage-door opener.

The dog should have been in a pet carrier, but Stanley didn't have a carrier, had no need for one because he had no need for a pet.

He hadn't seen Dr. Graham in several years, but the receptionist remembered him. "Max's daddy, right?"

"That's right." He'd always thought it was stupid to refer to oneself as an animal's parent, but Carol had thought it was great fun.

The receptionist leaned on her counter and smiled at the dog resting happily in Stanley's arms, getting his coat all dirty. "I see you have a new baby."

"She's not mine. I found her. I want Doc Graham to see if she's chipped."

"One would hope," said the receptionist, taking in the dog's lack of collar. "Doctor's giving O'Malley an exam right now, but after that he can fit you in. Just take a seat."

So Stanley took a seat, the dog still in his lap. She was so happy to be there, she offered a public show of affection.

"None of that," he said, moving his face out of range and putting up a hand. "You use that tongue to lick your butt."

The dog whined, her feelings hurt.

"It's okay. You're a good dog," he said and patted her head.

Which, of course, made her want to lick him again.

He was still trying to keep out of range of the scruffy dog's tongue when a woman left with an Irish Setter in tow. It was a beautiful animal with a silky coat. The woman gave Stanley a polite smile, then took in the condition of the dog in his lap, and her smile changed to a disapproving frown.

"I found her," Stanley said and then felt stupid. He didn't have to explain himself to strangers.

The woman wasn't interested, anyway. She and the beautiful O'Malley kept walking.

The receptionist showed Stanley and the dog to an exam room, and he set the animal on the stainless-steel exam table. She seemed perfectly content to sit there. No antsy squirming, no whining. This dog had probably never been to a vet, never had shots. Never had a chip put in. Stanley frowned.

He was still frowning when Dr. Graham entered the room. He was still a young man, not yet out of his forties. No paunch. Happily married. Stanley remembered he had a couple of kids. Life was still good for Doc Graham.

The vet greeted him like an old friend. "Stan, it's been a long time. How are you?"

"I'm okay," Stanley lied, then got right to the point. "I found this dog. I want you to see if she's chipped."

"Sure," said Dr. Graham. "How's Carol?"

"She's dead."

The doctor's easy expression turned to embarrassment. "I'm sorry. I didn't know."

Stanley frowned. He'd put an announcement in the obituaries.

But, then, who liked to read the obituaries? And why would someone Doc's age even bother? Stanley sure never had.

"Just tell me who owns this mutt."

"Sure thing. Where'd you find her?"

"On my doorstep."

Dr. Graham checked. "Nope, not chipped."

"Great. And she didn't have a collar."

"She might have slipped it." The vet shook his head. "Hard to imagine anyone not wanting this little cutie."

"I don't suppose you'd like her," Stanley ventured.

The doc shook his head. "I already have two rescues. My wife said that's enough. I guess you can take her to the animal shelter, ask if anyone's been looking for her."

Stanley did. No one had been looking for the dog. And seeing all the mutts in cages, he knew he couldn't leave her there.

"You have to belong to someone," he said as he started up the car. "We'll make some posters."

The dog whined.

"Hey, it's the best I can do."

And if nobody responded to those, well, that was it. The dog would have to go to the shelter.

"I can't keep you. I'm done with dogs," he explained as they pulled into the supermarket parking lot.

But he wasn't so heartless that he was going to make this one starve. They made a quick stop at the store where he purchased a double-bowl dog dish and a flea collar. And a regular collar. And a chew toy.

Okay, enough was enough.

Back at the house he filled the dish with food and water and then watched as his houseguest tucked in, vacuuming up everything as if she hadn't eaten in days. Maybe she hadn't. She obviously hadn't been bathed.

"Okay, you are getting a bath," he informed her. "I'm not having you stink up the whole house."

So upstairs they went to the guest bathroom where he filled the tub with warm water, then lowered the animal in. She stood patiently, shivering and looking miserable while he soaped and rinsed her, then drenched him by shaking off the water.

"Thanks, I needed that," he grumbled.

She wagged her tail, then showed her gratitude by trying to lick his face yet again as he toweled her off.

"None of that, now. We're not going to go getting attached."

The dog cleaned up well. With her coat white once more she looked good enough to enter a dog show.

"There," he said. "That's what you're supposed to look like. Okay, now, time to get your picture taken."

Getting the dog to sit still for a picture was a challenge. She obviously didn't know the command to sit. But she was smart, and it didn't take too many times of saying *Sit* and pushing her rump down, followed by praise and pets, for her to catch on. She was a natural model and sat observing him at work with his cell-phone camera, head cocked.

"Who do you belong to?" he wondered. "They must be going crazy looking for you." He certainly couldn't imagine a family moving away and abandoning the animal.

And yet people pulled that crap all the time. Pets and kids. You shouldn't have one if you weren't willing to invest the time.

He loaded the picture onto his computer. It didn't take long to make a poster, and it didn't take more than a few minutes to put some up around the neighborhood. *Did You Lose Me?* it asked. His phone number was under the dog's picture. He figured he'd get a call by the next day at the latest.

Meanwhile, though, the dog made herself at home after they got back to the house, settling in at his feet as he looked for a good movie to watch. Later, he let her out in the back yard, where she proved she was housebroken.

Good. She could sleep inside. He set out a folded blanket for her in a corner of the kitchen and gave her the chew toy he'd bought to keep her happy.

She didn't stay happy for long. He'd only gotten halfway upstairs when she appeared, ready to follow him to bed.

"Oh, no. Back down you go."

Back down they both went and into the kitchen again, where Stanley settled her on the blanket with her toy and a firm "Stay."

Of course, this wasn't a command she'd learned, either. He was just climbing into bed when she padded into the bedroom and sat by the foot of the bed, looking up at him. Waiting for an invitation.

Oh, for crying out loud. "You have a bed," he reminded her as he got out of his. "Come on, back into the kitchen with you."

She trotted after him, and he settled her yet again, this time with a piece of beef jerky.

Which she ate in a gulp and then was ready to go back to the bedroom with him.

He turned, held out a hand and said, "No."

She looked at him as if he was speaking a foreign language.

"Yeah, I'll bet, whoever owned you, you didn't hear that word from them very often."

You had to show a pet who the big dog was. He took her by her new collar and led her back to the blanket, said, "Sit" and shoved her rump down. Held up his hand and once more said, "Stay."

She looked at him and thumped her tail. *Yes, sir.*

"Okay, lie down," he said and extended her front paws out in front of her. "There you go. Good dog."

She wasn't interested in being good. It took several more tries and some whining to get her to stay put. Finally, it looked like she had the idea, and he trudged off to bed.

He wasn't alone for long. He'd just turned off the light when she jumped up on the bed and curled up against his leg.

"Okay, fine. It's probably only for one night. You may as well enjoy your visit."

He was drifting off to sleep when a voice whispered, "Name her Bonnie."

Oh, boy. There went his imagination again. Well, he wasn't listening to it. There would be no dog-naming. You named a dog, and it was yours.

"I'm calling you Dog," he informed his houseguest the next morning as he poured food in her dish. "You probably already have a name, anyway. There's no point in getting you confused."

Hopefully, someone would call, and then he and Dog could both get on with their lives.

"CAN WE HAVE Christmas lights like next door?" Brock asked as Lexie made his lunch.

"*May we have Christmas lights?*" Lexie corrected. Okay, really, who talked like that these days? Still, good grammar was important, and she was, after all, a teacher.

"May we have Christmas lights?"

Lexie flipped over his grilled cheese sandwich and contemplated. Those lights had lured her little boy right out of the yard. She'd brought him in and set him in a kitchen chair for six minutes (match the time to the age) and forced him to contemplate his disobedience.

Lights had been his downfall. Would it be good parenting to put some up? Even though she taught little children and had a college degree that proclaimed her an expert in early-childhood development, she often felt totally adrift when it came to parenting her own child. Parenting was such a huge responsibility. What if she screwed it up?

"Our house would look pretty with Christmas lights," Brock continued.

Yes, it would. So should she acquiesce, or shouldn't she? She had disciplined him, and they'd had a talk about how important it was not to go wandering off and scaring Mommy.

Brock had agreed that it wasn't good to scare Mommy. He'd learned his lesson. No more wandering off.

She did enjoy holiday lights, especially the ones that dangled like icicles. When her father was alive, he'd put them up every year. Those lights had turned their modest tract home into something magical and had brought a warm glow to a dark night. How could she not do the same for her child?

But she'd never put up Christmas lights before, and she had no idea how to go about it. Still, how hard could it be? She was sure she'd find a tutorial on YouTube or wikiHow.

"Stanley has lights," Brock pointed out.

Yes, Stanley, the next-door neighbor, Brock's new best friend. He'd come home with a wealth of information about the man. Stanley, it appeared, could take kids or leave them.

"But he likes me," Brock had concluded after sharing.

"How do you know that?" she'd asked.

"'Cuz he talked to me."

Well, there you had it. And it was more than she could say.

Brock was looking at her eagerly. It was their first Christmas in their new house. Their very own house. They needed to make it special.

"All right," she said, setting his plate in front of him. "We'll go to the hardware store after lunch. How does that sound?"

"That sounds good," he said with a grin and dug into his sandwich.

She sliced half an apple for him and added the slices to his plate, then ate the other half herself.

"An apple a day keeps the doctor away," her grandma used to tell her when she was growing up. She eventually did a little research on the health benefits of apples and learned that apples did, in fact, provide not only fiber but vitamin C, antioxidants and potassium. Ever since then, she'd become an apple-a-day girl, and Granny had approved.

Actually, Granny had approved of almost everything Lexie did. She was a good student and had graduated from college with honors. The only dumb thing she'd done was plan a future with the wrong man. Maybe someday she'd get a chance to do that right.

Although she had no idea where she'd find a new prospect. Not at work. Most of the teachers at school were women. There were two men on staff, but one was middle-aged and married, and the other was gay. No single dads had come across her path, though several rom-coms had convinced her they would. Lexie had a theory about that. Men didn't tend to get discontent in their marriages until their children were older than kindergarten. The novelty hadn't yet worn off.

Oh, listen to her. What a cynic she'd become.

But she wasn't a cynic, not really. She'd hung her mistletoe, and she still had hope. Maybe she'd try online dating again. Every man out there wasn't still living with his parents or fresh out of a relationship and bitter. Right?

After lunch she and Brock got in her well-seasoned Chevy Volt and drove to Family Sam's Hardware Store. According to Lexie's new friend Shannon, Family Sam had been divorced three times and wasn't on speaking terms with two of his offspring. But what could you do? It would be poor marketing, indeed, to change his store name to something more accurate. Grumpy Old Guy Supplies? Divorced with Drill Bits?

The temperature had dropped to freezing overnight and hadn't warmed up much since. Sidewalks and roads were still slippery. The car slid a little as Lexie backed it out of the driveway.

Maybe this was not a good idea. She didn't have snow tires yet.

But there was Brock, squirming in anticipation in his seat and asking if they could get lights just like the ones Stanley had.

"I like those pretty colors," he informed her.

"Then, that's what we'll get," she said and kept the car backing down the driveway. She'd go slowly. They'd be fine.

Everyone in town seemed to be taking advantage of a rain-free Sunday afternoon on this holiday weekend to dress up their houses, and Lexie and Brock passed several homes where people bundled in coats and scarves and gloves were busy stringing lights. Many yards had inflatable snowmen and Santas and reindeer laid out, waiting to get blown up come dark.

This was Lexie's favorite time of year. She loved the atmosphere of celebration and happiness, loved the sights and the sounds, the Christmas pageants and winter concerts, the gatherings, the hopefulness of it all. If only it could be Christmas all year long, how much happier people would be!

The hardware store was a beehive of activity, with men in jeans and jackets and boots in the lighting and plumbing aisles or poking around among the nuts and bolts, and couples checking out various displays of decorations.

One couple was looking at artificial trees, and Lexie felt a twinge of wistfulness. That had been her when she'd first got engaged, standing with Mistake Man, choosing their first tree together. Oh, the visions she'd had of a growing family gathered around it, opening presents!

If only she hadn't wanted that big, expensive, blow-out wedding and waited so long. They'd have gotten married and...then divorced. Things hadn't worked out with a diamond on her finger. It was foolish to think a band of gold would have made any difference.

"Can we get a tree?" Brock asked.

"*May we get a tree?*" she corrected.

"May we get a tree?"

"We're going to get one, but remember, we're getting a real tree this year," she said. "That's why we're waiting."

"I like that one," he said, pointing to the tree the couple was checking out.

"I do, too, but you'll like a real one even more," she assured him.

Speaking of real trees, better get a tree stand while supplies lasted.

"A real tree," Brock repeated, following her down the aisle.

With the tree stand taken care of, they moved on to the Christmas lights. The selection was already looking a little picked over. Good thing they'd come when they had.

"Miss Bell, Miss Bell!" called a childish voice.

Lexie turned to see one of her students running toward her, his parents following behind.

"Hello, Henry. How are you?" Lexie greeted him.

"I know my numbers now," the little boy informed her. "My daddy helped me."

"Very good," Lexie said.

As she greeted Henry's parents, who'd come up behind him, she heard Brock saying to the little boy "My Stanley helped me."

Helped him what? And *his* Stanley? With one short conversation he'd adopted their reclusive neighbor.

She sighed inwardly. It would be so nice for Brock to have a daddy, one that came with a grandpa. But she didn't have a magic wand she could wave and instantly produce one. They were doing fine on their own. Not every child had a daddy. Not every child had a mommy. And not every child had a grandpa. These days families came in all varieties.

It was time to have that chat, as her son was obviously hoping for the traditional kind of family, using Stanley as a stand-in.

A moment of chitchat and Henry and his mama and daddy went on their way, leaving Lexie and Brock alone with the lights.

"Brockie," she said gently, "it's a little early to be claiming Stanley for your own."

"But he likes me," Brock insisted, looking up at her with those beautiful brown eyes.

What was not to like? "I know, sweetie. But he's not related to us, and we don't know him that well."

"We could. He could be my new grandpa."

"Maybe someday you'll have a grandpa again," she said. "Meanwhile, let's be happy with just the two of us. Shall we?"

Stanley looked down at his boots, a sure sign that he wasn't inclined to think this a good idea.

"There are all kinds of families," she said.

"Like Tommy Dinkler? He has two daddies. And two grandpas," Brock added jealously.

"Yes, and you have a mommy and a grandma and Uncle Fred and Aunt Rose and Auntie Jen and Auntie Angie."

Lexie could tell he was weighing the benefits of what his old kindergarten playmate in California had against what he had, and the scales still weren't balancing.

To distract him, she said, "Let's decide what lights we want. How does that sound?"

It sounded good enough for him to forget about daddies and grandpas.

They selected multicolored lights to cover the front roofline and then got a ladder. Lexie could already envision how charming their house would look all dressed up in colored lights.

As she was daydreaming, a man with a beautifully sculpted face and an equally well-sculpted body appeared behind the counter, dressed casually in jeans and a red flannel shirt. Where had he come from? She'd been in the store a couple of times since moving to town and had never seen him before.

Those gorgeous hazel eyes of his lit up at the sight of her, and she could feel sparks fly her way across the counter.

Lexie's gaze immediately zeroed in on the naked ring finger on his left hand. Sparks and a naked finger—a strong sign that her Christmas could get merry and bright.

"Hey, there," he greeted her as she wheeled up her long cart with the ladder and lights. "Getting ready for Christmas?"

"Yep. It's my favorite holiday."

"Mine, too," he said as he scanned the bar code on the ladder. "Are you new in town? I don't think I've seen you before."

"I've been in a couple of times."

"Must have been my day off. I'd have remembered you."

Brock had been dawdling nearby, checking out a display of prelit standing reindeer. Now he called for Lexie, racing to her, nearly knocking an older man in a jacket and baseball cap off balance and making him scowl.

"Mommy! Look at the reindeer," he cried.

"Brockie, you have to watch where you're going," Lexie scolded. "Say sorry to the man."

"Sorry," Brock mumbled, looking at his feet.

"No harm done," the man said, his scowl downgrading to a frown, and moved on.

The gorgeous man with the hazel eyes looked warily at Brock, and Lexie could feel the sparks die. He finished ringing up her sale with a much less friendly smile, and there was no more talk about the holidays.

Well, then, your loss, she thought as she handed over her credit card. She was incapable of falling for any man who didn't fall for her son. Like her mom told her after her breakup, she'd gotten an education in love. That conversation was embedded in her brain.

LEXIE'S MOTHER, aunt and cousins had all gathered on the back patio only hours after her fatal conversation with the man she'd thought she'd be marrying. It was a beautiful summer day, the sun sparkling off the water in the pool. The gardenias were in bloom and scenting the whole back yard. It was an idyllic setting for a meltdown.

Which Lexie was in the middle of having. "I can't believe this. I thought he loved me. We finally had all the money we needed for the wedding, and I was about to start making reservations, order the invitations, shop for my wed…wed…"

Instead of finishing the sentence she broke into fresh tears. There would be no wedding-gown shopping, no reservation-making, no ordering of invitations. No perfect beach ceremony in Hawaii. No perfect life with her perfect man. Who, it turned out, wasn't so perfect after all.

"I'm sure he did love you," Aunt Rose said in an effort to console her.

"He just found someone he loved more," added her cousin Angie.

"Oh, that was helpful," her other cousin, Jen, said, frowning at Angie.

Mom patted Lexie's arm as Aunt Rose poured more lemonade into her glass. "These things happen. He wasn't the right one. Better to find out now than later."

Lexie hadn't wanted to find out at all. She'd been perfectly happy in her ignorance.

"I thought he *was* the right one," she protested. "We had so much in common."

They both liked movies and street tacos and hanging out at the beach. Come to think of it, he'd also liked checking out the other women at the beach. Lexie looked darned good in a bikini if she did say so herself, but that never stopped his eyes from wandering. Hmm.

He'd always say it was her he loved and it meant nothing. Looking back, she realized it had actually meant something. He wasn't ready to get married.

"I always thought he was conceited," Jen said.

"And not half as smart as you," put in Angie.

Except Lexie hadn't noticed that anything was wrong, so how smart was she, really? Well smart enough to say adios. Most mistakes deserved a second chance, but not cheating.

"Darling, someone better will come along," Mom said.

"How will I recognize him?" Lexie said miserably. "Obviously, I don't know how to pick the right man."

"You will after this," her aunt assured her.

"Try to think of it as an education in love," said her mother.

This particular education was ten times more costly than her college tuition. She was paying for it with her heart.

She could still see him sitting there in their apartment living room, right next to her on the sofa. He'd taken both her hands in his and said, "Lex, I have something to tell you."

She'd wanted to say, "I have something to tell you, too." After the latest deposit she'd made in their joint savings account, they finally had enough money for their dream wedding. She'd planned to tell him that and then mention the other little surprise that neither of them had planned on just yet. But the sadness in his eyes stopped her.

"I've met someone," he'd said.

"Good riddance if he's been cheating on you," said her cousin Angie, bringing her back into the moment.

"For sure," Jen agreed.

"I know it doesn't look like it right now, but this is a blessing in disguise. You can do better. You deserve better," said her mother.

Yes, she did.

"And next time you'll know better," put in Aunt Rose. "Take your time. Be picky. You owe it to yourself and the baby."

"Now, there's something to celebrate," said Jen. "I think we should have a baby shower."

"I think we should spend that money and go to Hawaii," said Angie. "Let's all go on your honeymoon!"

"Good idea," said her aunt. "You girls go and have a good time and forget about…"

"He-who-shall-not-be-named," said Jen.

The three cousins did fly to Hawaii. They shared a room at a fancy resort, played on the beach and drank fancy drinks with little umbrellas in
them—virgins for Lexie and the baby. The whole time she tried not to be
jealous of the couples she saw walking the beach, holding hands. It should
have been her.

It would be someday, she told herself. But she was going to hold out for
someone special, who understood the meaning of commitment.

"There's someone for everyone," her mom kept telling her. "You'll find
yours. And the next time it will be the right choice because you'll be wiser."

LEXIE WAS, INDEED, wiser now, and she knew better than to get taken in by
a handsome face. She was looking for more than a great smile and a beautiful body. She wanted a beautiful heart.

Another store employee, a teenage boy with a crop of pimples, carried
the ladder to her car for her, Brock bouncing along next to her as if he had
springs in his shoes, chanting, "We got lights. We got lights."

The only thing they didn't *got* was a rope to secure the ladder on the top
of the car, which she now realized they needed.

"I should have thought of that," she said, frowning at the car and ladder,
both of which had disappointed her.

There was nothing for it but to hurry back inside the store to purchase
some rope.

"I'll wait here," her ladder Sherpa promised.

"Thanks," she said. "Come on, Brockie. Let's go."

She took her son's hand, and they hustled back across the parking lot. It
had been salted to take care of ice and keep customers from slipping, but
there were a few dips and dents in the asphalt.

Lexie's foot found one. Her ankle turned in a direction no ankle was ever
meant to turn and, like a puppet with its strings cut, she went down, landing on her side. *Ow. Ow, ow...* No, more than *ow*. Paaain. And cold, hard
ground, people (including her own son) gawking.

Oh, and look, the stars had come out early. There they all were, dancing right in front of her eyes.

CHAPTER EIGHT

"MOMMY, YOU FELL!" Brock exclaimed, squatting down next to her and looking at her with concern.

The ladder Sherpa joined them. "You okay, lady?"

She would be if she could breathe. "I...oh...my...ankle."

"We can put a SuperBob bandage on it," Brock said. "SuperBob makes everything better."

A couple who looked to be somewhere in their forties rushed up. "I'm a doctor," said the man. "Are you hurt?"

Her pride. "I'm fine," she said, gritting her teeth. She'd endured un-medicated childbirth. She could survive anything. *Deep breaths. No, pant.*

Never mind the breathing. Whimper.

A large man with salt-and-pepper hair and a scruffy beard of the same color, wearing boots, jeans and an old army jacket trotted up to them. "What happened here?" he demanded. Was this Family Sam, himself?

"She slipped," said the woman.

"We salted the parking lot. You couldn't have slipped on ice," the big man informed Lexie. Yep, Family Sam, worried about a lawsuit.

"What about the rope?" asked the pimply teenager.

"I was coming back in to get rope to tie down the ladder," Lexie ex-plained. And never mind the rope. She needed painkillers.

"For God's sake, go get some rope," the big man growled at his em-ployee. "Get Carl to help you tie it down. Here, let's get her up," he said to the doctor.

"Can you stand?" the doctor asked Lexie.

She bit down on her lip and nodded. She didn't have much choice. She couldn't lie there in the parking lot.

They managed to get her up on her own two (at this point, one and a half) feet.

"There, good as new," said the big man.

"Would you like me to examine it?" the doctor asked her.

No, what she wanted was to get away. This was all so embarrassing. "I'm sure it's fine."

"You might have a chip fracture," the doctor warned.

"She's fine. Aren't you?" The big man gave her a fatherly pat on the shoulder and smiled. He had a big, toothy grin. It made her think of the Big Bad Wolf. *Grandpa, what big teeth you have!*

Lexie wasn't one to make waves. "I'm sure it's nothing," she said. Except this *nothing* sure hurt.

"Yes, you're young," said the big man, as if that made her invincible.

The teenager was back, another man with him (not the handsome one with the hazel eyes). "Ah, there's your rope. Get that ladder secured, boys. On the house," the big man said to Lexie.

"Thank you," she said between gritted teeth.

"It's the least you can do, considering she slipped in your parking lot, Sam," the woman with the doctor said, frowning at the big man.

So it was indeed Family Sam himself to the rescue. Except Lexie was sure he was more concerned with avoiding an insurance claim than rescuing a hapless customer who took a spill in his parking lot.

"You really should get that x-rayed," the doctor advised her.

She was aware of Family Sam's fatherly smile fading. "If your insurance doesn't cover it, you just send the bill to us," he told Lexie and gave her another fatherly pat.

"A lot cheaper than a lawsuit," the woman taunted.

"Let me help you to your car," said Family Sam, edging Lexie away from the Good Samaritans. "You go home and put some ice on it, and it will be good as new."

She wasn't so sure. Putting any weight on her foot brought tears to her eyes and made her gasp.

By the time she got home her ankle had swollen up like a softball. The doctor was right. She needed someone to look at it.

"I'll get you a SuperBob bandage," Brock offered.

"That's very sweet of you," she said, happy to encourage her son's chivalry. But SuperBob wasn't going to cut it.

She called her friend Shannon. "Are you busy?"

"Absolutely, binging on Hallmark holiday movies," Shannon replied. "You and Brock want to come over and join me?"

"Actually, I think I need a ride to the emergency room." No way did she want to drive anymore and keep putting pressure on her poor, swollen right ankle.

"The emergency room! Oh, no! What's wrong? Is it Brock?"

"No, he's fine. It's me. I fell in Family Sam's parking lot and twisted my ankle. It's kind of a mess, and I think I need to get it looked at. I'm sorry to bug you," Lexie hurried on. "I just couldn't think who else to call."

She sounded pathetic and desperate. She was.

"I love bugs. I'll be right over."

True to her word, Shannon was at Lexie's house in less than fifteen minutes. Brock let her in, informing her that Mommy fell, and she hurried to where Lexie sat, icing her injury.

"I hope it's just a sprain," Lexie said, lifting the package of frozen peas for show-and-tell. Although, she was beginning to have her doubts. She'd sprained her ankle once in PE in middle school, trying out for the volleyball team. (Which was when she realized she wasn't and didn't want to be a jock.) It hadn't felt anything like this.

"Mommy says it hurts," Brock offered.

Shannon took one look at the purple balloon at the end of Lexie's leg with its tiny cartoon character bandage and made a face. "I bet it does. You definitely need to go to the emergency room," she told Lexie. "Guess what?" she said to Brock. "We get to take your mom to the hospital. She's got a big owie, and we're going to have a doctor fix it."

Lexie got her coat back on and Brock all bundled up, and then, with Shannon's help, hop-hobbled out to her car, which looked almost as old as Lexie's. Teaching was a noble profession, but not the way to get rich quick. Or even slow.

"After the doctor makes you better, can we put up our Christmas lights?" Brock asked. "May we?" he quickly corrected himself.

"Let's talk about that when we get back," Lexie said. Maybe Family Sam would send someone over to hang her lights. Maybe he'd feel bad enough or at least worried enough to offer that service for free.

Woodland General Hospital was a twenty-five-year-old facility but had tried to disguise its age with a fresh coat of paint. The emergency room had updated flooring and new chairs in the waiting area—just enough window dressing to tell patients *We're on top of things.*

The waiting area was sparsely populated, with a couple in their early twenties seated side by side, both wearing sweatshirts over pajama bottoms and busy on their phones, and two older women, maybe sisters, looking at them in disgust. Whether the problem was the pj's or the phones or the fact that neither looked sick, who knew?

One of the women did give Lexie a sympathetic look as she limped over after giving her information at the reception desk and getting a lovely plastic bracelet. Between the limp and the yelps, she looked pretty pathetic.

"Who knows?" Shannon said as they settled into their chairs with the stiff, Naugahyde cushions. "You might meet a gorgeous nurse. Or a doctor."

"Emergency-room speed dating?" Lexie joked, with a smile and a shake of her head.

"Stranger things have happened, and speed dating is better than no dating. Someone's getting happy doing Eventbrite singles' events. Not me, though. So far that's been a bust."

Which was a mystery to Lexie. With her pretty face and great curves her friend should have been a regular man magnet.

Shannon sighed. "I tend to meet my men…hmmm. Where do I meet men? Oh, yeah. Nowhere. I swear, I don't think there's one decent single man in this whole town."

"There's got to be some somewhere."

"I don't know. It's like mining for gold when the mine's gone dry. Or dead. Or whatever it is mines do."

"There's always Bumble or Hinge," Lexie said, pushing away the memory of her failed matchup attempts.

Shannon rolled her eyes. "Been there, done that. They always look so promising until you scratch beneath the surface. I found one cheater with a white no-tan line where his wedding ring had been, one condescending mansplainer, one stoner who asked to borrow money so he could pay for our drinks. And a partridge in a pear tree."

"There are still good men out there," Lexie insisted.

"Let me know when you find one, and ask him if he's got a brother."

"Grandpa Stanley is a good man," piped up Brock, who wasn't so busy playing an educational game on his tablet that he couldn't keep track of the conversation.

"Grandpa Stanley?" Shannon asked.

"Our neighbor," Lexie explained. "He's an older man."

"How much older?"

"Way much older."

"Oh, well. Hold out for a doctor, then."

The nurse who settled them in their curtained cubicle looked barely out of high school let alone college, the doctor was a woman, and the X-ray technician was middle-aged and wore a wedding ring.

"Strike three," Shannon said after he'd finished with them.

"That's okay. I'm not desperate."

"I am. It's been way too long since I've had *s-e-x*."

"What's that?" Brock asked.

"Nothing you'd be interested in," Lexie told him.

"I just read about a new dating app," Shannon said.

"Yeah?" Lexie prompted.

Shannon brought the site up on her phone. "*Chemistry you can't flunk,*" she read. "*We'll find your perfect match.*"

"I'm not sure there is such a thing," Lexie said.

She'd revved up her hope after the father fail had left and tried one of those sites but had quickly learned that people weren't exactly truthful about themselves online. The real thing rarely matched his picture, which was usually off by several years or pounds, and those dates often lacked conversation. Which always surprised her when it seemed the same men could chat up a storm from the safety of their keyboards. She'd finally concluded that if anything was going to happen for her, it would have to happen organically.

Whatever that meant.

The lack of eligible men on the hospital staff wasn't the bad news. The bad news was the result of the X-ray. Lexie did, indeed, have a chip fracture. This discovery was followed by the gift of a blue walking boot that was big and clunky and made her feel like Frankenstein's monster as she walked out of the hospital.

It could be worse. Her insurance would not only cover the visit and the boot but also a visit to a specialist, which would be next on the list.

"I can take you after school tomorrow if they can fit you in," Shannon said as they left with Lexie's new fashion accessory, a referral and a prescription for pain meds.

"Thanks." Lexie sighed. "I guess I should be grateful I didn't break it."

"I'm hungry," Brock announced.

"We'd better stop at Daisy's Dairy Delights on the way home," Shannon said. "My treat. How does a burger and a chocolate-mint shake sound?" she asked Brock.

"Yay!" he cheered.

So after picking up Lexie's pain meds, which Lexie was determined to take only at night and only for a couple of days, they fueled up at Daisy's.

"Thanks for coming to the rescue," she said when Shannon finally dropped them off.

"Happy to do it. I remember what it was like being new in town. Do you need a lift to school tomorrow? You sure aren't going to be able to drive wearing that thing."

"We can walk. It's only a couple of blocks," Lexie said. And it was, after all, a walking boot.

"It's supposed to rain tomorrow. I'll pick you up," Shannon insisted.

It was going to be bad enough wearing the boot around the classroom. Lexie took her up on the offer.

"Can we hang up our Christmas lights now?" Brock asked as Lexie hung up their coats. "May we?" he corrected himself.

Trying to climb up the ladder (still on her car roof) with the big boot didn't seem like a wise idea. Lexie's spirits, already a little low, took the elevator to the basement. Bad enough she had this stupid fracture. Now she had to disappoint her son.

Temporarily, she told herself. She'd find someone to hang the lights. Check with the hardware store. Put out a call on the Fairwood community page on Facebook. Maybe she could ask one of the teachers at school. Perhaps Ed Murrow would be willing to help her out. He was probably around fifty and seemed pretty handy, surely not too old to go up a ladder.

"Can we?"

She didn't bother to correct his grammar. Somehow, it didn't seem right when she had to disappoint him.

"Not today, honey. I can't go up a ladder with my hurt foot." Lexie stuck out her walking boot as a visual reminder. "But I'm sure we can find someone to help us later this week," she added, falling back on her mother's child-rearing philosophy that if you had to deprive a child of a treat you needed to have Option Number Two handy.

Option Number Two offered hope to take away the sting of disappointment. Anyway, they still had plenty of time until Christmas. The window of Christmas-light opportunity was far from closing.

Brock wasn't on board with Option Number Two. His eyebrows took a dip right along with the corners of his mouth.

"Oh, no. Here comes Prince Thundercloud. We don't like to see him, do we?" Lexie said. "He makes Mommy sad."

This ploy usually worked, but not today. Prince Thundercloud refused to leave.

"You promised," Brock said, his voice filled with umbrage.

"Yes, I did, and I will find a way to make sure we get our lights up. Meanwhile, I need to see an attitude adjustment," she said firmly. "Okay?"

Brock was still looking far from happy, the ghost of Prince Thundercloud lingering.

"Let's make you some ants on a log," she said, and started for the kitchen.

He nodded and followed her there, stood silently by while she washed a couple of celery stalks and cut them into pieces.

She set the peanut-butter jar on the kitchen bar along with the box of golden raisins and handed over a dull knife. "How about you get the log ready?"

He took the knife and globbed peanut butter onto the celery. "I could hang up the lights. I watched Grandpa Stanley do it."

Grandpa Stanley again. "Honey, he's not your grandpa."

"He could be."

Yes, and there could be a reindeer out there somewhere with a red nose. "Here, let's put some ants on your log," she said and opened the box of raisins.

He reached in and took several, spacing them out along the middle of the celery log, concentrating on his task.

"Very good," she said when he was done.

He took a bite. "I bet Grandpa Stanley would like to help us."

"Maybe, when he knows us better."

Okay, the ants weren't cutting it. They needed a better distraction. "How about we give Grandma a call and see how she's doing?" Lexie suggested.

Talking to her mother had been easy when she was a child, a trial when she was a teenager and a lifeline once she hit her twenties. Since losing her father, it had become a duty.

Not that she didn't love her mother or want to talk to her, but conversation since Daddy's death felt like trying to chat about the weather with a fellow passenger in one of the *Titanic*'s lifeboats. Still, those calls kept them connected and, Lexie hoped, reminded them that they still had each other.

"I'm sure Grandma would like to hear about how we decorated the house," she said, reaching for her cell phone.

Brock said nothing.

Lexie had about resigned herself to leaving a message on her mother's voice mail when Mom answered. "Hello, honey." She sounded as chipper as Brock.

"Hi, Mom. We thought we'd call and check in."

"That was sweet of you. How are you doing?"

"We've been having adventures. We got the house all decorated for Christmas. Here, I'll let Brock tell you all about it."

He took the phone and said a dutiful, "Hi, Grandma. We got lights. But Mommy can't hang them up because she's hurt and has a big blue shoe on her foot. I'm going to ask Grandpa Stanley to put them up for us." There was a pause, and then he held the phone out to Lexie. "Grandma wants to talk to you."

"What is Brock talking about?" her mother demanded.

"I took a fall in the hardware-store parking lot and wound up with a chip fracture."

"Oh, Lord. What next?" Her mother's favorite phrase. Ever since Daddy died she'd turned into an Eeyore. "Are you in a cast?"

"No, a walking boot." Too bad in a way. If she'd been in a cast, preferably full-body, maybe her mother would have roused herself from her doldrums and offered to come help her.

"What were you doing at the hardware store?" As far as Mom was concerned, hardware stores were the domain of contractors and bored husbands.

"We were getting the lights."

"That Grandpa Stanley's going to hang," Mom said as if Brock had just told her that a tall, invisible rabbit named Harvey was helping them out. "Who is Grandpa Stanley?"

"The older man next door," Lexie explained as Brock skipped out of the kitchen. "Brock finally met him and has taken a liking to him."

"Have *you* met him?"

"Not yet."

"I'm going to Grandpa's," Brock called from the front hall.

Going to Grandpa's? "Oh, for heaven's sake. Mom, I have to call you back."

"Alexandra, what's going on?" her mother demanded.

"Brock, you stay right here," Lexie called.

No answer. Of course not. Her son was a mini-man on a mission. Once she got him back home he was going to be sitting on that kitchen chair for a lot longer than six minutes.

"Brock's on his way next door."

"To Grandpa's," her mother said, half disgusted, half confused.

"He knows he's not supposed to go out without me." That was it. She was going to have a lock installed at the top of the front door. "I'll call you later," she said and ended the call.

She clumped through the house as fast as she could, stopped at the coat closet only long enough to pull down her son's parka. Of course a little boy making a break for it wouldn't stop for something so insignificant as a coat.

Pulling her sweater tightly about her, she made her clumsy way down the front-porch steps and started across the lawn. Why was it, when you got pregnant, that no one ever warned you how hard parenting was?

Oh, yes, because then the entire race would die out.

Chip fractures, runaway sons… Honestly, could this day get any worse?

CHAPTER NINE

STANLEY WAS VERY BUSY—watching a hockey game on TV—when his door-bell rang. And rang. And rang.

Dog, his temporary houseguest, was thrilled with the idea of company and jumped off the recliner where she'd been sitting with him, raced to the door and began to bark.

Who the heck was on his front porch this late on a Sunday? Girl Scouts? Blue Birds? Someone selling magazines to put himself through college? What-ever they were selling, Stanley wasn't interested.

Okay, maybe if it was cookies, but it wasn't Girl Scout cookie season.

"I don't want any," Stanley called. Which was stupid. Nobody could hear him over the TV and the barking dog.

The doorbell continued to ring.

With a scowl, he pushed out of his recliner and lumbered over to the door. People should leave a man alone on the weekend when he was trying to rest.

He looked out one of the tall narrow windows that flanked his front door. No one selling anything. But something just as irritating.

He opened the door and frowned down on the kid from next door. What was he doing wandering around the neighborhood? It would be dark soon. And where was his coat? What kind of woman let a kid this age wander around the neighborhood without a coat? Or even with a coat?

Dog didn't care about any of those details. She was happy to greet their visitor, jumping up and pawing him.

The little boy giggled and knelt down to pet her, dropping the box he'd been holding. "What's your dog's name?"

"Dog. Does your mother know you're out?"

The boy nodded. He picked the box back up. It was a shiny cardboard one with a picture of a house lit with colored lights.

He offered it to Stanley. "Mommy can't hang up our Christmas lights. Will you?"

Stanley frowned and hid his hands behind his back. "Why can't your mom hang them?" What did he look like, the neighborhood handyman?

A soft chuckle floated on the air behind him.

His frown got longer. No, no, no. He did not hear a thing.

"She's hurt."

"Well, then, your dad."

"I don't have a daddy."

"Brock!" called an angry voice.

Stanley looked to see his neighbor coming his way. She was a pretty young woman, slender with long, reddish hair. She was carrying the boy's coat, but she herself was only in jeans and a thin sweater. And a blue walking boot. So that was why she couldn't hang the lights.

"Brock Arthur Bell," she scolded the boy, who gave a start and dropped the box. "What did I say about leaving the yard?"

The kid's lower lip began to wobble. "I just wanted to ask Grandpa Stanley to hang up our lights."

Grandpa Stanley?

The woman joined them on the porch and began stuffing her son into his red parka. "I'm sorry Brockie bothered you," she said to Stanley. "He was so enthralled with your Christmas lights that he wanted to put some up on our house. I'm afraid I fell in the parking lot at Family Sam's and fractured my ankle, so I don't want to try going up a ladder."

You can.

It felt like Carol was hovering right behind his shoulder. "I did not hear that," Stanley informed her.

"Excuse me?" The neighbor woman's face was turning red, probably not from the cold.

"Nothing," Stanley said. Meanwhile, the boy was kneeling in front of the dog, laughing while Butt Breath slobbered all over his face. "Dog, stop that," Stanley commanded, pulling on her collar.

Good grief. Dogs and kids and helpless neighbors. He had no idea what he had done to deserve this invasion of his privacy.

"I'm so sorry we bothered you," said the woman. "Come on, Brockie. We need to go home."

"But what about the lights?" The kid's face was scrunching up like he was going to cry. Next to him the dog whimpered in sympathy.

Stanley could hear the TV blasting at him from the living room. Some choir was singing "Deck the Halls." What the devil had happened to his hockey game? As if he couldn't guess. Carol again.

"Oh, for crying out loud," he muttered and scooped up the box. "I'll get my coat." He'd put the lights up, and then he'd be done with the neighbors.

"We have a ladder," Brock said, pointing to their car.

"So I see," Stanley said.

"You don't need to," she began.

"Yeah, I do," Stanley said, resigned.

"Well, thank you," she said. "It means a lot to my son. Come on, Brockie," she said to the kid, holding out her hand.

He didn't take it. "Can I walk over with Grandpa Stanley?"

Stanley was going to have to put a stop to this *grandpa* crap.

"May I?" his mother corrected, and Stanley suddenly remembered playing Mother, May I? as a kid.

This mother looked at him as if assessing his ability to get her son from his front lawn to hers. He obviously passed the test because instead of saying "No, you may not," she said, "All right. But once we're back at the house, you stay right in front of it. Do you understand me?"

The kid nodded eagerly and grinned.

Stanley, on the other hand, didn't. First he was the neighborhood handyman, now he was the nanny next door.

He grabbed his coat, Dog dancing at his heels, and then trudged next door with both Dog and Kid tagging along. It was freeze-your-ass-off cold out, and the air was damp, and Stanley had already hung one set of Christmas lights. Which he hadn't wanted to do. Wasn't Sunday supposed to be a day of rest?

There was no rest for his ears. The boy kept up a steady line of chatter. "We went to a hospital, and Mommy got her foot x-ed."

"You mean *x-rayed*."

Brock nodded. "Shannon took us. She's nice."

Mommy had a friend. Maybe that would lessen the amount of harassment she and the kid gave Stanley in the future.

"My grandma's in California," Brock continued. "My grandpa died, and he's with the angels."

So the boy was looking for a grandpa substitute. Well, he'd have to look somewhere else. At this point in life the last thing Stanley needed to be bothered with was a kid.

"Here," he said, handing over the box of lights. "Take these, and go wait on the porch." *And give me a minute of peace.*

The boy obeyed, walking off with the box, and Stanley trudged to the car and retrieved the ladder with Dog supervising.

"We're not going to get involved with these people," Stanley said to her.

As if the dog was staying? No, that wouldn't happen. Somebody would call and take her off his hands.

Back at the house, the kid was sitting on the front porch, his feet planted on the first step, his arms wrapped around the box of lights like it held treasure. Stanley supposed, in a way, it did. Kids were so easily pleased. Things that seemed small to grown-ups were huge to them.

He thought back to his own childhood, what a big deal it always was decorating the tree with his mom and dad and brother every year. And oh, the excitement of hanging up those Christmas stockings!

And oh, how pissed he'd been when he learned that his parents had lied to him about Santa Claus! He'd been all of five, and the news had been a crushing blow. Dad had lost his job at the plant, and they'd had to come clean. There would be no visit from Santa that year. There was no Santa, anyway, never had been. Stanley had been stunned, unable to take it in, even when he saw the proof of it on Christmas morning. The only presents under the tree had been socks and pajamas, new pants for his brother and him, along with boring knitted scarves and hats and winter coats a size too big from their grandparents. The Christmas stockings had felt like a joke, with hardly anything in them. An orange each and some Life Savers and a candy cane. No little toys, no fat bonbons. Not even any nuts. How could his parents have deceived him so?

"Life's tough," his dad had snapped when he made the mistake of complaining.

Christmas dinner had been at his grandma's. Turkey. Even back then he hadn't liked it. Grandma Clark had tried to save the day by serving cake and homemade fudge and sending some home with them. But it was too little too late.

If you asked Stanley, the whole Santa thing was sick and wrong, anyway. Better to give the kids presents and take credit for it yourself. Why should a fat man from an old poem get the glory? It was dumb. And scarring.

His neighbor came out on the porch to join her son, a jacket on over the sweater, as Stanley was setting up her ladder. She began helping the boy take the lights out of the box.

"It's awfully kind of you to do this," she said to Stanley.

He hadn't had much choice. He grunted and walked over to them. "You've barely got enough to do the front of your roofline," he informed her, look-ing at them.

"That will be enough," she said. "I really appreciate you helping us. If it wasn't for this boot I'd do it myself, but I was a little nervous about going up the ladder with it. I was going to find someone to help me," she added.

"Well, you did," Stanley said resentfully. He took the light string and started for the ladder. The kid moved to stand at the foot of it, watching as Stanley climbed.

It looked like he wasn't the only one who was going to be watching Stan-ley's every move. The woman stayed there on the porch.

"I'm Lexie Bell," she said.

"Stanley Mann," he replied. Not that he wanted to make her acquain-tance, but he did have some manners, after all.

"It's nice to finally meet you," she said. "We moved here from Califor-nia, and it's taking longer than I thought to get to know our neighbors."

What was he supposed to say to that? Nothing, he decided and kept working.

He was spared from any more conversation when her cell phone rang. She pulled it out of her coat pocket and said, "Hello, Mom. No, he's fine. Our neighbor's here now, helping us hang our lights. Isn't that kind of him?"

Kind, yeah, that was him.

She moved to the far end of her porch, still talking away on her phone. These millennials—or whatever the heck she was—they ought to just have their phones implanted in their hands and be done with it.

She was gone, but her kid was still right there at the foot of the ladder. "I like you," he said.

Oh, brother. "Don't be so quick to like people you don't know," Stanley said. He wasn't in a hurry to like this kid or his mom. And he sure wasn't in a hurry to get better acquainted with them.

"Do you like me?" Brock prompted.

"I'll let you know," Stanley said, stretching to secure another section of lights.

"When?"

"When what?"

"When will you let me know you like me?"

"Later," Stanley said and worked a little faster.

Lexie Bell had just finished her conversation when Stanley came down from the ladder. He plugged in the lights in the outdoor socket, and the roofline of their house suddenly glowed with all manner of jewel colors.

The boy jumped up and down and clapped his hands, and Lexie beamed at Stanley as if he'd worked a miracle.

"Thank you," she gushed. "How can we ever repay you?"

By not bugging me. "No need," he said. "If you open your garage door I'll put this ladder away."

"Oh, sure," she said and hurried inside.

A moment later, the door made its slow ascent, showing a garage filled with packing boxes, stacked every which way, and a Chevy compact. It probably didn't have any cardboard under it to catch oil drips.

Not his problem.

Lexie stood in the doorway, which looked like it led to the kitchen, same as Stanley's house. "Put it anywhere," she said.

Stanley leaned the ladder against the wall. "There you go," he said and started to hurry away before she could find something else to say and trap him there in some verbal spiderweb.

"Thank you again so much!" she called after him.

The kid, who was turning into his shadow, started to run after him.

"Brock Arthur Bell, you come here right now!" she called.

"I have to go," the kid said to him.

"Good," Stanley muttered. He beat it back home, Dog trotting next to him. Back in the house the TV was still going, and the hockey game was playing once more. Of course.

He got a towel and wiped off Dog's muddy paws, then wandered through the dining room on his way to the kitchen to make himself something hot to drink. He couldn't help seeing the house next door through the sheers covering the window. Those lights did look nice. Lexie Bell should have bought enough to do the porch railing as well.

Not his problem.

"Brockie, you need to remember what we talked about on Saturday, about staying in the yard," Lexie said firmly as she sat across from her son at their little dining table.

He nodded but looked confused. "I didn't wander off."

True, he hadn't. And he had told her where he was going.

"But you didn't wait to ask my permission, did you?" she pointed out. "You just left, and without your coat."

His gaze dropped, a sure admission of guilt.

"You knew I didn't want to bother Mr. Mann." Brock looked momentarily confused. "Stanley," she clarified.

"He didn't mind," Brock said.

Oh, good grief, she was getting nowhere. "Well, it was still wrong to go running off like that without waiting for my permission. You need to spend some time thinking about that."

He heaved a sigh. "I don't want to sit on the thinking chair."

"Well, you have to," Lexie said firmly.

"I just wanted lights," Brock grumbled and made his way to the designated chair to begin his little-boy torture session.

"I know. But I want you to think about what you did wrong. Okay?" He plopped onto the chair, his back turned toward her, shoulders hunched.

"You'll thank me someday." Had she just said that? She was turning into her mother.

That was okay. She was glad her parents had worked so hard to discipline and mold her. All those times she was sent to her room, deprived of candy for a week, grounded—how she'd resented them! But she'd learned to respect her elders and work hard, and she knew that was thanks to her parents working so hard to turn her into a civilized, responsible human being. She wanted the same for Brock, wanted him to grow up to be a good man.

Her son, a grown-up. That felt a hundred years away. Only a hundred years to go until Brock was civilized and responsible. A long, lonely haul when you were doing the parenting all by yourself.

Millions of women managed it somehow, she reminded herself. She would, too.

Brock's time-out ended and, after another little talk, they feasted on chicken strips, mashed potatoes and carrots for dinner. And chocolate milk. Punishment was over. It was time to end the day on a good note.

Bath time was followed by story time and bedtime prayers. "God bless Mommy and Grandma and Grandpa in heaven and Dog and Grandpa Stanley," Brock concluded.

Lexie hoped their neighbor didn't mind being dubbed an honorary grandpa. At some point she'd have to explain to Mr. Mann about her father's death. She hoped he'd understand and that he wouldn't mind. He wasn't much of a talker.

Or a smiler. It didn't bode well for understanding.

Oh, well, the world was full of grandpas. They'd find a better one somewhere.

"How's your foot feeling?" Shannon asked when she picked up Lexie and Brock for school on Monday.

"Not too bad, really," Lexie said. The pain meds worked wonders.

"Let me know when you want me to take you to the specialist."

"I can probably get an Uber," Lexie said.

"Sure, why not? You're rolling in the big bucks, right?" Shannon teased.

"I don't want to be a pain."

"You won't be. Give me chocolate for Christmas, and we'll call it even," Shannon said with a smile. "You know, the kids are going to find that boot fascinating," she predicted.

She was right. They did and, of course, wanted to hear all about Lexie's fractured ankle. "Did you cry when you fell down, Miss Bell?" Mirabella, one of her favorite students, asked.

"I wanted to," Lexie said.

"But you didn't?" Mirabella was amazed.

"Maybe a little. It's okay to cry when you're hurt, isn't it?"

All the students nodded.

"I cried when my turtle died," volunteered a little boy named Jonathan.

"That's okay because it's hard to lose pets we love. I bet you gave him a very happy life while he was here with you," Lexie said.

"I did," Jonathan replied and looked up adoringly at her. Adoration, one of the perks of teaching little ones.

Later, in the teachers' lounge, her coworkers were equally fascinated as well as sympathetic. "You poor girl. Are you going to have to have physical therapy?" asked Mrs. Davidson.

"Probably, but first I have to see a specialist. I need to call and schedule that," Lexie said, thankful for the reminder.

She brought up the information on her phone and called the specialist the emergency-room doctor had recommended. Happily, the doctor could squeeze her in that afternoon.

True to her word, Shannon drove her to the doctor, who did, indeed, prescribe physical therapy.

"We can see you tomorrow afternoon," the receptionist at Healing Help Physical Therapy assured Lexie when she called them.

"No problem running you there," Shannon assured her. "I can play *Cookie Jam* on my phone while I'm waiting."

Thank God for Shannon.

Except late that night Lexie got a text from her.

Puking big time and have a fever. Going to have to call in sick. Sorry I can't take you to school or PT. Don't hate me. ☹

Her poor friend. She should take her some chicken soup.

Sadly, she couldn't deliver it since she couldn't drive. Not to Shannon's, not to school. Not with this big, clunky boot.

Lexie frowned at her Frankenstein's monster footwear. Well, they didn't call it a walking boot for nothing. She'd walk to school and then she'd have to take an Uber to physical therapy.

She heard a soft pattering against her bedroom window. It was starting to rain, something they didn't get a lot of in Southern California. She shut her eyes and envisioned a not-so-brisk three-quarter-mile morning walk to school in chilly, damp weather.

Ho, ho, ho.

IT WAS EARLY MORNING, and Stanley was wheeling his garbage can to the curb when he saw the neighbor and her boy walking his way. It was cold and gray, not what you'd call a nice morning for a walk. But with that gigantic blue boot on her right foot she'd have trouble driving.

She was young and fit, and the school wasn't that far away. The rain would probably hold off.

He quickly turned to walk back up his driveway before he got trapped in conversation.

Too late. "Grandpa Stanley!" the boy called. "Grandpa Stanley!"

This was followed by his mother calling, "Brock, no. Leave Mr. Mann alone."

Stanley picked up his pace.

Stanley! What do you think you're doing?

It was just the wind, but it sure sounded like Carol. Stanley didn't want to, but he turned around.

"Hi, kid," he said to Brock. Okay, he'd been friendly. Now it was time to go inside. A wet drop on his nose confirmed that, yes, he didn't need to be standing around in his driveway.

Except here came Lexie Bell, hobbling up behind her son. Couldn't be much fun walking around in that thing.

"I'm afraid Brock's taken a shine to you," she said, half apology, half what-else he wasn't sure. Carol had been the one who read body language and translated conversational subtleties.

"I guess," he said, at a loss for any better way to respond. Two more wet drops fell, hitting the bald spot on top of his head.

"Well, have a nice day," she said and started walking away. "Come on, Brockie."

There. The woman was perfectly fine walking to school. A little rain never hurt anyone. Anyway, her coat had a hood, and that tote bag she was carrying looked waterproof.

Her son stayed put. "Shannon was going to drive us to school but she got sick. I don't think I like the rain," he added, scrunching up his face.

"It does that here in Washington," Stanley informed him.

"Brockie, come on," called Lexie Bell.

The boy heaved a dramatic sigh and started to trudge off after his mom.

Stanley frowned. Guilt was an uncomfortable thing.

Then he called, "Hey, you two. Come back here."

What a way to start his day.

CHAPTER TEN

"THIS IS SO nice of you," Lexie Bell said to Stanley as they drove off down the street. "I hope it's not too much trouble."

It was a pain in the butt. "You don't want to be walking around in the rain in that thing," he said.

"No, I don't. I really appreciate the lift. My friend was going to give me a ride this morning, but she's sick."

Which meant the woman would need a ride home, too. He sighed inwardly, resigned to his fate.

"What time do you get off?" he asked.

"Oh, Mr. Mann, you don't have to come get me," she protested.

If he didn't, he'd hear about it from Carol.

"It'll probably rain all day. You don't want to walk home in it. You don't even have an umbrella," he pointed out.

"You're right. It didn't rain that much where we lived. I guess I should invest in one now that we're up here."

"Yeah, you should," he agreed. "So, what time are you done with school?"

"You really don't have to bother. I have physical therapy scheduled right after. I'll just get an Uber."

"You're going to pay someone?" When she could get a ride for free? Stanley, not one to waste money, was horrified.

"Well, yes."

He shook his head. "Don't do that. What time do you get off?"

"I'll be ready to leave at three thirty. I'll pay you," she quickly offered.

"No need," he said.

Paying him would make about as much sense as calling some sort of taxi service. Who had that kind of money to fritter away?

He pulled into the drop-off lane and stopped, and she slid out.

"This was so kind of you. Thank you," she said as she opened the back door for her son.

"Thanks, Grandpa!" he called and hopped down.

"You go on in," she said to the boy. "I want to talk to Mr. Mann for a minute."

"Okay. Bye!" Brock said and ran off toward the front entrance.

"I wanted to explain about Brock," she said to Stanley. The few drops of rain had turned into a shower. She put up the hood of her coat. "My father died two years ago. He was the only grandpa Brock had. I'm afraid he wants a grandpa desperately."

"Doesn't your ex have a dad?" There had to be an ex somewhere in the picture. The kid hadn't been hatched.

"I'm afraid there isn't an ex. Well, there is, but he's not part of our lives and neither are his parents," she said, her face reddening. "We were engaged but..."

Stanley held up a hand. He wasn't into soap operas. "That's okay. I get the picture."

"Anyway, I appreciate you being so nice to him."

Nice to him? Stanley was doing his best to discourage the kid. Now he had two pests in his life, Mama Pest and Baby Pest.

"You'd better get inside before you drown," he said.

"And I should let you get going. Thanks again."

He nodded. She shut the door, and he got out of there.

Back home, Dog was waiting at the kitchen door to greet him, tail wagging, when he came in from the garage. She'd already devoured all the food in her dog dish.

"You'd think nobody had ever fed you," he said to her.

Maybe nobody had in a while. Her owners had to be going crazy looking for her. Stanley checked his voice mail. Someone should have seen those posters.

No messages.

"Where the heck are your owners?" he asked the animal.

She sat on her rump, swept the floor with her tail and yapped.

He pointed a finger at her. "You're not staying." He called the animal shelter to see if anyone had been in looking for a white West Highland terrier. No. He looked down at the dog, who looked up at him and wagged her little tail some more. "I don't want another dog," he informed her.

She cocked her head at him as if trying to understand.

He ignored her and made himself some coffee. At least there was coffee. That was something in his life that hadn't been turned upside down.

LEXIE HAD PACKED the children's day with activities ranging from working on learning the alphabet and all the sounds the various letters made to running one of their favorite math drills, which involved marching around the room, air punching while counting by twos. The story-time selection was *The Ninjabread Man*, a tale about a sensei's creation that comes to life and runs away.

Next came a craft project. She'd copied a pattern of a bell on red and green construction paper so the children could make their own Advent calendars.

"We're going to make paper chains to hang from our bells," she said, showing them the one she'd made as a sample.

"Bell, that's your name, Miss Bell," one of the children piped.

"Yes, it is. And what letter does the word *bell* start with?"

"*B!*" they chorused.

"And that makes the sound..."

"*Buh,*" came another chorus.

"Very good. Now, starting December first, every day we'll take off one link in our chain. Then we'll count how many links we have left, and that way we'll know how many days we have until Christmas."

The children wriggled with excitement.

"But we won't be in school until Christmas," Mirabella said, worried.

"No. But you'll all get to take your bells home with you when we leave for our winter break, so you can still take off the links," Lexie said.

She set them to work with safety scissors, cutting out the bells—a good motor-skills exercise for little hands. As the children worked she walked around the room, stopping at desks to help guide some of those little hands, offering compliments and encouragement as she went. "Good job following the lines, James... That's looking nice, Ilsa."

In addition to the Advent bells and Santa, Lexie had come up with a new favorite character, the Gingerbread Boy. She'd decorated the room with plenty of them before leaving school for Thanksgiving break, Brock helping her. There would be a hunt for the Gingerbread Boy, more stories about him, and on the last day of school, the children would find and decorate gingerbread boys (gluten-free for the children with allergies so everyone could enjoy the treat), all with the help of her two room mothers. It would be a month of learning, of course, but also of festivity. After all, Christmas was about joy, right?

The Christmas bell project went off without a hitch, and names were written on the bells and paper chains made, attached and counted. Lots of good learning there. By the end of the morning class, Lexie and her students were smiling. She took some ibuprofen and made her way to the teachers' lounge, humming "Joy to the World."

The afternoon slipped by as quickly as the morning had, and before she knew it, the school day was at an end and it was time for the children to collect their coats from their cubbies and line up at the door to go home. Another day successfully logged in. Lexie's ankle was screaming. Time for more ibuprofen.

She found her neighbor waiting for her when she and Brock walked outside. The rain had stopped but the trees were drippy, and the sky was still gray.

This was a variant Lexie hadn't thought to plan for when she took the job in Washington. Gray skies were rare in her corner of California. She'd never considered how much emotional warmth the sun provided. This constant gray was gloomy and made her feel a little gloomy, too.

Or maybe it was only that her ankle hurt.

"You're right on time," she said to Mr. Mann as she opened the back door for Brock. Rather an inane thing to say. Like he was a taxi driver or something. "Thank you for coming to get us."

"Where's the physical therapy place?" he asked, cutting to the chase.

"It's on Emerson Street. Do you know where that is?" Of course, he probably did. She was willing to bet he'd lived in this town for decades.

"Yeah, it's right around the corner from Main."

Main was the downtown street where the bank, the grocery store and drugstore and gas station were. It was dressed up for the holidays, the small trees in giant pots stationed along the sidewalk, all individually decorated. At the far end of Main were Daisy's Dairy Delight and a Taco Bell. Did every town in American have a Main Street? Probably.

On the corner of Main stood Great Escape, a small independent bookstore. The window display showed a Christmas tree made entirely of books with several teddy bears sitting nearby, each with a book propped in its lap.

Lexie had been in a couple of times since moving to town. On her last visit she'd learned that the owner, an older woman, had sold the store, and it would be passing into new hands soon. Lexie had been a little sad to learn this. She'd liked the woman and had been hoping to become better acquainted with her.

She'd also liked to have become better acquainted with her uncommunicative neighbor, to have been able to chat with him and ask him about his wife, and how long he'd lived in Fairwood. But Brock kept up a steady stream of chatter, telling Lexie all about his day, so Mr. Mann was neglected. He didn't seem bothered by that, though; he simply drove silently along.

He waited in his SUV while she met with the physical therapist for an assessment and was given her first easy exercises to do, Brock sitting on a chair nearby, then following her into the little gym area, taking it all in.

"I'll do exercises, too, Mommy," he promised as they left.

"That's a good idea," she said. "You can get strong ankles right along with me."

Back in the vehicle, conversation once more was between her and Brock with Mr. Mann their silent chauffeur.

He didn't speak until he'd pulled up in front of their house. "I'll give you a lift tomorrow if it's raining."

He sounded grudging, and she hoped it wouldn't rain.

"Well, thank you again," she said as she let Brock loose. "And please thank your wife for being so willing to share you with us."

The smile he'd almost been growing shriveled. "My wife's dead."

Something heavy landed in Lexie's chest, and she could feel her cheeks blazing. "I'm so sorry."

"It happens." He looked straight ahead, his face set in grim lines.

She couldn't think of anything to say, so she shut the door and gave a limp wave, which he didn't see, then followed Brock up the walk to the house. The poor man. No wonder he was so unhappy and unfriendly and un...everything.

It explained a lot. It also left her feeling at a loss for what to say next time she saw him. Where did they go from here? He obviously didn't want to talk about his wife. He obviously didn't like to talk at all. Awkward.

Oh, please don't let it rain tomorrow.

IT RAINED.

Once more she found herself being chauffeured to school by her neighbor.

Their parting the day before hung between them like a thick, black curtain, and Lexie felt nervous about trying to part it.

She wanted to ask about his wife—how she'd died, when she'd died, what she'd been like when she was alive. But Lexie could imagine how that would go over. Perhaps it was just as well that Brock kept up a running commentary all the way to school, telling Mr. Mann about his teacher and the boy in his class who'd lost a tooth and gotten five dollars from the tooth fairy.

"Tooth fairy," Mr. Mann had grunted in disgust. Obviously, not a fan.

Brock moved on from the tooth fairy to Santa Claus and how he wanted to ask Santa for a dog, but Mommy said they couldn't have one yet.

"Every kid should have a dog," Mr. Mann said.

Oh, fine. Now her neighbor wanted to talk?

"Santa knows we're waiting until you're a little bit older," she said to Brock, and Mr. Mann shook his head in disgust.

Obviously an expert on children. "Do you have children, Mr. Mann?" she asked. Sweetly, of course. Manners were important.

"No," he said shortly.

No wife, no children. Did he have any family nearby? Did he have friends? She hadn't seen any signs of visitors at his place since she'd moved in.

Brock kept chattering. Fortunately, it was enough to keep the two grown-ups from having to make conversation. But she had to say something about his wife. Had to.

Once they reached the school, she sent Brock on ahead again. "I just wanted to say I'm sorry about your wife," she said.

"Things happen." If it wasn't for the scowl on Mr. Mann's face she'd have thought he'd resigned himself to his loss.

"It doesn't make it any less awful when they do," Lexie pointed out.

He didn't agree or disagree. Instead, he asked, "Do you have physical therapy today?"

"No, not until later in the week. And if it's not raining we can walk home after school today."

He nodded. She shut the door. He drove off. She breathed a sigh of relief and shot up a quick prayer for sun come afternoon. Stanley Mann was not proving to be a comfortable person to be around.

He was the antithesis of her own father, who had been upbeat and happy, determined to always look on the sunny side of life, as he liked to say. He was like those men you saw in old paintings from the fifties that made life look so perfect. To be with him anywhere was to feel at home. Mr. Mann would not have made it as a subject for any such painting. The way he reined in his lips so severely it was as if he thought his face would crack if he smiled. Had he always been like that? Surely not.

She thought about her mother. She'd smiled plenty when Daddy was alive, but when they lost him it was like she'd put her smile in the coffin with him.

Lexie sighed as she trudged into school. Life could be so hard sometimes.

But it wasn't awful all the time, and seeing the happy faces of her students reminded her that there was still much to appreciate. Life was what you made it, right? Life could be good in spite of the bad.

Mr. Mann's troubles were forgotten as she got busy with the children. There was music time, some math and language drills, and playtime when the children could go to different activity stations where they could enjoy dramatic play with various costumes, work on floor puzzles, bake imaginary cakes, or enjoy a taste of science, examining shells and rocks with magnifying glasses. She also provided a reading corner with favorite books, and a blocks center where children could create walls and houses. As always, the day went by in a hurry.

The sun did come out later, and her neighbor took her at her word, leaving her to walk home after school. Clomping along in a walking boot may not have been the perfect ending to a perfect day, but it sure beat another awkward ride with Mr. Mann, and she was relieved.

She also felt a little guilty that she was relieved. Okay, so he wasn't the happiest person on the planet. It was understandable. The poor man had lost his wife. He needed to feel like someone cared.

"I think we should make some fudge when we get home," she said to Brock, who was skipping along beside her. "What do you think?"

"I like fudge," he said.

Maybe Mr. Mann liked fudge, too. Happily, she wouldn't have to ask him to run her to the store. She'd shopped before Thanksgiving, and she had everything she needed.

After a snack—that apple-a-day thing—she let Brock help her assemble the ingredients for chocolate-mint fudge, one of her favorites. Soon the house was filled with the aroma of chocolate. *The first baking smells of the Christmas season*, she thought and smiled. Maybe fudge would help their neighbor smile, too.

Okay, probably not, but she'd give him some, anyway.

As it cooled she got Brock started on his small amount of homework. Then she called Shannon to see how she was feeling.

"I think I'm going to live," Shannon said. "I'm planning on going to school tomorrow. Want a ride?"

"That would be great." Lexie suspected Mr. Mann would like a break from her as much as she would from him.

"I feel bad you had to walk to school in that boot," Shannon continued.

"I didn't. My neighbor wound up giving me a ride."

"Which neighbor? I thought you didn't know any of them."

"I don't really. It was the older man next door."

"You mean the hermit? Interesting. I guess he's not such a hermit after all."

"Oh, yes, he is."

But Lexie supposed that was what happened when you didn't have people in your life. What if Mom turned into a hermit? She'd never been as outgoing as Daddy. The last thing Lexie wanted to see was her mother becoming the female version of the never-smiling Stanley Mann. Hopefully, spending the holidays with her daughter and grandson would help Mom rediscover life.

Maybe having people to interact with would do the same thing for her reclusive neighbor. Fudge was a good way to begin.

While Brock dawdled over his homework Lexie walked next door to deliver her gift. His Christmas lights had come on, but no porch light glowed to encourage drop-in visitors.

She knocked on the door and immediately heard his dog barking. The porch light didn't come on, and the door didn't open. She knocked again. The dog barked. She could see lights on inside. She was sure he was home. She rang the doorbell. The only one interested in her presence on the front porch was the dog. Obviously, Mr. Mann had looked out the window and saw it was her and was deliberately hiding.

Rather a lowering thought, but she told herself not to take it personally. He probably wouldn't have opened the door even if Joseph, the Virgin Mary and all the shepherds were standing on his doorstep. Oh, well. She'd tried.

She was bending over to lay the plate on the porch when the light suddenly came on, and the door opened. There, with his dog prancing and barking at his side, stood Stanley Mann. Not smiling.

"Did you need something?" He made it sound like a crime if she did.

"No, I just wanted to give you some fudge." She held out the plate. "As a thank-you. For being so kind to us. It's been so nice to find a helpful neighbor."

He scratched an ear. "Uh, thanks."

As he reached to take the fudge the little dog rose up on her hind legs to greet Lexie. "What a sweetie," Lexie said, bending to pet her. "What's her name?"

"Dog," he said.

"Dog," she repeated. What kind of name was that?

"I found her. I'm waiting for whoever owns her to claim her."

"What if no one does?"

"Someone will." His tone of voice added *Someone better, or else.*

For a moment, Lexie was tempted to offer to take the dog, but she resisted, determined to stick to her resolve to wait until her son was a little older and would be more responsible in helping care for one.

Maybe Mr. Mann would decide to keep the dog after all. Maybe, come summer, he'd let the pup come over for playdates with Brock. Maybe by then they'd be good friends.

By this time next year I'll be married. That sure hadn't happened. Ah, yes, Lexie was so good at inventing perfect scenarios that didn't come to pass. She liked to think of it as being hopeful, but it was probably more a case of self-delusion.

Mr. Mann didn't appear inclined to stand around chatting. "I'd better get back," Lexie said. "I left Brock working on his addition, and I know he'll be needing help. Thanks again for everything."

"You're welcome," he said and managed a nod.

"Oh, and I don't need a ride to school tomorrow."

"Good."

Had he meant that as in good for her, or as in good for him? She decided not to ask. "Well, good night," she said and took a step back.

"Good night," he said, then he called the dog back in and shut the door.

CHRISTMAS LIGHTS, LIFTS *to school, fudge*, Stanley thought. *What next?*

CHAPTER ELEVEN

SNOW, THAT WAS what was next. At least according to Carol, who entered the quiet nothingness of his slumber to give him a weather prediction. She was still wearing that Santa hat, and now she had on her favorite jacket with the faux-fur trim, along with mittens, some sort of ski pants and boots. Carol had never skied. Was she taking up cloud-skiing?

"It's going to dump," she warned.

He didn't care. "If it does, I'm good. I've got snow tires."

And, speaking of good, Carol sure looked cute all dressed up like a snow bunny. Tonight she looked about thirty. Her hair was long again, hanging to her shoulders, and her cheeks were rosy. She perched on the edge of the bed. If he sat up and reached out, he could touch her.

He tried, but she danced away and floated up to hover in a corner by the ceiling.

"Your little neighbor will probably need you to drive her to physical therapy," she said. "And don't forget to shovel Mrs. Gimble's walk."

He and Carol had watched over the old woman ever since she'd lost her husband ten years earlier, and that wasn't going to change. Mrs. Gimble's daughter had moved back east with husband number two, and Mrs. Gimble was pretty much on her own. If Carol were still around she'd have been popping over there with cookies or to share a cup of tea, letting Mrs. Gimble ride shotgun when she went to the bookstore. Stanley had limited his involvement, but the old woman could hardly shovel snow by herself, so him doing it was a given.

"You'd better shovel Lexie Bell's as well so she can get to her mailbox," Carol continued.

"What, are you trying to kill me?" he protested. Hmm, probably not in good taste considering the fact that she was already dead.

"Your heart is fine, and you need the exercise. You're gaining weight. You've been eating too much junk food, Stanley."

"Not that much," he lied.

"Anyway, it's nice to help the neighbors, isn't it?"

Yeah, but how nice was up for debate.

"The lights you hung look lovely," she said, floating back down and hovering just out of touching range. "You have a good heart, Manly Stanley."

"Not so good anymore," he said. "It broke the day I lost you."

"I know," she said softly. "But it will mend. And I'm happy to see you've found someone to keep you company," she said, pointing to where Dog slept down by his feet. "A Westie, too."

Stanley crossed his arms over his chest. "I'm not keeping her. I told you before you di—er, left, no more dogs."

"Now, darling, you can't give up on enjoying animals simply because you know they'll leave you."

"Everyone I love leaves me," he said on a sob, feeling very sorry for himself.

"And new *everyone*s come into your life," she pointed out.

"No one can replace you," he said, offended by how casually she dismissed her departure and his loss.

"I didn't say that. Stanley, you're being awfully difficult tonight."

"I am not," he insisted. "But you're not here anymore, and I can do what I damn well want."

"Am I going to have to get angry with you? Remember, I can be very scary when I'm angry."

He knew. He'd already seen.

Oh, no, there came the creepy red-hot flaming eyes again, and she was right in his face, and he didn't want to grab her anymore. And he sure didn't want her to grab him. He crab-walked to the other side of the bed.

"Carol, you gotta stop doing this," he protested.

She settled back on the foot of the bed, and the red died back to blue. "I want you to be happy, Stanley."

"How can I be happy without you?"

"By looking to the future instead of the past," she said. "You can do it. I have confidence in you."

"Will you come and visit me every night?" If she did maybe he could get through the days.

"No, dear. I'm only here to get you started down the right path."

She was beginning to fade.

"Don't go, Carol," he begged. "Let's talk some more."

But it was too late. She vanished, and it was only him and Dog, who was lying at the foot of the bed, whimpering in her sleep, her little paws pumping like she was chasing something. Maybe she was chasing Carol.

Like me, he thought. "If only you were real," he murmured and lay back down, burrowing into his pillow.

He shut his eyes.

A voice whispered, "Name the dog Bonnie."

Oh, brother, he thought. Easy for her to tell him to keep the dog. She wasn't the one who'd have to walk the silly thing and shovel the turds out of the back yard.

The next morning he awoke to a wet tongue licking his chin and bright eyes looking eagerly at him.

"You only like me 'cause I feed you," he informed the dog.

Man's best friend, that was what people said, but really, a dog would go with anyone who'd feed it. And if you and your dog were marooned somewhere with no food, Fido would have no problem taking a chunk out of your leg. Dogs bit and growled and peed on carpets. Got sick. Cost a fortune in vet bills. You had to let them in and out, take them for walks, buy them food and flea collars and dog licenses. They cost a small fortune, and then they died. That was the reality of dogs.

He pushed aside thoughts of wagging tails and furry faces at the window looking for his return after a day of work. No dogs.

He let Dog out to go do her thing. She didn't stay out long.

"I know it's cold," he said as he let her in, "but you've got fur."

The silly thing just wriggled and barked, anxious to be petted.

"Yeah, you're a good dog," he admitted and obliged her.

He wiped her paws, filled her dog bowl, then checked for messages on his phone. Still no one calling to thank him for finding their beloved pet.

He poured himself a cup of coffee, then went to his computer to check the weather. The forecast had changed since the last time he'd checked. Carol was right. Snow was predicted for that very day.

"We'd better stock up," he said to Dog, who'd come to sit at his feet and keep him company.

Even though Stanley was in the store by nine, there was already a crowd. He wasn't the only one who'd seen the forecast. Although the Pacific Northwest usually experienced mild winters, every once in a while it got a dumping, and when that happened it was Snowmaggedon, and everyone panicked.

Grocery-store shelves would get wiped clean faster than you could say "Where's the bread?"

Stanley didn't need to panic. He had all-wheel drive on his SUV, and his snow tires were on. Not that he wanted to go anywhere. No, he'd be perfectly happy tucked in his house. No need to interact with anyone. Snow was the solitary man's friend, and he could hardly wait to leave this crowd of panicked shoppers and get back home to enjoy his solitude.

He got milk for his cereal and more dog food, then rounded out his shopping by adding other essentials such as pizza and chips. And peppermint ice cream. Carol was going to come around whether he ate it or not, so what the heck. He went back home, put away his groceries, checked the news on his computer, read a Lee Child thriller and threw some clothes in the wash. Colors and whites together. Who cared if his white T-shirts didn't sparkle?

By midmorning the snow had arrived, drifting down in big, soft flakes that hugged the lawn, the streets and the rhododendron bushes in front of the house. His new neighbor would probably be getting out of school early.

"Walking in the snow in that boot will be awful," Carol whispered.

"She'll get a ride," Stanley said.

What if she doesn't?

"Oh, for crying out loud," he muttered and looked up the number for the school.

Early dismissal at noon. He left a message for her at the school office that he'd be coming to get her and the kid. Come noon he was waiting for them.

The kid spotted him first and raced up, slipping and sliding as he went, his backpack bouncing. He yanked open the rear door and jumped onto the back seat. "It's snowing!"

"Yeah, it is," Stanley agreed, not feeling the same enthusiasm.

"My teacher said we should all go home and make a snowman. I want to make a snowman. Will you help me?"

"There's not enough snow for one," Stanley said. If this kept up it wouldn't be long until there was, but he kept that information to himself.

"When there is?" Brock persisted.

"I got stuff to do," Stanley informed him. He had to finish his book.

He checked his rearview mirror to see how the kid was taking this. He'd fallen back against the seat and was looking like Stanley had announced the end of the world. Too bad. Stanley wasn't going to freeze his ass off making a stupid snowman. Bad enough that he'd be out shoveling the white stuff the next morning.

Lexie had reached them now and settled into the front next to Stanley.

"Oh, my gosh, you are a lifesaver. My friend offered to drive us home, but since she doesn't like driving in the snow, I was planning to walk to save her the extra distance."

"In that thing?" Stanley said, motioning to her booted foot. "You don't want to do that."

"You're right, I don't. Thank you."

"No problem," he said. Just a pain in the butt.

Happily, she didn't ask about Carol, and the conversation on the way back was mainly between her and the kid, who was still carrying on about making a snowman.

"I think we'll need a little more snow on the ground, Brockie. Let's wait till tomorrow. Will it stay?" she asked Stanley.

"Probably for a day or two. It never lasts long."

Although it would be fine with him if it did. He was stocked up on food, and he could hole up with his book and his TV cop shows. The world would settle under a blanket of quiet, and nobody would bug him. Well, once he had the walkways shoveled.

That evening, on his way to the kitchen to heat up some canned clam chowder, he glanced out the dining-room window and saw Lexie Bell's Christmas lights reflecting onto the snowy roof. He had to admit, there was something about holiday lights on a quiet winter's night that lulled you into thinking all was well with the world. Carol would have been at the window, enjoying the sight.

Carol. A familiar sadness fell over him, and suddenly the sight wasn't enjoyable. He heated up the chowder, then ate it right from the pan as he watched the news on TV. Things were never well in the world, and snow and colored lights couldn't change that.

"You can still make things well in your world," Carol whispered as he fell deeper into sleep later that night. Yeah, that was Carol. The glass was always half-full.

But for Stanley the glass had broken the day she died.

Early the next morning he groaned as he walked out with his snow shovel, Dog watching from the safety of the garage. There had to be six inches of the stuff. By the time he got done with his neighbors he wouldn't have any energy left for his own front walk.

So what? He didn't need to shovel his. He wasn't expecting company, and he sure wasn't going anywhere.

Anyway, two front walks were enough. "I'll probably have a heart attack," he grumbled.

Although maybe that wouldn't be such a bad thing. Then he could die and be with Carol.

Oh, boy, she'd be pissed if she heard him say that. Best not to even think it.

I should move to a condominium, he thought. *Or the Caribbean. No snow-shoveling needed there.*

Mrs. Gimble came to her front door as he was moving the last shovelful of the stuff from her walk. She wore slacks and a blouse with a cardigan that she was pulling across her chest for warmth.

"Stanley, you are a dear," she said. "Thank you so much."

"No problem," he told her. "I need the exercise." According to Carol, anyway.

"I won't need the walk cleared for myself, of course," she said. "I'm not poking my nose out the door until this stuff is all gone."

A good idea. Mrs. Gimble was now a little stick of a woman. If she slipped and fell, those twig legs of hers would snap like dry kindling.

"Of course, my Meals on Wheels lady will appreciate being able to get to the door. That is, if you wouldn't mind shoveling the front steps while you're at it."

Like he had a choice? "Sure," he said and got to it. There weren't that many stairs, anyway.

With Mrs. Gimble taken care of he turned his attention to the pest on the other side. He'd get her taken care of, then he could go in and... What did he have to do today? Work a sudoku puzzle, check his investments online. Try and find something on the sports channel, eat a solitary lunch. His usual routine.

He frowned. Carol and her lecture about life being like a savings account—she of all people should know how little he cared about what he had in savings now that she was gone. He had no purpose, no life. No one needed him.

Dog was waiting by the garage door and wagged her tail and barked as he trudged past, on his way to take care of House Number Two. Well, okay. Someone needed him. At least for a little while.

LEXIE WAS RELIEVED that school was canceled. She sure hadn't wanted to walk to work, but the idea of riding with Shannon had made her anxious. The thought of Shannon even driving herself anywhere was not a good one, and Lexie was glad they could both stay safe at home. Shannon had made it safely to her place the day before but confessed to having almost collided with another sliding car before she safely slipped into her own driveway. She'd laughed about the adventure, but it had sounded hair-raising to Lexie.

Getting to enjoy the pretty, white stuff here in her neighborhood was a treat, though. *A snow day will be fun*, she thought, as she took a picture to text to her cousins in California. She and Brock could bake cookies, and he could try his hand at making that snowman he'd been talking about ever since he'd seen the first flakes.

She only wished she could show him how. This was his first year with snow, and she hated that she couldn't get out and enjoy it with him. She'd bought boots for both of them, but while his would fit great, hers would be useless.

"Breakfast," she called as she set Brock's bowl of oatmeal on the kitchen eating bar.

"Grandpa Stanley's outside," he cried as he raced over from the living-room window. He climbed onto a bar stool. "Can I go outside and help him?"

"May I go outside and help him?"

"May I?"

"What's he doing?"

"He's shoveling."

Shoveling. Lexie hurried to the window and looked out. Sure enough, there was Mr. Mann, working away, removing snow from their front walk. He was too old for that sort of thing. He'd have a heart attack.

She clomped out onto the front porch. "Mr. Mann, what are you doing?" she called.

"What's it look like I'm doing?" he called back, irritated.

"You don't need to do that."

"If I don't, who's going to?"

Not her. Not only was she on the injured list, she also hadn't thought to buy a snow shovel. Stupid.

"I'll get it done," she called. Surely she could find someone to hire. "Please don't go to all that trouble."

He kept shoveling. "Too late now. I'm half-through."

Brock was back. "I'm done with breakfast. Can I... May I go out and help Grandpa Stanley now?"

"I don't think he needs any help, Brockie." She wasn't sure he'd appreciate the company, either.

"Then, I'll watch."

"You can watch, but don't bother him," Lexie said. "Okay?"

Brock nodded eagerly.

"All right, then, let's get you dressed."

Brock ran for the stairs with a whoop, and Lexie followed, her gait uneven and clunky. Stupid boot. Stupid ankle.

At least she wasn't in a cast, she reminded herself. It could be worse. Things could always be worse.

Brock rushed through getting dressed and could barely stand still long enough for his toothbrush to finish its allotted two-minute brushing time. At last he was ready to go, racing down the stairs.

He danced from one foot to the other as she got him into his coat and hat and boots and tied on his muffler. He took his mittens and ran out the door and down the steps hollering, "Hi, Grandpa Stanley."

Mr. Mann didn't say anything, just acknowledged his presence with a nod and kept shoveling. Brock was going to drive him nuts.

"Brockie, see if you can make a snowman," she called from the front door. That would give him something to do besides bother their neighbor.

"Okay," Brock called back cheerfully and informed Mr. Mann, "I'm going to make a snowman."

Mr. Mann grunted something. It might have been *Good*. Or he might have been swearing under his breath.

It was obvious he wasn't wild about children. Happily, Brock was oblivious. He bounded into the middle of the yard, scooped up a handful of snow and sent it flying skyward. Then he knelt down and began pushing it around, a little human bulldozer.

Lexie had never made a snowman. Her parents had been warm-weather people, beach lovers. It hadn't occurred to them to take her someplace where there was snow, and it hadn't occurred to her to ask. She'd been happy enough with the beach, with weekends and vacations spent at her aunt and uncle's place in Santa Monica, hanging with her cousins, enjoying bodysurfing and bonfires and boys. Now that she was in the Northwest, though, she intended to learn how to cross-country ski. And make snowmen.

With her son happily playing in the snow, Lexie retreated back inside where it was warm. She'd watch from the window.

She took a picture of him, texted it to her mom and then settled on the couch where she could keep an eye on her son and started checking out craft ideas online. Oooh, she could make bottle-brush trees. How cute would those be sitting on her counter? And how cute was this reindeer treat jar? She could make it with Brock. All she'd need would be pipe cleaners, googly eyes and pom-poms.

She looked out the window to make sure he was still safe in the front yard and not bothering Mr. Mann. All was well out there. She returned her attention to her cell phone. Tea-light snowmen. How adorable!

THE KID WAS jabbering away. Stanley tuned him out. Thank God he was almost done with the front walk. He was sweating like a gym rat on a treadmill. As soon as he got back in the house he was going to grab some coffee and his book and not move. Well, after he made sure Dog did her thing.

Dog. Why hadn't anybody called him about the animal?

He gave his shovel one final push and dumped the load of snow on the lawn. Okay, mission accomplished.

As he turned to walk back to his house the Bell kid appeared in his line of vision. He'd plopped down in the snow in front of a small mound and was crying. Oh, good grief. What was the kid's problem?

Stanley walked over to where the boy sat. "What's wrong?"

"My snowman," the boy wailed.

"That's a snowman, huh?"

"I can't make him right."

There was an understatement. "Don't you know how to make a snowman?" Everyone knew how to make a snowman, for crying out loud.

The kid looked up at him, his mouth trembling, tears leaking out of his eyes, and shook his head.

"Did you ever make a snowman?"

Another shake of the head. "We never had snow where I lived." The words came out as a whimper.

Stanley remembered crying over a snowman once, too. He'd been a little older than this kid. His dad had gotten another job, and they'd moved to a new house in a new neighborhood that came complete with a neighborhood bully. The kid had knocked Stanley's snowman down and stomped it to death. It had been a crushing blow to see his work of art reduced to nothing but broken mounds and a carrot.

His old man came home from work at his new job and, after hearing about what had happened, had gone out with Stanley and helped him build a bigger, better one. He'd also given Stanley a few pointers in the manly art of boxing that served him well the next time the bully came around.

Who was showing this boy how to build snowmen and take on bullies?

Stanley laid his shovel aside. "Here, kid. You're going about it all wrong. You got to start with a ball and then roll it and make it bigger. Look."

He demonstrated. Hmm. Bending over wasn't quite so easy when you'd grown a gut.

He stood up. "Now, you keep rolling that around until it gets real big. That'll be his bottom."

"Okay," Brock said eagerly.

The eagerness didn't last, and kid was ready to quit way too soon.

"No, no. You gotta make his snow butt bigger," Stanley said.

"Snow butt," the boy repeated and burst into giggles.

Rolling such a big snow butt turned out to be a challenge, so Stanley helped him.

"Okay, there you go," he said when they were done. "Now we make his middle."

So it was back to rolling another ball of snow around the yard and then picking up some snow from Stanley's yard because it was fresh and untrammeled and why not.

"My mommy doesn't know how to make snowmen," Brock confided.

"I guess we'll have to teach her," Stanley said. "My dad taught me how to make snowmen."

"I wish I had a daddy," Brock confided. "Mommy says that sometimes things don't work out with daddies."

Not even an ex in the picture. *Good grief, this younger generation*, Stanley thought, forgetting he grew up in the era of drugs, sex and rock and roll.

"My mommy teaches kindergarten," Brock went on. "I'm not in kindergarten now. I'm in first grade. My classroom is next to Mommy's. My teacher's name is Mrs. Beeber. She has white hair like you."

"That means she's wise," Stanley said.

Brock considered this and nodded. "She's very smart. Like you."

Smart. Stanley smiled.

"Okay, this is big enough for his middle," he decided. "Let's put it on and see how he looks."

"Wow!" cried Brock as Stanley settled the second ball on the snowman. "Our snowman is really big."

"Yep. Nobody's gonna knock this guy over," Stanley said. "Now we just have to make his head."

Brock was dancing up and down by the time they settled the head in place.

"Arms," Stanley said and made his way over to the maple tree, the boy by his side. He broke off a couple of small branches. "These should work."

They did indeed. Old Frosty was coming to life.

"He needs a face," Stanley said, stepping back to admire their handiwork.

"How will we do that?"

"Well, you can use a carrot for his nose."

As if on cue, the kid's mom came out on the front porch.

"Mommy, we need a carrot," Brock cried, running up to her.

"And a scarf," Stanley called. "And you got any prunes?"

She looked at him, puzzled. "Prunes?"

Of course, the young had no need of prunes. "Never mind. I'll get some," he said and hurried back to his house.

Dog was dancing at the kitchen door when he went in, happy to see him. "You want to come see the snowman?" he asked the dog.

The bark and the tail wag looked like a yes.

Stanley grabbed a box of prunes. "Okay, come on, then."

Back outside they went, the dog bounding along, leaping as high as possible in an effort to clear the snow. Brock was already waiting, carrot and scarf in hand, his mom watching from the porch huddled inside a coat.

"So, we put the nose in the middle of the face," Stanley said, lifting the boy up so he could have the honors. "Then the eyes. Here you go."

Two prunes served as eyes, and six more made a smile. They wrapped the scarf around the snowman's neck, and that was that.

Lexie already had her phone poised. "Let me get a picture."

So Stanley and Brock stood by the snowman. Brock caught hold of Stanley's hand. Nobody had held his hand since Carol had died. It felt strangely comforting.

"That's perfect," she said happily.

Brock beamed up at Stanley. "Thank you, Grandpa."

"You did good," Stanley said and left it at that. "Now, get inside before you turn into a Popsicle."

"I can't turn into a Popsicle," Brock said with a giggle. "I'm a boy."

"And I'm an old man, and this cold is getting into my bones."

Stanley picked up his shovel, called Dog to come and walked back across the yards to his garage. He didn't realize it until he'd put away the shovel and gotten back inside the house: he was smiling.

He reined it in. He'd probably live to regret his good deed. Now the kid would really be a pest.

Sure enough, that afternoon his doorbell began ringing. Incessantly. And there was the kid again, this time with a plate of cookies cut in the shape of trees, frosted with green frosting and smothered in sprinkles.

"Mommy and me just made these," he informed Stanley. "I decorated them."

Stanley could tell. You could barely see the frosting under all those sprinkles.

Carol used to make those cookies. Stanley's thank-you was gruffer than intended, mainly because he was trying not to cry.

The boy's eyes got big. He looked like he wasn't sure whether he should smile or run away. He chose Door Number Two and scrammed.

Stanley felt suddenly sour. "Good. Maybe now the kid will leave us in peace for a while," he said to Dog, who was, as usual, standing right there next to him.

Dog didn't care about the complexities of human relations. Her eyes were on the plate of cookies. Her tail gave a hopeful wiggle.

"No, you can't have a cookie. They're not good for you." Stanley was going to have to buy some dog treats.

Dog treats. What was he thinking? This animal was not staying.

Except another check of his still-empty voice mail told him otherwise. "What's your story?" he asked Dog as he gave her another piece of jerky.

She stood on her hind legs and put her front paws on his pants.

He picked her up and carried her to his recliner. "What am I going to do with you?"

"Keep her," said Carol, who visited him that night to tell him how happy his kindness to the neighbors had made her.

"I always liked you in red," he said, taking in her red sweater. Darn, but she looked cute in that Santa hat.

She perched on the edge of the bed, her favorite spot. "Never mind my sweater."

"You're right. How about you take it off?"

She merely smiled and shook her head at him. "Your little neighbor's going to want to get a tree, you know."

"So?"

"She can't drive. Remember?"

Stanley frowned. "She'll find someone to take her."

"Who? She's new to the area with no family around, and she doesn't know anyone."

She has a job; she knows people.

"Stanley, she's taken a liking to you."

"That doesn't mean I have to be at her beck and call," he insisted.

"Stanley." It was the wifely-warning voice.

The best defense was a good offense. "Darn it, Carol. Enough already. What do I look like, Santa Claus?"

"No, you look more like the Grinch." Oh, no. Her eyes were starting to glow red again.

"I already risked a heart attack shoveling their walk."

"And made a snowman. And you enjoyed it."

"No, I didn't," he lied. "It was cold. Those two are pests."

"They need a father figure," Carol insisted.

"Well, that's not me." For crying out loud. What did he know about being a father figure?

As usual, she read his mind. "You were doing a pretty good job this afternoon."

"Carol, stop. Please. Leave me alone."

"Fine!" she snapped and vanished in a huff.

Crap. Now she wouldn't come back.

"Wait!" he cried. "I didn't mean it. Come back."

She didn't. He blinked awake and once more caught a hint of the scent of peppermint.

"I'm going crazy," he muttered.

Either that or he was developing a hyperactive conscience. Neither theory appealed.

It was only three in the morning. He got up, used the bathroom and then went back to bed. He punched his pillow, wishing he hadn't said what he'd said to Carol.

But, come on, hadn't he done enough of the holly-jolly Christmas crap? He wasn't a people person. He wasn't Saint Stanley. She knew that, and she would just have to be okay with it.

From the look of things the next morning, she wasn't.

CHAPTER TWELVE

CAROL HAD HANDED Stanley a lemonade when he'd come in from edging the lawn and demanded to know what he'd been doing flirting with Mrs. Gimble's daughter.

What the heck? "I was just talking to her."

Mrs. Gimble's daughter stopped by to see her mother every once in a while. They'd known her for years. Known the whole family ever since they moved to the neighborhood. It was hardly flirting to talk with the woman.

"And laughing."

"So? She said something funny."

"What?" Carol demanded.

"I don't remember. Good grief, Carol. She said hi. What was I supposed to do, turn my back on her?"

Carol's answer to that question was succinct. "Yes."

"You're always telling me to be more social," he reminded her.

She scowled and marched off to the living room, plopped on the couch and picked up her copy of *Woman's Day*. She began turning pages like she wanted to rip them out. Like she wanted to rip the magazine in two.

He followed and sat in the nearest chair, waiting for her to say something more. She would. He knew she would.

"There's social, and there's *social*."

"I don't understand."

"Oh, Stanley, don't be so dense," she said irritably. "She's divorced, you know."

"So? A lot of people are divorced."

"And she's looking for a replacement for her husband."

"So?"

"So, she was flirting with you. And you were flirting right back!"

"Oh, come on. We've known her since she was a kid. And I'm married."

"That doesn't mean anything. Ellie Jordan's husband left her for one of his college students, and one of Amy's friends had her husband stolen by her best friend. Who was divorced."

"Oh, come on, Carol, the woman doesn't want me," he said, amused. And a little flattered that she was jealous, he had to admit.

But it was silly for her to be. Even in his prime he'd never been more than average-looking. And now he supposed he was turning into an average middle-aged man. His hair was starting to thin, and his pectoral muscles were melting and sliding down, above the beginnings of a pot belly.

"You're still a nice-looking man."

He gave a snort.

"Are you getting a midlife crisis or something?"

"What?" He felt like he'd landed on an alien planet and was trying to learn the language and customs of its people.

"You've been being very secretive. Off running errands for hours. It doesn't take hours to go to the hardware store."

"It can," Stanley insisted.

Her eyes narrowed. "Is there someone else?"

"No," he said, shocked. "I'm working on something with John. And why would I want another woman when I've got you?"

Her gaze slid away from him. "I'm not exactly a size ten anymore."

So what if she wasn't quite as slender as she'd once been? "You still look great in a pair of shorts."

"And I'm getting gray hairs."

A few silver strands? So what? He loved those silver strands slipping into her hair.

"They make your hair sparkle in the sunlight."

He moved and sat beside her and put an arm around her shoulder. "If anyone needs to be worried about getting replaced, it's me."

"Women never trade their husbands in for younger men," she said irritably.

"Now, that was a sexist remark," he teased.

"It's true."

"Well, I'm not planning on trading you in, and I hope you're not planning on ditching me. I did see that new fifth-grade teacher eyeing you at the end-of-year party at Geri's house."

She made a face. "I'm being serious."

"So am I."

"I'm getting old," she said miserably.

"We both are. It happens. But we're still here, and we're both healthy, and we've got a lot of years left. And you really do look great."

She heaved a sigh. "I know I'm being completely illogical, but I'm having a hard time. I'll be fifty next month. Fifty, Stanley. I'll be half a century old. That's when things start to fall apart. You begin to become invisible. People throw over-the-hill parties for you and buy black balloons like it's some kind of joke, but I don't think it's funny."

"Well, then, I'll make sure nobody gives you black balloons."

She wasn't listening. "I'm getting wrinkles."

"Those are laugh lines."

"No, they're wrinkles," she insisted. She bit her lip and fell silent.

There was more going on here, something deeper. He knew it.

"What else is bothering you?"

She looked down at her hands. Sighed. "I think I'm done having periods."

Now he really had no idea what to say.

"Do you know it's been almost a year since my last period?"

He hadn't exactly been keeping track. Still, he remembered that first missed period. For a while there she'd thought that maybe, just maybe, a miracle had happened and she'd actually gotten pregnant. A home pregnancy test said no to that. Then the night sweats and mood swings had come, an unpleasant explanation of what was really happening.

She hadn't enjoyed the last few months at all. But lately, it seemed like those uncomfortable times were subsiding.

"What does that mean?" he asked. "Are you done with the night sweats?"

Her lower lip wobbled. "It means I'm done, period."

"Okay," he said slowly. Done, period. Done with periods. He wasn't getting it.

"It means I can never ever get pregnant."

They hadn't gotten pregnant the whole time they'd been married. This was nothing new.

But it was obviously something that still troubled her. He felt at a loss, unsure of what to say to make her feel better.

Tears began to slip down her cheeks. "I know it's silly, but at the back of my mind, I always had this fantasy that..." She took a shaky breath. "This is all so final. I just...have to adjust, that's all. I'm sorry. I'm not even being rational."

He snugged her up against him. "How you feel is how you feel. I'm sorry..." Now he was finding it hard to speak. "Aw, Carol, we should have tried harder to adopt. We shouldn't have given up. If I'd realized."

She shook her head. "No, don't you feel guilty because I'm having a meltdown. I'm the one who said no more. I know I need to be grateful that I'm still here. I love my job. I love my students."

"And they love you," he said. Many had come back to see her as young adults, telling her what college they'd chosen to attend or about that business they were starting. "You've guided a lot of kids over the years."

She nodded and took a swipe at her wet cheeks. "I know," she whispered.

"And you've got the nieces. They love you like crazy."

She nodded.

"So do I."

But it hadn't been enough. What they'd had hadn't been enough.

What came out next he really didn't want to ask because he was afraid of the answer he'd get. He asked, anyway. "Are you sorry you married me?"

She looked at him in surprise. "No, of course not."

"You could have married anyone." Maybe even married someone with kids. Her whole life could have been different.

She put a hand to his cheek. "I didn't want *anyone*. I wanted you. And we have been happy."

He felt so relieved to hear her say it that he almost cried. "We'll keep being happy," he said.

He'd work harder at doing things she wanted to do. He'd even take those ballroom-dancing classes she'd been wanting to take. Anything.

"I know. I'm being squirrelly," she said. "But I keep thinking what a turning point this is. It's like seeing a door closing."

"Which means another one's opening," he said. "Fifty's not that old, babe. You're still beautiful and healthy, and you love your work. You matter to all those kids you teach. You matter to your family. You matter to me."

She sniffed. Smiled at him. "Stanley, you are a dear."

"Age is just a number. You've got lots more years ahead of you, and you're going to be better with each one."

"Well, I don't know about that."

"I do. The best is yet to come."

"You're right," she said with a determined nod.

And now he had to make sure what he predicted happened. He already had a great surprise for her, but he knew he had to do more, so he did a very un-Stanley thing. He organized a birthday party, inviting the families and neighbors and friends.

"No black balloons or over-the-hill jokes," he instructed everyone.

"Stanley, no way can you do this all by yourself," Amy informed him. "I'm taking care of the food."

He hadn't been pleased with her assessment of his competence, but deep down he suspected she was right. Still, this was his idea, his wife, darn it all. So he asserted himself.

"I'm getting the cake," he insisted. "And I'm grilling burgers."

"Fine," she said, allowing him that much. "I'll take care of everything else."

He ordered a big sheet cake from the local bakery with lots of red frosting roses. He also ordered a dozen red roses from the local florist to be delivered on the big day.

He'd half wanted to surprise Carol, but he suspected she'd want to look her best, so he gave her a few days' notice. "We got company coming Saturday afternoon."

"We do?"

He could see the excitement in her eyes. Carol loved having company. He felt downright proud of himself.

"Yep. Thought you'd want to get your nails done or something."

"I just might," she said. "And what's this party for?" she asked coyly.

"Someone special I know is having a birthday," he answered.

"You're throwing me a party? Oh, Stanley, that is so sweet of you," she said and hugged him.

"I thought so," he said, making a joke of it.

But his stress levels had been no joke. Calling people and organizing the whole thing, figuring out how much hamburger and how many buns to buy, borrowing card tables and chairs to set up in the back yard—he was glad he didn't have to do this on a regular basis.

The big day came, and the hordes of guests arrived, bringing gifts and cards, crowding onto the patio and spilling into the back yard, guzzling beer and soda pop by the gallon. Kids running everywhere. Chaos. Stanley was glad to be tied to the barbecue where he didn't have to be in the middle of it all.

Carol was in her element, beaming as if he'd given her diamonds. Well, wait until she saw the surprise.

After dinner, as she was cutting her birthday cake, he slipped inside the house and called his buddy John. "Okay, bring it over."

"Be there in ten," said John.

Stanley wandered back out onto the patio. He checked his watch a couple of times and finally, with a couple of minutes to go, sauntered up to where Carol stood talking with one of her former students, her sister positioned next to her.

"Time for presents," he said. "Come on out to the front."

"Presents, yes, good idea," said Amy. "Don't you want her to open them here?"

"Not this one," he said and took his wife's hand.

"Hey, everyone, presents," Amy called and started a parade of people following them through the house and out onto the front porch.

Right on cue, John drove up to the curb in a refurbished shiny red 1969 Ford Mustang sporting a big red bow on its hood.

Carol gasped and covered her mouth with both hands. It was exactly the reaction Stanley had been hoping for, and his heart swelled.

"Happy birthday, babe," he said as all their friends oohed and aahed and clapped.

"Oh, Stanley," she breathed.

"Now you know where I was and what I was up to."

"You are amazing," she said and hugged him.

"Let's go check it out," he said.

"Oh, yes!"

She ran down the front walk, him strolling after, feeling very proud of himself.

She walked around the hood, and John got out and handed her the keys.

"John, it looks great."

"Yeah, well, you should have seen it when we first got it," he said.

Stanley joined them. "Take it for a spin."

She took the keys, hopped in and started it up. He hadn't seen her this happy in a long time.

The windows were already down to take advantage of the July sunshine. Stanley leaned his arms on the window of the driver's side. He motioned to the radio.

"Turn the radio on," he suggested.

She did and her favorite rock-and-roll classics station started playing the Eagles' "Life in the Fast Lane."

"Yow!" she squealed and cranked it up. "Get in, Stanley."

He ran around to the passenger side, hopped in, and she laid rubber, and they roared off with everyone clapping and waving.

"Stanley, this is the best present ever," she said, her voice filled with joy. "I feel like I'm eighteen again."

"You look as good as you did at eighteen," he said.

She smiled and shook her head. "You are so full of it, but you know what? I don't care. You're right. Fifty is just a number."

"It's a good number. We're gonna have another fifty together."

And he was determined to make sure they were good ones. "I still have some vacation time left," he said. "We should take a road trip before school starts again. See how this baby handles on the open road."

"That's a great idea."

"Where do you want to go?"

"Let's drive down the coast." She pointed a finger at him. "I'm doing all the driving."

"Absolutely," he said. "It's your car."

THEY TOOK THEIR drive down the coast that summer, visiting beach towns along the way. They had such a good time they took another road trip the next year. And the year after. And for her fifty-fifth birthday they took a cruise in the Caribbean and swam in turquoise-blue waters. They both had so much fun they signed up for another cruise, this time to Alaska, where they gaped at the glaciers in Glacier Bay and took a dogsled ride in Juneau and rode an old-fashioned train to Skagway. All memorable experiences made doubly memorable because he was with her.

They'd even taken a trip or two with friends.

Then for her sixtieth he'd thrown another party.

"You're becoming a real party animal," Amy had teased him.

Not really. He did it because Carol loved to entertain, and he loved Carol. If it weren't for her he'd probably be a hermit.

CHAPTER THIRTEEN

STANLEY HAD AWAKENED shivering, with Dog licking his face. All the bedcovers were pulled off him and dangling from the opposite side of the bed. For a moment there he thought *Carol*. But no, he'd done that himself, tossing and turning after she left in a huff.

He'd pulled on his bathrobe and went downstairs, turned up the thermostat and walked through the living room on the way to the kitchen just like he did every morning. And everything had looked the same, just like it did every morning.

Until this. There was his sudoku-puzzle book lying facedown on the floor, half-torn.

"Dog, you won't get any treats if you pull stunts like this," he scolded as he picked it up.

The dog looked at him as if to say *What are you talking about?*

He held it for her to see. "Half-torn."

She whimpered and started for the kitchen and the back door.

"I should make you stay out there," he muttered as he followed her.

But he didn't have the heart to get mean with her. She hadn't chewed up so much as a sock since she'd been with him. Everyone was allowed one mistake. Still, it was very strange.

He felt cold as he opened the door for the dog, but that was only a bit of wintry gust coming in. That was not Carol. And ghosts couldn't move things. Could they?

He needed coffee. He let the dog out, then flipped on the kitchen light.

Except it didn't come on. The coffee maker was dead, too. A tree must have fallen in the night and caused a power outage. No underground lines in the town of Fairwood, so that stuff happened a lot.

He went back to the living room and peered out the window. The house across the street had sold but was still standing vacant, so no lights were on there. The millennial workaholics were already gone. They never left any lights on in their place, so you couldn't judge by them. But farther down across the street he could see lights coming from inside the house. Same was true for Mrs. Gimble. Even Lexie Bell had power.

He went out to the garage. Once there he found no problem in the fuse box. Something was amiss.

Or, rather, someone. "Okay, Carol," he said as he went back into the house. "Not funny. Put the power back on. I want my coffee."

Nothing happened.

"This isn't fair. Come on."

Nothing happened.

"Okay, okay. I'll take her tree-shopping."

Suddenly everything began to hum back to life.

"But only if she asks."

The power flickered.

"I said I'd do it!" he shouted.

The power clicked back on and the microwave began to flash the time. It was stuck at 3:00 a.m., probably about the time he'd been having his nocturnal squabble with Carol.

Coincidence, he told himself. It was all coincidence.

He reset that and the clock on the stove and made himself some coffee, using what was left in the coffee canister, which had run mysteriously low. He let the dog back in and fed her, then got dressed in his favorite old sweats and Seahawks sweatshirt and sat down at the computer to check his stocks and read the morning's news. Dog settled at his feet.

All nice and cozy. Why did some people think you needed a whole troop of extras in your life, anyway? Besides, what was the point? He could barely stand his own company these days. Why would anyone else want to hang out with him?

"We're fine just the two of us, aren't we?" he said to Dog.

Just the two of them. The minute the words were out of his mouth he knew he was going to keep the animal. Unless, of course, her owners called to claim her. No one had called yet. At this point, it was likely no one would.

"Their loss, right, girl?" he said to the dog, and she agreed by nudging his hand.

He got the hint and petted her. "I should name you. You want a name?"

Name her Bonnie.

Okay, he could do that.

He didn't see Carol that night, but she did whisper in his ear, "You're making progress, Manly Stanley."

Bah, humbug.

By Monday morning the snow was beginning to melt, and the snowman in the Bell yard was slumping and falling apart. The streets and sidewalks were still slushy, though.

Stanley was backing his car out of the driveway to make an early-morning run to the store to replenish his supply of coffee when he spotted the pests next door walking down the street. Lexie Bell had tied a plastic bag around her injured foot. How long did she think that was going to last? That walking boot would tear the plastic to shreds in no time.

Accepting the inevitable, he let down his window and called them over. "You don't want to walk to school in this," he said.

She smiled as she got in. "You're right. We don't. I should sign Brock up to take the school bus, I guess, but that seems silly when we live so close."

"Not close enough for walking in this mess," Stanley said.

"My friend Shannon offered to give us a ride, but I think the streets are still kind of slippery, and I didn't want to make her drive any farther than she had to."

"Better to stay off the streets if you don't know how to handle snow and ice," Stanley said. But slush was no problem, especially for someone like him, who'd lived in the area all his life.

"You know how, don't you, Grandpa?" piped the kid.

"You bet your a—" *Ass* was probably not a good word to use in front of a little boy. Although he'd hear worse on TV. Still, Stanley censored himself. "Boots," he finished. Then, just to be clever, refined it to "You bet your snow boots."

"I'm wearing my snow boots," Brock said.

"So I see."

"It's awfully kind of you to come to our rescue. I'm sure this will be completely gone tomorrow, and then I'll get a ride with my friend," said Lexie Bell.

Stanley nodded. That suited him fine.

"How's the ankle doing?" he asked.

"I guess I need to resign myself to the fact that it's not going to heal overnight. The physical therapist thought the doctor might let me graduate to a brace before Christmas, which would really be great. I sure hope I can get back to physical therapy soon."

"Make an appointment for today. I'll take you."

Oh, no. Had that really just come out of his mouth? He wished he could stick out his tongue and pull the words right back like a frog catching flies. Carol was probably dancing for joy on some cloud.

"I couldn't ask you to drive me."

"You didn't. I volunteered." Like a dope. "Give 'em a call."

She did. "They can take me at four."

"I'll pick you up at school at quarter till," he said.

"That will be great," she said.

For her, not for him. What a pain in the butt.

But at three forty-five there he was, sitting outside the school, waiting when she and her kid emerged together.

"I can't tell you how much I appreciate this," she gushed. "You're being so kind to us."

He could hardly say the reason for that was because his wife's ghost was making him, so he said nothing.

"It's really great to start getting to know our neighbors."

Who said that was what they were doing?

"It's hard starting over in a new place," she confided.

Stanley didn't look her way, but he could still see her out of the corner of his eye. She was smiling at him like they were now best friends. He hunched into his coat like a turtle pulling into its shell.

"I guess that's the one thing I miss about California," she continued. "All my old friends. And my family. My aunt and uncle are there, and my cousins. And my mom." She sighed. "It's been two years since Daddy died, and she hasn't been doing very well without him. Of course, I get that. It hasn't been easy not having my father around. But still."

Why was this woman telling him all this? He wasn't a counselor. He kept his mouth shut, determined not to encourage any more sharing. It didn't work. She shared, anyway.

"I tried to get her to come up this summer and see the new house, but she made up some lame excuse."

"Maybe she wants to be alone," Stanley said, forgetting that he wasn't going to say anything. Well, the woman needed someone to defend her. "Not everyone wants to be around people." He sure didn't.

Yet here he was, chauffeuring Lexie Bell and her boy all over town.

"But I'm not people. I'm her daughter," Lexie protested. "Oh, well. She's coming up for Christmas. We'll make sure she has a wonderful time. Won't we, Brockie?"

"Yep," agreed the kid.

Whether the woman wanted it or not. Stanley thought of his sister-in-law. Any day she'd be calling him, determined to make sure he had a wonderful time at Christmas. Heaven help him.

He parked in front of Healing Help Physical Therapy, kept the engine running so he could keep the heat on, and prepared to wait in the SUV and read some more of the Lee Child thriller, which he'd brought along.

But then the kid said, "Come on, Grandpa," when he saw Stanley not moving to get out.

Stanley frowned. Surely his presence wasn't needed in there.

It won't hurt you to go in.

"Fine," he muttered, and turned off the ignition, grabbed the book, and got out.

"I hate you to have to wait," Lexie said as they entered.

This required a polite response. "It's okay. I brought a book," he said, and held up the paperback.

Stanley soon realized he wouldn't be doing much reading. Instead of following his mom around, the kid opted to wait in a chair next to Stanley while she got put through her paces on the equipment. Even though the boy had a spelling assignment, which he should have been fine doing on his own, he was determined to bring Stanley into the experience.

"*Lap,*" he said out loud, as he filled in blanks in one column to match the words in another. "*Nap. Cat.* Do you have a cat, Grandpa?"

"No, I already have a dog," Stanley said. Yep, that confirmed it. Bonnie was staying.

"Dog," Brock said and giggled.

"Her name's Bonnie now."

"Bonnie." The boy considered this. "That's a nice name."

"That's what my wife thinks—er, would think."

Brock looked at him. "What's her name?"

"Carol."

"Grandma Carol," the kid said, trying it out.

"She's gone." It still hurt to say it.

"Is she in heaven with my grandpa?" Brock asked.

"She should be." Stanley wished she'd hurry up and go there.

Except then he wouldn't see her again. Fresh sadness settled over him.

Their conversation was cut off by the appearance of a man leaving. He was Stanley's age and wore a jacket over a pair of jeans and old army boots. George Mathews from the bowling league. Stanley braced himself.

He smiled at the sight of Stanley. "Stan, haven't seen you in ages. What are you doing here?"

"Waiting for someone. Why are you here?"

George rubbed his shoulder. "Stinkin' rotator cuff. Hoping they can get me good as new in time for the spring league. When are you coming back?"

"I don't know." *Probably never.* "Kind of busy these days."

"Yeah? Who's this?"

"This is Brock," Stan said.

"Hello, there, Brock."

"My mommy's getting therapy," Brock told George. "Grandpa Stanley and me are waiting for her."

"Didn't know you had kids," George said to Stanley.

"Just friends," Stanley said. They weren't really friends, but he could hardly say *pests*.

"Grandpa and me made a snowman," Brock continued.

"Pretty cool," said George. Then, to Stanley, "Wish my grandkids were still at an age where they liked to do that. They're all in high school now, and all they want to do is look at their phones." He shook his head, then said, "Oh, well. What are you gonna do? Enjoy this while it lasts, my man. They grow up way too fast. And hurry up and get your butt back to the alley."

"Will do," Stanley lied, and George gave him a friendly salute and left.

Then it was back to spelling. Stanley half listened and idly watched as a therapist worked with Lexie. The guy looked to be about her age, and there seemed to be some friendly chatting going on. She was a pretty little thing so he was hardly surprised to see the guy showing some interest.

She seemed nice enough. What had happened with her and Brock's dad?

What did it matter? It was none of Stanley's business. The kid had fallen quiet. Stanley opened his book in the hopes of getting a chance to read some of it.

The silence didn't last. "My bonus word is *antlers*," Brock informed Stanley. "Reindeer have antlers. Reindeer pull Santa's sleigh."

Santa again, Stanley thought in disgust. He was spared from any conversation about reindeer and Santa as Lexie was done and ready to leave.

Stanley was ready also. He'd go home, drink some eggnog, make himself some toast with peanut butter, read his book in peace and quiet.

So, why, when he was anxious to get home, he opened his big mouth and asked Lexie Bell if she needed to run any errands, he would never know.

"I could stand to get a few things at the grocery store," she said.

What the heck. He could stand to buy a few more cookies.

So they went to the grocery store. She purchased the kind of good things responsible parents bought: apples, lettuce, milk. He bought chocolate chip cookies and chips. Why not? Bonnie didn't need lettuce and neither did Stanley. Bonnie. He doubled back and purchased a box of dog biscuits.

"Thanks for being willing to detour," Lexie said as they left the store. "I was pretty well stocked up, but I don't like to run out of produce."

"Can't have that," he agreed. Hey, he managed a carrot once in a while. Their route home took them by the tree lot.

"Trees!" cried Brock. "Can we get our Christmas tree now?"

"Oh, sweetie, not now," said his mom. Stanley could hear the embarrassment in her voice.

"But you promised," the kid said.

"I know. And we will."

"When?"

"When I get things worked out," she said.

"I want a tree," Brock whined.

"You getting a live tree?" Stanley asked. *Oh, yeah. Open the door wide to more errand-running.*

"I was planning on it. I'm sure my friend can take us later this week. Or I can get an Uber."

That again. This woman needed to learn the value of a dollar.

"Wait too long and all the good ones will be gone," Stanley said. Good grief. Just whip him with a string of Christmas lights and be done with it. He could feel her gaze on him. "May as well stop now. I've got rope in the back."

"Really?" She sounded so...grateful.

"Why not?" *Because I want to go home and relax, that's why not.* Well, it was too late now. He could almost see Carol smiling.

"That would be fabulous."

"Yay!" hooted Brock from his seat in the back.

And so it was that Stanley Mann found himself walking through a forest of cut trees in Grandma's Memories Tree Lot, helping Lexie Bell and her son pick out the perfect tree for their new home, offering sage advice and tapping various candidates on the ground to see if any needles fell off. Boy, did that bring back memories.

CHAPTER FOURTEEN

OVER THE YEARS Stanley and Carol had all kinds of trees: ones so tall he had to saw off several inches once they got them home in order to fit inside, cheap ones, pricey ones, flocked, and bare. Some they found at tree farms and cut themselves, most they picked up at tree lots. One year Carol wanted a Charlie Brown tree, and they found a perfect candidate when they were snowshoeing in the Cascades.

"That one is perfect!" she'd cried. "It's so scruffy and sad."

There was an understatement. "It's half-dead," he'd pointed out.

"Then, let's take it home and give it a purpose before it goes to tree heaven."

Both families had teased them about it. "This the best you could do?" joked his brother-in-law, Jimmy.

Carol had jumped to his defense. "It was exactly what I wanted. You know, you don't have to be perfect to be loved."

Thank God for that, Stanley had thought. With his hermit tendencies he was hardly the perfect man for Carol.

They finally switched to artificial trees. Less hassle, but it was never quite the same as getting a real one.

The first Christmas tree they ever bought was at a tree lot that turned out to be run by one of Carol's old boyfriends.

"Carol," he'd greeted her as they walked onto the lot. "Merry Christmas. How are ya?"

"I'm good, Dan."

"You look good," he said, sounding way too friendly for Stanley's taste.

She put an arm through Stanley's and moved him front and center. "This is my husband, Stanley."

Dan stuck out a mittened hand. "Nice to meet ya."

"Same here," Stanley lied as he took it.

Was this the jerk she'd told him about? Couldn't be. The guy wasn't as tall as Stanley, but judging from his shoulders and those tree-trunk thighs, he probably worked out. Stanley vowed to join the gym in the New Year.

"I heard you got married," Dan said. "You're a lucky dog," he told Stanley. "Half the guys in our class wanted to date her."

"You got to," she said, her voice light.

"Yeah, for about two seconds. You happy? I'm still single," he added with a grin.

Stanley frowned. Was that supposed to be funny?

"I'm ecstatic," she replied and hugged Stanley's arm.

"Well, darn. Guess I'll have to settle for selling you two a tree."

"That's what we're here for," she said.

"You got any fresh ones?" Stanley asked.

"They're all fresh," Dan the Tree Man replied, insulted.

Stanley walked up to one, grabbed it by the trunk and gave it the old needle test, banging it on the ground. A shower of needles fell.

"Hey, not so hard," protested Dan.

"Fresh, huh?" Stanley challenged.

The guy frowned at him. "Any tree's gonna lose needles if you treat it like it's a hammer."

Carol moved on to another. "Here's a pretty one. I bet it's fresh," she said, ever the diplomat.

Before Stanley could touch it Dan grabbed it and gave it a gentle tap. "See? Perfectly fresh."

"We'll take it," Carol said.

"I think we got took," Stanley muttered as he tied it on the roof of the GTO. "He could have at least given you a discount for old times' sake."

"Maybe he would have if you hadn't insulted him."

"I didn't insult him. I just tested to see if the needles would stay on. It's not fresh if they fall off. I don't care what he said."

"I think you were a little jealous."

"So you went out with him, huh?"

"Not for long, so there's no need to be jealous."

"I wasn't."

"Good. Because he's not half as cool as you. Or as...manly. Manly Stanley," she finished with a grin. Then she sobered. "There's no one I'd rather be with than you."

"Sometimes I wonder why," he admitted.

"Well, for one thing, you're easy to talk to. You actually listen. And that's more than I can say for a lot of the guys I dated."

Stanley had never been one to talk about himself a lot. He preferred to listen, especially to Carol. He appreciated her wit and her positive take on life, always enjoyed hearing the stories about the shenanigans of her pupils at school. She was so easy to be with.

Obviously, other men still wanted to be with her.

"That Dan wasn't the jerk you told me about, was he?"

"No. Who knows where *he* is."

Her comment got him wondering. He looked at her suspiciously. "Wait a minute. You knew your old boyfriend had this tree lot?"

"Yeah. Amy told me."

Stanley frowned. The last thing he'd have chosen was to go see some old boyfriend of Carol's.

"He wasn't really a boyfriend," she explained. "More like a friend I went out with a couple of times."

Had the guy kissed her? It didn't matter, Stanley reminded himself. He was the one who'd gotten her, and he was the one who was kissing her now.

"It's nice to give old friends business," she said.

Stanley wasn't so sure he wanted to bring any old *friends* into their life.

He gave the rope a final tug. "If any needles fall off, we're not doing business with him next year."

She just giggled.

Now that they had a tree, they had to get ornaments. Together they picked out red and blue and gold balls at the hardware store to go with the ornaments Carol already had. Her collection had been acquired over the years, all of them from her grandmother.

"She gave me one every year, starting when I was a baby. They all mean something to me," Carol said as she hung up a pink one that said *Baby's First Christmas*. "I love having special mementos to mark the years."

He liked the idea of that and vowed right then to find something special for her, something to mark their first year of marriage.

They'd hung the lights, the chains of gold beads that her mother had passed on to her and all their new ornaments and were admiring their handiwork when she said, "I have one more."

She disappeared down the hall to their bedroom and came back with a little wrapped box that he hadn't seen anywhere.

"Where'd that come from?" he asked.

"Santa's elves. Open it."

He did and found a metal Hot Wheels ornament shaped like a GTO. It was even red like his car. "Wow," he said. "This is really cool." How he wished he'd thought ahead to do something for her!

"Your first memory," she said. "Where do you want to hang it?"

He picked a bough at the front of the tree, smack-dab in the middle. "Here, where I can see it every day and think about what a great wife I have. Not that I need a reminder," he hastily added.

"I should hope not," she teased.

The tree made their small apartment festive. So did the cookies she baked—sugar cookies cut out to look like trees, frosted with green frosting and decorated with colored sprinkles.

"My family makes these every year," she said when he came into the kitchen to sample one.

"My mom makes these. I love 'em," he said and took a bite. "Oh, man, that's good."

"Lucky for you I like to bake," she said.

"I'd be a lucky man to have you even if you didn't like to bake," he said and slipped an arm around her waist.

Christmas Eve was spent visiting with both the families, opening presents, eating two Christmas dinners and attending a candlelight service, but Christmas morning was theirs alone. Stanley made his one specialty—pancakes from a mix—and they enjoyed them with hot chocolate.

After breakfast they opened the presents they'd bought each other. She'd given him a tool set, and he'd given her some Jean Naté perfume and a book by Elizabeth Peters, one of her favorite authors.

But the gift she was most thrilled with was the one he'd made over in his dad's garage. It was a flat wooden heart. In the middle was carved *Stanley + Carol. Forever.*

"Oh, Stanley, I love it," she cried, throwing her arms around him.

"Where are you going to hang it?" he asked, echoing her question to him when she'd given him his ornament.

"Right here, next to yours." She hung it and turned to him. "I do so love you."

"I love you more," he said and kissed her.

He never got tired of kissing her. Or making love to her. Being together, loving each other, that was the best Christmas present of all.

After, as they lay there, her in his arms, he kissed her hair and asked, "Happy?"

"Very," she said. "This is a perfect Christmas."

"Yes, it is," he agreed and thought how it didn't matter what was under the tree. He was holding the best present a man could have in his arms.

CHAPTER FIFTEEN

THE FIVE-FOOT TREE Lexie finally settled on was nice and full and had good color. Stanley, assisted by one of "Grandma's" helpers, loaded it onto the SUV and tied it down.

"Can we decorate it tonight?" Brock asked.

"May we decorate," his mother corrected.

"May we?"

"It's getting a little late," said Lexie. "Let's do that tomorrow. Mr. Mann, would you like to come over and help us and stay for dinner?"

A home-cooked meal? It had been a long time since he'd had one of those.

But it came at a price. Going next door for dinner was probably not a smart idea. He'd only get further enmeshed with these two.

"I make great lasagna," she said. "And I'd like to thank you for how much you've helped us."

Oh, man. Lasagna.

"My cheese bread kills."

"Kills?"

"It's really good," she explained.

Cheese bread, too. Really good cheese bread.

"And Caesar salad." She pointed to the grocery bag at her feet. "I've got romaine."

Who cared about the salad?

Cheese bread and lasagna, though. *Say yes,* urged Stanley's taste buds.

"Okay," he said.

"Great. Does six o'clock work for you?"

"Sure." What the heck, he had to eat. And it was only dinner.

And tree-decorating. He shouldn't have listened to his taste buds.

"More progress," whispered Carol later as he was drifting off to sleep.

That wasn't what Stanley called it. He called it *entanglement.* More involvement, more having to pretend he was happy with the season, happy with his life. He should have declined the offer.

"Lasagna, Stanley. Your favorite."

There was that. But this wasn't just about lasagna. This came with social strings attached. Ugh. Cheese in a mousetrap, that was what Lexie Bell had offered him.

Carol's final words were "Don't show up empty-handed," and that popped his eyes back open.

He had no idea what he should bring to his neighbor. Not cookies, since she baked. Not wine, since she had a kid and he wanted to bring something they could all enjoy. What, then?

This social stuff had been Carol's department, not his. Not only did he have no idea what to bring but he also had no idea what he and this young woman would find to talk about stuck together for a whole evening. She was Twitter and Facebook, and he was TV and puzzle books.

What was the point? He didn't need to go over to Lexie Bell's house. He could buy lasagna in the freezer section of the grocery store.

That settled it. He was staying home. Happy with his decision, he finally fell asleep.

His dreams that night put him in a winter wonderland, but Stanley found himself poorly dressed for the weather in nothing but his tighty-whities and a Santa hat, standing at the top of a mountain. Next thing he knew he was sledding down the slope on some kind of racecourse, out of control. In and out of trees he careened, branches whapping him as he went. Somewhere along the way he lost his Santa hat, and that seemed to bother him even more than the fact that the rest of his clothes were missing.

He shot out of the trees into the open where crowds of cheering people stood on both sides of the course, rooting for him. There was his bowling team. Unlike him, they were dressed.

"Go, Hambone!" yelled George Mathews.

Standing next to George was Frosty the Snowman. "You're gonna freeze your ass off," he called.

Stanley already was. He rushed past a herd of senior church ladies, waving, each one holding a casserole dish.

And there was the Grinch. "You're headed for disaster if you go next door, fool," he called.

Carol elbowed her way through the crowd, pushing the Grinch aside. "Don't listen to him, Stanley!"

A finish line just like the ones in the Winter Olympics loomed ahead, and there, along with a crowd of elves, stood Lexie Bell and her kid, both dressed in red parkas and ski pants and snow boots, both wearing reindeer antlers.

"You can do it, Mr. Mann," Lexie called. "Strong finish!"

Except at the last minute he fell off his sled and someone else swooshed by him. Santa Claus.

"Ho, ho, ho! I won," he taunted. "You are such a loser, Mann."

Suddenly a crowd of little demons wearing Santa hats and bearing huge pitchforks were surrounding him. "You're a loser," heckled one. "Nobody really wants to see you." He gave Stanley a poke with his pitchfork, making Stanley yelp.

"It's too late for you," jeered another. "You're never gonna change." He, too, gave Stanley a poke.

"Cut that out!" Stanley protested.

"Why?" joked the first one. "Your attitude sucks, and you deserve it."

A third demon stuck his pitchfork right through Stanley's hind end, turning him into a kebab. He lifted Stanley in the air like some sort of prize, and they began to parade off through a snowy forest.

"Where are you taking me?" Stanley cried. Amazingly, he wasn't in pain, but the humiliation sure stung.

"Someplace you'll feel right at home," said one.

They marched him to the edge of a precipice. A huge fire raged below them.

"Toss him in," cried one of the demons, and the one who had him skewered hurled his pitchfork like a javelin, sending Stanley the Kebab flying, screeching all the way.

He awoke just before he hit the flames and bolted upright in bed, startling Bonnie awake. It felt like the Little Drummer Boy was banging around in his chest. He swallowed and drew the dog up against him.

"What the heck did that mean?" he asked.

The dog had no answer. She flattened out against him and went back to sleep.

He knew, though. *Bad dreams. Not playing fair. Dirty pool, Carol.*

He lay back down, pulled the covers up to his ears, rolled onto his side and muttered, "I'm not going."

Then came the whisper. "Don't be a chicken."

His eyes popped open, and he searched the darkness for some hint of Carol. He sniffed. No peppermint in the air. Still, she was there somewhere, he knew it, waiting for him to shut his eyes again so she could catch him unawares.

Okay, if she wanted to play that game he'd wait her out. He'd stay awake. He turned on the bedside lamp, picked up his book and began to read. After ten minutes his eyelids drooped.

No, no, stay awake. He blinked and stared at the page. The printing was beginning to blur. His eyelids felt like they had ten-pound weights attached to them.

The weights won and he was back on that snowy mountain, all by himself. It was such a vast expanse of nothing, and looking around, he felt small and scared. Abandoned.

Carol didn't show herself, but he could sense her next to him. "You don't have to feel like this, Stanley. You can have people in your life."

Next thing he knew he was walking toward a lodge nestled among snow-covered fir trees. The lights inside beckoned him, and as he drew closer he could hear laughter and Christmas music. He smiled and picked up his pace. Once on the porch, he opened the door and was greeted with a blur of light that seemed to reach out and warm him.

He never saw beyond the light, but he woke up feeling... He wasn't sure what he felt. A little nervous, half-wishing he could stick with his decision to back out of that dinner invitation. But he knew he wasn't going to, because mixed in there somewhere was a feeling of anticipation, a thought that yes, homemade lasagna and cheese bread that *killed* would probably top what he found in the supermarket freezer. And the girl would need help putting up that tree.

Someone needing him. The thought made him feel rather...mellow.

After breakfast he went to the grocery store and bought a two-liter bottle of root beer. And vanilla ice cream. It seemed like the right kind of thing to take over to Lexie Bell and her kid. After all, who didn't like root-beer floats?

THE SUBJECT OF romance (or the lack thereof) was one that two single women were bound to discuss frequently. As Shannon drove Lexie and Brock to school, she informed Lexie that she was meeting up with someone she'd found on her new favorite online-dating site.

"So, he's got potential?" Lexie asked.

"I hope so. From the looks of him I think he could have. You really should check out that site. The people on it are more...real."

"I'll see how it works for you," Lexie said.

So far she hadn't had much luck when it came to online dating. She'd taken a couple of stabs at it, had a few dates, but nothing had worked out.

Of course, she wanted to find someone fabulous to share her days. And nights. Someone who would love both her and her son. But she was beginning to think that in order to change her luck she'd need to find a four-leaf clover, wear a rabbit's foot every day, hang a lucky horseshoe over her front door (where did you even find a horseshoe if you were a city girl?), capture a ladybug and get it to show her the end of the rainbow. Maybe then romantic good fortune would smile on her.

"I'll find out if he has a friend," Shannon promised.

Lexie wasn't holding her breath.

Oh, well. She had her son, she had her house, she had her teaching job, and she was making friends and had found a great bestie in Shannon. Her life was good. And if it never got better than that, so what? *Good* was a lot more than many people had.

And so what if she didn't have a date that night? So what if the company coming for dinner at her house was old enough to be her father? At least she had company coming.

She started baking the lasagna at five, and by five thirty she and Brock had set the table and she'd made the cheese mixture for her cheese bread. When their neighbor knocked on the door at six, the lasagna was out of the oven and the house smelled like an Italian restaurant.

He handed over a large bottle of root beer and a freezer bag with a carton of ice cream in it. "Thought you guys might like root-beer floats."

"That will be perfect for dessert," Lexie said.

Especially since they'd eaten all the cookies she'd baked. When she'd extended her dinner invite she hadn't thought ahead to dessert. Even when she was cooking she hadn't. Probably because she'd been thinking about horseshoes and four-leaf clovers.

"May I take your coat?" she offered. Except her hands were full. "Umm. Just a minute. Brockie, you can put the pop and the ice cream on the kitchen counter. Okay?"

"Okay," he said eagerly and started to dash toward the kitchen with the goodies she'd handed him.

"Walk," she called. "You don't want to shake the pop."

Brock slowed down, and Lexie took Mr. Mann's coat and hung it in the hall closet. "Come on in and sit down," she said, motioning to the living-room couch.

He nodded, came in and perched on the edge of her couch, set his hands on his thighs as if bracing to get right back up again. Looked around. He didn't say anything more, and she wondered if he'd used up all his words for the day just telling her about the root beer and ice cream.

"Dinner's almost ready," she told him and went to the kitchen. "I hope you're hungry," she called.

"I am."

She'd hoped he'd add something more, but that was the end of that conversation. There was really nothing cozy about being with Mr. Mann, and yet Lexie still felt drawn to him. She was sure that, deep down, like her, he was looking for connection.

Brock took over the conversational duties. He went in the living room and perched on the couch next to Mr. Mann. "Do you like cheese bread?"

"I do."

"I do, too," Brock said. "I helped set the table."

"It's good that you help your mom," said Mr. Mann.

Their tight-lipped neighbor was voluntarily saying something. Brock obviously knew how to draw him out.

She set out the food and summoned her son and her guest to the table. She watched Mr. Mann out of the corner of her eye once he dug into the lasagna. Would they possibly connect over pasta and tomato sauce?

He chewed, nodded his approval like some judge on a cooking-competition show and swallowed. "Really good."

It had been a long time since she'd had a compliment. She grinned and actually wiggled a little in her seat, like a child who'd just been patted on the head.

"My wife used to make lasagna," he volunteered. "This is almost as good as hers."

Thinking this was a possible invitation to offer condolences, Lexie said, "I am sorry about your wife."

He'd almost been smiling. The smile factory shut down, and he took another bite.

"How long has she been gone?"

"Three years."

"I don't think my mom is ever going to get over losing my dad," Lexie said. Not that she had herself, but she was doing better than her mother.

"You don't," Mr. Mann said simply.

"I worry about her," Lexie confessed. "She doesn't do any of the things she used to or see her old friends."

"Maybe she doesn't want to."

"But she needs a life."

"Yeah, well, everybody's got the right to live their life the way they want."

He said this with so much authority it was almost enough to convince Lexie that he was right. Almost, but not quite.

"When you have other people in your life, you have to keep living," she insisted.

"Maybe not everyone needs other people in their life," he said.

"Everyone needs someone," Lexie insisted. "It's why we're all put here together in the first place."

Mr. Mann merely shrugged and bit off a chunk of cheese bread.

"My grandma's coming to visit for Christmas," Brock announced.

Mr. Mann grunted. "Figures. That's when everyone's supposed to get happy, whether they want to or not."

After finishing his sentence, he did a very odd thing. He shot a quick look up toward the ceiling. What on earth was he looking for up there?

"Isn't Christmas a perfect time to get happy? To think about the good things in your life?" Lexie countered. "Christmas carols, presents, peace on earth, goodwill toward men?" He wasn't on board yet. "Christmas cookies?" she prompted.

He almost smiled at that. "Yeah, cookies are all right."

"I like cookies," Brock said.

"We need to make more, don't we, Brockie?" Lexie said. "Do you have a favorite cookie, Mr. Mann?"

His expression turned wistful. "My wife always made these chocolate cookies with a chocolate-peppermint frosting. They were the best."

"If you find that recipe, I'd love to try them," Lexie said.

He shrugged. "I don't know where she kept it." And he obviously didn't want to go looking.

She didn't press him. Instead, she moved them on to new conversational territory. "I'm glad you brought makings for root-beer floats, since I didn't have anything for dessert tonight."

"We used to have those sometimes when I was a kid growing up. When I was a teenager we got 'em a lot. Hamburger joints, the best place to take a date when you didn't have a lot of money." A smile tugged at the corner of his lips. "I used to take my wife to a place in Ballard called Zesto's."

"You fell in love over root-beer floats," Lexie finished for him, hoping to hear more.

"Long before that. I fell in love with her the first time I saw her."

"That is so sweet."

"She was sweet." He lost his smile and stuffed the last of his cheese bread in his mouth.

"I bet she was." And now it was time to move on before the poor man shut down. "Brockie, help me clear the table, and we'll get those floats made."

Mr. Mann dutifully ate his, but his smile stayed in hiding.

After dinner it was time to set up the tree, and she was glad of his help, both in bringing it in and getting it straight in the tree stand. Brock stood by, anxiously awaiting the moment when they could begin to decorate.

He was thrilled when Mr. Mann handed him a section of the lights and said, "Okay now, your mom will tell us where she wants these. Hold it up high."

So the two of them did Lexie's bidding, moving the string up and down and around the branches as she directed.

"And now the ornaments," she said, and Brock dived for the box she'd brought in from the garage.

"I guess it's kind of silly to put up a real tree and bother with lights when you can get artificial ones with the lights already on them," she said as she handed a glass snowflake ornament to Mr. Mann. "And it's a lot cheaper in the long run." She was still in sticker shock over how much she'd spent at the tree lot.

"Easier, too," he said.

"But I thought it would be fun to pick out a real tree."

"It is," he agreed. He half smiled. "I remember a couple times going with the wife to a tree farm and cutting our own tree. Your boy would love that."

"Next year we'll probably buy an artificial one that we can bring out every year," she said. "That will be more budget-friendly. And being on a beginning-teacher's salary, budgeting is important."

"You'll make more as time goes on."

And Brock would keep growing and needing more. Not that she'd ever begrudge him a penny. She watched as her son looked for the perfect spot to hang the little *Baby's First Christmas* ornament her parents had given her five years earlier, and her heart tightened. Her boy was the best thing that had ever happened to her.

She grabbed her phone and took a picture, capturing his look of concentration as he hooked it on a bough. Then caught him again as he beamed at her.

At last the tree was done, a happy one sporting colored bulbs and balls, homemade works of art, and the Patience Brewster ornaments Lexie had collected over the years.

"Our tree looks pretty," Brock said, taking it all in. He turned to Mr. Mann for confirmation. "Doesn't it?"

Their guest nodded approvingly. "Yeah, it does. Don't forget to keep water in the tree stand," he cautioned Lexie. "You're putting it up pretty early, and you don't want it to dry out and become a fire hazard."

"I won't forget," she promised.

Then he was out of things to say. He cleared his throat. "Guess I'll get on home. Bonnie needs to go out."

"Bonnie? Oh, your dog. You named her."

He shrugged. "Nobody's called to claim her. Looks like she's mine. Well," he finished briskly, "thanks for the dinner."

"Would you like to take some home with you?" she offered.

"No, that's okay."

"It'll only take a minute to wrap a piece."

He was already moving toward the door. "No, thanks."

She followed him and pulled his coat out of the closet, and he shrugged into it, gave a brisk nod, said good-night and then was gone.

But he'd come over and helped them decorate their tree. They'd actually had a conversation. Maybe, just maybe, she had made a friend in the neighborhood.

She got Brock in the tub and went back downstairs to put away the ornament boxes, humming as she went.

Her cell phone rang. *Mom*, she thought with a smile.

"Mom, we've just had the nicest time with our neighbor," she said. "He came over for dinner and helped us put up our tree."

"That was nice of him," Mom said.

"He's a little gruff and hard to get to know, but I think he's got a good heart. You'll get to meet him when you come up for Christmas."

"About Christmas," Mom began, and Lexie's smile fell away.

Oh, no. Don't say it.

CHAPTER SIXTEEN

"DARLING, I'M NOT feeling up to making the trip," Mom said.

An avalanche of disappointment dumped itself onto Lexie. It wasn't as if she was asking Mom to fly to Europe or drive twelve hours. It was barely over a three-hour flight from LAX to Sea-Tac airport, and then only another forty minutes to Fairwood, and Lexie had planned to pick her mother up at the airport. All Mom had to do was sit on a plane and then sit in the car.

"Oh, Mom. You promised."

"I know. I'll come up in the summer."

"It won't be the same. I wanted you to share Christmas with us in the new house. Brockie will be so disappointed."

Her mother's only response to this bit of guilting was to sigh.

It took a lot to make Lexie mad, but she could feel her temper rising. There was mourning, and there was selfishness.

But you could hardly call your mother selfish, especially when she wasn't normally. Not that anything had been normal since Daddy died.

Lexie tried begging. "Mom, please. We've both been looking forward to you coming up." The Christmas before had been hard. She'd been hoping they could make some new, happy memories this time around.

"I know you have, but I'm not feeling well."

Not feeling well. What did that mean? "As in you're sick?"

"I'm not myself. I'll make it up to you next year. I really will. I'm just not in a holiday mood."

Lexie took a deep breath. It was what it was, and there would be no changing her mother's mind about coming up. *Okay, adapt or die.*

"All right. I understand. We'll come spend Christmas with you."

They could have their own little Christmas early, enjoy their tree, then go to Mom's. The tickets would cost a small fortune, but that was what plastic was for.

"No, I don't want you to do that."

"Mom, you can't be alone on Christmas," Lexie protested.

"Your Aunt Rose will look in on me."

Look in on her. Like she was an invalid. Maybe in a way she was. She and Daddy had been a unit. They'd done everything together. One would take a breath, and the other would exhale. It was a wonder her mother was breathing now.

"You enjoy your holiday in your new house," Mom said. "We can Zoom on Christmas Day."

"That's hardly the same as having you here," Lexie grumbled.

Then she frowned. Maybe she was the one who was being selfish.

She gave up. "All right, we'll Zoom."

"I've disappointed you, haven't I?" Mom's voice was filled with regret.

"Yeah, you have," Lexie said. She wanted to add *I lost him, too. Snap out of it, Mom. You've still got people who need you.* She bit down on her lip. Hard.

"I'm so sorry. You know I love you more than anything."

Except Daddy and his memory.

Lexie sighed. "I love you, too."

And because she did, she was going to have to be patient and let Mom work out her issues. Heaven knew she'd had issues of her own when her relationship with the husband fail ended. It took time to get over losing someone, and when you'd been with that someone as long as her mother had been with her father, the time increased exponentially.

Once Lexie had her baby who needed her, she'd had to close the door on the past and move forward. It was the same when her father died. She still missed him, but she had to keep living, and she was determined to make life good for her son. She wished her mom could share that determination.

Maybe Mom thought Lexie didn't need her. If she did, she was wrong. A girl always needed her mother, no matter what age she was or where she was in life.

And Brock needed his grandma. Not that sleepwalking woman he'd come to know, but the energetic, involved woman she'd always been.

When Lexie was growing up Mom had dished out the fun like cookies: water-balloon fights in the summer and experiments in making Popsicles and ice cream; crazy Halloween parties where she'd don a sheet with holes to see out of, pretend to be a ghost and chase Lexie and her friends all over the house.

Then there was Christmas. Every year Lexie not only got treats in her Christmas stocking but there was always a letter from Santa, thanking her for minding her parents and telling her how proud they were of her. The Christmas stockings continued even when she was a teenager, and in addition to candy, teen-girl treasures such as nail polish, lip gloss and gift cards for token amounts started appearing. And always there was Santa's letter, encouraging Lexie to remember how loved she was and to always let her light shine. Daddy had always been the one to sneak outside Christmas Eve night and jingle some bells and call "Ho, ho, ho!" but Mom had been the architect of those letters. Lexie had saved every one of them.

After Brock was born Mom had started the tradition with him, too, but then Daddy died and so did the tradition of the letters from Santa. So did the laughter. Lexie had hoped this would be the year her mother took even a tiny step toward living her life again. It wasn't going to happen.

She said goodbye with as little rancor as possible and then went to fish Brock out of the tub. She put on a smile for her son and pretended everything was fine. She listened to his prayers and felt like she had an anvil on her chest when he asked God to bless Grandma. He was looking forward to his grandmother coming up for Christmas. It was not going to be fun breaking the news to him that she wasn't coming.

Lexie decided that news could be postponed. Who knew? Her mother could change her mind at the last minute. Or not.

Either way, she had to keep moving forward, and she'd make the holiday special for her son, no matter what.

She tucked Brock in, kissed him good-night, then went downstairs and made herself a mug of hot chocolate. Then she grabbed the TV remote and brought the Hallmark channel to life. At least there things turned out the way you wanted.

STANLEY LOVED LASAGNA, but lasagna didn't love him anymore. By the time he got home, he had a three-alarm fire going in his gut. He popped a couple of antacids and washed them down with a glass of milk.

"I shoulda stayed home," he said to Bonnie, who had trailed him out to the kitchen in the hopes of getting a dog treat.

But she'd already had her treat for the day. "I'm not going to spoil you," he told her.

And yet there she was, looking up at him with those bright little eyes.

"Okay, one more, but that's it," he said.

He dug one out of the box. Made her sit for it, then handed it over. She snapped it up and downed it in only a couple of chomps. Kind of like he'd devoured that lasagna earlier. A home-cooked meal had been a real treat.

Speaking of home-cooked meals. He frowned when his phone rang and the caller ID told him it was his sister-in-law, Amy, again.

"She's a pest," he informed Bonnie. A much more irritating pest than his neighbors would ever be. He knew she wouldn't give up calling him, though, so he decided to take the call and be done with it. "Hello, Amy."

"Oh, my gosh, you actually answered your phone. I'm in shock," she said.

Her greeting didn't produce any warm fuzzies. Quite the opposite. The cold pricklies took over.

"What do you want?" As if he couldn't guess.

"To see you."

Not really. They'd always rubbed each other the wrong way. Amy was only calling him out of a misplaced sense of duty.

"I look the same," he said. A little heavier, but she didn't need to know that.

"Funny, funny," she said, not in the least amused. "I let you off the hook for Thanksgiving, but I'm not going to for Christmas. You need to come down for Christmas dinner."

No, he didn't. It would be a repeat of Thanksgiving, only substitute red velvet cake for pumpkin pie. He still didn't like turkey, and he wasn't so crazy about cake that he was willing to drive all the way to Gresham for it.

"You can spend the night, you know," she added as if reading his mind.

"I'll pass, but thanks for the offer." There. Nice and polite.

There was momentary silence on the other end of the call as Amy worked out her next plan of attack. Then, "You know Carol wouldn't want us to lose touch."

Stanley rubbed his forehead. Amy was probably right on that one. Except he'd only gone to all those gatherings to please Carol and to make sure she got her family fix.

"Yeah, well, maybe next year," he said. Maybe by next Christmas Amy would have forgotten him. He only heard from her on Thanksgiving and Christmas, and if he kept turning her down, eventually those calls would dry up.

"I don't know why I bother," she said in disgust.

"Me, either," he said. "It's okay by me if you don't."

That pissed her off, and she ended the call, leaving Stanley to listen to the dial tone. He smiled and went in search of his recliner and TV. Amy was probably envisioning him feeling all hurt and insulted that she'd ended the call without so much as a goodbye and good luck. Actually, he felt amused. Amy always was a drama queen. She was probably working herself into a lather now and putting on a good show for her husband. The thought made him chuckle.

Carol wasn't laughing when Stanley rolled over in bed and found her head on the pillow next to his. "That wasn't very nice."

Oh, no. Not having this discussion.

He rolled away, facing the window only to find her already on that side of the bed, bending over him. She was wearing a silky blue nightgown that matched her eyes. *Wow.*

"Is that new?" he asked.

"New in your dreams. Now, don't change the subject."

"Oh, come on, Carol. You know your sister is a pain in the butt. The only reason she's bugging me to come visit is out of guilt. I'm not driving all the way to Gresham on Christmas Day. It's a long trek." And when you moved that far away you couldn't expect people to come visit.

"It is a distance," Carol admitted. "But she does care about you, Stanley."

He supposed, when it came right down to it, she did. He shouldn't have been so ungrateful.

But he still wasn't driving all that way for Christmas dinner.

"So what *are* you going to do?"

"I'll think of something."

"Maybe something with your neighbor," she suggested.

"Maybe," he said, not making any promises.

Carol smiled at him and bent over, close enough to kiss him. Maybe she was going to. To be able to kiss her one more time would be a taste of heaven.

"Lexie and Brock have taken quite a liking to you, Manly Stanley."

"Huh?" He pulled his thoughts back into the conversation with an effort.

She drifted away to the far end of the bedroom. "Did you have a good time tonight?"

"It was okay."

"Enjoyed the lasagna?"

"Almost as good as yours, babe. And the cheese bread was really good."

"It was kind of you to help set up their tree."

"Lexie could hardly haul it in with that boot of hers."

"And stay to decorate it."

"I was only being polite."

Carol grinned at him. "Oh. Was that it?"

"Yes."

"Admit it, Stanley. You enjoyed yourself."

"I guess. But I'm not making a habit of hanging out with those two."

Carol's expression became stern, and suddenly the bedroom felt cold. Stanley pulled the covers up to his chin.

"You've been making such progress. Don't disappoint me."

"I would never want to disappoint you," he said earnestly. He'd lived to make her happy.

"I know," she said. "And I know you're doing these things now to make me happy, but it's not about me, really."

"Of course it is. Who's haunting who?"

She giggled. "I am having fun. But this is about you, darling. I am going to make sure that you wind up with a good life."

"I'm fine," he insisted. He wasn't, and they both knew it. He'd never be fine without her.

"You're surviving. It's not the same as really living. You have to start participating in life."

"I am, already. What more do you want?" he demanded, irritated.

"I want you to start allowing yourself to enjoy being part of the human race." He opened his mouth to speak, but she held up a transparent hand. "I know you're not an extrovert, but you're not really a hermit, either. I'm not going to rest until you realize that there's a part of you that needs people, that wants people in your life. This is all a little bit like starting an exercise program. You're doing these things because you have to. I want to see you come to realize you don't have to but that you like to. You've made a beginning. Don't drop the ball now."

"Oh, for crying out loud," he muttered.

"Good night, Stanley. Pleasant dreams," she said and vanished in a cloud of sparkles.

Pleasant dreams. After that little speech, he'd probably have nightmares. He got up, went downstairs to the kitchen and took two more antacids.

CHAPTER SEVENTEEN

SHANNON CAME OVER for dinner and a crafting night after taking Lexie to her physical-therapy appointment on Monday. Lexie served up homemade veggie soup and used up the last of the French bread to make more cheese bread. She'd ordered online what they needed for their pine-cone center-piece project, and the box of supplies had come that very afternoon.

Once Brock was in bed and it was just the two women, Lexie asked how Shannon's date with her latest possible match had gone. "Spill. I want deets."

Shannon squirted a dab of hot glue on the back of a pine cone. "He's really nice."

Nice. Where were the rave reviews? "And?" Lexie prompted.

"He likes to play tennis, so that's good, and he's a foodie."

"Sounds like you guys have got stuff in common."

"We do, but I don't know if he's a keeper."

"If he's really nice..."

"There's more to life than nice," Shannon said, concentrating on securing her pine cone to its base. "I want to feel some sizzle when I'm with someone."

"So he didn't kiss you?"

"He did, and it was okay."

Just okay: that wasn't okay. "No fire, huh?"

"Barely a spark. He wants to see me again, but I'm gonna cool things."

"You're not going to just ghost him, I hope," Lexie said.

"No. I'm gonna use the *f*-word."

"Men hate it when you only want to be friends."

"I know," Shannon said with a sigh. She picked up another pine cone and examined it. "But what can you do? I mean, he *would* make a great friend. But I want a great friend plus great sex. I want to end up with somebody who sets me on fire, who sets the whole bed on fire. Is that asking too much?"

"I don't think so," Lexie said.

Except maybe it was. Could a man be fun to be with, great in bed and undyingly loyal all at the same time? She wasn't sure. She heaved a sigh.

"Yeah, maybe I'm dreaming," Shannon said.

"There's nothing wrong with dreams," Lexie was quick to say.

Except she wasn't so sure they came true. Her big dream had turned into a nightmare. She'd found someone she thought was perfect and gave him her heart, and look what had happened.

"If you really believe that, how come you're not looking harder?" Shannon challenged.

"I guess I'm not as brave as I once was."

Having her little boy to love had gone a long way toward helping her heal, but there was still a fissure that could crack her poor heart in two if she entrusted it to someone only to get rejected again. She longed to have a wonderful man in her life, really wanted that happy ending, that one true love like her mother and grandmother had both found, but maybe there was no such thing anymore. Maybe nobody really cared about *happily ever afters*. Maybe there was only *happy* now. Maybe you had to think of love like it was chocolate. You enjoyed it while it lasted, and when it was gone, it was gone.

You could always go out and get more chocolate. How many times could you go out and find true love? And if it kept vanishing and you had to go looking time after time, was it really love?

She frowned at her half-finished wreath. "Why is love so complicated?"

"I don't know," Shannon said. "I asked my mom that once."

"What did she say?"

"She said 'Don't ask me.' Mom's been married twice, and it's not looking good for Number Three."

"Some people figure it out. My parents did. And I think our neighbor did. His wife's been gone three years, but I can tell he still misses her. He can hardly bring himself to talk about her."

Similar to her own mother. But at least Mr. Mann was getting out there and making an effort in his own stiff way.

"That's so sad. And so romantic all at the same time."

Stanley Mann, romantic. Lexie had trouble envisioning it. He could barely manage friendly.

Getting to know him was like befriending a feral animal. There was a lot of coaxing involved. But the coaxing was working. He was warming to her and Brock and each time he was with them he revealed a little more of himself. There was a lot of good hiding under that crusty exterior.

INCH BY INCH, Lexie Bell and her kid kept encroaching further into Stanley's life. First it was cookies, rides, tree-shopping, then it was tree decorating. Next the kid was asking if Bonnie could come over to his yard and play.

The dog needed something to do besides watch TV and supervise Stanley as he worked his sudoku puzzles, so he let her go. But then he found himself walking over to say it was time for Bonnie to come home. And standing on the front porch, yakking with Lexie Bell. Not about anything much—him asking if she was keeping her tree watered, if she needed anything from the store. Her talking about Brock, how he was liking school and starting to make friends. Oh, and his Winter Holiday program was coming up at school. Would Stanley like to go? Not really, but he'd wound up saying yes, anyway.

He wasn't sure, but right after he'd agreed he thought he heard his wife whisper, "Good for you, Stanley."

Good for somebody. Those two were sucking up his time faster than a new vacuum cleaner.

They weren't the only ones. It seemed that Mrs. Gimble was somehow starting to take up more of his time also. It all began with a conversation at her mailbox. Even though she had someone to deliver meals, she was itching to bake. Could he pick up some vanilla extract at the store? Why not? He had to go to the store, anyway. Next he got a call. She was out of her pain medicine, and the friend who usually picked it up for her was sick. Was he, by any chance, going by the drugstore? And, while he was out... She'd reserved a book at the library. Would he mind picking it up?

Yeah, he minded.

Okay, not that much. He had to go out sometimes, himself, so really, it wasn't that big of a deal to run errands for the old woman.

Or for Lexie. It seemed like every day she was wanting to bake something Christmassy: red velvet cupcakes for the teachers' lounge, gingerbread cookies for her class. Oh, but she needed gluten-free flour. If he was going to the store...

He always got a treat as a reward, so why not? Good grief. He was no better than his dog. Anything for a treat.

But who could blame him? It felt like forever since he'd enjoyed home-baked goods. Carol had been quite the baker. And a great cook. He sure missed her chicken pot pie.

Had she been whispering to Lexie Bell in her dreams? he wondered when Lexie invited him for dinner on Thursday after he'd dropped off white chocolate chips. "I'm making a chicken pot pie," she said as they wound up having yet another front-porch yakfest.

The very mention of his favorite dish made his mouth water. "You know how to make that?"

"My mom's recipe. Flakiest crust you'll ever eat," she added.

He had to eat, and Carol wanted him to get out more. He agreed to dinner.

"Do you like it?" Lexie asked when he sat at her dining table, wolfing it down.

He nodded, swallowed. "It's as good as what my wife used to make."

She smiled at that. "I'm glad to hear it. My mom taught me how to make pie crust. She always said the secret to good crust is not handling it a lot, but I watched a cook online who said the secret is really in chilling it."

He nodded. He didn't care what the secret was. All he was interested in was the end result.

"Well, it's good," he said.

"I added thyme."

"Like in the old Simon and Garfunkel song."

She looked questioningly at him.

"Parsley, sage, rosemary and thyme?" he prompted. "'Scarborough Fair'?"

She nodded and pretended to know what he was talking about.

"Never mind," he said.

"We have pudding for dessert," Brock volunteered, not wanting to be left out of the conversation. "I held the beaters."

"That's good. You'll be able to cook for yourself when you move out."

Brock looked as puzzled now as his mother had over the mention of the Simon and Garfunkel song.

"When you grow up and have a house of your own," Stanley explained.

"I'm going to live with Mommy all my life and take care of her," Brock said.

Stanley chuckled at that. "Yeah, I said that when I was your age, too. Then I grew up and met a girl."

Brock made a face. "Girls."

"Yeah, I said that, too," Stanley told him.

"I like Shatika Wilson," Brock confessed after a moment. "She has a turtle *and* a cat."

"A wealthy woman," Stanley observed.

"Can we have a cat?" Brock asked Lexie.

"May we have a cat?" she said. "And now you want a cat instead of a dog?"

"We have Bonnie. I don't need a dog anymore."

Lexie looked at Stanley as if to say *What can you do?*

Yeah, what could you do? The kid had adopted both him and his dog.

"How did your day go, Mr. Mann?" Lexie asked.

Still calling him Mr. Mann while her kid called him Grandpa Stanley. It seemed a little weird. "Call me Stanley," he said.

She looked pleased. "Stanley. How did your day go?"

"It was all right. Had to run an errand for Mrs. Gimble. You haven't met her yet."

"She waved at me once this fall when she was at her mailbox," Lexie said.

"She doesn't get out much," Stanley said.

"That's too bad."

He shrugged. "It happens when you get older." A lot of stuff happened when you got older. Aches and pains, hemorrhoids, wrinkles. Potbellies. He'd put some work into that, he thought, and half smiled.

Losing the love of your life. His smile vanished, and his throat suddenly felt tight.

He cleared it. "How was your physical therapy?" he asked. Her friend had taken over chauffeur duties, and that had been a relief. One less thing he had to do.

He could almost hear Carol mocking "Yes, because you are so busy."

"I have another doctor appointment for right before Christmas. I'm hoping I'll be able to get out of this boot and into a brace."

"If you need a ride."

"I'm sure Shannon can take me."

Yep, she didn't need him for that. Oddly, he felt a little...hmm, what? Rejected? Nah.

"Well, if she can't and you need someone," he told her. What was he saying?

"Thanks."

"You should have my phone number for just in case you, uh, have an emergency or something," he said.

She smiled at him as if he'd given her a bouquet of roses. "That's so nice of you."

He wished she'd quit saying stuff like that. It was embarrassing.

"Well, you never know when you might need something."

She happily put his number in her phone and then gave him hers, too. "Just so you have it," she said. "Not that I'd be any help in an emergency," she added, sticking out her booted foot as exhibit A.

"I may have a cookie emergency," he joked. She giggled, and it lifted the corners of his mouth.

"Now, how about we have our pudding?" she said.

"Yes!" Brock hooted.

So pudding it was. Chocolate, with freshly whipped cream, not the crap from a can. Someone had raised this girl right.

"Good," Stanley said in approval after the first bite. "Nice to see someone using real whipped cream."

"Oh, yes. Another thing my mom taught me," Lexie said.

She suddenly looked sad. What was that about?

None of his business, that was what.

After dinner Brock asked Stanley if he'd play Candy Land with him.

Stanley had played the classic board game as a kid, himself. "That game's been around forever," he said.

"No, it hasn't," Brock said. "We just bought it this summer."

"I mean the game itself." He turned to Lexie. "The woman who invented it had polio. She came up with it when she was in the hospital, made it up to entertain the kids who were in there."

"So can we... May we play?" Brock asked.

"Yeah, I guess I've got time for a game," Stanley said.

With a whoop, Brock ran to fetch the game from a cupboard.

"It's really nice of you to stay and play with him," Lexie said.

Stanley shrugged like it was no big deal.

"I never knew the history of that game," Lexie continued as she began to clear the table. "That is so inspiring."

"She was a teacher, just like you."

"Except I'll probably never do anything big like that."

"You never know. You're still young. You got lots of time. Anyway, you're already doing something big. You're teaching kids. And you're raising one."

She sighed. "It seems like such an overwhelming job sometimes. I wish I wasn't doing it alone."

"So why are you?" None of his business.

Lexie concentrated on rinsing off a plate and loading it in the dishwasher. "I think I might have mentioned that things didn't work out with Brock's dad," she said, lowering her voice. She cast a look to where the boy was rummaging through a pile of games and card decks. "We finally had enough money for our wedding in Hawaii when he, uh, found someone else."

"What about the kid?"

Why was he asking this stuff? It was as if he was channeling Carol.

She lowered her gaze and bit on her lip. Her words came out as a whisper. "He didn't want to be a father."

Stanley had no patience for men who committed to a woman and then bailed. Even worse to bail on his child.

"Sounds like a shit to me," he said.

Carol would have come up with something softer, more comforting, like *You poor girl. I'm so sorry that happened to you.* Stanley scratched the back of his neck, suddenly uncomfortable.

"What he did was shitty," Lexie said. "But it showed me that he wasn't the kind of man I wanted. Of course, before everything blew up I thought he was perfect. Pretty stupid."

"There's no such thing as perfect. There's only the one who's perfect for you." Gack. What was he now, Oprah?

"I wish I could find that person. I'm not sure I will. I'm beginning to think there aren't any good men out there."

What a bunch of baloney. "How hard are you looking?" Stanley asked.

Her only answer was a shrug.

The kid was back at the table now, game in hand. "I like this game," he informed Stanley. "Do you?"

"I did when I was your age. Haven't played it in a long time."

"I'll help you," Brock said.

And so, Stanley Mann, the guy who'd never had kids, found himself absorbed in saving King Kandy from the ravenous candy snake. It wasn't exactly sudoku, so why the heck was he grinning?

The kid wasn't grinning when he lost.

"Hey, now," Stanley chided. "No pouting."

This made the corners of Brock's mouth slide lower.

"Sometimes you lose. That's what makes you strong. And you don't always lose. Sometimes you win."

"That makes me happy," Brock said. "Can we play again?"

"Only if you promise not to pout if you lose."

The kid nodded eagerly.

He did win the second game. "I won!" he crowed.

"Yep. See? Sometimes you win, and sometimes you lose, but no matter what you always got to man up and be a good sport."

"Man up and be a good sport," Brock repeated with a nod.

"And now it's time for my little man to have a bath," Lexie said.

"But I want to play with Grandpa Stanley," Brock protested.

"A good man always minds his mom," Stanley said.

That was all it took. The boy raced for the stairs.

"You are so good with him," Lexie said.

Stanley shrugged. "Kids aren't my thing. That was my wife."

"They may not be your thing, but my boy sure likes you. Thank you for being so good to him. To both of us."

Okay, this was getting uncomfortable. "No problem. I better get going. Bonnie needs to go out."

She looked a little shocked by his abruptness. "Oh, sure. Of course."

"Thanks for dinner," he said and started for the door.

"You're welcome anytime," she said. Then added "Oh, wait." She hurried to the fridge and pulled out a plastic leftover container. "Take some of this home. Brock and I can never eat it all."

Well, why not? "Thanks."

It was nippy out, and it smelled like snow. If the weather did turn, maybe Lexie would need a ride to school in the morning. Or to her next physical-therapy appointment, since that friend of hers didn't drive in the snow.

The woman needed more than some old guy to drive her around, he thought as he walked across her lawn to his. She needed a young buck she could do things with, grow old with.

"What a good idea," Carol whispered in his ear.

"Hey, it was just a thought," he said.

And thoughts were not the same as doing things. No way was he going to interfere in Lexie's life and play matchmaker. That was chick stuff.

Cupid's a man.

Stanley frowned. He knew where tonight's encounter with his wife was going to go.

CHAPTER EIGHTEEN

SURE ENOUGH, Stanley was barely settled in his recliner, looking for a good cop show on TV, when the screen went wonky and flipped from a murder scene to a cutesy café all decked out for Christmas. This looked suspiciously like the kind of movies his wife loved to watch every holiday season. There was the requisite adorable waitress, serving a customer a piece of pie, and here through the door came the man who would wind up falling in love with her. Stanley knew how these TV movies went. He'd watched enough of them with Carol.

"Oh, no," he said and aimed the remote. Back to the murder scene. The detective was squatting next to the bloodied body. "It looks like—"

Before Stanley could learn what it looked like he was back to the café. "Love," said the adorable waitress's friend.

"Come on, Carol," he said, exasperated. "I got the message already."

The TV settled down, and the murder investigation began in earnest. Obviously, she'd gotten the message, too.

Okay, maybe not. Here she came again, in the middle of the night. This time she was perched on a little pink cloud, dressed in a short pink dress with lots of ruffles, and she held a bow and an arrow with a heart-shaped tip. Oh, boy. Just as he feared.

"Babe, you know I love you," he said. It was how he'd always prefaced a refusal to cooperate. "I always have, I always will."

"I know," she said and smiled at him.

That sweet smile. It could still make his heart do a backflip.

"We had a lot of happy years together, didn't we?"

"Yes, we did. Carol, I still miss you so much."

"I know, darling. But try to remember how happy we were, how blessed to have had a lifetime together."

It had been a good life.

"And now you have this lovely young woman who needs a father figure and a little boy who calls you Grandpa."

Stanley rubbed his chin. Only a few days ago he would have replied *The kid's a pest*, but he'd gotten used to having the boy around. And he had gotten a kick out of playing Candy Land with him. Playing a kids' board game, after all these years. Who'da thought it?

"I know you're coming to care about those two. Don't you think Lexie deserves to be as happy as we were?"

"Well, sure. But, come on, Carol, what do you expect me to do about it? I'm not in the matchmaking business. That's stuff women do. And Cupid's not a guy," he hurried to add. "He's a naked baby."

"Actually, in mythology he's a youth, the son of Mercury, the winged messenger of the gods, and Venus, the goddess of love."

"Whatever he is, I ain't him," Stanley said.

Uh-oh. Her eyes were starting to take on that creepy red glow again. And was she actually getting bigger?

He squeezed his own eyes shut. "Don't be doing that, Carol. Please."

"Stanley!"

He opened one eye and ventured a look. Yep, still scary-looking. He slammed his eyelid back down.

Her voice softened. "I'm not asking you to set up a date or anything. Just if you happen to see someone nice, mention Lexie. Now, how hard is that to do?"

"Just mention her, huh?"

"And see if he's interested. You don't even have to give out her phone number. In fact, you shouldn't because you never know."

"Oh, so I'm supposed to see somebody nice, hook him up with Lexie but not give him her phone number because he might not be nice."

She frowned. "Stanley, you are being difficult."

"No, I'm being smart. It's never a good idea to try and set people up. Remember that book-club friend of yours you tried to match up with my poor old buddy Mickey?"

"Well, how was I to know she had a drinking problem?"

"That's my point. You can't always know about people."

She sighed, and he ventured another look. Good, she was back to the genial woman he knew and loved. No more fiery eyes, and she'd shrunk back down to size.

"All right, Manly Stanley. You know best."

"You bet I do," he said.

"And I know you want to see your new friend happy. She's benefiting so much from having you in her life. I'm proud of you, darling."

He'd always loved to hear her say that. It left him feeling all warm and gooey.

He smiled wistfully at her. "I wish I could hold you again."

"You are. In your heart." She blew him a kiss and was gone.

Yes, she would be in his heart for the rest of his days. But he sure missed being able to hold her in his arms.

Everyone needs someone to love.

It was the last thing he heard before he fell into a dreamless sleep.

And it was the first thing inside his head when he woke up in the morning. "Lexie's nice enough," he said to Bonnie as he dished up her dog food, "and I get what Carol's saying, but I don't know anybody the girl's age. What am I supposed to do, put an ad in the paper? She's young. She knows how to use the internet. She can find someone there."

But how did you really know about people you met on the those dating sites? Hard enough to find out about someone when you saw them in person. Hiding behind a computer screen, people could tell all kinds of lies about themselves.

"Not my problem," he explained to the dog.

Bonnie wagged her tail, a sure sign of agreement, and dug into her breakfast.

Yep, not his problem.

But then he found himself in the supermarket meat section, and there was Jayce Campbell, putting out packages of steak.

Nice-enough fella, and friendly. Always used to chat up Carol. The first time Stanley had come in the store after losing her, Jayce had asked about her. He hadn't gotten all sloppy sentimental on hearing she was gone; he'd shaken his head and said, "That sucks." Then he'd given Stanley a free steak and suggested he get a case of beer. "That's on me, too."

Stanley had never seen a ring on the guy's hand. He could almost feel Carol prodding him. The guy was okay—not bad-looking, either. Maybe Lexie would like him.

But Stanley was not in the matchmaking business.

"Hey, Mr. Mann," Jayce greeted him. "How's it goin'?"

"It's goin'," Stanley replied.

"Steak tonight?" Jayce asked.

"Yeah. Give me a good one."

"They're all good here. You know that," Jayce said with a grin as he handed over a nice rib eye.

"That'll work," Stanley said.

He could have sworn he felt a poke in the ribs.

Say something.

He'd imagined that.

Stanley!

Shit. What was he supposed to say? He didn't know how these millennials or Gen Xers or whatever this guy was thought. How was Stanley supposed to start a conversation about his love life?

He stalled. "Give me another one while you're at it."

"Sure," said Jayce and handed over a second package. "You having company or stocking up?"

"Stocking up." Okay, if there was a way to smoothly transition from talking about steak to women Stanley didn't know it. He took the blunt approach. "Got a woman in your life?" Maybe he should have been more general. Maybe the guy was into men.

"You know somebody?"

Stanley shrugged, keeping it casual. "Got a nice neighbor. She's new in town."

"Yeah? Is she quiche?"

Quiche. *Real Men Don't Eat Quiche.* Stanley remembered that expression. So, Jayce was asking...what?

"Is she hot?" Jayce clarified.

That term Stanley knew. "Yeah, she's pretty cute. She's looking to hook up. You interested?"

Jayce's eyes lit up like Stanley had just offered him a winning lotto ticket. "Sure. Why not? Got a number for her?"

Lexie wouldn't want him passing out her phone number like it was a party favor. "Tell you what. Give me yours, and I'll pass it on."

"Okay," Jayce said and did. "Tell her to call me if she's interested."

That had been simple enough. Stanley smiled as he made his way to the checkout stand. He'd done a favor for his neighbor and made Carol happy. All in a day's work.

LEXIE WAS SURPRISED when Mr. Mann stopped by her house Saturday morning. Lately he'd only been coming over to fetch Bonnie or drop off some grocery item she needed, so him popping over to visit felt about as natural as Scrooge dropping by with presents.

Brock had been right there the minute he heard their neighbor's voice. "I have a wiggly tooth," he informed Mr. Mann, then opened his mouth and demonstrated.

"You sure do," Mr. Mann agreed. "Want me to yank it out?"

Brock took a step back and shook his head violently. "Mommy says it will fall out all on its own. When it does I'll put it under my pillow for the tooth fairy."

"When I was your age and had a loose tooth, we tied a string around it, then hooked the other end to a doorknob and slammed the door," Mr. Mann said. "Came right out."

Brock's eyes got big, and he took another step back.

Okay, that was probably enough reminiscing about past tooth experiences. "Is there something we can do for you, Mr. Mann?"

"Stanley," he reminded her.

"Stanley," she said. That whole first name thing was going to take some getting used to. Her grandma had always told Lexie it was disrespectful to call her elders by their first names.

"Uh, no. I just, uh, happened to, uh, be talking to a guy at the grocery store and, uh, mentioned you."

"Mentioned me?" Where was he going with this?

"He works in the meat department. Nice guy, not married. I told him you were new in town." Stanley produced a slip of paper with a name and phone number on it. "He said to call him if you're interested."

So Stanley Mann was playing matchmaker. How sweet, Lexie thought, touched.

"That's awfully kind of you," she said and took it.

"Maybe you can meet for coffee or drinks or something."

"Maybe we can," she agreed. "Thanks."

He nodded, cleared his throat. "Well, uh, see you two later." Then he turned and went down the front-porch steps, looking like a man anxious to escape.

Lexie smiled as she shut the front door. A nice man. Wouldn't that be a change.

She did call later that day.

A sexy, low voice answered, making her body vibrate like a tuning fork, and she had an instant image of a cowboy on the cover of a romance novel. Was the rest of him as gorgeous as his voice?

"I'm Lexie Bell," she said. "My neighbor, Stanley Mann, told me about you."

Jayce Campbell gave a half chuckle. "He's a cool old dude. He said you're new in town."

"I am."

"That can be a pain in the ass. But hey, I can fill you in on everything you want to know."

"I'd like that."

"What are you doing tonight?"

"Tonight?" she repeated. Gosh, instant date.

"Sure. Why not? I'm in-between."

In between what? Well, women. Duh. All right, he was in-between and so was she, so why not?

"Okay," she said.

"I can pick you up."

The few first (and usually last) dates she'd had she'd chosen the place to meet and had arrived separately. She wasn't going to change that strategy, no matter who had recommended this man.

"I'll meet you," she said. "Where's a good place?"

"Smokey's. That place is lit."

"All right." Hopefully, Shannon could stay with Brock. "What time?"

"Seven?"

"Seven it is," she said. It would give her time to feed Brock before she left. "How will I recognize you?"

"I'm pretty tall. I'll be wearing jeans and a leather jacket. But don't worry, I'll spot you. I'll be looking for the best-looking woman in the place."

Flattery and he hadn't even seen her. She hoped he wouldn't be disappointed. She hoped *she* wouldn't be disappointed.

"All right. See you later," she said. And just like that she had a date.

She was grinning like she'd won a prize at the fair when she ended the call. Until she looked down and saw the stupid boot on her foot. Yeah, that was attractive. She should have told him she'd be the one in a walking boot.

Oh, well. There wasn't much she could do about the boot. She wouldn't be in it forever, and any man with a brain would understand that.

She called Shannon. "Any chance you can come over and hang out with Brockie for a couple of hours tonight? I have—wait for it—a date."

"A date? You met somebody? You used that dating app and didn't tell me?"

"I didn't. Actually, it's someone my next-door neighbor knows."

"The old guy set you up?" Shannon sounded disbelieving.

"He said he's nice. And he sounds nice."

"Here's hoping," Shannon said, although she sounded dubious.

That didn't stop Lexie from being excited. She fed Brock his dinner, then put on leggings and a long red tulip-edged sweater. It had a cute faux-fur trim and a scooped neckline. Sexy but not desperate. Perfect. She'd like to have worn some stylish boots with her outfit, but that wasn't an option so she settled for a black ballerina flat. The shoe didn't quite tie the sexy bow around her outfit, but oh, well.

Brock was playing with the vintage candles on the coffee table when she came downstairs. "You look pretty, Mommy," he told her.

"Thank you, sweetie." At least she passed a first grader's inspection.

"I wish I could go meet your new friend," Brock said.

"I'm going to see if he's someone you'll like," Lexie said. No way was she bringing around any man she hadn't checked out thoroughly. It would be a long time before Brock got to meet her new friend.

"This guy is going to fall crazy in love with you," Shannon predicted before Lexie left.

"Thanks for the vote of confidence." With her track record, Lexie would take all the votes she could get.

It was drizzling when Lexie's Uber pulled up in the graveled parking lot of Smokey's. It looked like a log cabin on steroids, with a big front porch. That was where the resemblance ended because the windows sported all manner of neon signs advertising different brands of beer. And dangling from the roofline was a neon cowgirl in a short skirt, holding a big glass, one booted foot kicking back and forth.

The minute Lexie got out of the car she heard country rock blaring out at her, and as she got closer to the door she could also hear loud conversation mixed with laughter. This was obviously the place to come for fun in Fairwood.

The inside was rough-hewn timber with pictures of mountain scenes and cowboys riding broncos hung on the walls, along with old Marlboro posters of cowboys smoking cigarettes. She could smell barbecue and grease.

Several couples already had taken over tables in the dining area, and the bar section was packed with singles—guys in jeans and T-shirts or casual shirts with the sleeves rolled up. Some of the women milling about wore jeans so tight Lexie wondered if they could even sit down. Others were in short, tight skirts and shimmering holiday-festive tops. Killer heels, stylish boots—totally on fleek, nothing like the ugly blue Frankenstein boot on Lexie's right foot. She suddenly didn't feel quite so sexy.

Speaking of sexy, here came a built-to-order guy in jeans, a gray T-shirt and a leather jacket—a real drool-maker with a perfect square chin, brown hair and eyes, and a mouth that she just knew would be capable of all kinds of amazing things. This couldn't be Jayce Campbell. She couldn't be that lucky.

He came up to her, smiled and asked, "Are you Lexie?"

Lucky Lexie. "I am," she said and wished she could hide her big, booted foot.

The Frankenstein boot didn't seem to bother Jayce. He looked her up and down and the smile went from friendly to bedroom ready. "Yaas."

Her thoughts about him exactly. *Wow.*

One of her grandma's favorite sayings popped into her head. *If something looks too good to be true, it probably is.*

No, no, Lexie wasn't going to go there. It was important to give people a chance. Between Granny's pearls of wisdom and her own past disappointment, Lexie was already prone to giving up on finding her Mr. Forever. She was not going to do that with this guy even before the drinks arrived, for crying out loud.

The host led them across a peanut shell–covered floor—peanuts on the floor, what was with that?—and seated them at a booth where a red candle bowl tried to cast some light on the scarred wooden tabletop.

He took off his jacket, slouched against the wall and put a leg up along the bench, making himself at home. He idly pointed in the direction of her foot. "What happened to your foot?"

"Chip fracture," she said.

"Yow," he said and made a face. "How long are you stuck in that thing?"

"I hope to be out of it by Christmas."

"No dancing for you tonight, I guess," he said and she felt that she'd disappointed him.

"You like to dance?" she asked.

"Hey, good foreplay," he said with a wink.

No points in the suave department for Jayce Campbell. Lexie didn't smile back, but he failed to notice. He was focusing on their waitress, checking her out from boobs to butt.

She set down water for both of them and a red plastic bowl filled with peanuts in the shell, obviously the source of the mess on the floor. "Can I get you guys started with something to drink?"

"Hale's pale ale for me," he said and looked to Lexie. "What do you want?"

Someone with a little more class. Maybe she *should* give Shannon's dating app a try.

"White wine?" she asked the waitress hopefully. This didn't look like a white-wine kind of place.

"You got it," the woman said and left them.

Lexie took a peanut from the bowl and shelled it, searching for a conversation topic that might give them a fresh start on the right foot. "I like your sleeve," she said, nodding at the herd of longhorn steers stampeding up his arm.

She put the shell back in the plastic bowl. He took it out and tossed it on the floor. "Meat's my thing. So, you met very many people since you moved here?"

"A few."

"It's gotta be hard being new in town. Not that I ever had to move. I've lived here all my life. Went to Fairwood High. Lettered in baseball. My batting average was over three hundred."

Even though Lexie wasn't into baseball she assumed that was a big deal. "Did you play in college, too?"

"Didn't go. Too expensive. Just as well. I'm not a college kind of guy."

Lexie had been a college kind of girl. She'd loved taking classes, enjoyed all the social aspects. She'd especially enjoyed taking English lit and history classes.

"I wanted to get out and start earning money. Wound up working at the store, and that's fine with me."

Okay. Earning money was good.

"What do you do when you're not working?" she asked.

"Same as anybody else, I guess. I work on my car. I'm fixing up a Dodge Charger I found in some old guy's field a couple years ago. That thing is going to be dope when I'm finished." He gave her a grin. "Maybe I'll take you for a ride when I get it done."

She wasn't into cars any more than she was into baseball, but she knew he thought he was offering her a big treat, so she smiled politely and said, "Thanks."

"When I'm not doing that I like to game, like to watch TV."

"What do you watch?" She had a suspicion the Hallmark channel didn't make his top list.

"Cop stuff. *Game of Thrones.* Anything with some action. How about you?"

"I like mysteries, rom-coms. PBS always has something good on." Everybody liked PBS.

"Boring," he sneered.

Okay, it was now official. This date was going to end up in Nowhere Land.

Their drinks came, and they ordered barbecued ribs and steak fries. Ribs. Something in common. Oh, boy, what a stretch.

"So, nobody in your life right now?" he asked.

She shook her head.

"Maybe we can fix that."

No, *they* couldn't.

He talked some more about himself—his job, his favorite sports team, the Christmas cookies his mom made every year. Then he actually got around to asking Lexie about herself. Did she bake? No hidden agenda there.

"I like to bake."

He flashed her that sexy grin again. Except now the sexy shine had worn off.

"Well, whaddya know? I like to eat," he said.

Oh, boy. How soon could she leave?

They finished their meal, and the waitress offered dessert.

"I'll pass," Lexie said.

"Guess we're done here," Jayce said to the waitress.

The bill came, and Lexie offered to pay half.

"Nah, it's on me," he said and whipped out his plastic.

Okay, he wasn't stingy. That was a good thing.

But it wasn't enough.

Lexie quickly took out her phone to request an Uber.

"Hey, I can drive you home," he offered once he realized what she was doing.

"No, that's okay. But thanks."

By the time the bill was paid her ride was five minutes away. It couldn't get there soon enough.

As they walked out the door, she started to make her escape, but he said, "I'll walk you to the car. Where is it?"

"Looks like it's over there."

At the dark end of the parking lot. Ugh. Was he going to want to kiss her? Of course he was, and the last thing she wanted was to waste time smearing lips with this tool. Funny how, when she'd first seen him, that had seemed like a great idea. Now, uh, no. And what if he got pushy? She mentally prepared to knee him in the groin.

"Next time I'll pick you up," he said as they started off the porch.

Not a chance. She quickened her pace, and clumped off the last step. "Thanks again for dinner."

"Whoa, what's your hurry?" He edged her against the wall and moved in close to her and slid a hand around her middle.

It might have been a turn-on if he hadn't already turned her off permanently. "The driver's waiting," she said crisply.

"He'll wait," Jayce said, edging closer. "How about a little taste to tide me over until next time?" His mouth went for her lips and his hand went for a boob.

Okay, enough of this. She dodged his mouth and gave him a shove. "No. I'm done here."

He stumbled back, half-laughing. "Oh, I get it. Next time we party. You can come to my place or I can come to yours. I'm easy."

But she wasn't. "No next time," she informed him.

He frowned. "I thought you wanted to hook up."

"What?"

"That's what the old man said. Sounded like you were thirsty, looking for some action."

"I'm not that thirsty," she said firmly.

He looked at her in total disgust. "Well, sooorry. Guess I got it wrong."

"Somebody sure got it wrong." And that somebody was going to get an earful.

CHAPTER NINETEEN

SHANNON HAD JUST gotten Brock into bed when Lexie walked back in the house. "Hey, Cinderella, midnight's a long ways away," she greeted Lexie. "Was Prince Charming that big of a frog?"

"Afraid so. Nothing in common at all, and on top of that he was ready for a parking-lot sex party."

"Wow. Locked and loaded, huh?"

Lexie shook her head. "Stanley Mann apparently told him I was looking to *hook up*."

"So your neighbor is some kind of dirty old man pimp?"

"I don't think so, but he sure isn't a very good judge of character."

"Oh, I don't know. He's latched on to you, and I'd say that makes him a pretty good judge of character."

"Aww, thanks. Since you're here, how about some popcorn and Hallmark?" Lexie suggested. There was no point in having the whole evening be a waste.

"Sounds good to me," Shannon said. "Let's find a Christmas movie. Even if we haven't met the perfect man in real life, at least we can pretend they exist."

Lexie made popcorn and brought out the eggnog Stanley had picked up for her at the store, and they settled in to watch a movie. She found herself actually feeling jealous as the perfect romance played out before her. The hero wasn't full of himself, and the couple's first meet was sweet and involved no mention of *good foreplay*.

It's fiction, she reminded herself. Real life was always messier. And boy, was hers a mess. What *had* Stanley Mann been thinking when he set her up with Mr. Meat Market?

She spotted her neighbor taking Bonnie for a walk the next afternoon and called him over for a front-porch visit. "Mr. Mann," she began.

"Stanley," he corrected.

She ignored the correction. "I met your friend from the meat market." Her tone of voice was a dead giveaway that her neighbor's good deed was not going to go unpunished.

He looked at her warily. "Yeah?"

"Yeah."

"You two didn't hit it off?" he guessed.

"No, we did not. What did you tell him about me?"

He picked up his dog as if for protection. "Nothing. I told him you were new here and that you were nice."

"What else?" she prompted.

"Nothing. Like I said, that you were new here and you were looking to hook up."

"You really told him that?"

"Well, yeah." Bonnie was starting to lick his face, and he put her back down, patting her head. An avoidance tactic if ever Lexie had seen one.

"Well, that's what he was ready to do," she said with a frown.

Stanley straightened and mirrored the frown. "So what's the problem?"

"I don't have sex the second I meet someone," she informed him. Had she just said that to a man old enough to be her father, a man she barely knew? She could feel her cheeks heating up.

Stanley's bushy eyebrows shot up toward his receding hairline. "Is that what he thought?"

"That's the impression you gave him."

Now he was nonplussed. "I don't understand."

Okay, what they had here was a generation gap, and Lexie had fallen right through it. "Mr. Mann——"

"Stanley," he corrected. He was starting to sound grumpy now.

"I don't know what *hooking up* meant in your day but in mine it means *sex*."

His eyes doubled in size, and his cheeks flushed pink.

He dropped his gaze and mumbled, "Well, uh, all you kids do that. Right? Maybe that's how he got confused."

All you kids? Now she was offended.

"Not all of us," she informed him. "I'm an adult and I have standards. I have a son to think of. I'm not going to fall in bed with somebody I have nothing in common with." Hmm. That didn't quite come out right.

He took a step backward as if fearing she might slap him. "I thought he was an okay guy. My wife liked him. Thought I was doing you a favor."

It was the thought that counted, she reminded herself. And Jayce probably wasn't such a bad man when it came right down to it. It wasn't his fault that Stanley Mann had accidentally painted her out to be the thirstiest girl in Fairwood, so there was no point scolding Stanley.

"I appreciate the thought," she said, opting for magnanimity. Still, the words came out as stiff and cold as an icicle.

"I'll have a talk with him," Stanley said, now looking ready to flay the meat man.

Lexie sighed and shook her head. "Never mind. It was just a miscommunication."

Stanley looked relieved. Then embarrassed all over again.

He nodded. "Okay, well, uh, that's good," he said. Then he turned and fled down her steps and down the front walk.

Lexie felt bad as she watched him go. Poor Stanley had simply been trying to do a good deed, and she'd verbally smacked him. She could see that wall he'd had around him when they first met going right back up.

STANLEY DID GO to the store first thing Monday, ready to punch Jayce's lights out, only to discover that the kid felt the same way toward him.

"Jeez, Mr. Mann. You set me up with an iceberg."

"I set you up with a nice girl," Stanley protested. What was wrong with this kid? Didn't he know a great woman when he saw one?

"I don't want a nice girl. I wanna have a good time."

Jayce was looking at Stanley like he was clueless. Maybe he was. Or maybe this young fool didn't know a good thing when he saw it.

"You're just lucky I don't clobber you," Stanley said. "And I will if you ever come around her," he muttered as he wheeled his cart off. Without so much as a package of hamburger in it.

"That's why you don't mess around in people's lives," he grumbled that night, turning his back on Carol, who was hovering by the bed. She'd at least had the good sense to abandon the Cupid getup.

"You tried," she said. "It's not your fault you had a little miscommunication."

"Little?" He pulled the covers up over his ears.

He could still hear Carol, though. "I think it was sweet of you to try."

"Well, I'm done with that stuff."

"Everything we do in life doesn't turn out perfect, you know that."

He acknowledged her observation with a grunt.

"But other things do, so it all balances out."

He wasn't going to acknowledge the truth of that. It would only lead to her thinking up more things for him to do. He kept quiet.

"Good night, darling. Pleasant dreams," she whispered.

He didn't have to turn over to know she was gone. He felt her absence. Just as he'd felt it the moment he lost her.

He did have pleasant dreams, though. He dreamed they were in the Cascade Mountains, walking hand in hand on the bank of the Wenatchee River. He was carrying a wicker picnic basket in his other hand. The sun was out, the birds were singing, Carol was smiling at him.

"Life can be a beautiful thing," she said. "Every minute of it."

He set down the picnic basket and drew her to him. "I like this minute," he said and kissed her.

"Oh, yes," she said happily. She pointed to a flat, grassy spot. "Let's have our picnic right here."

Carol magically produced a blanket and laid it out, and they sat down to enjoy their feast. The picnic basket was full of everything Stanley liked: ham sandwiches, deviled eggs, home-baked cookies and a thermos of hard lemonade.

"Tomorrow let's go to that antique store I saw in Cle Elum and see what nostalgic goodies we can find," she said.

"You mean junk," he said, and she laughed at him.

"No, I mean treasures," she said.

"You're the only treasure I need," he told her.

"And you're mine. I love you, Stanley."

He awoke the next morning, smiling and content. Until reality rushed in and reminded him that he wasn't picnicking in the mountains, and his wife was dead. There were no more tomorrows left for them.

Meanwhile, today, here was his dog licking his face.

"You need to go out, don'tcha?" he said to her, and she gave him a yip and a tail wag.

He pulled on his bathrobe, went downstairs and let her out, then got his coffee going. Today he was going to stay in the house all day and do nothing. With nobody and for nobody. Especially the pest next door.

Once Bonnie was inside he filled her dish with food, and she fell on it as if it were her last meal. When she was finished she came and sat next to him as he ate his morning cereal, leaning against his leg. He reached down and scratched behind her ears. She thanked him by licking his hand.

Somebody still appreciated him. He didn't need to go looking for more *somebody*s to add to his life and more things to keep him running in all directions. He had plenty to do.

He finished his breakfast, brushed his teeth, changed a light bulb in the living-room lamp, took out the garbage. Worked a sudoku puzzle. Yep, he had plenty to do.

Later that afternoon he took Bonnie for a walk, and they just happened to pass Lexie Bell's house. He knew she was home from school because both her living-room and kitchen lights were on. She hadn't needed him to pick her up. If it had snowed would she have called him? What was she doing in there? Baking? What did he care if she was?

Back in the house, he gave Bonnie a treat and fixed a treat for himself, a mug of instant hot chocolate and some packaged chocolate chip cookies. "So what if they're not home-baked? They're cookies, right?" he said to Bonnie.

She didn't appear to have an opinion one way or another. She merely looked at him, hoping for another dog treat.

"I think these cookies and what I'm giving you have something in common," he told her. "They're both as hard as hockey pucks."

There was more to life than cookies. And homemade lasagna. And cheese bread that *killed*.

And enjoying them with someone. For a moment he could almost see Carol at the stove, an apron tied over her sweatshirt and jeans, pulling a pot pie from the oven. They'd eat at the kitchen table, talking about how their day had gone, then move into the living room to watch TV. Sometimes they'd stay at the table and play a game of gin rummy.

He never ate dinner at the table anymore.

He was about to read a little before watching the evening news when his phone rang. It was Lexie Bell. He wasn't going to answer it. He'd had enough drama. Let her call someone else with her latest...whatever.

After several rings the phone quieted, and Stanley opened his book.

He'd barely started reading when the phone began to ring again. Nope, not answering.

But this time he did abandon his book to check his voice mail when whoever was calling gave up on him answering.

A little boy's voice said, "Grandpa Stanley, my Winter Holiday program is tomorrow night at seven o'clock. You are coming, right? I'm gonna be a snowflake."

Oh, boy. He looked down at Bonnie, who was studying him, awaiting his decision.

"He can be a snowflake without me," Stanley said. And that was that.

Until Carol rang in on the matter. She came for a visit around midnight, dressed like Mrs. Claus, with a white wig complete with a bun on her head and old-fashioned wire-rimmed glasses. She wore a high-collared blouse that looked like it belonged in a museum and a red skirt and red-and-white-striped apron complete with ruffles.

He recognized the getup immediately. It was one she used to wear on the last day of school before winter break. She always sent the kids home with candy canes and a Christmas card, each one with a special greeting written especially for the child.

"I'd forgotten about that outfit," he said to her.

"It's still in the red bin in the guest-room closet," she said. "Maybe you can find someone who will appreciate it. Another teacher, perhaps."

He knew exactly where she was going with this but refused to follow. "Maybe," he said, not committing to anything.

"You are going to go to the school program, aren't you?"

"I've gone to more than my fair share of those over the years," he reminded her. It was one of the obligations of being married to a teacher.

"Yes, but someone has invited you specifically to this one. You don't want to disappoint Brock."

"The kid won't know if I'm there or not," Stanley said.

"Children always know."

Stanley pulled his pillow over his head.

Of course, a small thing like a pillow didn't stop her. Her voice came through loud and clear. "Go, darling. Make the effort. You'll be glad you did."

He would not. He didn't say it, though. Instead, he clamped his lips tightly shut. The last thing he wanted was to argue with her.

"Pleasant dreams," she whispered and left.

He did dream, but it wasn't pleasant. He found himself floating over the grade-school auditorium. Adults were milling around, kids racing here and there, wearing elf hats and reindeer antlers.

Everyone was laughing and whooping it up except for one little boy, sitting in a dark corner of the stage. He was wearing white pants and a white sweatshirt topped with some kind of giant plastic blue-trimmed snowflake that had a hole for his face. The face wasn't smiling. In fact it was crying.

"Grandpa Stanley didn't come," the kid wailed.

Stanley woke up with his bushy eyebrows pulled together and his mouth drawn down at the corners. School programs. Bah, humbug.

But the next night found him walking into the school gym along with about a million parents and their noisy offspring. There were rows and rows of metal chairs and, beyond them at the far end of the gym, a stage had been set up. On it was a backdrop of wooden trees painted to look snow-covered. They didn't look very well constructed to Stanley. Whoever had been in charge of props could have used some help.

A boy dressed in a suit with a little red bow tie went racing past him and managed to tromp on his foot in the process, making the corn on his middle toe very unhappy. A small band consisting of some of the older kids was stationed in front of the stage, and they were playing an off-key rendition of "Deck the Halls." Stanley was no musician, but he knew bad when he heard it. His ears joined the protest along with his throbbing toe. *Why are we here?*

Good question. All this happy exuberance—it was the emotional equivalent of having to get dressed up in a suit and wear a necktie. Uncomfortable and suffocating. Where was the exit?

Don't you dare.

He knew that voice. He decided he didn't dare. If he ducked out he'd hear about it come bedtime. He found a seat on the end of one of the rows of metal chairs a ways back from the front, sat down and braced himself for the torture that lay ahead.

He'd barely gotten seated when a middle-aged woman wearing a black parka over red pants and enough perfume to burn every hair in Stanley's nose laid a bejeweled hand on his shoulder and pointed to the seats next to him.

"Are those taken?" she asked. She had a sonic-boom voice that bounced down to Stanley and slapped him in the ears.

She wouldn't believe him if he said *Yes, by the Invisible Man and his wife.* He had no choice but to say "No."

"Wonderful," she enthused. "Come on, Gerald," she said to the man behind her, a tank wrapped in jeans and a fur-lined parka with a head the size of a giant pumpkin.

Stanley himself wasn't exactly svelte, but this man made him look downright emaciated.

Before Stanley could stand up to give her room the woman started side-stepping her way to her chair. In the process she managed to tread on Stanley's other foot, making him wince. He was still trying to get up and out of the way when the tank barreled through, and he got the foot with the corn. Stanley's eyes crossed, and he sucked in air.

"Sorry," the man mumbled as he sat down, his shoulder butting right up against Stanley's.

"No problem," Stanley said, making the extreme effort to be polite and hoping Carol was still around and watching. This was too cozy for comfort.

He gave his chair a little scoot sideways to buy them both some breathing room. It didn't help all that much. He gave it another scoot. Scooting wasn't really helping. The best solution would be to move.

The woman struck up a conversation before he could, leaning across her husband and saying, "We came to see our granddaughter. She's one of the Sugar Plum Fairies. She's taking ballet lessons."

Stanley nodded.

"Who are you here to see?" the woman asked.

Stanley could have said *the neighbor kid*, but instead, to his surprise, out popped, "My grandson." Well, he was Grandpa Stanley, wasn't he?

"These programs are such fun, and the children are so sweet."

Stanley thought of the urchin who'd tromped on his foot and said nothing. The rows were filling up now, and the place was buzzing with excitement as if they were all at the 5th Avenue Theatre in Seattle, waiting for the curtain to go up on a musical.

"Kind of hot in here, isn't it?" said the man next to Stanley and proceeded to struggle out of his coat. He only got Stanley in the ribs once.

Okay, time to move. Stanley saw a seat on the end in the row in front to his left. A pretty, slender woman was in the seat next to it. She probably wouldn't elbow him in the ribs or tread on his foot.

He had just stood up when a good-looking man seated himself next to the woman and kissed her. Okay, so much for that seat.

Stanley looked farther afield. Good grief. The place was now a sea of parents and grandparents. Only a couple of seats available, all smack-dab in the middle of a row. How many feet would he trample getting to one? He gave up the idea, covered his aborted move with a stretch and sat back down.

And just in time. Here was the principal of the school, taking the mike, tapping on it and asking, "Is this on?"

The thing let out a squeal, and people yelped and covered their ears. Yes, it was on.

Take two worked better, and she was able to welcome everyone to their holiday celebration. "The children have worked very hard, and I know you'll all love the show they put on."

Stanley had to admit, the show was creative. A little girl and boy dressed in winter garb came on stage, both dragging sleds and announcing to the crowd that they were lost.

"How will we ever find our way to Grandma's house?" asked the girl.

"Maybe the reindeer will guide us," said the boy.

Cue the reindeer. A couple dozen little ones, all wearing antlers, filed on stage. And there, herding them, was Lexie Bell. So this was her class.

They sang—surprise, surprise—"Rudolph the Red-Nosed Reindeer," complete with hand motions. Cell phones were pulled out, cameras flashed. The kids finished their song and departed to enthusiastic applause.

But the two stars of the show were still lost, so then it was time for the Sugar Plum Fairies to guide them to Grandma's. Six little girls in frilly skirts leaped and twirled, one losing her balance and nearly taking out the rest.

"Oh, no!" gasped the grandma seated near Stanley, and he figured her granddaughter must have been the off-kilter fairy. There wouldn't be any more bragging from Grandma.

Cell phones were busy capturing the dance. The poor stumble fairy would probably be all over the internet by morning.

More students got involved. A choir sang "Winter Wonderland," and a student recited a poem about Christmas being a time for good cheer. "To lonely ones and sad ones, and those we hold most dear," she finished and curtsied.

Oh, brother.

Finally, the snowflakes made their appearance, singing "Let It Snow." To Stanley's surprise there was one solo at the end, and the kid who stepped up to sing the last *Let it snow* turned out to be Brock. He threw his arms wide, half-singing, half-shouting, and it came out loud and clear.

"That's my grandkid," he said to the Sugar Plum Fairy grandparents as they all applauded. Stretching the truth a little? Yeah, but so what?

"Isn't he cute," the woman said half-heartedly.

Actually, he was.

The two lost kids found their way to Grandma's, and the program ended with all the children singing "We Wish You a Merry Christmas," as the band slaughtered the song.

Then the performance was over, and kids were racing everywhere, looking for their parents. And Brock was racing toward Stanley. He felt an odd sensation of pride, which was stupid since he was no relation to this boy. Still, it warmed him when Brock plowed into him and hugged him.

"You came, Grandpa!"

"Wouldn't miss it," Stanley lied.

Lexie joined them. "Thank you for coming out. It meant so much to Brock."

It looked like he was out of the doghouse. Funny saying, that, considering the fact that you never saw a dog in a doghouse anymore. Only men who messed up.

A LITTLE CHRISTMAS SPIRIT

"Did I do good?" Brock asked Stanley eagerly.

"Yeah, you did."

The kid was looking up at him with adoring eyes. Lexie Bell was looking at him gratefully. He felt like he'd just bowled a perfect game. Stupid, really.

He cleared his throat. "Do you need a ride home?" he asked her.

"No, we're fine. My friend Shannon will run us home. I have to stay and visit with the parents, anyway. You won't want to wait that long."

Yeah, he had to get home. He wasn't disappointed. It was no big deal.

He nodded. "Okay, then."

"I'm making chicken and noodles for dinner tomorrow," she said before he could walk off. "If you'd like to join us, that is."

Yep, all was forgiven.

"Sure. Uh, I'll bring ice cream."

And so he had a dinner invitation for the following night. His calendar was filling up.

"Something going two nights in a row. Aren't you turning into the social butterfly, Manly Stanley?" Carol teased that night.

She'd lost the Mrs. Santa outfit and was back in that red sweater again. Carol always could fill out a sweater.

He smiled at her. "You look awful cute tonight, babe."

"And you looked cute in that sports jacket."

"Nobody else was wearing one. I thought parents dressed up for stuff like that."

"Not anymore. Nobody dresses up for anything. A shame, really," she said with a sigh. "I'm glad you did, though. And I'm proud of you for going. You made the night special, for both of them."

"Yeah, I guess I did that," Stanley said. "You know, Carol, I think I'll give your Mrs. Claus outfit to Lexie. I bet she'd like it."

Surprisingly, Carol didn't say anything.

He looked around. She was gone.

He sighed and smiled and let himself drift into sleep.

The next day he drove to the grocery store and bought some peppermint ice cream. "I'm going to the neighbor's for dinner. Gotta bring something," he told the checker.

"Uh-huh," he replied in a voice that said *Big deal*.

Considering how much trouble Stanley had been in only a few days ago, it was.

He was still feeling pretty darned good when he went to Lexie's house for dinner. The lights he'd strung for her were on and gave the place a festive air. Next year she should hang some along her porch, too, and the rest of her roof. He could help her with that.

She greeted him wearing jeans and the boot. But on her other foot was a big, floppy slipper made to look like a unicorn.

"Interesting," he said, pointing to it as he stepped through the door.

"It's fun to have something fanciful to wear," she said.

Was that what you called it.

The house smelled like...cookies? "Something smells good," he said as she took his coat.

"Oh, I have a candle burning," she told him. "Cinnamon."

That was disappointing. He'd been hoping for cookies. But he'd brought cookie deprivation on himself. He was the one who'd opened his big mouth and said he'd bring the ice cream.

Brock was on hand to take it from him and put it away for later.

"We have cookies to go with our ice cream," Lexie informed him.

No cookie deprivation after all. Here was good news, indeed. But he felt like he needed to earn that treat. And really clear the air about that little misunderstanding.

"I, uh, talked to Campbell. He won't be bothering you again."

Her cheeks turned pink.

"I'm sorry about—"

She cut him off. "Let's forget it. Okay?"

Fine with him. "Okay."

The dining table was already set, and in the middle of it sat something he hadn't seen the last time he was over—a circle of gold-tipped pinecones of varying shapes and sizes hugging a fat, red candle. As he got closer he could tell the candle was the source of the cinnamon he'd smelled.

"That's nice," he said.

"I made it."

Impressive. "Yeah?"

"I like to make things," she said.

Obviously. Food, pretty decorations. Lexie Bell was a nice young woman. She deserved to find some nice man and be happy. Not that Stanley would be assisting with that search. Ever again.

He enjoyed the dinner, especially the cookies, little round ones dusted with powdered sugar.

"My wife used to make these," he said. The memory made him wistful but, surprisingly, not horribly sad.

"My grandma made them. So does my mom. We call them snowball cookies," Lexie said.

"I hope it snows again," Brock said. "I want to make another snowman."

"We might get some more," Stanley said. The kid would probably need help with that snowman.

"I want to make snowballs, too," Brock said and popped half a cookie in his mouth.

"Yeah? How come?" Stanley asked.

"So I can have a snowball fight," Brock crowed.

"Be careful what you wish for, kid. Getting hit in the face with a snowball hurts."

"Who would throw a snowball in someone's face?" Lexie said, shocked.

"Your brother," Stanley said, remembering.

Brock frowned at that. "I don't want a brother."

"At the rate we're going you won't have to worry," Lexie muttered, then blushed.

"Brothers are okay," Stanley said.

"They are?"

"Sure. You always have somebody to play with right there with you in the house," Stanley told him.

"Then, I do want a brother. Maybe I'll ask Santa for a brother."

Stupid custom, thought Stanley.

"I think Santa specializes in toys," Lexie told her son.

"I like toys, too. When are we going to see Santa, Mommy?"

"Soon," Lexie said.

"Will you take us to see Santa, Grandpa Stanley?" Brock asked.

Stanley gave a snort. "There's no such thing."

Silence fell over the room, the kind of silence you heard right before a big storm broke.

Uh-oh. What had he just said?

The one thing you should never, never say to a kid, that was what. What had he been thinking? The truth was, he hadn't. He'd been feeling at home and so comfortable he'd let his guard down.

Lexie looked at him in shock. Brock blinked. Then blinked again. Then the storm broke.

CHAPTER TWENTY

THE KID BURST into noisy tears and pushed away from the table so hard it knocked over his half-melted ice cream, sending a pink puddle spreading across the tabletop. Then he bolted.

"Uh, I'll get that," Stanley said, reaching for a napkin.

"Don't bother," Lexie said stiffly. "I'll take care of it later. After..."

After she first cleaned up the mess Stanley had made. He scratched the back of his head, suddenly at a loss for how to explain what he'd just done.

"Mr. Mann, how could you?" she scolded, looking at him like he'd just committed a murder.

Maybe, in a way, he had.

"I guess I shouldn't have said anything." There was a bright remark.

"I guess not," she snapped. "Children have to grow up so quickly these days. Brock's going to have enough hard truths to hear later. He shouldn't have to..." Her lower lip began to wobble.

Great. Now she was going to cry, too.

"It's just as well," Stanley said. "After all, it's true."

Not the right thing to say. "Maybe you should go home now. I'll probably be busy with Brock for quite a while," she said with a Frosty the Snowman accent.

An arctic chill invaded the room. Warm welcome had turned into winter cold shoulder. Like Stanley had meant to make her kid cry, for crying out loud.

The ice cream was dripping onto the carpet now, but Lexie didn't notice. She turned her back on him and rushed up the stairs after her son. The party was over.

Just as well. He'd had enough drama with these two. He grabbed his coat and marched out the door.

LEXIE RACED UP the stairs after her son, steaming as she went. Where did Stanley Mann get off, telling her child there was no such thing as Santa! How could he have been so thoughtless and mean?

She found her son sprawled across his bed, his face buried in his pillow, sobbing his heart out. She wanted to cry, too. He was just a little boy. To take the joy of Santa away from him had been wrong. Sick and wrong.

Brock was a human earthquake, his little body heaving and rolling with sobs. What could she say to her son to take away the sting of harsh reality? She laid a hand on his back, and he rolled over and looked at her, tears racing down his cheeks, his face red from crying.

"There has to be a Santa," he wailed and threw himself into her arms.

Her poor little boy. He so hadn't been ready for this.

She kissed the top of his head and stroked his hair and searched her mind for the right words.

"Grandpa Stanley doesn't have it quite right," she said. "There really was a real Santa once."

Brock pulled away enough to look up at her half doubtful, half hopeful. "There was?"

"His name was Nicholas. He was a bishop."

Brock's brows pulled together, and he looked at her in confusion. "What's a bishop?"

"Like a minister," she improvised. "He was a very kind man, and he loved to help people who didn't have any money. He especially liked to help children and would leave little gifts for them."

"Like Santa?" Brock asked, hope returning.

"Like Santa. People called him Saint Nicholas. You could say he was the first Santa."

Now came the smile. Brock sat back on his knees and began to bounce excitedly, turning the bed into a trampoline. "There is a Santa!"

Her son was so anxious to be a believer. She should let him.

But then, if he learned the truth yet again, maybe from some older child on the playground or one of her cousin's children, he'd be doubly disillusioned. "We did get our idea of Santa from him, but Santa is pretend, sweetie. He's a fun friend mommies invent so their little boys can have a special present under the tree. He's a game you and I play so I can find extra ways to do nice things for you."

"But I saw Santa last year. I asked him for Legos."

"And he told me," Lexie said. Okay, stretching the truth a little, but a woman had to do what a woman had to do. "He was pretending, too, all so you could have a happy Christmas Day."

Brock frowned, processing this.

She pulled him close and put an arm around him. "Santa is something fun mommies and daddies have been doing for a long time. Grandma and Grandpa played the Santa game with me, and their mommy and daddy played the Santa game with them. Someday, when you're grown up and have children you'll play the Santa game with them, and they'll have fun finding that special present under the tree just like you do."

Her son didn't say anything, just sat there, still processing this huge turn of events.

"It is fun to pretend, isn't it?" she prompted.

He nodded, slowly. "Will I still get my Christmas stocking?"

The treats for it were already hidden in her closet. "Of course."

"And the extra present under the tree?"

It was ordered and supposed to ship soon. "Yes. So you see, the only difference is when you go see Santa, you'll know it's a game."

"Can we still go see Santa?"

"Of course we can."

He smiled. Finally. "Good. Because I want to tell him I want a Junior Handyman tool set."

"I'm sure you'll get it," she said. "Now, how about a bath and a bedtime story?"

He nodded, slid off the bed and started for the bathroom, his earlier misery forgotten.

Lexie was finding it harder to let go of her emotions. Seeing her son so upset had been distressing. Thank you, Stanley Mann.

She should never have baked him cookies or invited him to dinner, should never have invited him to Brock's school program. If she'd known what it would lead to she'd never have accepted so much as one kind gesture from him.

But later, after her son was in bed and she was sponging up the mess on the carpet, she was able to admit that her neighbor wasn't a monster. Under that gruff exterior beat a kind heart. He wasn't the Grinch, out to ruin Christmas. He was simply a grumpy, lonely old man who needed love.

Which he was more than welcome to look for somewhere else. He wasn't all bad, but he was bad enough, and they really didn't need him in their lives, spreading negativity over everything.

She shouldn't have rushed so quickly to attach herself and her son to him. She certainly didn't do that with men her own age. Maybe with Stanley she'd figured since he was older he was harmless. Ha!

There had been plenty of red flags—his standoffishness, his sour attitude and rare smiles. She'd been so excited to befriend her neighbor, so desperate for a male figure in her son's life, she'd ignored those red flags.

Well, she was done with that. From now on she was going to ignore Stanley Mann.

ENOUGH WAS ENOUGH. Lexie Bell the pest could live her life, and Stanley would live his. He'd known all along it would be a dumb idea to get involved with those two, and he'd been right. Well, he'd had enough of them. And he'd had enough of cookies and fudge and cheese bread. And stringing lights and decorating trees. And Christmas.

Oh, no. What was that he heard? Voices. He went to the living-room window and twitched the curtain.

Carolers were coming down the street. He turned off all the lights and retreated to his recliner. They continued to come closer, approaching like a freight train. "Fa-la-la-la-la."

Oh, cut it out.

Soon he could tell they were on the sidewalk right in front of his house. He could hear them out there, gustily singing that it was the season to be jolly. Bonnie heard them, too, and began to bark.

"Stop that," he commanded. "Don't encourage them."

This was no season of joy. He was now more miserable than ever.

Santa. Ugh. Santa was a crock, and Christmas was nothing but a stupid holiday full of commercialism and fat guys who pretended they could bring you what you wanted. Well, he wanted his old life back, and neither Santa nor anybody else was going to make that happen. He went in search of ice cream.

The ice cream didn't make him feel any better. Neither did his encounter with Carol that night. Bad enough that the kid was upset and that Lexie Bell wanted to strangle him with a string of Christmas lights, but Carol had to weigh in as well.

"Stanley, what on earth were you thinking?" she scolded. Tonight she was dressed like an old-time schoolmarm. She held a ruler and was slapping it on the palm of her hand. He half expected her to whack him with it.

"I don't know." But he did. He'd been remembering his own disappointment on learning there was no Santa. Santa was a crock. "Parents shouldn't lie to their kids," he muttered.

"It's pretending, Stanley. It's no different than a child having an imaginary friend."

"I never had an imaginary friend," he argued.

"Don't be obtuse. You shouldn't have said what you said, and you know it."

"It just slipped out. Okay?" he said defensively.

"You need to make it up to that girl."

"Carol," he said sternly. "I'm done. She as much as kicked me out. What do you want me to do?"

"I want you to think of something. That's what I want you to do."

"I'm tired of thinking. I'm just plain tired."

"Well, then, I'll leave you to get some rest," she said in a huff.

And with that she was gone without leaving behind so much as a hint of peppermint.

After she left he tossed and turned, and once he finally made it into what should have been a restful sleep, he found himself far from resting. He was having Christmas dinner with Ebenezer Scrooge. The only other dinner guest was the Grinch. The scarred, old wooden table they sat at had nothing but a soup tureen, cracked bowls, and three spoons. No tablecloth, no pinecone centerpiece, no candles.

"You're one of us now," said Ebenezer. He pointed to the tureen. "Have some gruel."

"Gruel for Christmas dinner?" Stanley protested.

"You expected me to roll out the red carpet?" sneered Scrooge, and the Grinch laughed.

The room was cold, and the fireplace in the corner only a blackened mouth.

"Can't you light a fire?" Stanley begged. "It's cold in here."

"Coal costs money. Why should I spend money on the likes of you?" his host demanded.

"You're supposed to be a changed man," Stanley protested. "A man who keeps Christmas well."

"Don't believe everything you read," said Scrooge.

Stanley looked to the Grinch for confirmation.

He merely shrugged. "People never really change, you know."

"They can," Stanley insisted. "You two are a couple of downers. I'm not like you, and I don't like you. I'm leaving."

That made them both laugh. The Grinch laughed so hard he fell off his chair.

Stanley pushed away from the table and marched across the room, which, he suddenly realized, looked mysteriously like a dungeon. The door was thick and heavy with a barred window that looked out on nothing but darkness. He grabbed the metal handle and pulled, but it refused to budge.

"We're locked in," Scrooge informed him. "Locked in by our own bad attitudes."

Stanley gave another tug. The door still wouldn't budge. He ran to the one window in the room. It was barred.

He grabbed the bars and rattled them, crying, "I want out! Let me out!"

He was still crying "Let me out!" when he woke up.

CHAPTER TWENTY-ONE

ON FRIDAY THE last of the afternoon light shone on a truck with a U-Haul trailer attached pulling into the driveway of the house across the street from Lexie's. It was followed by a car.

"Look, Mommy!" Brock cried. "Kids!"

Lexie joined him at the living-room window and looked out. Sure enough, two little girls had jumped out of the truck and were running across the yard to the front door where a tall, lean man with brown hair and glasses stood, opening it. A woman got out of the car and followed them. The girls looked somewhere around Brock's age, and the adults looked to be in maybe their late thirties or early forties.

New neighbors! Maybe they were actually nice. One could hope.

"Can I go over and play?" Brock asked.

May I go over and play?

"May I?"

"Let's give them a chance to unpack first," Lexie said.

Brock's pout showed what he thought of that idea.

"I tell you what, though. We can make some cupcakes to welcome them to the neighborhood and take them over later. How does that sound?"

"Yes!" he hooted and raced for the kitchen.

Yes! Lexie thought. *Oh, please let these people be normal.*

After the requisite handwashing, she put her son to work helping with the baking. The thought occurred that, nice as it was to have him enjoying helping her in the kitchen, it would be equally nice if he had a father with whom he could share these kinds of bonding moments. Or a grandpa.

The image of her son and Stanley Mann standing by the snowman they'd made popped into her mind. She erased it with the memory of Stanley Mann making her son cry when he killed Santa. There would be time for male bonding later. With someone else.

Brock was getting very good at cracking eggs into a bowl (and then fishing out the eggshells) and enjoyed using the mixer under her close supervision. She'd gotten giant marshmallows and chocolate chips to make snowmen to top the cupcakes and Hershey's Kisses for their hats. The project kept Brock occupied for a good couple of hours. After dinner they had to decorate a little box to put the cupcakes in, and that took more time. But then Brock's patience was at an end, and he was begging to go meet the neighbors.

Lexie hoped they'd given the newcomers sufficient time to at least catch their breath. She also hoped they'd appreciate getting a treat and a welcome to the neighborhood. She knew she would have appreciated such a gesture when she'd moved in.

They bundled up and crossed the street to the house that had stood empty for so long, Brock carrying his box decorated with red construction paper and cut-out white snowflakes as carefully as if he were a Wise Man bearing a gift for the Christ Child. The day was clear and the ground dry, which made walking so much nicer. Like her house, this one had a long front porch. There was something about a front porch that was so welcoming. Maybe the neighbors, themselves, would be as well.

As they approached the front door she could hear children laughing inside. Laughter was always a good sign. It meant the people were happy.

There was never any laughter coming from Stanley Mann's house.

She shoved away the thought. That was his own fault.

Lexie rang the doorbell and heard high-pitched voices accompanied by a stampede of feet.

"I'll get it!"

"No, I will! Daddy, Arielle's shoving!"

The two little girls they'd seen earlier opened the door, each fighting for the best hold on the doorknob. They both had ponytails and big eyes and looked like Disney princesses in the making. Each stared curiously at Lexie.

"Who are you?" asked the smaller of the two girls.

Brock said, "I'm Brock. We brought snowman cupcakes." He held out the box.

The taller one was quick to take it. "Thank you."

They'd been taught manners. That was a good sign.

The woman Lexie had seen earlier appeared at the door. She was slender, and her hair was perfect. There was no wedding band or glinting diamond on her left hand, but from the suspicious way she eyed Lexie it was clear that she wasn't going to be inviting Lexie in for a chat.

So a girlfriend, and an insecure one at that. Lexie's pleasant vision of neighboring back and forth vanished with a poof.

She made the effort to be neighborly, anyway. "I'm Lexie Bell, and this is my son Brock. We live across the street," she added, pointing to her place, "and thought it would be nice to welcome you to the neighborhood."

"I'm Isobel," said the littler girl.

"I'm Arielle," said her sister. She handed the box over to the woman. "You want to see our rooms?" she asked Brock.

"Let's get your room squared away before you start having company," the woman said to her in a tone of voice that brooked no argument. She gave Lexie a smile that almost moved the meter up to polite. "Thanks for these. The kids will enjoy them."

"Our pleasure. Welcome to the neighborhood," Lexie said.

"Thanks," said the woman and shut the door.

Of course there was no *Looking forward to getting to know you*. No *We'll have to have coffee sometime*. No nothing. Lexie found herself feeling cranky as they walked back across the street.

"Can I go over... May I go over and play tomorrow?" Brock asked.

"We'll see," Lexie answered and sighed inwardly. Apparently they were doomed to have sucky neighbors.

Still, she found herself looking out her window at the house across the street a lot after they got home. Not spying. She just happened to look that way once in a while.

She could see lights on inside, people moving about. Around ten the woman got in the car and left. So together but not living together yet. But obviously serious since she was helping her boyfriend move.

Oh, well, so what if he'd been nice-looking, if he had kids. There were other nice-looking men out there who liked kids.

Somewhere.

Meanwhile, she'd live her life, and the neighbors would live theirs. They'd wave occasionally. Maybe the kids would play together. But that would be it.

Except the next afternoon there was the man, standing on her front porch. He smiled at her. It wasn't a sexy smile like Jayce the Meat Man's, but it was a friendly one, set in a nice face with kind, gray eyes, a face that said *You'll like me once you get to know me*.

"Hi, I'm Truman Phillips," he said. His voice was warm, and it, too, promised she'd like him.

"I'm Lexie Bell," she said.

"The Cupcake Queen. Those were spectacular."

Not simply *good* but *spectacular*. Why did he have to have a girlfriend?

"It wasn't much," Lexie said modestly.

"It was great, and the girls and I appreciated the gesture. And the sugar. We drove straight here yesterday—seventeen hours—and the girls had been up since the crack of dawn. It was a long day, and I was bushed before we even started unloading. The place is chaos."

"Maybe you and your girlfriend could use some help," Lexie offered. "I'm pretty good at putting away dishes." Where was the girlfriend today? Lexie had seen no sign of her car.

Not that she'd been spying. It was just a casual observation she'd made.

"No girlfriend," he said. "It's just my daughters and me. My old college pal, Margo, lives up here, though. She helped us get our stuff unloaded. You must have met her when you dropped off the cupcakes."

"I did."

No girlfriend. Oh, happy day! Truman Phillips was easy to look at, and he had two nice little girls. How was he single? *Why* was he single? What happened to the mom? It was hardly something you could ask a new neighbor, but she was dying to know his story.

"Well, if you could use some help," she offered again.

He looked as if she'd offered him an all-expenses-paid vacation to the Caribbean. "Really?"

"Sure." The sound of voices had brought Brock downstairs from his room. "Brockie, would you like to go to Mr. Phillips's house and help them?"

He immediately began jumping up and down. "Yes!"

"It looks like you've got some helpers," she said to Truman.

"Great. We could use it. Margo had things going on this weekend, and I wasn't looking forward to unpacking the kitchen stuff alone. We only got as far as setting up the beds last night."

"Moving is exhausting," Lexie said as she took Brock's coat from the hall closet. "But it's also an adventure."

"That it is, and the girls and I were ready for one."

"You sure your husband won't mind?" Truman asked as they crossed the street.

"It's just Brock and me."

He nodded, taking that in.

The moment they were in the house Arielle had Brock by the hand and was towing him up the stairs, her sister following with a squeal.

"They're excited!" Truman explained.

"Of course they are. How old are they?"

"Arielle is ten going on sixteen, and Isobel is seven."

"They're sweet."

"They are," he agreed as he led the way to the kitchen. "They have their moments, but they're good kids. When you've got good kids it makes everything bearable."

Had Truman Phillips's life been unbearable with his ex? Lexie was dying to know.

He gestured to her foot. "Are you sure you're okay to do this?"

"Oh, yes," she assured him. "It's only a chip fracture, and I'm hoping to lose the boot and get into a brace by Christmas."

"I bet you're ready for that. I broke a leg once. Was stuck in a cast for an eternity and a half. I hope you don't have the kind of job where you have to be on your feet a lot."

"I do. I'm a teacher."

He looked impressed. "There's a noble occupation. Where do you teach?"

"Fairwood Elementary."

"Any chance either of my girls will have you?"

"I'm afraid not. I teach kindergarten."

"Is your son in your class?" Truman wanted to know.

"He's in first grade."

"So just one grade behind Isobel." Childish laughter drifted down to where they sat. "Looks like the kids are getting along well," Truman said. "It'll be nice for the girls to know someone when they start school. It's hard starting halfway through the year."

"It is unusual to see kids moving in partway through the school year," Lexie said, avoiding a direct question. Was that still being too nosy? Not compared to asking what happened with his ex, which was what she really wanted to do.

"It just worked out that way. I bought the bookstore in town. It took a while to get all the proverbial ducks in a row."

A man who loved books. It was all Lexie could do not to sigh like a girl who'd just gotten a chance to meet her favorite rock star.

"I've been in there a few times and loved the friendly vibe."

"Hopefully, we can keep that going."

"What made you decide to buy a bookstore?" she asked.

"Books are what I do. I owned a store in Los Angeles and it was great, but I really wanted the girls to grow up in a small town. My friend told me about Great Escape and got me in touch with the owner. I came up and checked it out. Checked out the school and was impressed. Everything fell together."

"It sounds like it," Lexie said. Upstairs she could hear little feet running and more squeals. Brock was probably in heaven. Play buddies, at last. Maybe things were falling together for her and Brock as well.

"You like it here? Are the neighbors nice?" Truman asked.

What to say to that? "It's a quiet neighborhood." She'd tell him about Mr. Mann when the time was right.

He nodded. "Well, at least we have a kid across the street for the girls to play with."

And a woman for you to play with.

Don't be in a rush, she cautioned herself.

But after organizing spices and pots and pans together, and after he'd sprung for pizza delivery, it only seemed right to invite him for dinner the following night as she was getting ready to leave. Not rushing. Just being neighborly.

"That'd be great. What can I bring?"

It was easy to see where his girls got their good manners.

"Nothing but your appetite."

"I can do that."

He called for the girls, and they ran to the head of the stairs, Brock with them. They all looked overheated, their faces red, hair damp. All three were smiling.

"Time for us to go home, Brockie," Lexie said.

"I don't want to go," he protested.

"Can he stay and help us?" asked little Isobel.

"No, but we'll see you all tomorrow. You're coming over to our house for dinner," Lexie said to her.

"Yay!" hooted Brock.

"Can we have spaghetti?" Isobel asked.

"Isobel," her father chided.

"It's okay. We like spaghetti," Lexie said. Except she had no makings for sauce and no hamburger in the house. She'd have to make a run to the grocery store.

She'd get an Uber.

CHAPTER TWENTY-TWO

I THINK MY family all need books for Christmas, Shannon replied when Lexie texted her about her new neighbor.

Your book binge won't be able to compete with my cheese bread, Lexie texted back.

Or your cuteness. Should I hate you? ☺

LOL. Maybe.

But she wouldn't once the monster box of Godiva chocolates Lexie had bought her got delivered.

Call me after. I need deets!

Maybe there wouldn't be that many deets to share. Maybe Truman Phillips wasn't looking to jump into something. And even if he was, he might not want to with her. Maybe he was simply happy at the thought of not having to deal with making dinner for his kids.

Or maybe there really was such a thing as Santa, and he'd delivered a great man just in time for Christmas. One could always hope.

Lexie made it to the grocery store on her own just fine without any help from a certain neighbor—thank you, Uber—and was able to serve the requested spaghetti along with her killer cheese bread and a salad. Truman had come bearing eggnog ice cream, which paired quite well with Christmas cookies, and everything was consumed with much chatter and giggles. It was a happy time, and she could tell by the appreciative look in Truman's eyes as he watched her that he was interested in her. Sooo...maybe he was looking to jump into something. Or at least walk into something.

After dinner, Brock and the girls played Candy Land, which gave the adults time to visit. Truman, Lexie learned, was a big fan of PBS and every British mystery he could get his hands on. Naturally, owning a bookstore, he loved to read.

"So far my girls are big readers, too," he said, looking fondly to where the kids sat at the table playing.

"It sounds like you're doing everything right as a parent," Lexie said.

"I'm trying."

He looked wistful, and she couldn't help asking, "What happened with their mom?"

His lips crumpled up like he was trying to swallow something distasteful.

Lexie immediately regretted her nosiness. "I'm sorry. I shouldn't have asked."

"Don't be. She had some problems. She'd always been kind of a, uh, partyer, which, I confess, I thought was exciting when I first met her. But somewhere along the way the partying got wilder, and then completely out of hand. Drugs. She's in rehab. Again."

"Oh, I'm really sorry," Lexie said.

He looked so sad. She wished she could think of something else to say but found herself at a loss.

"This stuff happens. I'm just grateful it didn't happen when she was pregnant with either of the girls." He shook his head. "When we first got together she loved being with a *smart man*," he said, using air quotes. "And, of course, I loved how vivacious she was. I guess we're your typical case of opposites attract. Nobody tells you that opposites also can drive each other crazy. We were like puzzle pieces that seemed like they should fit together but didn't. Anyway, I couldn't stand to see what she was doing to herself, and I sure couldn't let the girls be around that."

"Of course not. Do they miss their mother?"

"Sometimes. We've been separated for four years now, so they were little when we were still together. They know Mommy has some troubles and include her in their bedtime prayers."

"Children are so forgiving," Lexie said.

She could easily picture the two little girls kneeling by their beds, hands clasped just like Brock did, asking God to bless Mommy—a Hallmark movie, a Debbie Macomber novel and a Thomas Kinkade painting all rolled into one.

"So far so good. I make it a point to never bad-mouth their mother. It's hard not to sometimes, but I want the girls to understand that everyone has faults."

Like Stanley Mann. Lexie felt a sudden poke to her conscience.

"And if you were to cut everyone out of your life who wasn't perfect, you'd wind up with nobody in it."

Another poke. Ouch!

"Not that she gets to be around them when she's messed up like this," he hurried to say. "We're taking it one day at a time. If all goes well with rehab, we're talking about her coming up to visit this summer. We'll see."

"You are a good man," Lexie said, impressed.

"I try the best I can. It's hard to keep all the balls in the air sometimes. Margo's always been supportive. She's got someone in her life now, but she's determined to make time to watch out for us."

Which explained her not-so-welcoming attitude when Lexie showed up at his door.

"So that's me. What about you?"

Fair was fair. She'd stuck her nose into his love fail. It was only right that she share hers. She looked over to make sure Brock wasn't listening. Of course he wasn't. He was having too much fun with his new friends.

She summed up the sad story in one sentence. "He cheated when we were engaged, and we broke up."

"Maybe it's a good thing you realized what you were about to get into before you actually got married," Truman said.

She nodded. "It is. It hurt, though."

"Does he see Brock?"

She shook her head. "He gave up parental rights."

Truman shook his head in disgust. "You really did have a lucky escape."

"I guess I did," Lexie said. "Anyway, I got a great little boy out of the deal, so I'm not complaining. And I love my job and my house. And I like this town. We only moved in a few months ago, so I'm still getting to know people."

"I think I'm going to like it here," Truman said. "I sure have a nice neighbor," he added, making her blush.

Happy holidays! she texted later to Shannon.

OMG! For me, too. Chocolates just arrived. You are the best.

No, you are. Shannon had been a lifesaver for her.

Now bring me a perfect man. ☺ And tell me about yours? How was din-din?

He loves my cheese bread.

And you, I bet.

Maybe.

Who knew? One thing she knew for sure. Truman Phillips was one neighbor she was really going to enjoy.

About that other neighbor. Truman's words hovered over her like a pesky ghost.

STANLEY HAD SEEN the new neighbor when he was out walking Bonnie. He'd also seen Lexie over there on Saturday, taking the man goodies. He supposed she'd never bring him anything again.

On Sunday he watched from his dining-room window as the man and his girls trooped across the street to her place, probably for dinner. Stanley supposed, now that she'd found someone her own age who also had kids, that there'd be a lot of that. She had no need of him anymore.

Even if she needed him, she didn't want him. After his goof he wouldn't be getting invited over for dinner. Or needed to run errands. He certainly wouldn't be invited to any more school programs.

What did he care? He was fine on his own.

He was lying. He already missed being part of Lexie and Brock's life. Spending time with them had become a habit, and now that she'd broken the habit he found himself feeling…empty. Even Carol didn't seem to be speaking to him.

"What do you think I ought to do?" he asked Bonnie.

She gave a yap and wagged her tail. *Give me a dog treat.*

Life was simple when you were a dog, he reflected as he tossed her a treat. You ate, you barked, you pooped, you chased a squirrel or two, and then you slept. You didn't think about people you missed or people you'd managed to irritate and alienate. You simply wagged your way through the day.

It was so much more complicated for human beings. Maybe humans thought too much. Maybe, like dogs, they needed to simply go by instinct.

Stanley's instincts told him that if he ever wanted the human equivalent of a dog treat he was going to have to apologize to Lexie for upsetting her kid. He still didn't think he'd done anything all that wrong, but sometimes you had to apologize even when you felt you shouldn't have to.

He went in search of his phone, Bonnie trotting after him.

"You gonna make sure I do this?" he said to her. He sure needed someone to give him courage.

He could feel his heart rate speeding up as he made the call. What should he say? How should he begin? That ringing felt like a countdown. Before a bomb was due to go off.

The ringing stopped, and his call went to her voice mail. Then came the tone that signaled it was time for him to talk. His brain chose that moment to take a nap.

"Uh," he said. There was a great beginning. Good grief. He tried again. "Uh. Lexie." *I miss your cookies. I miss hanging out with you and Brock. I don't mind driving you places. I'm sorry about the Santa thing. It's for the best, though.* No, not that. That was stupid. Start with...not about missing cookies. That would put him right on the same level as Bonnie. May as well bark. And it wasn't about the cookies. It was about what they'd meant, that someone cared.

He was still choosing his next words when the beep that said *You're done, fool,* went off. He clicked off his portable phone with a scowl and went in search of peppermint ice cream.

His last words before nodding off that night were, "Sorry, Carol, I just can't get it right."

For a minute there, he thought he felt a gentle touch on his cheek. But he knew he'd only imagined it. Carol was still silent, and his life was empty once more.

LEXIE'S DOCTOR GAVE her permission to ditch the walking boot, and she came home with a lightweight brace, which meant she could start wearing cute shoes again. And driving!

"Just in time for Christmas," she told Shannon, who'd driven her. "And a nice present for you, too. Now you don't have to take me everywhere."

"I didn't mind," Shannon assured her. "And you'd do the same for me. Only I might not spend as much on chocolate for you," she joked.

"With all those rides you've given me I owe you chocolate for life," Lexie said.

"I like the sound of that."

"Want to stay for dinner?"

Shannon shook her head. "I can't. I'm meeting another potential Mr. Perfect."

"Oh?" Lexie prompted.

"He seems promising, but then they always do until you spend some time with 'em. I think my New Year's resolution is going to be to quit trying so hard, let things happen naturally. And enjoy my life just as it is."

"That sounds like a good plan."

"Unless, of course, tonight's man du jour turns out to be great. Then, forget the resolution," Shannon finished with a grin.

"You never know. You can find love anywhere." Maybe even across the street.

It was way too early to tell, but a girl could hope.

Free to drive, Lexie decided it was time to make good on her promise to take Brock to see Santa. She fed him a quick meal of mac and cheese and chicken fingers, then got him dolled up in his slacks and red sweater, and off they went to the nearby mall where Santa was making an appearance.

"Come up with me," Brock said when it was his turn to sit with Santa.

"Well, who have we here?" the man greeted him and added the requisite "Ho, ho, ho!"

"I'm Brock, and this is my mom," Brock said. "I know we're just pretending, but I still like you."

The man shot an amused look at Lexie. "Well, now, that's good to hear. I like you, too, young man. I think I need to bring you something extra special for Christmas. What do you think?"

"I want a Junior Handyman tool set. I thought you should let Mommy know in case she forgot."

"I bet she remembered," said Mall Santa.

"I bet she did, too," Brock agreed.

Mall Santa smiled up at Lexie. "And what would you like for Christmas, young lady?"

My mother to be with me, a good man. Neither were things she could ask for in front of her son.

The first wasn't going to happen: she was resigned to that. But the good man? She pictured Truman's smile and felt as warmed as if she'd consumed a hot buttered rum. Maybe the New Year was going to be a happy one.

Meanwhile, she had her pretty new house, a good friend in Shannon, and her adorable boy. She had much to be grateful for.

"You know, Santa, I think I'm good," she said.

"Well, then, let's take a picture together," Mall Santa suggested. "Ho, ho, ho! Merry Christmas."

Yes, it is looking merry, she thought when Truman came by that evening with a book for her. "A thank-you for dinner," he explained as he handed it over.

It was wrapped in red ribbon, but she could easily see the title: *Living Your Best Life Yet*.

"Not that you aren't," he hurried to add, "but I thought you might like this. It's by a woman named Muriel Sterling. She's pretty popular with a lot of my women readers. She actually lives here in Washington, in a town called Icicle Falls. Her family owns a chocolate company."

"Ooh, I like her already," Lexie said. "Thank you. I love self-improvement books." And she was more than ready to live her best life yet.

"Good. Well, I guess I'd better get back over to the house. I promised the girls I'd send out for pizza again." He didn't move.

"Do you normally eat this late?"

"For a while. Have to keep the bookstore open, and until I find an employee, that job falls on me. I gave them cheese and crackers and some apple slices at the store, so they're not starving."

"An apple a day, that's what my grandma used to say." Who cared? What a dumb remark.

"So did mine," he said, smiling. "I'm a big believer." Still he stood there. "I guess you and Brock have already eaten."

Never turn down an opportunity to be with a great guy. "We have, but there's always room for pizza."

His smile grew. "Yeah?"

"I could come over and help you finish unpacking," she offered.

"That would be great," he said.

Yes, it would. She called up the stairs, and her son came racing down them. "How would you like to go over to Mr. Phillips's house for pizza?" Lexie asked him.

"Yes!" he whooped and yanked the closet door open.

"I guess that settles it," she said and reached for her coat.

Winter darkness had fallen, and the Christmas lights Stanley had strung for her sparkled like jewels. His lights were on, too. His house looked deceptively festive. What was he doing in there, all by himself?

Who cared?

And what would her grandma say about her attitude? She already knew what Truman would say, and she suddenly felt a little small.

Once inside his house, though, she quickly became absorbed with the children and helping organize more of the chaos scattered around the Phillips's house and forgot about Stanley Mann. Laughter and pizza. Merry Christmas from Truman's home to hers.

While the children raced around, the two adults talked about the holidays, both past and present. Truman's plans included spending some time with his old friend on Christmas Eve and doing an online chat with his family back home on Christmas morning.

"Then I guess the girls and I will tuck in for the day," he finished.

"You're more than welcome to come over to my house in the afternoon," Lexie said. "As it turns out, it's just going to be Brock and me."

"No family coming to visit?"

She sighed, then told him about her mother.

"That's too bad," he said.

"Hopefully, by next year it will be different. I still wish I could get her to come up this year. I think it would do her good. But there's not much I can do if she doesn't want to."

"It sounds like she needs more time," Truman said. "When you've gone through something bad, it can take a while to see anything good in life."

Like Stanley Mann? Why, oh, why, did he keep coming to mind? She pushed him firmly out and kept him out for the rest of the evening. She had other things to think about besides him.

Once the house was pretty much squared away, she decided she really didn't have an excuse to hang around any longer. They'd been at the kitchen table relaxing with glasses of soda pop, but now the glasses were empty.

"I should go," she said, and got up and set hers on the kitchen counter.

He set his down, too, and they stood there, looking at each other. The heat growing between them was enough to start a whole troop of little elves running around in her tummy.

"It's probably too soon to kiss you," he murmured and moved closer.

"Probably," she agreed. *Darn.*

"But we have spent a lot of hours together," he pointed out.

And unpacking a lot more than dishes. They'd already shared so much of their personal lives.

"But we still don't know each other very well." And they had children. They needed to be cautious and responsible.

She didn't make a move to leave.

He inched a little closer. "What else do you want to know?"

"What are you like when you're not being so..." *Perfect.* "Nice. Do you lose your temper?"

"When I'm tired. Sometimes I yell. Mostly, though, I give myself a time-

out. Send the girls to their rooms, chill and reassess. I swear if I hit my finger with a hammer. But I've never hit a woman, never spanked my girls."

She bit her lip. "Ever cheated?"

His eyes popped wide. "No. Good God, no."

"Sorry. I had to ask."

"Understandable. How about you? Do you have a fatal flaw I should know
about?" he asked. "I can't imagine you do."

She thought of how long it had taken to forgive the man who had once
wanted to be her husband and then dumped her, and of how upset she'd
been with Stanley.

"I hate to confess it, but I think I have a hard time forgiving and letting go."

"That's understandable, too" he said. "But if there's one thing I've learned,
it's that you can't move on to what's better until you let go of what was bad."

"How true. You know, you are a very wise man."

He also looked good in his jeans and shirt with its sleeves rolled up. They
showed off his strong arms. And those lips sure knew how to smile. What
else were they good at?

She closed the last few inches between them. "I think moving on to what's
better sounds like an excellent idea."

He raised an eyebrow, half smiled. "Yeah?"

"Oh, yeah."

He took off his glasses and set them on the counter. "Should we pretend
it's already New Year's Eve and about to strike midnight?"

"I think we should."

He slipped his arms around her waist. She slid her hands up his chest,
and they pretended.

Truman was a fabulous pretender.

Later that night, as she snuggled in her bed, it wasn't sugar plums Lexie
dreamed about.

MONDAY WAS THE last day of school before Christmas, and Lexie had a party
with her students. Before they arrived she sprayed a cinnamon-scented air
freshener around the room and sprinkled cookie crumbs on their desks.
When they came in she informed them that the Gingerbread Boy had been
to school.

"Is he still here?" asked one of the children, looking eagerly around.

"No, but I think some of his friends might be. Shall we look for them?"

The search was mounted, with the children exploring every corner of
the classroom. Alas, the Gingerbread Boy's friends were nowhere to be

found in class. Which meant coats had to be donned, and the children had to be taken outside to search the playground. While they conducted their search, the two room mothers came in and set up for a party, decorating and distributing Lexie's baked, wrapped gingerbread boys. When the children returned they found a giant cardboard Gingerbread Boy waving at them, and edible ones at each desk. Then there were stories to read, songs to sing and a game to play. The children left for their holiday break happily wound up and buzzing.

Her own son was buzzing at the end of the school day, also, full of details about his class holiday party. "We played pin the hat on Santa," he told her.

"And did you get the hat on the Santa's head?"

Brock shook his head. "I pinned it on his shoulder. Teacher said it looked good there. Emily thinks Santa is real."

Oh, dear. She hoped Brock hadn't passed on what he'd learned from their neighbor.

"Did you tell her he wasn't?" Lexie asked nervously.

Brock shook his head. "I didn't want to make her cry."

Like *someone* had made him cry. Lexie's brows dipped into an irritated V.

"I don't think she's big enough to know yet," Brock continued. "Not like me." He was silent a moment, then asked, "Can Grandpa Stanley come over and play Candy Land?"

"You want to see Grandpa Stanley?" Lexie asked, surprised.

"I miss him."

Faults and all. Her son was more forgiving than she was. What did that say about her?

More important, what did that say to her?

Stanley Mann had a crusty exterior, but inside he had a soft heart. That had been evidenced in the things he'd done for her and her son. She contrasted that to herself, all sweet and kind on the outside, but when it came to forgiving a grumpy old man who'd made a misstep, she had a heart as hard as a lump of coal.

This had to be a lonely time for the man. She could fix that. It was the season of peace on earth, goodwill toward men. Even curmudgeons.

The next day, with Brock riding shotgun, she drove to the supermarket—it felt so good to be able to drive herself!—and picked up buttermilk, red food coloring, and cake flour. She'd make red velvet cupcakes and take some to Stanley and maybe even invite him over for dinner.

On her way back she happened to drive by the bookstore. What a coincidence! Ha.

"This is the bookstore Mr. Phillips bought. I bet he and the girls are in there working. Should we go in and say hi?" she said to Brock.

As expected, her son said an emphatic *yes*, so they parked the car halfway down the block and made their way to the store. Walking with that light brace felt so good.

Once they got to the store she saw the sign on the door. *Closed, but not for long. Please join us for our grand reopening February 1.* Darn.

Oh, well, she had cupcakes to bake.

"I guess they're not open yet," she said to Brock.

He had his face pressed to the window. "But I see Mr. Phillips."

She joined him at the window. Indeed, Truman was there with the former owner. They both were seated in armchairs, and each had an iPad and the woman had a notebook and pencil. They were obviously working. The girls were over in the children's book section, reading.

"Come on, Brockie, let's go. They're not open," Lexie said.

Too late. He was already knocking on the window.

"Brockie, don't bother them. They're busy." Casually dropping by to purchase a book was one thing, but ignoring a Closed sign and hovering at the window probably looked more like stalking.

But Truman was on his way to the door.

"We came to see you," Brock told him once he'd opened it.

"Well, come on in."

"You're closed," Lexie protested. "And you're obviously busy. I thought you were open for business."

"We will be. And June and I were just going over a few things," he said. "We could probably use a break."

He ushered Lexie in and introduced her to the former owner, June Yates.

"Oh, yes, you've been in before," June said with a smile. "Nice to see you."

The girls came over, each with a book in hand. "Hi, Brock," said Isobel. "I'm reading this." She held up a Dr. Seuss book. "We have a whole bunch. Want to come see?"

He nodded eagerly and ran for the books.

"I shouldn't be bothering you," Lexie said to Truman.

"It's no bother. Sorry we're not open for business. I'm going to do a little remodeling."

"Feel free to show her," said June.

"I'll give you the two-minute tour," he said to Lexie.

It wasn't a large store, but he had good ideas for making better use of the space. "These——" he said, pointing to two rows of shelves "——we're going to put on rollers and make them movable. That way we can push them aside and make extra room for seating when we have author events."

"That's a great idea."

They moved to the children's book section. "Going to have different bookcases here, too. They'll be circular and rotate. Then, right there we'll make a space for story time. I'm hoping to find someone who'd like to come in on a Saturday afternoon once a month and read to the kids. Know anyone who might be interested in that?" he asked, raising both eyebrows.

Reading to children? Gee, twist her arm. "I think I might know someone," she said with a smile.

Brock held up a book to her. *Splat the Cat*. "Can we get this?"

She turned to Truman. "I know you're not officially open, yet but can you ring up a sale?"

"I'll do better than that. How about I give that to you for Christmas, Brock?" he asked.

Brock hugged the book to him. "Yes! Thank you."

"How will you make any money if you keep giving away your books?" Lexie protested.

"I'm sure you'll be a loyal customer," he said.

He had that right.

They stayed a few more minutes, then Lexie herded her son toward the door, saying to Truman, "We need to let you get back to work."

He walked them to the door. "I'm looking forward to Christmas," he said to her.

"Me, too," she told him.

As she was about to follow her son out, he caught her hand and drew her close enough so he could whisper in her ear. "And maybe celebrating New Year's Eve."

His breath tickled, and those little elves all began to dance around in her tummy again.

"That sounds like an excellent idea," she said.

Brock grabbed her other hand and pulled. "Come on, Mommy. I want to go home and read my new book."

"See you later," Truman said.

Oh, yes.

"I like our new friends," Brock said as they drove home.

"Me, too," Lexie said. This was going to be such a good Christmas.

Back at the house, Brock dived into his book, reading aloud to Lexie as she put together the cupcakes. By the time they were out of the oven and cooled, he'd had enough of Splat and was ready to help frost and decorate. Of course, many sprinkles were needed on the top of each one.

"Can I take some to Grandpa Stanley?" Brock asked as they decorated.

"This time I'm going to make the delivery," she told him. "I need to talk to him."

ONCE ON HIS front porch she found she wasn't quite sure what to say. She thought back to that voice mail he'd left. He hadn't known, either.

Maybe the best approach was to simply say *Let's start again. Why don't you come over for dinner on Christmas Day?*

She rang the doorbell. A moment later she could hear his dog barking on the other side of the door. Stanley was taking his time opening it. Maybe he was hiding in there.

Meanwhile, her phone was going off. It was Aunt Rose's ringtone. Her aunt rarely called. Curious, Lexie pulled the phone out of her coat pocket and took the call. At the rate Stanley was going she'd have plenty of time to talk.

"Hello," she said as she rang the doorbell again.

"Lexie, dear, I'm at the emergency room with your mother. You need to get down here right away."

CHAPTER TWENTY-THREE

STANLEY STILL REMEMBERED how it all happened.

As usual, he'd balked at the idea of having a party. This time Carol wanted to have one to celebrate Halloween. He especially hated Halloween parties. Dressing in silly costumes that made you look like a dork, playing those goofy games she and her sister always came up with.

"Why don't we go out instead," he'd suggested. "Have dinner, take in a scary movie."

"We can do that anytime. Halloween only comes once a year."

There was something to be grateful for.

"Come on, Stanley, don't be a party pooper."

"I'm not a party pooper," he insisted. He hated it when she called him that. Just because he didn't want to play stupid games with a houseful of people didn't make him a party pooper.

"Yes, you are," she insisted.

"Can't we just have one couple over and watch movies?" he suggested.

"We did that last year. And the year before."

"And it was fun, right?"

"It was. But I miss having a party. I want to play dark tag again."

Oh, Lord, chasing each other around in a pitch-dark room. They'd played that game plenty when they were young, but they weren't young anymore. People in their sixties should have a little more decorum, if you asked him. Not that Carol was asking.

"Somebody's bound to run into something and get hurt or wreck the furniture. Remember the last time we played that? Jimmy ran into the curio cabinet and broke the glass. And it wasn't cheap to repair."

"We'll move it."

Yes, moving furniture around, that would be fun. "Don't you think we're a little too old for some of these games?"

She frowned at him. "Darn it, Stanley, we're not that old yet."

"I am," he said.

"Is this the same man who once told me age is just a number?"

"The number's gotten bigger since you turned fifty," he argued.

"We're not dead yet."

He sighed. This was a losing battle. May as well give up and give in.

She smiled, knowing what that sigh signified. "It will be fun," she promised.

"Fun," he repeated, unconvinced.

Carol didn't ask much of him, and she did everything he liked with him: fly-fishing, snowshoeing, bowling. (She hadn't ever mastered the game and opted out of joining a league with him, but she'd still hit the alley once in a while on a Saturday night.) Car shows, of course. So if she wanted to have a party once in a while and play some crazy games, the least he could do was be a good sport and go along with it.

Anyway, she was right. He did always manage to have a good time once things got going. Especially if he and some of the guys could slip away for a game of Ping-Pong. You were never too old for that.

Carol loved decorating, and soon ceramic figures of ghosts and witches and pumpkins started appearing all over the house, and she set out a miniature patch of honeycomb pumpkins on the dining table as a centerpiece. She also drafted him to help her carve pumpkins for the front porch the week before the party.

That he could get into. He'd loved carving pumpkins as a kid, and he enjoyed creating a couple of downright creepy faces, one traditional with triangle eyes and nose and a crooked mouth; the other he made to look like the famous painting she'd showed him once called *The Scream*.

"That is truly terrifying," she said, looking at it.

"Maybe it will scare everyone away," he joked.

"Ha-ha," she said, unamused.

They set their creations up that very night, lining the steps to the front porch, then lit the candles and stepped back to check out how they looked.

"They look great. I think we are now ready for Halloween," she said, smiling.

"Yep," he agreed and slipped an arm around her.

Christmas was her favorite holiday, but Halloween came in a strong second. Carol not only enjoyed finding an excuse to entertain a mob, she also loved handing out candy to the kids who came trick-or-treating.

"Don't you look pretty!" she'd say to all the little princesses. To the Darth

Vaders and ghosts and monsters she'd say, "You look so scary!" And she'd always beg the little witches not to turn her into a toad, which would make them giggle. "You won't do that if I give you candy, will you?" she'd ask. Of course, they'd promise not to because Carol was always generous with the candy. And she guarded the candy bowl like a dragon, getting after Stanley every time he raided it.

At least he'd get plenty of treats at the party. It would be his reward for having to walk around dressed like a giant salami.

They'd finished dinner and were loading the dishwasher together the Friday night before the big bash when she said, "I think I'll go pick up the last of the food I need for the party."

"Just wait until tomorrow," he advised. "You've got all day."

"I want to bake some more cookies and make a pumpkin roll."

"That doesn't take all day to do," he pointed out.

"But I don't want to be pooped by the time everyone gets here."

"You already look pooped. Stay home and relax. You can send me to get the stuff tomorrow."

She refused to take him up on the offer. Even after all the years they'd been together he still managed to come home with a brand she didn't like or the wrong size of something.

"Okay, then, I'll go with you. I don't like you driving at night."

"I'm a better driver than you are," she said.

Stanley's night vision wasn't as good as it once was, but he could handle driving to the grocery store.

"I won't be that long," she assured him. "And I'd rather do it by myself. You get antsy after a while."

Only because it took her a million years to decide between ice cream flavors, and she had to inspect every apple in the produce section. They invariably ran into someone she knew, and that meant standing around talking, blocking the aisle. She'd take forever.

"Come on, babe, stay home. I found a movie for us to watch."

"I'll be back in plenty of time to watch a movie," she assured him.

But she wasn't. She didn't come back at all.

Instead two policemen showed up on his doorstep, looking for Carol's next of kin, politely asking if they could come in.

No! Stanley already knew they were there with bad news. *Don't give it to the old guy on the doorstep.*

His heart shut down; his brain shut down. He could hardly breathe. He stood back and let them in, managed to lead them into the living room.

"I'm afraid there's been an accident," said one of the cops.

"An accident," he repeated. "Is she alive?"

"I'm sorry, sir. She died while paramedics were attempting to revive her."

Stanley's mind kept rejecting the image. Not Carol. She was too full of life. She couldn't be dead. Not so suddenly, with no warning.

"What do I do now?" he asked.

Of course, they thought he was talking about procedure. He was talking about the rest of his life.

Amy was almost as much of a wreck as Stanley, so it fell to her husband, Jimmy, and Carol's best friend, Lois, to make the calls canceling the party. Other family members stepped in and helped with funeral arrangements. Stanley filled out forms, barely seeing what he was writing. Her wrote her obituary for the paper. How did you sum up a person's life in only one paragraph? Especially a person like Carol, who was so kind and thoughtful, who made life special for everyone who knew her?

Women started showing up with casseroles; cards flowed in. He couldn't bring himself to read any of the cards, and the food got dumped in the garbage.

The church was packed for her memorial service. So many of her former students came to pay their respects and sing her praises. The woman who'd never had a child of her own had touched hundreds of lives.

Afterward family and close friends came to the house to help consume the latest offering of casseroles, along with cakes and pies, telling him how sorry they were, how great Carol was. They clustered in groups and chatted like they were at a cocktail party. Carol would have loved seeing the house full of people. But Carol wasn't there, and Stanley just wanted them to all go away.

"Life goes on," said one of the neighbors, and it was all Stanley could do not to punch him.

"You'll see her again one day," Georgia Wallis, one of the church ladies, assured him, giving him a hug.

Easy for Georgia to dish out the platitudes. Her husband was still hale and hearty. She had no idea how it felt to lose the love of your life. And he didn't want to see Carol one day. He wanted to see her now.

But, like his insensitive neighbor had said, life did go on. Stanley just didn't want to be a part of it. He sold the mangled Mustang for scrap, made her sister and mom take away her clothes and lotions, and he hid her jewelry box under the bed. Then he turned into a robot, going through the motions of everyday life.

He found it impossible to feel thankful on Thanksgiving, and he didn't open a single Christmas card that came. He didn't put up a tree, and he didn't put up lights. Too many reminders of his life with Carol.

Memories flooded him, anyway: buying their first tree, Carol baking cookies, her delighted expression when he gave her the ornament he'd made for her, sitting next to her on the sofa watching Christmas movies.

Christmas morning he looked at the spot where they had always put the tree and cried.

HE DIDN'T CRY anymore, and he was seeing Carol again—a lot sooner than Georgia had predicted. Funny how, even as a ghost, she managed to bring out the best in him.

Or had been until he blew it with the Santa thing. Just when he was beginning to almost enjoy life. He just wasn't equipped to live without Carol.

CHAPTER TWENTY-FOUR

STANLEY CAME TO the door, leery of what he'd find. He looked out the side window and saw Lexie standing on the porch, yakking on her phone. Good grief, you couldn't even go to somebody's house without…

Never mind the device. She was here, and she had a paper plate with cupcakes on it. The block of cement that had been sitting in his chest since that ill-fated dinner crumbled. It looked like he was forgiven. He'd still say he was sorry, though.

He opened the door just as the plate fell from her hand, sending cupcakes tumbling in all directions.

She looked at him bleakly. "My mom," she said. Then the poor kid broke into tears and hurled herself against him.

It had been a long time since Stanley had held a crying woman, but his arms remembered what to do, and they quickly responded to the need and wrapped around her.

"It's okay," he said, patting her back, even though it obviously wasn't. "Tell me what's going on."

"She's in the emergency room. She's had a heart attack." Lexie pulled away. "I have to get to her." She turned and started back to her house at a run.

Stanley followed, not quite so fast. *He* was going to have a heart attack trying to catch up with Lexie. She wasn't wearing that big, clunky boot anymore, just a brace. The girl could really move now.

She slowed when she got to her front porch, hesitated at the front door. Whirled around, panic on her face. "What am I going to tell Brock?"

"Tell him she's sick."

"What if she…"

Stanley had been down this road. He understood the shock and fear that rode on your shoulders with every step.

"You don't know what if. Take this one minute at a time."

Lexie nodded, bit her lip, opened the door.

Brock came bounding up. "Grandpa Stanley! Did you come to play with me?"

"No, I came to help you and your mom. You're going to be taking a trip." To Lexie he said, "Go pack what you need. I'll see how soon I can get a flight out for you two."

She looked at him gratefully. "Thank you. So much."

"What are neighbors for?" he replied.

"Are we going someplace?" the boy asked.

"We have to go see Grandma," Lexie said. Her lower lip trembled, but she managed to fake calm and added, "She's not feeling well. Come on, let's get some clothes packed."

They went upstairs, and Stanley returned to his house and went to work on the phone. He was able to book a flight and pay for it in record time. He pulled on his coat, told Bonnie to behave while he was gone, then grabbed his car keys and backed his SUV out of the garage.

By the time he got to Lexie's house she was packed and ready to go.

He handed over her flight information. "The car's waiting. Come on."

She bit her lip and nodded, hustled her son out the door.

As soon as she had Brock and herself buckled in, Stanley took off, resisting the urge to speed. The last thing they needed was to get stopped by a cop. Or, worse, get in an accident.

He hoped Lexie's mom would be okay. Why did things like this always seem to happen during the holidays?

"I can't thank you enough for this," Lexie said, tears making her voice waver. "We're always imposing on you."

"It's not imposing if I offer."

"Especially after..."

He knew where she was going and cut her off. "I was wrong."

"You're a rock," she said.

It was what Carol used to tell him. Steady Stanley, always there when you needed him. No one had needed him for a long time. Except now someone did, maybe would continue to need him for some time. He sure wasn't going to let her down.

"Oh, God," Lexie whimpered. "First my dad. Now... I don't want her to—" She bit the words off, looked to the back seat where her son sat, hugging his little backpack.

"It's gonna be okay," Stanley assured her.

Yeah, as if he knew? But it was no use her spending the whole flight down in a panic.

"This is not how I pictured Christmas," she said miserably.

He sighed. "Stuff happens."

She bit her lip, nodded.

"Does Grandma have a cold?" Brock asked.

Tears were leaking out of the corner of Lexie's eye. "No, honey, she's sicker than that."

"Are we going to make her chicken soup?" he asked.

"Maybe," Lexie said and wiped her cheek.

Poor kids, Stanley thought.

At the airport he unloaded her carry-on for her, wishing he could do more. Of course, there wasn't more you could do when somebody was going through something like this.

"I'll keep an eye on the house," he told her.

"Thanks," she said. "I do have something coming." She lowered her voice and leaned in. "It's Brock's present from Santa. Even though he knows the truth, he's still looking forward to that extra gift under the tree. Could you keep an eye out for it?"

"Sure," Stanley promised.

"Although we probably won't get back in time," she said, and her lower lip began to wobble.

"I'll bring it in," he promised. Then added, "You can do this."

She dashed away the last of her tears, nodded. "Thank you for everything. I'll pay you back for the tickets."

"No need. Think of it as a Christmas present."

She shook her head. "No, that's too much."

Considering the Santa mess it was a small-enough penance. "I don't think so. I hope your mom does okay."

"Me, too," she said. Then she surprised him by leaning over and kissing him on the cheek. "Thank you again. For everything. Come on, Brockie, we have to hurry," she said to her son and pulled him through the entrance.

"Bye, Grandpa," the kid said as he followed her. "We have to go help Grandma get better."

"You will," Stanley said and hoped he was right.

And then they were gone. Stanley stood there a moment, trying to process everything that had just happened. He wasn't sure he could.

He got back in his SUV and drove home. Bonnie was waiting to greet him, tail wagging.

He picked her up, and she immediately got busy trying to lick his face. "You're a good dog," he told her. "Let's find you a dog treat, and then we're going to put up our Christmas tree."

He could have sworn he smelled peppermint when he went into the garage to bring in the big artificial tree they'd bought that last Christmas before Carol died. He couldn't help smiling.

"I know, babe. Better late than never."

Once he had the tree and the bin with the ornaments set out in the living room, he put on her favorite radio station that played Christmas music all day long. A chorus began to sing "We Need a Little Christmas."

Yes, they did.

THE FLIGHT TO LAX was torture. Lexie longed to lay her head on the drop-down tray and wail, but mommies didn't get to enjoy that luxury. She tried to keep the tears dammed and pay attention when her son was talking to her, but it was a challenge.

Brock was oblivious to his mother's consternation, enjoying the view out the window and the novelty of airplane food. She kept him busy with coloring and let him play some games on his tablet. He only began to get squirmy toward the end of the flight.

"When will we see Grandma?" he asked.

"Soon," she said and hoped it would be soon enough.

It was dark by the time the plane landed. She called her uncle as soon as passengers were allowed to turn on their cell phones.

"I've got Jen with me. We'll pick you up in the loading zone," he told her.

If she'd been coming in under normal circumstances she'd have been delighted to see her cousin. Like her, Jen was a teacher.

"How's Mom?" she asked her uncle.

"She's going to be okay," said Uncle Fred. "They ran an EKG and took an X-ray. Did a blood test. Looks like it wasn't a heart attack after all."

Lexie sagged in relief. No heart attack. Her mom was all right.

But if not a heart attack, why was she in the hospital? "Then, what was it?" Lexie asked.

"Some kind of panic attack."

Panic attack. That was what Lexie had just had. Honestly, she was going to let her mother have it.

People ahead of her were taking down their carry-ons, starting to move up the aisle. "We're getting off now," she said to her uncle and ended the call.

"Was that Grandma?" Brock asked.

"No, that was Uncle Fred. He's going to take us to Grandma." *Who is fine. Thank God!*

Her uncle and cousin were waiting in Uncle Fred's Lexus when Lexie and Brock emerged from inside the terminal. At the sight of her he hopped out and took her luggage. "It's good to see you, Lexie. Sorry we got you down here for nothing, but when it happened your aunt was terrified."

Poor Aunt Rose. Lexie could only imagine.

"I'm glad everything's okay," her cousin said, hugging her. "Angie and I are taking you to Back on the Beach tomorrow for chill time."

After the stress of the last few hours, she'd need it.

"So don't commit matricide," Jen teased.

Lexie giggled. She felt practically giddy with relief. "How did you know that's what I was thinking?"

"Because that's what I'd be thinking," said her cousin.

Once at the hospital, Uncle Fred and Jen took Brock to find a treat in the hospital cafeteria, which was open late, and Lexie went in search of her mother and aunt. She found Mom waiting to be discharged, sitting up in a hospital bed in her emergency-room cubicle, still wearing the latest style in hospital-gown ugly, Aunt Rose seated in a chair nearby.

There was only a two year difference between the sisters, and Mom was the youngest, but no one looking at them would think that. Aunt Rose was fit with tanned, youthful skin, thanks to fills from her dermatologist. Her hair was stylishly cut and highlighted. Mom's hair, on the other hand, was now a drab dirty-blond streaked with gray. She looked gaunt, and the lines around her mouth had turned into crevices. She'd aged overnight. Still, Lexie couldn't imagine a better sight.

"Oh, Lexie, darling," she greeted her daughter. "You shouldn't have come all this way."

Lexie hurried to the bedside and kissed her. "Are you serious? Not come when I think you're having a heart attack?"

Both her mother and aunt looked embarrassed at this.

"I'm sorry to have worried you," Aunt Rose said, "but it looked serious, and I knew you'd want to know what was going on."

"Of course I would," Lexie said. "What happened?"

"We were at my house, just looking through some old pictures, and suddenly your mother couldn't breathe. And she had pain in her chest."

"I feel so foolish," Mom added. "I had no idea a panic attack could mimic a heart attack. I don't even know why I panicked. One minute I was looking at pictures of all of us at the beach, and the next your aunt was calling 9-1-1."

Pictures of all of us. There was a big clue. Her father had to have been in them. Poor Mom.

"The important thing is that you're okay," Lexie said. She took her mother's hand and gave it a squeeze. She could feel the tears rising.

"Where's Brock?" Mom asked.

"He's here. Uncle Fred and Jen took him to the cafeteria to get something to eat."

"Oh, dear. I've turned your life upside down," Mom fretted.

"No, you haven't," Lexie lied.

But the next day when it was just her and her cousins at the popular Santa Monica beachfront restaurant, she did some serious venting. "I don't know how to help her," she finished and took another bite of her grilled fish taco. It didn't taste so good anymore.

Lexie's cousin Angie pointed a perfectly manicured finger at her. "You're definitely going to have to have a come-to-Jesus meeting. Your mom's got to get a grip."

Lexie pushed away her plate. "How do you get a grip on losing the most important person in your life?"

Neither cousin had an answer for that.

Once back at the house, she found her mom and Brock at the kitchen table, working a puzzle together. The sun was shining in through the window, creating a nimbus around them. Her mom wasn't exactly exuberant, but she didn't look totally miserable, either. Lexie came to a decision.

Later that night, after Brock was sound asleep in Lexie's old bed, she made peppermint tea and then settled them on the living-room couch. "I've booked a flight home for tomorrow," she said.

Disappointment was plain on her mother's face. "So soon?"

"Yes, so soon. Tomorrow is Christmas Eve, and I want to be back at the house for Christmas. All Brock's presents are there. Plus I have red velvet cupcakes on the counter going stale and a turkey in the fridge that needs to be cooked."

Mom sighed and set her mug of tea on the coffee table. "Of course."

Lexie laid a hand on her mother's. "And you're coming with us."

"Oh, darling, I'm not up to it."

"I think you are," Lexie said, determined to be firm. "And besides, we should be together. You scared the crap out of me, Mom," she added softly.

"I didn't mean to scare you," Mom said, sounding defensive.

"I know, but you did. And, frankly, I've been worried about you."

"I'm fine," Mom insisted.

Right. Lexie had just witnessed an example of how fine her mother was.

"No, you're not. And I'm sorry you're having such a hard time. I've had a hard time, too, but I have a son who needs me to be there for him, and I need you there for me. I need my mom back."

Her mother's lower lip began to wobble, and she put a hand to her chest.

Lexie scooted next to her and wrapped an arm around her shoulder. "Take a deep breath, Mom. It's okay."

"It's not," her mother said, her voice tripping over a sob.

That was all it took. The dam broke, and Lexie started crying also. They sat there together for a long time, holding each other and sharing a fresh helping of grief. At last Lexie went in search of tissues so they could mop their wet faces and blow their noses.

"We both have to keep living," she said after her second nose blow. "Daddy would want us to, you know that."

"I…can't," her mother said softly.

"You have to try, at least for Christmas. Can you do that? Please? For us?"

Mom bit her lip.

"And to honor Daddy?"

A fresh tear slipped down her mother's cheek.

"Our flight leaves at six." It meant they'd get in late but Lexie didn't care. At least she'd found a flight out and getting home late was preferable to not getting home at all.

Mom sighed, nodded. "I'm tired. I think I'll go to bed."

Lexie felt tired, too. And drained. She went to bed shortly after her mother. Curled up next to her little boy in the bed that had once been hers, she let out a deep sigh and shot up a quick prayer of thanks that Mom would be with them for Christmas.

Her mother didn't initiate any conversation on the way to the airport, but she managed a smile or two for Brock and put an arm around him as they waited in the airport terminal to board their plane.

It's a beginning, Lexie thought.

Their plane landed at Sea-Tac at nine that night, and it took another forty-five minutes for their Uber ride to get them home. By the time they arrived, Brock was cranky and yawning, and her mother looked ready to drop. Lexie felt overwhelmed with relief and happiness at the sight of their house. Home sweet home.

As they went up the front walk she realized she'd never even told Truman that she'd had to fly back to California. If she hadn't booked that return flight, he'd have come over the next day with the girls and wondered what kind of flake invited him for dinner and then wasn't around to serve it. Living so close, she'd never even thought about exchanging phone numbers, so she couldn't have texted him.

Truman and his girls. Would Mom be up for being sociable with strangers? Lexie hoped so.

The front porch was bare of packages. Stanley must have intercepted Brock's present and taken it to his house. She'd call him once she had her son and her mother settled in.

Inside, she sent Brock straight to bed, skipping the nightly bath routine, then gave her mother a quick tour of the house.

"It's very nice, darling," Mom said. "You've done a lovely job decorating."

"I'm glad you're sharing our first Christmas in it," Lexie told her.

"I am, too," Mom said, and Lexie hoped she really meant it.

Whether she was glad or not, she needed it. There was nothing in the old house but sadness. Her mother hadn't even bothered to put up a tree.

Not that Christmas was about trees. Or presents. But it was about hope. Maybe Mom could find enough to take her into a better New Year.

She settled her mother in the guest bedroom, then called Stanley. She'd seen a light on in his house so hoped it was okay to call him after ten at night.

He picked up on the second ring. "How's your mom?" he asked, and the concern in that gruff, old voice warmed Lexie's heart.

"She's fine. It turned out she had a panic attack, not a heart attack."

"Good," he said.

"I'm sorry to call you so late."

"I was up."

Great. She'd run right over. Then, once that final present was under the tree she, too, could go to bed.

"I didn't see anything on the front porch and figured you must have taken in Brock's present," she said. "Would you mind if I came over and got it now?"

There was moment of silence and that uneasy feeling of uh-oh tippy-toed up behind Lexie and said *Gotcha!*

Oh, no. Please don't say what I think you're going to.

CHAPTER TWENTY-FIVE

"IT DIDN'T COME," Stanley told Lexie. "I was watching," he added, in case she thought he hadn't been vigilant.

There was a long silence on the other end of the call, and he could envision the tears collecting in her eyes.

"But I, uh, have something. I'll bring it over."

He ended the call before she could tell him to forget it. His old Lionel train set was a leftover from his childhood that he'd never gotten rid of. From the late fifties, it was still in mint condition. Some of those old sets went for as much as ten thousand dollars. He figured his would fetch at least five, probably more.

But he'd never wanted to sell it. At first the thing had been a bit of nostalgia he couldn't bring himself to part with. Then he'd kept it, thinking he'd give it to his son one day. The son never arrived, and the train set eventually was forgotten.

Until after the Santa fiasco. Then, when the present for Brock never arrived, the idea of giving the train set to him had popped into Stanley's mind like a gift from... Santa.

Carol had probably planted the thought there. At least, he hoped she had. Maybe, if he put it to good use, she'd visit him again. He had a feeling those visits were coming to a close, but he longed to see her one last time.

He'd found the train set, checked to make sure everything was still working and cleaned it up, and now it was ready to go. Kids these days were into video games and drones and fancy games with lots of bells and whistles, so maybe this was a dumb idea. But maybe Brock was still young enough to think a train set was cool. After all, the boy liked to play Candy Land.

Stanley threw on his coat, picked up the giant cardboard box that contained all the smaller boxes with the engine and boxcars and passenger cars and the extra tracks and headed next door.

Lexie must have seen him coming, because by the time he got to her front porch she already had the door open.

"I'm sorry what you ordered didn't come, but maybe this will work," he said and moved past her into the living room.

The tree had a few presents around it, but she hadn't turned on the tree lights. In fact, the whole living room was a little dark, with only one light on.

She sighed. "*Guaranteed delivery before Christmas.* That's what they promised."

"Things don't always go the way you plan," he said. And he should know. He set the box down on the floor by the tree and knelt in front of it. "I need some light to work by."

She turned on some more lights, then came and knelt next to him, watching as he opened the box. "Oh, my gosh," she said as he took out the vintage engine. "How cute is that!"

"It was mine when I was a kid."

"It's an antique, then."

Just like him.

"We couldn't take it. It's probably valuable."

"Yeah, it is," Stanley agreed.

"There's probably someone in your family..."

He thought of Carol's prissy nieces and their spoiled little girls and shook his head. "No, there's not. They're into other stuff. It's not a fancy video game."

"No, it's not." She grinned. "It has...heart."

"Yeah, it does," he agreed and knew he'd found the right home for his childhood treasure.

Together, they laid out the tracks so the train would circle the tree and coupled the cars. She turned on the tree lights, and he plugged in the transformer and set the little Lionel chugging its way around.

"It's so cute. It looks like something out of an old movie," Lexie said, and Stanley saw that she was smiling. She turned the smile on him, and it felt like sunshine on his shoulder on a winter's day. "I can't thank you enough."

"This should square us," he said hopefully.

"It more than squares us," she said and stood up.

He stood, too. Time to go.

"It's been a long couple of days. I need to unwind," she said. "Would you like some eggnog?"

The warmth spread from his shoulder and wrapped around his heart. "Yeah." And if she'd had a long couple of days he knew exactly what she needed. "I have just the thing to go with it. I'll be right back," he said and grabbed his coat.

He speed-walked back across the lawns. He was tempted to run, but the temperatures had dropped, and the grass was frosty. The last thing he wanted was to slip.

Although if he fell and broke something, then it would be her turn to drive him around, he thought with a chuckle.

Once inside the house, he went to the cupboard where he kept the booze and grabbed a bottle of rum. Bonnie was sure he had to be looking for something for her and stood on her hind legs, dancing in anticipation.

"Okay, something for you, too," he told her and gave her a treat. "I won't be long," he promised, then hurried back out the front door.

Lexie grinned when he stepped back inside and held up the bottle. "Yes, that is exactly what I need," she said.

He followed her to the kitchen where she had two glasses of eggnog poured and added the rum.

She picked up her glass, and he picked up his. Then, before he could drink, she clinked them together. "To the New Year," she said.

"To the New Year," he echoed.

They wandered back into the living room, and she turned off all the lights except the colored ones on the tree, and they sat and watched the train circle it.

"You saved me, Stanley," she said. "If it wasn't for you, there'd have been no present from Santa under the tree."

"Yeah, but now the kid knows there's no Santa."

"He does, but we decided it's still fun to pretend, and I'd promised him there'd be an extra present for him. If I hadn't come through he'd have been crushed."

"My dad told me there was no such thing as Santa," Stanley volunteered.

"Were you disappointed?"

"You bet. It was a shock to hear it was all a big lie."

"That was what you thought, that your parents were lying?"

"Well, they were, weren't they?" he retorted.

"I prefer to think of it as pretending," she said.

He shrugged. "It wasn't a good time. The old man was out of work, money was tight. I guess the whole thing sort of stuck in my craw."

"Funny how those childhood experiences can do that," she said. "I had a great childhood. I sure hope I can give Brock one."

"Looks like you already are," Stanley told her. "You're a good mom."

"You really think so?"

"Sure. You kind of remind me of my mom. She was the best." Okay, they were getting kind of touchy-feely here. He downed the last of his eggnog and stood. "I better let you get to bed. Your boy will probably be up early."

She stood, too, and walked with him to the door. Before opening it she asked, "Stanley, do you have plans for tomorrow?"

He could have had plans. Now he almost wished he'd taken his sister-in-law up on her Christmas-dinner invitation.

"Not really," he said.

"Would you like to join us over here? I'm going to cook a turkey, and I've got the last of those cupcakes. The new neighbors are coming over."

"Sounds like a crowd," he said. She probably didn't need one more pie-hole to feed.

"It'll be a nice crowd. And I think my mom would like having someone her age to talk to. I know Brock would love to have you here. So would I."

Someone genuinely wanted his company. He smiled. "Okay."

"Great! Come on over around two."

Back home he let Bonnie out to do her thing, and while she was in the back yard, he set her present—a new chew toy—under the tree.

"We'll have Christmas morning together before I have to leave," he told her as they went up the stairs to bed.

It was a quiet bedtime. Carol still hadn't made an appearance. That night he slept dreamlessly, but he awoke feeling…not bad. Not bad at all. In fact, he decided, he was rather looking forward to the day, turkey dinner and all.

THE TRAVELING AND later bedtime had worn Brock out, but by six he was bouncing on Lexie's bed, waving his stocking around. "Mommy, it's Christmas!"

"Yes, it is," she said.

Her son was happy, her mother was with them, and the candy cane in the Christmas stocking was that they had company coming to join them. A true gathering of the neighbors, just like she'd envisioned when she first bought the house. She could hardly wait. She could especially hardly wait to see Truman. It was going to be a great day.

"Look what I got," Brock said and dumped the contents of his stocking on the bed.

Out fell mini candy bars (bought on sale after Halloween at fifty percent off and hidden away). Also a tiny metal car, a set of Christmas-themed finger puppets, gummy worms and a small travel game—all ordered online. Thank God those had come in time.

"That's quite a haul," she said.

There was something else, a folded piece of paper. It wasn't folded as neatly as she originally had done it, which meant Brock had looked at it.

He nodded happily. Then sobered. "Mommy, are you sure there's no Santa?"

She tousled his hair. "There can be if you want there to be."

The nod became very enthusiastic. "I do. Look what I got." He handed over the paper.

She already knew what the little note said since she'd been the one who'd written it.

She unfolded the paper and said, "Let's read it together."

"'Dear,'" she began.

"'Brock,'" he read. "'You are a good boy, and your M-m-m...'"

"'Mother,'" she supplied.

"'Mother l-l-lo...'"

"'Loves.'"

"'Loves you,'" he said and beamed. "I know these words! 'Merry Christmas. Santa.'"

"Well, what do you know," Lexie said.

His brow furrowed. "Did Santa really write me?"

"Let's not worry about who wrote that," she suggested. "Let's concentrate on what it says. You are a good boy, and your mother loves you. Now, your special gift from Santa is still coming but there's something else waiting for you. Should we go downstairs and see what's under the tree?"

His head nearly nodded right off his neck, and he bounced off the bed.

"Wait a minute," Lexie called. "Why don't you go knock on Grandma's door and tell her it's time to get up?"

"Okay!" He started for the door.

"First, come put everything back in your stocking."

This produced a slightly impatient frown, but he obeyed.

While he was busy restuffing his stocking, Lexie donned her brace. Then, as he ran off to wake Grandma, she raced down the stairs, turned on the tree lights and started the train going. She grabbed her phone so she could capture that most magical moment in childhood, when he first saw the tree with its presents and promise of fun.

"Grandma's coming," Brock hollered. This was followed by the thunder of little-boy feet coming down the stairs.

Lexie had her phone set to Video and caught the intake of breath and the wide eyes followed by the squeal and the excited rush to the tree. *God bless you, Stanley Mann*, she thought as her son fell in front of the track and watched in wonder as the little train chugged its way around the presents.

Stanley, himself, had turned out to be a gift. Under those crusty layers of gruffness the man was solid gold. Like the valuable train set he'd given her son, he was a keeper.

Lexie had coffee ready by the time her mother came down half an hour later, a bathrobe over her pajamas. She'd gotten as far as combing her hair and, knowing Mom, had also brushed her teeth. Her smile, however, was a pale shadow of what it had been when Lexie's father was alive. But she was there with them. That was what mattered.

The pile of presents under the tree was small. A game for Brock, a book Grandma had sent back when she hadn't planned on coming up, some socks decorated with dinosaurs, and from Lexie's cousins, who'd been dubbed aunties, Legos and a Harry Potter wizard training wand that came complete with lights and sounds.

Lexie loved the bracelet Mom had sent: rose gold with a heart bearing an *L*. And she knew she'd forever treasure the tree ornament made of Popsicle sticks, painted red and shaped into a sleigh, that Brock had made for her at school.

She baked coffee cake for breakfast and got the turkey in the oven, and by early afternoon the house was filled with an aroma that said *Let's eat*.

Her mother helped her in the kitchen, made punch and assisted Brock in setting the table for their holiday feast. As they worked, Lexie kept up a line of cheerful chatter, but it was as if Mom was wearing armor and the arrows of cheer bounced off.

Still, she was there. It was a beginning, and you had to begin somewhere.

Truman and his girls arrived a little before two, the girls wearing red-and-green Christmas dresses and Truman in jeans and a tan Nordic-looking sweater with a border of reindeer running across his chest. He sure looked like what Lexie wanted for Christmas, and her heart gave a squeeze as if those little elves had moved from her tummy to trampoline on it.

He came bearing gifts, a box of candy as well as gift cards to the bookstore for both Lexie and Brock.

"We picked out the candy," said Isobel, the younger sister.

"It was a good pick. We like chocolates," Lexie said to her. "You didn't have to do that," she told Truman as Brock led the girls into the living room to see his train, but she was pleased nonetheless.

"My mother always told me you should never show up to dinner empty-handed," he said.

"It sounds like you have a very smart mother."

"I do. I should have listened to her more often."

She imagined he was talking about his ex but didn't say anything, figuring that was a conversation they didn't need to keep going. Christmas wasn't the time to talk about past mistakes. It was about new beginnings waiting right around the corner.

"Speaking of mothers," Lexie said, "come on in and meet mine. She wound up coming to spend Christmas with us after all."

Introductions were made, and the grown-ups settled on the couch while the kids sat by the tree, following the progress of Brock's new train, which hadn't stopped running from the moment he first saw it.

Truman was polite to Mom, asking questions about where she lived, then following up with more questions when he learned she lived in Southern California. When that conversation dried up, he asked what she thought of Lexie's new house.

"It's very lovely, but the weather's so gloomy up here," Mom said.

"I hear it rains a lot in the Pacific Northwest," Truman said. "But, looking at how green it is here, I think I can live with that."

"It's gorgeous in the summer," Lexie put in. "You'd like it here then, Mom."

Her mother said nothing, refusing to be drawn into admitting that was a possibility. Honestly, it was as if Mom was determined to do all she could to toss the merry out of Christmas.

The doorbell rang, and Brock popped up. "It's Grandpa Stanley!"

Her mother didn't look all that thrilled at her grandson having a replacement grandpa, and now Lexie wondered if it had been such a good idea to invite Stanley for dinner after all.

Brock opened the door, and in stepped Stanley Mann, looking festive in slacks and a shirt under a red pullover sweater. He'd accessorized with a red bow tie. And something even more amazing—a big smile.

"Merry Christmas, Grandpa!" Brock hollered as if their neighbor had suddenly gone deaf. "I got a train for Christmas."

"You did?" Stanley said.

Brock took him by the hand and towed him into the living room. "Come and see."

"That's a nice one," Stanley said and winked at Lexie as she approached. "Something sure smells good," he said to her.

"Turkey and all the fixings," she replied. "Stanley, I want you to meet our new neighbors."

The girls said a polite hello, and the men shook hands. Then it was time to introduce Stanley to Mom.

"Good to meet you," he said to her. "You've raised a great daughter."

So polite and…sociable. Had Stanley been taken over by aliens?

Mom murmured her thanks but didn't do anything to keep the conversation going. That didn't appear to bother Stanley. He settled on the couch and observed the kids, chatted with Truman about trains and how nobody was interested in them anymore.

"Only old farts like me," he finished.

"Brock looks like a convert," Truman observed.

"That one is courtesy of Stanley," Lexie explained, and her mother looked over at him in surprise. "He pretty much saved the day."

Stanley waved away her praise, but the corners of his lips sneaked up.

"I had a Transformers train set when I was little," Truman reminisced. "I loved that thing. Wish I still had it. I think it would be worth something now." He nodded in the direction of the vintage Lionel set slowly making its way around the tree. "That one looks pretty valuable."

Stanley shrugged. "It's worth a few pennies." Lexie brought the video up on her phone of Brock's reaction to it and showed him. "And that's priceless," he said, watching it.

Yep, he'd been taken over by aliens.

Dinner was a boisterous and happy affair with the children at their own little table, in high spirits and giggling. Even Mom almost smiled a couple of times. Until after dessert. The children wolfed down their stale red velvet cupcakes, then pulled out Candy Land and set up camp in the living room while the adults lingered over coffee.

That was when Stanley casually said to Mom, "I hear you lost your husband."

Lexie's good spirits plummeted, and she braced herself.

Mom set down her coffee mug, stared at it. Said nothing. Lexie and Truman exchanged looks. *What do you do in a moment like this?*

Stanley appeared oblivious. "Hard," he said. "I lost my wife three years ago." He shook his head. "I still miss her."

"I'd rather not talk about my husband," Mom said stiffly.

"I can understand that," Stanley said. "What's worse is people butting into your life, wanting you to smile and come to big holiday gatherings and pretend like nothing happened."

Gift or not, Lexie was going to wring his neck.

Mom looked at him in surprise, then nodded. Then frowned at Lexie as if it was all her fault that Mom had scared her half to death only three days earlier.

"Exactly," she said.

"Yep, tough to move on," Stanley said. He punctuated this bit of wisdom with a slurp of coffee. "But, you know, life is like living off your savings account. Each day you take another withdrawal, and pretty soon there's nothing left. You gotta spend those days wisely, make the most of them, you know?"

Mom nodded thoughtfully. "That's an interesting point."

"I never thought of it that way," said Truman. "That was really profound."

Lexie said nothing. She was too surprised, both by Stanley's advice and her mother's reaction to it.

Stanley merely shrugged. "It's something my wife once told me."

"I wish I could have met her," Lexie said.

"You'd have liked her. You remind me of her, always happy and positive. We need more of that in this world. Kind of balances out all the grumps," Stanley concluded with another wink.

"Yes, we do," agreed Truman, and the way he looked at Lexie promised a very happy New Year.

BACK HOME THAT evening, Stanley turned on the lights on his Christmas tree. He put on a CD of Christmas songs, settled in his recliner with Bonnie and let the music wash over him. It had been a good day.

And to top it off, Carol paid him a visit later that night, perching on the end of the bed. She was dressed in a glowing white gown, and she looked like an angel, and his heart gave a squeeze at the sight of her.

"I thought you were mad at me, babe," he said.

She smiled at him, showing off her dimples. "You know I could never stay mad at you, Manly Stanley." She floated a little closer, and he caught a whiff of peppermint. "It looks like you had a nice day today."

"I did," he admitted and reached out to pet Bonnie, who was sleeping through the entire conversation.

"I'm glad to see you spending your life so wisely, darling."

"I'm trying," he said. Not defensively. He was, indeed, trying, and it felt good.

"It's going to be a wonderful year for you," she predicted. "Merry Christmas, Stanley, and have a happy life."

A LITTLE CHRISTMAS SPIRIT

"That sounds like good-bye," he said and felt panic stirring in him.

"I can't stay here forever. You know that."

"Just a little longer," he begged.

"You don't need me now. You're going to be fine on your own. I'll see you much later. I love you."

Then she was gone, just like that. But, thinking of her last words to him, he decided it was okay. It was time to let her go, time to move on.

Stanley settled his head back against his pillow and closed his eyes.

The next morning he woke up to see a thick, white carpet of snow on the lawn. Plenty for making a snowman.

"Come on, girl," he said to Bonnie. "Let's get going. We've got a life to live."

And like Tiny Tim would have said, *God Bless Us, Everyone.*

ONE YEAR LATER

THE TOWN OF Fairwood received a light dusting of snow on the first Saturday in December. It was enough to paint the trees white and provide a lovely backdrop as wedding guests drove up to the little church, but not so much that people would be afraid to drive. Even Shannon, who was one of Lexie's bridesmaids, had no trouble getting there.

The sanctuary was done up with poinsettias and greens and red and white candles and smelled like pine. The pews were filled with friends of the bride and groom from both Fairwood and California.

Lexie stood at the back of the church, wearing a faux fur–trimmed wedding gown. She also wore a pink-pearl necklace that had once belonged to Carol Mann. In one hand she held her bouquet, made up of red and white roses. The other hand rested on Stanley's arm. Out of the corner of her eye, she could see him running a nervous finger under the collar of his tux shirt.

When she'd asked him to walk her down the aisle he'd protested. There had to be someone else, someone more qualified.

There was, but as far as Lexie was concerned Stanley was the man she wanted for the job. Neighbor, friend, confidant, still sometimes cranky, he had come to mean the world to her.

She watched as her son, the ring bearer, followed Truman's daughters down the aisle. He was trying very hard not to step on the red and white-silk rose petals the girls had scattered, tiptoeing or leaping over them as he went and drawing some chuckles from the onlookers.

She could see her mother sitting in the front with her aunt and uncle. Mom still hadn't moved up from California, but she'd visited during the summer and had accompanied Lexie and Truman and the kids on their trip to Icicle Falls to meet Muriel Sterling and check out the Sweet Dreams Chocolate Company. She was back for the wedding and would be watching over the children while Lexie and Truman honeymooned in Hawaii, then staying clear through Christmas.

Up at the altar, Truman stood looking at Lexie with all the adoration a woman could ever want. Her heart squeezed in response.

Funny how once upon a wish Lexie had been so determined to have a fancy destination wedding. It turned out she didn't need it after all. She'd reached her destination when she moved to Fairwood, and there was no better place to start her new life with her wonderful man.

She smiled at Stanley, and he smiled back and patted her hand as if to reassure her.

She didn't need reassuring. She knew that she'd made the right decision. Her grandma would have approved.

The wedding consultant signaled that it was time for the bride to begin her walk down the aisle.

"You ready to do this?" Stanley asked her.

"Oh, yes," she said.

STANLEY SAT AT the reception table with Lexie's mother and her aunt and uncle.

"They make a charming couple, don't they, Meredith?" Lexie's aunt said to Lexie's mom.

"Yes, they do," said Meredith. "I'm glad she finally found someone." She turned to Stanley. "It was sweet of you to walk her down the aisle."

He felt embarrassed with Lexie's uncle right there at the same table. "Probably should have been her uncle," Stanley said.

"Fred wasn't offended. We all know how much you've done for her and how much you mean to her."

"You've been a gift," said her mom.

Now that she'd gained back some weight and the color had returned to her face, Meredith Bell wasn't a bad-looking woman. Stanley knew Lexie had hopes that something would happen between the two of them, but it wasn't going to. Carol had been the only woman for him.

That didn't mean he couldn't make room in his life for friends, though. And an adopted daughter and grandchild or two. Or three.

"She means a lot to me, too," he said.

Okay, getting too mushy here. He dug into his salmon.

It was hard not to feel mushy when it came time for toasts, but he kept his simple and to the point. Actually, he was amazed he even remembered the few words he wanted to say with so many people looking at him.

He cleared his throat. "To Lexie, the daughter I never knew I wanted, and to Truman, the only man who deserves her."

He knew he got it right when he saw Lexie dabbing the corner of her eye with her napkin.

Much later that night he came back home and settled in his recliner with Bonnie and a bowl of peppermint ice cream to listen to Christmas music and read.

We wish you a Merry Christmas, sang a choir.

No need to wish it. He fully intended to have one.

* * * * *

A Christmas Blessing
Sherryl Woods

Also by Sherryl Woods

Chesapeake Shores

Lilac Lane
Willow Brook Road
Dogwood Hill
The Christmas Bouquet
A Seaside Christmas
The Summer Garden
An O'Brien Family Christmas
Beach Lane
Moonlight Cove
Driftwood Cottage
A Chesapeake Shores Christmas
Harbor Lights
Flowers on Main
The Inn at Eagle Point

The Sweet Magnolias

Swan Point
Where Azaleas Bloom
Catching Fireflies
Midnight Promises
Honeysuckle Summer
Sweet Tea at Sunrise
Home in Carolina
Welcome to Serenity
Feels Like Family
A Slice of Heaven
Stealing Home

Molly DeWitt Mysteries

Tropical Blues
Rough Seas

Nonfiction

A Small Town Love Story:
Colonial Beach, Virginia

For a complete list of all titles by Sherryl Woods,
visit www.sherrylwoods.com.

CHAPTER ONE

GETTING CONSUELA MARTINEZ out of his kitchen was proving to be a much more difficult task than Luke Adams had ever envisioned. His housekeeper had found at least a dozen excuses for lingering, despite the fact that her brother was leaning on his car's horn and causing enough ruckus to deafen them all.

"Go, *amiga,*" Luke pleaded. "Enjoy your holidays with your family. *Feliz Navidad!*"

Consuela ignored the instructions and the good wishes. "The freezer is filled with food," she reminded him, opening the door to show him for the fourth time. Though there were literally dozens of precooked, neatly labeled packages, a worried frown puckered her brow. "It will be enough?"

"More than enough," he assured her.

"But not if you have guests," she concluded, removing her coat. "I should stay. The holidays are no time for a good housekeeper to be away."

"I won't be having any guests," Luke said tightly, picking the coat right back up and practically forcing her into it. "And if I do, I am perfectly capable of whipping up a batch of chips and dip."

"Chips and dip," she muttered derisively.

She added a string of Spanish Luke felt disinclined to translate. He caught the general drift; it wasn't complimentary. After all this time, though, Consuela should know that he wasn't the type to host a lot of extravagant, foolish parties. Leave that sort of thing to his brother Jordan or his parents. His brother thrived on kissing up to his business associates and his parents seemed to think that filling the house with strangers meant they were well loved and well respected.

"Consuela, go!" he ordered, barely curbing his impatience. "*Vaya con Dios.* I'll be fine. I am thirty-two years old. I've been out of my playpen for a long time."

One of the dangers of hiring an ex-nanny as a housekeeper, he'd discovered, was the tendency she had to forget that her prior charge had grown up. Yet he could no more have fired Consuela than he could have his own mother. In truth, for all of her hovering and bossiness, she was the single most important constant in his life. Which was a pretty pitiful comment on the state of his family, he decided ruefully.

Consuela's unflinching, brown-eyed gaze pinned him. Hands on ample hips, she squared off against him. "You will go to your parents' on Christmas, *sí?* The holidays are a time for families to be together. You have stayed away too long."

"Yes," he lied. He had no intention of going anywhere, especially not to his parents' house where everyone would be mourning, not celebrating, thanks to him.

"They will have enough help for all of the parties that are planned?"

Luke bit back a groan. "Consuela, you know perfectly well they will," he said patiently. "The place is crawling with your very own nieces and nephews. My parents haven't had to cook, clean or sneeze without assistance since you took over the running of that household forty years ago before they'd even met. When you came over here to work for me, you handpicked your cousin to replace you. Maritza is very good, yes?"

"*Sí,*" she conceded.

"This trip to see your family in Mexico is my present to you. It's long overdue. You said yourself not sixty seconds ago that the holidays are meant for families. You have not seen your own for several years. Your mother is almost ninety. You cry every time a letter comes from her."

"After all these years, I get homesick, that's true. I am a very emotional person, not like some people," she said pointedly.

Luke ignored the jibe. "Well, this is your chance to see for yourself how your mother is doing. Now stop dawdling and go before you miss your plane and before your brother busts our eardrums with that horn of his."

Consuela still appeared torn between duty to him and a longing to see her mother. Finally she heaved a sigh of resignation and buttoned her coat. "I will go," she said grudgingly. "But I will worry the whole time. You are alone too much, *niño.*"

It had been a long time since anyone had thought of Luke Adams as a little boy. Unfortunately, Consuela would probably never get the image out of her head, despite the fact that he was over six feet tall, operated a thriving ranch and had built himself a house twice the size of the very lavish one he'd grown up in.

"Ever since——" she began.

"Enough," Luke said in a low, warning tone that silenced her more quickly than any shout would have.

Tears of sympathy sprang to her eyes, and she wrapped her plump arms around him in a fierce hug that had Luke wincing. For a sixty-year-old woman she was astonishingly strong. He didn't want her weeping for him, though. He didn't want her pity. And he most definitely didn't want her dredging up memories of Erik, the brother who'd died barely seven months ago, the brother whose death he'd caused.

"Go," he said more gently. "I will see you in the new year."

She reached up and patted his cheek, a gesture she dared only rarely. *"Te amo, niño."*

Luke's harsh demeanor softened at once. "I love you, too, Consuela."

The truth of it was that she was about the only human being on the face of the earth to whom he could say that without reservation. Even before Erik's death had split the family apart, Luke had had his share of difficulties with his father's attempted ironclad grip on his sons. His mother had always been too much in love with her husband to bother much with the four boys she had borne him. And Luke had battled regularly with his younger brothers, each of them more rebellious than the other. Erik had been a year younger, only thirty-one when he'd died. Jordan was thirty, Cody twenty-seven. Consuela had been the steadying influence on all of them, adults and children.

"Te amo, mi amiga," Luke said, returning her fierce hug.

Consuela was still calling instructions as she crossed the porch and climbed into her brother's car. For all he knew she was still shouting them as the car sped off down the lane to the highway, kicking up a trail of dust in its wake.

Alone at last, he thought with relief when Consuela was finally gone from view. Blessed silence for two whole weeks. His cattle were pastured on land far from the main house and were being tended by his foreman and a crew of volunteers from among the hands. The ranch's business affairs were tied up through the beginning of the new year. He had no obligations at all.

He opened a cupboard, withdrew an unopened bottle of Jack Daniel's whiskey from the supply he'd ordered, ostensibly to take along as gifts to all the holiday parties to which he'd been invited. He pulled down a nice, tall glass, filled it with ice and headed for his den and the big leather chair behind his desk.

Uncapping the bottle, he poured a shot, doubled it, then shrugged and filled the glass to the rim. No point in pretending he didn't intend to get blind, stinking drunk. No point in pretending he didn't intend to stay that way until the whole damned holiday season had passed by in a blur.

Just as he lifted the glass to his lips, he caught sight of the wedding photo on the corner of his desk, the one he'd turned away so that he wouldn't have to see Erik's smile or the radiance on Erik's wife's face. He'd destroyed two lives that day, three if he counted his own worthless existence. Erik was dead and buried, but Jessie's life had been devastated as surely as if she had been in that accident with him.

A familiar knot formed in his stomach, a familiar pain encircled his heart. He lifted his glass in a mockery of a toast. "To you, little brother."

The unaccustomed liquor burned going down, but in the space of a heartbeat it sent a warm glow shimmering through him. If one sip was good, two were better, and the whole damned bottle promised oblivion.

He drank greedily, waiting to forget, waiting for relief from the unceasing anguish, from the unending guilt.

The phone rang, stopped, then rang again. The old grandfather clock in the hall chimed out each passing hour as dusk fell, then darkness.

But even sitting there all alone in the dark with a belly full of the best whiskey money could buy, Luke couldn't shut off the memories. With a curse, he threw the bottle across the room, listened with satisfaction as it shattered against the cold, stone fireplace.

Finally, worn out, he fell into a troubled sleep. It wasn't his brother's face he saw as he passed out, though. It was Jessie's—the woman who should have been his.

THE SKY WAS dark as pitch and the roads were icing over. Jessie Adams squinted through the car's foggy windshield and wondered why she'd ever had the bright idea of driving clear across Texas for the holidays, instead of letting her father-in-law send his pilot for her. She wasn't even sure how Harlan and Mary Adams had persuaded her that she still belonged with them now that Erik was gone.

She'd always felt like an outsider in that big white Colonial house that looked totally incongruous sitting in the middle of a sprawling West Texas ranch. Someone in the family, long before Harlan's time, had fled the South during the Civil War. According to the oft-told legend, the minute they'd accumulated enough cash, they'd built an exact replica of the mansion they'd left behind in ashes. And like the old home, they'd called it White Pines, though she couldn't recall ever seeing a single pine within a thirty-mile radius.

The bottom line was the Adamses were rich as could be and had ancestry they could trace back to the *Mayflower,* while Jessie didn't even know who her real parents had been. Her adoptive parents had sworn they didn't know and had seemed so hurt by her wanting to find out that she'd reluctantly dropped any notion of searching for answers.

By the time they'd died, she'd pushed her need to know aside. She had met Erik, by then. Marrying him and adjusting to his large, boisterous family had been more than enough to handle. Mary Adams was sweet as could be, if a little superior at times, but Erik's father and his three brothers were overwhelming. Harlan Adams was a stern and domineering parent, sure of himself about everything. He was very much aware of himself as head of what he considered to be a powerful dynasty. As for Erik's brothers, she'd never met a friendlier, more flirtatious crew, and she had worked in her share of bars to make ends meet while she'd been in college.

Except for Luke. The oldest, he was a brooder. Dark and silent, Luke had been capable of tremendous kindness, but rarely did he laugh and tease as his brothers did. The expression in the depths of his eyes was bleak, as if he was bearing in silence some terrible hurt deep in his soul. There had been odd moments when she'd felt drawn to him, when she'd felt she understood better than anyone his seeming loneliness in the midst of a family gathering, when she had longed to put a smile on his rugged, handsome face.

That compelling sense of an unspoken connection had been ripped to shreds on the day Luke had come to tell her that her husband was in the hospital and unlikely to make it. In a short burst riddled with agonized guilt, he'd added that he was responsible for the overturning of the tractor that had injured Erik. He'd made no apologies, offered no excuses. He'd simply stated the facts, seen to it that she got to the hospital, made sure the rest of the family was there to support her, then walked away. He'd avoided her from that moment on. Avoided everyone in the family ever since, from what Harlan and Mary had told her. He seemed to be intent on punishing himself, they complained sadly.

If Luke hadn't been steering clear of White Pines, Jessie wasn't at all sure she would have been able to accept the invitation to come for the holidays. Seeing Luke's torment, knowing it mirrored her own terrible mix of grief and guilt was simply too painful. She hated him for costing her the one person to whom she'd really mattered.

Searching for serenity, she had fled the ranch a month after Erik's death, settled in a new place on the opposite side of the state, gotten a boring job that paid the bills and prepared to await the birth of her child. Erik's baby. Her only link to the husband she had adored, but hadn't always understood.

She stopped the dark thoughts before they could spoil her festive holiday mood. There was no point at all in looking back. She had her future— she rested a hand on her stomach—and she had her baby, though goodness knows she hadn't planned on being a single parent. Sometimes the prospect terrified her.

She found a station playing Christmas carols, turned up the volume and sang along, as she began the last hundred and fifty miles or so of the once familiar journey back to White Pines. Her back was aching like the dickens and she'd forgotten how difficult driving could be when her protruding belly forced her to put the seat back just far enough to make reaching the gas and brake pedals a strain.

"No problem," she told herself sternly. A hundred miles or more in this part of the world was nothing. She had snow tires on, a terrific heater, blankets in the trunk for an emergency and a batch of homemade fruitcakes in the back that would keep her from starving if she happened to get stranded.

The persistent ache in her back turned into a more emphatic pain that had her gasping.

"What the dickens?" she muttered as she hit the brake, slowed and paused to take a few deep breaths. Fortunately there was little traffic to worry about on the unexpectedly bitter cold night. She stayed on the side of the road for a full five minutes to make sure there wouldn't be another spasm on the heels of the first.

Satisfied that it had been nothing more than a pinched nerve or a strained muscle, she put the car back in gear and drove on.

It was fifteen minutes before the next pain hit, but it was a doozy. It brought tears to her eyes. Again, pulling to the side of the road, she scowled down at her belly.

"This is not the time," she informed the impertinent baby. "You will not be born in a car in the middle of nowhere with no doctor in sight, do you understand me? That's the deal, so get used to it and settle down. You're not due for weeks yet. Four weeks to be exact, so let's have no more of these pains, okay?"

Apparently the lecture worked. Jessie didn't feel so much as a twinge for another twenty miles. She was about to congratulate herself on skirting disaster, when a contraction gripped her so fiercely she thought she'd lose control of the car.

"Oh, sweet heaven," she muttered in a tone that was part prayer, part curse. There was little doubt in her mind now that she was going into labor. Denying it seemed pointless, to say nothing of dangerous. She had to take a minute here and think of a plan.

On the side of the road again, she turned on the car's overhead light, took out her map and searched for some sign of a hospital. If there was one within fifty miles, she couldn't spot it. She hadn't passed a house for miles, either, and she was still far from Harlan and Mary's, probably a hundred miles at least. She could make that in a couple of hours or less, if the roads were clear, but they weren't. She was driving at a safe crawl. It could take her hours to get to White Pines at that pace.

There was someplace she could go that would be closer, someplace only five miles or so ahead, unless she'd lost her bearings. It was the last place on earth she'd ever intended to wind up, the very last place she would want her baby to be born: Luke's ranch.

Consuela would be there, she consoled herself as she resigned herself to dropping by unannounced to deliver a baby. Luke probably didn't want to see her any more than she wanted to see him. And what man wanted any part of a woman's labor, unless she happened to be his wife? Luke probably wouldn't be able to turn her over to Consuela fast enough. With all those vacant rooms, they probably wouldn't even bump into each other in the halls.

Jessie couldn't see that she had any choice. The snow had turned to blizzard conditions. The world around her was turning into a snow-covered wonderland, as dangerous as it was beautiful. The tires were beginning to skid and spin on the road. The contractions were maybe ten minutes apart. She'd be lucky to make it these few miles to Luke's. Forget going any farther.

The decision made with gut-deep reluctance, she accomplished the drive by sheer force of will. When she finally spotted the carved gate announcing the ranch, she skidded to a halt and wept with relief. She still had a mile of frozen, rutted lane to the house, but that would be a breeze compared to the five she'd just traveled.

A hard contraction, the worst yet, gripped her and had her screaming out loud. She clung to the steering wheel, panting as she'd seen on TV, until it passed. Sweat streamed down her face.

"Come on, sweet thing," she pleaded with the baby. "Only a few more minutes. Don't you dare show up until I get to the house."

She couldn't help wondering when that would be. There was no beckoning light in the distance, no looming shape of the house. Surely, though, it couldn't be much farther.

She drove on, making progress by inches, it seemed. At last she spotted the house, dark as coal against the blinding whiteness around it. Not a light on anywhere. No bright holiday decorations blinking tiny splashes of color onto the snow.

"Luke Adams, you had better be home," she muttered as she hauled herself out from behind the wheel at last.

Standing on shaky legs, she began the endless trek through the deepening snow, cursing and clutching her stomach as she bent over with yet another ragged pain. The wind-whipped snow stung her cheeks and mingled with tears. The already deepening drifts made walking treacherous and slow.

"A little farther," she encouraged herself. Three steps. Four. One foot onto the wide sweep of a porch. Then the other. She had made it! She paused and sucked in a deep breath, then looked around her.

The desolate air about the place had only intensified as she'd drawn closer. There was no wreath of evergreens on the front door, no welcoming light shining on the porch or from any of the rooms that she could detect. For the first time, she allowed a panicky thought. What if she had made it this far, only to find herself still alone? What if Luke had packed his bags and flown away for the holidays?

"Please, God, let someone be here," she prayed as she hit the doorbell again and again, listening to the chime echo through the house. She pounded on the glass, shouted, then punched the doorbell again.

She heard a distant crash, a loud oath, then another crash. Apparently Luke was home, she thought dryly, as she began another insistent round of doorbell ringing.

"For cripe's sakes, hold your horses, dammit!"

A light switch was thrown and the porch was illuminated in a warm yellow glow. Finally, just as another contraction ripped through Jessie, the door was flung open.

She was briefly aware of the thunderstruck expression on Luke's face and his disheveled state, only marginally aware of the overpowering scent of alcohol.

And then, after a murmured greeting she doubted made a lick of sense, she collapsed into the arms of the man who'd killed her husband.

CHAPTER TWO

"WHAT IN BLAZES...?"

Luke folded his arms around the bundled-up form who'd just pitched forward. Blinking hard in an attempt to get his eyes to focus, he zeroed in on a face that had once been burned into his brain, a face he'd cursed himself for cherishing when he had no right at all. He'd seen that precious face only minutes ago in the sweetest dream he'd ever had. For an instant he wondered if he was still dreaming.

No, he could feel her shape, crushed against his chest. He drank in the sight of her. Her long, black hair was tucked up in a stocking cap. Her cheeks, normally pale as cream, had been tinted a too-bright pink by the cold. Her blue eyes were shadowed with what might have been pain, but there was no mistaking his sister-in-law.

"Jessie," he whispered, worriedly taking in the lines of strain on her forehead, the trickle of sweat that was likely to turn to ice if he didn't get her out of the freezing night in a hurry.

When in hell had it turned so bitter? he wondered, shivering himself. There hadn't been a snowflake in sight when he'd sent Consuela off. Now he couldn't see a patch of uncovered ground anywhere. Couldn't see much of anything beyond the porch, for that matter.

More important than any of that, what was his sister-in-law doing here of all places? Was she ill? Feverish? She would have had to be practically delusional or desperate to turn up on his doorstep.

He scooped her up, rocking back on his heels with the unexpected weight of her, startled that the little slip of a thing he'd remembered was bulging out of her coat. She moaned and clutched at her belly, shuddering against him.

She's going to have a baby, he realized at last, finally catching on to what would have been obvious to anyone who was not in an alcohol-altered state of mind. No one in the family had told him that. Not that he'd done more than exchange pleasantries with any of them in months. And Jessie would have been the last person they would have mentioned. Everyone walked on eggshells around him when it came to anything having to do with his late brother. If only they had known, if only they had realized that his guilt was compounded because he'd fallen for Erik's wife, they would never have spoken to him at all.

"You're going to have a baby," he announced in an awestruck tone.

Bright blue eyes, dulled by pain, snapped open. "You always were quick, Lucas," Jessie said tartly. "Do you suppose you could get me to a bed and find Consuela before I deliver right here in the foyer?"

"You're going to have a baby *now?*" he demanded incredulously, as the immediacy of the problem sank in. He would have dropped her if she hadn't been clinging to his neck with the grip of a championship arm wrestler.

"That would be my best guess," she agreed.

Luke was so stunned—so damned drunk—he couldn't seem to come to any rational decision. If Jessie had realized his condition, she would have headed for the barn and relied on one of the horses for help. He had a mare who was probably more adept at deliveries than he was at this precise moment. His old goat, Chester, was pretty savvy, too. Jessie would have been in better hands with them, than she likely was with him.

"Lucas?" Her voice was low and sweet as honey. "Could you please..."

He sighed just listening to her. The sweetest little voice in all of Texas.

"Get me into a bed!"

The shout accomplished what nothing else had. He began to move. He staggered ever so slightly, but he got her into the closest bedroom, his, and settled her in the middle of sheets still rumpled from the previous night. And several nights before that, as near as he could recall. He'd ordered Consuela to stay the hell out of his bedroom after he'd found little packets of some sweet-smelling stuff in his sock drawer.

He stood gazing down at Jessie, rhapsodizing to himself about her presence in his bed, marveling at the size of that belly, awestruck by the fact that she was going to have a baby here and now.

"Luke," she said in a raspy voice that was edged with tension. "I'm going to need a little help here."

"Help?" he repeated blankly.

"My clothes."

"Oh." He blinked rapidly as he watched her trying to struggle out of her coat. Awkwardly, she shrugged it off one shoulder, then the other. When she started to fumble with the buttons on her blouse, his throat worked and his pulse zoomed into the stratosphere.

"Lucas!"

The shout got his attention. "Oh, yeah. Right," he said and tried to help with the buttons.

For a man who'd undressed any number of women in his time, he was suddenly all thumbs. In fact, getting Jessie out of her clothes—the simple cotton blouse, the oddly made jeans, the lacy bra and panties—was an act of torture no man should have to endure. Trying to be helpful, she wriggled and squirmed in a way that brought his fingers into contact with warm, smooth skin far too frequently. Trying to look everywhere except at her wasn't helping him with the task either. Every glimpse of bare flesh made his knees go weak.

The second she was stripped bare, he muffled a groan, averted his gaze and hunted down one of his shirts. He did it for his own salvation, not because she seemed aware of anything except the demands her baby was making on her body. Surely there was a special place in hell for a man whose thoughts were on sex when a woman was about to have a baby right before his eyes.

She looked tiny—except for that impressively swollen belly—and frightened as a doe caught in a hunter's sights. He felt a powerful need to comfort her, if only he could string an entire sentence together without giving away his inebriated state. If she knew precisely how drunk he was, she wouldn't be scared. She'd be flat-out terrified, and rightfully so. He wasn't so serene himself.

"Where's Consuela?" she asked, then let out a scream that shook the rafters. She latched on to his hand so hard he was sure that at least three bones cracked. That grip did serve a purpose, though. It snapped him back to reality. Pain had a way of making a man focus on the essentials.

The baby clearly wasn't going to wait for him to sober up. It wasn't going to wait for a doctor, even if one could make it to the ranch on the icy roads, which Luke doubted.

"Consuela's in Mexico by now," he confessed without thinking. "She left earlier today." When panic immediately darkened her eyes, he instinctively patted her hand. "It's going to be okay, darlin'. Don't you worry about a thing."

"I'm...not...worried," she said between gasps. "Shouldn't you boil water or something?"

Water? Water was good, he decided. He had no idea what he'd do with it, but if it got him out of this bedroom for five seconds so he could try to gather his scattered thoughts, it had to be good. Coffee would be even better. Gallons of it.

"You'll be okay for a minute?" He grabbed a key chain made of braided leather off his dresser and gave it to her. "Hang on to this if another pain hits while I'm gone, okay? Bite into it or something." It had worked for cowboys being operated on under primitive conditions, or so he'd read. Of course, they'd also been liberally dosed with alcohol at the time.

Jessie's blue eyes regarded the leather doubtfully, but she nodded gamely. "Hurry, Luke. I don't know much about labor, but I don't think there's a lot of time left."

"I'll be back before you know it," he promised. Stone-cold sober, if he could manage it.

He fumbled the first pot he grabbed, spilled water everywhere, then finally got it onto the stove with the gas flame turned to high. With a couple of false starts, he got the coffee going as well, strong enough to wake the dead, which was pretty much how he felt.

For a moment he clung to the counter and tried to steady himself. It was going to be okay, he vowed. He'd delivered foals and calves. How much different could delivering a baby be? Of course, mares and cows had a pretty good notion of what they were doing. They didn't need a lot of assistance from him unless they got into trouble.

Jessie, on the other hand, seemed even more bemused by this state of affairs than he was. She'd obviously been counting on a doctor, a team of comforting nurses, a nice, sterile delivery room and plenty of high-tech equipment. A shot of some kind of painkiller, too, more than likely. What she was getting was a drunken amateur in an isolated ranch house. It hardly seemed fair after all she'd already been through. After all he'd put her through, he amended.

An agonized scream cut through the air and sent panic slicing through him. He tore down the hall to the bedroom. He found her panting, her face scrunched up with pain, sweat beading up on her brow and pouring down her cheeks. Damned if he didn't think she looked beautiful, anyway. The door to that place in hell gaped wider.

"You okay?" he asked, then shook himself. "Sorry. Dumb question. Of course, you're not okay."

He grabbed a clean washcloth from the linen closet, dashed into the bathroom to soak it with cool water, then wiped her brow. He might not be exactly sober yet, but his brain was beginning to function and his limbs were following orders. For the first time, he honestly believed they could get through this without calamity striking.

"You're doing fine," he soothed. "This is one hell of a pickle, but nothing we can't manage."

"Did...you...call...a doctor?" she asked.

A doctor? Why hadn't he acted on that thought back when he'd had it himself? Maybe because he'd figured it would be futile. More likely, because his brain cells had shut down hours ago just the way he'd wanted them to.

"Next thing on my list," he assured her.

She eyed him doubtfully. "You...have...a list?"

"Of course I have a list," he said, injecting a confident note into his voice. "The water's boiling. The coffee's on."

"Coffee?"

"For me. You don't want me falling asleep in the middle of all the fun, do you?"

"I doubt there's much chance of that," she said, sighing as the pain visibly eased.

Her gaze traveled over him from head to toe, examining him so intently that it was all Luke could do not to squirm. Under other circumstances, that examination would have made his pulse buck so hard he wouldn't have recovered for days. As it was, he looked away as fast as he could. Obviously, this was some sort of penance dreamed up for his sins. He was going to be stranded with Jessie, forced to deliver his brother's baby, and then he was going to have to watch the two of them walk out of his life. Unless, of course...

"Luke, can I ask you a question?"

He was relieved by the interruption. There was only heartache in the direction his thoughts were taking. "Seeing how we're going to be getting pretty intimate here in a bit, I suppose you can ask me anything you like."

"Are you drunk?"

He had hoped she hadn't noticed. "Darlin', I don't think you want to know the answer to that."

This time he doubted Jessie's groan of anguish had anything to do with her labor pains.

"Luke?"

"Yes, Jessie."

"Maybe you'd better bring me a very big glass of whatever it was you were drinking."

He grinned at the wistful note in her voice. "Darlin', when this baby turns up, you and I are going to drink one hell of a toast. Until then, I think maybe we'd both better stay as far away from that bottle as we can. Besides, as best I can recall, I smashed it against the fireplace."

She regarded him with pleading blue eyes. "Luke, please? I'm not sure I can do this without help. There's bound to be another bottle of something around here."

He thought of the cabinet filled with whiskey, considered getting a couple of shots to help both of them, then dismissed the temptation as a very bad idea. "You've got all the help you could possibly need. I'm right here with you. Besides, alcohol's not good for the baby. Haven't you read all those headlines warning about that very thing?"

"I don't think the baby's going to be inside me long enough to get so much as a sip," she said.

As if to prove her point, her body was seized with another contraction. Going with sheer instinct, Luke reached out and placed his hand over her taut belly. The skin was smooth and tight as a drum as he massaged it gently until the muscles relaxed.

He checked his watch, talked to her, and waited for the next contraction. It came three minutes later.

He wiped her brow. "Hang in there, darlin'. I'll be right back."

She leveled a blue-eyed glare on him. "Don't you dare leave me," she commanded in a tone that could have stopped the D-Day invasion.

"I'm not going far. I just want some nice, sterile water in here when the baby makes its appearance. And we could use a blanket." And something to cut the umbilical cord, he thought as his brain finally began to kick in without prodding.

He'd never moved with more speed in his life. He tested the phone and discovered the lines were down. No surprise in this weather. He sterilized a basin, filled it with water, then cleaned the sharpest knife he could find with alcohol. He deliberately gave a wide berth to the cabinet with the whiskey. He was back in the bedroom before the next pain hit.

"See there. I didn't abandon you. Did you take natural childbirth classes?"

Jessie nodded. "Started two weeks ago. We'd barely gotten to the breathing part."

"Then we're in great shape," he said with confidence. "You're going to come through this like a champ." The truth was he was filled with admiration for her. He'd always known she had more strength and courage than most women he'd known, but tonight she was proving it in spades.

"Did you call a doctor?" she asked again.

"I tried. I couldn't get through. Don't let it worry you, though. You're doing just fine. Nature's doing all the work. The doctor would just be window dressing."

Jessie shot him a baleful look.

"Okay," he admitted. "It would be nice to have an expert on hand, but this baby's coming no matter who's coaching it into the world, so we might just as well count our blessings that you got to my house. What were you doing out all alone on a night like this anyway?"

"Going to your parents' house," she said. "They invited me for the holidays."

Luke couldn't believe that they'd allowed her to drive this close to the delivery of their first grandchild. "Why the hell didn't Daddy fly you over?"

"He offered. I'm not crazy about flying in such a little plane, though. I told him the doctor had forbidden it."

Luke suspected that was only half the story. He grinned at her. "You sure that was it? Or did that streak of independence in you get you to say no, before you'd even given the matter serious thought?"

A tired smile came and went in a heartbeat. "Maybe."

He hitched a chair up beside the bed and tucked her hand in his. He would not, *would not* allow himself to think about how sweet it was to be sitting here with her like this, despite the fact that only circumstance had forced them together.

"Can't say that I blame you," he said. "If you don't kick up a fuss with Daddy every now and then, next thing you know he's running your life."

"Harlan just wants what's best for his family," she said.

Luke smiled at her prompt defense of her father-in-law. One thing about Jessie, she'd always been fair to a fault. She'd even told anyone who'd listen that she didn't blame him for Erik's death, even with the facts staring her straight in the face. It didn't matter. He'd blamed himself enough for both of them.

"Dad's also dead certain that he's the only one who knows what's best," he added. "Sometimes, though, he misses the mark by a mile."

Her gaze honed in on him. "You're talking about Erik, aren't you? You're thinking about how your father talked him into staying in ranching. If Harlan had let him go, maybe he'd still be alive."

And if Luke had been on that tractor, instead of his brother, Erik would be here right now, he thought. He'd known Erik couldn't manage the thing on the rough terrain, but he'd sent him out there, anyway. He'd told him to grow up and do the job or get out of ranching if he couldn't hack it. Guilt cut through him at the memory of that last bitter dispute.

He glanced at Jessie. The mention of Erik threw a barrier up between them as impenetrable as a brick wall. For once, Luke was glad when the next contraction came. And the next. And the one after that. So fast now, that there was no time to think, no time to do anything except help Jessie's baby into the world.

"Push, darlin'," Luke coaxed.

Jessie screamed. Luke cursed.

"Push, dammit!"

"You don't like how I'm doing it, you take over," she snapped right back at him.

Luke laughed. "That's my Jessie. Sass me all you like, if it helps, but push! Come on, darlin'. I'm afraid this part here is entirely up to you. If I could do it for you, I would."

"Luke?"

There was a plaintive, fearful note in her voice that brought his gaze up to meet hers. "What?"

"What if something goes wrong?"

"Nothing is going to go wrong," he promised. "Everything's moved along right on schedule so far, hasn't it?"

"Luke, I'm having this baby in a ranch house. Doesn't that suggest that the schedule has been busted to hell?"

"Your schedule maybe. Obviously the baby has a mind of its own. No wonder, given the way you take charge of your life. You're strong and brave and your baby's going to be just exactly like you," he said reassuringly.

"I think I've changed my mind," she said with a note of determination in her voice. "I'm not ready for this. I'm not ready to be a mother. I can't cope with a baby on my own."

Luke laughed. "Too late now. Looks to me like that horse is out of the barn."

Moments later, a sense of awe spread through him at the first glimpse of the baby's head, covered with dark, wet hair.

"My God, Jessie, I can see the baby. Just a little more work, darlin', and you'll have a fine, healthy baby in your arms. That's it. Harder. Push harder."

"I can't," she wailed.

"You can," Luke insisted. "Here we go, darlin'." He slid his hands under the baby's tiny shoulders. "One more." Jessie bore down like a trooper and the baby slipped into his hands.

"Luke," Jessie whispered at once. "Is the baby okay? I don't hear anything."

The baby let out a healthy yowl. Luke beamed at both of them. "I think that's your answer," he said.

He surveyed the squalling baby he was holding. "Let's see now. Ten tiny fingers. Ten itsy-bitsy toes. And the prettiest, sassiest blue eyes you ever did see. Just like her mama's."

"Her?" Jessie repeated. She struggled to prop herself up to get a look. "It's a girl?"

"A beautiful little angel," he affirmed as he cleaned the baby up, wrapped her in a huge blanket and laid her in Jessie's arms.

Even though her eyes were shadowed by exhaustion, even though her voice was raspy from screaming, the sight of her daughter brought the kind of smile to Jessie's face that Luke had doubted he would ever see again.

She looked up at him, her eyes filled with gratitude and warmth, and his heart flipped over. A world of forbidden possibilities taunted him.

"She is beautiful, isn't she?" Jessie said, her gaze locked on the tiny bundle in her arms.

"Just about the most gorgeous baby I've ever seen," he agreed, thinking how desperately he wished he could claim her as his own. His and Jessie's. He forced the thought aside. "Do you have a name picked out?"

"I thought I did," she said. "But I've changed my mind."

"Oh? Why is that?"

"Because she rushed things and decided to come at Christmas," she explained. "I'm going to call her Angela. That way I'll always remember that she was my Christmas miracle." She turned a misty-eyed gaze on Luke. "Thank you, Lucas."

If he lived a hundred years, Luke knew he would trade everything for this one moment out of time.

Later the guilt and recriminations would come back with a vengeance. Jessie would remember who he was and what he had done to ruin her life. The blame, no matter how hard she denied it, would be there between them.

But right now, for this one brief, shining moment, they were united, a part of something incredibly special that he could hold in his heart all the rest of his lonely days. They had shared a miracle.

CHAPTER THREE

JESSIE FELT AS if she'd run a couple of marathons back-to-back, but not even that bone-weary exhaustion could take away the incredible sense of joy that spread through her at the sight of her daughter sleeping so peacefully in her arms. Her seemingly healthy baby girl. Her little angel with the lousy sense of timing.

For perhaps the dozenth time since dawn had stolen into the room, bathing it in a soft light, she examined fingers and toes with a sense of amazement that anyone so small could be so perfect. Her gaze honed in on that tiny bow of a mouth, already forming the instinctive, faint smacking sounds of hunger even as she slept. Any minute now she would wake up and demand to be fed.

"Luke, she's hungry," Jessie announced with a mixture of awe and pride that quickly turned to worry. Not once during all the hours of labor or since had she given a single thought to what happened next. "What'll we do?"

Given their past history, it was amazing how quickly she'd come to rely on Luke, how easily she'd pushed aside all of her anger and grief just to make it through this crisis. And, despite his less than alert state on her arrival, despite all the reasons he had for never wanting to see her again, he hadn't let her down yet.

Of course, judging from the way he was sprawled in the easy chair in a corner of the bedroom with his eyes closed, the last bit of adrenaline that had gotten him through the delivery had finally worn off.

Faint, gray light filtered through the frosted window and cast him in shadows. She studied him surreptitiously and saw the toll the past months—or some mighty hard drinking—had taken on him.

The lines that time and weather had carved in his tanned, rugged face seemed deeper than ever. His jaw was shadowed by a day or more's growth of beard. His dark brown hair, which he'd always worn defiantly long, swept the edge of his collar. He looked far more like a dangerous rebel than the successful Texas rancher he was.

If he looked physically unkempt, his clothes were worse. His plaid flannel shirt was clean but rumpled, as if he'd grabbed it from a basket on his way to the door. It was unevenly buttoned and untucked, leaving a mat of dark chest hair intriguingly visible. The jeans he'd hauled on were dusty and snug and unbuttoned at the waist.

Jessie grinned as her gaze dropped to his feet. He had on one blue sock. The other foot was bare. She found the sight oddly touching. Clearly he'd never given a thought to himself all during the night. He'd concentrated on her and seeing to it that Angela made it safely into the world. She would never forget what he'd done for her.

"Luke?" she repeated softly.

The whisper accomplished what her intense scrutiny had not. His dark brown eyes snapped open. "Hmm?" He blinked. "Everything okay?"

"The baby's hungry. What'll we do?"

"Feed her?" he suggested with a spark of amusement.

"Thanks so much." She couldn't keep the faint sarcasm from her voice, but she smiled as she realized how often during the night she'd caught a rare teasing note in Luke's manner. In all the time she'd lived with Erik she'd never seen that side of Luke. He'd been brusque more often than not, curt to the point of rudeness. His attitude might have intimidated her, if she hadn't seen the occasional flashes of something lost and lonely in his eyes. In the past few hours, she'd seen another side of him altogether—strong, protective, unflappable. The perfect person to have around in a crisis. The kind of man on whom a woman could rely.

"Anytime," he teased despite her nasty tone.

Once again he'd surprised her, causing her to wonder if the quiet humor had always been there, if it had simply been overshadowed by his brothers' high spirits.

Still, Jessie was in no mood for levity, as welcome a change as it was. "Luke, I'm serious. She's going to start howling any second now. I can tell. And this diaper you cut from one of your old flannel shirts is sopping. We can't keep cutting up your clothes every time she's wet."

"I have shirts I haven't even taken out of their boxes yet," he said, making light of her concern for his wardrobe. "If I lose a few, it's for a good cause. Besides, I think she looks festive in red plaid."

As he spoke, he approached the bed warily, as if suddenly uncertain if he had a right to draw so close. He touched the baby's head with his fingertips in a caress so gentle that Jessie's breath snagged in her throat.

"As for her being hungry, last I heard, there was nothing better than a mama's own milk for a little one," he said, his gaze fixed on the baby.

"I wasn't planning on nursing her," Jessie protested. "It won't work with the job I have. She'll have to be with a sitter all day. I need bottles, formula." She moaned. There were rare times—and this was one of them—when she wondered how she would cope. She'd counted on Erik to be there for her and the baby. Now every decision, every bit of the responsibility, was on her shoulders.

"Well, given that she decided not to wait for you to get to a hospital or to arrange for a fancy set of bottles," Luke said, still sounding infinitely patient with her, "I'd say Angela is just going to have to settle for what's on hand for the time being. Don't you suppose you can switch her to a bottle easily enough?"

"How should I know?" she snapped unreasonably.

Luke's gaze caught hers. "You okay?"

"Just peachy."

His expression softened. "Aw, Jessie, don't start panicking now. The worst is over."

"But I don't know what to do," she countered, unexpectedly battling tears. "I have three more classes to take just to learn how to breathe right for the delivery, and a whole stack of baby books to read, and I was going to fix up a nursery." She sobbed, "I... I even...bought the wallpaper."

Her sobs seemed to alarm him, but Luke stayed right where he was. Her presence here might be a burden, her tears a nuisance, but he didn't bolt, as many men might have. Once more that unflappable response calmed Jessie.

"Seems to me you can forget the classes," he observed dryly, teasing a smile from her. "As for the wallpaper, you'll get to it when you can. I doubt Angela will have much to say about the decor, as long as her bed's warm and dry. And babies were being born and fed long before anybody thought to write parenting books. If you're not up to nursing her yet, it seems to me I heard babies can have a little sugar water."

"How would you know a thing like that?"

"I was trapped once in a doctor's office with only some magazines on parenting to read."

His gaze landed on her breasts, then shifted away immediately. Jessie felt her breasts swell where his gaze had touched. Her nipples hardened. The effect could have been achieved because of the natural changes in her body over the past twenty-four hours, but she didn't think that was it. Luke had always had that effect on her. A single look had been capable of making her weak in the knees. She had despised that responsiveness in herself. She was no prouder of it now.

"I have a hunch that left to your own devices, the two of you can figure it out," he said. "I'll leave you alone. I've got chores to do, anyway."

He headed for the door as if he couldn't get away from the two of them fast enough. Jessie glanced up at him then and saw that, while his cheeks were an embarrassed red, there was an expression in his eyes that was harder to read. Wistfulness, maybe? Sorrow? Regret?

"You'll holler if you need me?" he said as he edged through the doorway. Despite the offer of help, he sounded as if he hoped he'd never have to make good on it.

"You'd better believe it," she said.

A slow, unexpected grin spread across his face. "And I guess we both know what a powerful set of lungs you've got. I'm surprised the folks on every other ranch in the county haven't shown up by now to see what all the fuss was about."

"A gentleman wouldn't mention that," she teased.

"Probably not," he agreed. Then, in the space of a heartbeat, his expression turned dark and forbidding. "It would be a mistake to think that I'm a gentleman, Jessie. A big mistake."

The warning startled her, coming as it did on the heels of hours of gentle kindness. She couldn't guess why Luke was suddenly so determined to put them back on the old, uneasy footing, especially since they were likely to be stranded together for some time if the snow kept up through the day as it seemed set on doing.

Maybe it was for the best, though. She didn't want to forget what had happened to Erik. And she certainly didn't want to be disloyal to her husband by starting to trust the man who rightly or wrongly held himself responsible for Erik's death. That would be the worst form of betrayal, worse in some ways perhaps than the secret, unbidden responses of her body. Luke had delivered her baby. She might be grateful for that, but it didn't put the past to rest.

"Well, Angela, I guess we're just going to have to make the best of this," she murmured.

Even as she spoke, she wasn't entirely certain whether she was referring to her first fumbling attempt at breast-feeding or to the hours, maybe even days she was likely to spend in Luke's deliberately ill-tempered company.

Days, she knew, she was likely to spend worrying over how great the temptation was to forgive him for what he'd done.

AN HOUR LATER, the chores done, Luke stood in the doorway of his bedroom, a boulder-size lump lodged in his throat as he watched Jessie sleeping. The apparently well-fed and contented baby was nestled in her arms, her tiny bottom now covered in bright blue plaid. Erik's baby, he reminded himself sharply, when longing would have him claiming her—claiming both of them—for his own.

Sweet Jesus, how was he supposed to get through the next few days until the storm ended, the phone lines were up and the roads were cleared enough for him to get word to his family to hightail it over here and take Jessie off his hands? He'd gotten through the night only because he'd been in a daze and because there were so many things to be done that he hadn't had time to think or feel. Now that his head was clear and the crisis was past, he was swamped with feelings he had no right having.

He forced himself to back away from the door and head for his office. He supposed he could barricade himself inside and give Jessie the run of the house. He doubted she would need explanations for his desire to stay out of her path. Now that her baby was safely delivered, she would no doubt be overjoyed to see the last of him.

Last night had been about need and urgency. They had faced a genuine crisis together and survived. In the calm light of today, though, that urgency was past. He could retreat behind his cloak of guilt. Jessie would never have to know what sweet torment the past few hours had been.

He actually managed to convince himself that hiding out was possible as morning turned into afternoon without a sound from his bedroom. He napped on the sofa in his office off and on, swearing to himself that he was simply too tired to climb the stairs to one of the guest suites. The pitiful truth of it was that he wanted to be within earshot of the faintest cry from either Jessie or the baby. A part of him yearned to be the one they depended on.

Shortly before dusk, he headed back to the barn to feed the horses and Chester. The wind was still howling, creating drifts of snow that made the walk laborious. Still, he couldn't help relishing the cold. It wiped away the last traces of fog from his head. He vowed then and there that no matter how bad things got, he would never, ever try to down an entire bottle of whiskey on his own again. The brief oblivion wasn't worth the hangover.

And he hoped like hell he never again had to perform anything as important as delivering a baby with his brain clouded as it had been the night before.

He lingered over the afternoon chores as long as he could justify. He even sat for a while, doling out pieces of apple to the goat, muttering under his breath about the insanity of his feelings for a woman so far beyond his reach. Chester seemed to understand, which was more than he could say for himself.

When he realized he was about to start polishing his already well-kept saddle for the second time in a single day, he forced himself back to the house and the emotional dangers inside. Chester, sensing his indecisiveness, actually butted him gently toward the door.

The back door was barely closed behind him when he heard the baby's cries. He stopped in his tracks and waited for Jessie's murmured attempts to soothe her daughter. Instead, the howls only escalated.

Shrugging off his coat and tossing it in the general direction of the hook on the wall, Luke cautiously headed for the bedroom. He found Jessie still sound asleep, while Angela kicked and screamed beside her. Luke grinned. The kid had unquestionably inherited Jessie's powerful set of lungs. Definitely opera singer caliber.

Taking pity on her worn-out mama, he scooped the baby into his arms and carried her into the kitchen. Once there, he was at a loss.

He held the tiny bundle aloft and stared into wide, innocent eyes that shimmered with tears. "So, kid, it looks like it's just you and me for the time being. Your mama's tuckered out. Can't say I blame her. Getting you into the world was a lot of hard work."

The flood of tears dried up. Angela's gaze remained fixed on his face so attentively that Luke was encouraged to go on. "Seems to me that both of us have a lot to learn," he said, keeping his voice low and even, in a tone he hoped might lull her back to sleep. "For instance, I don't know if you were screaming your head off in there because you're hungry or because you're soaking wet or because you're just in need of a little attention."

He patted her bottom as he spoke. It was dry. She blew a bubble, which didn't answer the question but indicated Luke was definitely on the right track.

"I'm guessing attention," he said. "I'm also guessing that won't last. Any minute now that pretty little face of yours is going to turn red and you're going to be bellowing to be fed. Seems a shame to wake your mama up, though. How about we try to improvise?"

Angela waved her fist in what he took for an approving gesture.

"Okay, then. A little sugar water ought to do it." Cradling her in one arm, he ran some water into a pan, added a little sugar and turned on the burner to warm it. Unfortunately, getting it from the saucepan into the baby required a little more ingenuity.

Luke considered the possibilities. A medicine dropper might work. He'd nourished a few abandoned animals that way as a kid, as well as an entire litter of kittens when the mother'd been killed. One glance into Angela's darkening expression told him he was going to have to do better than that and fast.

"Chester," he muttered in a sudden burst of inspiration. When the old goat had wandered into the path of a mean-spirited bull, Luke had wound up nursing him with a baby bottle for months while he recovered. Where the hell had he put the bottle?

Angela whimpered a protest at the delay.

"Shhh, sweetheart. Everything's going to be just dandy," he promised as he yanked open every single cupboard door in the kitchen. Consuela had the whole place so organized that a single old baby bottle should have stood out like a sore thumb. If it was there, though, he couldn't find it, which meant it was probably out in the barn. He couldn't very well take the baby out there looking for it.

"Damn!" he muttered under his breath.

Huge tears spilled down the baby's cheeks. Obviously she sensed that his plan was falling apart. Any second now she was clearly going to make her impatience known with angry, ear-splitting screams.

"Hey," Luke soothed. "Have I let you down yet?"

Spying Consuela's rubber gloves beside the sink, he had another flash of inspiration. He snatched them up, put another pot of water on to boil, then tossed the gloves in to sterilize them. He found a sewing kit in a drawer, extracted a needle and tossed that in as well.

So far, so good, he reassured himself. The problem came when he judged everything to be sterile. He couldn't poke a hole in one of the glove's fingers and then fill it with warm water while still holding the baby. He grabbed a roasting pan that looked to be about the right size, padded it with a couple of clean dish towels and settled the baby onto the makeshift bed. Judging from the shade of red that her face turned, she was not happy about being abandoned.

"It's only for a minute," he promised her as he completed the preparations by tying a bit of string tightly around the top of the glove. He eyed the water-filled thumb of the glove with skepticism, waiting for the contents to gush out, but it appeared the hole he'd made was just right. He held it triumphantly where Angela could see it. "There! Now didn't I tell you we could manage this? We're a hell of a team, angel."

He picked her up, then sank onto one of the hard kitchen chairs and offered her the improvised bottle. Her mouth clamped on it eagerly and within seconds she was sucking noisily. Luke regarded her with pride.

"You are brilliant," he applauded. "Absolutely the smartest baby ever born."

"You're pretty smart yourself," a sleepy—and damnably sexy—voice commented.

Luke's heart slammed against his ribs. He refused to look up, refused to permit himself so much as a single glance at the tousled hair or bare legs or full, swollen breasts he'd dreamed about too many times to count.

Unfortunately Jessie pulled out a chair smack in his line of vision. She was still wearing his shirt, which came barely to mid-thigh. Her shapely legs were in full view. How many times had he envisioned those legs clamped around him as he made love to her? Enough to condemn his spirit to eternal hell, no doubt about it.

"Feeling rested?" he inquired huskily, keeping his eyes determinedly on the baby he held.

"Some. When did the baby wake up?"

"About a half hour ago. She was hungry."

"So I see."

He could feel a dull, red flush climbing into his cheeks. "I didn't want to wake you. I figured we could manage. It gave me a chance to test that theory I read. Seems to be working. She likes it."

"I'm impressed."

He stood so suddenly that the makeshift bottle slid from Angela's mouth. She protested loudly. Luke shoved both baby and water into Jessie's arms.

"I have work to do." There was no mistaking the sudden expression of dismay in Jessie's eyes, the flicker of hurt at his harsh tone. He managed to grit out a few more words before fleeing. "Help yourself to whatever you need. I'll be in my office."

"Luke, you don't have to run off," she said quietly.

Something in her tone drew his gaze back to her face. The longing he read there shook him more than anything that had happened so far. "Yes, I do," he said tightly.

"Please, I'd like the company."

"No." He practically shouted the word as he bolted.

Her expression stayed with him. Had it truly been longing, he wondered to himself when he was safely away from the kitchen, a locked oak door between him and temptation. Surely he'd been mistaken. No sooner had he reached that conclusion than he cursed himself for a fool. Of course, Jessie was yearning for something right now, but not for him.

No, he told himself sternly, that look had been meant for her husband. It was only natural at a time like this that she would be thinking of Erik, missing him, wishing that he were the one beside her as she fed their first precious baby. Luke was nothing more than a poor substitute.

There was only one way he could think of to keep from making another dangerous mistake like that one. He had to stay inside this room with the door securely locked...and temptation on the other side of it.

CHAPTER FOUR

UNFORTUNATELY, TEMPTATION DIDN'T seem inclined to stay out of Luke's path. Only one person could be tapping on his office door not an hour after he'd stalked off in a huff and left her all alone with her baby in the kitchen. Since that display of temper obviously hadn't scared her off, he wondered if she'd have sense enough to take the hint and go away if he didn't answer. He waited, still and silent, listening for some whisper of movement that would indicate she'd retreated as he desperately wanted her to do.

"Luke?" Jessie called softly. "Are you asleep?"

Apparently she didn't have a grain of sense, Luke decided with a sigh. "No, I'm awake. Come on in."

She opened the door and stood at the threshold, shifting uneasily under the glare he had to force himself to direct her way. Despite his irritation, he couldn't seem to take his eyes off her.

She'd wound her long hair up into some sort of knot on top of her head, but it threatened to spill down her back at any second. Luke stared at it in fascination, wondering what she'd do if he helped it along, if he tangled his fingers in those silky strands and tugged her close. An image of their bodies entwined flashed in his head with such vivid intensity it left him momentarily speechless—and racked with guilt.

"Are you hungry?" she asked quietly, ignoring the lack of welcome. "I've fixed enough supper for both of us. I hope you don't mind."

Luke thought of all the reasons he should reject the gesture. If not that, then tell her to bring the food to him in his office. Sharing a meal seemed like a lousy idea. He had no business sitting down across from her, making small talk, acting as if they were a couple or even as if they were friends. Every contact reminded him of the feelings he'd had for her while she'd been married to his brother. Every moment they were in the same room reminded him that those feelings hadn't died. He owed it to her—to both of them—to keep his distance.

Just when he planned to refuse her invitation to supper, he caught the hesitancy in her eyes, the anxious frown and realized that Jessie was every bit as uncertain about their present circumstances as he was. There apparently wasn't a lot of protocol for being stranded with the man responsible for a husband's death, especially when those feelings were all tangled up with feeling beholden to him for delivering her baby.

"Give me a minute," he said with a sigh of resignation.

He watched as she nodded, then closed the door. He shut his eyes and prayed for strength. The truth of it was it would take him an hour, maybe even days to be ready for the kind of time he was being forced to spend with his brother's widow. He had only seconds, not enough time to plan, far too much time to panic, to think of all the dangers represented by having Jessie in his home.

As soon as he'd gathered some semblance of composure, he got to his feet, gave himself a stern lecture about eating whatever she'd fixed in total, uncompromising silence, and then racing hell-bent for leather back to the safety of his den. That decided, he set out to find her.

When he reached the kitchen, where she'd chosen to serve the dinner on the huge oak table in front of a brick fireplace that Consuela had persuaded him to build, the first words out of his mouth were, "I don't want you waiting on me while you're here."

It was hardly a gracious comment, but he had to lay down a few rules or it would be far too easy to fall into a comfortable pattern that would feed all the emotions that had been simmering in him for years now.

She leveled her calm, blue-eyed gaze on him. "We both have to eat. It's no more trouble to fix for two people than it is for one," she said as she dished up a heaping spoonful of mashed potatoes. She passed the bowl to him.

Luke didn't have an argument for that that wouldn't sound even more ungracious than he'd already been, so he kept his mouth clamped shut and his attention focused on the food. The potatoes were creamy with milk and butter. The gravy was smooth and flavored with beef stock, just the way he liked it. The chicken fried steak was melt-in-the-mouth tender. The green beans had been cooked with salt pork.

"When did you have time to do all this?" he asked. He studied her worriedly, looking for signs of exhaustion. She looked radiant. "You're not even supposed to be on your feet yet, are you?"

"There wasn't much to do. Consuela saw to most of it. I've never seen so many little prepackaged, home-cooked meals. She must have been stocking your freezer for a month. How long is she going to be gone, anyway? Or has she abandoned you for good, because of your foul temper?"

"I wouldn't blame her if she had, but no." Luke allowed himself a brief, rueful grin. "She figured company might be dropping by during the holidays, but I doubt she imagined it happening quite this way."

"Neither did you, I suspect." Jessie's penetrating gaze cut right through him. "You'd holed up in here for the duration, hadn't you? You were planning to spend the holidays with your buddy Jack Daniel's." She gestured toward the cabinets. "I saw your supply."

Luke winced at the direct hit. "I've only touched one bottle and I smashed it halfway through," he said defensively.

"Too bad you didn't do it sooner," she observed.

"If I'd known you—and especially Angela—were coming, I would have."

"Now that we are here, what happens next?"

He regarded her cautiously. "What's your real question, Jessie? You might as well spit it out."

Her glance went back to the cabinet. "Are you planning to finish off the rest?"

"Not unless I'm driven to it," he said pointedly.

This time Jessie winced. "Believe me, I know what an imposition this is. We'll be out of your hair as soon as the roads are passable." She glanced toward the windows, where the steadily falling snow was visible. "When do you suppose that will be?"

Luke shrugged. "Don't know. I haven't heard a weather report."

"Are the phones still out?"

"Haven't tried 'em since last night."

"Don't you have a cellular phone? That ought to be working."

To be perfectly honest, Luke hadn't given his cellular phone a thought. He still wasn't used to carrying the damned thing around with him. Keeping track of it was a nuisance. It was probably outside on the seat of his pickup. "I'll check next time I have to go to the barn."

"I could get it. I need to get the rest of my clothes from my car."

Luke cursed himself for not thinking of that. Of course, she'd had luggage with her if she'd been intending a stay at White Pines for the holidays.

"I'll get 'em," he said, pushing away from the table, leaving most of his food uneaten. The excuse was just what he needed to escape this pleasure-pain of sitting across from her in a mockery of a normal relationship between a man and a woman.

"Finish your supper first."

"I'm not hungry," he lied. "I'll get something later. Besides, I'm sure you're anxious to call the folks with the good news. They'll be thrilled to know that you and Erik have a daughter. Doubt they'll be quite so thrilled to hear where you had it though. Dad will want to fly in a specialist to check you and the baby out. He'll probably have a med-evac copter in here before the night's out."

Though he couldn't quite keep the bitterness out of his tone, Jessie grinned at his assessment. "He probably will, won't he? But not even Harlan Adams can defy nature. Nobody's going to be taking off or landing in this blizzard."

"They will if Daddy pays them enough," Luke retorted dryly.

"Well, I won't have it," Jessie retorted with a familiar touch of defiance. "Nobody needs to risk a life on my account. The baby and I are perfectly fine here with you and I intend to tell Harlan exactly that."

Luke had to admire the show of gumption. Obviously, though, Jessie hadn't had to stand up to his father when he got a notion into his head. To save her the fight she couldn't win, he found himself saying, "Maybe it would be best not to make that call, then."

Jessie actually looked as if she was considering it. "But they'll be worried sick about me not showing up last night," she said eventually. "I have to let them know I'm okay."

So, reason had prevailed after all. Luke was more disappointed than he cared to admit.

"Darlin', they've seen the weather," he said, beginning a token and quite probably futile argument, one he had no business making in the first place. Perversity kept him talking, though. "Their phone lines are probably down, too. They'll understand that you probably had to stop along the way and can't get through to let them know."

"Not five seconds ago you were telling me I didn't know your daddy. Now who's kidding himself? Harlan probably has a search party organized. The Texas Rangers are probably out on full alert, sweeping the highways for signs of my car."

There was no denying the truth of that. Luke stood. "Then I suppose we'd better head them off at the pass. I'll get the phone."

He grabbed his heavy sheepskin jacket from the peg by the back door, realizing as he did that Jessie must have hung it there. As he recalled, he'd merely tossed it in that general direction when he'd heard the baby crying earlier. As he pulled it on, he could almost feel her touch. He imagined there was even the faint, lingering scent of her caught up in the fabric.

Outside, the swirling snow and bitter cold cleared his head and wiped away the dangerous sense of cozy familiarity he'd begun to feel sitting at that old oak table with Jessie across from him. He took his time getting Jessie's belongings from her car, then lingered a little longer in the cab of his truck.

As he'd suspected, the cellular phone was on the passenger seat. All he had to do was pick it up and dial home. There wasn't a doubt in his mind that his father would find some way to get Jessie out of his hair before dawn. He would be alone again and safe.

Christmas was only three days away, New Year's a week after that. Surely he could get through so few days without resorting to his original plan of facing them stinking drunk. And heaven knew, Jessie would be better off with his family where the celebrations would be in high gear despite the weather, despite his family's private mourning, where there would be dozens of people to fuss over Angela.

Feeling downright noble about the sacrifice he was making, he actually managed to pick up the phone. But when it came to dialing it, he couldn't bring himself to do it. He thought of the incredible, once-in-a-lifetime miracle he and Jessie had shared. He remembered how it had felt to hold Angela in his arms, to have those trusting, innocent eyes focused on him. Jessie and Angela's unexpected presence had been a gift from a benevolent God, who apparently didn't think his soul was beyond repair.

Would it be so wrong to steal a few more hours, maybe even a day or two with Jessie and Angela? Who could possibly be hurt by it?

Not Erik. He was way past being hurt by anything, not even the knowledge that his brother coveted his widow.

Not Jessie, because Luke would never in a million years act on the feelings she stirred in him.

Not the baby. There was no way he would ever allow anything or anyone to harm that precious child. His paternal instincts, which he'd not even been aware he possessed, had kicked in with the kind of vengeance that made a man reassess his entire existence.

So the only person who might be harmed by his deception would be himself. He stood to lose big time by pretending for even the briefest of moments that Jessie and Angela were a part of his life. Emotions he'd squelched with savage determination were already sneaking past his defenses. The mere fact that he was considering hiding the cellular phone was proof of that.

And yet, he couldn't bring himself to let them go just yet. He'd fallen for Angela as hard as he'd fallen for her mother. Looking into those big blue eyes, he'd felt a connection as strong and powerful as anything he'd ever felt before in his life. He couldn't sever it, not until he understood it.

Likewise, he couldn't watch Jessie disappear until he had finally processed this terrible hold she had on him. From the moment he'd set eyes on her, he'd been riveted. If a bolt of lightning had struck him at that instant, he doubted he would have noticed.

Over time he'd grown to admire her sharp wit, bask in her sensitivity, but in that first instant there had been only a gut-deep attraction unlike anything he'd ever experienced before or since. She had the same effect on him now. He was a man of reason. Surely he could analyze their relationship with cold, calculating logic and finally put it to rest.

He gripped the phone a little tighter and glanced around at the drifts of snow that were growing deeper with each passing minute. A quick toss and no one would find the sucker before spring.

Just as he was about to act on his impulse, that reason of which he was so proud kicked in. What if there was a genuine emergency? The cellular phone might be their only link to the outside world. Instead of burying it in snow, he tucked it into the truck's glove compartment, behind the assortment of maps and grain receipts and who-knew-what-else had been jammed in there without thought. Then he turned the lock securely and glanced guiltily back at the house, wondering if Jessie would guess that he was deliberately keeping her stranded, wondering what her reaction would be if she did know.

Even through the swirling snow, he could see the smoke rising from the chimney, the lights beckoning from the windows. An unexpected sense of peace stole over him. Suddenly, for the first time since he'd built it simply to make a statement to his father—a declaration of independence from Harlan Adams and his need to maintain a tight-fisted control over his sons—the huge, far-too-big monster of a house seemed like a home.

JESSIE COULDN'T IMAGINE what was taking Luke so long. Surely Luke hadn't lost his way in the storm. Though the snowfall was still steady, it was nowhere near as fierce and blinding as it had been.

And he knew every acre of his land as intimately as he might a woman. His voice low and seductive, he'd boasted often enough of every rise and dip, every verdant pasture. He'd done it just to rile his father with his independence, but that didn't lessen the depth of his pride or his sensual appreciation for the land. No, Luke wasn't lost, which meant he was dallying intentionally.

While he was taking his sweet time about getting back, she was tiring quickly. The last burst of adrenaline had long since worn off. She had already cleaned up the remains of the supper they'd barely touched, washed the dishes and put them away. For the past five minutes she'd been standing at the back door, peering into the contrasting world of impenetrable black and brilliant white.

She thought she could see Luke's shadow in the truck and wondered for a moment if he had a bottle stashed there. That array she'd found in his cupboard had worried her. She had never known him to take more than a social drink or two before, had never seen him as on-his-butt drunk as he'd been the night before when she'd arrived.

When at last he climbed out of the truck and headed for the house, she watched his progress with a critical eye. He didn't seem to be staggering, no more so than anyone would be in the deep snow. Shivering at the blast of frigid air, she nonetheless planted herself squarely in the middle of the open doorway, so he couldn't pass by without her getting a whiff of his breath.

"Everything okay?" she called as he neared.

"Fine. Get back inside before you freeze."

Jessie didn't budge. "You took so long I got worried."

He brushed past her, bringing the fresh scent of snow and the tingle of icy air into the house with him. There was no telltale trace of liquor mingling with the crisp winter aromas. She sighed with relief as she closed the door tightly against the night.

"Couldn't find the phone," he announced as he plunked her bags in the middle of the floor. "I'm always forgetting it someplace or another. It'll turn up."

Jessie regarded him suspiciously. His tone seemed a little too hearty. "What about a CB? You must have one and I know your folks do."

"Mine's on the fritz. Haven't seen any reason to get it fixed since I got the phone."

He was deliberately avoiding her gaze. "Luke?" she began quizzically.

He glanced her way for the briefest of seconds. "What?"

Jessie debated calling him on what she suspected were a series of lies, then chastised herself for being far too suspicious. What possible motive would he have for lying? There wasn't a doubt in her mind that he wanted her gone just as badly as she wanted to go. Getting him to the dinner table hadn't been easy. Getting him to stay there had been impossible. He'd seized the first excuse he could to escape. Obviously he wasn't anxious to close the gap that had formed between them when Erik had died on this very ranch.

Last night's emergency and Luke's gentle, caring response to it had been an aberration brought on by extraordinary circumstances. Now they were back to the status quo. She couldn't help the vague feeling of disappointment that stole through her.

Finally she shook her head. "Nothing. I'll take my things to the bedroom." She glanced at him. "Or would you rather I take them to one of the guest suites upstairs?"

Luke seemed unduly angered by the question. "I can take them and you'll stay in the room you're in now."

"But there's no reason for me to put you out of your own room, when there are bedrooms galore upstairs." Left unspoken was the fact that every time she thought about having delivered her baby not simply in Luke's house, but in his bed, an odd sensation stirred in the pit of her stomach. It was a sensation that wouldn't bear too close a scrutiny.

Luke's jaw took on the stubborn set that was a family trait. Erik had been equally bullheaded, his chin perpetually at the same defiant tilt. Yet Erik had been easily swayed, easily reasoned with. Luke, to the contrary, was no pushover.

"Jessie, you'll stay downstairs for as long as you're here," he insisted. "You won't have to climb stairs."

"But I'll be in your way," she protested.

His gaze settled on her. "You won't be in my way," he said with soft emphasis. "This is the way I want it."

She retreated from the argument she clearly had no way of winning. It was his house. She'd stay where he wanted her. "I'll be going to my room, then."

Before she could reach for her bags, Luke shot her a warning look, then picked them up and preceded her down the hall. Inside the room with its dark wood and masculine decor, he deposited the suitcases, then whirled to leave, practically colliding with her in his haste. Jessie's hands immediately went out to steady herself, landing on his chest. Luke jerked as if he'd been brushed by a branding iron. Their gazes clashed, then caught.

"Sorry," she murmured, pulling her hands away.

"Are you okay?"

"You just startled me when you turned around so fast. I stumbled a bit, that's all."

Luke shook his head ruefully. "I'm not used to having to watch out for other people underfoot. It's one of the habits that comes from living alone. Well, not alone exactly. Consuela's here, but she's used to dodging me. To hear her tell it, I've got all the grace of a bull in a china shop. Did I tell you she went to visit her family in Mexico?"

Listening to him, Jessie couldn't stop the smile that tugged at the corners of her mouth. "Lucas, you're babbling," she teased. "Are you nervous for some reason?"

"Nervous?" he repeated the word as if he were testing it. "What would I have to be nervous about?"

"That's what I was wondering. It's not as if we're strangers." Jessie blushed despite herself. "Especially after last night."

A dull red flush crept up Luke's neck. "Maybe it would be best if we didn't talk too much about last night."

"But what you did for me..." She tried to think of the right words to express her gratitude.

"I did what anybody would have under the circumstances."

"That's not true. Luke, if you hadn't been here, if you hadn't been who you are..."

"Who I am? You mean Erik's brother," he said on an odd, flat note.

"No," she said emphatically. "I mean the kind of man you are, completely unflappable, gentle, competent." She trembled when she thought of the tragedy his presence and his calm, quick actions had averted. "My God, Luke, you delivered my daughter, and if you were even half as terrified as I was, you never let on to me."

"Try three or four times as terrified," he corrected. "I just talked a good game."

Jessie reached up and rested her hand against his stubbled cheek, felt a faint shudder whisper through him, saw his eyes darken. "Don't joke," she chided. "I'm serious. I'm trying to thank you properly for what you did, for bringing my baby safely into the world. I'll never forget it."

"There's no need for thanks," he said, brushing aside her gratitude.

"There is," she insisted, trying to think of an adequate way of showing him how grateful she was. The perfect gesture suddenly came to her and she blurted it out impulsively, not pausing to think of the implications. "In fact, I would be honored if you would consider being Angela's godfather. I know that's what Erik would have wanted, too."

Luke's eyes turned cold and he broke away from her touch. "You're wrong, if you think that," he said flatly. "I'm the last man in the world Erik would want anywhere near you or your daughter."

Too late, Jessie realized she couldn't have shattered the quiet moment any more effectively if she'd tossed a live hand grenade into the room. By mentioning Erik, by reminding Luke of his brother, she had destroyed their fragile accord.

"Luke, that's not true..." she began, but she was talking to herself. Luke had fled from the room as if he'd just been caught committing a crime and a posse of lawmen were after him, guns already blazing.

Troubled, Jessie stared after him. Not until she heard her daughter whimper did she move. Picking Angela up from her makeshift bed, a blanket-lined drawer, she paced the floor with her until she quieted.

"You know something, angel? Your uncle Luke is a very complicated, perplexing man."

No one knew more clearly than she did how dangerous those two traits could be in a man, especially for a woman who enjoyed nothing more than solving puzzles.

CHAPTER FIVE

THERE WAS A huge stack of unpaid bills on Luke's desk. Normally he hated sitting there with a calculator, checking the totals against his own records, writing the checks, meticulously balancing the books. The process bored him. The mistakes irritated him. If he'd wanted to do this much math, he'd have been a damned accountant.

Tonight, though, the tedium of the assignment drew him. In fact, he hadn't been able to leave that bedroom fast enough to get to his office and shut the door behind him. Only a vague sense of the absurdity of the action kept him from bolting it.

At any rate, as long as he had to concentrate on numbers written out in black and white, numbers that either added up or didn't, he wouldn't have to think about the woman in his bedroom who made no sense to him at all.

What had possessed Jessie to suggest that he be godfather to Angela? Couldn't she see how inappropriate that was? Couldn't she guess how deeply hurt the rest of the family would be over her choice? Hell, they probably wouldn't even show up for the baptism. They'd be certain she'd placed the baby's very soul in jeopardy by selecting her father's killer as the baby's godparent.

Okay, she was grateful for his help in delivering the baby. He could understand that. He didn't think thanks were necessary, but if Jessie did, she could have found a dozen ways of thanking him that wouldn't turn the entire family inside out. A framed snapshot of the baby would have sufficed. A dutiful note would have covered it.

Instead, with all the impulsiveness and generosity he'd always admired in her, she had made a grand gesture that would have ripped the family apart. They would have chosen sides. In the end, more than likely Jordan and Cody would have backed Jessie's choice. His parents would have been appalled.

Even he cared enough for the family's feelings to want to avoid deliberately causing them any more anguish.

Fortunately, his head at least had been clear. He'd said no before she could get too carried away with her planning.

He raked his hand through his hair and muttered an oath under his breath. A tiny part of him regretted the necessity for declining her offer. Being godparent to the baby he'd helped deliver would have bound him to Jessie and Angela. It would have kept him on the fringes of their lives. It would have placed him where no one would have questioned his involvement, where he could watch out for them.

Where he could torture himself, he added bleakly. Saying no had been the right decision, the only decision.

Determinedly, he picked up the first invoice from the pile on his desk and went to work. Sometime between the first bill and the second, he fell soundly asleep. The next thing he knew it was morning and the very woman who'd been tormenting him in his dreams was hovering around in his office as if she belonged there.

"What the hell are you doing?" he asked crankily, rubbing his aching shoulders as he eyed Jessie warily. For a woman who'd just had a baby less than forty-eight hours before, she was damned energetic. Normally he'd consider that an admirable trait, but at the moment it seemed a nuisance to have her bustling around as if he weren't even there. "Jessie, whatever you're up to, give it a rest."

"I'm getting some light in here. It's dark as pitch." She drew back the draperies with a flick of her wrist, revealing the blinding glare of sunlight on snow.

"Beautiful, isn't it?" she asked cheerfully. "I'll be back in a minute with your breakfast. You really shouldn't sleep at your desk, Lucas. It's bad for your back."

Given the fact that every muscle between his neck and his butt ached like the very dickens, Luke couldn't argue with her. If she hadn't taken off, though, he would have had a few things to say about her intrusion into his domain. He figured they could wait until she returned. If she brought strong, black coffee with her, he might even moderate his protest to a dull roar.

He stood up cautiously, testing to see if any of his parts actually worked. His legs held him upright, which was better than he deserved. He stretched carefully, slowly working the kinks loose. By the time he heard Jessie's returning footsteps, he was feeling almost civilized. That didn't mean he intended to tolerate her sudden burst of uninvited activity.

Unfortunately for his resolve, the aroma of coffee preceded her into the room. Oblivious to whatever order there might be to his desk, she brushed piles of papers aside and deposited a tray laden with pancakes, eggs, bacon and a pot of coffee. Luke glanced at the new disarray, considered bellowing in outrage, then took another whiff of that coffee and poured himself a cup instead. He sipped it gratefully as he sank back into his leather chair.

Maybe the bustling wasn't so bad, after all. Only trouble now was, she didn't go away. In fact, she seemed to be waiting for something. She hovered at the edge of his desk, her gaze fixed on him as if trying to determine how to broach whatever was on her mind.

"Coffee's good," he said, watching her uneasily. "Thanks."

"You're welcome."

"Don't worry about the dishes. I'll bring them back to the kitchen and wash up when I'm done," he said, hoping she'd take the hint and leave.

She actually grinned at that. "Trying to get rid of me?" she inquired.

Almost as if to taunt him, she pulled up a chair and sat down. What astonished him was the fact that even though she was wearing her oversize maternity clothes, she managed to look as sexy as if she'd been wearing something slinky. His imagination was perfectly capable of envisioning every curve under her shapeless top. As if it might make a difference, he turned his attention to the food she'd brought. He poured syrup on the pancakes and cut into the eggs.

"I told you yesterday that I didn't want you waiting on me," he reminded her even as he took his first bite of pancakes. They were light as air. He knew for a fact that Consuela hadn't left these, which meant Jessie had been cooking. "You need to rest. Taking care of a new baby is tiring. I want you concentrating on Angela."

"Angela's fine. She's been fed. Now she's sleeping. That's what newborns do."

He snapped a piece of crisp bacon into crumbs and prayed for patience. "So, rest while you have the chance. Read a book. The library next door is filled with them."

"Maybe later."

He could see he was getting nowhere. Maybe if he divided up the chores and took the lion's share himself, she'd restrict herself to doing only what she'd been assigned.

"Okay, here's the deal," he said. "I'll fix breakfast and lunch. You can deal with supper, since Consuela already has those dishes prepared and ready to pop into the oven. I'll clean up. Agreed?"

"That hardly sounds fair," she said. "I'll cook all the meals. You clean up."

"No," Luke insisted, his voice tight. "We'll do it my way. And since you've already done breakfast today, I'll handle dinner. You're done for the day. Go take a nap."

"I wonder why I never noticed before what a bully you are," she commented, her expression thoughtful.

The observation didn't seem to trouble her a bit, but he found it insulting. "I am not a bully. I'm just trying to divvy things up fairly."

"You have an odd notion of fair," she observed. "Oh, well, never mind. I won't argue for the moment. Maybe you should consider the pancakes a bribe," she suggested.

Luke's gaze narrowed. "A bribe? For what?"

"So you'll do what I want, of course."

"Which is?"

She opened her mouth, seemed to reconsider, then closed it again. "No, I think we'll wait and talk about it later. I think you could use a little more buttering up." She stood and headed for the door.

Luke stared after her in astonishment. "Jessie!"

His bellow clearly caught her by surprise. She halted in the doorway and looked back. The glance she shot him couldn't have been more innocent if she'd been a newborn baby.

"Yes?" she said.

"What kind of game are you playing here?"

"No game," she insisted.

"You want something, though. What is it?"

"It can wait. Enjoy your breakfast."

"Tell me now," he ordered.

She smiled. "I don't think so."

She closed the door with quiet emphasis before he could even form another question. Suddenly, despite himself, he found himself laughing.

"Well, I'll be damned," he said aloud. "Maybe I underestimated you, after all, Jessie Adams. Seems to me you have gumption to spare, more than enough to take on the Adams men."

On the other side of the door, Jessie heard the laughter and the comment. "You ain't seen nothing yet, Luke Adams," she murmured sweetly.

Unlocking the puzzle that Luke represented had become a challenge she couldn't resist. And drawing Erik's family back together seemed like the best Christmas gift she could possibly give to all of them. She'd come to that conclusion during a long and restless night.

Erik wouldn't have wanted his death to split them apart. He wouldn't have wanted the unspoken accusations, the guilt and blame to stand between Luke and his parents. Whatever had happened on Luke's ranch that day, Erik would never have blamed the big brother he'd idolized. He would have forgiven him. As much as Erik had craved his independence, he had loved his family more. If he hadn't, he might have fought harder to break free from Harlan's influence.

If, if, if...so many turning points, so many choices made, a few of them deeply regretted.

If she had accepted Harlan's offer to fly to his ranch, then the storm and her unexpected labor wouldn't have forced Jessie into accepting Luke's help and his hospitality. If that wasn't a sign from God, she didn't know what was. Obviously, He had given her a mission here and the most readily accessible place to start was with Luke. After all, Christmas was a time for miracles.

With the snow plows uncertain, she figured she had a few days at least to utilize her powers of persuasion. By the time the roads were cleared, she was determined that she and Angela wouldn't be going on to Harlan and Mary's alone to celebrate the new year and a new beginning. Their son would be with her.

BY LATE THAT AFTERNOON, Jessie's plans and her temper were frayed. She hadn't seen more than the flash of Luke's shadow the entire day. He'd managed to sneak lunch onto the table and disappear before she could blink. She'd passed his office, just in time to see him vanish into the library. She'd bundled up and trailed him to the barn, only to see him riding away on horseback. A gimpy old goat had been gamely trying to follow him.

Shivering, she had trudged back inside only to hear Angela screaming at the top of her lungs. Nothing she'd done had settled the baby down. Angela was dry and fed. For the past twenty minutes, Jessie had been rocking her in front of the fire in the kitchen. Angela's great, hiccupping sobs continued unabated.

"A few more minutes of this and you'll have me in tears, too," Jessie murmured in distress. "Come on, sweetheart. You're tired. Go off to sleep, like Mommy's little angel."

Blessed silence greeted the suggestion. Five seconds later, Angela screamed even louder than before. Obviously she'd only taken time off to rev up her engine.

Jessie could feel the first, faint beginnings of panic. Already uncertain

about her mothering skills, her inability to soothe her baby seemed to confirm just how unprepared and inept she was.

Because the rocking seemed to be making both of them more jittery
than serene, she stood and began to pace as she racked her brain for some
new technique to try.

She tried crooning a lullaby, singing an old rock song at full volume, rubbing her back. She was at her wit's end when she heard the back door slam.

Luke hesitated just inside the threshold. "What's all this racket?" he demanded, but there was a teasing note in his voice and a spark of amusement
in his eyes. "I could hear both of you all the way out at the barn. Chester
took off for parts unknown. The horses are trying to hide their heads under
the hay."

"Very funny," Jessie snapped just as Luke reached for the baby. She re-
linquished her all too readily.

"Come here, angel," he murmured consolingly. "You were just missing
Uncle Luke, weren't you?"

Jessie's traitorous daughter gulped back a sob, then cooed happily. Held
in the crook of Luke's arm, she looked tiny, but thoroughly contented. Jessie wanted to warn her that a man's arms weren't a guarantee of protection,
but maybe that was a lesson it was too soon to teach. If the feel of Luke's
strength could silence the baby's cries for now, Jessie had no complaints. She
felt the oddest, most compelling yearning to have his arms around her as
well. With her hormones bouncing around in the wake of the baby's birth,
she seemed to be more insecure than ever.

Luke glanced her way. "Stop hovering. We're doing fine. I'm going to
start supper and Angela's going to help, aren't you, munchkin?"

Jessie sank gratefully onto a kitchen chair and watched Luke's efficient
movements as he pulled packages from the freezer with one hand, all the
while carrying on a nonsensical conversation with the baby. Jessie sighed
with envy as she watched him.

"How do you do that?" she asked.

He shrugged. "Maybe it's like a horse. If it knows you're afraid, it'll buck
you off sure thing. If you handle it with confidence, it'll go along with you."

Jessie sorted through the metaphor and came to the conclusion he thought
she was scared to death of her own daughter. "In other words, I'm lousy
at this."

He shot a glance over his shoulder at her. "Did I say that? I thought I was
saying that she senses you're not sure of yourself."

"Well, I'm not."

"You will be."

"How did you get to be so good with babies?"

"Three younger brothers, I suppose. All three of them had very different temperaments. Jordan was the charmer from day one. He could wheedle anything out of anybody. He gurgled and smiled and cooed. Even Daddy wasn't immune to him. It's no wonder he's been such an incredible business success."

"And Cody?"

"He's the flirt. There hasn't been a woman born he couldn't win over. Daddy couldn't handle him worth a lick. Come to think of it, Mama could never handle him either, but he could always make her think she'd won. He wrapped Consuela around his little finger and, believe me, she's no patsy."

"What about Erik? What was he like?" Jessie asked cautiously, keeping her gaze on Luke's face. His expression didn't change, but he did hesitate. For a moment she almost regretted bringing him up.

"Erik was the diplomat," he said eventually. "He was the master of compromise. If Mama gave him two chores, he'd make her settle for one. If Daddy ordered him to be home at midnight, Erik would compromise for twelve-thirty. He never, ever accepted their first offer. If he'd been in the foreign service, it was a skill that would have served him well. As it was, he compromised himself into waiting for the life he really wanted by offering to prove himself first as a rancher."

There was a note of sorrow in his voice that resonated deep inside Jessie. "He wanted so badly to be a teacher in junior high, the age when kids are testing themselves, and he would have been good at it, too," she said. "He just wanted to please your father."

"He should have known that nothing would impress Daddy except success," Luke said bitterly. "If Erik had stuck to his guns and gone on to be a teacher, if he'd won recognition for that, it would have pleased Daddy more than seeing him trying to be a rancher and failing."

Jessie felt a surge of anger on Erik's behalf. "Don't belittle your brother for trying. At least he admitted that he was staying at the ranch in an attempt to gain your father's approval. You won't even admit that's what you're doing." She waved her hand to encompass the kitchen, the whole house. "Isn't that what all of this is for, to impress your father, to prove you could start from scratch, without a dime of his money and have a bigger, more impressive ranch?"

As if she sensed the sudden tension, Angela whimpered. Luke soothed her with a stroke of his finger across her cheek and a murmured, "Shh, angel. Everything's okay. Your mama and I are just having a slight differ-ence of opinion."

His angry gaze settled on Jessie. "I bought this ranch because ranching is what I do. I built this house because I needed a home."

"How many bedrooms, Luke? Five? Seven? More than there are over at White Pines, I'll bet. And how many rooms do you really live in? Two, maybe three, if you don't count the kitchen as Consuela's domain?"

"What's your point?"

"That you're every bit as desperate for approval from Harlan as Erik ever was. You're just determined to do it by besting him at his own game."

"Or maybe I was just planning ahead for the time when I have a family to share this ranch with me," he said quietly, his gaze pinned on her. "Maybe I was thinking about coming in from the cold and finding the woman I loved in front of the fire, holding my baby."

The softly spoken remark, the seductive, dangerous look in his eyes held Jessie mesmerized. His voice caressed her.

"Maybe I was imagining what it would be like when this was no longer just a house, but a home, filled with warmth and laughter and happiness. Or didn't you ever stop to think that I might have dreams?"

"So why don't you do something to turn it into a home?" she taunted be-fore she could stop herself.

The look he shot her was unreadable, but there was something in the coiled intensity of his body language that sent a thrill shimmering straight through her.

"Perhaps I have," he said, his challenging gaze never leaving hers.

Then, while Jessie's breath was still lodged in her throat, he pressed a kiss to the baby's cheek, handed her back to her mother and sauntered from the room with the confidence of a man who'd just emerged triumphant from a showdown at the OK Corral.

That was the last she saw of him until after the supper she'd been forced to eat alone. She'd spent most of the evening the same way, alone in the kitchen, pondering what Luke had said—and what he hadn't. With the radio tuned to Christmas carols, her mood was a mix of nostalgia and wistful-ness and confusion.

She hadn't especially wanted to spend the holidays with Erik's family, hadn't been much in the mood for celebrating at all in fact, but now that Christmas was only two days away, she couldn't help thinking of the way it had been the year before. She wondered if she would ever recapture those feelings.

The whole family and dozens of friends had been crowded around a gigantic tree, its branches loaded with perfectly matched gold ornaments and tiny white lights, chosen by a decorator. Mary had played carols on the baby grand piano, while the rest of them sang along, their voices more exuberant than on key.

Jessie remembered thinking of all the quiet Christmases as she'd been growing up, all the times she'd longed for a boisterous houseful of people. With her hand tucked in Erik's, she'd been so certain that for the first time she finally understood the joy of the season. Her heart had been filled to overflowing. In agreeing to go to White Pines this year, perhaps she'd been hoping to reclaim that feeling for herself and eventually for her baby.

It seemed unlikely, though, that it would have been the same. Erik had stolen her right to be there from her, wiped it away in an instant of carelessness that she'd never really doubted for a moment was as much his fault as Luke's. Sometimes, when it was dark and she was scared, she blamed Luke, because it hurt too much to blame her husband.

Everything Luke had said earlier was true. Erik had hated working on the ranch, whether his father's or his brother's. He'd had other dreams, but his father had been too strong and Erik too weak to fight. He'd preferred working for Luke, who tolerated his flaws more readily than his father did. He'd accepted his fate by rushing through chores, by doing things haphazardly, probably in a subconscious bid to screw up so badly that his father or Luke would finally fire him.

Well, he'd screwed up royally, all right, but he'd died in the process, costing both of them the future they'd envisioned, costing Angela a father and her the extended family she'd grown to love. Sometimes Jessie was so filled with rage and bitterness over Erik's unthinking selfishness that she was convinced she hated him, that she'd never loved him at all.

At other times, like now, she regretted to her very core all the lost Christmases, all the lost moments in the middle of the night when they would have shared their hopes and dreams, all the children they'd planned on having.

"Jessie?" Luke said, interrupting her sad thoughts as he stood in the kitchen doorway, his hands shoved in the pockets of his jeans. "Are you okay?"

"Just thinking about last year and how much things have changed," she admitted.

Luke's eyes filled with dismay. "I'm sorry. I know facing a Christmas without Erik is the last thing you expected," he said, regarding her worriedly. "Why don't you come on in the living room? I've started a fire in there."

Without argument Jessie stood and followed him. She was frankly surprised by the unexpected invitation, but she had no desire to spend the rest of the evening alone with her thoughts, even if being with Luke stirred feelings in her that she didn't fully understand.

When Luke stood by the fireplace, Jessie crossed over to stand beside him. He looked so sad, so filled with guilt, an agonizing of guilt that had begun some seven months ago for both of them. Instinctively she reached for him, placing her hand on his arm. The muscle was rigid.

She tried to make things right. "I don't blame you for the way things are, Luke. I wanted to. I wanted to lash out at someone and you were the easiest target. You were there. You could have stopped him." She sighed. "The truth is, though, that Erik was always trying to prove himself, taking chances. You couldn't have kept him off that tractor if you'd tried."

He shrugged off her touch. "Maybe not, but I blame myself just the same. Look what I've cost you."

Jessie wanted to explain that it wasn't Erik she missed so much as the feeling of family that had surrounded them all that night as they sang carols. To say that aloud, though, would be a betrayal of her husband, an admission that their life together hadn't been perfect. She owed Erik better than that. He had given her the one thing she'd never had—the feeling of belonging to a family with history and roots.

"Regrets are wasted, Lucas. We should be concentrating on the here and now. It's almost Christmas, the season of hope and renewal," she said.

She glanced around the living room, which looked as it would at any other time of the year—expensive and sterile. It desperately needed a woman's touch. Even more desperately, it needed to be filled with love.

"You'd never even know it was the holidays in here," she chided him. "There's not so much as a single card on display. I'll bet you haven't even opened them."

"Haven't even been out to the mailbox in days," he admitted.

She lifted her gaze to his. "How can you bear it?" Before he could answer, she shook her head. "Never mind. That was what the cabinet full of liquor was all about, wasn't it?"

"Sure," he said angrily. "It was about forgetting for a few blessed days, forgetting Christmas, forgetting Erik, forgetting the guilt that has eaten away at me every single day since my brother died right in front of my eyes."

Jessie flinched under the barrage of heated words. "Sounds like you've been indulging in more than whiskey. You sound like a man who's been wallowing in self-pity."

"Self-loathing," Luke said.

"Has it made you feel better?" she chided before she could stop herself. She'd been there, done that. It hadn't helped. "Has anything been served by you sitting around here being miserable?"

He didn't seem to have an answer for that. He just stared at her, his expression vaguely startled by her outburst.

"Don't you think I feel guilty sometimes, too?" she demanded. "Don't you think I want to curl up in a ball and bemoan the fact that I lost a husband after only two years of marriage? Well, I do."

She was on a roll now, releasing months of pent-up anger and frustration. She scowled at him. "But I for one do not intend to ruin the rest of my life indulging in a lot of wasted emotions. I cried for Erik. I grieved for him. But a part of him lives on in Angela. I think that's something worth celebrating. Maybe you're content to spend the holidays all shut up in this bleak atmosphere, but I'm not."

Oblivious to his startled expression, oblivious to everything except the sudden determination to take charge of her life again, starting here and now, she declared, "The minute I get up tomorrow morning, I am going to make this damned house festive, if I have to make decorations from popcorn and scraps of paper."

She shot him a challenging look. She had had it with his veiled innuendoes and sour mood. "As for you, you can do what you damned well please."

CHAPTER SIX

SITTING RIGHT WHERE he was, staring after Jessie long after she'd gone, Luke realized he hadn't given a thought to Christmas beyond being grateful that he wouldn't be spending it with his family, enduring their arguments and silences, their grief. Consuela had dutifully purchased his gifts to everyone, wrapped them and sent them over to White Pines. He'd merely paid the bills.

Now, though, he would have had to be denser than stone to miss Jessie's declaration that the atmosphere around his house was awfully bleak for the season. That parting shot before she'd gone off to her room had been a challenge if ever he'd heard one. Just thinking about it was likely to keep him up half the night, wondering how he could give them both a holiday they would never forget. There was no question in his mind that with Jessie and Angela in the house, it would be wrong, if not impossible, to ignore the holiday—the baby's first.

A week ago he hadn't expected to feel much like celebrating, but for the past forty-eight hours his mood had been lighter than it had been in months. Part of that was due to Angela's untimely, but triumphant, arrival. She was truly a Christmas blessing. A far greater measure of his happiness was due, though, to this stolen time with Jessie and his sense that she truly didn't blame him for Erik's accident.

He finally admitted at some point in the middle of the night that instead of getting her out of his system, he was allowing her to become more firmly entrenched in his heart. He could readily see now that his initial attraction to Jessie had been pure chemistry, tinged with the magical allure of the forbidden. In some ways, his conscience insisted, she was even more out of reach to him now.

But he knew in his gut that the attraction went beyond her being unavailable to him. Traits he'd only suspected before were clear to him now. He was coming to know her strengths and her weaknesses in a whole new way and nothing he'd discovered disappointed him.

In addition to being beautiful and warmhearted, she was also quick-tempered. In addition to being strong and brave, she was also willful and stubborn. She had a quick wit and a ready laugh, but she could also be a bit of a nag when she believed in her cause. In his view the positives outweighed the negatives. The contrariness only made her more interesting.

Those discoveries solidified his long-held belief that she and Erik had been mismatched from the start. As much as he had adored his younger brother, he'd also recognized that Erik was weak, too weak to stand up to their father, too weak to provide much of a challenge to a woman like Jessie.

He'd wondered more than once what had drawn them together in the first place. Observing them in years past with a sort of detached fascination, he had had no problem guessing why Erik had chosen a woman with Jessie's strengths. Less clear was why she had fallen in love with his brother. The past couple of days had given him some insight into that.

He was beginning to realize that far from being the gold digger she had appeared to some distrusting family members at first glance, Jessie had simply craved being part of a family with history and roots. On the surface, anyway, his family was storybook caliber with its strong men, boisterous affection, deep-rooted ties to the Texas land and abiding sense of loyalty. Erik had been her passport to all of that.

He couldn't help wondering, though, why she had chosen to move across the state after Erik's death, when she could have stayed at White Pines, claimed her rightful place in the family she'd obviously grown to love, and been doted on.

As he understood it, his parents had begged her to stay, especially after they'd learned she was pregnant. Even though it had meant giving up something desperately important to her, Jessie had insisted on going.

Whatever her reasons, he admired her for standing up to them. He also knew she hadn't taken a dime when she'd left. It was yet more testament to her character, proof that she had married Erik for love, not for money.

Lingering in the barn, Luke was leaning against a stall door, still contemplating Jessie, when Chester butted him from behind. The old goat was obviously tired of being ignored. Luke turned on him with mock indignation.

"Hey, what was that all about? Goats who get pushy don't get treats."

Chester didn't get the message. He nudged Luke's coat pocket trying to get at the sections of apple he knew were there. Luke dug them out and fed them to him.

"So, what do you think, Chester? What can I do to make this holiday special?"

Since the goat didn't seem to have any sage advice, Luke headed back toward the house. He was almost there when inspiration struck. He might not be able to deliver a load of gifts or even an album of Christmas carols, but he could certainly come up with a tree.

He detoured to the woodpile for an ax, then headed into the stand of pine trees on the ridge behind the house. He'd planted most of them up there himself, full-grown pines that had cost a fortune. He supposed he'd done it just because his parents had no similar trees, despite the name of their home. The gesture had been some sort of perverse link to his past.

He surveyed the cluster of trees critically, dismissing several as too scrawny, a few more as misshapen, though they'd all seemed perfect to him when he'd chosen them from the nursery. Finally his gaze landed on a tree that was tall and full and fragrant.

He worked up a sweat and an appetite chopping it down, then dragging it through the snow all the way back to the house. Propped up against the back porch railing, the tree seemed ever-so-slightly larger than it had on the ridge. He eyed it uneasily and decided he might have been just a little opti-mistic about fitting it into the house. Still, there was no denying that it was impressive. It made a statement, one he hoped that Jessie couldn't mistake.

After stomping the snow off his boots and dusting it from his clothes, he snuck inside to make sure that Jessie was still in bed. During the night as he'd been sitting awake in the living room staring into the fire, he'd heard her pacing the floor with the baby. Hopefully, she was catching up on lost sleep this morning.

He tiptoed down the hall as silently as a man his size could manage, then edged the bedroom door open a crack. Down for the count, he decided, after watching the soft rise and fall of her chest for several seconds more than was entirely necessary.

Angela, however, was another story. In her makeshift bed, a drawer they had lined with blankets, she was cooing to herself and waving her arms as if to let him know she was ready for an adventure. Luke couldn't resist the invitation. There was something about holding that tiny bundle of brand new life in his arms that filled him with a sense of hope.

Swearing to himself that he was only picking the baby up to keep her from waking Jessie, he carried her, bed and all, into the kitchen. Those serious eyes of hers remained fixed on him trustingly all the way down the hall. He was certain they were filled with anticipation, indicating she was ready to try anything. He figured she was destined to break a good many hearts with what seemed to him her already-evident daredevil nature.

"Now, then, sweet pea, can you be very quiet while I bring the tree in? Just wait till you see it. It's your very first Christmas tree and, if I do say so myself, it's just about the prettiest one I've ever seen."

Angela seemed willing to be temporarily abandoned. Luke was on the porch and back in a flash, lugging the tree through the kitchen and into the living room. He found the perfect spot for it in the nook formed by a huge bay window. As soon as he'd put it down, he went back into the kitchen for the baby. This time he plucked her out of her bed and carried her in his arms, admiring the simple red plaid sleeper Jessie had apparently stitched up from another one of his old shirts.

"So, what do you think?" he asked as he stood before the tree, admiring the sweep of its branches against the ten-foot-high ceiling. Placing it in a stand, assuming he even had one that would fit its thick trunk, definitely would require a little trimming at the top.

Angela seemed fascinated. He echoed her approval. "Pretty awesome, huh? Wait till you see it with lights and decorations. You won't be able to take your eyes off it."

The only problem was the lights, the decorations and the tree stand were all stored upstairs. He had a hunch she wouldn't tolerate being put back in that drawer again. "Now that is a quandary," he said to Angela. "But we can solve it, can't we? I'll just settle you right here on the floor so you can see, put some pillows around you in case you happen to be precocious enough to roll over. I think that's a little advanced even for someone of your brilliance, but there's no point in taking chances."

Angela's face scrunched up the instant he deposited her among the pillows. He propped her up so she had a better view of the tree, an arrangement which seemed to improve her disposition. "Now don't let me down, angel," he cajoled. "No crying, okay? I promise I'll be back before you can say Santa Claus."

He darted worried glances over his shoulder all the way out of the room. The baby seemed to have settled into her nest without a fuss. He doubted her contentment would last, though.

Thankfully, Consuela was the most organized human being he'd ever met. The Christmas decorations were tidily stacked and labeled in a storage closet, where he'd insisted they remain this year. She'd succeeded in sneaking a fat, pine-scented candle and a table decoration into the dining room, but that was all she'd dared after his firm instructions.

Luke managed to get all the boxes into his arms at once, then juggled them awkwardly as he made his way back downstairs. The boxes began to wobble dangerously halfway down. The top one tumbled off, then the one after that. There was no mistaking the tinkling sound of glass breaking. Mixed with his muttered oaths and Angela's first faint whimpers, it was apparently more than enough to wake Jessie.

He'd just turned the corner to the living room when she came staggering out of the bedroom, sleepily swiping at her eyes. "What's going on? Where's Angela?"

Luke stepped in front of her and blocked her view of the living room. "Everything's under control. Why don't you go back to bed? You must be exhausted after being up half the night."

"I'm awake now. What broke?"

"Nothing important."

"What's all that stuff you're carrying?"

"For someone who's half-asleep, you ask a lot of questions. Did you get a job I don't know about as a reporter?"

Ignoring the question, she blinked and took a step closer. Her heavy-lidded gaze studied the boxes. When the contents finally registered, her face lit up with astonishment. "Christmas decorations?"

Luke sighed. So much for his surprise. "Christmas decorations," he confirmed, then shifted out of her way so she could see past him.

"I thought Angela should have a tree for her first Christmas," he admitted sheepishly. "You made it pretty clear last night how you felt about the lack of holiday spirit around here. I decided you were right."

Jessie's eyes widened. "Luke, it's…"

"Awesome?" he suggested, after trying to study the tree objectively. Despite the impressive size of the room, the tree took up a significant portion of it.

"Huge," Jessie declared.

"I know. It didn't look nearly as big outside."

Before he realized what she intended, Jessie turned and threw her arms around his neck. "Thank you," she said, kissing him soundly.

Her lips were warm and pliant against his, impossibly seductive. The impulsive gesture almost caused him to drop the remaining boxes. "Jessie!" he protested softly, though there was some doubt in his mind if he was warning her away to save the decorations or his sanity.

She regarded him uncertainly for the space of a heartbeat, but apparently she chose to believe he was worried about the ornaments. She claimed several of the boxes and carried them into the living room. Then she took a thorough survey of the tree and pronounced it the most incredible tree she had ever seen. The glint of excitement in her eyes was enough to make Luke's knees go weak. If she ever directed a look half so ecstatic at him, he could die a happy man.

"Don't do a thing until I get back," she demanded as she headed from the room.

"Where are you going?"

"To get dressed and to make hot chocolate."

He thought she looked exquisite in her robe, a pale pink concoction that was all impractical satin and lace. As for the hot chocolate, he was plenty warm enough as it was. "Not on my account," he said.

"On mine," she said, visibly shivering. "I'm freezing in this robe."

The innocent comment lured him to look for evidence. He found it not in the expected goose bumps, but in the press of hard nipples against the robe's slinky fabric. "I'll turn the heat up," he countered eventually. Anything to keep her in that softly caressing robe.

Apparently she caught the choked note in his voice or the direction of his gaze, because her expression faltered a bit. A delectable shade of pink tinted her cheeks. "It'll only take a minute," she insisted. "Besides, we can't possibly decorate a tree without hot chocolate. I'm pretty sure there's a law to that effect."

Luke found himself grinning at the nonsense. "Well, we are nothing if not law abiding around here. I'll test the lights while you're gone."

"But don't start stringing them on the tree, okay? I want to help."

"You mean you want to give orders."

She grinned back at him and his heart flipped over. "Maybe," she admitted. "But you wouldn't want to end up with blank spaces and have to do it all over again, would you?"

He shot her a look that was part dare, part skepticism. "Who says I'd do it over?"

"It is Angela's first tree," she reminded him in that sweet, coaxing tone she used so effectively. "You want it to be perfect, don't you?"

He laughed. "So that's how it's going to be, is it? One teeny little mistake and you're going to accuse me of traumatizing the baby's entire perception of Christmas?"

He glanced down at Angela and saw that she'd fallen fast asleep amid her nest of pillows. "Look," he said triumphantly. "She's not even interested."

Jessie waved off the claim. "She won't sleep forever. Test the lights, but that's all, Lucas."

"Yes, ma'am."

When she'd gone, Luke tried to recall the last time he'd taken orders from anyone. Not once that he could think of since moving out of his father's house. More important, this was absolutely the only time he'd ever taken orders and actually enjoyed it.

SOMETHING HAD CHANGED OVERNIGHT, Jessie decided as she searched through her luggage for the festive red maternity sweater she'd bought for the holidays. She'd fallen in love with the scattered seed pearl trim around the neckline. Except for its roominess, it made a stylish ensemble with a pair of equally bright stirrup pants and dressy flats.

Suddenly she was overwhelmed by the Christmas spirit. It wasn't just the sight of that incredible tree. It was Luke's thoughtfulness in getting it for her. There was no mistaking that the tree and his shift in mood were his gifts to her.

She thought she'd seen something else in his eyes, as well, something she didn't dare examine too closely for fear she would confirm the attraction that had scared her away from White Pines.

Twenty minutes after she'd left him, she was back with a tray filled with mugs of steaming hot chocolate topped with marshmallows, and a plate of Christmas cookies she'd found in a tin, plus slices of her own homemade fruitcake. It made an odd sort of breakfast, but who cared? It fit the occasion. She also brought along the radio, which she immediately tuned to a station playing carols.

"Now?" Luke asked dryly, when she had everything set up to her satisfaction.

Jessie surveyed the ambience and nodded. "Ready. Did you check the lights?"

"All the strands are working," he confirmed. "More than we could possibly need even for this monster. I suspect half of them were used outside last year." He regarded her with a teasing glint in his eyes. "I assume you have a blueprint of some kind for their placement."

"Very funny."

He held out the first strand. "It's all yours."

Jessie's enthusiasm faltered slightly as her gaze traveled up the towering tree. "You have to do the first strand. I can't reach the top."

"I brought in a ladder."

She shot him a baleful look. "Never mind. Heights make me dizzy." So did Luke, but that was another story entirely. She was finding the powerful nature of her reactions to him increasingly worrisome.

"Are you sure you can trust me to do it right?" he teased.

"Of course," she said blithely. "I'll be directing you."

To his credit, he actually took direction fairly well. He seemed to lose patience only when she made him shift an entire strand one level of branches higher. "It'll be dark there, if you don't," she insisted.

"There are going to be a thousand lights on this tree at the rate we're going," he argued. "Nobody's even going to see the branches."

She turned her sweetest gaze on him. "The baby will like the lights."

The argument worked like a charm. Luke sighed and moved the strand.

"I'd better check the fuses before we turn this thing on," he complained. "It'll probably blow the power for miles around."

"Stop fussing. It's going to be spectacular. Let's do the ornaments next."

"Where did you intend to hang them? There's no space left."

She hid a grin at the grumbling. "Lucas, I could do this by myself."

He actually chuckled at that. "But you'd miss half the fun."

Jessie narrowed her gaze. "Which is?"

"Bossing me around."

"You have a point," she said agreeably. "But admit it, you're getting into the holiday spirit."

The teasing spark in his eyes turned suddenly serious. There was an unexpected warmth in his expression that made Jessie's pulse skitter wildly.

"I suppose I am," he said so quietly that she could practically hear the beating of her heart. "Can I tell you something?"

Jessie swallowed hard. "Anything."

"It's the first Christmas tree I've ever decorated."

She stared at him incredulously. "You're kidding."

He shook his head. "Mother always hired some decorator, who'd arrive with a new batch of the most stylish ornaments in the current holiday color scheme. We were never even allowed to be underfoot. By January second, it was all neatly cleared away, never to be duplicated."

"That's terrible," Jessie said. "I just assumed..."

"That we had some warm family tradition, like something out of a fairy-tale," he concluded. "You were there. You saw the fuss Mother made over choosing the design for the tree."

"I thought maybe it was something she'd started to do after you were all older and the family started doing more formal entertaining during the holidays."

"Nope. Not even when we came home from school with little handmade decorations. Those went on Consuela's tree. I think she still has them all. Mother paid a fortune for the perfect tree. She wasn't about to have the design marred by tacky ornaments made by her children."

Jessie's heart ached for the four boys who'd been deprived of the kind of tradition she'd always clung to. When she looked his way again, Luke's thoughtful gaze was on her as if he was waiting for her reaction to having one of her myths about his family shattered.

"Where are those decorations now?" she asked, clearly surprising him.

"In Consuela's suite, I suppose. Why?"

"Can you find them?"

He gave her an odd look. "Jessie, there's no need to get all sentimental about a bunch of construction paper and plaster of paris decorations."

"I want them on this tree," she insisted.

Luke shook his head at what he obviously considered a fanciful demand. "I'll take a look later."

"Promise?"

"I promise." He played along and solemnly crossed his heart. "What about you, Jessie? What was it like at your house?"

"Quiet," she said, thinking back to those days that had been a mix of happy traditions and inexplicable loneliness. "There were just the three of us. By the time I was adopted, my parents were already turning forty. There were no grandparents. I always thought how wonderful it would be if only there were aunts and uncles and cousins, but both of my parents had been only children."

"Is that why you were coming back to White Pines this year? Did you want to maintain the ties so your baby would eventually have the large family you'd missed?"

"That was part of it. That and wanting her to know she's an Adams. I don't have that sense of the past that you have. I suppose it can be a blessing and a curse—Erik certainly saw it that way—but I envy it more than I can tell you."

"Why didn't you ever search for your biological parents?"

She recalled how badly she'd once wanted to do exactly that. "I thought about it right after I learned I was adopted," she admitted. "But my parents were so distressed by the idea that I put it aside."

He paused in hanging the decorations and studied her from atop the ladder. "Is it still important to you?"

Jessie felt his gaze on her and looked up at him from her spot on the floor amid the rapidly emptying boxes. "I think it is," she said quietly. "It's as though there's a piece of me missing and I'll never be whole until I find it. It's funny. I thought Erik and your family could fill that space, but I was wrong. It's still there."

Luke climbed down from the ladder, then hunkered down in front of her and rested his hands on her knees. His gaze was even with hers and filled with compassion. "Then do it, Jessie. Find that missing part. I'll help in any way I can."

Something deep inside her blossomed under the warmth of his gaze. And for the first time she could ever recall, it seemed there was no empty place after all.

CHAPTER SEVEN

THOUGH IT TESTED her patience terribly, Jessie agreed with Luke's idea that they not turn on the tree lights until evening. The decision to wait left her brimming with an inexplicable sense of anticipation, almost as if she were a child again. She could recall year after year when she'd huddled in her bed, pretending to sleep, listening for the sound of reindeer on the roof, the soft thud of Santa landing on the hearth after a slide down the chimney. She wanted those kinds of memories for her daughter, those and more.

She wanted Angela to grow up with memories of Christmas Eves gathered around a piano singing carols, of midnight church services, and of the chaos of Christmas morning with dozens of cousins and aunts and uncles. She couldn't give her those things, but Erik's family could. And as difficult as it might be at times to be around Luke without touching him, without openly loving him, she would see to it that the connection with the Adamses was never severed.

She glanced up to find Luke's gaze on her. She smiled, her eyes misty. "We'll make it sort of a Christmas Eve ceremony," she said, wondering at the magic that shimmered through her at the hint they were starting a tradition of their own. The memory of it was something she could hold tight, something no one could criticize or take away from her.

And yet, judging from the intent way Luke studied her, there must have been a note of sadness in her voice she hadn't realized was there.

"Are you sorry you're not spending Christmas Eve at my parents' house?" he asked.

There was an odd undercurrent to the question that Jessie couldn't interpret. Was he regretting not acting more aggressively to get her out of his hair? Or was the question exactly what it seemed? Was he worrying about her feelings?

"It's not the Christmas I was anticipating," she admitted, and saw the immediate and surprising flare of disappointment in his eyes. She hurried to reassure him. "It's better, Luke. No one could have done more to make this holiday special. You made sure I had a healthy baby. And how could I possibly regret the first Christmas with my daughter, wherever it is?"

Luke glanced at the baby she held cradled in her arms. Angela had just been fed and was already falling asleep again, her expression contented.

"She is what this season is all about, isn't she?" he said. "They say we don't always do so well with our own lives, but we can try harder to see that our children experience all of the magic of the holidays, that they get everything they deserve out of life."

His bleak tone puzzled her. "Luke, you sound as if your life is over and hasn't turned out the way you expected. That's crazy. There's still lots of time for you to fulfill all your dreams."

His inscrutable gaze met hers. Something deep in his eyes reached out and touched her. It was that odd sense of connection she'd felt so often in the past, as if their souls understood things they'd never spoken of.

"I'm not so sure about that," he said quietly. "I think maybe I missed out on the one thing that makes life worth living."

"Which is?" she asked, her voice oddly choked.

"Love."

Something in the way he was looking at her turned Jessie's blood hot. Her pulse thumped unsteadily. There was no mistaking the desire in his hooded eyes, the longing threading through his voice.

Nor was there any way to deny the stubborn set of his jaw that said he would never act on whatever feelings he might have for her. Fueled by guilt or conscience, he had declared her off limits.

Which was as it should be, Jessie told herself staunchly. Yet she couldn't explain the warring of regret and relief that his silent decision stirred in her. Stranded here with him, she didn't dare explore any of her feelings too closely, but she had been reminded sharply of all of them. Most especially she had remembered how a simple glance could warm her, how easily the soft caress of Luke's voice could send a tremor of pure bliss rippling through her.

At White Pines, with Erik alive, those responses had been forbidden. She had felt the deep sting of betrayal every time she hadn't been able to control her reaction to her husband's brother. Now it seemed the denials had gone for naught. Luke had reawakened her senses without even trying. He, thank goodness, appeared far more capable of pretending, though, that he hadn't. The charade of casual distance between them would be maintained to protect them both from making a terrible mistake.

"I think I'll put Angela down for a while," she said, practically dashing from the room that vibrated with unspoken longings.

Only after she had the baby safely tucked into her makeshift bed again, only after she was curled up in a blanket herself did she give free rein to the wild fantasies that Luke set off in her. Dangerous, forbidden fantasies. Fantasies that hadn't died, after all, not even after her attempt to put time and distance between herself and this complex man who'd found a spot in her heart with his unspoken compassion and strength of character.

"Oh, Lucas," she whispered miserably. "How could I have done it? How could I have gone and fallen in love with you?"

There was no point in denying that love was what she was feeling. She had fought it practically from the moment she'd first set eyes on him. She had run from it, leaving him and White Pines behind. But three nights ago, when Luke had been there for her, when he had safely delivered her baby and treated her with such tenderness and compassion, the powerful feelings had come back with a vengeance.

That didn't mean she couldn't go on denying them with every breath left in her. She owed that to Erik.

More than that, she knew as well as Luke obviously did, the kind of terrible price they would pay, the loss of respect from the rest of the family if he ever admitted what she was beginning to suspect…that he was in love with her as well.

LUKE WAS SLOWLY but surely going out of his mind. There wasn't a doubt about it. Another few days of the kind of torment that Jessie's presence was putting him through and he'd be round the bend. His body was so hard, so often, that he wondered why he hadn't exploded.

All it took was a whispered remark, an innocent glance, a casual caress and he reacted as if he were being seduced, which was clearly the farthest thing from Jessie's mind. There were times it seemed she could barely stand to be in the same room with him. She'd bolted so often, even a blind man would have gotten the message.

He couldn't understand why she, of all the women in the world, had this mesmerizing effect on him. Maybe guilt had made all of his senses sharper, he consoled himself. Maybe he wouldn't be up to speed and ready to rock and roll, if there weren't such an element of danger involved. He was practically hoarse from telling himself that Jessie was not available to him ever, and his body still wasn't listening!

It had been tough enough with Erik alive. His sense of honor had forbidden him from acting on his impulse to sweep Jessie into his arms and carry her off to his own ranch. Erik and Jessie had made a legal and religious commitment to love each other till eternity. Luke had witnessed their vows himself, had respected those vows, in deed, if not always in thought. He'd been tormented day in and day out by the longings he could control only by staying as far from Jessie as possible. With her right here in the home in which he'd envisioned her so often, his control was stretched beyond endurance. He was fighting temptation minute by minute. Each tiny victory was an agony.

A lesser man might not have fought so valiantly. After all, Erik's death had removed any legal barriers to Luke's pursuit of Jessie. But he knew in his heart it hadn't diminished the moral commitment the couple had made before God and their family and friends. Maybe if Luke told himself that often enough, he could keep his hands off her for a few more days.

But not if she impulsively threw her arms around his neck again, not if he felt the soft press of her breasts against his chest, or the tantalizing brush of her lips against his. A man could handle only so much temptation without succumbing—and hating himself for it forever after.

The safe thing to do, the smart, prudent thing would be to retrieve that blasted cellular phone from his truck and call his parents.

And he would do just that, he promised himself. He would do it first thing Christmas morning. Tomorrow, Jessie would be out of his home, out of his life. She would be back where she belonged—at White Pines—and back in her rightful role as Erik's widow, mother of Harlan and Mary's first grandchild.

Tonight, though, he would have Jessie and Angela to himself for their own private holiday celebration. Just thinking about sitting with Jessie in a darkened room, the only lights those on the twinkling tree they'd had such fun decorating, made his pulse race. They would share a glass of wine, listen to carols, then at midnight they would toast Christmas together.

And tomorrow he would let her—let both of them—go.

That was the plan. If he had thought it would help him stick to it, he would have written it down and posted it on the refrigerator. Instead, he knew he was going to have to draw on his increasingly tattered sense of honor. He stood in his office for a good fifteen minutes, his gaze fixed on Erik and Jessie's wedding picture just to remind himself of the stakes. He figured his resolve was about as solid as it possibly could be.

He tried to pretend that there was nothing special about the evening by choosing to wear one of his many plaid shirts, the colors muted by too many washings, and a comfortable, well-worn pair of jeans. Consuela would have ripped him to shreds for his choice. His mother would have declared herself disgraced. He considered it one small attempt to keep the atmosphere casual.

There were more. He set the kitchen table with everyday dishes and skirted the temptation of candles with careful deliberation. He would have used paper plates and plastic knives and forks if he'd had them just to make his point.

Still, there was no denying the festive atmosphere as he heated the cornish game hens with wild rice, fresh rolls and pecan pie that Consuela had left for his holiday meal. The wine was one of his best, carefully selected from the limited, but priceless, assortment in his wine cellar. The kitchen was filled with delicious aromas by the time Jessie put in an appearance.

She'd dressed in an emerald green sweater that had the look of softest cashmere. It hung loosely to just below her hips, suggesting hidden curves. Her slacks were a matching shade of wool. She'd brushed her coal black hair and left it to wave softly down her back.

"Something smells wonderful," she said peering into the oven. The movement sent her hair cascading over her shoulder. She shot him an astonished look. "Cornish game hens? Pecan pie?"

"Consuela," he confessed tightly as he fought the desire to run his fingers through her hair.

Her gaze narrowed speculatively. "She must have suspected you'd be having a special guest here for the holidays."

Was that jealousy in her voice? Luke wondered. Dear heaven, he hoped not. Jealousy might imply that his feelings were returned and he knew without any doubt that all it would take to weaken his resolve was a hint that Jessie felt as he did.

"Not suspected," he denied. "Hoped, maybe. Consuela is a hopeless romantic and my bachelor status is a constant source of dismay to her. She stays up nights watching old videos of Hepburn and Tracy, Fred Astaire and Ginger Rogers. I think she's worn out her tape of *An Affair to Remember*. She wakes me out of a sound sleep with her sniffling."

Jessie smiled. "A woman after my own heart. Maybe we should watch an old movie tonight. Does she have *It's a Wonderful Life* or *Miracle on 34th Street?*"

"I'm sure she does, but I refuse to watch them if you're going to start bawling."

"Can't stand to see a woman cry, huh?"

Certainly not this one woman in particular, he thought to himself. He would shift oceans, move continents if that's what it took to keep Jessie happy. His brother had broken her heart.

As soon as the disloyal thought formed, Luke banished it. Jessie had loved Erik. Their marriage had been solid. It wasn't for him to judge whether Erik's decisions had disappointed her. He dragged himself back to the present and caught Jessie studying him curiously.

"Nope, I never could stand to see a woman cry," he said, deliberately keeping his tone light. "I'm fresh out of hankies, too."

Jessie grinned. "No problem. I saw boxes of tissues stashed in the bathroom closet."

Luke heaved an exaggerated sigh of resignation. "I'll find the tapes right after dinner."

Dinner was sheer torture. Jessie found the candles Luke had avoided and lit them. The kitchen shimmered with candlelight and the glow from the fireplace. It was the kind of romantic lighting that turned a woman's complexion delectably soft and alluring, the kind of lighting that stirred the imagination. Luke's was working overtime. He could barely squeeze a bite of food past the lump lodged in his throat.

"You're awfully quiet," Jessie observed.

"Just enjoying the meal," he claimed.

She eyed his full plate skeptically. "Really?"

He was saved from stammering out some sort of explanation by the sound of whimpers from the bedroom. "Angela's awake," he announced unnecessarily and bolted before Jessie could even react.

With the baby safely tucked against his chest, it was easier somehow to keep his emotions in check. Right now he figured Angela was as critical to his survival as a bulletproof vest was to a cop working the violent streets.

"She's probably hungry," Jessie said when the two of them were settled back at the table.

The innocent observation had Luke's gaze suddenly riveted on Jessie's chest. So much for keeping his attention focused elsewhere.

"She's not making a fuss yet," he replied in a choked voice, clinging to the baby a trifle desperately. "Enjoy your dinner."

Jessie seemed about to protest, but finally nodded and picked up her fork. Luke kept his gaze firmly fixed on the baby.

"How are you doing, sweet pea? Ready for your very first Christmas? It's almost time for the big show, the lighting of the tree."

"It's amazing the effect you have on her," Jessie commented. "It must be your voice. It soothes her."

Luke grinned. "Can't tell you the number of women I've put to sleep by talking too much."

Blue eyes observed him steadily as if trying to assess whether he was only teasing or boasting. Apparently she decided he was joking. To his amazement, he could see a hint of satisfaction in her eyes.

"I doubt that," she countered dryly. "I suspect it's the kind of voice that keeps grown-up women very much awake."

"You included?" The words slipped out before he could stop them. His heart skidded to a standstill as he watched the color rise in her cheeks. Those telltale patches were answer enough. So he hadn't totally misread those occasional sparks of interest in her eyes. Nevertheless, a few sparks weren't enough to overcome a mountain of doubts.

Jessie seemed to struggle to find her voice. When she finally did, she said dryly, "Now that's the famous Luke Adams ego that's legendary around these parts."

"That's not an answer," he taunted, enjoying the deepening color in her cheeks.

"It's as close to one as you're likely to get," she taunted right back.

Luke chuckled. "Never mind. I already have my answer."

Jessie's gaze clashed with his, hers uncertain and very, very vulnerable. Luke finally relented. "You're immune to me. You've seen me at my worst."

"Bad enough to terrify the angels," she confirmed, her voice laced with unmistakable gratitude for the reprieve he'd granted.

She stood up with a brisk movement and reached for the baby, making her claim on the armor he'd clung to so desperately. "I'll feed her now," she said.

"You haven't had dessert," Luke protested, not relinquishing the baby. At this rate they'd be engaged in a tug-of-war over the child.

"We'll have it in front of the tree," Jessie said determinedly and held out her arms.

Reluctantly, he placed Angela in her mother's arms and watched them disappear down the hallway to the bedroom. Only when the door shut softly behind them did he breathe a heartfelt sigh of relief.

The reprieve, however, didn't last nearly long enough for him to regain his equilibrium. The clean-up kept him occupied briefly. Fixing coffee and pie to take into the living room took only moments longer.

In the living room, he plugged in the tree and turned on the radio, once again tuning it to a station playing carols. The room shimmered with a thousand twinkling colored lights. Luke was certain he had never seen a more beautiful tree, never felt so clearly the meaning of Christmas.

As he anticipated Jessie's return, he fingered the carved wooden figures in the crèche he'd placed beneath the tree, lingering over the baby Jesus.

His thoughts were on another baby, one he wished with all of his jaded heart was his own.

He was standing, still and silent, when he sensed Jessie's approach. He heard her soft, indrawn breath. The faint scent of her perfume whispered through the air, something fresh and light and indescribably sexy.

"Oh, Luke, it's absolutely spectacular," she murmured. "The whole room feels as if it's alive with color."

He glanced down and saw reflected sparks of light shimmering in her eyes. Her lush mouth was curved in the sweetest smile he'd ever seen. Angela was nestled in her arms, spawning inevitable comparisons to the most finely drawn works of Madonna and child. In motherhood, even more than before, Jessie was both mysterious and beautiful, so very beautiful that it made his heart ache.

Nothing in heaven or hell could have prevented what happened next. Luke felt his control slipping, his resolve vanishing on a tide of desperate longing. He lowered his head slowly, pausing for the briefest of instants to gauge Jessie's reaction before gently touching his mouth to hers.

The kiss was like brushing up against fire, hot and dangerous and alluring. He lingered no longer than a heartbeat, but it was enough to send heat shimmering through him, to stir desire into a relentless, demanding need. The temptation to tarry longer, the need to savor, washed over him in great, huge, pulsing waves.

This one last time, though, the determination to cling to honor was powerful enough to save him, to save them both. He drew back reluctantly, examining Jessie's dazed eyes and flushed cheeks for signs of horror or panic. He saw—or thought he saw—only a hunger that matched his own and, to his deep regret, the grit to resist, the impulse to run.

"Merry Christmas," he said softly before she could flee.

She hesitated, her eyes shadowed with worry. "Merry Christmas," she said finally, apparently accepting the truce he was offering in their emotional balancing act.

Luke hid a sigh of relief. She hadn't run yet and he had just the thing to see that she didn't. "I found Consuela's tapes. What'll it be?"

Jessie blinked away what might have been tears, then said, "*Miracle on 34th Street,* I think."

"Good choice," he said too exuberantly. He slid the tape into the VCR and flipped on the TV while Jessie settled herself and the baby on the sofa.

Luke warned himself to sit in a chair on the opposite side of the room, warned himself to keep distance between them. He actually took a step in that direction, before reversing and sinking onto the far side of the sofa.

Jessie shot him a startled look, then seemed to measure the space between them. Apparently it was enough to reassure her, because slowly, visibly she began to relax, her gaze fixed on the TV screen where the holiday classic was unfolding.

They could have been watching *Doctor Zhivago* for all Luke saw. He couldn't seem to drag his gaze or his thoughts away from Jessie. Each breath he drew was ragged with desire. Each moment that passed was sheer torment as his head struggled between right and wrong.

And yet, despite the agony of doing what he knew deep in his gut was right, he thought he had never been happier or more content. The night held promise tantalizingly out of reach, but it shimmered with possibilities just the same. A few stolen hours, he vowed. No more. He would soak up the scent of her, the sight of her so that every fiber of his being could hold the memory forever.

Her laughter, as light as a spring breeze, rippled over him leaving him aroused and aching. Tears spilled down her cheeks unchecked, luring his touch. His fingers trembled as he reached to wipe away the sentimental traces of dampness. At his touch, her gaze flew to his, startled...hopeful.

That hint of temptation in her eyes was warning enough. If Jessie was losing her resolve tonight, then being strong, being stoic was going to be up to him.

He withdrew his hand and thought it was the hardest thing he had ever done. Only one thing he could imagine would ever be harder—letting her go. And tomorrow, just a few brief hours from now, he would be put to the test.

CHAPTER EIGHT

CHRISTMAS MORNING DAWNED sunny and clear. The snow shimmered like diamonds scattered across white velvet. Sparkling icicles clung to the eaves. The world outside was like a wonderland, all of its flaws covered over with a blanket of purest white.

For once Jessie had apparently gotten up before Luke. She hadn't heard him stirring when she fed Angela at 6:00 a.m. Nor was there any sign of him in the kitchen when she went for a cup of coffee before showering and getting dressed. Usually starting the coffeepot was the first thing he did in the morning. Today it hadn't even been plugged in. Jessie checked to make sure the electric coffee machine was filled with freshly ground beans and water, then plugged it in and switched it on.

After tying the belt on her robe a little more securely, she sat down at the kitchen table to wait for the coffee to brew. Her thoughts promptly turned to the night before. Every single second of their holiday celebration was indelibly burned on her memory: the delicious dinner, the sentimental old movie, the shared laughter, the twinkling lights of the tree, the kiss.

Ah, yes, the kiss, she thought, smiling despite herself. She wasn't sure which one of them had been more shocked by its intensity. Even though Luke had initiated it, he had seemed almost as startled as she had been by the immediate flaring of heat and hunger it had set off. Though his mouth against hers had been gentle and coaxing, the kiss had been more passionately persuasive than an all-out seduction. Fire had leapt through her veins. Desire had flooded through her belly. If he had pursued his advantage, there was no telling how far things might have gone.

Well, they couldn't have gone too far, she reassured herself. She had just had a baby, after all. Still, there was no talking away the fact that she'd displayed the resistance of mush. And once again Luke had proven the kind of man he was, strong and honorable.

His restraint, as frustrating as it had been at the time, only deepened her respect for him. She added it to the list of all of his admirable traits and wished with all her heart that she had met him first, before Erik, before any possibility of a relationship had become so tangled with past history and old loyalties, so twisted with guilt and blame.

Almost as soon as she acknowledged the wish, guilt spread through her. How could she regret loving Erik? How could she possibly regret having Angela? Life had blessed her with a husband who had loved her with all his heart, no matter his other flaws. She had been doubly blessed with a daughter because of that love. What kind of selfish monster would wish any of that away?

"Dear God, what am I thinking?" she whispered on a ragged moan, burying her head on her arms.

There was only one answer. She had to find some way to get away from Luke, to put her tattered restraint back together. She had to get to White Pines before she made a terrible mistake, before the whole family was ripped apart again by what would amount to a rivalry for her affections.

Despite their occasional differences, she knew how deep the ties among Erik's family members ran. They would consider themselves the protectors of Erik's interests. Luke would be viewed as a traitor, a man with no respect for his brother's memory. They would hold her actions against him, blaming him alone for their love when the truth was that she was the one who was increasingly powerless to resist it. She wouldn't allow that to happen.

An image came to her then, an image of Luke returning from his pickup, his expression filled with guilt as he'd sworn he couldn't find his cellular phone. More than likely she'd been in denial that night, longing for something that could never be, or she would have known what that expression on his face had meant.

Anger, quite possibly misdirected, surged through her. It gave her the will to act, to do what she knew in her heart must be done. She stood and grabbed Luke's heavy jacket, poked her bare feet into boots several sizes too large, snatched up his thick gloves, and stomped outside.

She was promptly felled by the first drift of snow. She stepped off the porch and into heavy, damp snow up to her hips. She dragged herself forward by sheer will, determined to get to the truck, determined to discover if Luke had deliberately kept her stranded here.

Her progress could have been measured in inches. Her bare skin between the tops of the boots and the bottom of the coat was stinging from the cold.

Still, she trudged on until she finally reached the pickup and tugged at the door. The lock was frozen shut.

Crying out in frustration, Jessie tried to unlock it by scraping at the ice, then covering the lock with her gloved hands in a futile attempt to melt the thin, but effective coating of ice. She tried blowing on it, hoping her breath would be warm enough to help. When that didn't work, she slammed her fist against it, hoping to crack it.

Again and again, she jiggled the handle, trying to pry the door open. Eventually, when she could barely feel her feet, when her whole body was shuddering violently from the cold, the lock gave and the door came free. She jumped inside and slammed the door, relieved to be out of the biting wind.

Remembering that Erik had always left the keys above the visor, no matter how she'd argued with him about it, she checked to see if Luke had done the same. No keys. She doubted Luke was any more security conscious than his brother had been. She checked under the floor mat, then felt beneath the front seat.

That's where she eventually found them, tucked away almost beyond her reach. Her fingers awkward from the gloves and the cold, she finally managed to turn on the engine. It might take forever for the truck to warm up, but she intended to spend as long as it took to thoroughly check the pickup for that cellular phone.

It didn't take nearly as long as she might have wished. To her astonishment and instantaneous fury, she found it on the first try, right in the glove compartment. Luke hadn't even bothered to lock it, though it was obvious to her that he had made a passing attempt to hide the phone under some papers. Clutching the phone in her hand, she sank back against the seat and simply stared at it.

"Luke," she whispered, "what were you thinking?"

She was so caught up in trying to explain her brother-in-law's uncharacteristic behavior that she didn't hear the crunching of ice or the muttered oaths until Luke was practically on top of her. Suddenly the passenger door was flung open—the damned lock didn't even stick under his assault—and Luke jumped into the seat beside her.

Jessie shot him an accusing look. His gaze went from her face to the cellular phone and back again. He muttered a harsh oath under his breath.

"It was here all along, wasn't it?" she asked in a lethal tone.

He didn't even have the decency to lie. He just nodded.

"Why, Luke?" Her voice broke as she asked. Unexpected tears gathered in her eyes, threatening to spill over. She felt betrayed somehow, though she couldn't have explained why. Maybe it was because she had expected so much more of Luke. The hurt cut deeper and promised worse scars than anything Erik had ever done.

Luke shoved his hand through his hair and stared off into the distance. He didn't speak for so long that Jessie thought he didn't intend to answer, but eventually he turned to face her, his expression haggard.

"I couldn't make the call," he said simply. "I just couldn't make it."

"Do you hate your family so much?" she demanded. "How could you let them worry about me? How could you leave them wondering if there'd been an accident? My heaven, they must be out of their minds by now."

He shot her a look filled with irony. "Do you really think that was what it was about?"

"What else?" she demanded, her voice rising until she didn't recognize it. "What else could have made you do something so cruel?"

Before she could even guess what he was about, he reached out and clutched the fabric of the coat that was several sizes too large for her. He dragged her roughly to him. This time when he claimed her mouth, there was nothing sweetly tentative about it. The kiss was bruising, demanding. It was the kiss of a desperate man, a man who had kept his emotions on a tight leash for far too long.

Jessie recognized the passionate claiming even before she felt the raging heat. Even as a protest formed in her head, exhilaration soared in her heart. Furious with herself for the weakness, she gave herself up to the magic of that kiss. His cheeks were stubbled, his skin cold, except where his mouth moved against hers. There, there was only the most tempting heat and she couldn't deny herself the pleasure of it.

As if he sensed that she wasn't fighting him, as if he realized that she was fully participating in this conflagration of sensation, Luke's rough touch became a softer caress. Demand gave way to the gentler persuasion. Out-of-control hunger turned to a far sweeter coaxing.

Jessie was captivated, her body aswirl with a riot of new feelings, more powerful than anything she'd ever felt with Erik. Not even her carefully cultivated battle against disloyalty could keep her from giving her all to this one devastating kiss.

This man, though, this timing...she couldn't help thinking how wrong it was, when she could think at all. A spark of pure magic scampered down her spine, chased by a shiver of doubt. She suspected they could thank bulky coats and thick gloves for checking their actions, more than they could credit either of them with good sense.

Eventually Luke cupped her face in his gloved hands. With his eyes closed and his forehead barely touching hers, he sighed heavily.

"Oh, Jessie, I never meant for this to happen," he said on a ragged, desperate note.

"But it has," she said, not sure whether that was cause for regret or joy. Only time would tell. "Now what?"

Luke released her and sank back against the passenger seat, his gaze fixed on the ceiling. "You take that phone and you go inside and call the folks. Daddy will find some way to pick you up before the day is out."

Somehow shocked at his matter-of-fact dismissal, Jessie stared at him. "You want me to go?" she whispered, devastated. "Now?"

"Especially now." His gaze determinedly evaded hers.

"But why? It's all out in the open at last. The way you feel. The way I feel. It was all there in that kiss. Don't tell me you can still deny it. There's no turning back now, Lucas. We have to deal with it."

If he was shocked by her feelings for him, he didn't show it. Instead, the look he turned on her was every bit as cold as the world outside that truck. "We are dealing with it. You're going and I'm staying. That's the way it has to be, the way it was meant to be."

Jessie shivered, chilled as much by his tone as the howling wind. "You can't mean that."

"I've never meant anything more," he insisted, his expression as steady and determined as she'd ever seen it. "Go to White Pines. It's where you belong."

A great, gnawing sensation started in the pit of Jessie's stomach. She sensed that if she did as he asked, if she left him here alone and went to be with his family, taking her place there as his brother's lonely, tragic widow, that would indeed be the end of it. Whatever might have been between them would die. Harlan, Mary, Jordan and Cody would be united in their opposition. The family and all of its complicated antagonisms and hurts would be like an insurmountable wall.

Well, she wouldn't have it. Maybe what she thought she felt for Luke was wrong. Maybe what he felt for her was some sort of terrible sin. Maybe they were both betraying Erik.

In a perfect world, her marriage would have fulfilled all of her dreams. It would have lasted a lifetime. And no man would ever have come along who was Erik's equal. She would have dutifully mourned until the end of time.

But her marriage hadn't worked. Erik had died. And Luke Adams was twice the man Erik had been. That wasn't her fault. It wasn't Erik's. In his own way, Erik had tried to make her happy. He had never realized that she couldn't be happy as long as he was so obviously miserable with the choices he alone had made for his life.

Nor, though, was the fault Luke's. Their feelings simply were there. He had done nothing to exploit them.

And she couldn't believe a benevolent God would have conspired to force her here to have her baby, if something more hadn't been meant to come of it. If there was one thing Jessie believed in with all her heart, it was fate. Surely God had brought them together not just to forgive, not just to rid themselves of guilt, but to love.

"I will only go to White Pines if you will come with me," she announced, her chin set stubbornly.

Luke stared at her, an expression of incredulity spreading across his handsome face. His mouth formed a tight line. Disbelief sparked in his eyes. "No way."

"Then Angela and I are staying."

"No way," he repeated more firmly, reaching for the cellular phone that had started them inevitably down this path and now lay forgotten in her lap.

Jessie's hand closed around it first and before Luke could react, she opened the car door and threw it with all her might. Landing silently, it disappeared slowly, inevitably in a soft drift of snow.

Luke's shocked gaze followed its path, then returned to her face. His jaw worked. Jessie waited for an explosion of outrage, but instead his lips curved into an unexpected smile. Amusement sparkled in his eyes. He seemed to be choking back laughter.

"The situation is not amusing, Lucas."

"It's not the situation, it's you. I can't believe you did that," he said at last.

She glared at him, not entirely sure what to make of this new mood. "Well, believe it."

"We might not find it till spring."

"So what?"

"You were the one who mentioned how cruel it was to leave my parents wondering and worrying about you."

Jessie's determination faltered ever so slightly. Apparently she was every bit as thoughtless as he was. "The phone lines are bound to be up soon. We'll call then."

He regarded her quizzically. "And if there's an emergency?"

"What kind of emergency?" She couldn't seem to keep a faint tremor out of her voice.

"The house burning down. The baby getting sick."

Jessie felt the color drain out of her face. "Oh, my God," she murmured, clambering out of the pickup. She tumbled into the snow, then struggled back to her feet. Before she could steady herself, Luke was beside her.

"You okay?"

"We have to get that phone."

He gave her an inscrutable look. "I'll get it. You go on inside. Despite the charming winter attire you appropriated from me, you're not really dressed for this weather."

She eyed him distrustfully. "You'll bring it inside?"

"Hey, I'm not the one who tried to bury it. I knew exactly where it was in case we really needed it."

She scowled at him. "Don't start trying to make yourself into a saint now, Lucas. It's too late."

He turned back and, to her astonishment, he winked at her. "It always was, darlin'."

LUKE RETRIEVED THE cellular phone and barely resisted the urge to roll in the snow in an attempt to cool off his overheated body. The effect Jessie had on him was downright shameful. His blood pounded hotly through his veins just getting a glimpse of her. The kiss they had just shared could have set off a wildfire that would consume whole acres of prairie grass.

Damn, why had she been so willing? Why hadn't she smacked him, put him in his place, blistered him with scathing accusations? The instant he had hauled her into his arms, he'd half-expected the solid whack of her palm across his cheek. When it hadn't come, he'd dared to deepen the kiss, dared to pretend for just a heartbeat that he had a right to taste her, a right to feel those cool, silky lips heat beneath his, a right to feel her body shuddering with need against his.

The truth of it was, though, that he had no rights at all where Jessie was concerned. Even though she seemed to feel that that kiss had opened up a whole new world for the two of them, he knew better. He knew it had paved the way to hell, destroying good and noble intentions in its path.

He stuck the phone in his pocket and continued on to the barn, where he fed Chester and the horses. Chester nudged his hand away from his pocket, searching for his treat. Instead, there was only the phone.

"Sorry, old guy. I left the house in a hurry. I forgot your apple. I'll bring two when I come back later."

The old goat turned a sympathetic look on him, as if he understood the turmoil that had caused Luke to fail him.

"Good grief, even the animals are starting to pity me," he muttered in disgust and made his way back to the house, where he found Jessie singing happily as she worked at the stove.

The table had been set with the good china. Orange juice had been poured into crystal goblets. The good silver gleamed at each place. Luke eyed it all warily.

"It's awful fancy for breakfast, don't you think?"

"We're celebrating," she said airily.

He wasn't sure he liked the sound of that. It hinted that she wasn't letting go of the momentary craziness that had gripped the two of them in the pickup. "Celebrating what?"

She cast an innocent look in his direction. "Christmas, of course," she said sweetly.

"Oh."

She grinned. "Disappointed, Lucas?"

"Of course not." He glanced around a little desperately. "Where's Angela?"

"Sleeping."

"Are you sure? Maybe I should go check on her. She doesn't usually sleep this late."

Jessie actually laughed at that. "Surely a grown man doesn't have to rely on a three-day-old baby to protect him from me, does he?"

Luke felt color climb up the back of his neck and settle in his cheeks. "I just thought she ought to be here," he muttered. "It is her first Christmas morning."

"She'll be awake soon enough. Sit down. The biscuits are almost ready."

He stared at her incredulously as she bent over to open the oven door. The view that gave him of her fanny made him weak.

"When did you have time to bake biscuits?" he inquired, his voice all too husky.

"You were in that barn a long time," she said. She glanced over her shoulder. "Cooling off?"

Luke stared at her. What had happened to the sweet, virtuous woman who'd arrived here only a few days earlier? What did she know about her ability to drive him to distraction? *Get real, Lucas,* he told himself sternly. *She was as responsible for the heat of that kiss as you were.*

"Jessie," he warned, his voice low.

"Yes, Lucas?"

She sounded sweetly compliant. He didn't trust that tone for a second. "Don't get into a game, unless you understand the rules," he advised her.

"Who made up these rules? Some man, I suspect."

"Oh, I think they pretty much go back to Adam and Eve," he countered. He fixed his gaze on her until her cheeks turned pink. "I figure that gives 'em some credibility. People have been living by 'em for centuries now."

Jessie shook her head. Judging from her expression, she seemed to be feeling sorry for him.

"You are pitiful, Lucas," she said, confirming his guess.

He stared at her, a knot forming in his stomach. "Pitiful?"

"You don't know what to do about how you feel, so you start out hiding behind an itsy-bitsy baby and now you want to put God and the Bible between us."

"Right's right," he insisted stubbornly.

"And what was meant to be was meant to be," she countered, looking perfectly confident in making the claim.

Obviously she wasn't worried about the two of them being stricken dead by a bolt of lightning. Luke couldn't understand it. How could she be so calm, so sure of herself, when he'd never felt more off balance, more uncertain in all of his life?

"Whatever that means," he grumbled.

"It means, Lucas, that you might as well stop fighting so hard and accept the inevitable."

He studied her worriedly. "Which is?"

"Angela and I are in your life to stay."

He swallowed hard. "Well, of course you are," he said too heartily. "You're my sister-in-law. Angela's my niece."

Ignoring his comment, Jessie dished up scrambled eggs, bacon and golden biscuits. Only after she'd seated herself across from him did she meet his gaze.

"Give it up, Lucas. It's a battle you can't win."

Determination swept through him. "Try me," he said tightly.

To his annoyance, Jessie actually laughed at that. "Oh, Lucas, I intend to."

CHAPTER NINE

WITH JESSIE'S CHALLENGE ringing in his ears, Luke retreated to the barn. He figured it was the only safe place for him to be and still be within shouting distance of the house in case of a crisis. Inside, even in his office with the door shut, he couldn't escape Jessie's unrealistic expectations for their future. As brief as her presence had been, she had pervaded every room, leaving him with no place to hide from her or his unrelenting thoughts about her.

What she wanted from him, though, was impossible. How could they possibly have a relationship without bringing the wrath of the entire family she admired so much down on them? Couldn't she see that they were as doomed in their way as Romeo and Juliet had been? Or had she considered and then dismissed the problems? Could he possibly be that important to her?

He hunkered down on a bale of hay and distractedly tossed apple sections to Chester. The goat seemed to accept the unexpected largesse as his due. When Luke grew distracted and forgot to offer another chunk of apple, Chester butted him gently until he remembered. He scratched the goat behind his ears and wished that all relationships were this uncomplicated.

Dealing with goats and horses and cattle was a hell of a lot less troubling than dealing with a woman, Luke concluded when Chester finally tired of the game and wandered off. Food, attention, a little exercise, a few animal or human companions and their lives were happy. Women, to the contrary, sooner or later always developed expectations.

To avoid dealing with Jessie's fantasies, he considered saddling up one of the horses and riding off to check on the cattle. He manufactured a dozen excuses why such a trip was vital to the ranch's operations, even though he had a perfectly capable foreman in charge, a man who could probably account for every single head of longhorn cattle on the ranch without Luke's help.

Unfortunately, he could see through every excuse. He had no doubts at all that Jessie would be even quicker to see them for what they were: cowardly reasons to bolt from all the emotions he couldn't bear to face. While being someplace else—*anyplace else*—held a great deal of appeal at the moment, Luke wasn't a coward. Which meant, like it or not, staying and seeing this through.

Finally, tired of having only Chester and the horses for company when the most beautiful, if unavailable, woman in the world was inside, Luke heaved himself up and headed back to the house. Maybe Jessie had come to her senses while he was gone. Maybe his body had become resigned to celibacy.

And maybe pigs could fly, he thought despondently.

He found her sitting in front of the fireplace in the kitchen mending one of his shirts. As an inexplicable rage tore through him, he yanked the shirt out of her hands.

"What the hell are you doing?" he demanded.

Jessie didn't even blink at his behavior. "There was a whole basket of mending sitting in the laundry room waiting to be done," she said calmly as if that were explanation enough to offer a man who'd clearly lost his mind.

"Consuela's the housekeeper around here, not you."

"Is there some reason I shouldn't help her out?"

"It's her job," he insisted stubbornly.

Jessie merely shook her head, gave him that exasperating look that was filled with pity, and reached for another shirt. "It's my way of thanking her for all the meals she fixed before she left."

"She fixed them for me," Luke said, clinging to his stance despite the fact that even he could see he was being unreasonable. There was a quick and obvious remedy for what ailed him but he refused to pull Jessie into his arms, which was clearly where his body wanted her, where his long-denied hormones craved her to be.

One delicate eyebrow arched quizzically at his possessive claim on the meals Consuela had fixed. "Does that mean I'm no longer allowed to eat them?" Jessie inquired. "You planning to starve me into leaving?"

"Of course not," he snapped in frustration. "Just forget it. I'm going to my office."

"On Christmas?"

"If you can sew on Christmas, I can work."

"I'm not sure I see the connection," she commented mildly. She shrugged. "Whatever works for you."

Luke clenched his fists so tightly, his knuckles turned white. Why had he never noticed that Jessie was the most exasperating, the most infuriating woman on the face of the earth? She was so damned calm and...reasonable. He didn't miss the irony that he considered two such usually positive traits to be irritating.

To emphasize his displeasure, he plunked the cellular phone on the table in front of her. "Call my parents," he ordered tightly, then stalked away.

With any luck at all, Jessie would be tired by now of his attitude, he thought with only a faint hint of regret. After all, how long could a woman maintain this charade of complacency in the face of such galling behavior? She'd be packed and gone by the time he emerged from his office. His life could return to normal.

He glanced over his shoulder just as he headed through the doorway. She was humming to herself and, if he wasn't mistaken, there was a full-fledged smile on her face. He had the sinking realization that she wasn't going anywhere.

JESSIE WASN'T ENTIRELY sure why she was being so stubborn. One devastating, spine-tingling kiss hardly constituted a declaration of love.

Still, with every single bit of intuition she possessed, she believed that Luke was in love with her. That kiss was a symptom of stronger emotions. She was certain of it. She simply had to wait him out. Sooner or later, he would see that she wasn't afraid of the consequences if she stayed. He would see, in fact, that she welcomed them. Eventually he would realize that together they could even conquer all of the opposition they were likely to arouse.

The unexpected ringing of the cellular phone startled her so badly, she pricked her finger with the needle she'd been using to stitch buttons back onto Luke's shirts. Should she answer it? Or take it to Luke in his office? Of course, by the time she carried it through the house, whoever was calling would probably give up thanks to her indecisiveness.

It was guilt over her own failure to call Harlan and Mary that finally convinced her to answer on the fifth ring.

"Hello," she said tentatively.

"Who the hell is this?" Harlan Adams's unmistakable voice boomed over the line.

An odd mix of pleasure and dismay spread through her. "It's Jessie, Harlan. Merry Christmas!"

"Jessie?" he repeated incredulously. "You're okay. What the devil are you doing over at Lucas's? Why haven't you called? My God, woman, Mary's been out of her mind with worry."

Jessie decided that rather than responding to the questions and the barely disguised accusations Harlan had thrown out at her, she'd better go on the offensive immediately.

"I went into labor on the way to your house," she explained. "I was scared to death I'd deliver the baby in a snow drift. Luke's ranch was the only place nearby. You have a beautiful granddaughter, Harlan. I've named her Angela."

As she'd expected, the announcement took the wind out of his sails. "You've had the baby? A girl?"

"That's right."

"Mary," he called. "Mary! Get on the other line. Jessie's at Luke's and she's had the baby!"

Jessie heard the echoing sound of footsteps on White Pines's hardwood floors, then the clatter of a juggled, then dropped, phone. Finally, Mary's breathless voice came over the line. "You had the baby?"

"A girl," Jessie confirmed. "Angela. She is so beautiful, Mary. I can't wait for you to see her."

"But why are you at Luke's? Why not a hospital?"

"Angela was too impatient to get here. With the blizzard and everything, I figured this was my best bet."

"But the doctor did get there in time?" Mary asked worriedly.

Jessie hauled in a deep breath before blurting, "Actually, Luke delivered her. He was incredible. Calm as could be. You would have been so proud of him. I don't know what I would have done without him."

The explanation drew no response. Jessie could hear Mary crying. Eventually, Harlan spoke up.

"I don't get it, girl. That was three days ago. Why haven't you called before now?"

"The phone lines are down and Luke had misplaced the cellular phone. He hunted all over for it. It finally turned up this morning, buried under some papers." It was a stretch of the truth, but Jessie had no intention of filling them in on her own battle with Luke over this very phone.

"No wonder we couldn't reach him," Harlan grumbled. "That boy would lose his head if it weren't tacked onto his neck."

Jessie sighed. She'd never noticed that Luke was particularly absentminded, not about anything that mattered. The observation was just another of Harlan's inconsequential put-downs, uttered without thought to their accumulated cutting nature. She'd practically bitten her lower lip raw listening to him do the same thing to Erik. If she had thought it would help, she would have told him to stop, but she had known the order had to come from Erik.

"Well, it doesn't matter now," Harlan said. "Now that we know where to find you, I'll have my pilot pick you up in an hour. There's a landing strip not far from Luke's. He should be able to get you there."

"No," Jessie said at once.

"Beg pardon?" Harlan said, sounding shocked by her unexpected display of defiance.

"Jessie, darling, you must be anxious to be away from there," Mary protested. "We know how difficult it was for you to see Luke after what happened to Erik. Please, let Harlan send for you. We want you here with us and we can't wait to see the baby. You should be with family now."

"Luke is family," she reminded them.

"Yes, but…well, under the circumstances, you must be under a terrible strain there."

"No," Jessie insisted. She took a deep breath and prepared to manufacture an excuse that not even strong-willed Harlan Adams could debate. "The baby has no business being dragged around in weather like this, not for a few more days anyway. By then the roads will be clear and I can drive the rest of the way."

"Oh, dear," Mary promptly murmured. "She is okay, isn't she?"

"She's just fine, but she's a newborn and it's freezing outside. I'll feel better about bundling her up and taking her out in a few days, I'm sure."

"Well, of course, you must do what you think is best for the baby," Mary conceded eventually, but there was no mistaking her disappointment.

"Nonsense," Harlan said, heading down the single track his mind had chosen with dogged determination. "I'll send a doctor along in the plane to check her out. The baby ought to be seen by a professional as soon as possible, anyway. I'm sure Luke did his best, but he's not a physician. Don't worry about a thing, Jessica. I'll have Doc Winchell at Luke's before nightfall. Then you can all come back together. We'll have you here in time for the party Mary has planned. It'll be a celebration to end all celebrations."

"But, Harlan, it's Christmas," Jessie argued. "You can't expect the doctor or the pilot to disrupt their plans with their families to make a trip like that."

"Of course I can," Harlan countered with the assurance of a man used to having his commands obeyed. "You just be ready. I'll call back when they're on their way. Put Lucas on."

Defeated, Jessie sighed. "I'll see if I can find him."

She took the phone she deeply regretted answering down the hall to Luke's office. She tapped on the door, then opened it. He was leaning back in his leather chair, staring out the window. There was something so lonely, so lost in his expression that her heart ached. If only he would let her into his life, then neither of them would be alone again.

"Luke, your parents are on the line," she said and held out the phone.

He searched her face for a moment, his expression unreadable. Finally, he took the phone and spoke to his father.

"She's fine, Daddy. The baby's fine. I'm sure it's not the way Jessie would have preferred to deliver her baby, but there were no complications. She came through like a real trooper. She was back on her feet in no time. And the baby's a little angel."

He closed his eyes and rubbed his temples. "No, Daddy, I'm sure Jessie hasn't been overdoing it. She knows her own strength." His expression hardened and his gaze cut to Jessie again. "No, she didn't mention that you were sending Doc Winchell. I'm sure she'll be relieved. Right. We'll be expecting him."

Most of Harlan's side of the conversation had been muffled, but Jessie heard him asking then if Luke intended to come to White Pines with her.

"No," Luke said brusquely. "I told Mother before that I have things to do here." His expression remained perfectly blank as he listened to whatever his father said next. Finally he said, "Yes, Merry Christmas to all of you, too. Give my best to Jordan and Cody."

He hung up the phone and turned back to the window. "Shouldn't you be packing?" he inquired quietly.

Tears welled up in Jessie's eyes. She hadn't expected him to be so stubborn. For some reason, she had thought when the time came, he would realize that he belonged at White Pines for the holidays every bit as much as she did. More so, in fact.

"I'm not leaving you here," she insisted.

He turned to confront her. "You don't have a choice. Harlan's taken it out of your hands. I told you that was exactly what would happen if you called him. It's for the best, anyway. It's time you were going."

"I didn't call. They called here." Jessie lost patience with the whole blasted macho clan of Adams men. "Oh, forget it. You can't bully me, any more than your father can. If I want to stay here, I'll stay here."

He regarded her evenly. "Even if I tell you that I want you to go?"

"Even then," she said, her chin tilted high.

"Why would you insist on staying someplace you aren't wanted?"

"Because I don't believe you don't want me here. I think you want me here too much," she retorted.

"You're dreaming, if you believe that," he said coldly.

Jessie's resolve almost wavered in the face of his stubborn, harsh refusal to admit his real feelings. "I guess that's the difference between us, then. I believe in you. I believe in *us*. You don't."

"That's a significant difference, wouldn't you say?"

"It's only significant if you want it to be."

"I do."

A tear spilled over and tracked down her cheek. "Damn you, Luke Adams."

"You're too late, Jessie," he told her grimly. "I was damned a long time ago."

For all of her natural optimism, for all of her faith in what a future for the two of them could hold, Jessie couldn't stand up to that kind of bleak resignation.

"Angela and I will be gone before you know it," she said, fighting to hold back her tears as she finally admitted that she was defeated.

In the doorway she paused and looked back. "One of these days you're going to regret forcing us out of your life, Luke. You're going to wake up and discover that you've turned into a bitter, lonely old man."

That said, she straightened her spine and walked away from the man she'd come to love with all her heart. Regrets? Luke was filled with them. They were chasing through his brain like pinballs bouncing erratically from one bumper to the next.

Was he doing the right thing? Of course, he was, he told himself firmly. He had to let Jessie go. He had to let her walk out of his life, taking the baby who'd stolen a little piece of his jaded heart with her. They weren't his to claim. They were Erik's and they were going home, where they belonged. They were going to a place where he no longer fit in.

He would have stayed right where he was, hidden away in his office, but Jessie was apparently determined to make him pay for forcing her out of his life. She appeared in the doorway of his office, bundled up, her long hair tucked into a knit cap, her cheeks rosy, either from anger or from a trek outdoors. He suspected the former.

"We're leaving," she announced unnecessarily.

Luke had seen Doc Winchell arrive in a fancy four-wheel-drive car a half hour earlier cutting a path through the fresh snow. He'd been expecting to see it driving away any minute now heading back to the airport. He'd been listening for the sound of the back door slamming shut behind them, then the roar of the car's engine. The silence had taunted him. Now, though, it seemed they were finally ready to go, and he was going to be forced to endure another goodbye.

"Have a safe trip," he said, refusing to meet her condemning gaze.

"Aren't you going to come and say goodbye to Angela?"

"No," he said curtly and felt his heart break.

"Lucas, please."

She didn't know what she was asking, that had to be it, he decided as he finally got to his feet and followed her into the kitchen.

Doc Winchell, who'd been the family physician ever since Luke could recall, beamed at him. "Lucas, you did a fine job bringing this little one into the world. Couldn't have done better myself. We'll get her weighed and checked out from head to toe tomorrow, but she looks perfectly healthy to me."

Luke kept his gaze deliberately averted from the bundled-up baby. "She really is okay, then?"

"Perfect," the doctor confirmed.

"Being out in this weather won't hurt her?"

"The truck's heater works. She's wrapped up warmly. She'll be fine."

"What about flying?"

"It shouldn't be a problem and I'll be right there to keep an eye on her."

Luke nodded, his hands shoved in his pockets to keep from reaching out to hold the baby one last time. "Take good care of her, Doc. She's my first delivery." He grinned despite himself. "Hopefully, my last, too. I don't think I ever want to know that kind of fear again."

As if she sensed that Angela was his Achilles' heel, Jessie plucked the baby up and practically shoved her into Luke's arms. He had to accept her or allow her to tumble to the floor. One look into those trusting blue eyes and he felt his resolve weaken.

"Say goodbye, Angela," Jessie murmured beside him. "Uncle Luke isn't coming with us."

As if she understood her mother, Angela's face scrunched up. Her tiny lower lip trembled. Huge tears welled up in her eyes.

Luke rocked her gently. "Hey, little one, no tears, okay? Your uncle Luke will always have a very special spot in his heart, just for you. You ever need anything, anything at all, you come to me, okay, sweet pea?"

As always, the sound of his voice soothed her. She cooed at him. His effect on her gave him a disconcerting sense of satisfaction. He felt as if his sorry existence meant something to somebody.

Jessie seemed to guess what he was feeling. Her gaze, filled with understanding and a kind of raw agony, was fixed on his face. Luke couldn't bear looking into her eyes. She knew too well why he was pushing them away. He looked back at Angela's precious little face instead.

"Goodbye, sweet pea. You take good care of your mommy, okay?"

He held the baby out until Jessie finally had no choice but to claim her.

"Goodbye, Lucas," she said, her voice laced with all the regret he was feeling. "I will never, ever forget what you did for us."

He wanted to tell her it was nothing, but he couldn't seem to force the words past the lump lodged in his throat. He just nodded.

Jessie reached up then and touched her hand to his cheek, silently commanding him To look at her. When he did, she said softly, "If you ever, *ever* change your mind, I'll be waiting."

"Don't wait too long," he warned. "Don't waste your life waiting for something that can never be."

For an instant he thought she was going to protest, but finally she sighed deeply and turned away. She walked out the kitchen door and never looked back.

It was just as well, Luke thought as he watched her. He would have hated like hell for her to see that he was crying.

CHAPTER TEN

THE COMMOTION CAUSED by their arrival at White Pines was almost more than Jessie could bear, given her already-confused and deeply hurt state of mind.

Harlan gave Doc Winchell the third degree about the baby's health. Mary claimed Angela the minute Jessie set foot across the threshold. Jordan and Cody studied the new baby with fascination, offering observations on which family members she most resembled. A handful of strangers, visiting for the holiday, chimed in.

They had almost nothing beyond the courtesies to say to Jessie, and not one of them asked about Luke. It was hardly surprising, she concluded, that he had refused to set foot in the house at White Pines.

As she stood apart and watched them, Jessie couldn't help wondering why she'd once wanted so desperately to be a part of this family. It suddenly seemed to her that she'd mistaken chaos and boisterous outbursts for love.

Of course, back then she'd had Erik as a buffer. He'd seen to it that she was never left out of the conversation. He'd insisted that she be treated with respect. She had basked in his attention and barely noticed anyone else.

Except Luke.

Thinking of him now, all alone again on his ranch, she regretted more than ever leaving him, despite his cantankerous behavior. She should have risen above it. She should have listened to her heart.

Suddenly she couldn't stand all the fussing for another instant. Reaching for Angela, she startled them all by announcing that the baby was tired from the trip and needed to be put down for a nap. To her astonishment, no one argued. She would have to remember that tone of voice for the next time someone in the family tried to steamroll over her.

"I found an old crib in the attic," Mary said at once. "I had Jordan set it up in your old suite. As soon as the rest of the roads have cleared and it's safer to drive, we'll go into town for baby clothes and new sheets and blankets. In the meantime, I've had Maritza wash a few things I saved from when the boys were babies."

Jessie fought a grin as she tried to imagine sexy, irrepressible Cody, the tall, self-assured Jordan or Luke ever being as tiny as Angela was now. "Thank you," she said. "I'm sure we'll be fine."

Cody separated himself from the others as she started up the stairs. "How is Luke?" he asked, walking along with her. Lines of worry were etched in his brow that she was sure hadn't been there mere months before. He was only twenty-seven, but he seemed older, wearier than he had when she'd left.

"Stubborn as a mule," she said. "Lonely."

"Why didn't he come with you?"

Jessie met Cody's concerned gaze and gave him the only part of the real answer she could. The rest was private, just between her and Luke. She couldn't say he was staying away because of her. "Because he blames himself for Erik's death, and he thinks the rest of you do, too."

Cody couldn't have looked more shocked if she'd announced that Luke was locked away at home with a harem.

"But that's crazy," he blurted at once. "We all know what happened was an accident. Nobody blames Luke. Hell, if anybody was at fault it was Daddy. He's the one who backed Erik into a corner and made him try to be something he wasn't. Any one of us could have taken a spill on that tractor. Accidents happen all the time on a ranch."

Jessie couldn't have agreed with him more, but she was startled that Cody recognized the truth. Of all of them, he had always seemed to be the least introspective. Cody seemed imperturbable, the one most inclined to roll with the punches. She'd always thought he accepted things at face value, including Harlan's own view of himself as omnipotent. Obviously she'd fallen into the trap of viewing him merely as the baby in the family. The truth was he'd grown into a caring, thoughtful man.

"That's what I tried to tell Luke, but the accident didn't happen here. It happened on his land. He seems to think he should have prevented it somehow." She looked into Cody's worried eyes. "Talk to him. Maybe you can get him to see reason. I couldn't."

Cody looked doubtful. "Jessie, if you couldn't reach him, I don't see how I can. You were always able to communicate with him, even when the rest of us were ready to give up in frustration."

Jessie sighed. "Well, not this time."

At the doorway to the suite she had shared with Erik she paused. Cody leaned down and brushed a light kiss across her cheek. "I'm glad you're back, Jessie. We've missed you around here. I think the last ounce of serenity around this place vanished the day you left."

She was startled by the sweet assessment of her importance to this household where she'd always felt like an interloper. "Thanks, Cody. Saying that is the nicest gift anyone could have given me."

He grinned. "Don't say that until you've opened those packages downstairs. Something tells me everyone's gone overboard in anticipation of your return and the arrival of the baby." He winked at her. "One thing this family is very good at is bribery."

"Bribery?"

"So you'll stay, of course. You don't think Daddy will be one bit happy about his first grandbaby growing up halfway across the state. He's going to want to supervise everything from cradle to college. Hell, he'll probably try to handpick her husband for her. Just be sure he doesn't make her part of some business deal."

Before Jessie could react to that, Cody was already thundering down the stairs again.

"Cody, for heaven's sakes, remember where the dickens you are," Harlan bellowed from somewhere downstairs.

"I'm just in a hurry to get another slice of Maritza's pie," Cody shouted back, unrepentant.

"No more pie until dinner," Mary called out. "There won't be a bit left for the rest of us."

"Mother, Maritza's been baking for a month," Cody retorted. "There must be enough pies in the kitchen to feed half of Texas. You've only invited a quarter of the state at last count. One slice won't be missed."

Jessie stood for a moment longer, listening to the once-familiar bickering and decided that this, too, was what it meant to be part of a family. Somehow, though, with neither Erik nor Luke here the atmosphere had lost something vital—its warmth.

Feeling thoughtful and a little lonely, she opened the door to her suite, took a deep breath...and walked back into her past.

THE HOUSE WAS EMPTY. Luke found himself wandering from room to room, hating the oppressive silence, hating the sense of loneliness that he'd never noticed before. He'd always been a self-contained man. Hell, any cowboy worth his salt could spend days on end in the middle of nowhere, content with his own thoughts.

Suddenly he didn't like his own company all that much. In a few short days, he'd grown used to Jessie invading his space at unexpected moments. He'd come to look forward to his own private time with Angela, their one-sided conversations, her sober, trusting gaze.

He stood at the doorway to his own bedroom and tried to force himself to cross the threshold. For some idiotic reason, he felt as if he were trespassing on Jessie's private space, rather than reclaiming his own.

She'd left the room spotless, far neater than it had been when she'd arrived. The bed had been made up with fresh sheets. He knew because he'd heard the washing machine and dryer running and investigated. He'd found sheets and towels in the dryer, a load of his clothes in the washer.

He sighed. He almost wished she had left the old sheets on. Perhaps then, when he finally crawled back into that lonely bed of his, he might have been surrounded by her scent. Now, he knew, it would smell only of impersonal laundry detergent and the too-sweet fabric softener.

As he stood there he caught the glint of something gold on the nightstand beside the bed. The last rays of sunshine spilled through the window and made the metal gleam, beckoning him. Instinctively he knew whatever it was, it wasn't his. Puzzled, he crossed the room to see what Jessie had left behind.

Even before he reached the nightstand, he realized what it was: a ring. Her wedding ring. His heart skipped a beat at the sight of it. He picked up the simple gold band and let it rest in the palm of his hand. Even though he knew what it said, he read the engraved message inside: Erik and Jessica—For Eternity.

What had she been thinking? he wondered. She must have taken it off when she was cleaning and simply forgotten it, he decided because he wasn't sure he wanted to consider any other implications. He didn't want to believe that she'd been deliberately making a statement, leaving him an unmistakable message that would force him to act or forever damn himself for his inaction.

Eventually he pocketed the ring and returned to the kitchen and poured himself a cup of coffee. He put the ring on the table in front of him as he sipped the rank brew that had been left since morning.

What the devil was he supposed to do now? He could mail it to her at White Pines. Unfortunately, the arrival of her wedding ring in the mail might stir up a hornet's nest, if anyone in the family happened to notice. Heaven knew what interpretation they might place on her leaving it behind. He hadn't even figured out his own interpretation of its significance.

If an outsider saw him, he'd think Luke had lost his mind, Luke acknowledged dryly. He was studying that tiny ring as if it were a poisonous snake,
coiled to strike. The truth was, though, that the ring's presence in his bedroom was every bit as dangerous as any rattler he'd ever encountered.

"Seems to me like there are two choices here," he finally muttered, his
gaze fixed on the gold band. "Send it off and quit worrying about it or call
her up and ask what the devil she had in mind. Sitting here trying to make
sense of it isn't accomplishing a blessed thing."

It was also leading him to talk to himself, he noted ruefully.

He carried the coffee and the ring into his office, where he'd left the
cellular phone. He sat behind his desk for several minutes, trying to figure
out what he could say that wouldn't make him look like an idiot. Finally he
just dialed the damn number, taking a chance that Jessie would be in her
old suite and that it would still have the private line Erik had had installed.
She answered on the first ring.

"Jessie?"

There was the faintest hesitation before she asked, "Lucas? Is that you?"

Something inside him suddenly felt whole again at the sound of her voice.
It was a sensation that probably should have worried him more than it did.
"Yeah, it's me," he confirmed. "How was your flight? Any problems?"

"No, everything went smoothly. Angela never even woke up."

"That's good. I imagine everyone there made quite a fuss when they saw
her."

"That's an understatement," she said. "According to Cody, your father
will probably want to plan out her entire life, up to and including her choice
of a husband."

Luke found himself laughing at the accuracy of his youngest brother's assessment. "Listen to him. He has the old man pegged."

That said, he suddenly fell silent.

"Luke?"

"Yes."

"Was that all you wanted, to see if we'd arrived okay?"

He sighed. "No." Without quite realizing that he'd reached a decision
on his approach, he blurted out, "Actually, I wanted to let you know that
you'd forgotten your wedding ring. You must have taken it off when you
were cleaning or something."

"I didn't forget it," she said, a note of determination in her voice.

Her response left him stymied. "Oh," he said and then fell silent again, struggling with the possibilities, fighting a flare of hope he had no business at all feeling. Finally he asked, "Why, Jessie?"

"Think about it, Lucas," she said softly and he could almost see her smiling. "You're a bright man. You'll figure it out."

"Jessie..."

"Goodbye, Luke. Merry Christmas."

She hung up before he could get in another word. He sat staring stupidly at the phone in his hand. He closed his eyes and wished with all his heart that he'd gone to the Caribbean for the holidays. Or maybe taken a trip to Australia. Or even the South Pole.

Then he remembered that Jessie would have found the house empty when she'd gone into labor on the highway. Who knew what might have happened then. He couldn't regret having been here for her. No matter how much pain his feelings for her caused him in the future, he couldn't regret these few days they'd had.

He just had to figure out how to make them last a lifetime.

JESSIE GENTLY PLACED the telephone receiver back in its cradle and turned to the wide-awake baby on the bed beside her.

"That was your uncle Luke," she whispered, unable to keep a grin from spreading across her face. Just hearing his voice made her pulse do unexpected somersaults.

Angela understood. Jessie was absolutely certain of it. She waved her little fist in the air approvingly.

"How long do you figure it's going to take him to show up here?" Jessie wondered aloud.

She was far more confident now that he would turn up than she had been when she'd ridden away from his ranch with Doc Winchell. Leaving her own car there had been her ace in the hole. If Luke didn't make the trip to White Pines, after all, she knew she could always go back to get her car and have one last chance at making him see what they could have together.

She rolled onto her back, only to have her wedding picture catch her eye. It was still sitting on the dresser, just as it had while she and Erik had lived in this suite.

"You understand, don't you?" she whispered with certainty. "You've forgiven Luke and me for falling in love and that's all that really matters."

A soft tap on her door quieted her. "Jessie?" Mary called softly. "We'll be serving dinner in half an hour."

"I'll be right down," she promised.

"Bring the baby. I've found a carrier for her. I'll leave it outside the door."

"Thanks, Mary."

Jessie listened as her mother-in-law's footsteps faded, then she glanced down at her daughter. "Showtime, angel. It's time to go and dazzle your family."

The baby waved her arms energetically, an indication that she was more than ready for anything the Adams clan had in mind for her—now or in the future. Jessie wished she could say the same.

She had no sooner reached the bottom step, when Jordan appeared to take the carrier from her. At thirty, he was a successful businessman, one of the few to weather the Texas oil crisis and come out ahead. He was considered one of the state's most eligible catches, but he had remained amazingly immune to any of the women who chased after him.

"You look lovely, Jessie." He glanced down into the carrier, his expression faintly nervous as if he weren't too sure what to do with a baby. He seemed worried she might be breakable. "Everyone's anxious to see the newest addition to the family."

Jessie hesitated. "By everyone, I assume you mean that this isn't just a family celebration tonight."

Jordan's mouth quirked in a grin that reminded her so much of Luke, she felt her heart stop.

"Nope. The usual cast of thousands," he said. He leaned down and whispered, "Stick close to me and I'll protect you from the multitudes."

"And what about your own date?" she whispered right back. "I know perfectly well you must have one here. I've never seen you without a beautiful woman on your arm."

A flicker of something that might have been sadness darkened his eyes for just an instant, before his ready smile settled firmly back in place.

"I decided even I deserved a night off," he replied.

"Tired of small talk?" Jessie asked.

"Tired of all of it," he admitted. When Jessie would have questioned him further about whether this indicated an end to his days as Houston's most available playboy, he prevented it by taking her arm and propelling her into a room already crowded with guests.

"Behold the heir apparent," he announced, holding the baby carrier aloft as everyone applauded. That said, he seemed only too anxious to turn the baby over to the first person who asked to hold her. He wandered off without a second glance, his duty done.

For the second time since her arrival at White Pines, Jessie was gently shunted aside by people anxious to get a glimpse of the newborn. She heard the story of her being stranded at Luke's ranch told over and over. She heard her own bravery magnified time and again.

What she never heard, though, was any mention of Luke's incredible role in any of it. Just when she was prepared to climb halfway up the stairs and demand that everyone listen to her version of the events, Harlan folded a strong arm around her shoulders and called for silence.

"A toast," he announced. "Everybody have some champagne?"

Glasses were lifted into the air all around them.

"To Jessie and Angela," he said. "Welcome home."

The toast echoed around the room, as heartfelt from strangers as it was from the family. Even so, the welcome left Jessie feeling oddly empty. White Pines no longer felt like home. What saddened her more was that she wasn't sure whether it was the loss of Erik or the absence of Luke that made her feel that way.

When the cheers had died down, Harlan announced that the buffet supper was ready. The guests moved swiftly into the huge dining room to claim their plates and a sampling of the food that Jessie knew Maritza and the rest of the staff had been preparing for weeks now. She recalled from past years how bountiful and diverse the spread would be, but her own appetite failed her.

She surveyed the room until she finally spotted Cody holding her daughter and went to join them.

"I'll take her," she offered. "Go on and have your dinner."

Cody grinned. "I don't mind. I'm practicing my technique. I figure if I can charm 'em when they're this little, I'll have no problems with the grown-up ladies."

"Well, Angela's certainly fascinated," Jessie agreed as she observed her daughter's fist tangled in Cody's moustache. The baby tugged enthusiastically and Cody winced, but he didn't give her up. He simply disengaged her fingers as he chattered utter nonsense to her. Like Luke, he seemed totally natural and unselfconscious with the infant in his arms.

"You might have to work on your conversational skills," Jessie teased, after listening to him.

"You're not the first woman to tell me that," he admitted with a wicked grin that probably silenced most women on the spot, anyway. Jessie was immune to it, but she found herself amused by his inability to curb the tendency to flirt with any female in sight.

"I guess it's what comes from spending most of my days with a herd of cows," he added. "They're not too demanding."

"And what about Melissa?" she inquired, referring to the young woman who'd been head over heels in love with Cody practically since the cradle. "Is she too demanding?"

Cody's eyes lit up at the mention of the woman everyone assumed he would one day marry, if he ever managed to settle down at all. "Melissa hangs on my every word," he said confidently.

The touch of arrogance might have annoyed some people, but Jessie knew that Cody's ego wasn't his problem. The young man was simply a textbook case of a man who was commitment phobic. Melissa had contributed to the problem by wearing her heart on her sleeve for so long. Cody tended to take her for granted, certain she would be waiting whenever he got around to asking her to marry him.

One day, though, either Melissa or some other woman was going to turn Cody inside out. Jessie smiled as she envisioned the havoc that would stir.

"What are you grinning about?" Cody asked.

"Just imagining how hard your fall is going to be when it comes. Yours and Jordan's."

"Won't be any worse than Erik's," he teased. "Or Luke's," he added, shooting her a sly look.

Jessie swallowed hard. "Luke's?" she said, feigning confusion.

"I'm not blind, Jessie. Neither is anyone else around here, for that matter. Why do you think they were so appalled when they realized where you were when you had the baby? Luke never did have much of a poker face."

She was stunned. "What are you saying?"

"That my big brother is crazy in love with you. Always has been. Luke may be the strong, silent type, but he's transparent as can be where you're concerned."

Even as her heart leapt with joy at his confirmation of her own gut-deep assessment of Luke's feelings, Jessie denied Cody's claim. "You're wrong," she insisted.

Cody shook his head, clearly amused by her protest. "I'm not wrong. Why do you think he's not here?"

"I explained that earlier. It's because he's feeling guilty about Erik's death."

"He's feeling guilty, all right, but it's not because of Erik's death. At least, that's only part of it," he told her emphatically. "Luke's all twisted up inside because he's in love with Erik's widow."

Jessie practically snatched Angela out of Cody's arms. When she would have run from the room, when she would have hidden from Cody's words, he stopped her with a touch.

"Please, Jessie, I didn't mean to upset you. I, for one, think it would be terrific if you and Luke got together. Erik's gone. We can't wish him back. And if you and Luke can find some kind of happiness together, then I say go for it. Jordan agrees with me. He seems to be looking for happy endings these days. Don't say I told you but I think the confirmed bachelor is getting restless," he confided. "He needs you and Luke to set an example for him."

Once more, Cody had startled her, not just with his assessment of the undercurrents that she thought had been so well hidden in the past, but with his blessing.

"I don't know what the future holds," she said quietly, the words as close to an admission about her own feelings as she could make. "But I will always be grateful to you for speaking to me so honestly."

Cody draped an arm around her shoulders and squeezed. "Hey, Luke might be stubborn as a mule, but he is my big brother. I want him to be happy. As for you, the whole family lucked out when Erik found you. We want to keep you. And there's Angela to think of," he said, touching a finger gently to the baby's cheek. "She deserves a daddy and I think Luke would make a damned fine one."

Only after he had walked away did Jessie whisper, "So do I, Cody. So do I."

CHAPTER ELEVEN

LUKE COULD SEE only one way to push Jessie out of his life once and for all. If she had chosen Erik because she wanted a family to call her own, if she clung to him now for the same reason, then he would give her one. Not his, but her own. Her biological family.

He'd been awake half the night formulating his plan. First thing in the morning on the day after Christmas, he was on the phone to a private investigator he'd used once when he'd suspected a neighbor of doing a little cattle rustling from his herd. He supposed finding a long-lost family couldn't be much trickier than tracing missing cattle.

"Her adoptive family's name was Garnett," Luke told James Hill, dredging up the surname from his memory of the first time Jessie had been introduced to the family, practically on the eve of the wedding. Erik hadn't risked exposing her to too many of his father's tantrums or too many of his mother's interrogations. It was probably one of his brother's wisest decisions. Jessie might have fled, if she'd realized exactly what she was getting into. The surface charm of the family disintegrated under closer inspection.

"What else can you tell me about her?" Hill asked.

"What do you mean?"

"Where was she born? Where did she grow up? Her birth date? Anything like that?"

Luke listened to the list and saw his scheme going up in flames. For the first time he realized how very little he actually knew about Jessie. He'd fallen in love with the woman she was now. It had never crossed his mind that he might want to be acquainted with the child she had been or the lonely teenager who'd longed to discover her real family.

"I don't know," he confessed finally.

"You'll have to find out something or it'll be a waste of my time and your money," the private investigator informed him. "With what you're giving me, I can't even narrow the search down to Texas."

Luke sighed. "I appreciate the honesty. I'll see what I can find out and call you back. Thanks, Jim."

"No problem. If I don't talk to you before, have a Happy New Year, Luke."

"Same to you," he said, but his mind was already far away, grappling with various ideas for getting the information he needed about Jessie without her finding out what he was up to. He didn't want her disappointed if he failed to find answers for her.

To his deep regret, he could see right off that there was only one way. He would have to follow her to White Pines. The only way he could ask his questions was face-to-face, dropping them into the conversation one at a time over several days so she wouldn't add them up and suspect his plan. If the thought of seeing her again made his palms sweat and his heart race, he refused to admit that his reaction to the prospect of seeing her had anything at all to do with his decision to go. The trip was an expediency, nothing more.

For the second time that morning, Luke made a call he'd never in a million years anticipated making.

"Hey, Daddy, it's Luke."

"Hey, son, how are you?" Harlan asked as matter-of-factly as if Luke initiated calls to White Pines all the time. If he was startled by Luke's call, he hid it well.

"I'm fine."

"What's up?"

He drew in a deep breath and finally forced himself to ask, "Can you send the plane for me? I'm coming home."

Dead silence greeted the announcement, and for the space of a heartbeat Luke thought he'd made a terrible mistake in calling, rather than just showing up. It had been less than twenty-four hours since he'd flatly declared he wouldn't be coming to White Pines. If his father started one of his typical, if somewhat justifiable, cross-examinations, Luke didn't have any answers he was willing to share. He waited, unconsciously holding his breath, to see how his father would handle this latest development in their uneasy relationship.

"I'll have the plane there in an hour," his father said finally. It was as though he'd struggled with himself and decided to give his son a break for once.

Luke heaved a sigh of relief. "Thanks."

"No problem," Harlan said. He paused, then added, "But if you go and change your mind on me, though, I'm warning you that you'll pay for the fuel."

Luke laughed at the predictable threat, relieved by it. Obviously Harlan hadn't mellowed that much. "That's what I love about you, Daddy. You never allow sentiment to cloud your thinking about the bottom line."

By THE TIME Jessie got downstairs for breakfast on the morning after Christmas, only Mary remained at the table. She looked as stylish and perfectly coiffed as she had the night before, despite the fact she couldn't have had more than a few hours sleep.

Last night, surrounded by family and old friends, by the famous and the powerful, she had been in her element. She was equally at ease at the head of the table with only her daughter-in-law to impress. Jessie found that polish and carefully cultivated class a bit intimidating.

Her reaction to Mary Adams had a lot to do with the older woman's unconscious sense of style. In fact, Jessie couldn't ever recall seeing Erik's mother in anything more casual than wool slacks, a silk blouse and oodles of gold jewelry. Nor had she ever seen her with a single frosted hair out of place. Mary eyed Jessie's jeans and pale blue maternity sweater with obvious dismay.

"We must take you shopping," she announced, without a clue that her expression or her innuendo were insulting.

"I have plenty of clothes," Jessie protested. "Unfortunately, the baby arrived before I'd planned, so I didn't bring anything except maternity clothes along. The pants can be pinned to fit well enough."

"Not to worry," Mary said cheerfully. "I'll ask Harlan if the plane's free. The pilot can take us over to Dallas for the day. We can shop the after-Christmas sales at Neiman-Marcus. I have half a dozen things that I need to return and you certainly won't be needing those new maternity outfits we gave you now."

She shook her head, an expression of tolerant amusement on her face as she confided, "Harlan hasn't gotten my size right once in all the years we've been married. I've become used to these post-holiday exchanges."

Jessie tried again. "Maybe another day," she said a little more forcefully. Deliberately changing the subject, she asked, "Where are Jordan and Cody this morning?"

"Jordan's already flown back to Houston. He had business to attend to, or so he claimed. He's probably chasing after some new woman. I think Cody is off somewhere with his father," she said without interest.

She regarded Jessie thoughtfully. "That shade of blue isn't quite right for you. I believe something darker, perhaps a lovely royal blue, would be perfect with your eyes."

Jessie had been so certain she'd ended the subject of the shopping excursion. Apparently she hadn't. "I'm not sure I have the energy yet to keep up with you," she confessed as a last resort.

Finally something she'd said penetrated Mary's self-absorbed planning.

"Oh, my goodness, what was I thinking?" Mary said, looking chagrined. "Of course, you must be exhausted. I remember when the boys were born, I didn't even leave the hospital for a week and here it's only been a few days since Angela was born. How on earth are you managing? Young women today are much more blasé about these things than my generation was."

Since Mary's question seemed to be rhetorical and she appeared to have fallen deep into thought, Jessie concentrated on spreading jam on her perfectly toasted English muffin. She'd once wondered if the kitchen staff at White Pines had been told to toss out any that weren't an even shade of golden brown. Her own success was considerably more limited. She burned as many as she got right in the old toaster she had in her apartment.

"A nanny," Mary announced triumphantly, capturing Jessie's full attention with the out-of-the-blue remark.

"A nanny?" Jessie repeated cautiously.

"For Angela."

She'd hoped for a new tangent, but this one was pretty extreme even for Mary. "Please, it's not necessary," she said firmly. "I can take care of the baby perfectly well. Besides, you couldn't possibly find anyone on such short notice. And I'll be going back home next week, anyway."

"Nonsense," Mary said dismissively. "You'll be staying right here."

When Jessie started to argue, Mary's expression turned intractable. It was a toss-up whether Luke and the others had gotten their stubborn streaks from Harlan or their mother. The combined gene pool was enough to make Jessie shudder with dread.

"I won't take no for an answer," Mary said just as firmly. "Even if you insist on going back to that tiny little apartment and that silly job eventually, you have to take a few weeks of maternity leave. You'll spend it right here, where we can look after you."

Jessie bristled at having the life she'd made for herself dismissed so casually, but she bit her tongue. She honestly hadn't given any thought to the fact that she was entitled to maternity leave. It was on her list of things to worry about closer to the baby's arrival. Angela had thrown that timetable completely off.

"I don't know how much time I'm entitled to," she admitted.

"I believe I've heard six weeks is the norm," Mary said distractedly, jotting herself a note on the pad she always had at hand at breakfast for writing down the day's chores. She dispensed them to the staff as merrily as if they were checks. They weren't always received in quite the same spirit, but Jessie doubted if Mary noticed that.

Her mother-in-law glanced up from her notes. "Of course, three months would be better. Why don't I have Harlan call your boss and make the arrangements?" She made another note.

The thought of Harlan Adams negotiating anything with her boss gave Jessie chills. "Absolutely not. I'll make the call later today. After that I suppose we can talk more about how long I'm staying."

She gazed directly at Mary and tried to recall the precise tone of voice she'd used so successfully the evening before. "But no nanny. It wouldn't be fair to hire someone and then turn right around and fire them again."

"Well, of course not," Mary agreed far too readily. "We'll send her home with you. It will be our gift."

Jessie felt as if she were losing control of her life. "You said yourself that my apartment is tiny. When you visited, you complained you could barely turn around in it. It can hardly accommodate a live-in nanny."

Mary didn't even bat an eye at that complication. "Then we'll find you someplace larger," she said at once. She picked up her cup of tea. "If you decide to go back, of course."

"I thought we had settled that," Jessie began, then sighed. Clearly she would be better off saving this particular fight for another day. She didn't have the strength for it this morning. She stood. "I think I'll go back up and check on Angela."

"No need, Jessica. I believe Maritza's sister is sitting with her now."

She had married into a household of control freaks, Jessie decided, fighting her annoyance. Erik had quite likely been the only one in the group whose personality didn't demand that he take charge of every single situation. She had learned her lesson from observing him, though. If she didn't stand up to them, they would dismiss her opinions and her plans as no more than a minor nuisance.

"There's no need for her to stay with the baby," she told Mary forcefully. "I have a few letters to write this morning and some calls to make, so I'll be with her."

With that she turned and headed for the stairs, fully expecting yet another argument. For once, though, Mary was silent. Well, almost silent, Jessie amended. She thought she heard her mother-in-law sigh dramatically the instant she thought Jessie was out of earshot.

Back in her suite, she found a beautiful, young Mexican woman sitting right beside Angela's crib. Apparently she had taken her instructions to watch the baby quite literally, because she didn't even look away when Jessie entered the room.

"Buenos dias," Jessie said to her.

The young woman glanced her way and smiled shyly.

"Do you speak English?" Jessie asked.

"Yes."

"What's your name?"

"Lara Mendoza."

"Lara, thank you for looking after the baby. I'll stay with her now."

Lara seemed alarmed by the dismissal. "But it is my pleasure, *señora*. It is as Señora Adams wishes."

Jessie bit back a sharp retort. "It's not necessary," she insisted gently. "I'll call for you, if I need you, Lara."

Lara's sigh was every bit as heavy as the one Jessie had heard Mary utter. Apparently she was testing everyone's patience this morning.

Still, she had to admit that she was relieved to be on her own. Perhaps the decision to come to White Pines had been a bad one, after all. All of the things she'd hated most—the control, the dismissal of her opinions, the hints of disapproval—were coming back to her now.

She realized that for all of her hopes and dreams when she'd married Erik, this still wasn't her family. Jordan and Cody seemed to like her well enough. Even Harlan appeared to be fond of her. But Mary was another story. Every time her mother-in-law addressed her, Jessie couldn't help concluding that the older woman found her sadly wanting.

Suddenly she was filled with a terrible sense of despondency. Perhaps there was no place she really belonged anymore, not here and certainly not with Luke. He'd made that clear enough. Perhaps it was time she accepted the fact that she and Angela were going to have to make it entirely on their own.

A tap on the door interrupted her maudlin thoughts. She eyed the door suspiciously. She didn't think she could take another run-in with Mary just yet.

"Who is it?" she called softly, hoping not to wake the baby.

"Open the door and find out," a masculine voice said.

The sound of that unmistakable voice gave her goose bumps. She practically ran to fling open the door, relieved and elated by his timely arrival.

"Luke," she cried and propelled herself into his arms without considering his reaction.

Despite his startled grunt of surprise at her actions, he folded his arms around her and held her close. Suddenly she no longer felt nearly so alone. Breathing in the familiar masculine scent of him, crushed against his solid chest, she felt warm and protected and cherished. Those feelings might be illusions, but for now she basked in them.

After what seemed far too brief a time, Luke gently disengaged her and stepped back just far enough to examine her from head to toe. His expression hardened, as if something he saw angered him. She couldn't imagine what it could be.

"What's this?" he demanded, rubbing at the dampness on her cheeks. "What's wrong, Jessie?"

Jessie hadn't even been aware that she'd been crying before his arrival. Or maybe they were tears of joy at seeing him. Or perhaps simply the overly emotional tears of a woman who'd just given birth. She couldn't say. She just knew that at this moment she had never been more grateful to see someone in her life.

"Jessie? What's going on?" he asked as he led her away from the door and shut it behind him. A worried frown puckered his brow as he waited with obvious impatience for answers. "What has my family done to you now?"

"Nothing," she said. "Everything. Oh, Luke, they're taking over. I'm trying so damned hard not to let them. I am not a weak woman. You know that."

"No mistake about it," he agreed.

Jessie barely noticed the sudden return of a twinkle in his eye. She was too caught up in trying to explain her frustration. "But they're bulldozing right over me," she said, giving full vent to her exasperation. "They don't listen to a word I say. They don't even hear me."

To her astonishment, Luke chuckled. "Darlin', that's nothing to get all stressed out about. That's just Mother and Dad. Talk louder and stand your ground. Sooner or later, they'll get the message."

Jessie recognized the wisdom of his advice. She'd even seen how well it worked in action. She'd just lost her strength to fight there for a minute. She gazed up at Luke, tears still shimmering in her eyes, and offered a watery grin. "Quite a welcome, huh?"

He grinned. "Can't say I've ever minded having a woman hurl herself into my arms," he teased.

His gaze captured hers and held. Suddenly the teasing light in his eyes died out, replaced by something far more serious, something far more compelling. Jessie's breath snagged in her throat.

"Luke," she began huskily, then cleared her throat and tried again. "Luke, what are you doing here? Yesterday you flat-out refused to come. Did something change your mind?" She thought of the ring she'd left behind and the odd call he'd made the day before when he'd discovered it.

"I suppose you could say I came to take the pressure off you."

She regarded him uncertainly. It wasn't exactly the response she'd been anticipating. "In what way?"

He shrugged. "With me around, Daddy will be so busy trying to take charge of my life again, he won't have time to go messin' in yours."

"That's what you think," she said dismally. "Harlan could fiddle with the lives of an entire army platoon without missing a beat. As for your mother..." She sighed heavily.

Luke grinned. "Don't I just know it," he said, matching her sigh with apparent deliberation. "Maybe we should both just hide out in here for the duration."

An intriguing idea, Jessie thought. She was stunned, however, that Luke had suggested it, even in jest. Or, perhaps that was the point. Perhaps he intended to tease and taunt her as he might a younger sister, robbing her of any notions that he thought of her in any kind of sexual way. She searched his gaze for answers, but whatever emotions had been swirling there a moment before had given way to pure amusement.

"I have an idea," he said. His voice had dropped to a daring, conspiratorial note.

"What?" she asked suspiciously.

"I saw this very bored young woman sitting right outside your door. I have a feeling she would be more than glad to babysit for a bit."

Jessie rolled her eyes. Obviously Lara had decided to stay within shouting distance. "I'll bet," she muttered. "She's there under orders from your mother."

Luke chuckled. "Don't look a gift horse in the mouth. Let's let Lara do her thing. You and I can go to lunch."

"I just ate breakfast," Jessie protested.

"Obviously you haven't noticed the roads into town. By the time we get there, it will definitely be lunchtime."

"Won't your family be expecting you to eat lunch here? Have you even seen your father or mother yet? Or Cody?"

"Not hide nor hair of them. I snuck in the back way," he admitted. "You can help me keep it that way a little longer. Are you game?"

Jessie would have hopped a bus to nowhere if it would have gotten her away from White Pines for a little while, long enough to get back her equilibrium. A trip into town with Luke sounded perfect.

"You tell Lara," she said. "I'll get my coat."

As he started toward the door of the suite, Jessie called after him, "Luke?"

He glanced back.

"I don't have any idea what really brought you here, but I'm very glad you came."

An oddly wistful expression came over his face for an instant. It was gone in a heartbeat.

"Maybe I just heard your prayers for a knight in shining armor," he taunted. "My armor's a bit tarnished, but I can still stand up to a common enemy."

Hearing him expressing the view of Harlan and Mary that she'd been thinking to herself only a short time earlier made Jessie feel suddenly guilty. For all of their bossiness, they had always been kind to her. The huge pile of Christmas presents stacked in the corner—everything from a silver teething ring to a car seat for the baby, from a golden locket to a filmy negligee and robe for her—attested to their generosity.

"They're not that bad," she countered.

"Don't need a hero, huh? Want me to head on home, then?"

Jessie had the feeling he would be only too relieved to comply. For a multitude of reasons, she wasn't sure she could bear it if he left.

She leveled a challenging glare at him. "Just try it, Lucas. You'll have to walk through me."

He winked at her. "An interesting idea."

That wink stirred ideas in Jessie that could have gotten her arrested in some parts of the world, she was sure. Harlan and Mary would certainly have been scandalized by her thoughts. She grabbed her coat before she was tempted to act on any one of them.

As if he'd read her mind, Luke inquired lazily, "In a hurry, darlin'?"

"You have no idea," she replied in a choked voice.

"Oh, I'll bet I do." He touched a finger lightly to her lips. "Hold those thoughts."

Jessie had no problem at all complying with that rather surprising request. She doubted she could have banished them with a solid whack by a crowbar. What she couldn't comprehend to save her soul was why Luke had suddenly taken it into his head to torment her like this. Whatever his reasons, though, she intended to make the most of his presence.

He might walk away from her and from White Pines eventually, but if he went this time it wouldn't be without putting up the fight of his life for his heart. Jessie intended to claim it, this time for good.

CHAPTER TWELVE

LUKE WAS HAVING a great deal of difficulty remembering what it was that had originally brought him to White Pines. Sitting across from Jessie in a booth at Rosa's Mexican Café, his mind kept wandering to that desperate, hungry kiss they had shared in his truck. Just thinking about it aroused him. She had been hot and yielding in his arms, every bit as passionate as he'd ever imagined.

Now, as he watched her gasp with each bite of Rosa's lethally hot salsa, he was just as fascinated by her passion for the spicy food. Her eyes watered. Sweat beaded on her brow. He thought she had never been more appealing, though he wondered if she was going to survive the meal.

"They have a milder version," he said, taking pity on her.

She waved off the offer. "This is delicious," she said as she grabbed her glass of water and gulped most of it down before reaching for another chip and loading it with the salsa. "The best Mexican food I've ever had. I wonder why Erik never brought me here."

Luke didn't have an answer to that, but he couldn't help being glad that they were sharing her first experience with Rosa's Café, a place he'd always preferred to the fanciest restaurants in the state. Rosa, yet another of Consuela's distant cousins, had been bossing him around since his first visit years before. Coming here felt almost more like coming home than going to White Pines. He was delighted that Jessie liked it.

In fact, he was discovering that he was captivated by her reactions to everything. It seemed to him that in many ways Jessie took a child's innocent delight in all of her surroundings. Her responses to the simplest pleasures gave him a whole new perspective on the world, as well. Each time he was with her, his jaded heart healed a bit. Each time she chipped away at his resolve not to get more deeply involved with his brother's widow.

Remembering his resolve reminded him at last of why he'd broken his

A CHRISTMAS BLESSING

vow never to return to White Pines. He had come not simply to see Jessie again and indulge his fantasies about her, but to ply her for information about her past. It was a mission from which he couldn't afford to be distracted. He wanted to give her the gift of her family before he walked out of her life.

"It doesn't bother you at all, does it?" she asked, snagging his attention.

"What?"

"The food."

"Why? Because it's hot? I grew up on Mexican food. Consuela put jala-peño peppers in everything. I'm pretty sure she ground them up and put them in our baby food."

Jessie grinned. "No wonder you're tough as nails. This stuff will defi-nitely put hair on your chest, as my daddy used to say."

There it was, Luke thought. The perfect opening. "Tell me about your family," he suggested. "Did you always know you were adopted?"

She shook her head. "No, I didn't have a clue until I was a teenager. One night I was talking about a friend who was adopted and who'd decided to search for her birth mother, and my mother suddenly got up and ran from the room. I had no idea what I'd said to upset her so. Daddy looked at me like he'd caught me torturing a kitten or something and went rushing after her. I sat there filled with guilt without knowing why I should feel that way."

Luke couldn't begin to imagine her confusion and hurt. "Is that when they told you?"

"Later that night. I'd cleaned up the supper they'd barely touched and done the dishes when they finally came into the kitchen and told me to sit down. They looked so sad, but stoic, you know what I mean?"

Luke nodded. He'd actually seen a similar look in her face the day before, when he'd sent her away. He wondered how much of this she'd shared with Erik. A pang of pure jealousy sliced through him, and he cursed himself for being a selfish bastard, for wanting more of her than his brother had had.

Oblivious to his reaction, Jessie went on. "Anyway, they told me then that they had adopted me when I was only a few days old. They said they didn't know anything at all about my birth mother, that they hadn't wanted to know. They'd made sure the records were sealed and never looked back."

"You must have felt as if your whole world had been turned on its ear," Luke suggested.

"Worse, I think. It wasn't just that I wasn't who I'd always thought I was—Dancy and Grace Garnett's daughter. It was that they had lied to me for all those years. If you knew how Dancy and Grace preached about honesty above all else, you'd know how betrayed I felt when I learned the truth. It was as though they weren't who they'd claimed to be, either." She looked at him. "Am I making any sense here?"

"Absolutely." Since she seemed to be relieved to be sharing the story with him, Luke remained silent, hoping that would encourage her to go on.

"I begged them to let me find my biological mother, but Grace started crying and Dancy got that same accusing look on his face again."

Even now, she sounded guilt ridden, Luke noticed. "Do you realize that when you talk about them in casual conversation, you refer to them as Mother and Father, but just now, talking about that time, you instinctively started calling them by their first names?"

She seemed startled by the observation. "I suppose that's true. Like I said, I started thinking about them differently then." She gave him an imploring look. "Please, believe me when I say that no one could have had more wonderful parents. I loved them with all my heart. I grieved when they died. But something changed that night. I didn't want it to, but it did."

"Not because they were your adoptive parents, but because they'd lied."

She nodded. "The very thing they'd always told me was one of the worst sins a person could commit."

Luke felt a shudder roll through him and wondered if his own devious plan would fall into the category of lying and whether she would forgive him when she discovered what he was up to.

"But you gave up the idea of looking for your birth parents, didn't you?"

"At first I was so angry that I didn't care what they wanted, but then, after a few days, I realized how deeply hurt they would be. I told myself that they were my real parents in every way that mattered, so, yes, I dropped the idea."

"Where would you have looked?" he asked.

"Dallas, I suppose. It was the closest big city." She shrugged. "I was sixteen. This hit me out of the blue. I had no idea how to start."

"And they never told you anything more, just that you had been born in Texas?"

"Nothing." She sighed and broke the chip she was holding in two and put it aside.

When she glanced up again, Luke saw that her eyes were shimmering with unshed tears. His resolve stiffened. He would find her biological parents for her. She would have her family. She would have an identity that belonged to her, something he realized with sudden intuition was probably just as important to her as family.

No longer would she be Grace and Dancy Garnett's adopted daughter. Or Erik Adams's widow. Or even Angela Adams's mother. She would know her roots, her heritage. That, above all, was something Luke could understand. It was something no one in his family ever lost sight of. He'd been raised on tales of his ancestors and their struggles and accomplishments. They'd been held up as role models, tough in body and indomitable in spirit. Luke and his brothers had been expected to surpass their examples. The pressure had been unceasing.

It was odd, he thought. Jessie had so little family history. He sometimes thought he and his brothers had had too much. The legacy had shaped them into the men they were. He had wanted to shape his own legacy. Cody had fought to claim the one they shared. Jordan was, quite possibly, the most fiercely independent of all of them.

He reached across the table and claimed Jessie's hand. It was cold as ice. Clearly startled by his touch, she met his gaze.

"Just wanted to bring you back to the present, darlin'," he said softly.

Color rose in her cheeks. "Oh, Luke, I'm sorry. I never talk about the past like that. I can't imagine what got into me. You've probably been bored to tears."

"Anything but," he assured her, resisting the urge to run straight to the pay phone and call Jim Hill with the few bits of new information he had. He needed one last thing, though, the only thing he could think of that might help and that Jessie was sure to know, despite her doubts about so much else. He needed to find out her exact birthday. He knew how old she was— twenty-seven. And he recalled that her birthday was sometime in summer.

In fact he would never forget the celebration they'd thrown at White Pines her first year there. Erik had insisted on a real, old-fashioned Texas barbecue with neighbors coming from miles around and a live band for square dancing. He remembered every minute of it. That, in fact, was the night he'd realized that he was falling for his brother's wife, that what he'd dismissed as attraction went far deeper.

Jessie had been his partner for a spinning, whirling, breath-stealing square dance. Her cheeks had been flushed. Her bare shoulders had shimmered with a damp sheen of perspiration. Her lush lips had been parted, inviting a kiss. He had obliged before he'd realized he was going to do it. The quick, impulsive kiss had been briefer than a heartbeat, but it had shaken him to his core. Jessie had looked as if she'd been poleaxed.

The band had shifted gears just then and played a slow dance. Jessie had drifted into his arms, innocently relaxing against him, oblivious he was certain to the fact that his body was pulsing with sudden, urgent need. Desperate to keep her from discovering just how badly he wanted her, he had spotted Erik across the dance floor and maneuvered them into his brother's path. Erik had been only too eager to claim his wife.

If there had been regret in Jessie's eyes, Luke had blinded himself to it. He'd taken off right after that dance and from that day on he'd steered as far away from Jessie as he possibly could without drawing notice.

Glancing at her, he wondered if she recalled that night as vividly as he did. Bringing up the memory was one way to learn the last piece of information he figured he could get for the detective—or so he told himself.

"Hey, darlin', do you recall that shindig we threw for your birthday your first year at White Pines?"

Her blue eyes sparkled at once. "Goodness, yes. I'd never had such a lavish birthday party. Your parents actually had a dance floor installed under the stars, remember?"

"Oh, I remember," he said, his voice dropping a seductive notch.

"I'd never square danced before."

"You sure took to it."

"It was exhilarating," she said softly, and her eyes met his, her expression nostalgic.

If she was saying more than the obvious, Luke couldn't be sure. He decided for his own sanity it would be best to steer away from the minefield of any more intimate memories.

"Was that July or August? All I remember was how hot it was." Of course, he conceded to himself, his memory of the temperature might have had nothing to do with the weather. Jessie could have had his blood steaming with a look back then. She still could, he admitted. Air-conditioning hadn't been manufactured that could cool him off in her presence.

"August second," she said. "It was the day before my birthday."

That nailed it down, Luke thought, rather proud of himself. He glanced at his watch, then slid from the booth. "Excuse me a second, Jessie. There's a phone call I was supposed to make. I just now remembered it."

She regarded him oddly, but said nothing. Feeling like a sneak, Luke practically raced to the phone booth. He reached the detective on the third ring.

"I was able to come up with a little more information," he said and gave him what he had. "Does that help at all?"

"Some," Hill said. "I ran the name through the computer after we talked, just to see if anything turned up based on what you had this morning."

Luke sucked in a breath. "And?"

"Nothing much beyond the usual, social security number, credit rating, that kind of thing. There was one thing I found a little odd, though."

"What?"

"Looks to me as if she's been investigated before. There are some inquiries on the credit history."

"Couldn't that have been for a car loan or a job reference or something?"

"Possibly. It just didn't seem to track that way."

"How recently?"

"A few years back."

Luke felt his heart begin to thud dully. "In the fall?"

"As a matter of fact, yes. Most of the inquiries seemed to be around September or October."

Erik and Jessie had been married on November first. Her name had started coming up at White Pines only a month or two before as someone about whom Erik was serious.

"Do you know something about that?" Hill asked.

"Not for certain, but I'd put my money on Daddy," Luke said, fighting his anger. He'd known that Harlan suspected Jessie's motives in marrying Erik, but he'd had no idea he'd gone so far as to check her out. "My guess is that Harlan was doing some checking before Erik and Jessie got married. He probably wanted to be sure that the Adams name wasn't about to be sullied or that she wasn't going to take Erik for a fortune."

The detective didn't react to Luke's explanation except to say, "Maybe you can get the information you're after from your father, then. He was probably pretty thorough. Do you want me to wait until you check it out?"

"No, get started. Even Daddy probably couldn't bust his way into sealed adoption records."

"What makes you think you can?"

"Because you're going to tell me exactly how to go about it, and then I'm going to tell Jessie. She's probably the only one who can get through the legal red tape."

"If she wants to," Hill reminded him.

Luke thought of the sad expression he'd seen on her face earlier. "She'll want to," he said with certainty.

"She might not like what she finds."

"I'll be with her every step of the way," he vowed. "It'll be okay."

"You're the boss," the detective said. "I'll be in touch as soon as I have anything. Where will I find you?"

"At White Pines."

"Home for the holidays?"

"Exactly," Luke said dryly. "Just your typical family get-together."

It would be a lot less typical when he cornered his father about having Jessie investigated before the wedding. He was filled with indignation on her behalf. In fact, he might very well do something he'd been itching to do for years. He might wring Harlan's scrawny old neck.

LUKE'S EXPRESSION LOOKED as if it had been carved in stone when he came back from making that phone call. Whatever it had been about, the call had obviously upset him.

Jessie watched his profile warily on the ride home, wondering if she should try to probe for an explanation for his change in mood. She supposed she ought to be used to his sullen silences, but having caught a few tantalizing glimpses of the other, gentler side of his nature, she wasn't sure she could bear this return to an old demeanor, an old distance between them.

"Bad news?" she inquired eventually.

"You could say that," he said tersely.

"Can I help?"

He glanced her way. "Nope. I'll take care of it."

Jessie's gaze narrowed. "You jumped in this morning when you saw I had a problem," she reminded him. "Why won't you let me return the favor?"

"Because I can solve this myself."

"I could have solved my problem myself, but that didn't prevent you from butting in, because you cared."

Luke's gaze settled on her and his mouth curved into the beginnings of a smile. "You saying you care, Jessie?"

"Well, of course I do," she said hotly. "Luke, you know how I feel about you…" At the warning look in his eyes, her voice trailed off. Then, irritated with him and herself, she added determinedly, "And about what you did for me and Angela."

"Let's not start that again."

"Well, dammit, it's not something I'm ever likely to forget."

"Stop cursing. It's out of character."

She lost patience with all the verbal tap dancing. "Lucas, you are the most exasperating, mule-headed man it has ever been my misfortune to know. It's no wonder I'm cursing."

He grinned at her outburst. "I care about you, too," he conceded, his voice gentler. "If I really needed help with this, Jessie, I swear you'd be the first person I'd turn to."

Ridiculously pleased, she said, "Really?"

"Cross my heart."

"So does it have something to do with the ranch?"

He laughed. "Give you an inch and you go for the whole damned mile, don't you?"

"You know a better way to get what you want?"

An oddly defeated expression passed across his face. "No, darlin', I can't say that I do."

"Luke?"

"Drop it, Jessica. There's nothing for you to worry about." He glanced at her. "Except maybe how you're going to bring Mother and Daddy to heel."

She heaved a sigh. "I'd rather tackle your problem."

"No," he said with a grim note in his voice. "I can just about guarantee that you wouldn't."

Before Jessie could respond to that cryptic remark, he'd parked the fancy four-wheel-drive car in front of the garage and climbed out. Before she could move, he had her door open. He reached out, circled her waist with his hands and lifted her down from the high vehicle.

He was close enough that she could feel his warmth, close enough that his breath whispered against her cheek. She would have given anything to stay just that way, but the reality was they were at White Pines and there were far too many prying eyes.

Besides, judging from the grim, determined set of Luke's jaw, he would not have allowed it.

"Come on, darlin'. Let's go show 'em who's in charge of our lives."

"I was thinking maybe I'd slip away and take a nap," Jessie said wistfully.

"Resting up before the big battle," Luke noted. "A good idea."

"You could do the same," she suggested daringly, casting a sly look up at him. If the way his jaw was working was any indication, he did not mistake the seductive intent of the invitation.

"Darlin', believe me, that would be a declaration of war," he advised her.

Jessie was up for it. And Luke, she knew with every fiber of her being, was tempted. She winked at him. "One of these days you're going to take me up on it," she taunted him.

"Not in this lifetime," he said emphatically.

Jessie just grinned. She had a feeling deep inside that he was wrong. He was going to cave in far sooner than he thought. She could hardly wait.

CHAPTER THIRTEEN

WITH JESSIE RESTING in her suite, Luke paced up and down in his own, trying to cool off before confronting his father with what he'd discovered. Walking into a room and hurling accusations after months of separation would hardly get their relationship back on track. Still, he couldn't help wondering if Harlan made a habit of investigating any woman with whom any of his sons were involved. If that were the case, Jordan and Cody would probably send him into bankruptcy. Luke took a sort of grim pleasure in the prospect. He'd often wondered if his father would ever have to pay the price for his attempted control of his sons.

When he finally considered his temper calm and his approach reasonable, he bounded down the stairs two at a time and headed straight for Harlan's office.

He found his father seated behind a massive desk piled high with files and spread sheets. Wearing a pair of reading glasses, he was squinting at a computer screen, a sour expression on his once-rugged face. Except for the glasses and perhaps a new wrinkle or two, the scene of his father engrossed in work was so familiar that it made Luke's heart ache.

The glasses and the faint signs of aging, though, reminded him of just how long he'd been away. It wasn't just since Erik's death, but all the years since he'd declared his independence from Harlan's manipulations and moved to his own ranch. He wondered how many other subtle changes there had been since he'd gone.

Harlan glanced up at Luke's entrance. "So, there you are," he said.

His pleasure at seeing Luke was betrayed by his eyes, even though his tone was neutral. He almost sounded uncertain, Luke thought with surprise. It was a far cry from the usual arrogance. He couldn't help welcoming the change.

"About time," Harlan grumbled, his tone more in character. "I wondered where the hell you'd disappeared to. Your mother didn't even know you'd arrived. Wouldn't have known it myself except one of the trucks was missing."

"I had an errand in town. Jessie came along and we had lunch," he added with his usual touch of defiance. Even after all this time, it was a knee-jerk reaction, he realized with a sense of chagrin. If his father commented on the weather, Luke found some reason to counter his claim.

His father nodded, ignoring the testiness. "Fresh air probably did her good. She looked a mite peaked to me last night."

"She just had a baby," Luke reminded him.

His father's expression finally shifted to permit a small hint of approval. "Cute little thing, isn't she?" he said with a note of pride. "Looks like an Adams."

"I was thinking she looked like Jessie," Luke countered, just to be contrary...again.

Harlan shrugged, not rising to the bait. "Who can tell at that age?" he admitted. "You boys all looked exactly alike when you were born." His expression turned thoughtful. "Not a one of you turned out the same, though, in looks or personality. I never could make sense of how that happened."

"We all got your stubborn streak, though," Luke reminded him.

Harlan chuckled at that. "I like to blame that particular trait on your mama. Makes her crazy."

"I can imagine."

Harlan settled back in his chair and studied Luke intently. "You look tired. Why'd you really come home, son? You have something on your mind?"

"I just thought it was about time for a visit," Luke replied noncommittally.

"Your mother's going to be mighty glad to see you."

Luke doubted it. Mary Adams was too caught up in her own social whirl and in her husband to pay much mind to the comings and goings of her sons. He was more interested in his father's reaction. They had never parted without some sort of petty squabble, probably just the clash of two strong wills. Since Erik's death the tension had been greater than ever.

"And you?" he asked, watching his father's expression closely.

His father seemed taken aback by the question. "That goes without saying," he said at once. "This is your home, boy. Always will be."

Luke sighed, relieved yet still incapable of fully believing the easy answer. "I wasn't so sure you felt that way after the way Erik died," he said cautiously. "It's understandable that you might blame me for what happened."

"Is that what's kept you away from here?"

Luke shrugged. "Part of it."

"Well, you were wrong. Your brother died because he was a reckless fool," his father snapped angrily, "not because of anything you did."

Luke was startled by the depth of emotion. He suspected there was a heavy measure of guilt behind the anger, but hell would freeze over before Harlan would admit to it. Still, the reaction worked to his advantage. With his father's usual control snapped, it seemed like the perfect moment to get an honest answer from him.

"I wonder how he would have felt if he'd known you had Jessie investigated," Luke inquired casually, his gaze pinned to his father's face. "It might have given him the gumption to go after the life he really wanted."

Harlan's skin turned ashen. "What the devil do you know about that?" he demanded indignantly, unsuspectingly confirming Luke's suspicions. "And what business is it of yours, if I did?"

Luke refused to be drawn into an argument over ethics, morality or just plain trust. He had his own agenda here. "Find out anything interesting?" he inquired lightly.

"Nothing worth stopping the wedding over, which you obviously knew already." He leveled a look at Luke. "Like I asked before, what business is this of yours? It happened a long time ago. If anyone should have told me to mind my own business, it was Erik, but he never said peep."

"Maybe because he was too damned trusting to suspect you'd do something like that. I'm not nearly so gullible where you're concerned. I know how manipulative you can be. I like Jessie. I don't like to think that you don't trust her."

"Is that it?" Harlan demanded with a penetrating look. "Or is it something more?"

Luke felt as if he were standing at the edge of a mine field with one foot already in the air for his next fateful step. "Like what?"

"Like maybe your interest in her is personal."

"Well, of course it's personal," he snapped, hoping to divert his father from making too much of his defense of Jessie by admitting straight out that he cared for her as he would for any other family member. It was a risky tactic. It appeared his father had been far more attuned to the undercurrents around White Pines than he'd realized.

"She's my sister-in-law," he pointed out. "She just delivered my niece in my bed a few days ago. I'd say that gives me cause to take an interest in her."

"And that's all there is to it?" Harlan inquired, skepticism written all over his face.

"Of course." Luke uttered the claim with what he hoped was enough vehemence. His father still didn't exactly look as if he believed him, but to Luke's relief he appeared willing to let the matter drop.

"You found out she was adopted, didn't you?" Luke prodded.

"Already knew that. Erik told us."

"Did you find out anything about her family?"

"Now who's asking too many questions?"

Luke scowled at him. "Just answer me. I have my reasons for asking."

"So did I," Harlan said testily.

Luke stood. "Never mind. I can see this was a waste of time."

"Oh, for goodness' sakes, settle down. Yes, I found out about her family. They were good, decent, church-going people. Paid their bills on time. Gave her a good education. There was nothing to find fault with there."

"I meant her biological family."

An expression of pure frustration spread across his father's rough-hewn features. "Couldn't get anywhere with that. Didn't seem worth chasing after, once I'd met her. My gut instinct is never wrong and it told me right off that Jessie's honest as they come. If I hadn't known it before, there was no mistaking it when she walked away from here without a cent after Erik died. She's a gutsy little thing, too stubborn for her own good, if you ask me."

"An interesting assessment coming from you," Luke observed.

Harlan's expression turned sheepish. "So it is."

Luke decided he'd better get out of his father's office before Harlan picked up the issue of Luke's feelings for Jessie and pursued it. He'd diverted his father once, but Harlan was too damned perceptive for Luke to keep his emotions hidden from him for long. A few probing questions, a few evasive answers and the truth would be plain as day.

"I think I'll go hunt down Mother," he told his father.

"I believe you'll find her in the parlor reading or planning some social schedule," Harlan said with a grimace. He turned back to his computer and sighed. "You know anything about these danged things?"

"Enough to get by," Luke said.

"Maybe you could give me a few pointers later. At the rate I'm going, this year's records won't even be programmed before next year."

Surprised by the request, Luke nodded. "I'd be happy to." It was the first time he could ever recall his father admitting that one of his sons might have an expertise he didn't. That single request went a long way toward mending fences, hinting that perhaps they could finally find a new footing for their relationship, one of equals. Respect was all he'd ever really craved from his father. He'd known he had his love, but true respect had been far harder to come by.

Just as Luke reached the door, his father called after him. "It really is good to have you home again, son. This house was built for the whole family. Never realized how empty it would be one day."

Luke felt an unexpected lump form in his throat. He'd discovered the same thing about his own house recently, as well. For a few brief days it had felt like a home. "Thanks, Daddy," he said. "It's good to be here."

Oddly enough, he realized as he walked away, it was true. It was unexpectedly good to be home. He wondered just how much of that could be attributed to Jessie's presence upstairs and whether from now on "home" to him would always be wherever she was.

THAT NIGHT AS he dressed for dinner, Luke conceded that his prediction of his mother's reaction to seeing him had been right on target. She had been superficially pleased when she'd greeted him, but within minutes she'd been distracted by a flurry of phone calls from friends confirming holiday plans. He'd been only too glad to escape to his suite, where he waited impatiently for some news from Jim Hill. He doubted his mother had even noticed when he left the parlor.

Upstairs, he spent a restless hour wishing he still had a right to head out to his father's barns and work the horses. He needed some hard exercise to combat the stress of being home again, of being so close to a woman he hungered for and couldn't have. His shoulders ached with tension. His nerves were on edge. He would have gone out and chopped wood, if he hadn't seen a woodpile big enough to last till spring.

He supposed the real truth was that he'd been feeling tense and out of sorts ever since Jessie had appeared on his doorstep. It was as if he were being ripped apart inside, torn between desire and honor. If he'd thought his emotions were frayed at his ranch, he realized now that the necessity for watching every word, every glance while under his father's roof only compounded the problem. His conscience, never something he'd worried too much about before Erik's marriage to Jessie, was taking a royal beating.

Eventually he tired of pacing. Worn out by tangling with his own thoughts, he started back downstairs. Outside Jessie's door, he heard Angela crying and Lara's unsuccessful attempts to quiet her. He hesitated, wondering where Jessie was. Perhaps she had already gone downstairs.

He tapped on the door and opened it. The young Mexican girl, her cheeks flushed, her hair mussed, was frantically rocking the crying baby. The jerky movement was not having a soothing effect. Quite the contrary, in fact.

"What's the problem?"

"I cannot get her to sleep," Lara whispered, sounding panicked. "No matter what I do, she cries."

"Where's Jessie?"

"With the *señora*."

"Has the baby been fed?"

"*Sí.* Only a short time ago."

Luke crossed the room in a few quick strides, then reached down and took the baby from Lara. She fit into his arms as if she belonged there, her warm little body snuggling against his chest. Her gulping cries turned to whimpers almost at once.

"Shh," he whispered. "It's your uncle Luke, sweet pea. What's with all the noise? Were you feeling abandoned there for a minute?" He glanced at Lara and saw that an expression of relief had spread across her face. "How was she while we were out this afternoon?"

"Like an angel, Señor Luke. She slept most of the time. I thought she would go to sleep again as soon as she had eaten."

Luke rubbed the baby's back. A tiny hand waved in the air, then settled against his cheek. As if she found the contact familiar and comforting, she quieted at once. That strange sense of completeness stole over him again.

Luke made a decision. "Lara, why don't you take a break for a few hours. I think our little angel ought to join the rest of us for dinner."

"But *la señora* said..."

Luke tried to recall exactly how many times he'd heard his mother's edicts repeated in just that way by Consuela, by his father, even his teachers. Mary Adams's influence had been felt everywhere in his life, at least when she chose to exert it. "Let me worry about my mother. Have your dinner. Go on out for the evening. We can manage here."

"*Sí,* if that is your wish," she said with obvious reluctance.

"It is," he assured her.

He found a soft pink baby blanket, obviously a new addition since he doubted there would have been anything pink in the assortment of items his mother had saved from her sons. Wrapping Angela loosely in the blanket, he cradled her in one arm and gathered a few spare diapers and a bottle with his other hand. He eyed a can of baby powder, debated a couple of toys, but abandoned them when he couldn't figure out how to pick them up.

"Remind me to get you one of those fancy carry things," he told the baby, who regarded him with wide-eyed fascination. "I don't have enough hands to carry this much paraphernalia. Things were a whole lot less complicated at my house, before you got outfitted with the best supplies money could buy."

Angela gurgled her agreement.

"You know what I love most about you, sweet pea? You go along with everything I say. Be careful with all that adoration, though. It'll give a guy a swelled head. I don't want to give away any trade secrets. After all, we men should really stick together when it comes to women, but for you I'll make an exception. If there's any heartbreaking to be done, I want you to be the one who does it. You need advice about some jerk, you come to me. Is it a deal?"

The baby cooed on cue. Luke grinned.

"You understood every word, didn't you? Well, now that we've settled how you should go about dealing with men, let's go find your mama and your grandparents. Not that I'm so crazy about sharing you, you understand, but the truth is I'm not always going to be around. You need to have other folks you can count on, too. Your mama's one of the best. And nobody on earth will protect you from harm any better than your granddaddy. He's fierce when it comes to taking care of his own. Just don't let him bully you."

Angela yawned.

"Okay, okay, I get the message. I'm boring you. Let's go, then."

Downstairs, he located the rest of the family in the parlor. He found the varying reactions fascinating—and telling. His mother looked vaguely dismayed by the sight of Angela in his arms, just as she had when any of her own children had slipped downstairs during a grown-up party. His father grinned, unable to hide his pleasure or his pride, just as he had when showing off his sons to company. Jessie seemed resigned at the sight of her daughter comfortably settled against Luke's chest.

"Where on earth is Lara?" his mother demanded at once. "I am paying that girl to look after the baby."

Before Luke could say a word, Jessie jumped in. "Don't blame Lara. I suspect your son is responsible for this. Is that right, Luke?"

Luke shrugged, refusing to apologize. "She was crying."

"Babies cry," his mother said irritably. "Picking them up will only spoil them."

"Oh, for goodness' sakes, Mary, she's a newborn," Harlan countered. "There's nothing wrong with giving her a little extra attention. Besides, I want to get to know my first grandbaby. Bring her here, Luke."

He eagerly held out his arms. Luke placed the baby in them and wondered at the oddly bereft feeling that instantly came over him. He moved over and took a seat by Jessie, gravitating almost unconsciously to her warmth as an alternative to the strange sort of serenity he felt when holding the baby.

As soon as he sat down, though, he realized his mistake. Jessie represented more than warmth. She exuded heat and passion, at least to him. His body responded at once, predictably and with the kind of urgency he hadn't known since his teens.

"Sherry, Lucas?" his mother asked.

"Hmm?" he murmured distractedly.

"She's asking if you would like a drink," Jessie explained as if she were translating a foreign language. There was a look of knowing amusement in her eyes he couldn't mistake.

"No thanks," he said.

"I'm very surprised to see you here, Lucas," his mother commented.

"But we're delighted, aren't we, Mary?" his father said, a warning note in his voice.

His mother seemed startled by the sharp tone. "Well, of course, we are. I'm just surprised, that's all. He hasn't been here for months. And," she added pointedly, "he told me quite plainly that he couldn't get here over the holidays. As I recall, he told you the same thing just yesterday."

Luke refused to be drawn into a quarrel. "Plans change," he said.

"Will you be staying long?" his mother asked.

"Mary!" Harlan protested. "You'll make the boy think we'd rather he stayed home."

His mother flushed. "Well, of course, I didn't mean that. For goodness' sakes, Harlan, I was just trying to think ahead and make some plans. I was wondering if we should have another party, perhaps for New Year's Eve."

Luke shuddered at the thought. "Not on my account," he said with absolute sincerity.

"I think a quiet celebration is more in order this year," Harlan said, regarding him with something that might have been understanding. "I think we had enough chaos around here last night to last till next year."

"Chaos?" Mary repeated, red patches of indignation in her cheeks. "I worked for weeks to make sure that we had a lovely party for our friends on Christmas and you thought it was chaos?"

Harlan sighed. "I didn't mean any disrespect, dear. Your parties are always well attended. They're the high point of the social season around the whole state of Texas. Everyone knows that. I just think one is enough." As if he sensed that his fancy verbal footwork hadn't yet placated her, he added, "Besides, I know firsthand how much the planning takes out of you."

Mary sighed heavily, her expression put-upon. "I suppose a quiet family occasion would be nice for a change. Perhaps for once Jordan and Cody can be persuaded to leave their current paramours at home."

"I doubt that will be a problem," his father said. "Jordan claims to be fed up with the social whirl and Cody's trying to put a damper on Melissa's enthusiasm for a spring wedding. I suspect they'll be happy to come alone."

"That was certainly the impression I got from them, too," Jessie chimed in. "I never thought I'd see the day when those two would turn up anywhere without a woman, but they seemed almost relieved to be on their own last night."

After the initial awkwardness and minor bickering, the rest of the evening settled into something astonishingly comfortable. Dinner passed quickly with quiet conversation about old friends and plans for the next few days of the holidays.

"The McAllisters' annual party is tomorrow night," Mary reminded them. She looked at Luke and Jessie. "I'm sure you'll both want to come."

"Not me," Jessie said at once. "I'm not quite up to partying yet, but the rest of you go."

Luke noticed that Jessie claimed a lack of energy only when it suited her purposes. She'd always hated the stuffy McAllisters and the collection of rich and powerful they dutifully assembled periodically to prove their own worth to the neighbors.

"I believe I'll stay here, too," he said, studiously avoiding Jessie's gaze.

His mother opened her mouth to protest, but to his surprise, his father defended his decision. "Mary, leave him be. If it were up to me, I'd stay home, too, but I know you won't have it."

"Well, for goodness' sakes, it's social occasions like this that make the kind of business contacts you need," his mother grumbled. "I should think Luke would be aware of that, as well."

Luke settled back in his chair, his decision reinforced by his father's surprising understanding. "I prefer to make my business contacts in an office, Mother. That way there's no confusing my intent. As I recall, the last time I tried to do business at one of these social occasions, Henry Lassiter thought I was going to trade a herd of cattle for his daughter's hand in marriage."

Next to him, Jessie choked back a laugh. Her eyes sparkled with undisguised merriment. "How on earth did you extricate yourself from that?"

"Thank goodness I didn't have to," he said, laughing at the memory.

"Janice Lassiter was as appalled as I was. She told her father in no uncertain terms that she was not a piece of property he could trade in to get a prize bull and a few cows. I have to admit I found her a bit more intriguing after she said that."

To his surprise his mother's mouth curved into a smile. "You never told us that story."

"Of course not," Luke said. "Do you realize how embarrassing it was to realize that I'd made some innocent remark that got mistaken for a marriage proposal? It's not something a man wants getting around."

Jessie leaned close and whispered, "There are some women who might even take you up on an innocent remark even without the offer of the cattle. Those are the ones you really have to watch your step with."

Luke shifted and stared at her, his blood suddenly thundering in his veins. He could feel his cheeks flush and prayed that his very observant father was watching something else at the moment. If Luke meant anything at all to Angela, who was sound asleep in her grandfather's arms, the little munchkin would wake up and start screaming right now to divert attention.

She didn't, which meant he had to hide his reactions as best he could.

Why had he never noticed that sweet, demure Jessie was a master of torment? She must have had poor Erik in a daze from the day they'd met. Or perhaps his brother had been made of sterner stuff than he'd ever realized.

"Watch yourself, darlin'," he murmured in an aside he hoped couldn't be overheard. "You're just begging for trouble."

Jessie turned her deceptively innocent gaze on him. "Who's going to give it to me, Lucas?"

Good question. For him to tangle with her in the way he longed to, the way she was taunting him to, he was the one who would be in real trouble. Up to his neck in it, as a matter of fact, and drowning fast.

CHAPTER FOURTEEN

IF IT WEREN'T for the half dozen servants scattered around, Luke and Jessie would have had the house to themselves the following evening, once his parents had gone off to the McAllisters' party. For some reason, Jessie found being alone with Luke at White Pines oddly intimate and very disconcerting. Acknowledging her feelings for Luke at his ranch had been one thing. Admitting them here, where she and Erik had spent their entire married life, was something else entirely.

Frankly, she was still surprised that Luke had conspired to be alone with her. When she'd left his ranch, she had been all but certain she would never see him again unless she arranged it. Now, not only had he followed her to White Pines, he seemed unwilling to let her out of his sight. She couldn't believe it was because he'd had a change of heart about their relationship. He was still jumpy as a june bug around her. To be truthful, she wasn't much better.

Sitting across from Luke in the huge, formal dining room, with the table set with fancy china, sterling silver and fine crystal, Jessie felt as if the atmosphere were suddenly charged with electricity. In his kitchen she had been comfortable, even sure of herself. Here she felt as if she were on a first, very nerve-racking date. She wondered if he felt the same uncertainty, the same shivery anticipation.

If he did, it wasn't apparent, she decided with some regret. He'd worn slacks and a white dress shirt, left open at the throat just enough to reveal a sexy whorl of crisp, dark hair and tanned skin. With his hair neatly combed, his cheeks freshly shaved, he looked as confident as Jordan, as sexy as Cody and as at ease as Erik. The combination was enough to make her palms sweat.

Luke lifted his glass of wine and took a slow sip, his gaze never leaving her face. The intensity of that look was deliberate. There was no mistake about it. Jessie could feel her cheeks flush. Her pulse skittered wildly.

CHRISTMAS BLESSING

"Everything okay?" he inquired in a lazy drawl that sent fire dancing through her veins.

"Of course," she responded in a choked voice. "Why?"

"You look a little…feverish."

Oh, sweet heaven, she thought desperately, wishing she could pat her cheeks with a napkin dipped in the crystal goblet of ice water. The man was deliberately turning the tables on her. She swallowed hard and searched her soul for the confidence to play his game and win. "No," she said eventually, her voice shaking. "I'm fine."

He nodded politely, but there was a knowing gleam in his eyes. "If you say so."

"I do," she said adamantly.

"Okay."

Fortunately, Maritza came in with the main course just then—beef Wellington. "It is your favorite, Señor Luke, *sí?*"

Luke grinned at her, his attention diverted at last. Jessie used the reprieve to draw in a deep breath and surreptitiously fan herself with her napkin.

"Absolutely," he told the housekeeper. "And not even Consuela does beef Wellington better than you do."

"I will not tell her you said so," Maritza said, her cheeks rosy with pleasure at the compliment.

"Thank you," Luke said, his expression absolutely serious. "She'd put me on a diet of canned soup for a month, if she found out."

When the housekeeper had retreated to the kitchen, Jessie said, "You're very kind to her."

He seemed surprised by the comment. "Why wouldn't I be? She's terrific. The whole family is. Did you know that Rosa who owns the café we went to is another cousin? I believe Lara is Rosa's daughter or maybe she's a second cousin. I've lost track of all the connections."

"And you're nice to all of them." Seeing his skepticism, Jessie tried to analyze what she'd seen in their rapport. "I can't explain exactly," she finally admitted. "It's not that you're just polite, that you say what's expected. You genuinely appreciate what they do. I'm sure that's why Consuela chose to go with you when you left White Pines. I suspect you make her feel like part of the family, while your mother treated her like hired help."

Luke shrugged off the compliment. "Consuela is family to me," he said with surprising feeling. "She's the one who really raised me, raised all of us, for that matter. Mother's single goal in life was to make Daddy's life easier, to give him whatever he wanted. She gave him four sons, then did everything she could to see that we stayed out of his way. If I'm ever fortunate enough to have children, I made a promise to myself that they will never feel the way we felt as kids, as if we were a nuisance to be tolerated."

Jessie was appalled by the assessment, by the trace of bitterness in his voice. Obviously his resentments ran deeper than she'd ever realized.

"Your father certainly never treated any of you that way as far as I could tell," she argued. "He's obviously very proud of all of you."

Luke's expression was doubtful. "You can say that after the way he manipulated Erik, the way he's always tried to control the rest of us?"

Jessie found herself smiling at the concept that anyone on earth could manipulate or control Luke. "I don't see that he exactly has you under his thumb."

"Because I rebelled."

"Don't you suppose the struggle to become your own man made you stronger?"

His gaze narrowed. "What's your point?"

"That if Harlan had made it easy for you, you might not have fought half so hard to get your own way. All of this could have been yours. You would have had a nice, comfortable life without really struggling for it."

"Are you saying he deliberately battled with us over every little thing just to make us fight back?"

Jessie shrugged, refusing to spell it out any more clearly. She wanted him to look at his past from a fresh perspective and draw his own conclusion. "You know Harlan better than I do."

Luke's expression grew thoughtful. "I never thought about it that way before," he conceded. "I always wanted my own place. I didn't want to follow in his footsteps and simply claim what he'd already built. The harder he fought to keep me here, the harder I fought to go."

"And you succeeded in making the break," she pointed out. "You have a successful ranch of your own now, one you can be especially proud of because you know it's the result of your own hard work, isn't that right?"

He nodded slowly. "Jordan made the break, as well. He and Daddy used to stay up half the night fighting over his future. Daddy was fed up with him wildcatting at oil wells all over hell and gone. Told him it was time to settle down back here. Swore he'd cut him out of the will, if he didn't stay."

He paused, then suddenly grinned. "I just remembered something. I was here the night Jordan packed his bags and stormed out to move to Houston. He told Daddy he could take his inheritance and shove it. I came down when

I heard all the commotion and found Daddy standing at a window watching him go. There were tears in his eyes and the strangest look on his face."

"What kind of look?" Jessie asked.

"I realize now that it was satisfaction, maybe even that pride you're so sure he feels for us. He was actually glad that Jordan was going after his dream," he said, a note of astonishment in his voice. "Jordan even admitted to me later that he'd had an awfully easy time landing his first desk job in the oil business. He always had a hunch that Daddy had made a call or two."

"Could be," Jessie said. "Too bad he hasn't tackled Jordan's social life. It's time he settled down. I think he's finally ready."

"Really?" Luke shook his head, clearly bemused by the discoveries he was making once he looked past those deeply ingrained resentments. "That would be something to see. I think Jordan's going to surprise us all when he finally falls in love."

"What about Cody? How did Harlan deal with him?" Jessie asked.

"In his heart, Cody was the one who always wanted White Pines," Luke said. "Unlike Jordan or me, Daddy kept pushing him toward the door. The harder he pushed, the more Cody dug in his heels and made himself indispensable around here. The next thing we knew he'd built himself a little house down the road and was acting as foreman."

Three brothers, Jessie thought, all a little stronger because Harlan had had the wisdom to make them fight for their choices in life, rather than handing them a future on a silver platter.

And then there was Erik.

"Erik was the only one the technique backfired with," she said softly. "He was never like the rest of you. He was gentle, eager to please. You said yourself the other day that he was the diplomat. Whenever Harlan pushed him, he backed down, tried to find a middle ground, hoping to win his father's approval. Instead, Harlan just grew more and more impatient with him."

Luke reached for her hand. Jessie supposed he meant it only as a gesture of comfort, but it made her senses spin. She couldn't have pulled away, though, if her life had depended on it. Fortunately, she supposed, Luke broke off the contact all too soon.

"I suppose the real skill in parenting is understanding each child's personality," Luke said thoughtfully. "Daddy said just last night how amazed he was at how different we were. Maybe if he'd recognized that sooner, Erik wouldn't have suffered so, trying to be something he wasn't. And you wouldn't have lost him."

Jessie took a deep breath and met Luke's gaze. It was time to tell him everything and see where it led them. "I suspect I was destined to lose him one way or another. At least this way he never had to lose me to another man."

Luke choked on the sip of wine he'd just taken. His eyes watered as he stared at her with astonishment written all over his face. "What are you saying?" he demanded.

Jessie drew in a deep breath. She wasn't going to let him mistake her meaning with subtleties. "That I was in love with you long before Erik died," she admitted boldly.

Luke was shaking his head before she completed the sentence. "Don't say that," he protested.

"Why not? It's true." She leveled a gaze into his troubled eyes. "Why do you think I left here after Erik died?"

"Because you couldn't bear to be around me, knowing I'd caused his death," Luke said.

Jessie decided she'd already opened the door. It was time to walk through it.

"No," she told him softly, but adamantly. "Because I was filled with guilt over my feelings for you. From the day Erik and I moved into White Pines, I felt this connection to you. I didn't want it. I couldn't explain it. I certainly could never have acted on it, but it was there, just under the surface, tormenting me."

Tears welled up in her eyes, spilled down her cheeks. "You have no idea how guilty I felt when he died. A tiny part of me was actually glad that I would never have to make a decision to leave him. I don't think I could have, no matter how badly I wanted to. I could never have hurt him that way. For all of his weaknesses, Erik was good to me. He deserved better than he got from me. He deserved my whole heart, instead of just a piece of it."

She thought back to the few moments she'd had with Erik at the hospital after Luke had come to tell her that her husband was dying. Alert for just a heartbeat, he'd turned that gentle, understanding gaze of his on her.

"Be happy, Jessie," he'd whispered, clutching her hand in his.

"Not without you," she'd insisted, as the life slowly seeped from his body with each weakening beat of his heart.

He'd squeezed her hand fiercely. "Tell him, Jessie." Then more emphatically, he'd said, "Tell Luke."

At first she hadn't realized what he meant. "What?" she'd pleaded. "Tell Luke what?"

He'd struggled for air, then managed to choke out two words. "Love him."

"Of course, I will tell him that you love him," she'd soothed, caressing his cheek.

He'd smiled faintly at that. "Not me. You."

Remembering how stunned she'd been, how consumed with guilt, Jessie thought no man had ever displayed more love, more generosity than Erik when he'd clung to her hand and said, "'S okay, Jessie."

"Oh, Erik, forgive me," she'd pleaded.

That sweet smile spread across his face one last time. "Nothing to forgive," he'd whispered. "I love you."

She gazed across the table at Luke and wondered how much she should tell him about Erik's final words. Would they free him to love her?

Or, as they had with her, would they merely renew his own deeply ingrained sense of guilt? Knowing that Erik had guessed how they felt about each other, even if neither of them had ever acted on those feelings, was a heavy burden. She could attest to that. It had driven her from White Pines.

In the end she kept silent and the moment to confide passed.

"You're not in love with me," Luke said sharply, cutting into her reverie.

Jessie's head snapped up. She almost choked on the bubble of hysterical laughter that formed in her throat. He seemed to think by saying it enough, he could make it true.

"Lucas, that is not for you to say."

He slammed his glass of wine onto the table with so much force, it was a wonder the crystal didn't shatter. Wine splashed in every direction. He glared at her. "I won't have it, do you understand me?"

She gave him a compassionate look. "Maybe you can control your feelings, maybe you can sweep them under the carpet and pretend they don't exist, but you can't do the same with mine. I won't allow that."

His expression turned thunderous. "You won't *allow* it?" he repeated slowly.

Jessie held her ground. "They're my feelings."

"They're crazy."

She shrugged. "Maybe so. In fact, at this precise moment, I'm almost certain you're right about that. I would have to be crazy to fall in love with such a mule-headed male." She gave him a resigned look. "But, then again, there's no accounting for taste when it comes to matters of the heart."

She watched Luke's struggle to get a grip on his temper. In a perverse sort of way, she almost enjoyed it.

"Jessie, be reasonable," he said with forced patience. "It's not me you're in love with. It's the family. I'm taking care of that."

She went perfectly still. "You're taking care of that?" she repeated care-fully. "What exactly does that mean? Did you suggest Harlan and Mary adopt me? What?"

A dull red flush climbed up Luke's neck. "No, I...um, I spoke with a private investigator."

Stunned, she just stared at him. Dear heaven, it was worse than she thought. "About?"

He winced at her curt tone. "It was supposed to be a surprise."

"Tell me now." She bit off each word emphatically. She couldn't think when she'd ever been so furious. He'd denied that this had anything to do with his family. So, if she was interpreting all of the stuttered hints and in-nuendoes correctly, he had decided to get himself off the hook with her by presenting her with her biological parents. Definitely a tidy solution from his point of view. "What exactly is this investigator investigating?"

Luke heaved a sigh. "He's looking for your mother."

At one time that announcement would have thrilled her. She would have leapt from the table and thrown her arms around him for being so thought-ful. Now all she felt was empty. He was expecting her to trade her very real, very deep love for him for a stranger's possible affection. Couldn't he see it wasn't the same at all?

He seemed genuinely puzzled by her lack of response. "I thought this was what you wanted. You said... You told me how much you'd wanted to find your biological family."

"I did. I still do," she said wearily. When she could manage it without weeping, she met his gaze. "But not if it's going to cost me you."

The instant the words were out of her mouth, she ran from the room. Upstairs in her suite, she sent Lara away and took Angela in her arms.

"Can't he see it, angel? Can't he see that the two of you are the only fam-ily I need?"

WELL, THAT HAD certainly gone well, Luke thought in disgust. Maybe he was every bit as bad as Harlan, trying to manipulate lives and control feel-ings. He'd only wanted to give Jessie the possible—her real family—to make up for the fact that he could never give her the impossible—himself.

After apologizing to Maritza for spoiling the meal she'd worked so hard to prepare, he slowly climbed the stairs. His thoughts were in turmoil... again.

What could he say to Jessie to make her see that it wouldn't work? No matter how badly he wanted her, no matter how much she professed to love him, Erik would always be between them. There would never be a moment when their passion could flower, free from guilt and the overwhelming sense of having betrayed a man they had both loved. If their own consciences didn't destroy them, the disappointment and indignation of the rest of the family surely would.

He paused outside Jessie's suite and listened. He could hear the faint sounds of movement, the murmur of voices. Or was it only one voice? Jessie's, perhaps, as she soothed Angela back to sleep?

Unable to help himself, he quietly opened the door a crack and peered inside. The suite's bedroom was in shadows. A silver trail of moonlight splashed across the bed.

In a corner of the room the whisper of the rocker drew his attention. Jessie was holding the baby to her breast, nursing her. The glow of moonlight made her skin incandescent. Luke's gaze was riveted, his body instantly throbbing with an aching need.

He realized after a moment that the yearning he felt went beyond the physical. He wanted to claim Jessie and the baby as his own with a fierceness that staggered him. He wanted the right to be in that room beside them, to drink in the incredible sight of mother and child in an act as old as time. He wanted...so much more than words could possibly express.

He could deny it from now to eternity and it wouldn't change the truth. Somehow Jessie had realized that and made peace with it, while he still struggled. He knew, even if she did not, that love did not always conquer the obstacles in its path. She would come to see him as a sorry prize, if he cost her the love of his family.

Suddenly he sensed her gaze was on him. When she looked up, he could see the sheen of dampness on her cheeks, and a dismay worse than anything he'd felt over betraying Erik cut through him.

"I'm sorry," he said in a ragged whisper.

The rocker slowed. "For?" she asked cautiously.

The simple question stymied him. For making her cry? For loving her? For refusing to go down a path that could only lead to worse heartache?

"For everything," he said at last.

He turned away then, a dull sensation of anguish crushing his chest. Knowing he was closing the door on so much more than just the sight of the two people he loved most in the world, he quietly pulled it shut.

Even then, though, he couldn't move. In the gathering silence, he heard Jessie whisper his name. It was no louder than a sigh of regret, but to his ears it seemed louder than a shout. He resisted the longing to open that door—the only shield between him and a wildly escalating temptation—for a single heartbeat, then two.

"Luke?"

He closed his eyes and tried to shut out the sound of her voice, but the echo of his softly spoken name was already in his head, driving him crazy. A sigh shuddered through him and he knew he was lost. He opened the door, stepped inside, then closed it.

And as he did, he knew with every fiber of his being that nothing in his life would ever be the same.

CHAPTER FIFTEEN

JESSIE WATCHED WITH bated breath as Luke closed the door to the suite behind him. Her heart seemed to have stilled and then, as he took the first step toward her, it began to thunder mercilessly in her chest.

Dear heaven, how she loved him. Earlier tonight she'd been sure that she had lost him forever. She had run out of ways to combat his stubbornness, or so she had thought.

Apparently all it had taken was the whispered cry of his name on her lips, a soft command he'd been unable to resist. He crossed the room, reluctance still written all over his hard, masculine face, and sank slowly to the edge of the bed beside the rocker, careful not to allow his knees to brush against hers. Too careful. It told her how deeply his feelings for her ran and how much he feared losing control.

His gaze remained fixed on the baby in her arms. A soft, tender smile tugged at the corners of his lips. If she could have, without disturbing Angela, she would have touched a finger to that normally stern, unforgiving mouth. She would have tried to coax that smile to remain in place.

"Was it so very difficult?" she inquired dryly.

His gaze found hers. "What?"

"Walking into this room."

"Not difficult," he said, the smile coming and going again like a whisper. "Dangerous. When I'm around you, I can't think. My common sense flies out the window. No one has ever had such control over me."

"I don't think feelings are something you can dictate with common sense," she said.

"Maybe not, but actions are." He studied her with a rueful expression. "You have the lure of a siren, Jessie. You and your baby."

"Is that so terrible?"

"I've told you all the reasons it is."

"Reasons, yes, but you've never said what was in your heart."

Luke sighed and looked away. When he eventually settled his gaze on her again, there was an air of acceptance about him that she hadn't seen before. It gave her hope.

"My heart," he began, then shook his head. "I'm not sure I can find the words."

She leveled a look at him, then said quietly, "Then show me."

A soft moan seemed ripped from somewhere deep inside him. "Jessie, don't..."

"It's just the two of us here in the dark, Lucas. You can show me what's in your heart. There's no one to object."

She thought she detected the faint beginnings of another wry smile.

"Not just two of us, Jessie. Angela's right here with us. Hardly a proper audience for all I'd like to do to you, all the ways I'd like to show you how I feel."

Jessie wasn't about to let him seize an easy excuse for maintaining the status quo. Her entire body shook with her desperate yearning for his touch.

"She's ready to be put down for the night," she countered. "I'll take her into the other room. After that, Luke, no more objections. No more excuses."

She tucked the baby into her crib, caressing the soft, sweet-smelling cheek with a delicate touch. Suddenly she was overwhelmed with emotions—love for this precious new life, love for the man who waited in the next room. Her fear of the future was diminishing day by day.

Finally it was her love for Luke that drew her back. She was lured by the promise of warmth, by the deep sense of honor that made Luke the man he was, a man worthy of loving. There would be no passion between them, she thought with deep regret. Not tonight. Physically for her, it was too soon. Perhaps emotionally, as well, though she didn't think so.

But there would be commitment at last. She could sense it with everything in her. He would no longer deny his feelings. And with Luke by her side, they could fight the rest of the inevitable battle with his family together.

He stood when she entered, then met her halfway across the room. Fighting, then visibly losing one last battle with himself, he opened his arms to her. Jessie moved into the embrace with the sense that she was finally, at long last, home to stay. The serenity that swept through her was overwhelming.

"It won't be easy," he said, his chin resting atop her head as she nestled against his chest.

"Easy is for cowards," she said bravely.

"Anything this difficult may be for fools," he said dryly.

She stepped back and looked up at him. "Do you love me?"

He cupped her face in his hands, then slowly, so very slowly lowered his head until his mouth covered hers. The answer was in his kiss, a consuming, breath-stealing kiss that seemed to last forever and said *yes, yes, yes* with each passing second. The touch of his lips branded her, the invasion of his tongue claimed her as intimately as she knew his body would some day. Relief and so much more washed through her, filling her with wild exhilaration.

Convinced at last, she dared to insist on an answer to her earlier question. "Do you love me?"

"I thought I'd just told you," he said, a satisfied smile on his face.

"That was just a clue," she said, deliberately dismissing the kiss to taunt him. "A very good clue, but not conclusive. I want proof, Lucas."

His eyebrows rose fractionally. "Oh, really? How far can I actually go under the circumstances."

"I'll let you know when you've reached the limit."

"That's what I'm afraid of, we'll reach yours and test mine beyond endurance."

She stripped him of his shirt with slow deliberation. When his torso was bare, she caressed the hard muscles of his arms in a deliberately provocative gesture, following the shape, learning the texture of his skin. "I'd say you're strong enough to take it."

His gaze narrowed. "Do you have a wanton streak I ought to know about?"

"I suppose that's one of the things you'll learn eventually," she taunted him, delighting in the flare of heat in his eyes, the unmistakable catch of his breath that hinted of sudden urgency.

He reached for the buttons of her blouse then and easily freed them. Beneath the cotton, her breasts were fuller than ever and extraordinarily sensitive. He swallowed hard as his tanned, callused finger traced the pale, rounded flesh, arriving in time at the already throbbing nipple. He leaned down and flicked over the sensitive bud with his tongue. A gasp rose in Jessie's throat as she clung to his shoulders.

With her eyes closed and her head thrown back, there was no knowing where his caresses would come next or how shattering they would be. With each exquisite, daring touch, her body responded in ways she'd never expected it to.

Far too soon, she realized the torment she was putting him—putting both of them—through. There would be no tumbling into bed, no tangling of bared arms and legs, no press of bodies on fire. She had underestimated how difficult it would be to call a halt. Her newly awakened body throbbed with need. Luke's muscles were tensed with the effort of holding back. His eyes glittered with dangerous emotions.

She covered his hands with her own and stilled his touch.

"Enough?" he asked, his voice hoarse.

"Not nearly enough," she replied, still wondering at the discovery that there could be so much more than she had ever experienced with Erik. "But we're dangerously close to the point when I'll lose all reason."

"How long will it be before I can hold you through the night?" he asked, his voice filled with hunger and perhaps just a touch of awe that such a day would, indeed, finally come. They'd reached a turning point and moved on. There would be no going back from this night. They both recognized that.

"There's been no one in my life, Luke. Not since Erik. I saw no need to ask the doctor about this," she confessed with regret. "A few weeks, I believe."

Luke's expression turned grim. "Just about long enough to put out the wildfire we're about to touch off when everyone figures out what's going on."

Jessie's confidence faltered for a moment. He still hadn't said the words she'd demanded of him. Every action, every touch told her he loved her, but she wanted him to say the words, wanted to hold the sound of them in her heart. "Luke, exactly what is going on?"

He glanced from her bared breasts to her face and back again. "I'd say that's plain enough."

"Just sex?"

"Darlin', there's no such thing as *just sex,* where you and I are concerned. I knew the instant I laid eyes on you years ago that it would be like this between us."

"You know what I mean," she said impatiently.

He pulled her back against him, close enough she could feel his warmth, could feel the steady, reassuring beat of his heart.

"We'll work all of that out," he promised. "One step at a time, Jessie, we'll find our way."

He still couldn't seem to bring himself to say the words. But for now, it was close enough. It was a vow that whatever lay ahead, they would face it together.

HARLAN WAS STILL at the breakfast table when Luke arrived downstairs in the morning. He knew the instant he looked into his father's eyes that he was upset about something. Luke had a sinking feeling deep in his gut that he knew what that something was. He had thought he heard his parents come in the night before just as he'd slipped from Jessie's room well after midnight. He'd been all but certain he had gotten past them undetected, but perhaps he hadn't been as stealthy as he'd imagined.

His father put the paper aside and waited while Luke poured himself a cup of coffee. Luke deliberately took his time.

When he was finally seated, he met his father's gaze. "Everything okay?"

"I was about to ask you the same question."

"Oh?"

"I saw you leaving Jessie's room last night. I wondered if there was something wrong with her or the baby."

The question might have been innocuous enough, but Luke knew his father better than that. Harlan never inquired casually about anything. And their earlier conversation had already demonstrated Harlan's suspicions. Luke could have manufactured a discreet answer, but he had a hunch his father had already figured out the implications of catching him in that upstairs hallway.

"They're fine," he said, focusing his attention on buttering his toast.

"Then there must have been some other reason for you to be sneaking out with half your clothes in your hand."

So, Luke thought dully, there it was, out in the open. Spelled out in his father's words, it sounded sordid, and his love for Jessie was anything but.

"I love her," he declared defiantly, meeting his father's gaze evenly. "And she loves me."

Harlan sighed deeply, but there was little shock in his eyes. Instead, his gaze hinted of sorrow and anger. "I was afraid of this," he said.

"There's nothing to be afraid of. We're just two people who fell in love. You could be happy for us."

"She's your brother's widow, dammit!"

Luke bit back an expletive of his own. "Erik is dead, Dad. Denying our feelings won't bring him back."

The quietly spoken remarks did nothing to soothe Harlan's temper. "How far has it gone?"

"Not far. She just had a baby."

His father scowled at him. "I meant before."

Luke felt a rough, fierce anger clawing at his stomach. How readily his father was willing to condemn him for a sin he hadn't committed. He supposed that was the price he had to pay for declaring his independence. Despite Jessie's analysis last night, he knew that Harlan would never totally trust him because of that.

"There was nothing between us when Erik was alive," he declared quietly. *"Nothing!"*

"Who the hell are you trying to kid, son? I saw the way the two of you looked at each other. I knew in my gut that was what drove you away, what drove both of you away. You were running from feelings you knew weren't right."

He stared hard at Luke. "Whose baby is it?" he demanded. "Erik's or yours?"

For the first time in his life, Luke honestly thought he could have slammed a fist into his father's face and enjoyed it.

"How dare you?" he said, his tone lethal. "Neither Jessie nor I ever did anything to deserve a question like that. It doesn't say a hell of a lot about your opinion of Erik, either. Whether you choose to believe it or not, he and Jessie had a good marriage. She's not the kind of woman to turn her back on her vows. And I would have rotted in hell before I would have done anything, anything at all to take that away from him."

"Instead, you took away his life."

The cold, flatly spoken words slammed into Luke as forcefully as a sledgehammer. Though he had blamed himself too damned many times in the middle of the night for not doing more to save Erik, the doctors had reassured him over and over that his brother had been beyond help. Hearing the accusation leveled by his father, the same man who'd absolved him from guilt only a day or two before, made him sick to his stomach.

He refused to dignify the accusation with a response. Instead, he simply stood and headed for the door. "I'll be gone before Mother gets down." He glanced back only once, long enough to say, "If Jessie so chooses, she and your granddaughter will be going with me. You can put us all out of your head forever."

"Lucas!" his father called after him. "Dammit, son, get back here!"

Luke heard the command, but refused to acknowledge it. He could not, he *would not* submit to more of his father's disgusting accusations. Nor would he allow Jessie to be put through the same ordeal.

He had known this was the reaction they would face. It was one reason he had fought his feelings so relentlessly. It was why he'd struggled against Jessie's feelings as well, but no more. Those feelings were out in the open now and the fallout had begun. That didn't mean he had to linger at White Pines until his parents poisoned the happiness he and Jessie were on the threshold of discovering.

He was still trembling with rage when he slammed the door to Jessie's suite behind him.

Visibly startled by his entrance and by his obviously nasty temper, Jessie motioned him to silence. "I've just gotten the baby back to sleep," she whispered as she led him into the bedroom. "What on earth's wrong?"

"Pack your bags," he ordered at once. His plan to give her an option in the matter had died somewhere between the dining room and the top of the stairs. He intended to claim what was his and protect them from the righteous indignation they would face if they remained here.

"Why?"

"We're going to my ranch."

To her credit Jessie held her ground. "Why?" she repeated, her voice more gentle. Worry shadowed her eyes.

Luke muttered an oath under his breath and began to pace.

"Lucas, sit down before you wear a hole in the carpet. Besides you're making me dizzy trying to follow you."

"I can't sit. I'm too angry."

"It's barely seven o'clock in the morning. What could possibly have set you off this early in the day?"

"I just came from having a little chat with Dad. Apparently he saw me leaving your room last night and jumped to all the worst conclusions."

"Meaning?"

He frowned at her. "He assumes you and I are having an affair."

"Luke, if it weren't for certain circumstances, we would be," she said pointedly.

"He assumes it has been going on for some time." When she showed no evident reaction to that, he added, "He wonders if perhaps Angela is mine."

Jessie's eyes widened. Her mouth gaped with indignation. Patches of color flared in her cheeks. She flew out of the rocker and headed for the door.

Luke stared after her. "Where the devil are you going?"

"To have a few words with your father. I will not allow him to insult Erik's memory, to insult all of us with such a disgusting allegation."

Luke caught her elbow and hauled her back into the room. "It won't help. He's in a rage. He won't listen."

"Oh, he'll hear me," she insisted in a low tone. "Let me go, Luke."

"Not until you calm down." After a moment, she stopped struggling. Her utter stillness was almost worse. "I'm sorry, Jessie. I knew this was the way he would take it. God knows what Mother will have to say when she finds out. She'll probably insist on going into seclusion from the shame of it all. I think the thing to do is get away until they've had a chance to settle down and digest the news. Maybe then we can have a conversation that won't deteriorate into a lot of ugly name calling."

Jessie's chin tilted stubbornly. "I won't leave. Not like this."

"There's no choice. You have no idea what it's going to be like around here in a few hours. I won't let you go through that."

"I'm not leaving," Jessie repeated adamantly. "I thought Angela would bring this family back together. It seemed to me just yesterday that you and your father were putting past differences behind you. I can't allow our feelings to ruin your chances for a reconciliation."

Luke stared at her incredulously. "Jessie, what the hell is going on here? You fought like crazy to get me to acknowledge my feelings for you. Finally, just last night, we agreed to stop fighting how we feel and try to build a future. Now you're willing to put that at risk so my father and I can get along? I don't get it. Where are your priorities?"

"Where they've always been," she said quietly. "With family. Nothing's more important, Luke. Nothing."

He took a step back and studied her as if she were an alien creature. He didn't understand how he had gotten it so wrong. She was still the woman he loved, all right. Her hair was tousled and just begging for him to run his fingers through it. Her cheeks were rosy, her eyes glinting with determination. She was the most incredible mix of soft curves and fierce convictions he'd ever met.

Right now, though, it seemed to him their dilemma came down to a choice between family and him. If he understood her correctly, she was choosing his family.

Raking his fingers through his hair in a gesture of pure frustration, he shook his head. "So that's it, then? After all this, you're choosing them over me."

He had to admit that Jessie looked shocked by his assessment.

"That isn't what I'm saying at all," she protested. "I'm saying we need to stay here and work it out."

"Not me," Luke said stubbornly. "You can make peace with the devil, if that's what you want, but I'll be damned if I'll hang around with people who think so little of you and of me. Frankly, I'd think you'd have more pride, too."

With one last look in her direction, he turned and stalked from the room. Just as he had with his father earlier, he ignored her plea for him to return. As far as he could tell, there was nothing more to be said.

Only after he had his bag packed and was outside did he allow himself to stop for an instant and think about what was happening. When he did, this great empty space seemed to open up inside him.

They had been so close. He had actually begun to believe that dreams could come true. In the end, though, Jessie's love hadn't been as strong as he'd thought.

He threw his bag onto the passenger seat of one of his father's pickups and dug the keys out from under the mat. He'd hire someone to drive it back from his ranch tomorrow. He sure as hell wasn't about to ask Harlan to have the pilot fly him home.

Besides, the long, tedious drive would do him good. He'd have time enough to figure out how he was going to survive not having Jessie and Angela in his life.

He was just about to turn onto the driveway, when a bright red pickup skidded to a halt behind him, blocking his way. Cody leapt from the truck before the engine quieted.

"Luke, what the hell are you doing?" his youngest brother demanded.

"What does it look like? I'm stealing one of Daddy's trucks and going home."

"Without Jessie?" Cody inquired softly.

Luke stilled and stared at his brother. "What do you know about Jessie and me?"

Cody rolled his eyes. "Hell, Luke, anyone who isn't blind could see how the two of you feel about each other. Don't abandon her now."

"You've got it backward. She made the decision to stay."

"You're the one in the truck, about to head down the driveway," Cody contradicted. "That constitutes abandonment in my book. I thought you had more guts."

A dull throbbing was beginning at the base of Luke's skull. "Whatever you have to say, Cody, spit it out. I want to get on the road."

His brother shot him a commiserating look. "I talked to Jessie a little bit ago. She wasn't making a lot of sense, but I got the gist of it. I know what Daddy said. It was a lousy thing to say. There's no getting around that."

"So you can see why all I want to do is get the hell away from here."

"Sure can," Cody agreed.

Luke was startled by the unexpected agreement. He studied Cody suspiciously.

"Of course, Jessie also told me a story. She said you'd remembered how Daddy taught us to be strong, how he made us fight for the things we wanted in life. She told me some cockamamy theory that he deliberately puts road-blocks in our paths just so we have to scramble over them. It's his way of finding out how badly we want something."

Luke closed his eyes. He recalled the exact conversation all too vividly.

"Isn't Jessie worth fighting for?" Cody asked softly. "Seems to me like she is."

His brother's words reached him as nothing else had. Cody was right. He was running away from the most important fight of his life. Luke sighed and cut the pickup's engine.

"When did you grow up and get so damned smart?" he asked as he climbed from the truck and snagged his brother in a hug.

"Not me," Cody denied. "It was Jessie. She gave me all the arguments I'd need."

"She could have tried them on me herself."

Cody grinned. "She said you were too mad at her to listen. She figured since I was neutral, I might have a shot at getting through that thick skull of yours."

"Daddy's never going to approve of me being with Jessie," Luke said. "Mother's going to go ballistic."

"Ought to make life around here downright interesting," Cody said. "Maybe I'll move back to the main house just to watch the fireworks. Jordan will probably want to come home, too."

"Only if you both intend to stand beside me on this," Luke warned.

A crooked grin on his face, Cody held up his hand for a high-five. "That's what brothers are for."

Luke realized that was something he was finally beginning to under-stand, thanks to Jessie. It killed him to admit it, but it just might be that she was a hell of a lot smarter than he was when it came to matters of fam-ily and the heart.

CHAPTER SIXTEEN

HER HANDS CLUTCHED tightly together, Jessie stood at the window of her room and watched Luke and Cody's sometimes heated exchange below. When Luke finally shut off the truck's engine and emerged, a sigh of relief washed through her. She had been so afraid that the desperate call she'd made to Cody had been too late. She'd also known he might be her only chance to make Luke see reason.

She knew from her own conversation with Cody on Christmas that he had given her relationship with Luke his blessing. It had been her first hint that not every member of the Adams clan would be opposed to the feelings she and Luke shared.

This morning she had sensed that even more than Cody's ability to stand up to Luke, what was needed was someone who wouldn't be passing judgment on the original cause of the disagreement between father and son.

As she watched Cody and Luke enter the house, she prayed that all of Cody's skills at persuasion wouldn't be wasted the instant Luke ran into his father.

Drawing in a deep breath, she decided that this was not a battle Luke should have to take on alone. It was their fight. Plucking Angela from her crib, Jessie emerged from her suite and started downstairs.

Halfway down she realized Luke was waiting at the bottom of the steps, his gaze fixed on her. Her pulse skittered wildly as she tried to anticipate what he would say to her. Beside him, Cody shot her a wink and an irrepressible grin.

"I think I'll join Daddy for some coffee," Cody said. "I want a front row seat for the next act."

Jessie smiled at him. "Thanks for coming so quickly."

"No problem. Nothing like tangling with big brother here to get my adrenaline jump started in the morning. Can't wait to get to Daddy now.

I might even try to persuade him to let me buy that new tractor I've been wanting."

After he'd gone, Luke finally spoke. "I'm sorry," he said. "I shouldn't have run out and left you to deal with Daddy." The apology seemed to have been formed at some cost. He was watching her uneasily.

Jessie reached out and touched his cheek. "You thought I'd chosen them over you, when nothing could be further from the truth. I chose us, Lucas. We can't have a future if we don't settle this with everyone now. It will eat away at us, until we're destroyed. Hiding away on your ranch is no solution, and in your heart, I think you know that."

His lips curved in what might have been the beginning of a smile. "You play dirty, though, Jessica. Threw my own words back in my face."

"No, I didn't." She grinned unrepentantly. "I had Cody do it. If I could have gotten him here fast enough, I would have had Jordan add his two cents."

He cupped her face in his hands. "You are worth fighting for, Jessie. Never doubt that. The way I felt when I climbed into that truck, the empty space inside me where my heart had been, I hope to God I never feel that way again."

"You won't," she whispered. "I promise."

Angela stirred in her arms just then. Luke glanced at the baby and his expression softened. "Come here, sweet pea," he said and claimed her.

A look of resolve came over his face as he clasped Jessie's hand. "Shall we go face the enemy on his own turf?"

She halted in her tracks, forcing him to a stop. "We won't get anywhere, if you keep thinking of your father as the enemy."

"How else should I be thinking of him? He's standing square between me and the woman I love."

The declaration made her smile. "Try thinking of him as a father who's defending the honor of his son who died."

Luke sighed heavily. "In too many ways that makes it all the harder, darlin'. It's almost impossible to fight a ghost."

Jessie said nothing, just squeezed his hand. She thought she knew how to disarm Harlan Adams, though. And when the time came, she would use Erik's own words to do it.

WITH ANGELA IN his arms and Jessie at his side, Luke felt his strength and courage returning. He felt whole again. That gave him the resolve he needed to walk back into that dining room and face his father.

His lips twisted into a grim smile as he overheard Cody and Harlan arguing over the need for a new tractor. Cody was cheerfully enumerating a list of reasons to counteract every one of Harlan's opposing arguments. Their words died the instant Harlan spotted Luke and Jessie in the doorway.

"Cody, go and take care of that matter we were discussing," his father ordered brusquely.

For an instant, Cody looked confused. "I can buy the tractor?"

His father shrugged. "Might as well let you do it now, before you drive me crazy."

The tiny victory gave Luke hope. He could see once again that sometimes all Harlan really wanted was a good fight. He wanted to be convinced that a decision was right. If his sons couldn't make a strong enough case, they lost. It might have been pure contrariness, but he sensed that it really was his father's way of seeing that they learned to fight for what they believed in. Maybe underneath that tough exterior, his father really did want only what was best for his sons.

Luke made up his mind then and there that his case for claiming Jessie and Angela as his own would be a powerful one.

"Thought you'd taken off," Harlan said, his tone cool.

His avid gaze carefully avoided Luke and settled on his granddaughter. Luke watched him struggling with himself, fighting his obvious desire to stake his claim on the baby he believed Luke had no right to.

Luke kept his voice steady. "I decided running wouldn't solve this problem."

"Did you reach this decision all on your own, or did Jessie's refusal to go force you into it?"

Luke shot a wry look at his father. "Does it really matter? I'm here now." He glanced at Jessie, seated so serenely beside him. "We're here now."

"You two are going to break your mother's heart," his father said bluntly.

"Why?" Luke demanded. "We've done nothing wrong. Neither of us ever betrayed Erik. We never even let on to each other how we felt until a few days ago. I've been fighting it ever since, out of a sense of honor. It made me crazy, thinking of how Erik would feel if he knew. I couldn't even grieve for him the way I should, because I thought I didn't have the right."

He felt Jessie's gaze on him, warming him with her compassion.

"I think there's something both of you should know," she said softly.

Luke started to silence her, but she cut him off. "No," she insisted. "This is my fight, too."

She leveled a look at Harlan. "I'm fighting for a future for me and for Angela. That doesn't mean we're turning our backs on the past. It doesn't mean we care any the less for Erik. Neither of us will ever forget that he's Angela's father. Choosing to be together just means we're moving forward. That's something Erik understood."

Harlan's face turned practically purple with indignation. "How dare you tell me what my son would or would not have understood! Do you think you knew him any better than I did?"

"Yes," Jessie said.

The quiet, single-word response seemed to startle Harlan as a full-fledged argument might not have. Luke was astonished by her quiet serenity, her composure and their effect on his father.

"Okay, go on and say your piece," Harlan grumbled. "Get it over with."

"I was with Erik when he died," she reminded them. "He knew he wasn't going to make it."

Luke saw tears forming in her eyes, watched as they spilled down her cheeks. She seemed oblivious to them. Her entire focus seemed to be on making Harlan hear what she had to say.

"He knew," she said softly. "He knew how Luke and I felt about each other, possibly even more clearly than I'd admitted up to that point."

"Dear God!" Harlan swore. "That's what killed him, right there. Knowing his wife was in love with another man would be enough to cost any man the will to live."

Jessie shook her head. "No, he gave us his blessing. He said he wanted me to be happy."

"You're making that up," Harlan said. "Damned convenient, since he's not here to speak for himself."

If Luke hadn't seen the agony in her eyes, he might not have believed her himself. He could tell, though, that the memory of those final moments with her husband had tormented her for months now, twisting her up with guilt and self-recriminations.

"It's true," she said evenly. "And if you don't believe me, you can call Doc Winchell. He was right by Erik's side at the end. He heard every word."

A stunned silence settled over the room. Harlan was clearly at a loss. Luke was torn between anguish and an incredible sense of relief that his brother had known about his feelings for Jessie and forgiven him for them. It was as if the last roadblock to his complete sense of joy had been removed. He could feel tears sliding down his cheeks. Unashamed, he let them fall as he watched his father. Not until this moment had he realized how desperately he wanted forgiveness from him, not just for his brother's death, but for this, for loving Jessie.

Harlan finally sank back, his shoulders slumped in defeat. "I don't suppose there's anything I can do to stop you from getting on with a life together," he said grudgingly. "You're both adults. You'll do what you want whether I approve or not."

Luke thought he heard an underlying message in his father's words, a cry for reassurance that their love was deep enough to be worth the cost. He nodded.

"That's true, Daddy. We can get married the way we want. No one can stop us. We can raise Angela and any other children we might be blessed with. We can live happily ever after." He looked straight into his father's eyes then. "But it won't be the same if you're not in our lives. We don't need your approval, but we do want your love."

Jessie's hand slid into his. He folded his own around it and held on tight as they waited for his father's decision. He knew giving in wouldn't come easily to him. It never had. But, as Jessie had reminded him time and again, his father was a fair man.

"It'll take a bit of time," Harlan said eventually. "Some getting used to." A tired smile stirred at the corners of his mouth. "I suppose there's something to be said for keeping Jessica and Angela in the family. She could have gone off and married some stranger."

Luke grinned at him. "I knew you'd find a way to put a positive spin on this sooner or later."

Harlan sighed heavily. "I just hope that's argument enough to keep your mother from going straight through the roof."

Luke stood and settled the baby against his shoulder. "Maybe I'll leave that one to you."

"Sit down!" Harlan ordered.

Luke grinned at them despite himself. "Bad idea, huh?"

Jessie patted his hand. "Remember, Luke, it's a family matter."

For better or worse, it looked as if the whole clan was going to be together through thick and thin. He just hoped like hell that Cody and Jordan settled down soon and took some of the pressure off him. He glanced at Jessie.

"Happy? You got what you wanted."

"We got what we needed," she corrected. "I love you, Luke Adams."

"I love you. And I'll find your family for you, if it's the last thing I do."

"No need," she said. "I've found the only family I'll ever need."

"If you two are going to keep this up, I'm going to leave the room and take that grandbaby of mine with me," Harlan warned. "It's not proper for her to be a witness to your carrying on."

Luke was already leaning toward Jessie to claim a kiss. "Goodbye," he murmured, distractedly.

"'Bye," Jessie said just before her lips met his.

Luke was hardly aware of Harlan's exaggerated sigh or of the moment when his father lifted Angela out of his arms. He had something far more important on his mind—the future.

* * * * *

Christmas In
Snowflake Canyon
RaeAnne Thayne

Praise for RaeAnne Thayne's
Hope's Crossing series

"A heartfelt tale of sorrow, redemption and
new beginnings that will touch readers."
—*RT Book Reviews* on *Sweet Laurel Falls*

"Plenty of tenderness and Colorado sunshine
flavor this pleasant escape."
—*Publishers Weekly* on *Woodrose Mountain*

"Thayne, once again, delivers a heartfelt story of a
caring community and a caring romance between
adults who have triumphed over tragedies."
—*Booklist* on *Woodrose Mountain*

"Readers will love this novel for the
cast of characters and its endearing plotline...
a thoroughly enjoyable read."
—*RT Book Reviews* on *Woodrose Mountain*

"Thayne's series starter introduces the Colorado
town of Hope's Crossing in what can be described
as a cozy romance...[a] gentle, easy read."
—*Publishers Weekly* on *Blackberry Summer*

"Thayne's depiction of a small Colorado mountain
town is subtle but evocative. Readers who love
romance but not explicit sexual details will delight
in this heartfelt tale of healing and hope."
—*Booklist* on *Blackberry Summer*

Also available from RaeAnne Thayne
and Harlequin

Willowleaf Lane
Currant Creek Valley
Sweet Laurel Falls
Woodrose Mountain
Blackberry Summer

Dear Reader,

I don't think any of you who regularly reads my books will be surprised to learn I love the holidays. I've written many stories centered around this time of year, when family and friends draw closer to share traditions, memories, music, food.

Despite all the glittery magic and shining joy, I'm sure I don't have to tell you the holidays can be chaotic and stressful, too—a time of unreasonable expectations and unrealized potential. Nothing will ever be as ideal as we imagine and for some of us (me!) that can be as hard to swallow as last year's peppermints.

But how boring is perfection, really? It is our flaws and our failings—and the dignity and grace with which we strive to overcome them—that make each of us beautifully human. This is the lesson both Dylan Caine and Genevieve Beaumont, the hero and heroine of *Christmas in Snowflake Canyon,* must learn.

This year I'm resolved to give myself a break. My tree can be a little lopsided, each ribbon doesn't have to be precisely measured and curled, nobody but me will know if I use store-bought cookie dough in my gifts to neighbors. Instead, I intend to take every occasion to pause, to breathe, to remind myself to savor the tiny joys of each day. It's my wish that you might do the same.

All my very best,

RaeAnne

A deep and loving thank-you to my parents,
Elden and RaNae Robinson, for making each of
my childhood holidays wonderful. Also, special thanks
to a dear octogenarian aunt Betty Grace Hall—
who constantly urges me to write faster so she can
live long enough to see what happens to all my people.

CHAPTER ONE

IF HE HAD to listen to "The Little Drummer Boy" one more time, he was going to ba-rum-bum-bum-bum somebody right in the gut.

Dylan Caine huddled over a whiskey at the crowded bar of The Speckled Lizard, about two seconds and one more damn Christmas carol away from yanking the jukebox plug out of the wall. Some idiot had just played three versions of the same song. If another one flipped, he was going to knock a few heads and then take off.

His brother was now—he checked his watch—ten minutes late. The way Dylan figured, it would serve Jamie right if he bailed. He hadn't wanted to meet at the bar in the first place, and he certainly wasn't in any mood to sit here by himself listening to a bad version of a song he'd never liked much in the first place.

On this, the evening of Black Friday, the Liz was hopping. A popular local band was supposed to be playing, but from the buzz he'd heard around the bar, apparently the bass player and the lead singer—married to each other—had shared a bad Thanksgiving tofurkey the day before and were too busy yakking it up to entertain the masses.

Those masses were now growing restless. He no longer liked crowds under the best of circumstances, and a bar filled with holiday-edgy, disappointed music fans with liberal access to alcohol struck him as an unpleasant combination.

Somebody jostled him from behind and he could tell without turning around it was a woman. The curves pressing into his shoulder were a good giveaway, along with a delectable scent of cinnamon and vanilla that made him think of crisp, rich cookies.

His mouth watered. He'd been a hell of a long time without...cookies.

"Pat, where's my mojito? Come *on*. I've been waiting *forever*."

The woman with the husky voice squeezed past him to lean against the bar, and from the side, he caught only an equally sexy sleek fall of blond hair. She was wearing a white sweater that was about half an inch too short, and when she leaned over, just a strip of pale skin showed above the waistline of a pair of jeans that highlighted a shapely ass.

The longtime Lizard bartender frowned, his wind-chapped face wrinkling around the mouth. "It's coming. I'm shorthanded. Stupid me, I figured when the band canceled, nobody would show up. Give me a sec. Have some pretzels or something."

"I don't *want* pretzels. I want another mojito."

She had obviously already had a mojito or three, judging by the careful precision of her words. The peremptory tone struck a chord. He looked closer and suddenly recognized the alluring handful: Genevieve Beaumont, spoiled and precious daughter of the Hope's Crossing mayor.

She was quite a bit younger than he was, maybe six years or so. He didn't know her well, only by reputation, which wasn't great. He had always figured her for a prissy little society belle—the kind of vapid, boring woman who wasted her life on a solemn quest for the perfect manicure.

She didn't look it now. Instead, she looked a little tousled, slightly buzzed and oddly delicious.

"If somebody plays another damn Christmas carol, I swear, I am going to *scream*. This is a freaking bar, not Sunday school."

"Hear, hear," he murmured, unable to hold back his wholehearted agreement.

She finally deigned to pay attention to anything but herself. She shifted her gaze and in her heavily lashed blue eyes he saw a quick, familiar reaction—a mangle of pity and something akin to fascinated repugnance.

Yeah, he hated crowds.

To her credit, she quickly hid her response and instead offered a stiff smile. "Dylan Caine. I didn't see you there."

He gave her a polite smile in return. Completely out of unwarranted malevolence, he lifted what remained of his left arm in a caricature of a wave. "Most of me, anyway."

She swallowed and blinked but didn't lose that stiff smile. If anything, it seemed to beam unnaturally, like a blinking string of Christmas lights. "Er, nice to see you again," she said.

He couldn't remember ever having a conversation with the woman in his life. If he had, he certainly would have recalled that husky voice that thrummed through him, as rich and heady as his Johnnie Walker.

"Same," he said, which wasn't completely a lie. He did enjoy that little strip of bare skin and a pair of tight jeans.

"Are you visiting your family for the holidays?" she asked, polite conversation apparently drilled into her along with proper posture and perfect accessory coordination, even when she was slightly drunk.

"Nope." He took a sip of his whiskey. "I moved back in the spring. I've got a place up Snowflake Canyon."

"Oh. I hadn't heard." She focused on a point somewhere just above his right ear, though he noticed her gaze flicking briefly, almost against her will, to the eye patch that concealed a web of scar tissue before she jerked it away.

He fought the urge to check his watch again—or, to hell with Jamie, toss a bill on the bar for his tab and take off.

Though they certainly weren't society-conscious people like the Beaumonts, Dermot and Margaret Caine had drilled proper manners in him, too. Every once in a while he even used them. "Don't think I've seen you around town since I've been back. Where are you living these days?"

Her mouth tightened, and he noticed her lipstick had smeared ever so slightly on her lower lip. "Until three days ago, I was living in a beautiful fifth-floor flat in Le Marais in Paris."

Ooh là là. Le Marais. Like that was supposed to mean anything to him.

"Somebody should really do something about that music," she complained to Pat before Dylan could answer. "Why would you put so many freaking versions of the same song on the jukebox?"

The bartender looked frazzled as he pulled another beer from the tap. "I *had* to spring for that stupid digital jukebox. Worst business decision of my life. It's completely ruined the place. It's like karaoke every night. Here's a little secret you might not know. We have a crapload of people in Hope's Crossing with lousy taste in music."

"You could always take it out," Dylan suggested.

"Believe me, I'm tempted every night. But I paid a fortune for the thing. Usually I just end up forking over some of my tips and picking my own damn songs."

He finally set a pink mojito in front of Genevieve. She picked it up and took a healthy sip.

"Thank you," she said, her sexy voice incongruously prim, then gave Dylan that polite, empty smile. "Excuse me."

He watched her head in the direction of the gleaming jukebox, wondering what sort of music she would pick. Probably something artsy and annoying. It better not be anything with an accordion.

He checked his watch, which he really hated wearing on his right arm after a lifetime of it on the left. Jamie was now fifteen minutes late. That was about his limit.

Just as he was reaching into his pocket for his wallet, his phone buzzed with an incoming text.

As he expected, it was from Jamie, crisp and succinct:

Sorry. Got held up. On my way. Stay there!

His just-older brother knew him well. Jamie must have guessed that after all these months of solitude, the jostling crowd and discordant voices at The Speckled Lizard would be driving him crazy.

He typed a quick response with one thumb—a pain in the ass but not as bad as finger-pecking an email.

You've got five.

He meant it. If Jamie wasn't here by then, his brother could drive up to Snowflake Canyon to share a beer for his last night in town before returning to his base.

The digital jukebox Pat hated switched to "Jingle Bell Rock," a song he disliked even more than "The Little Drummer Boy."

"Sorry," the bartender said as he passed by on his way to hand a couple of fruity-looking drinks to a tourist pair a few stools down.

Dylan glanced over at the flashing lights of the jukebox just in time to see Genevieve Beaumont head in that direction, mojito in hand.

Uh-oh.

More intrigued by a woman than he had been in a long time, he watched as she said something impassioned to the professionally dressed couple who seemed to be hogging all the music choices.

He couldn't hear what she said over the loud conversation and clinking glasses wrapping around him, but he almost laughed at her dramatic, agitated gestures. So much for the prissy, buttoned-up debutante. Her arms flung wide as she pointed at the jukebox and then back at the couple. From a little impromptu lipreading, he caught the words *bar, idiot* and *Christmas carols.*

The female half of the couple—a pretty redhead wearing a steel-gray power suit and double strand of olive-sized pearls—didn't seem as amused as Dylan by Genevieve's freely given opinion. She said something in response that seemed as sharp as her shoes, judging by Genevieve's quick intake of breath.

The woman brandished a credit card as if it was an AK-47 and hurried toward the digital piece of crap, probably to put in the Mormon Tabernacle Choir singing "Away in a Manger" or something else equally inappropriate for the setting.

Dylan chuckled when, after a quick, startled second, the mayor's genteel daughter rushed forward like a Broncos tackle, her drink spilling a little as she darted ahead, her body blocking the woman from accessing the jukebox.

"Move your bony ass," he heard the woman say, quite unfairly, in the personal opinion of a man who had just had ample evidence that particular piece of Ms. Beaumont wasn't anything of the sort.

"Make me," Gen snarled.

At that line-in-the-sand declaration, Dylan did a quick ninety-degree swivel on his barstool to watch the unfolding action and he realized he wasn't the only one. The little altercation was beginning to draw the interest of other patrons in the bar.

Nothing like a good girl fight to get the guys' attention.

"I have the right to listen to whatever I want," Madame Power Suit declared.

"Nobody else wants to listen to Christmas music. Am I right?"

A few nearby patrons offered vocal agreement and the color rose in the redhead's cheeks. "I do," she declared defiantly.

"Next time, bring your iPod and earbuds," Genevieve snapped.

"Next time be the first one to the jukebox and you can pick the music," the woman retorted, trying to sneak past Genevieve.

She shoved at Genevieve but couldn't budge her, again to Dylan's amusement—until the man who had been sitting with the carol-lover approached. He wore a dress shirt and loosened tie but no jacket and was a few years older than his companion. While he carried an air of authority, he also struck Dylan as similar to the bullies in the military who had no trouble pushing their weight around to get their way.

"Come on. That's enough, girls. What's the harm in a few Christmas carols? It's the day after Thanksgiving, after all."

"I believe this is between me and your girlfriend."

"She's not my girlfriend. She's my associate."

"I don't care if she's Mrs. Santa Claus. She has lousy taste in music and everybody in the place has had enough."

The other woman tried again to charge past Genevieve with her credit card but Genevieve blocked access with her own body.

"Do you have any idea who you're messing with?" He advanced on her, his very bulk making him threatening.

"Don't know, don't care."

He loomed over her, but Genevieve didn't back down. She was just full of surprises. On face value, he wouldn't have taken her for anybody with an ounce of pluck.

"She happens to be an assistant district attorney. We both are."

Oh, crap.

Genevieve apparently meant it when she said she didn't care. "I hate attorneys. My ex-fiancé was an attorney," she snapped.

The guy smirked. "What's his name? I'd like to call the man and buy him a drink for being smart enough to drop-kick a psycho like you."

Genevieve seemed to deflate a little, looking for a moment lost and uncertain, before she bristled. "*I* drop-kicked *him,* for your information, and I haven't missed him for a minute. In my experience, most attorneys will do anything necessary to get their way."

"Damn straight," the woman said. She planted her spiked heel on Genevieve's foot hard and when the effort achieved its desired result—Genevieve shrieked in surprise and started to stumble—the woman tried to dart around her. But the former head cheerleader of Hope's Crossing High School still apparently had a few moves. She jostled with the woman and managed to slap away her hand still gripping the credit card before she could swipe it.

"That's assault!" the woman declared. "You saw that, didn't you, Larry? The stupid bitch just hit me."

"That wasn't a hit. That was a slap. Anyway, you started it."

"True story." A helpful bystander backed her up.

The woman turned even more red in the face.

"Okay, this is ridiculous. Let her pass. Now." Larry the Jerk reached for Genevieve's arm to yank her away from the jukebox. At the sight of that big hand on her white sweater, Dylan rose, his barstool squeaking as he shoved it back.

"Sit down, Caine," Pat urged, a pleading note in his voice. Dylan ignored him, adrenaline pumping through him like pure scotch whiskey. He didn't necessarily like Genevieve Beaumont, but he hated bullies more.

And she did have a nice ass.

"You're going to want to back down now," he said, in his hardest former-army-ranger voice.

The guy didn't release Genevieve's arm as he looked Dylan up and down, black eye patch and all. "Aye, matey. Or what? You'll sic your parrot on me?"

Dylan was vaguely aware of an audible hiss around him from locals who knew him.

"Something like that," he answered calmly.

He reached out and even with only one hand he was able to deftly extricate Genevieve's arm from the man's hold and twist his fingers back.

"Thank you," she answered in surprise, straightening her sweater.

"You're welcome." He released the man's hand. "I suggest we all go back to our drinks now."

"I'm calling the police," the woman blustered. "You're crazy. Both of you."

"Oh, shut up," Genevieve snapped.

"You shut up. You're both going to face assault charges."

"I might not be a lawyer but I'm pretty sure that wasn't assault," Genevieve responded sharply. "This is."

Dylan hissed in a breath when Genevieve drew back a fist and smacked the woman dead center in her face.

Blood immediately spurted from the woman's nose, and she jerked her hands up, shrieking. "I think you just broke my nose!"

The contact of flesh on flesh seemed to shock Genevieve back to some semblance of sobriety. She blinked at the pair of them. "Wow. I had no idea I could do that. I guess all those years of Pilates weren't completely wasted."

The words were barely out of her mouth when the woman dropped her hands from her nose and lunged at her, and suddenly the two of them were seriously going at it, kicking, punching, pulling hair.

Why did they always have to pull hair?

Dylan, with only one arm and skewed vision, was at a disadvantage as he reached into the squirming, tangled pair of women to try breaking things up. Larry, without a similar limitation, reached in from the other side but the women jostled into him and he stumbled backward, crashing into a big, tough-looking dude who fell to the floor and came up swinging.

Everybody's nerves were apparently on edge tonight, what with dysfunctional family dinners, early-morning shopping misery, puking-sick musicians. Before he knew it, the guy's friends had entered into the fray and what started as a minor altercation over Christmas carols erupted into a full-fledged, down-and-dirty bar fight involving tourists and locals alike.

Dylan did his best to hold his own but it was harder than he expected, much to his frustration.

At one point, he found himself on the ground, just a few feet from the conveniently located jukebox power cord. He did everybody a favor and yanked it out before leaping to his feet again, just in time to see his brother wading into the middle of the fray, along with Pat and the three-hundred-fifty-pound Speckled Lizard cook, Frankie Beltran, wielding a frying pan over her head.

"I can't leave you alone for a *minute*." Jamie grabbed him by the shirt and threw him away from the fight that was already abating.

His own adrenaline surge had spiked, apparently, leaving him achy and a little nauseous from the residual pain. He wiped at his mouth where one of the tourists—a big dude with dreads and a couple of tattoos—had thrown a punch that landed hard.

There was another new discovery that sucked. A guy had a tough time blocking with his left when he didn't have one.

"If you'd been here on time, you could have joined in," he answered.

"You ought to be ashamed of yourself, hitting a wounded war hero!" The woman who had started the whole thing had apparently turned her ire to the tourist who had punched him. Even though Pat tried to restrain Genevieve, she leveraged her weight back against the bartender to kick out at the dreadlocked snowboarder.

He wasn't quite sure how he felt about Genevieve Beaumont trying to protect him.

"How the hell was I supposed to know he was a wounded hero?" the snowboarder complained. "All I saw was some asshole throwing punches at my friends."

A commotion by the door to the tavern announced the arrival of two of Hope's Crossing's finest. The crowd parted for the uniformed officers, and Dylan's already-queasy stomach took another turn.

Two people he did *not* need to see. Oh, this wasn't going to end well.

He had dated Officer Rachel Olivarez in high school a few times. If he remembered the details correctly, he'd broken up with her to date her sister. Not one of his finer moments.

If that wasn't enough, her partner, Pete Redmond, had lost his girlfriend to Dylan's older brother Drew. He doubted either one of them had a soft spot for the Caines.

He should have remembered that particular joy of small-town life before he moved back. Everywhere a guy turned, he stumbled over hot, steaming piles of history.

Rachel spoke first. "What's our problem here, folks?"

"Just a little misunderstanding." Jamie gave his most charming smile, still holding tight to Dylan. Predictably, like anything without a Y chromosome, her lips parted and she seemed to melt a little in the face of all of Jamie's helicopter-pilot mojo for just a moment before she went all stern cop again.

"They always are," she answered. "Genevieve. Didn't expect to see you here. You're bleeding."

She said the last without a trace of sympathy, which didn't really surprise Dylan. Genevieve didn't have many friends in Hope's Crossing.

"Oh." For all her bravado earlier, her voice came out small, breathless. Rachel handed her a napkin off a nearby table and Genevieve dabbed at her cheek, and her delicate skin seemed to turn as pale as the snowflakes he could see drifting past the open doorway.

Rachel turned to him. "You're bleeding, too," she said, with no more sympathy.

"Oh, I think I've had worse," he said, unable to keep the dry note from his voice.

"This is all just a misunderstanding, right?" Jamie aimed a hopeful charmer of a grin at Rachel. "No harm done, right?"

"No harm done?" The woman holding a wad of napkins to her still-streaming nose practically screamed the words. She held up a hank of red hair Genevieve had pulled out from the roots, and for some strange reason, Dylan found that the most hilarious thing he'd seen in a long time.

"What do you mean, no harm done? I've got a court date Monday. How am I supposed to prosecute a case with a broken nose and half my hair missing?"

"Why don't you shave the rest?" Genevieve suggested. "It can only be an improvement. It will save you a fortune on hair spray."

"Can you really be as stupid as you look?" Larry shook his head. "We're district attorneys. Do you have any idea what that means? We decide who faces criminal charges. Officers, I insist you arrest both of these people."

Rachel didn't look thrilled about being ordered around. "On what charges, Mr. Kirk?"

"Assault, disturbing the peace, drunk and disorderly. How's that for starters?"

"It was just a bar fight," Jamie protested. "The same thing happens a couple times a week here at the Lizard. Isn't that right, Pat?"

"Don't bring me into this," the bartender protested.

"So are you pressing charges, Ms. Turner?" Officer Redmond asked.

"Look at my nose! You're damn right I'm pressing charges."

"Pat?"

The bartender looked around. "Well, somebody needs to pay for these damages. It might as well be Mayor Beaumont."

"Oh! That's *so* unfair!" Genevieve exclaimed. "If you hadn't bought that stupid digital jukebox, none of this would have happened."

"You probably want to keep your mouth shut right about now," Dylan suggested. "I'll pay for the damages."

He ignored Jamie's rumble of protest.

"That's all I care about," Pat answered, reaching out and shaking Dylan's hand firmly, the deal done. "Caine is right. We have bar fights in here a couple times a week. As long as somebody replaces those broken tables, I won't press charges."

"It doesn't matter whether you press charges or not. You still have to arrest and book them for assault," the prick of an assistant district attorney said.

"Sorry, Dylan, Ms. Beaumont, but I'm going to have to take you in." Despite her words, Rachel didn't sound at all apologetic.

"You can't do that!" Genevieve exclaimed.

Rachel tapped the badge on her chest. "This sort of says I can."

The officer reached around and started handcuffing Genevieve. With all her blond hair, silky white sweater and that little stream of blood trickling down her cheek, she looked like a fallen Christmas angel.

"Stop this. Right now," she said, all but stamping her foot in frustration. "You can't arrest me! My father will never allow it!"

"Believe it or not, there are still a few things around Hope's Crossing William Beaumont can't control."

Like most of the rest of the town, it sounded as if Rachel had had a run-in or two with Mayor Beaumont, who tended to think he owned the town.

"Why aren't you arresting her?" she demanded with a gesture to the assistant district attorney. "She's the one who wouldn't stop playing the stupid songs on the jukebox. *And* I think she broke my foot with that hideous shoe."

Rachel seemed unaffected as she turned her around and started reciting her Miranda rights. Her partner turned his attention to Dylan.

"Turn around and place your hands behind your back," Pete ordered.

"I'll do my best, Officer," Dylan answered. He twisted his right arm behind his back and twisted his left, with the empty sleeve, as far as he could.

"Dylan," Jamie chided.

Redmond apparently realized the challenge. "Um, Olivarez, what am I supposed to do here?"

Rachel paused in mid-Miranda and looked at her partner in annoyance that quickly shifted to more of that damn pity when she looked at Dylan.

"You could always let me go," he suggested, fighting down the urge to punch something all over again. "I was only coming to the rescue of a damsel in distress. What's the harm in that?"

"Or not," she snapped, and before he realized what she intended, she reached for the cuff on Gen's left wrist and fastened the other side onto his right.

Oh, joy. Shackled to Genevieve Beaumont. Could he stoop any lower?

"You can't do this!" she exclaimed again. "I've never been arrested before. I can't believe this is happening, all because of some stupid Christmas carols."

"I like Christmas carols," Rachel said.

"So do I," Genevieve answered hotly. "Believe me, I do. But not on a Friday night when I only wanted a few drinks and some good music."

"You can explain that to the judge, I'm sure. Come on. Let's go."

She headed for the door, pushing her still-protesting prisoner ahead of her. Dylan, by default, had to go with them.

When she opened the door, a blast of wind and snow whirled inside, harsh and mean.

He was aware of Genevieve's sudden shiver beside him and some latent protective instinct bubbled up out of nowhere. "It's freezing out there. At least let the woman put on her coat."

Rachel raised an eyebrow at him, as surprised as he was by the solicitude. Genevieve apparently didn't even notice.

"That's right. I can't leave without my coat. And my purse. Where's my purse?"

"I'll get them," Jamie offered.

"Where are they?" Pete asked.

"I was sitting over there." She gestured toward her table. It seemed a lifetime ago that she had pressed her chest against his shoulder so she could bug Pat about her mojito. "My coat should be hanging on the rack. It's Dior. You can't miss it."

Jamie found the coat and purse quickly and handed them over. "I can't say this is how I expected to spend my last night of leave."

"Sorry."

"No worries. I'll call Andrew. He'll have you out in an hour or two."

The only thing worse than the lecture in store for him from Pop would be the similar one their older brother would likely deliver.

"If they send me to the big house, take care of Tucker for me, will you?"

Jamie threw him a look of disgust. "This isn't a joke, damn it. You're under arrest. These are serious charges."

"It was just a bar fight. Drew can handle that in his sleep. On second thought, Charlotte can take care of Tuck. He likes it at her place."

His brother shook his head. "You're insane."

He must be. Despite the indignity of being shackled to Genevieve Beaumont and hauled out through the biting snow to the waiting patrol car, Dylan was astonished to discover he was enjoying himself more than he had in a long, long time.

CHAPTER TWO

THIS WAS A *DISASTER*. A complete, unmitigated catastrophe.

The rush that had carried her through the altercation—had she *really* punched a woman in the nose?—was beginning to ebb, replaced by hard, terrifying reality.

Her father was going to kill her.

Her mother was going to pop a couple of veins and *then* kill her.

She slumped into the seat, wondering just how her life had descended into this misery. A week ago, she had been blissfully happy in Paris. Long lunches with her friends at their favorite cafés, evenings spent at Place Vendôme, afternoon shopping on the Rue de Rivoli.

Okay, maybe, just maybe, she should have been looking for work during some of those long lunches. Maybe she should have tried a little harder to turn her two internships into something a little more permanent.

She had always figured she had plenty of time to settle down. For now, she only wanted to grab as much fun as she could. What else was she supposed to do after her plans for her life disintegrated into dust like old Christmas wrapping paper?

She had been in a bit of a financial hole. She would be the first to admit it. She liked nice things around her. She would eventually have climbed her way out of it.

How was she supposed to do that now, with a record? She slumped farther back into the seat, vaguely queasy from the scent of stale coffee and flop sweat that had probably seeped into the cheap leather upholstery along with God knows what else.

Her father would see her arrest as just more proof that he needed to tighten the reins.

She burned from the humiliation that had seethed and curled around in her stomach since that afternoon. Her parents were treating her as if she were twelve years old. She was basically being sent to her room without supper in a grand sort of way.

She should have known something was up when they sent her a plane ticket and demanded she come back to Hope's Crossing, ostensibly for Thanksgiving with them and her brother, Charlie. Stupid her. She hadn't suspected a thing, even though she had picked up weird vibes since she arrived home Wednesday.

Thanksgiving dinner had been a grand social affair, as usual. Her parents had invited several of their friends over and Genevieve had endured as best she could and escaped to her room at the earliest opportunity.

Then this morning after breakfast, William had asked her to come into his study. Her mother had been there, looking pale and drawn. As usual, sobriety wasn't agreeing with Laura.

It certainly hadn't agreed with Genevieve as she had sat, sober as a nun, while William outlined the financial mess she was in and then proceeded to give her the horrifying news.

He was closing her credit accounts, all of them, and withdrawing her access to her trust fund.

"I've been patient long enough." His grim words still rang in her ears, hours later. "For nearly two years, I've let you have your way, do what you wanted. I told myself you were healing from a broken heart and deserved a little fun, but this is becoming ridiculous. It stops today. You're twenty-six years old. You graduated from college four years ago and haven't done a damn thing of value since then."

Her father had thrown her one miserable bone. Her grandmother Pearl had left her hideous house to her only son when she died in the spring. If Genevieve could take the house, fix it and sell it at value within three months, she could take the earnings back to Paris to seed the interior-design business she had been talking about for years.

And if she could turn a profit within the first year of her business, her father would release the rest of her trust fund permanently.

William had been resolute, despite her best efforts to cajole, plead or guilt him into changing his mind. She was stuck here in Hope's Crossing—this armpit of a town where everyone hated her—throughout the winter.

Furious with all of them, she had packed her suitcase, grabbed the key to Pearl's house and left her parents' grand home in Silver Strike Canyon—the second biggest in town, after Harry Lange's.

Yet another big mistake. Pearl's house was far, far worse than she had expected. Was it any wonder she had gone to the Lizard with the intention of getting good and drunk?

True to form, she had taken a lousy situation and made it about ten times worse. She could only blame it on mental duress brought on by hideous pink porcelain tubs and acres and acres of wallpaper.

That was really no excuse. What had she been thinking? She didn't pick fights, take on annoying people, *punch* someone, for heaven's sake! She had just been so angry sitting there in the Liz, feeling her life spiral out of control, certain that she would have to spend the next several months in this town where everybody snickered at her behind their hands.

Now she was sitting in the backseat of a police squad car, handcuffed to Dylan Caine, of all people.

He shifted in the seat and she was painfully aware of him, though she couldn't seem to look at him. He used to be gorgeous like all the Caine brothers—tough, muscular, rugged. They all had that silky brown hair, the same blue eyes, deep creases in their cheeks when they smiled. Keep-an-eye-on-your-daughters kind of sexy.

He was still compelling but in a disreputable, keep-an-eye-on-your-wallet kind of way. He hadn't shaved in at least three or four days and his hair was badly in need of a trim. Add to that the scars radiating out around his eye patch and the missing hand and he made a pretty scary package.

Each time she looked at him tonight—damaged and disfigured—sadness had trickled through her, as if she had just watched someone take a beautiful painting by an Italian master and rip a seam through the middle.

Yes, that probably made her shallow. She couldn't help herself.

He did smell good, though. When he shifted again, through the sordid scents of the police car, she caught the subtle notes of some kind of outdoorsy scent—sandalwood and cedar and perhaps bergamot, with a little whiskey chaser thrown in.

"I'm sorry you were arrested, but it's your own fault."

He scoffed in the darkness. "My fault. How do you figure that, Ms. Beaumont?"

"We are handcuffed together," she pointed out. "I think you could probably call me Genevieve."

"Genevieve." He mocked the way she had pronounced her own name, as her Parisian friends had for the past two years—Jahn-vi-ev, instead of the way her family and everyone she knew here had always said it, Jen-a-vive—and she felt ridiculously pretentious.

"You didn't have to come riding to my rescue like some kind of cowboy stud trying to waste his Friday-night paycheck. I was handling things."

He snorted. "Last I checked, *Genevieve,* that bitch looked like she was ready to take out your eyeball with her claws. Trust me. You would have missed it."

Like he missed being able to see out of two eyes? She wanted to ask but didn't dare.

"You wouldn't be here if you had just minded your own business."

"It's a bad habit of mine. I don't like to watch little cream puffs get splattered."

It annoyed her that he, like everybody else she knew, thought so little of her.

"I'm not a cream puff."

"Oh, sorry. I suppose it would be *éclair.*"

He said the word with the same exaggerated French accent he had used on her name, and she frowned, though she was aware of a completely inappropriate bubble of laughter in her throat. It must be the lingering effect of those stupid mojitos.

"I believe the word you're looking for is *profiterole.* An *éclair* is oval and the filling is piped in while a *profiterole,* or cream puff, is round and the pastry is cut in half then some is scraped away before the rest is filled with whipped cream."

It was one of those inane, obscure details she couldn't help spouting when she was nervous.

He snorted. "Wow. You are quite a font of information, *Genevieve.* This evening is turning into all kinds of interesting."

She couldn't see his features well through the snow-dimmed streetlights but she was quite certain he was laughing at her. She hated it when people laughed at her—one of the biggest reasons she hated being here in Hope's Crossing.

Before she could respond, the vehicle stopped and she saw the solid, somehow intimidating shape of the police station outside the ice-etched window.

A moment later, the door on her side of the vehicle opened and Pete Redmond loomed over her. "You two having fun back here?"

Dylan didn't answer, making her wonder if he *had* been having fun.

"What do you think?" Genevieve tried for her frostiest tone. Pete had tried to ask her out once when she was home for the summer, before her engagement to Sawyer.

"I think you're in a pickle, Ms. Beaumont," he answered.

Oh, she could think of a few stronger words than that.

"I think we all need to suit up for the you-know-what to hit the fan after Mayor Beaumont gets that phone call," the female police officer with the split ends and the improper lipstick shade said as she helped pull Genevieve out of the backseat and Dylan, by default, after her.

Her stomach cramped again, just picturing her father's stern disapproval. What if he decided her latest screw-up was too much? What if he decided not to give her the chance to sell Pearl's house as her escape out of town?

She might be stuck here forever, having to look for excitement at a dive like The Speckled Lizard.

A sudden burst of wind gusted through, flailing snow at them, rattling the bare branches of a tree in front of the station. Gen shivered.

"Let's get you two inside," the female officer said. "This is shaping up to be a nasty one. We're going to be dealing with slide-offs all night."

Despite the nerves crawling through her, the warmth of the building seemed almost welcoming.

She had never been inside a police station. Somehow she expected it to be...grittier. Instead, it looked just like any other boring office. Cubicles, fluorescent lighting, computer monitors. It could be a bland, dreary insurance office somewhere.

She was aware of a small, ridiculous pang of disappointment that her walk on the wild side had led her to this. On the other hand, she was still shackled to the scruffy, sexy-smelling, *damaged* Dylan Caine.

The officers led them not to some cold interrogation room with a single lightbulb and a straight-backed chair but to what looked like a standard break room, with a microwave, refrigerator, coffee maker.

Yet another illusion shattered.

"Have a seat," Pete said.

"Can you take these off now?" Dylan raised their joined arms.

The female officer seemed to find the whole situation highly amusing, for reasons Gen didn't quite understand.

"I don't know about that," she said slowly. "We wouldn't want the two of you starting any more fights. Maybe we should leave it on a few more minutes, until we give Chief McKnight time to assess the situation."

Genevieve drew in a breath. The McKnights. She couldn't escape them anywhere in this cursed town.

"What about our phone calls?" Dylan said. "I need to call my attorney, who also happens to be my brother Andrew. I'm sure Ms. Beaumont wants to call her father."

"You don't speak for me," she said quickly. "I don't need to call my father."

"But you're going to need an attorney."

She was exhausted suddenly after the ordeal of the evening and the cut on her cheek burned. Her brain felt scrambled, but she said the first thing that came to her mind. "I'll use yours. Andrew Caine is my attorney, too."

Her father would find out about this, of course. She couldn't hide it. For all she knew, somebody had already told him his only daughter had been scrapping in a bar like some kind of Roller Derby queen. But she couldn't endure more of his disappointment tonight, the heavy, inescapable weight of her own failure.

"Seriously?" Officer Olivarez—now, there was a mouthful—looked skeptical. "You're sure you don't want to call Daddy to bail you out?"

"Positive." She looked at the two officers and at Dylan. "I think we can all agree, the last thing any of us needs tonight is for my father to come down here. Am I right?"

"I doubt anything you do will stop that," Dylan drawled.

He was right. Someone at the Lizard had probably already dropped a dime on her. Wasn't that the appropriate lingo? William was probably already on his way over but she wasn't going to be the one to call him.

"Andrew Caine is my attorney. End of story," she declared. "Now will you please take these things off?"

After a pause, the female officer pulled out a key to the handcuffs and freed them. Instead of elation, Genevieve fought down an odd disappointment as she rubbed the achy hand that had been cuffed with her other one.

"You can call your brother over there." Officer Olivarez gestured with a flip of her braid to a corded phone hanging on the wall.

Dylan headed over and picked up the phone receiver, and after an awkward moment where he tried to figure out what to do with it, he draped it over his shoulder so he could punch the numbers with his remaining hand.

Poor guy. Even something as simple as making a phone call must be a challenge with only one hand.

The two officers started talking about a sporting event Genevieve didn't know or care anything about. She couldn't hear Dylan's conversation with his brother, but judging by the way his expression grew increasingly remote, it wasn't pleasant. After a few minutes, he hung up.

"Well? Is he coming to get us out?"

"He'll be here. He wanted to know if we had been booked yet."

The two officers exchanged glances. "Chief McKnight wants us to hang on until he gets here. It's kind of a sticky situation, what with the district attorney's office being involved."

"What does that mean?"

"Once we book you, you have to go into the system," Pete Redmond explained, not unkindly, and she was a little sorry she hadn't agreed to go out with him all those years ago. "That means your arrest will always be on record, even if you're not charged."

"The police chief is on the phone with the district attorney, trying to iron things out."

"How long will that take?" she asked.

"Who knows?" Pete said.

He started to explain the judicial system to her but she tuned him out. He was saying something about bail hearings when she heard a commotion through the open doorway.

"Where the hell is my daughter?"

Merde. Any alcohol that hadn't been absorbed into her system by now seemed to well up in her gut.

Dylan gave her a careful look and shoved a garbage can over with his foot. "You're not going to puke on me now, are you?"

She willed down the gorge in her throat. "I'm fine. I won't be sick."

She was almost positive that was true, anyway.

"Good. Because I have to say, that would just about make this the perfect date."

An inelegant snort escaped before she could help it. Again, she blamed the mojitos, but her father walked in just in time to catch it.

He stood in the doorway and glowered at her, and she was filled with such a tangle of emotions, she didn't know what to do with them—anger and hurt and an aching sort of shame that she was always a disappointment.

"Genevieve Marie Beaumont. Look at you. You've been back in town less than forty-eight hours and where do I find you but in the police station, associating with all manner of disreputable characters."

Beside her, Dylan gave a little wave. "Hey there, Mayor Beaumont."

Some of her father's stiff disapproval seemed to shift to an uncertain chagrin for a moment and it took her a moment to realize why. She had heard enough in her infrequent visits home to know that Dylan was considered a hero around town, someone who had sacrificed above and beyond for his country.

"I didn't, er, necessarily mean you by that general statement."

"I'm sure," Dylan said coolly.

"Yes, well." Her father cleared his throat and turned back to Genevieve. "I'm doing what I can to get you out of here. I've already been on the phone with the district attorney to see if we can work things out with his people before this goes any further. I'm quite outraged that no one called me first. That includes you, young lady. I realize you haven't been in trouble with the law before but surely you know the first thing you should always do is call your attorney."

"You're not my attorney." Her words came out small, and, as usual, her father didn't pay her any mind.

He went on about his plan for extricating her from the mess as if she had said nothing.

"You're not my attorney," she said in a louder voice. "Andrew Caine is."

Her father didn't roll his eyes, but it was a close thing. "Don't be ridiculous. Of course I'll represent you."

"I thought attorneys weren't supposed to represent family members."

"That's people in the medical profession, my dear," he said indulgently, as if she were five years old. "Attorneys have no such stricture. If you would prefer, I can call one of my associates to represent you. Either way, we'll have these ridiculous charges thrown out and pretend this never happened."

She could just cave. It would be easy. Her father would take care of everything, as he had been doing all her life—as she had *let* him do, especially the past two years.

He couldn't have it both ways, though. He couldn't one moment tell her he was cutting her off financially to fend for herself and then still try to control the rest of her life.

"I have an attorney," she said, a little more firmly. "Andrew Caine."

Her father gave her a conciliatory smile that made her want to scream. "You're overwrought, my dear. I'm sure this has been an upsetting evening for you. You're not thinking clearly. Mr. Caine is a fine attorney, but how would it look if you had someone else represent you?"

As if she had finally found a little backbone?

She was spared from having to answer by the arrival of the police chief of Hope's Crossing, Riley McKnight.

William spotted him at the same time. "Finally!" he exclaimed and headed out to apprehend the police chief, leaving her and Dylan alone.

An awkward silence seemed to settle around them like the cold snow falling outside. "Wow. Your dad..."

"Is incredibly obstinate. Either that or he has selective hearing loss," she finished for him.

"I was going to say he's concerned about you. But those work, too."

She could feel her face heat. "He's tired of cleaning up my messes. Can you tell?"

"Caught a hint or two. What kind of messes, *Genevieve?*"

Oddly, she didn't mind his exaggerated French pronunciation of her name this time. It was actually kind of…sexy. "It's a very long and boring story." One she didn't feel like rehashing right now. "Listen, I *am* sorry you were messed up in this whole thing. I had a bit too much to drink and I guess I went a little…crazy."

"I would describe it as completely bat-shit, but that's just me."

"I did, didn't I?" It wasn't a completely unpleasant realization.

"I wish I'd thought to shoot some video of you punching that woman. I haven't enjoyed anything that much in…a long time."

She was glad, suddenly, that she'd given him something to find amusing.

"Thank you for trying to protect me."

He shrugged, looking embarrassed. "I would say *anytime* but I'm afraid you might take me up on that," he answered, just as Andrew Caine walked in.

"Take you up on what?"

"Nothing. Never mind. What the hell took you so long? Did you stop off for Thanksgiving leftovers at Pop's on the way?"

Andrew Caine looked very much like she remembered Dylan looking before his accident. Gorgeous. Brown hair, blue eyes, chiseled features.

Tonight, Andrew's short brown hair was rumpled a little on one side and she wondered if Dylan's call had caught him in bed, or at least dozing on the couch while a basketball game played or something. His blue dress shirt was tailored and elegant but a little wrinkled, as if he had yanked it out of the laundry hamper at the last minute.

"Tell me why I never get calls about you during business hours. I ought to leave your ass in here overnight. Hell, I should leave you here all week-end. It would serve you right."

"Guess it's my turn for the annoying family lectures," Dylan murmured in an aside to her.

A little laugh burbled out of her; she couldn't help it, and he gazed at her mouth for a moment before jerking his gaze back to his brother.

"A bar fight at the Lizard. Really. Couldn't you try for something a little more original?"

Dylan shrugged and aimed his thumb at Genevieve. "She started it."

"Tell me you weren't fighting with Genevieve Beaumont." Andrew narrowed his gaze. "Pop is seriously going to kill you. And then Mayor Beaumont will scrape up what's left of you and finish you off."

"That's not what I meant." Annoyance flickered across his expression. "I haven't sunk that low."

"It was all my fault," Genevieve said. "I...lost my head and your brother stepped in to try to calm the situation."

"It obviously didn't work."

"Well, no," she admitted.

"What's this I hear about you scalping a county prosecutor and breaking her nose?"

She had actually physically attacked another human being. She flushed, hardly able to believe she had actually done that. She didn't know how to respond. Fortunately, Dylan's brother didn't seem to require a response.

"Never mind," he said. "I'm sure your father will fix things for you. Where is he?"

She gestured to the back of the police station. "He's talking to Chief McKnight. But he's not my attorney. You are."

The man's eyebrows rose just about to his hairline. "Since when?"

"Now. I want to hire you." Of course, she didn't have much money to pay him right now but she would figure something out.

"You really think your father will go for that?"

"I'm twenty-six years old. I make my own decisions." Most of them had been poor the past few years but she decided not to mention that. "I would like to hire you to represent my interests. That's all that really matters, isn't it?"

He studied her for a long moment and then shook his head. "Sure. Far be it from me to turn away business, especially when it's guaranteed to piss off William Beaumont. No offense."

"None taken," she assured him.

"I'm going to assume I'm entitled to some kind of referral bonus for steering new clientele your way," Dylan said.

Her new attorney frowned at his brother. "You can assume you're entitled to shut your pie hole and let me see if I can get you and your new friend here out of this mess."

CHAPTER THREE

"THAT'S IT? We're really free to go?"

An hour later, Jahn-Vi-Ev Beaumont looked at Andrew as if he had just rescued a busload of puppies from a burning building.

Dylan wasn't quite sure why that made him want to punch something again.

"For now. Between your father and me, we were able to work the system a little to get you both out of here tonight. You're still facing charges for felony assault. It's a very serious accusation."

"But at least I don't have to spend the night in jail. I couldn't have done that." She shuddered. "I don't even have any moisturizer in my purse!"

Dylan just refrained from rolling his eyes. He noticed Andrew was trying hard to avoid his gaze. "Maybe you should think of that next time before you start barroom fights," his brother suggested mildly.

"I won't be starting any more fights. You can be sure of that. I never want to walk into the Lizard again."

"Good idea. I can't guarantee you're not going to serve any jail time for this. Felony assault is a very serious charge, Ms. Beaumont."

To Dylan, this seemed like a lot of wasted energy over a couple of punches.

"I know."

"Your father says he can give you a ride home."

She looked through the glass doors to where Mayor Beaumont waited, all but tapping his foot with impatience. "Do I have to go with him?" she asked, her voice small.

"No law says you do."

"Can't you give me a ride to my car? I'm parked behind the bar."

Did she really think her attorney's obligation extended to giving his clients rides after a night in the slammer? And why was she so antagonistic toward her family? It didn't make sense to him. Seemed to him, the Beaumonts were the sort who tended to stick together. Just them against the poor, the hungry, the huddled masses.

"How much did you have to drink tonight? Maybe you'd better catch a ride all the way."

"Three—no, three and a half—mojitos. But that was hours ago. If you want the truth, I'm feeling more sober than I ever have in my life."

He had a feeling she would want nothing so much as a stiff drink if she could see herself right now, her hair a mess, dried blood on her cheek from the cut, her sweater fraying at the shoulder where the district attorney must have grabbed a handful.

"Maybe you'd be better off catching a ride with your father."

"Would you want your father to give you a ride home from the police station right now?" she demanded of Dylan. When he didn't answer, she nodded. "That's what I thought. I won't drive, then. You can just give me a ride to my grandmother's house. Either that or I'll sneak out the back and walk."

Andrew sighed. "I'll take you to your grandmother's house. I have to drop my idiot brother off, too. But you can't just ditch your father. You have to go out there and tell him."

So much for his puppy-saving lawyer brother. Now she looked at Andrew as if he were making her pull the wings off butterflies. Dylan didn't have a whole lot of sympathy for her. *Don't do the crime if you can't do the time, sister.*

"Fine," she said and tromped out of the room in sexy boots that had somehow lost a heel in the ruckus.

The minute she left, Andrew turned on him. "Gen Beaumont. Seriously? I do believe you've hit a personal low."

"Knock it off," he growled. Funny. While he might have said—at least *thought*—the same thing, he didn't like the derision in his brother's voice when he said her name.

"What were you thinking, messing with Gen Beaumont?"

"I was *not* messing with her." He didn't want to defend himself, but he also didn't want to listen to his brother dis her, for reasons he wasn't quite ready to explore.

"Yeah, I should have stepped back. It was stupid to get involved, but I could see that if I didn't, somebody would end up seriously hurt. Probably her."

"She's a walking disaster. You know that, right? From what I hear, she's been leaving a swath of credit-card receipts across Europe, embroiled in one financial mess after another."

His family was going to make him crazy. For months they had been nagging him to get out of his house in Snowflake Canyon, to socialize a little more, maybe think about talking to somebody once in a while besides his black-and-tan hound dog. But the minute he ventured into social waters, they felt compelled to yank him back as though he were a three-year-old about to head into a school of barracudas.

"Relax, would you? I'm not going to get tangled up with her. I know just what Genevieve Beaumont is—a stuck-up snob with more fashion sense than brains, who wouldn't be caught dead in public with someone like me. Someone less than perfect."

He heard a small, strangled sound behind him and Andrew's expression shifted from skepticism to rueful dismay. Dylan didn't need to look around to realize Gen must have overheard.

Shoot.

He turned, more than a little amazed at the urge to apologize to her. "Gen."

She lifted her slim, perfect nose a little higher. "I'm ready to go whenever you are. I finally persuaded my father I didn't need a ride," she said to Andrew before turning a cool look in Dylan's direction. "I'll wait by the door. That way I don't have to be around someone like you any longer than necessary."

With one last disdainful glance she picked up her purse and her Dior coat and walked back out of the office with her spine straight and her head up.

"There you go. See?" Dylan said after she had left, shoving down the ridiculous urge to chase after her and apologize. "Nothing to worry about. Now she won't be speaking to me anyway."

"And isn't that going to make for a fun ride home?" Andrew muttered, shrugging into his own coat.

She refused to look at Dylan Caine as his brother drove through the dark, snowy streets of Hope's Crossing. Since Thanksgiving had come and gone, apparently everybody was in a festive mood. Just about every house had some kind of light display, from the single-strand, single-color window wrap to a more elaborate blinking show that was probably choreographed to music.

"I'm living in my grandmother's house," she reminded Andrew from her spot in the second row of his big SUV that had a Disneyland sticker in the back window and smelled of peanut butter and jelly sandwiches.

"Got it."

"You know where that is?"

"Everybody knows where Pearl lived."

Genevieve looked out the window as they passed a house with an inflatable snow globe on the lawn featuring penguins and elves apparently hanging out in some kind of wintry playground. She thought it hideous but Grandma Pearl would have loved that kind of thing. She felt a pang of sorrow for the woman who had taught her to sew and could curse like a teamster, especially when she knew it would irritate her only son.

Gen had flown home for her funeral in April, wishing the whole time that she had taken time to call her grandmother once in a while.

Grandma Pearl's house squatted near the mouth of Snowflake Canyon on a wooded lot that drew mule deer out of the mountains. It was just as ugly as she remembered, a personality-less rambler covered in nondescript tan siding.

"You have the key?" Dylan asked.

"Yes," she answered, just as curtly.

He opened his door on the passenger side of the front seat. "You don't have to get out," she said quickly. "I don't want to be seen with you, remember?"

He ignored her and climbed out of the SUV and held her door open in a gesture that seemed completely uncharacteristic. She thought about being childish and sliding out the other side, but she figured she had already filled her Acts of Stupidity quota for the day.

Aware of his brother waiting in the car, she marched up the sidewalk to the front door, where she at least had had the foresight to leave a porch light burning before leaving for the bar.

"I'm good. Thanks. You can go now."

"Genevieve. I'm sorry you heard that."

"But not sorry you said it."

"That, too," he said.

She still burned with humiliation, though she wasn't sure why. Everyone saw her that way. Why did it bother her so much that he did, too?

"Forget it," she said. "I have. Do you think I really care about your opinion of me? After tonight, we won't have anything to do with each other. We don't exactly move in the same social circles."

"Praise the Lord," he said in an impassioned undertone, and she almost smiled, until she remembered he despised her.

"Good night, Dylan."

"Yeah. Next time, try to have a little self-restraint."

She nodded and quickly unlocked the door, hurried inside and closed it shut behind her.

She had to will herself not to watch him walk back to his brother's waiting vehicle. Instead, she forced herself to focus on the challenge ahead of her—the horrible green shag carpeting, dark-paneled walls, tiny windows.

She was so tired. Exhaustion pulled at her, and she felt as if her arms weighed about a hundred pounds each. Mental note: lingering jet lag and adrenaline crashes didn't mix well.

She headed straight for the hideous pink bathroom and managed to wrestle her clothes off with those giant, tired arms then stepped into the shower.

At least she had hot water. Always a plus. Actually, the house had a few things going for it—decent bones and a fantastic location at the mouth of the canyon, to start. The half-acre lot alone was worth at least a couple hundred thousand. If she could transform the house into a decent condition, anything else would be a bonus.

She stood under the hot spray until the water finally ran out, then toweled off, changed into her favorite pair of silk pajamas and climbed into the bed, grateful for the sheets she had thought to bring down from her parents' house.

She could do this. Yes, it was overwhelming, especially on an extremely limited budget. Difficult, but not impossible.

If she pulled this off, she might be able to leave Hope's Crossing with a nice chunk of cash, at the very least, and maybe pick up a little hard-earned pride along the way.

She supposed it was too much to hope that she might even earn her family's respect—or anything but contempt from a tough, hardened ex-soldier like Dylan Caine.

OVER THE WEEKEND, Dylan tried not to give Genevieve Beaumont much thought. He was surprised at how difficult he found that particular task.

He would think of her at the oddest times. While he cleared snow off his long, winding driveway in Snowflake Canyon with the thirty-year-old John Deere he had fixed up. While he went through the painstaking effort of chopping wood for the fireplace one-handed and carried it into the house—also one-handed. While he was sitting by said fire with a book on his lap and Tucker curled up at his feet.

Monday morning his cell phone rang early, yanking him out of a vaguely disturbing but undeniably heated dream of her wearing a demure, lacy veil that rippled down to a naughty porn-star version of a wedding gown made out of see-through lace.

His phone rang a second time while he was trying to clear that vaguely disturbing image out of his head.

"Yeah?" he growled.

"Cheerful this morning, aren't we?" His father's Ireland-sprinkled accent greeted him. "I suppose I might be a mite cranky, too, if I had spent my weekend on the wrong side of the law."

Dermot made it sound as if his youngest son had been riding the range holding up trains and robbing banks. Dylan imagined his father viewed the transgressions the same.

"Not the *whole* weekend," he answered, sitting up in bed and rubbing a little at the phantom pains in his arm. His now-narrowed world slowly came into focus. "Only Friday night. I spent the rest of the time shoveling snow. How about you?"

"You didn't come to dinner last night."

Dermot threw a grand Sunday dinner each week for any of Dylan's six siblings who could make it and their families. The combined force of all those busybodies was more than he could usually stand.

"I came to dinner on Thanksgiving, didn't I? I figured that would be sufficient. Anyway, it took me a couple hours to clear the snow and by then I figured you'd be eating dessert."

"Nothing wrong with coming just for the dessert. It was a delicious one. Erin brought that candy-bar cake you like so much and we had leftover pie from Thanksgiving."

His stomach rumbled at the mention of the signature recipe Andrew's wife made. "Sorry I missed that."

"She left a piece especially for you as she knows how you favor it. You can stop by the house when you're in town next."

That was an order, not really a suggestion, and Dylan made a face he was quite glad his pop couldn't see.

"I'm to give you an important message from your brother."

"Which one? I have a fair few."

"Andrew. He tried to call you earlier but couldn't get through. He said the call went straight to your voice mail, and he left orders for me to try again."

Dylan hadn't heard his phone but sometimes the cell-tower coverage up here could be sketchy. He checked his call log and saw he had three voice-mail messages, no doubt from Andrew.

"What's the message?"

"You're to meet him at the district attorney's office at noon. Don't be late and wear a tie if you can find one."

Now, *that* sounded ominous. He had always hated dressing up, something

Pop and all five of his brothers knew. A lifelong healthy dislike had become infinitely more intense over the past year.

"A tie." Another of his many nemeses. He defied anybody to knot a damn Windsor one-handed.

"Do you have one?" Dermot asked when he didn't respond. "If you don't, I can run one of mine up to you."

"I can find one. You don't need to drive all the way up here." He didn't know whether to be touched or guilty that his father was willing to leave the Center of Hope Café during the breakfast rush to bring his helpless son a necktie.

"Did Andrew tell you *why* I'm supposed to meet him wearing a tie?"

"Nary a word. All I know is he was heading into court and ordered me to make sure I personally delivered the message. If you didn't answer your phone this morning, I was under orders to drive up Snowflake Canyon to drag you down. You'll be there, right?"

"I'm not five years old, Pop. I'll be there."

A guy might have thought multiple tours in Afghanistan would be enough to convince his family he could take care of himself.

Then again, since he had come home half-dead, they could possibly have room for doubt.

"See that you are," Dermot said. He paused for a moment, long enough for Dylan to accurately predict a lecture coming on.

"I'm disappointed in you, son. Surely you know better than to find yourself in a fight at a place like The Speckled Lizard, no matter the provocation."

"Yes. I've heard the lecture now from both Jamie and Andrew, thanks, Pop."

"What were you thinking to drag that pretty young Genevieve Beaumont into your troubles?"

He snorted at the blatant unfairness of that. "Who dragged whom? You obviously didn't hear the whole story. I was minding my own business, waiting to share a drink with my brother. I can't help it if the woman is bat-shit."

"Watch your mouth," Dermot said sharply. "That's a young lady you're talking about."

He shuddered to think what Pop would say if he knew the kind of semi-pervy dreams Dylan was having about that particular young lady, crazy or not.

"Right. A young lady with a particular aversion to Christmas carols and a right hook that needs a little work."

"Ah, well. She's a troubled girl who could use a few friends in town. You treat her kindly, you hear me?"

When Dermot was riled, the Irish brogue he'd left behind on the shores of Galway when he was just a lad of six peeped out like clover in July.

"I hear you."

"Now you had best be hurrying along if you're to make it to meet your brother on time."

"Yeah. Message received. I'm up. I'll be there. I'm heading into the shower right now."

"See that you are." Dermot's voice was stern but he tempered it to add, "And I'll expect to see both of my sons here afterward for a bite and any news from court."

He hung up with his father and slid out of bed. After letting Tucker out with a quick check to make sure he didn't have to plow again in order to make it down to the main canyon road, he hurried into the shower, trying to pretend he wasn't wondering whether Genevieve would be there.

"No. Hell no. Are you freaking kidding me? That's the stupidest thing I ever heard. Absolutely not."

Through her own shock at the proposal Andrew Caine had just laid out for the two of them, Genevieve found Dylan's reaction fascinating.

"Geez, Dyl. Don't hold back," his brother said with a raised eyebrow. "Seriously, why don't you tell us how you really feel?"

"You want to know how I really feel? I feel like I've just been steamrolled."

"Come on. It's a hundred hours of community service. It's not like you're being sentenced to hard labor on the chain gang. I hope I don't need to tell you how far I've had to bend over in the last forty-eight hours to make this deal happen. You're lucky you're not serving hard time for assaulting two officers of the court."

Beside her, she was aware of Dylan's hand clenching on his thigh. Despite the evidence of his frustration, she couldn't help thinking he looked quite different from the disreputable hellion who had brawled at The Speckled Lizard just a few nights earlier. Though his hair still needed a trim, he had shaved off the stubble that had made him look so dangerous, and he wore tan slacks, a light blue dress shirt and a shiny hammered silver bolo tie that gleamed in the fluorescent lights.

She wouldn't have taken him for the cowboy sort but the look somehow worked.

"I'll do the community service," he growled to his brother. "I've got no problem with that. Just not there. This is a damn setup, isn't it? They got to you, didn't they?"

Andrew Caine looked slightly bored. "Who's *they?*"

"Charlotte and Smoke Gregory. Since the moment the two of them hooked up, they've been trying to drag me into this stupid Warrior's Hope business. I won't do it. Have the judge throw me in jail for contempt if you have to, but I'm not going out there."

"What's the problem?" Genevieve asked. "I think it's a fantastic deal! My father has been calling me all weekend to warn me I could be going to prison if I didn't let him take over my defense. I'm really glad I didn't listen to him."

"Thank you. It's always nice to hear from a client who appreciates all my hard work."

"You're welcome."

From what she understood, Andrew had worked some kind of attorney magic. They only had to plead guilty to misdemeanor assault and disturbing the peace charges and they would in turn be sentenced to a hundred hours of community service. If they were able to finish the hours before the New Year, their guilty pleas would be set aside and nothing would remain on their records.

"I'm not doing it," Dylan said, his jaw set.

"Don't be an asshat," his brother said. "How hard can it be? It's basically two weeks' effort to keep from going to jail. Only an idiot would refuse a sweet deal like this."

"I don't want to work at A Warrior's Hope," he said through clenched teeth. "Charlotte and Spence know that."

Genevieve didn't know much about the organization, though she had heard it started up this summer while she had been in Paris.

When she arrived at the airport before Thanksgiving, she had been surprised to find Charlotte Caine, Dylan's once-fat sister, at the baggage claim along with the town's disgraced hero, former baseball star Spencer Gregory, helping a guy in a wheelchair in a Navy cap pick up his luggage.

She wasn't sure what she found more stunning: how much weight Charlotte had lost or that she was apparently hooking up with Smokin' Hot Spence Gregory, at least judging by the way they held hands like a couple of teenagers at the movies and even shared a quick kiss in a quiet moment.

Her parents had treated Charlotte and Spence with stiff politeness, not bothering to hide their disapproval. She thought it was because of Spence's past but quickly found out otherwise. Spence had apparently been exonerated of all charges, something else she hadn't heard about in Paris. Instead, her father had spent the first ten minutes in the backseat of the car service grousing about A Warrior's Hope.

From their complaints, she figured out Charlotte and Spence had started the organization to provide recreational therapy to wounded veterans. Her father seemed to think Harry Lange was crazy to condone and even encourage it, which was one of the few times she had ever heard William complain about Harry.

She wasn't necessarily looking forward to helping out with the charity but it beat multiple alternatives she could think of, not the least of which was scrubbing toilets at the visitors' center.

"You don't have a lot of options here, Dylan," Andrew Caine went on. "The assistant district attorneys are pushing hard for jail time, especially since this isn't your first brush with the law in Hope's Crossing. Because I happen to be damn good at my job, I was able to talk them down off the ledge. Wounded war hero, bad press, yadda yadda yadda. This is a good deal. As your attorney and as your big brother, I have to advise you to take it. Both of you. You would be stupid to walk away."

"I'm taking it," Genevieve assured him quickly, before she could change her mind. Both of the Caine brothers shifted their gazes to her and she couldn't help compare the two. Even though he had cleaned up, Dylan still looked dangerous and rough, probably because of the eye patch, while Andrew had an expensive haircut and wore a well-cut suit.

He was just the kind of guy she should find attractive—well, except for the wedding ring, the reportedly happy marriage and the two kids.

Somehow she found Dylan far more compelling, though she was quite sure all either Caine saw when they looked at her was a ditzy socialite.

I know just what Genevieve Beaumont is—a stuck-up snob with more fashion sense than brains, who wouldn't be caught dead in public with someone like me. Someone less than perfect.

She pushed the memory away. "Do you, er, have any idea what kind of things we might be required to do?" she asked Andrew.

She didn't have a lot of experience with people with disabilities or, for that matter, with warriors of any sort. Unless one counted women fighting over the sales rack at her favorite department store in Paris, which she doubted anyone would.

"You'll have to work that out with Spence and his staff. From what I understand, they have another group arriving for a session in a few days, and because of the holidays, they are in need of volunteers."

"Sure. Why not," Dylan said shortly. "Might as well waste the time and money of everybody in town."

"*You* might think it's a waste of effort, but not everybody agrees with you," Andrew answered. "Most people in Hope's Crossing think it's a great program. They are jumping at the chance to help make a difference in the lives of people who have sacrificed for the sake of their country."

The attorney's voice had softened as he said the last part, Gen noted. He was watching his brother with an emotion that made her throat feel tight. Dylan looked down at the hand clenched on his leg.

"I don't claim to be as smart as you. I don't have a couple fancy degrees hanging on my wall. But be honest, Andrew. Do you really think a week in the mountains can make any kind of *difference* for guys whose lives are ruined?"

Was that how Dylan saw his own war injuries? Andrew's jaw tightened, and she knew he was thinking the same thing.

"A hundred hours," the attorney said instead. "You can finish that in a few weeks and put this whole thing behind you. Or," he went on, "you can stand by your belief it's a big waste of time and choose jail time instead. Before you do that, ask yourself if you really want to break Pop's heart by spending the first Christmas in a decade when you haven't been in the desert or the hospital, not with your family but in a jail cell."

For just a brief moment, she caught a tangle of emotions in Dylan's expression before he turned stoic once more.

"At least tell me the truth." His voice was low, heated. "This was Charlotte's idea, wasn't it? She and Spence won't back off. They've been riding me about this for weeks."

"Neither of them had anything to do with it," Andrew assured him. "If you want the truth, Pop suggested it. When he mentioned it, I thought it was a good idea and brought it up with the D.A. They ran with it."

"Remind me to take you off my Christmas list for the next twenty years or so," Dylan growled.

"Like it or not, you're in a unique position to help here," Andrew said quietly. "Charlotte, Spence…everybody can give lip service about what it takes to walk that journey to healing but you're right in the middle of it. You understand better than anyone."

Genevieve's face and neck felt hot as the sincerity of the words seemed to arrow straight to her stomach.

She thought she enjoyed such a cosmopolitan life, but she suddenly realized she knew *nothing* about the world. She hadn't given men like Dylan a thought while she had been in Paris.

It made her feel small and selfish and stupid. He might think A Warrior's Hope was a waste of time, but she resolved in that moment on a hard chair in her attorney's office that she would do her best, even if the concept filled her with anxiety.

"Stand on your principles if you want," Andrew went on when his brother remained silent. "What do I care? I get paid either way, though I will point out that I'll be the one to get crap from Pop if you're enjoying the county jail's hospitality over the holidays."

"Yeah, boo hoo."

Andrew rolled his eyes. "Right. Or you can just yank up your skivvies, suck it up and keep in mind it's only for a few weeks. Lord knows, you've endured a hell of a lot worse than this."

That hand clenched again on his thigh, then he slowly straightened long fingers. She was certain he would stick to his guns and refuse to agree to the plea agreement and she didn't want him to. She hated the idea of him spending time in jail, especially when she knew the whole thing was her fault.

"What's the big deal?" she said quickly. "Like your brother said, it's only a few weeks. It might even be fun."

"There you go," Andrew said dryly. "Listen to the woman. Lord knows, you could use a little fun."

She knew he was mocking her, that he probably thought she was some useless sorority girl out to have a good time, but in that moment she didn't care. Not if it meant Dylan Caine wouldn't have to spend Christmas in jail because of her.

The silence stretched out among the three of them like a string of too-taut Christmas lights, crackly and brittle, but after a long moment Dylan's shoulder brushed hers as he shrugged.

"Fine," he bit out. "A hundred hours and not a minute more."

The attorney exhaled heavily, and she realized he had been as anxious as she was. He had just been better at hiding it. "Excellent." Blue eyes like Dylan's gleamed with triumph. "I'll run these over to the courthouse and let the district attorney and the judge know you've both agreed. The paper work should be in order by Wednesday and you should be able to start the day after."

"Great. Can't wait for all that fun to begin," Dylan said.

"Someone from A Warrior's Hope will be in touch to let you know details about what time to show up."

"Thank you," Genevieve said. "I appreciate your hard work."

A small part of her had to wonder if her father or someone else in his firm might have been able to get all the charges dismissed, but she wasn't going to let herself second-guess her decision to have Andrew represent her.

"I've got some papers I'll need you to sign. Give me just a moment."

He walked out of the office, and she shifted, nervous suddenly to be alone with Dylan. The events of Friday night seemed surreal, distant, as if they had happened to someone else. Had she really been handcuffed to the man in the backseat of a police car?

He was the first to break the silence. "I have to admit, I didn't really expect to see you here."

"Why not? Did you think I would have preferred jail? I've heard it's horrible. My roommate in college was arrested after a nightclub bust for underage drinking. She said the food was a nightmare and her skin was never the same after the scratchy towels."

"I guess taking the plea agreement was the right thing to do," he drawled. "I wouldn't want to ruin my skin."

He almost smiled. She could see one hovering there, just at the corner of his mouth, but at the last minute, he straightened his lips back into a thin line. It was too late. She had seen it. He *did* have a sense of humor, even if she had to pretend to be a ditzy socialite to bring it out.

"What I meant," he went on, "was that I figured you would have second thoughts and go with your own in-house counsel. I can't imagine the mayor is thrilled you're letting a Caine represent you."

An understatement. She had finally resorted to keeping her phone turned off over the weekend so she didn't have to be on the receiving end of the incessant calls and texts.

"He didn't have a choice, did he? I'm an adult. He might think he can dictate every single decision I make, but he's wrong. He might be forcing me to stay in Hope's Crossing but that doesn't mean I'm going to let him strong-arm me in everything."

"He's forcing you to stay home? How did he do that? Cut off your credit cards?"

Right in one. Her mouth tightened at the accuracy of his guess. She was angry suddenly, at her parents for trying to manipulate her, at herself for finding herself in this predicament, even at Dylan. He had a huge, boisterous family that loved him. Even more, they seemed to respect him. She had witnessed both of his brothers trying to watch out for him while he only pushed them away.

She and Charlie hardly spoke anymore, both wrapped up in their separate worlds.

"None of your business," she answered rudely. "Spending an evening handcuffed together doesn't automatically make us best friends. Anyway, I'm still mad at you for what you said about me to your brother."

Again that smile teased his mouth. "As you should be. If you remember, I did apologize."

She made a huffing noise but didn't have the chance to say anything else after his brother returned.

AN HOUR LATER, the deed was done.

"So that's it?"

"On the judicial end. Now we turn you both over to Spence and his team at A Warrior's Hope. You only need to fill your community-service hours. They'll give the judge regular updates on the work you do there and whether it meets the conditions of the plea agreement."

That wasn't so bad, she supposed. It could have been much worse. She could only imagine her father coming in and trying to browbeat the judge, who happened to be one of few people in town who stood up to William, into throwing out all the charges.

"Thank you," she said again to Andrew. "Dylan, I guess I'll see you Thursday at A Warrior's Hope."

He made a face. "Can't wait."

With an odd feeling of anticlimax, she shrugged into her coat and gathered up her purse.

"Wait. I'll walk out with you," Dylan said.

She and Andrew both gave him surprised looks. "Okay," she said.

Outside the courthouse, leaden clouds hung low overhead, dark and forbidding. They turned everything that same sullen gray. In the dreary afternoon light, Hope's Crossing looked small, provincial, unappealing.

She could have been spending Christmas in the City of Lights, wandering through her favorite shops, enjoying musical performances, having long lunches with friends at their favorite cafés.

Paris at Christmas was magical. She had loved every minute of it the year before and had been anticipating another season with great excitement.

Instead, she was stuck in her grandmother's horrible, dark house, surrounded by people who disliked her. Now she had to spend the weeks leading up to Christmas trying to interact with wounded veterans. If they were all as grim-faced and churlish as Dylan Caine, she was in for a miserable time.

"Where are you parked? I'll walk you to your car."

She blinked in surprise at the unexpected courtesy. "That midblock lot over by the bike shop."

"I'm close to that, too."

They walked in silence for a moment, past the decorated windows of storefronts. She would have liked to window-shop but she didn't have any money to buy anything, so she couldn't see much point in it.

"Your brother did a good job," she finally said, just as they passed Dog-Eared Books & Brew, the bookstore and coffee shop owned by Maura Mc-Knight. "We got off easier than I expected. We could have been assigned to pick up roadside trash or something."

"Is it too late for me to sign up for that?" he answered.

She made a face. "What's the big deal? Why don't you really want to help out at the recreation center? Your brother's right. You understand better than anybody some of the challenges wounded veterans have to face."

The clouds began to spit a light snowfall—hard, mean pellets that stung her exposed skin.

He was silent for a long moment, snow beginning to speckle his hair, and she didn't think he would answer. She was just about to say goodbye and head for her car when he finally spoke. "I believe Spence and Charlotte had good intentions when they started the program."

"But?"

"Nobody else on the outside understands what it's like to have to completely reassess everything you do, everything you thought you were. I hate bolo ties."

She blinked at the rapid shift in topic. "O-kay."

"I hate bolo ties but here I am." He aimed his thumb at his open coat, where she could see the string hanging around his collar, with that intricate silverwork disk at the center. "Andrew ordered me to wear a tie for the hearing. I can't tie a damn tie anymore. After trying for a half hour, I finally just stopped at that new men's store over on Front Street and bought this. It was either that or a clip-on, and I'm not quite there yet."

She didn't know what to say, especially as she could tell by his expression that he was regretting saying anything at all to her.

She decided to go back to the fashionista ditz he called her. "Personally, I like bolo ties. They're just retro enough to be cool without being ostentatious. Kind of rockabilly-hip."

He snorted. "Yeah. That was the look I was going for. The point is, a couple of days playing in the mountains wouldn't have a lot of practical value when the real challenges are these endless day-to-day moments when I have to deal with how everything is different now."

She couldn't even imagine. "I guess I can see that. But don't you think there could be value in something that's strictly for fun?"

"I don't find too many things fun anymore," he said, his tone as dark as those clouds as they walked.

"Maybe a couple days of playing in the mountains are exactly what you need," she answered.

"Maybe."

He didn't elaborate and they walked in silence for another few moments. As they walked past one of her favorite boutiques, the door opened with a subtle chime and a few laughing women walked out, arms heavy with bags.

She didn't recognize the blonde with the paisley scarf and the really great-looking boots, but the other one was an old friend.

"Natalie! Hello."

The other woman stopped her conversation and her eyes went wide when she spotted her. "Gen! Hi."

They air-kissed and then Natalie Summerville stepped back, giving a strange look to Dylan, who looked big and dangerous and still rather scruffy, despite his efforts to clean up for court.

"How *are* you?" Natalie asked. "I saw your mom at the spa the other day and she told me you were coming back for Thanksgiving."

Yet you haven't bothered to call me, have you?

Natalie had been a good friend once, close enough—she thought, anyway—that Genevieve had included her in her flock of seven bridesmaids. They had been on the cheerleading squad together in high school, had double-dated often at college, had even shared a hotel room in Mazatlán for spring break after junior year.

When she had been engaged, preparing to become Mrs. Sawyer Danforth of the Denver Danforths, Natalie had loved being her friend.

After Gen ended the engagement, she felt as if she had broken off with many of her friends, as well. Natalie and a few others had made it clear they didn't understand her position. She and Sawyer weren't married yet. Why couldn't he have his fun while he still could? She had overheard Natalie say at a party that Genevieve was crazy for not just ignoring his infidelity and marrying him anyway.

Sometimes she wished she had.

"Are you heading back to Paris soon?"

"I'll be here for a month or so. At least through Christmas."

She imagined word would trickle out in their social circle about her parents' mandate and her enforced poverty, if it hadn't already. Her mother was not known for her discretion.

"Great. Good for you."

"We should do lunch sometime," Genevieve suggested. "I hear there are a few new restaurants in town since I've been gone."

"Yeah. Of course. Lunch would be…great." Genevieve didn't miss that Natalie had on her fake voice, the one she used at nightclubs when undesirable men tried to pick her up.

"I'll call you," Natalie said, with that same patently insincere smile.

"Or I can always call you."

"My schedule's kind of crazy right now. I don't know if you heard but I'm getting married in February. I think you know my fiancé. Stanton Manning."

He had been one of Sawyer's friends and cut from the same impeccably tailored cloth. "Of course. Stan the Man."

Her face felt frozen from far more than the ice crystals flailing into her. Natalie had been one of her bridesmaids, for heaven's sake, but hadn't bothered to even let Genevieve know she was engaged.

If she were fair, she would have to acknowledge that she hadn't been her best self during the humiliation of her marriage plans falling apart. She had been the one to drop all her friends first and flee Colorado as quickly as possible.

"I hadn't heard," she said now. "Congratulations."

"Thanks. I'm counting down the days. You know how that is."

Natalie's friend poked her and she flushed. "We're honeymooning in Italy. He has an uncle who owns a palazzo on the Grand Canal in Venice with stunning views. It's going to be *unbelievable*. Oh, and we've already bought a house together in Cherry Creek. You'll have to see it next time you're in Denver. Stunning. Just stunning. Six bedrooms, five bathrooms. It's perfect for entertaining."

"I'm very happy for you," she said stiffly.

Okay, so Natalie was living the life she had expected, the one she had dreamed. Italian honeymoons, showplace houses, beautiful friends. She refused to let envy eat at her.

She gave Natalie another hug. "Seriously, I'm really happy for you. Be sure to tell Stanton congratulations from me, won't you?"

"Definitely." Natalie avoided her gaze and definitely didn't risk any glances in Dylan's direction. Her friend nudged her again and she gave that well-practiced smile again. "Well, we'd better go. We're meeting people at Brazen. See you, Genevieve."

"'Bye," she murmured.

Only after they walked away did she realize she hadn't introduced Dylan. Despite the cold wind that seeped beneath her jacket and whipped her hair around, Genevieve could feel her face heat. A lousy mood was no excuse for poor manners.

He was gazing at her with an expression she couldn't decipher but one that made her squirm. "Oh. You're still here."

"So they tell me."

"You didn't need to wait. I can find my own way to my car."

As if to illustrate, she set off at a brisk pace toward the parking lot, still a few hundred yards away. She had only made it past one more storefront when her heel caught on a patch of ice and she started to flounder.

In a blink, he reached out to block her fall with his arm and his body. Instead of tumbling to the sidewalk, she fell against him and for a moment she could only stare up at him, that strong, handsome face now dominated by the black eye patch. He was still gorgeous, she realized, a little surprised. And he smelled delicious, clean and masculine.

A slow shock of heat seemed to sizzle inside her, and she couldn't seem to make her limbs cooperate for a long moment. He gazed down at her, too, until a car passed by on Main Street, splattering snow, and she remembered where they were.

What was *wrong* with her? She couldn't be attracted to Dylan Caine. She wouldn't allow it. Genevieve jerked away from him, her face burning, and made a point to move as far away on the sidewalk as she could manage.

He watched her out of that unreadable gaze for a long moment. "Let's get out of this snow."

They walked in silence the rest of the way, until she reached the cute little silver BMW SUV her parents had given her when she graduated from college. At least they hadn't taken that away, too.

At her SUV, she unlocked the door and he held it open for her. Just as she was sliding in, Mr. Taciturn finally found his voice.

"Can I offer a little friendly advice?"

Her stomach tightened. "In my experience, when someone says that, a person usually can't do much to shut them up."

And the advice was rarely friendly, either, but she didn't add that.

"Don't I know it. I was just going to suggest that you might endure your hundred hours of service a little easier if you can get over being chickenshit."

"Excuse me?"

"You know. The whole disgusted, freaking-out thing if one of the guys looks at you or, heaven forbid, dares to touch you only to keep you from falling on your ass."

Her face heated all over again. "I don't know what you're talking about," she said stiffly.

She certainly couldn't tell him she had freaked out because of her own inconvenient attraction.

"Goodbye. I'll see you Thursday," she said, then slammed her door shut, turned the key in the engine and sped out of the parking lot without looking back.

CHAPTER FOUR

THREE MORNINGS LATER, Genevieve was still annoyed with Dylan, with Natalie, with her parents—with the world in general—as she dressed carefully for her first day at A Warrior's Hope. She really had no idea what to expect or what she might be asked to do, which made it difficult to determine appropriate attire.

She finally selected black slacks and a delicious peach cashmere turtleneck she'd picked up at a favorite little boutique in Le Marais. Probably overkill, but she knew the color flattered her hair and eyes.

Or at least it usually did. Unfortunately, it clashed terribly with the overabundance of Pepto-Bismol-pink in Grandma Pearl's hideous bathroom.

This was her least favorite room in the house. How was she supposed to apply makeup when this washed her out so terribly? If she could afford it, she would renovate the entire room, but she doubted her budget would stretch to cover new bathroom fixtures.

She was just finishing her second coat of mascara with one eye on her watch when chimes rang out the refrain of Handel's "Hallelujah Chorus." Grandma Pearl's ghastly doorbell. She shoved the wand back into the tube and hurried through the house, curious and a little alarmed at who might be calling on her this early in the morning.

"Good. You *are* home." Her mother beamed at her as soon as Genevieve opened the door.

"Mother! What are you doing here?"

"Oh, that awful doorbell! Why haven't you changed it yet?"

"I'm still trying to figure out how. Seriously, why are you here?"

"I'm on my way to the salon. When you were at the house the other day, I couldn't help noticing your nails. Horrible shape, darling. I thought I would treat you to a mani. I've already made the appointment with Clarissa. She had a tight schedule but managed to find room first thing this morning. Won't that be fun?"

Her mother gave her a hopeful look and Genevieve scrambled for a response. Since the end of her engagement—and the subsequent death of all Laura Beaumont's thinly veiled ambitions to push them both into the higher echelons of Denver society—Genevieve's interactions with her mother had been laced with heavy sighs, wistful looks, not-so-subtle comments about this gathering, that event.

Being married to one of the most financially and politically powerful men in small Hope's Crossing wasn't enough for Laura. She had always wanted more. When she was engaged to Sawyer and she and Laura worked together to create the wedding of the century, Genevieve had finally felt close to her mother.

She had missed that closeness far more than she missed Sawyer.

"I can't," she said regretfully. "I'm starting my community service today."

Laura gave a dismissive wave of pink-tipped fingers that looked perfectly fine to Genevieve. "Oh, that. Well, you can just start tomorrow, can't you? I'm sure they won't mind. I'll have your father give them a call."

This was her family in a nutshell. Her mother didn't understand anything that interfered with her own plans, and when she encountered an obstacle, she expected William Beaumont to step in and fix everything.

When Gen's younger brother, Charlie, had been arrested for driving under the influence in an accident that had actually resulted in the death of one of his friends, William had been unable to prevent him from pleading guilty. Charlie had served several months at a youth corrections facility, and Laura hadn't spoken to her husband for weeks.

Now both of their children had been embroiled in legal difficulties. She imagined Laura found it much easier to pretend the whole thing hadn't happened.

"I don't believe it's that simple, Mother," Gen said. "It's court-mandated. I have to show up or I could go to jail."

Laura pouted. "Well, what am I supposed to tell Clarissa? She's expecting us."

How about the truth? That you see the world only the way you want to see it?

"Tell her I have another obligation I couldn't escape. I'm sure she'll understand."

Laura gave a frustrated little huff. "I was looking so forward to finding a moment to catch up with you. We hardly talk when you call from France. I can't say I agreed with your father's decision to cut you off financially. I tried my best to talk him out of it. I told him you were having a wonderful time in Paris, that you needed this time and why shouldn't you take it? As usual, he wouldn't listen to me. You know how he can be when he's in a mood. Still, I told myself at least this would give me the chance to spend a little more time with you, darling."

Her parents drove her crazy sometimes...she couldn't deny that. These past two years away had helped her see their failings more clearly, but she still loved them.

"I'm sorry. I wish I could go," she said, not untruthfully.

"I understand. You have to do what you must. I'll see if I can reschedule for tomorrow."

"Mother, I'll be going to the center tomorrow, too. And the day after that."

"Every day?"

Laura obviously didn't quite grasp the concept of a commuted sentence. "I have a hundred hours of community service to complete in only a few weeks. Yes, I'll probably be going every day between now and Christmas."

"This is what happens when you decided not to have your father represent you. He could have had the whole misunderstanding thrown out."

Like Charlie's little "misunderstanding" that had killed one girl and severely injured another? William had been helpless to fix that situation. Charlie had taken full responsibility for his actions and had come out of his time in youth corrections a different young man, no longer sullen and angry.

"It's done now," she said. "I'm sorry, Mother, but I really need to go or I'll be late for my first day."

"Well, will you come back to the house instead of staying in this horrible place? Then I would at least have a chance to catch up with you in the evenings."

Again, her mother saw what she wanted to.

"I can't. My evenings will be spent here, trying to do what I can to prepare this house for sale. Dad didn't give me any other choice."

"He has your best interests at heart, my dear. You know that, don't you?"

"He might have *thought* he did. We have differing opinions on what the best thing for me might be."

Not that anything was new there. Her father had notoriously found her lacking in just about every arena. He thought she had been wasting her time to obtain a degree in interior design, nor could he see any point in the sewing she had always loved or the riding lessons she tolerated.

The only time either of her parents seemed to approve of her had been during her engagement.

"Will you at least go to dinner with us this weekend? With Charlie back in California for his finals week, the house is too quiet."

"I'll try," she promised. She ushered her mother out with a kiss on the cheek and firmly closed the door, practically in her face.

After Laura drove away, Genevieve hurriedly grabbed one of the totes she loved to make and headed out the door, fighting down a whirl of butterflies in her stomach.

For two days, she had been having second—and third and fourth and sixtieth—thoughts about this community-service assignment with A Warrior's Hope. She couldn't think of a job less suited to her limited skill set than helping wounded veterans. What did she know about their world? Next to nothing. Most likely, she would end up saying something stupid and offensive and none of them would want anything to do with her.

A hundred hours could turn into a lifetime if she screwed this up.

By the time she drove into the parking lot of the Hope's Crossing Recreation Center in Silver Strike Canyon, the butterflies were in full-fledged stampede mode.

She was five minutes early, she saw with relief as she climbed out of her SUV and walked into the building.

Construction on the recreation center had been under way during her last visit home for Pearl's funeral. The building was really quite lovely, designed by world-renowned architect Jackson Lange. Created of stone, cedar planks and plenty of glass, the sprawling structure complemented the mountainous setting well for being so large.

It also appeared to be busy. The parking lot was filled with several dozen cars, which she considered quite impressive for a weekday morning in December.

She wasn't exactly sure how A Warrior's Hope fit into the picture, but she supposed she had a hundred hours to figure that out.

The butterflies went into swarm-mode as she walked through the front doors into a lobby that wouldn't have looked out of place in one of the hotels at the ski resort.

She stood for a moment just inside the sliding glass doors, hating these nerves zinging through her. Spying a sign that read A Warrior's Hope at one desk, she drew in a steady breath in an effort to conceal her anxiety and approached.

The woman seated behind the computer was younger than Genevieve and busy on a phone call that seemed to revolve around airline arrangements. She held up a finger in a universal bid for patience and finished her call.

"Sorry," she said when she replaced the phone receiver on the cradle. "I've been trying to reach the airline for *days* to make sure they know we need special arrangements to transport some medical equipment when our new guys arrive next week."

"Ah." Gen wasn't quite sure what else to say. "I'm Genevieve Beaumont. I believe you were expecting me."

The woman looked blank for a moment then her face lit up. "Oh! You're one of the community-service people. Spence said you were coming today. Our computers have been down. No internet, no email, and wouldn't you know, our IT guy is on vacation. I've been so crazy trying to track down somebody else to help I forgot you were coming. I'm Chelsea Palmer. I'm the administrative assistant to Eden Davis, the director of A Warrior's Hope."

"Hi, Chelsea."

She didn't recognize the young woman and couldn't see any evidence Chelsea knew her—or *of* her—either.

"I don't suppose you know anything about computers, do you?" the woman asked hopefully.

Gen gave a short laugh. "On a good day, I can usually figure out how to turn them on but that's the extent of my technical abilities. And sometimes I can't even do that."

Chelsea gave her a friendly smile. She was quite pretty, though she wore a particularly unattractive shade of yellow. She could also use a little more subtlety in her makeup.

Gen certainly wasn't going to tell her that. Instead, she would relish the promise of that friendly smile. Around Hope's Crossing, she found it refreshing when people didn't know who she was. Here, many saw her as snobbish and cold. She had no idea how to thaw those perceptions.

She had loved that about living in Paris, where her friends didn't care about her family, her connections, her past.

"Thanks anyway," Chelsea said. "I'll figure something out. My ex-boyfriend works in IT up at the resort. He agreed to come take a look at things."

"Even though he's an ex?" She hadn't spoken with Sawyer since the day she threw his ring back at him.

"I know, right? But we left things on pretty good terms. He's not a bad guy.... He was only a little more interested in his video games than me, you know? I decided that wasn't for me."

"Understandable."

Chelsea's gaze shifted over Gen's shoulder and her face lit up. "Hey, Dylan! Eden said you would be stopping in this morning."

"And here I am. Hi. Chelsea, right?"

"One two-second conversation in line at the grocery store and you remembered my name."

Gen didn't like the way all her warm feelings toward the other woman trickled away. Friends weren't that easy to come by here in Hope's Crossing. She certainly couldn't throw one away because she was feeling unreasonably territorial toward Dylan, even if *she* had been the one shackled to the man.

She didn't blame Chelsea for that little moment of flirtatiousness. Dylan still needed a haircut. Regardless, he looked quite delicious. Even the black eye patch only made him more attractive somehow, probably because the eye not concealed behind it looked strikingly blue in contrast.

She thought of that moment when she had nearly fallen on the ice a few days earlier, when he had caught her and held her against his chest for a heartbeat.

And then the humiliation of his words, basically accusing her of being so shallow she recoiled in disgust when he touched her, which was *so* not true.

"Genevieve." He again said her name as her Parisian friends did and for some strange reason she found the musical syllables incredibly sexy spoken in that gruff voice.

"Is that how you say your name?" Chelsea asked in surprise. "I though it was Gen-e-vieve."

She managed to tamp down the inappropriate reaction to the man. "Either way works," she said to Chelsea. "Or you could simply call me Gen."

"Thanks. I'll do that."

The young woman turned her attention back to Dylan. She tucked her hair behind her ear—her *pointy* ear, Gen thought, before she chided herself for her childishness in noticing. She was a horrid person, as superficial as everyone thought.

"We're all so excited you're finally coming to help us," Chelsea said. "Eden has been over the moon since she heard about your, er, little brush with the law."

"Good to know I could make everybody's day," he said dryly, but Chelsea didn't appear to notice.

"It's going to be *perfect*," she exclaimed. "You're going to be great! Exactly what we need."

She had said nothing of the sort to Genevieve, yet another piece of evidence in what she was beginning to suspect—that her presence was superfluous here, an unnecessary addendum. The organizers of the program wanted Dylan to help out at A Warrior's Hope because of his own perspective and experience. She, on the other hand, was little more than collateral damage.

"Where is Eden?" she finally interjected.

"She's at the pool with Spence and our new program coordinator, Mac Scanlan."

"I thought Eden was in charge," Genevieve said.

"Technically, she is. She's the executive director, in charge of fundraising, planning, coordinating events etc. We just hired a new person to actually run the activities. He's spending the day familiarizing himself with the facilities. She told me to send you to the pool the minute you both arrive."

Which had been several minutes earlier, but who was counting?

"Thanks," Genevieve said.

"I'm supposed to make you ID badges first, but we'll have to do that later, when my system is back in action. You know where to go, right? Through the main doors there and down the first hall."

Dylan seemed reluctant to move. Apparently Genevieve would have to take the lead. She followed Chelsea's directions, aware of him coming up behind her.

"You made it," she said to Dylan as they entered the hallway.

"You didn't think I'd show?"

"Given your general reluctance to this whole idea, I guess I wouldn't have been surprised if you had decided you'd rather go to jail."

"I'm still not discounting that possibility."

She smiled a little. "I don't even know what I'm doing here. Chelsea's right. You are in a far better position than anybody else, especially me."

"So everybody says. I'm not seeing it."

"You know what it's like to be injured in battle, to have to rebuild your life."

"Right. I'm doing a hell of a job, aren't I?"

Genevieve flashed him a quick look. "Better than I would in your situation," she answered truthfully.

"You would probably start designing a fashion line for one-armed pirate wannabes and go on to make millions of dollars."

She laughed. "The only one-armed pirate wannabe I know doesn't seem particularly interested in fashion."

He gave her a mock offended look. "What do you mean? I wore a bolo, didn't I? I thought I was going for the hipster look."

"Or something," she answered.

He snorted but said nothing as they moved toward the door at the end of the hall where she could see the flickering blue of water.

"You were wrong the other day," she said when they nearly reached it.

He paused and gave her a curious look. "You'll have to be more specific. I'm wrong about a lot of things."

She fiercely wished she hadn't said anything but she couldn't figure out a way to back down now.

"Er, you implied I flinched away when you touched me—that I was, I don't know, disgusted or something because you're, er, missing your arm. That wasn't it. You just..." Her voice trailed off.

"I just..." he prodded.

"You make me nervous," she said in a rush. "It has nothing to do with any eye patch or...or missing hand. It's just...you."

His eyebrow rose and he studied her for a long moment, so long she could feel herself flush. "How refreshingly honest of you, Ms. Beaumont."

"I just didn't want you to think I'm— What's the word you used? Er, chickenshit."

He laughed as she pushed open the door to the pool area and the sound echoed through the cavernous space.

Several people congregating beside the pool looked over at the sound and Genevieve recognized Spence Gregory and Dylan's sister, Charlotte, as well as a man in a wheelchair and another woman she didn't know.

"I wasn't sure you would make it," Spence said to Dylan when they reached them, holding out his hand. After a slight pause, Dylan took it.

"Why does everybody keep saying that?" he asked.

"No reason." Charlotte hugged him and he gave her an awkward sort of pat with his right arm.

"I'm so glad you agreed to do this," his sister said.

"You made it impossible for me to refuse, didn't you?"

"Don't blame me. It was all Pop's idea, and Andrew's the one who ran with it. Though I probably should confess that Spence *might* have mentioned to Harry Lange how much we'd like to have you volunteer here and I believe Harry *might* have mentioned it to Judge Richards during one of their poker games."

Charlotte stepped away from her brother and gave Genevieve a cool smile. "Hello, Genevieve. We're glad you agreed to help, too. We have a strong core of volunteers already, but we're always glad for more."

Genevieve had enough experience with polite falsehoods to recognize one when she heard it. She supposed she shouldn't be surprised. Charlotte probably blamed her for her brother's troubles in the first place.

"I'm happy to help." She was an old hand at polite falsehoods herself.

Spencer Gregory stepped up. "Good to see you again. I didn't have the chance to say hello when we saw you at the airport last week."

He really was gorgeous up close. She didn't follow baseball but she knew Smokin' Hot Spence Gregory was a nickname given only in part for the man's fastball. Oddly, despite those long lashes and that particularly charming smile, he didn't make her nerves flutter at all, unlike others in the room she could mention.

"My father loved to tell business associates from out of town how you used to be our paper boy."

"I hope I was a good one."

"The best, according to my father."

Spence smiled and gestured to the other two people. "Dylan, Genevieve, this is Eden Davis, our executive director, and Mac Scanlan, who just started this week as our program coordinator."

"What is your role at A Warrior's Hope?" Genevieve asked, trying to keep things straight in her head.

"I'm the director of the entire recreation center. A Warrior's Hope is only one part of what we do here."

"But it was his idea and he's the fundraising genius behind it." Charlotte smiled with far more warmth than she had shown Genevieve. Spence aimed that charmer of a grin down at her, and even if she hadn't seen them together at the airport, she would have easily picked up that the two of them were *together*.

The once-fat-and-frumpy Charlotte Caine was involved with Smokin' Hot Spence Gregory. She still couldn't quite believe it.

"It's become Charlotte's baby, too. She organizes all the volunteers."

"What do you think we'll be doing?" she asked. "I'm really good at filing, correspondence, that kind of thing. And I've had a little experience with fundraising for a few charities my family supports."

"Just for the record, I'm not good at any of those things," Dylan offered.

Charlotte gave her brother a sly smile. "I've got just the project for both of you. Yesterday Sam Delgado, our contractor, and his crew put the finishing touches on several cabins for our guests. The first group to use them will be coming in first thing Monday morning. Before they arrive, we need to decorate the cabins for Christmas. That's where you two come in."

CHAPTER FIVE

THIS WAS HIS version of hell.

Yeah, he had spent a combined total of six of the past ten years in the Middle East through his various deployments, four of those in direct combat. He was a trained army ranger, sent in to dangerous hot spots for difficult missions.

He had seen and done things that kept him up nights—and had spent months in rehab, a very special kind of misery.

He would rather go back to living in a tent where the sand seeped into every available crevice, wearing seventy-five pounds of gear in a-hundred-twenty-degree weather without showering for weeks, than endure this torture his wicked sister had planned for him.

He stood in a large storage room in a back corner of the recreation center surrounded by boxes and crates.

"Isn't there something else I could be doing right now?" he asked, with more than a little desperation.

"I can't think of a thing," Charlotte said cheerfully. "We want these cabins to be perfect, a home away from home for these guys—and one woman—while they're here. We want to make this a perfect holiday."

He wanted to tell his sister she was wasting her time, but he had already tooted that particular horn enough.

"We'll do a fabulous job. Don't worry." Genevieve beamed with excitement. Why shouldn't she? This was probably right up her alley. Hang some lights, put up a few ornaments. Nothing so uncomfortable as actually *talking* to any wounded veterans—present company excluded.

He remembered what she had said earlier—that he made her nervous and it had nothing to do with his physical disfigurements.

He didn't believe her. Not really. How could he? She was a perfect, pampered little princess and he was scarred and ugly. They were Beauty and the Beast, only this particular beast couldn't be twinkled back into his old self, the one without missing parts.

"I'm sure you will, Genevieve," Charlotte was saying. "You have such an instinctive sense of style. When I heard about your little, uh, legal trouble, I knew you would be perfect to help us get the cabins ready for their first guests."

Genevieve looked surprised and flattered at Charlotte's words. "I graduated with a degree in interior design," she said. "Eventually I hope to open my own design firm."

"Then you really are perfect."

"I'll do my best. I saw some really beautiful lights in Paris. They had these little twinkly snowflakes and each one was unique. They were stunning. You don't have anything like that, do you?"

Charlotte pressed her lips together to keep in the smile he could see forming there. "We didn't buy our lights in Paris this year," she said with a dryness he wasn't sure Gen would catch. "You'll have to be content with the cheap ones from the big box store."

"I suppose we can make those work," she answered.

"You'll have to, I'm afraid."

"What about the trees?"

"Also from a big box store. But they're all prelit, which is a big plus."

"We'll make it wonderful. You'll see. Won't we, Dylan?"

"Wonderful," he repeated. Why did he suddenly feel as if he'd been dragged by a couple of high-school cheerleaders to help decorate for a homecoming dance?

He could really use a beer right about now.

"Aren't you supposed to be working?" he asked Charlotte, mostly to change the subject from snowflakes and Christmas trees. "Who's running Sugar Rush while you're here bossing around the reprobate help?"

Her haughty look rivaled anything Genevieve Beaumont might deliver.

"I have a staff, you know. They're very qualified to run the place without me."

"Even at Christmas, the busiest time of year?"

"Even then. I took today and Monday off so I can help Eden and Spence get everything ready for the group coming in next week."

She glowed whenever she talked about the things she loved: their family, her gourmet candy store in town, A Warrior's Hope...and Spencer Gregory and his daughter, Peyton.

He still wasn't sure how he felt about Spence and Charlotte together.

When they were growing up, the man had been one of his closest friends. They had gone on camping trips together, played ball, even double-dated a time or two.

Their lives had taken very different paths in the years since Spence's mom used to work at Pop's café, Dylan's to the military and Spence's to a life of fame and riches—and eventual scandal—in Major League Baseball. Dylan still wasn't convinced the guy was good enough for his baby sister but it was obvious the two were crazy in love.

"I hope this doesn't sound rude," Genevieve said, "but I have to say it. You look completely *amazing*."

Charlotte looked startled. "Thank you. Why would that be rude?"

"Just because...you know. How you were before."

Charlotte had always been amazing, as far as Dylan was concerned. Kind and funny and generous. Trust Genevieve not to be able to see past a few extra pounds.

"I just think it's fantastic. It must have been so difficult to lose all that weight when you spend all day surrounded by all those empty calories at your store," she went on. "How did you do it?"

Charlotte looked a little disconcerted by the blunt question. "Willpower, I suppose." Her gaze flickered to Dylan then back to Gen.

"The truth is, when Dylan almost died last year, I realized how off track my own life had become. While he lay in a hospital bed fighting to survive, I realized my own unhealthy habits were slowly killing me. I had been given the precious gift of life and I was wasting it. Dylan's challenges had been thrust upon him, but I was choosing mine every day. It was pretty sobering."

How had this become about him? Dylan shifted, wishing he could still tell his sister to shut up—though even when they were kids, if Pop had heard him, he would have had to scrub dishes at the café for a week.

He didn't like to think about that miserable time when antibiotic-resistant infections had ravaged his system and left him as weak as a baby—and he especially didn't like Charlotte giving Genevieve one more reason to see him as an object of pity.

He jumped up. "I'm going to start hauling some of these boxes down to the cabins."

"Oh, you don't have to do that," Charlotte said. "I can grab a couple of the guys who work at the recreation center to help."

"This is why I'm here, isn't it?"

Before she could argue—something his little sister had always been very

adept at—he stacked a couple of boxes and lifted them with his arm, bracing them against his chest with his prosthetic.

"Don't be a stubborn jerk," she said. "I'm sure there's a dolly or cart or
something. You don't have to carry all these boxes down to the cabins by
yourself."

"I've got it," he snapped and walked out before either she or Genevieve
could stop him.

It was going to take him the whole damn afternoon to carry all the boxes
down but he didn't care. He would take monotonous physical exertion any
day over seeing that pity in Genevieve's eyes.

WHEN HE RETURNED from carrying the first load of boxes to the five small
cabins along the river, he found Genevieve and Charlotte loading a couple
of wheeled carts with more boxes.

He frowned. "You didn't think I could carry them on my own?"

"This is about efficiency," his sister answered. "I won't let you spend four
of the remaining hours you owe us schlepping boxes back and forth when
the three of us can do it this way in a few trips."

Okay, she had a point, though he didn't want to admit it.

"Fine," he muttered, then directed his efforts to stacking the carts better for maximum-load capacity.

He ended up pulling one of the heavily laden carts while Genevieve and
Charlotte maneuvered the other one together and he tried not to notice the
nice rear view that had landed him in this mess in the first place.

He had to admit, his sister was right—as usual. They had all the boxes
transported to the cabins and dispersed among them in only an hour, with
Charlotte directing where everything should go.

The log structures weren't anything fancy, maybe a total of about six hundred square feet each. They seemed well laid out, with a large living area
combined with a kitchen then two separate bedrooms and a roomy bathroom. Probably because they were so close to the river and the inherent
flood potential, the cabins were built above grade but the cleverly designed
landscaping created a natural wheelchair ramp into each one, which made
it far easier to roll the carts to the porches.

The decor inside was what he considered Western chic—a lot of antlers, rich colors, cowboy themes. Each had big windows to provide warm
natural light, with sweeping views to the river on one side and the mountains on the other.

"That should be the last of it," Charlotte said as they carried the final box inside the cabin farthest from the main building.

Genevieve pulled off her fluffy mittens and looked around at the space. "Goodness, it's tiny. There's hardly room for a Christmas tree in here," she exclaimed.

Charlotte looked amused. "This is bigger than most base housing. Am I right, Dylan?"

He shrugged. He had always rented off-base when he wasn't deployed. Sometimes a guy needed a break from the life. "The whole place would fit inside your bedroom, right?" he asked Gen.

She frowned, giving the matter serious consideration. "My room at my parents' house, maybe. But I lived in much smaller places in Paris. You wouldn't believe how tiny the flats there are—and how much they charge for them. It's really quite absurd."

He didn't comment since his only experience with Paris was a layover once when he was en route to a mission in Central Africa.

"I was planning to put the trees up there in the corner between the sofa and love seat."

Gen moved to the spot and slowly revolved with her arms out, gauging the space. "That should work."

Charlotte glanced at her watch. "Actually, let me rephrase. I was planning on the two of *you* putting the trees up there. I've got to run."

A ridiculous little spasm of panic burst through him, in no small measure at the idea of being alone in these cozy little cabins with Genevieve.

He had to wonder if his sister wanted a little payback for her frustration with his attitude these past months since he had returned to Hope's Crossing.

"You two should be able to handle this without any problem. These are the keys to all six cabins. As you saw when we dropped off the boxes, the layout is the same, only the furniture and colors are different. You can set up the Christmas trees in the same spot in all of them. Just lock up when you're done. See you."

She left in a rush, leaving behind a long, agonizing silence.

Yeah. Definitely his version of hell. He couldn't imagine a deeper misery than an afternoon putting up Christmas decorations with Jahn-Vi-Ev Freaking Beaumont—even if she did look particularly lovely in a fancy little tilted knit hat that matched her scarf and roses in her cheeks from the past hour's exertion.

She gave him a sideways glance, and he thought he saw nerves in her gaze. Maybe she wasn't any more thrilled about being in an enclosed space with him right now.

She should be nervous. He was feeling particularly...predatory right about now.

"This is *tons* better than the things I expected we might have to do, don't you think? I mean, putting up Christmas decorations is fun. I thought I might have to, I don't know, help with therapy or something."

She tended to chatter when she was nervous. Under normal circumstances, that would have set his teeth on edge, but with Gen, he actually found it...endearing, though he wasn't quite sure why.

"Have you ever put up a Christmas tree before?" he asked gruffly.

She looked at the long box with the tree label. "Um. No. You?"

He shook his head. "I haven't spent a Christmas stateside in seven years—except for last year, when I was in the hospital."

"I'm afraid we're going to be in trouble. I've never needed a tree of my own. I came home from Paris for Christmas the past few years and never wanted to go to all the trouble to put one up since I was coming home anyway. Before that, my sorority mother or roommates always took care of it."

"Well, we're both obviously underqualified for this job. We'd better let Eden know she'll have to find some other criminals to help her out."

He supposed it *had* been a while since he had felt like joking about much of anything, and apparently he was out of practice, at least judging by the uncertain look Genevieve was sending him.

"Oh. We'll figure it out. Don't you think?"

Sure, they could figure it out. How hard could it be? But he had only one hand that worked and he couldn't imagine that would make the process easier.

After much debate that morning, he had ended up wearing one of his prosthetics. He didn't like either of them but this one was slightly less annoying than the other. He had also packed his Leatherman multitool, invaluable when driving in changeable Colorado weather situations, where a guy never knew what might happen.

Now in resignation, he pulled out the Leatherman and used it to rip the tape on the Christmas-tree box. Once open, the contents just looked like a big pile of green bristly branches.

Genevieve peered over his shoulder. "Is that the way it's supposed to look? It seems kind of...smushed. That can't be right."

"Let's hope it bushes out after we pull it out. Give me a hand here."

Together, they lifted the pieces out, power cords trailing, and set them side by side on the wood flooring of the kitchen.

Genevieve studied the sections then nudged one with her foot. "This looks like the biggest one. Don't you think it goes on the bottom?"

He fought a smile at her serious contemplation of the task at hand. "Good guess."

After struggling to figure what went where for a few more moments, Gen discovered a sheet of directions concealed under packaging in the box. The rest of the assembly went off without a hitch.

He maneuvered the tree into the corner where Charlotte had indicated, which had a conveniently located outlet. He crouched down and plugged it in and the seven hundred white lights lit up the small space.

"Oh. Look!" she exclaimed softly. "It's beautiful!"

He was looking, but not at the tree. The flickering lights reflected in her eyes and she seemed to glow from the inside out, with all that blond hair and the deliciously soft sweater that clung to her.

He was staring, he realized with dismay.

"Even for a cheap department-store tree?" he asked, his voice more caustic than teasing.

He was sorry for the words when her expression of joy seeped away and her features closed.

"I'm not saying a designer tree wouldn't look more real but this one will do for here."

He fought the ridiculous urge to apologize for shattering the magic like a cheap glass ornament. "Great. One down, five more to go."

An hour later, each of the cabins had a Christmas tree in the corner. They had developed a certain rhythm to it. He would open the box, she would separate the pieces and they would work together to assemble them. By the last one, she didn't clap her hands with glee when he tested the lights, only fluffed out a few of the crinkled branches.

"Now we can decorate them," she said. "What a relief they're already prelit. My dad used to complain so much about his struggles to string lights on the tree."

He had a tough time picturing the starchy mayor with his hands covered in sap, trying to twist Christmas lights around tree branches.

"I would have thought the Beaumont family hired somebody to do that kind of menial labor."

She leaned back against the kitchen counter, a pensive, almost sad look in her eyes. "We hired a decorator after we moved into the new house in the canyon when I was ten. In the early days when we lived over near Miner's Park, we always decorated it ourselves. It used to be a wonderful family time. The first Saturday afternoon in December, we would go up to Snowflake Canyon and cut down our Christmas tree. My mom would make hot chocolate and we would all bundle up and set out. Charlie was always so cute in his snowsuit."

It matched a lot of his own memories and he was aware of a familiar, hollow pain. His mother had died of cancer when he was a teenager, and he still sometimes fiercely missed her softness and warmth.

"After my dad would wrestle with the lights for a couple of hours, we would spend all evening hanging the decorations, making sure each strand of tinsel hung just so."

His mom hadn't been nearly as fastidious. Their tree had always been one big haphazard jumble of keepsakes, photographs, sloppy ornaments made by little hands. A glorious, magical shambles.

The Christmas after Margaret died, none of them had felt much like celebrating. A few days before Christmas, Charlotte had begged Pop to get a tree. He remembered finding her in the living room in tears with boxes of ornaments open around her.

Teenage boys weren't always the most emotionally sensitive creatures, but he had done his best to comfort her and had ended up helping her decorate the tree the best they could.

Come to think of it, that had probably been the last ornament he had hung.

"Yeah, I'm afraid tree decorating isn't really my thing," he said. "Since you seem to be all over it like sugar on a doughnut, maybe I'll go search out Eden and see if she wants to put me to work doing something else."

Anything else.

"You'll do no such thing." She frowned at him. "I can't decorate six trees by myself! They have to be done today and they have to be *perfect*."

"I really think this is a job you can handle better by yourself."

She narrowed her gaze. "Now who's being, er, chickenshit?"

He didn't want to do this. The very idea of spending even five minutes hanging Christmas decorations just about made his toes curl. But he was no coward.

He looked at the sprawl of boxes, at the bare Christmas tree, at the lovely woman standing in front of him with a barely suppressed crackle of excited energy at the prospect ahead of her.

He sighed and accepted his fate. "Fine. Where do we start?"

GENEVIEVE COULD THINK of far worse things than decorating six cute little cabins for the holidays.

As they started opening boxes to see what she had to work with, she wondered if adding a few festive touches to Grandma Pearl's house might brighten up the place.

Her grandmother had adored Christmas. Every year, she had turned the outside of her house into a blinking, tacky wonderland. Plastic Santas, snowmen, polar bears. Gen hadn't wandered into the storage room in the basement yet, but she could only guess that it would probably still be stacked high with boxes containing Pearl's huge crèche collection.

Her grandmother probably had a hundred different manger scenes. The Holy Family in a shelled-out coconut she had bought on a trip to Hawaii, a teak-carved set a friend carried home on her lap from Australia, chiseled ebony from Ghana dressed in tribal clothing.

A few were elegant, even artful, but most were tacky, brought home from Pearl's extensive travels to Branson, Mount Rushmore, Florida, Las Vegas.

And her grandmother hadn't been content to collect alone. From the time Gen was a little girl, her grandmother would give her a new Nativity set each year. She used to love decorating her bedroom with them, touching each figure, setting them around her bedroom. After she became a teenager, she had gotten tired of the hassle of it.

Maybe she would pick a few of her favorite sets from Pearl's collection— *not* the one that featured Homer and Marge Simpson, certainly—and set them out while she was living in her grandmother's house.

The garland for the tree in this cabin was made of red wooden beads strung together. It probably wouldn't have been her choice, but it fit the cozy setting.

She draped it carefully then stood back to gauge the results. "Does that look good?" she asked Dylan.

Her dour companion gave a cursory look. "Sure. Fine."

She sighed. They had been doing this for only twenty minutes and it felt like forever, especially with this uncomfortably awkward silence between them.

She would far rather be doing this with someone else. Eden, Charlotte. Even Mac.

"We ought to have some kind of Christmas music," she said suddenly.

"I won't sing, if that's what you're getting at."

She wouldn't be surprised if he sang beautifully, judging by his low, melodious speaking voice. At least when he wasn't grumping and grousing at her.

"I wouldn't dare ask," she retorted, stepping away from the tree and heading toward the well-outfitted entertainment center against the wall. She turned on the TV and found, as she suspected from the dish she had seen on the roof, that the cabin was connected to a satellite system. She flipped through channels until she found a station streaming Christmas music. A jazzy version of "Jingle Bells" filled the small space.

"Correct me if I'm wrong," Dylan said after a moment, "but isn't Christmas music what got us in this mess in the first place?"

"It's all about the venue, right? It wasn't appropriate at The Speckled Lizard on a night when I wanted to get sloppy drunk and stupid, but for decorating a Christmas tree, it's perfect."

He started indiscriminately tossing green and red balls on the tree. All her aesthetic senses recoiled from such haphazard decorating, but she forced herself to bite her tongue. She wasn't in charge here. He could decorate however he wanted. At least he was helping.

"Why did you want to get sloppy drunk the other night?" he asked after another silence that somehow didn't seem as uncomfortable with the Christmas music in the background.

"It's a long story."

He gestured to the tree and the overflowing boxes. "We've got nothing but time, sweetheart."

She knew he meant nothing by the endearment. Still, it helped her answer without the customary bitterness that ate away at her whenever she thought about her father's ultimatum.

"I'm not exactly thrilled about being back in Hope's Crossing."

He chuckled. "No kidding?"

"That afternoon, my parents gave me an ultimatum. I have to stay here until I manage to flip my grandmother's house, which is a complete nightmare. It's going to take me *forever*. Pearl had absolutely no design sense whatsoever."

"What do you mean? When we were kids, we always begged Mom and Dad to drive us past your grandmother's house to see her Christmas light display."

She shuddered. "Her *hideous* Christmas light display, you mean."

"Kids don't care about things like that. The bigger and brighter the better as far as the younger set is concerned."

"And some in the older set. Grandma Pearl, anyway. Her house is...well, something to behold. I packed my suitcase and moved in after my little chat with my dear parents. After just an hour, the magnitude of the task at hand sort of…smacked me in the face and I needed the escape."

"Ah. That explains a lot. In other words, it was an interior-design crisis. You should have explained that to the judge. 'Yes, I punched that woman, Your Honor, but there were extenuating circumstances. Two words—*shag carpeting.*'"

She laughed, amazed at further evidence that Dylan Caine had a sense of humor. "You can joke about it, but you wouldn't be laughing if you saw the place. Every time I walk through the door, I feel like I'm entering a time warp, discoing back to the seventies."

"I'm sure it's not that bad."

"Oh, it is."

She told him about some of the low points—the layers after layers of wallpaper, the tile in the bathroom, the blue carpet in a couple of the bedrooms.

"Where are you going to start?"

He seemed genuinely interested—either that or he was only trying to stave off boredom while they decorated the tree.

"I should really gut the place and start over, especially the bathrooms and the kitchen, but I don't have any kind of budget. I'm going to focus on fixes that are cheap. I'm renting a steamer to take off the wallpaper. I figure I can paint for the cost of a couple buckets."

"You ever painted a room?"

She made a face. "I have a degree in interior design. I know how to paint a room."

"You know how, but have you ever actually done it?"

"For your information, we had to as part of our course work." She didn't add that four of her fellow students had worked together on the assigned project, redecorating a few rooms at a group home in Denver for people with developmental disabilities.

She had mostly cleaned brushes and picked up lunch for the other three, but she figured she had absorbed enough information through the experience that she could pick things up as she went along.

"I'm a long way from painting, anyway. It's going to take me *weeks* to steam off the wallpaper."

"Weeks, huh?"

"I'm not kidding. I counted six layers of wallpaper. I think every time Pearl was in a mood, she would slap up another design on top of what was already there."

She went on about her plans for the house, and before she realized it, the tree was finished. She had jabbered the entire time, barely aware of it.

He was going to think she was the brainless debutante everyone else did.

"Sorry to ramble." To her astonished horror, she could feel heat soak her cheeks and knew she must be blushing. "I tend to get carried away."

"I didn't mind," he said gruffly. She had the strangest feeling he wasn't only saying the words to be nice. Dylan Caine was many things but she wasn't sure *nice* was among them.

"Well, I'm sorry anyway. See what being alone in that house for only a few days is doing for me? I'm turning into my grandma Pearl, ready to talk anybody's ear off."

"If you don't mind, I've got two of those for now and I'd like to keep it that way, all things considered."

How could he joke about his missing parts? She did not understand this man.

Needing a little distance, she took a look around the cabin and decided on a whim what else was needed.

"I'm going to go outside and cut some evergreens to arrange on the mantel, along with the lights your sister was talking about. That will make it perfect in here."

He looked wary. "Fresh pine boughs weren't on Charlotte's list."

"This is what you call improvisation," she said with a smile.

His gaze shifted to her mouth and stayed there for just an instant, long enough for heat to bloom inside her and her thoughts to tangle like strings of Grandma Pearl's Christmas lights.

She grabbed the pair of scissors Charlotte had provided them for cutting ribbons and hurried outside into the December afternoon.

The cold mountain air slapped more than a little sense back into her.

Any attraction to Dylan Caine was absolutely ridiculous. Two people could not be more opposite. He was gruff, rough-edged, slightly dangerous. He had seen things, probably *done* things she couldn't even imagine, and he had the battle scars to prove it.

She was, in his words, a cream puff. Why would a man like him ever be interested in her?

What had she done in her life that had any meaning? Beyond the project to help that group home where she had made only a halfhearted effort, what had she ever done for someone else?

Oh, her family donated to various charities. Her mother sat on some philanthropic boards in town and helped out with a few causes.

Those were her parents' efforts, desultory as they might be.

The past two years, Genevieve had spent in self-indulgence and self-pity. She was really rather tired of it.

Even if her parents hadn't reined her in, she wanted to think she soon would have come to that realization on her own—but she would have done it in her lovely little flat in Le Marais, not stuck here.

She sighed as she clipped another pine branch. She didn't have any business being attracted to the compelling, dangerous Dylan Caine, but they could at least be friends. She might be as crazy as Grandma Pearl but she thought he had enjoyed listening to her talk about the house.

She had a feeling maybe he needed a friend as badly as she did.

As MUCH AS he loved his baby sister, right now he wanted to wring her neck.

Was this what he had come to? Of all the assignments she might have found for him, why the hell would she put him to work hanging Christmas decorations with Genevieve Beaumont? Did she think he wasn't capable of anything more?

He glowered as he carried a couple of the empty boxes outside to the porch to be hauled away later.

It didn't help anything that when he looked at Gen, all he could see was someone beautiful and perfect, with a whole world of possibilities ahead of her. She might be going through a tough time right now—though, really, did she think dealing with her grandmother's ugly house was the worst thing that could happen to a person?—but life would even out for her. Her parents would probably come around and she would return to Paris to her life of frivolity and fun.

He shoved a smaller box into another one a little harder than he'd intended and it ripped just as Genevieve returned to the porch with her arms full of evergreens.

"Sorry it took me so long but I tried to cut from the side of the trees that faces away from the recreation center and the cabins."

"Won't those turn brown before Christmas?" Even from here, he could smell them—tart, crisp, citrusy.

She frowned and looked down at the boughs in her arms. "My parents always have a fresh-cut wreath and it's good from Thanksgiving until New Year's. I think they should be okay for a few weeks, don't you?"

With her cheeks flushed from the cold and her nose an even brighter pink, she looked fresh and sweet and not at all like the snobby bitch he wanted to believe her. She was also as unreachable as the Christmas star on top of the sixty-foot spruce in front of City Hall.

His stump ached suddenly from the cold and the exertion.

"How should I know?" he snapped, suddenly pissed at the whole damn world. "Do I look like a freaking expert on Christmas decorating?"

Her eyes went wide at his sudden attack, and her breath hitched in a little. He saw surprised hurt in her eyes for only an instant before she composed her lovely features into that cold, supercilious expression he was beginning to suspect she donned for self-protection.

"Sorry," she answered, her voice icicle-cool. "My mistake. Forget I asked your opinion."

She brushed past him on her way inside, stirring the air with the thick scent of pine mingled with the vanilla-and-cinnamon scent that was hers alone.

He probably should apologize for his bad temper, but he decided to let things ride. Better she think he was a bad-tempered bastard.

"I'll start opening the boxes in the next cabin over," he said curtly.

"Fine."

He might as well have been invisible for all the notice she paid him as she started arranging pine branches on the mantel.

After a moment, he turned and stalked down the sidewalk to the cabin next door.

He found the garland in the first box he opened. He should probably leave it for her to hang when she finished in the other cabin, but as he gazed down at the coil of intertwined thin ironwork stars of this one, he felt a ridiculous urge to atone somehow for hurting her feelings.

He picked it up and started draping it around the little tree, trying his best to imitate the artful way he had seen her hang the garland in the first cabin. It was harder than it looked, though he wanted to think he had done a passable job.

When she finally came in sometime later, her nose was a little pink, her eyes slightly swollen. She looked as if she had been fighting tears—or maybe even giving in to them—and his stomach felt hollow.

"I know. It looks terrible," he muttered.

Not only that, but hanging the garland by himself hadn't been nearly as enjoyable as decorating the other tree had been with both of them working together.

"I didn't say that."

"You didn't have to." He could either be miserable and short-tempered or he could try to get along with her. They still had four-and-a-half trees to go. It didn't have to be *complete* torture.

"I'm obviously not as gifted in this arena as you are," he said gruffly.

"Few people are," she said, voice smart as she stepped forward to reposition one section of garland.

She smelled delicious, he couldn't help noticing again as she nudged him out of the way so she could move another loop of garland.

He had to stop picking up those things, he told himself.

She was the perfectly beautiful Genevieve Beaumont, pampered and adored princess.

He was...not.

"There. That should do it," she said. "You had the basics down. Now it's only a matter of finessing the details, see?"

In her naturally husky voice, the benign words sounded vaguely sexual.

"Yeah. I can see that," he said. "That looks much better."

She offered a hesitant smile and his heart gave a hard little tug.

Kissing her right now would be a really terrible idea. The worst. So why couldn't he stop thinking about it?

He shoved away from the wall. "Since you're obviously better at this, why don't you finish up here and *I'll* go cut down some evergreens for this cabin and the others."

"Can you—" she began then stopped. Could he what? Clip the branches? It would probably be a little harder than it should be, especially with only a pair of scissors instead of pruning loppers, but he didn't doubt he could handle it.

"Yes," he said firmly. He held out his hand and she handed over the scissors, still looking a little doubtful.

He grabbed his jacket and waited until he walked outside to shrug into it and then headed toward the thick trees near the river.

He should have brought Tucker with him, he thought as he did his best with the scissors. The coon dog loved to be outside and adored any kind of running water. Sometimes he thought Tuck must have a little water dog in him, as much as he loved chasing skeeters in the little stream that trickled through Dylan's land in Snowflake Canyon.

He stacked the boughs he cut next to a little snow-covered bench beside the groomed trail that ran alongside the river. After he cut what he gauged the appropriate amount of pine boughs for the remaining five cabins, he returned to the bench for the rest.

No rush, he thought. They would be decorating the rest of the day. He figured he deserved five minutes to himself after being around Genevieve all morning.

He used one of the pine branches to sweep snow off the bench and then sat in the quiet little woods, listening to the river's music and the mournful wind in the treetops.

After only a few moments of peace, he heard the crunch of boot steps in snow and tensed, assuming Genevieve had come looking for him.

"It's restful here, isn't it?"

He jerked around at the male voice to find Spence Gregory walking toward him. So much for his mad special-forces skills. The ambush had taken more from him than several good friends and a few things he rather needed.

"Not bad," he answered. "It's a little cold this time of year for meditating on the meaning of life, but it will do."

Spence smiled as he crossed the last few feet between them, wiped off snow on the other side of the bench and sat down. "Don't you have some community service you're supposed to be doing?"

He should probably be embarrassed to be caught slacking, but something told him Spence understood. If he didn't, well, too damn bad.

"Just taking a breather. Genevieve wanted pine boughs to decorate the mantels." With his thumb, he pointed to the pile beside him.

"Sorry. I wasn't riding you," Spence assured him. "How's that working out? Genevieve Beaumont, I mean. I don't know much about her, but Charlotte seemed to think she would try to wiggle out of her sentence after the first hour."

He fought down his immediate urge to defend the woman, who had been working her butt off since they arrived. Just the fact that he *wanted* to defend her to his friend seemed wrong on multiple levels.

"She's fine," he said shortly. "I, on the other hand, am ready to poke one of those pointy star ornaments in my other eye. Come on, Spence. Can't you find something else for me to do? This is a nightmare assignment."

Spence gave a solemn look that didn't fool Dylan for a second, especially when he caught that little gleam of amusement in his friend's eyes. "I'm sorry. I tried, I really did, but Eden and Charlotte tell me decorating the cabins has to be the priority for now, at least until the new group arrives next week. After that, you'll have plenty of other things to fill your hours."

"Can't wait," he muttered.

He wasn't looking forward to any of it. He suspected Spence and Eden and the rest expected him to magically bond with the other veterans, simply because they had a small thing in common. He wasn't seeing it and really wished he could figure out a way to wriggle out of this whole thing.

"It should be fun," Spence said. "We've got a great group coming in. A couple of marines and the rest are army. None of them has been on skis or snowboards before."

He hadn't been skiing since his accident. It ought to be interesting to see how he would do on the turns when he could only plant one pole. He saw a lot of right turns in his future.

"You're wearing one of your prosthetics," Spence said after a minute.

Not his favorite topic of conversation. "For now. The thing is a pain in the ass. Or stump, anyway."

"How is your pain level these days? Charlotte worries about you."

Something else he didn't like to talk about. More than a year after the amputation, he had become used to the occasional phantom aches.

Unfortunately, he wasn't sure he would ever become accustomed to waking up each morning and seeing that empty space starting a few inches below his elbow.

"I'm fine," he said, rising and scooping up the greenery in one motion. "I'd better take these back before Gen has to come looking for me."

Spence gave him a curious look and Dylan realized using the shortened version of her name probably sounded far too familiar.

His friend said nothing, though, only nodded. "You probably don't want to keep a woman like her waiting."

Dylan scooped up the branches and headed through the snow back to the cabins.

CHAPTER SIX

"So. What do you think?"

Several hours later, the pale afternoon sun filtered in through the cabin windows, illuminating the cheery scene inside—the decorated tree, the red and green ornaments she had hung on ribbons in the windows, the mantelpiece covered in some of the cut pine boughs with white pillar candles popping through as well as a few scattered gold stars and little twinkly lights.

He had just finished hanging more greens that Gen had shaped into a wreath and adorned with red ribbons and more of those glittery gold stars.

The mission furniture in this cabin featured simple oak and wrought-iron accents, sparely elegant lines and simple design. With the ribbons weaving through the entwined elk-antlers chandelier above the small dining room, every inch of the cabin seemed festive and welcoming, even to his untrained eye.

He looked around at all the work they had both done with an odd sense of satisfaction. "It will do," he said.

She was silent and he saw her face fall. "Oh," she said.

He wasn't quite sure why until he realized that what he considered pretty high praise—especially given that he expected most of the guys participating in A Warrior's Hope would just be grateful for a comfortable bed—probably came across as faintly damning.

He cleared his throat and tried again. "You don't need me to tell you the place looks great," he said gruffly. "All six cabins are perfect. You did a good job."

Color seeped into her cheeks. "Thanks. You were really a huge help, too."

He doubted that. His job seemed to mostly consist of doing what he was told—hanging this ornament here, that ribbon there. He had to wonder what any of the guys in his unit would say if they knew he was putting up holiday decorations because of a bar fight over Christmas carols.

He hoped like hell they never found out.

"From here, it looks like the star on top of the tree is a little bit crooked," he said. "I'll see if I can straighten it out. Where's that step stool?"

She tilted her head with a frown that made her look a little like a puzzled kitten. "Are you sure? It looks okay to me."

"What do you mean? You don't trust the opinion of the man with one eye?"

Her color deepened and she looked flustered. "I didn't say that."

"Where's the stepladder? I'll adjust the star, and if you don't think I'm right, I can move it back where it is now."

"Sure. Okay."

She brought the small stepladder over. He climbed up and tweaked the star slightly, aligning the horizontal points until they looked level to him.

He stepped down again and went to stand by Genevieve. "Is that better?"

She tilted her head one way and then the other, then shifted to face him.

"You were right! It *was* crooked. Wow, that's *tons* better."

He had to chuckle at her reaction, as if he had just single-handedly— yeah, punny—saved Santa's sleigh from enemy combatants.

"I do what I can," he said modestly.

She smiled back at him and a subtle, seductive intimacy seemed to stretch between them, fragile and bright like those glass ornaments gleaming in the windows.

This wouldn't do. He cleared his throat. "I guess that about wraps things up for our first day. Eight hours down, ninety-two something to go."

"Oh, don't remind me." She looked daunted at the prospect of the hours stretching out ahead of them. He couldn't blame her for that.

"Sorry. For now, you should focus on what we accomplished today," he said. "More like what *you* accomplished. I'm sure everyone who stays here will feel welcome in Hope's Crossing."

She nudged his shoulder. "We did it together. We make a pretty good team, Caine."

She smiled, soft and pretty, and a fierce need twisted in his gut. For hours, he had been working closely with her, had been trying not to be intoxicated by the cinnamon-vanilla scent of her, had listened to that contralto voice talk about everything and nothing.

It was more than a guy could take. He wanted to kiss her. Right here, surrounded by all this holiday hoopla. He wanted to lick that sweet bottom lip, to trace his thumb over the arc of her cheekbones, to tangle his fingers in her hair....

He gazed at her and the moment seemed to freeze like the river's edge. It might have been the reflection of the lights from the tree—or maybe his overactive imagination—but he thought he saw something flicker in her eyes, something warm and almost...welcoming.

He leaned down an inch, not sure if he had the stones to take the chance and cover the rest of the distance between them. In the second or two while he was still trying to make up his mind, the door to the small cabin opened, sending a cold rush of air washing over him.

"Here you two are!"

Charlotte's voice effectively shattered that crystalline moment. Gen eased away from him, color rising on her cheekbones.

Yeah. He was going to strangle his sister one of these days.

"Hey," he said, trying for a casual tone.

Charlotte's gaze slid between him and Gen, and he saw concern there before she quickly masked it. Great. He had just given her something else to worry about.

"I checked every cabin and finally found you in the very last one."

"Funny. Seems like it might have made more sense to start with the one that had all the lights on."

She made a little-sister sort of huff. "Yes, but that would have been too easy. Besides, this way I got to look at all the other cabins. I was amazed. They look fantastic! The real greenery was a fantastic touch."

"Don't look at me." Dylan pointed to Genevieve. "It was her idea."

"You cut down most of the branches," Gen said, quick to give him credit where it certainly wasn't due.

"Yeah, but I wouldn't have had the first clue where to put them. That was all you."

"I get it," Charlotte cut in before Gen could add anything else. "It was a team effort. A great one. The cabins turned out better than I imagined—so good, in fact, I need to grab my camera and take some pictures for the website."

"I can do that, if you want," Genevieve offered. "Photography's kind of one of my things. I have a high-resolution digital SLR and a wide-angle lens that would really help capture the whole cabin."

Charlotte made a face. "I have no idea what half of that meant, so I guess that indicates you're far more qualified than I am to take pictures."

"I can bring it tomorrow, if you'd like."

His sister smiled. "That would be fantastic. In fact, if you don't mind, why don't you plan on bringing it with you every day while you're here?

We have a small digital camera and one of those GoPro cameras to capture live action when the guys are out on activities, but we could always use a few more photographs taken by somebody who knows what she's doing to use on the website and in our brochures."

"Sure. No problem."

Charlotte took another look around the cabin, focusing on all the clever little touches Genevieve had incorporated.

"I can't believe you're already done," Charlotte said. "I was afraid it might take the entire weekend to finish decorating all six of the cabins."

Gen had been a bit of a taskmaster but he really hadn't minded. "Does that mean we don't have to come tomorrow?" he asked, only half joking.

Charlotte made another one of those sibling noises of disgust. "Nice try. You're not getting off that easily. We have a million things to do before the new group arrives Monday."

Yeah, he was afraid of that. While they had been working on these cabins, it had been easy to focus only on the task at hand, not the bigger picture.

"This wasn't so bad, was it?" Charlotte asked.

"It had its moments," he answered. Including the one she had interrupted before anything could really begin. "Are we done here?"

"Yes. Actually, that's why I came looking for you, to let you know you could wrap things up and go for the day."

"Great." He grabbed his coat. "See you tomorrow."

He suddenly had a fierce craving to be sitting by his fire with a beer and the quiet, undemanding company of his dog.

GENEVIEVE WATCHED DYLAN rush off as if he couldn't stay here in this small cabin another moment. His sister watched him, too, a little frown rippling her forehead.

He had obviously reached the end of his patience with her. She wasn't sure how he'd endured her mindless chatter as long as he had.

He had almost kissed her. If Charlotte hadn't interrupted them, Gen knew he would have. She wasn't sure what she found more surprising, that he had thought about kissing her—or that she had wanted him to. For hours, she had been thinking about it, wishing for it.

This was completely ridiculous. She was crushing on Dylan Caine— shaggy, cranky, *damaged* Dylan Caine.

He was the exact opposite of the sleek, polished men she usually dated. Men like Sawyer, who used to put almost as much care and attention into his wardrobe and appearance as she did.

Maybe that was what drew her to Dylan, that he was so very different from her norm. He had done things she couldn't begin to imagine. He was tough, hard. Genuine. Unlike Sawyer, who had dreams of following in his father's congressional aspirations, Dylan was the sort of man who could never be a politician because he would say just what he thought, to hell with the consequences.

"Is he always so…abrupt?" she asked his sister now.

Charlotte watched after her brother. "I can't believe he made it this long, if you want the truth. I honestly thought he would be climbing the walls after the first hour. Was he a bear all day?"

Gen thought of that moment when he had stomped outside to gather more pine boughs. He had been gone a long time, so long she had been ready to go search for him in case he'd fallen in the river, when he returned with his arms full of greenery. After that, he had been more relaxed and comfortable, as if those few moments out in nature had centered him or something.

"He had his moments," she said. "I think mostly we managed to tolerate each other. He let me jabber on about whatever, inanities, really, though every once in a while I let him slip into those brooding silences of his."

His sister gave a surprised-sounding laugh. "How thoughtful of you."

Gen shrugged. "I figured it was the least I could do for a returning war hero and all."

When Charlotte laughed again, Gen wanted to bask in the warmth of it. She liked the other woman. In their interactions that day, she had been kind to her, even though Gen could tell she had great reservations about Genevieve's ability to contribute to A Warrior's Hope.

As far as she remembered, Charlotte had never been outright rude to her but she was usually cool—probably because Genevieve had never been particularly nice to her.

She thought of Natalie suddenly and the gulf between them now and felt a wave of loneliness. She had a few close female friends in Paris and she missed them fiercely.

She pushed it away. Once she straightened out her life and sold the house, she could return to Paris and her friends there.

"The problem is," Charlotte answered thoughtfully, "I think we've all indulged those brooding silences for too long, until now Dylan is more comfortable with his own company than engaging in polite conversation. He prefers to hide away at this dilapidated old cabin up in Snowflake Canyon where he doesn't have to talk—or *listen*—to anyone."

Gen didn't want to contradict his sister but she wasn't sure that was true.

When she thought about it, Dylan seemed to want her to keep talking. In a strange sort of way, he had almost seemed…*soothed* while he listened to her ramble on about living in Le Marais: her favorite candlelit bistro, the pâtisserie she loved, the best museums.

When she ran out of things to talk about and lapsed into silence while they worked, he would target a well-placed question about other countries in Europe she had visited, people she knew there, her plans for Pearl's house, and she would start up again.

Her throat hurt from all that talking, but she was pretty sure he had enjoyed listening to her more than he probably would admit. He had smiled several times and had even chuckled a time or two at one of her stories involving her elderly neighbor and the very large dog who shared her very small flat.

"I'm really hoping that being forced to work at A Warrior's Hope will, I don't know, help drag him out of himself, you know?"

Again, she didn't want to contradict his sister after really only a day spent in the man's company, but she knew a little about interfering family members. "I'm sure you have good intentions and want to help him. But really, if he enjoys being on his own in Snowflake Canyon and isn't hurting anybody by it, that's his call, isn't it?"

Charlotte blinked a little and Gen wished she hadn't said anything. She didn't want to ruin any chance she might have of a friendship with Charlotte. After a moment, the other woman's expression turned pensive.

"That's exactly what he says."

"He should know, don't you think?"

"I suppose you're right. I just can't imagine he's happy up there."

"Again, his call."

"You might be right," Charlotte said. "It's never easy watching someone you care about make choices you can't accept are good for him."

Was that how her parents felt? Were they acting out of a position of concern and not manipulation? She wasn't quite ready to accept that yet.

"Do you have a place to store all these empty boxes?" she asked.

"I was going to have a couple of the guys carry them back to the storage room in the main building, but we might as well take care of it. Do you mind helping me haul them back before you take off?"

"The carts should be down here somewhere. We can probably get them all in one trip."

Together, she and Charlotte loaded the empty boxes onto the two utility carts.

"Thank you again for all your hard work," Charlotte said after they pulled the carts back to the recreation center and stacked the empty boxes in the storage room.

She had accepted early in the day that her sweater was likely ruined. It was too bad, too, as it was one of her favorites. She supposed that served her right for ever being silly enough to think she could wear peach cashmere to work.

"I'm thrilled with the way the cabins look," the other woman said. "It's so much better than I ever imagined."

"You're welcome. Decorating is right up my alley. It's too bad you don't have a hundred more. That would probably fill the rest of the hours, wouldn't it?"

Charlotte laughed and Gen thought how pretty she was now that she had lost all that weight. No wonder Smokin' Hot Spence Gregory was dating her.

As soon as the thought flitted across her brain, she felt vaguely ashamed of herself for focusing on the superficial. She needed to train herself to look beyond appearances. Really, Charlotte had always been quite lovely, for a large girl.

"I'm afraid you've met and exceeded all our decorating needs. I'm sure we can find plenty of other things to keep you busy, and very few of them should be completely miserable."

"Something to look forward to," Genevieve said with a smile, picking up her purse. "I'll see you tomorrow."

She was almost to the door when Charlotte called her back. "Do you have plans tonight? I'm getting together with some friends for dinner. You could join us if you want."

For a moment, she didn't know what to say. She was a little embarrassed at how excited she was by the invitation. She thought of all those lovely long lunches in Paris when she and her friends would talk about food and fashion, history and even a little politics.

She found it difficult to come up with the perfect balance in her response. She didn't want to come across as giddily overenthusiastic, but she didn't want to be a snotty bitch, either.

Apparently, she mulled it too long. At her lingering silence, Charlotte's friendly smile slid away. "Well, if you want to come, we're meeting at Brazen, the new restaurant that opened this summer in the old firehouse at the top of Main Street."

"Brazen." Alex McKnight's restaurant. All her good feelings dissolved.

"Have you been there? The food is fantastic and the ambience is wonderful, with gorgeous views of downtown."

Alex would be there, and perhaps even her sister Maura. Maura's daughter, Sage, might even show up. The McKnights tended to run in packs.

Every time she thought about the family, she had a sick, greasy feeling in her stomach—part anger, part shame. She had treated them horribly. She knew that. She had been cold and downright mean, and she knew her mother had been worse.

Still, she couldn't help wondering if they had all been laughing at her behind her back for being so stupid she didn't know her fiancé was sleeping around during her entire engagement, with one of the McKnights and with many others.

"I'm sorry. I can't tonight. Maybe another time."

"Sure. It was last-minute anyway. I'm sure we'll have another chance."

She wanted to say yes. She would like to be friends with Charlotte—and not because she had developed a serious crush on the woman's brother. She liked her, and heaven knew, she could use a friend in Hope's Crossing since it appeared all her old crowd didn't have room for her anymore in their busy lives.

As much as she would like to go to dinner with Charlotte tonight, Gen knew she couldn't. Sometimes, the past dug in with sharp claws and wouldn't let go, no matter how hard a person tried to pry it loose.

HE WOULD RATHER be tortured than admit it, but by the afternoon of his second day working for A Warrior's Hope, Dylan almost wished he had a few more ornaments to hang.

Instead, he was in a large storage room behind the building with Mac Scanlan, the program director for the organization, trying to organize and inventory the huge volume of equipment, much of it apparently donated.

He didn't mind the work so much as the company. Mac seemed like a decent enough guy for a United States Navy combat diver, but he was chatty as hell.

Where Dylan hadn't minded Genevieve's prattle the day before—okay, he had actually enjoyed some of it—Mac was driving him crazy, asking questions about his deployments, his injuries and his recovery process.

Though he didn't give many precise details, Dylan picked up that he had lost the use of his legs during a covert operation during Gulf One when an underwater explosive had detonated at the wrong moment.

"That looks like all the regular skis," he said shortly after they had tallied a vast collection, some new and apparently donated by Brodie Thorne's sporting-goods store and some really nice gently used high-dollar equipment donated by people in town. "You've got enough here to open a ski swap."

"Good to have options so we can fit all sizes and abilities," Mac said. "Growing up here, you've probably got skis of your own, don't you?"

"Somewhere at my pop's house. I haven't been up in a few years."

"You're coming with us next week, though, aren't you? We plan to hit the slopes at least a couple times."

The guy was relentless about encouraging Dylan to participate in the activities of A Warrior's Hope.

"I'll cross that bridge."

"No reason you can't ski one-handed," Mac said. "Hell, I can do it with no legs. I've got a little ski seat I sit on. It's boss. Or you could snowboard. You can probably rip it up on a board."

He had never had much patience for snowboarding. Maybe he was a snob because he had always liked the purity of skiing, but he might have to reconsider.

"Yeah, maybe," he answered, which had become his answer to everything Mac threw at him.

For the past two hours, the man had seemed determined to wrest more out of him than a couple of syllables at a time and Dylan had become equally determined not to let him.

In the midst of the battle of wills, all he could think about was how much he had actually enjoyed the day before with Genevieve.

She had yammered on just as much as Mac and about far more ridiculous things. If he ever went to Paris, he wouldn't need to read a guidebook. She had told him more than a guy would ever have to know. Hell, he even knew exactly which shops sold her favorite scarves and which tried to pass off knockoffs from China as genuine antique Lyonnaise silk.

For some reason, he had enjoyed listening to her far more than he did being smacked in the face with all the things he couldn't do anymore.

The room was filled to the brim with sports equipment. Baseball bats, tennis racquets, climbing gear, canoes. Much of it was designed for use by people with various physical limitations.

He hated those adaptations.

All he could see when he looked at the rows of skis, the golf clubs, the fishing poles were all the things he had left behind. He wanted his old life back, when he could grab a fly rod any damn time he felt like it and head for a nearby trout stream to be alone with the current and the fish and his thoughts.

"You live in one of the most gorgeous places I've ever been, and that's saying something," Mac was saying. "What kinds of things do you like to do for fun?"

The man just wouldn't let up.

"Oh, you know. This and that," he said shortly. Right now he didn't do much, mostly puttered around his land in Snowflake Canyon, messing with the tractor, repairing the chicken coop that had been there when he moved in, tossing a stick one-handed for Tucker when they were both in the mood.

"After I was hurt, I spent the first five years in a bottle," Mac said into the silence. "Didn't want to do a damn thing."

Dylan tensed. Apparently the program director had been talking to Charlotte, who seemed to think he was turning into some self-pitying alcoholic. He wasn't. He knew when to stop and forced himself to do it, even when he didn't want to.

"That can happen," he said, hoping that would be the end of it.

It wasn't.

"One night I went out for a drive while I was loaded and crashed this really sweet van with hand controls the VA bought for me. Ended up with a broken arm and some cuts and bruises, but I was lucky I didn't kill anybody else. Nothing like wrapping a van around a tree to sober you up fast. I realized while I was stuck in the wreckage waiting for the fire department to cut me out that I wasn't ready to go. I could still think and talk and breathe, so why the hell was I feeling so sorry for myself? I went to AA, cleaned up my act, went back to school on the government's dime. Five years ago I met the love of my life, Luisa. She was a nurse at the VA and still has the most beautiful eyes I've ever seen. I told her so, she went out with me and we've been married for four years. She had a couple kids with her first husband who died a few years before I met her, so now I get to be a dad, too. Funny how life works out, isn't it?"

"Hilarious," Dylan muttered.

"It's been a great ride, man. I wouldn't change a thing."

He didn't believe that for a second. If Mac had a chance to go back to the moment before that underwater bomb exploded, Dylan didn't doubt he would do it in a heartbeat.

Just as Dylan would give anything to go back and redo a few of his own decisions the day his world changed.

"How's it going in here?"

He looked up to see Eden Davis in the doorway.

"We're just about wrapping up the inventory," Mac said. "I wanted to check the snowshoes you were telling me about. I think that's about all I have left."

"Think you can handle that yourself?"

"I should be able to."

"Great. I need to steal Dylan for a minute," she said. "We just finished buying the grocery staples to supply the cabins, and I think Genevieve could use some help sorting them and stocking the cupboards." He wasn't sure he really trusted himself to be alone with Gen in the cabins again. On the other hand, it beat the hell out of the alternative.

"You're the boss," he said.

"We took everything to the cabin closest to this building. You'll find her."

"Sure."

He headed down the trail through a light, pretty snowfall that gently landed on the pines, trying to tell himself his little surge of excitement was due to the reprieve Eden had granted him from listening to more of Mac's stories. It couldn't have anything to do with Genevieve.

He rapped on the door of the cabin, though he wasn't really sure why, since she didn't live there, then pushed open the door when she bade him come in.

"Oh. Dylan. Hi."

He registered how lovely she looked today, in a far more practical cotton shirt than the fuzzy peach sweater she had worn the day before. He had seen her only briefly that morning when they had both picked up their ID badges from the front desk, before Eden sent them in different directions.

Somehow he had forgotten that silky fall of hair; her soft mouth; the high, elegant cheekbones.

He forced himself not to stare, looking instead at the boxes and bags of groceries that covered just about every inch of the cabin.

"That would be a little food."

She tucked an errant strand of hair behind her ear with a frazzled sort of gesture. "I know, right? We filled three carts and spent a small fortune. You would not *believe* the price of milk these days."

"I do drink milk occasionally," he murmured. "Since I don't currently have a cow, I do have to purchase it."

"Oh. Of course. I guess I'm still thinking in liters and euros instead of gallons and dollars. It's hard to make the translations in my head."

"Understandable." He looked around at the bags of groceries. "So what is the plan here?"

"We bought the same thing for each cabin—cold cereal, snacks, that kind of thing. We'll have to divide everything evenly and then put it all away in the cabins."

He could think of worse tasks. Inventorying recreational equipment, for instance. "Let's unload everything onto the table and the bar and group the items together, then we can divvy things up into a couple empty boxes for each cabin."

"That's exactly what I was thinking. I hope we've got enough boxes."

They set to work stacking piles of items together. When six boxes were emptied, he set them along one wall and started dispersing one of each item to the boxes.

She didn't seem as talkative today. He missed her chatter, though he would rather be dragged behind a pair of those skis than admit it.

"Eden said we don't have to come in tomorrow," she said after several moments. "That will be nice. I have a million things to do, including a trip to the hardware store that will probably take me hours. I have so many things to buy for the house."

Here was the chatter he had missed.

"Oh?"

"I'm hoping to get some of the wallpaper down tomorrow and start painting. We'll see if I make it that far since it's my only day off for a while. Eden told me to expect a crazy day on Monday, shuttling the new guests here from Denver and helping them settle in. She said expect a ten-hour day."

"Can't wait," he muttered.

She paused in distributing bunches of bananas in the boxes. "I don't think it's been that terrible so far. In fact, I've quite enjoyed it."

"It's been less than two full days," he pointed out. "And you spent most of that time decorating and shopping. That's not really out of the norm for you, is it?"

He regretted the rather snarky words as soon as they were out, especially when her mouth tightened and she looked down at the bananas as if they were dipped in diamond dust.

"Now, if only we can spend a few days having our hair done and getting a massage, it will seem like every other day for me," she said quietly.

He sighed, feeling like the jackass that he was. "Sorry," he muttered. "That was out of line. You've worked hard."

He wasn't sure whether she accepted his apology or not as she picked up another bag and started sorting bagged baby carrots into the piles in silence.

"Tell me something," she finally said. "Were you this cranky before you, er, were injured?"

The unexpected question startled a laugh out of him. "Before I left my hand in an ambush in Helmand Province? I don't know. Probably."

She was quiet, her head angled to one side as she watched him. "You were in an ambush?"

He didn't want to talk about this. Hell, he didn't like *thinking* about it, though memories of that fateful evening would always haunt him.

Mac had been trying to weasel the information about his injuries out of him all morning, and he hadn't wanted to reveal a damn thing. For reasons he couldn't have explained, he wanted to tell Genevieve.

"Yeah. We were on the hunt for a group of insurgents responsible for several bombings focusing on girls' schools. They were killing their own people, just because a few girls wanted to learn how to read. We had solid information that the insurgents were in one particular village, so we were doing a house-to-house search."

He was quiet, focusing on the small bag of clementines in his hand, crisply orange and sweet smelling.

"Everybody in the whole village was acting suspicious. We knew we were onto something. Finally, somebody directed us to this cluster of houses, all connected to each other, on the outskirts of town. We were clearing it room by room when I found this kid. He couldn't have been more than twelve."

The kid—barefoot, big dark eyes—had a weapon, a big old Kalashnikov probably left over from the Soviet war.

Dylan should have shot him on sight but those big dark eyes had looked terrified as hell. He had tried to talk to him in his limited Persian and then had tried Pashto, trying to assure the kid they wouldn't hurt him if he handed over the weapon.

Instead, the kid had watched out of those big eyes, saying nothing. Dylan knew now he had only been waiting until the rest of the unit moved within range before he detonated the suicide bomb strapped beneath his robes, taking down the whole dilapidated series of buildings.

"What happened?" Gen asked softly.

"He was one of the insurgents."

"The little boy?"

He nodded. *There you go, Princess Jahn-Vi-Ev. That's the real world for you, at least in some of the planet's nastiest neighborhoods.*

"Beneath his robes, he was strapped with a shitload of explosives, which he detonated as soon as he could achieve maximum kills."

She made a soft sound of distress that seemed to drive sharp splinters into his heart. "Oh, no."

He should stop now. He had told her enough. She didn't need to hear the rest. He wouldn't tell her about the eighteen hours he had spent buried under rubble, listening to his friends' gurgling last breaths. Or the rabid fear that the rest of the insurgents would be the ones to dig him out and how much pain they would inflict once they found him.

He didn't need to tell her everything, but once he started, the words just seemed to ooze out of him like raw sewage.

"I lost five good friends that day. Good men and good soldiers. When more of our guys in the area finally dug me out, everybody kept telling me how lucky I was to survive. A miracle, they said. I've got to say, I'm not convinced."

Especially since he knew his stupid soft heart had been responsible for the whole FUBAR. He should have blasted the kid when he'd had the chance. The explosives would have gone off and Dylan still would have gone down but everybody else would have been out of range of the worst of the damage.

She had turned pale, clutching a jar of salsa to her chest as if it were her firstborn. "Oh, Dylan." Her voice sounded ragged, thin. "I'm so sorry."

He shrugged. After one quick look, he shifted his gaze back to the clementines and their sweet citrus scent that drifted in the air, unable to bear the pity in her eyes.

"I expect you'll hear worse from the guys who come through the program," he said. "My story is pretty classic, all things considered."

"Do you...? Are you still in pain?"

Her question took him by surprise. Few people asked him that. The ambush had been more than a year ago.

"Is that why I'm a grouchy bastard, you mean? Because I'm nobly and heroically coping with my battle scars?"

She made a small sound, not quite a laugh—but he wouldn't have expected that after the grim story he had just shared. "I didn't say that," she said as she moved closer to him to set the salsa in one of the boxes.

"That's not why I'm grouchy," he said. "But yeah, sometimes I feel a twinge or two."

The eye actually bothered him more than anything. Once in a while, he had headaches that made him want to rip off half his face, but he didn't want to tell her that.

"I'm so sorry," she said again. This time she rested her hand on his, where he still clutched the bag of fruit, and he wanted to drown in the warmth of her eyes.

He would never be able to eat an orange again without thinking of this moment, her fingers soft against the back of his hand, the heat of her seeping into him, the tug of emotions in his chest.

He wanted desperately to kiss her again, even though he knew it was completely idiotic. She was a pampered princess. Perfect hair, perfect clothes, perfect makeup, while he was a broken-down wreck of a man with no job, no prospects, nothing except a great dog and an equally broken-down wreck of a house.

He jerked his hand away and shoved the bag of fruit into one of the boxes. "Everybody's sorry. That doesn't ease the pain one damn bit, now does it?"

She gave him a long look. "No. I guess you're right. Biting everybody's head off is probably a much better pain reliever."

He almost smiled at her sarcastic response but managed to bite it back. He still couldn't believe he had shared that with Genevieve Beaumont, of all people. He hadn't told anyone in his family those details. Why her?

Needing to put a little emotional and literal distance between them, he focused on the task at hand. "Looks like we've sorted everything. I'll take one of these boxes over and start putting things away in the cabin next door. You can start in this one, since you're here."

Without waiting for an answer, he lifted the heavy box using his arm and propping it on the prosthetic. Ignoring the pain that was a little more than the twinge he had told her, he headed outside and away from her as quickly as he could manage it.

CHAPTER SEVEN

HER CELL PHONE rang just as she was climbing into her SUV to make the short drive from the recreation center back to her grandmother's house at the mouth of the canyon.

She was so exhausted, she just wanted to rest her head against the steering wheel and sleep for a few days.

She hadn't slept well the night before, troubled by angst that kept her awake and then nightmares when she finally did manage to close her eyes. Even if she hadn't already been feeling as if her bones were coated in lead, the afternoon with Dylan had been emotionally draining.

Every time she thought of him lying injured under rubble or grieving for his friends afterward, she wanted to cry. She *had* cried a few tears in the bathroom after he left the cabin but had quickly rinsed her eyes and then applied a few artful brushstrokes of makeup to conceal the evidence.

She couldn't imagine what he had endured. It seemed so real, so raw, completely out of her realm of experience. They were total opposites, as she had thought many times, which made this odd, tangled connection between them so disconcerting.

She knew he was attracted to her, but he didn't seem at all motivated to do anything about it. Maybe he wouldn't. He apparently preferred to ignore the currents zinging between them.

She only wished that she could do the same.

Depressed suddenly, she pulled out her phone and looked at the caller ID.

The mayor—just about the last person she felt like talking with right now. She wasn't at all in the mood to listen to her father lecture her about all the many ways she was wasting her life.

She turned off the sound and sent the call to voice mail. As she started the SUV, the phone vibrated with a second call, also from her father.

He would keep this up all day until she answered. Her parents were experts at relentless erosion tactics, wearing her down until she finally gave in.

Once in France, she had forgotten to charge her phone overnight and her battery died. Her mother had ended up calling poor old Madame Archambault—her neighbor with the big dog—and insisted she climb the three flights of stairs to Genevieve's flat to make sure she wasn't lying comatose from carbon-monoxide poisoning.

Intoxication au monoxyde de carbone.

She could turn her phone off, but if she did that, she suspected William might very well be waiting for her at Grandma Pearl's house by the time she drove down the canyon. She would rather talk to him on the phone than in person any day.

With a heavy sigh, she connected the call. "Hello, Father."

"Genevieve. Darling. There you are!"

"Yes," she answered. For a brief moment, she ached for the surreal but wonderful relationship they'd developed when she was engaged, when both of her parents had seemed to think she could do no wrong. For once.

"I dropped by your grandmother's house today but you weren't there."

Court-ordered community service, remember that? Of course he didn't.

"I'm sorry I missed you," she lied.

"I let myself in and took a look around."

He threw the words out between them like a dead rodent. Though he didn't add anything else, she heard the subtext anyway. *You haven't done much, have you?* No. She hadn't. She had been there only a week and had spent most of that time having estimates done and figuring out her budget. And staying out of jail.

"If you had waited until I was there, I could have showed you around and told you some of my plans."

"Your plans." He said the words mildly but, again, subtext was everything. They smacked of so much derision, her chest actually hurt.

"Now that I've done the initial survey work, I'm going to start taking the wallpaper down in a few of the rooms tonight. I'll be bringing in someone to strip the cabinets in the kitchen and I've picked out the new flooring."

"That all sounds...ambitious."

"It's going to be great when I finish. Just wait."

"I'm sure," he answered. "I had forgotten how small and depressing my mother's house was. Are you certain you wouldn't like to stay in your own room here while you're working on the renovations?"

She really longed for her little en suite bathroom with the jetted tub and the steam shower, but she wasn't going to cave on this. "Positive. I'm fine."

"If you change your mind you know you're always welcome."

"Thank you."

"The reason I called, actually, is that I have some good news."

"Oh?"

She could use a little good news right now after the difficult day.

"Yes. I had lunch today with Judge Richards. He indicated he might be amenable to changing the terms of your plea agreement."

"Change the terms." For a long moment, she didn't know what else to say.

"Yes. He's not willing to reduce your community-service hours but he says he has no problem with changing the venue to somewhere a little more... appropriate. Somewhere like the library or the fine-arts museum."

The words took a moment to sink through her exhaustion. Change the venue. Library or museum.

A few days ago, that would have been an immensely appealing offer.

"Why would Judge Richards be willing to do that?"

"It took some doing—I won't lie to you, but let's just say I called in some favors."

She could almost hear her father preening on the phone. She hated when he pushed his weight around town, especially on her behalf. It was more proof that he didn't think her capable of anything on her own.

As much as she might cringe at his efforts, she was also fiercely tempted by them. Volunteering at the library or the museum would be so easy. She could be done by Christmas and would enjoy being surrounded by books or precious artworks. Both the library and the art museum offered safe, serene environments, far removed from the kind of gritty details she had heard today.

The internal war only lasted a moment before shame washed over her for even being enticed. She thought of Dylan and everything he had lost and the courage it must take him every single day to climb out of bed and face the world, given his new limitations.

She could borrow a little of his strength and carry on with the current arrangement.

"I appreciate your efforts on my behalf, Father, but that's not necessary," she said quickly, before she could change her mind. "I'm content with the agreement as it stands."

"You don't know what you're saying." Her father's voice was slightly impatient—and more than a little patronizing. "Think this through before you make a hasty decision you'll regret later. Wouldn't you be more comfortable spending your hours at the library than working with rough soldiers who aren't fit to do anything worthwhile anymore?"

Appalled, she moved the phone away from her ear and stared at it. She wanted very much to hang up the phone. She loved her father but sometimes she didn't understand how he could be so callous, bordering on cruel.

"Yes. I would probably be more comfortable doing something more in my element," she said. "But maybe I'm tired of being comfortable."

"Now, Genevieve…"

He was ramping up for another lecture, she knew, and she didn't want to hear it.

"I've got to go," she said quickly. "I'm driving through the canyon and I'll probably lose you. Thank you for trying, but I signed a plea agreement and I intend to stick by it."

She hung up quickly before her father could start in again and turned her phone completely off so he couldn't try calling her back. She wasn't nearly as tired now as she backed out of the parking space and headed for the main road.

It was amazingly empowering to make a decision she could feel good about, for once, and she wouldn't let her father take that from her.

THE MOMENT HE drove up to his childhood home on Winterberry Road, Dylan knew he shouldn't have come.

The driveway was chock-full of vehicles and he ended up parking his old pickup behind Spence's Range Rover on the street.

He usually tried to avoid these Sunday dinners like the plague, but Pop's birthday was the next day. He kind of felt obligated to make an appearance. He loved his family, but they were easier taken in small doses. Having everybody together like this made for a loud, boisterous scene. He always ended up with a headache that lasted hours.

Still, after he shut off the engine, he sat in his truck for a long time, until Tucker whined a little and rested his chin on Dylan's thigh.

"Yeah. I know. We're here, right? We might as well go in."

He opened his door, dread heavy in his gut, and started up the sidewalk. The weather matched his mood, darkly ominous. Winter storm clouds obscured the tops of the mountains and the air smelled of impending snow. While nothing was falling yet, weather forecasters were predicting a few inches that night.

Despite the grim evening, Pop's house looked warm and inviting, with a big Christmas tree in the window dressed in thick gold ribbons and a hodgepodge of ornaments.

Charlotte had probably set it up for Pop, who was usually too busy this time of year to worry much about Christmas decorations while he catered holiday parties all around town.

"You're going to behave yourself, right?" he said to Tucker. The dog gave him a patient, what-do-you-think? sort of look. Dylan sighed and pushed open the door.

A wave of noise, heat and sumptuous smells just about knocked him off his pins. Roast beef, if he wasn't mistaken, and some of Pop's glorious mashed potatoes, as well as something chocolatey.

Tucker was completely at home here on Winterberry Road since he had lived here with Pop—and Charlotte, until she'd bought a house of her own—during Dylan's various deployments. The dog immediately headed to what he and his siblings had always called Mom's company room to plop down on his favorite spot by the gas fireplace that oozed out heat. A minute later, a rat-skinny little Chihuahua raced in and started licking Tuck's big, jowly face.

"Tina! Come back!" A little dark-headed boy ran after the Chihuahua, followed by Pop's plump tabby, who always acted more like another dog than a cat.

When his nephew Carter—his brother Brendan's son—spotted the coon dog, joy exploded on his four-year-old features.

"Tucker!" He clapped his hands and hurried in to throw chubby arms around the dog's neck. When Tina—his brother Drew's dog—decided she had spent long enough greeting Tucker, she scampered off, and Carter toddled after her with a cheery giggle.

Pop's Sunday dinners were always like this. Chaos and chatter, kids and animals chasing each other, delicious smells seeping out of the kitchen.

Curled up in a corner chair beside the fire was one of his favorite people on earth, his niece Faith.

She had a book on her lap, her legs tucked up beside her, and was wearing a cute little fluffy white snowman sweater that somehow made him think of Genevieve, until he pushed away the thought.

"Hey, Faith."

Her smile was soft, pretty, genuine. She looked at him without any kind of expectations, which was particularly refreshing in this family where everybody seemed to have some.

"Hi, Uncle Dylan. I knew you were here because of Tucker. Did Grand-pop know you were coming?"

He pretended to grimace. "Oops. I think I forgot to mention it to him. Do you think he'll have enough food?"

"You know he will. He always makes *tons*." She gave him a comforting sort of smile, looking so much like her mother that his heart gave a sharp twist for this poor motherless little girl and her brother, the little imp currently on Chihuahua patrol.

"What are you doing in here by yourself?" he asked.

"I got this book yesterday and I want to finish it. It's *so* good. It's about cats and they live in the forest and hunt together and talk to each other and stuff. You should read it!"

He smiled. "Sounds like it's right down my alley," he lied. "Maybe you could lend it to me when you finish."

"Sure," she said generously.

Right now he had a powerful desire to sit on the uncomfortable sofa by the fire while Faith read her book about cats beneath a big framed photo-graph of the whole Caine family under different circumstances.

There was his mom, sweet and pretty, though even then he could see signs of the cancer she fought for two years. And there was Charlotte, chubby and cute, and Pop with considerably more hair.

And him. He was there, too, a cocky-as-hell, good-looking teenager, smiling and whole.

"I wish I'd thought to bring along a book. I would sit here with you and read."

"You can borrow one of Grandpop's."

His chuckle sounded rusty but she didn't seem to mind. "Maybe I'll find one and come back when everybody starts getting too loud in the other room."

"Sure." She smiled happily at him, and his heart ached all over again for Brendan and his family.

"I guess I'd better go tell your grandpop happy birthday."

"Okay."

He kissed the top of her head, remembering the pictures she would color and send him every week during his long hospitalization. Some weeks they were the only thing that carried him through.

Knowing he couldn't delay anymore, he steeled himself and walked back to the huge great-room addition off the kitchen that he and his brothers had helped Pop build the summer he was twelve.

As he expected, the scene was chaos—a few people sitting at the table talking, a couple of boys cheering at a football game on the big-screen TV, still others—Pop included—working in the open kitchen.

His oldest brother, Patrick—a banker in Denver who must have driven out with his family for Pop's birthday—was the first to notice him.

"Well. Miracles never cease. Look who decided to come down from his mountain to be with us mortals."

Everybody snapped to attention at the grand announcement, including Pop, who looked beyond thrilled.

"Told you he would come," Charlotte said smugly. Dylan was almost certain money exchanged hands in a few corners.

They didn't need to make it seem as if he was a recluse. It hadn't been that long since he had come to one of the infamous Caine family Sunday dinners—and he'd been here on Thanksgiving, for heaven's sake.

"You know this doesn't count toward your community service, right?" Spence asked from the table where he was apparently hard at work snapping beans. Pretty humble work for somebody who should have been in the Baseball Hall of Fame.

"Yeah, yeah. Hey, Pop. Happy birthday."

He leaned in and gave his father an awkward, one-armed hug. Dermot threw his arms around Dylan's waist and hugged him back. "My birthday is complete now that you're here," he said when he pulled away, his eyes a little damp.

"Yeah, forget about Jamie and Aidan. Who needs them?" he said.

"We're calling Aidan on Skype later," Charlotte said. "He'll be here next week for Christmas anyway. And Jamie was just here for several days. He took Pop to Le Passe Montagne for his birthday before he left."

"I guess that counts. Smells great in here." He mustered a smile for Erin and Carrie, his two sisters-in-law—married to Drew and Patrick, respectively. Pop always did most of the work in the kitchen, even for his own birthday party, but Charlotte and the sisters-in-law all shared matriarch responsibilities.

He was grateful his brothers had married good women. The men in his family seemed to have inordinately good taste—and then worked hard to deserve their wives.

"How long before we eat?" he asked.

"As soon as you get over here and stir the gravy," Pop growled.

"There are nearly twenty people crowded into this house. I just got here. Why do I have to stir the gravy?"

"That's why," Dermot said briskly. "Because you just got here. Everybody else has been helping already. You know the rule in my kitchen."

"If you want to eat, you have to work," all the Caine siblings said in unison.

He sighed but moved obediently to the stove, picking up a wooden spoon from the drawer. Everything smelled delicious. His stomach growled. He probably hadn't had a decent meal since that Thanksgiving dinner—not counting the leftovers Pop had sent home with him.

He had cooking skills. All of them did. Dermot wouldn't have allowed his children to grow up without them. Their parents had taken that motto seriously—with seven children, they had to be organized and efficient in splitting the workload.

Pop had also made sure they all took a turn working at the café. He and Spence used to wash dishes together, back in the day.

His limited culinary skills had come in handy during a few meals when they only had MREs. He always kept a few extra spices in his ruck to dress things up.

He supposed he ought to start cooking more. TV dinners and a few doggie bags of food Dermot sent from the café just weren't enough all the time. He didn't really have a good excuse for why he didn't, other than he didn't feel like it most of the time.

When Pop judged the gravy to be ready—others might be in on the prep, but he always had the final vote—they all jostled to find spots to eat.

Even without Jamie and Aidan, the Caines overflowed the big twelve-place dining table. A second long folding banquet table had been set up in the sunroom for the kids.

He enjoyed the meal and even enjoyed the company. He was grateful to be seated between Erin and Carrie. Erin taught third grade at one of the two Hope's Crossing elementary schools while Carrie was a pediatrician in Denver.

They talked over him mostly about their Christmas preparations, which presents were already wrapped, the gifts they were giving to neighbors. He was content to listen to them and also grateful not to have attention focused on him for once.

His luck ran out just as the meal was winding down.

Erin was the first to go in for the kill. "So, Dylan. How are things going with your service work at A Warrior's Hope?"

He set down his fork, the last few bites of his lusciously juicy roast beef losing a little of its savor. "Fine, so far."

"The real work will start tomorrow, when our new guests arrive," Charlotte said from across the table.

He wasn't looking forward to that, but he supposed he would survive.

"How are things with Miss Priss of the mighty right hook?" Brendan asked.

"You mean Gen Beaumont?" he asked, a little more testily than he should have.

"Yeah," Brendan said. "You ready to strangle her yet?"

For a brief instant, his gaze connected with Charlotte's, and he saw that shadow of worry there again. She hadn't said anything to him since that moment the other day when she had walked into the cabin just as he was about to make the momentous mistake of kissing Gen. He had been waiting for a lecture, but for once his baby sister was minding her own business.

"Not yet," he murmured.

"I would be. From what I understand, she is a holy terror. The other guys at the station house were talking the other day about a time when she crashed her car into the ladder truck when she was about sixteen, I guess. It was a brand-new convertible and the ink was hardly dry on her license. I guess she hit the truck while trying to back out of a parking space at the hardware store during the Fill the Boot fundraiser—and then she threw a fit. The guys shouldn't have parked right there. It was all their fault. Blah blah blah. You would have thought the world had ended and the whole volunteer fire department had purposely set out to park in a spot they knew she would stupidly back into—like a big fluorescent green ladder truck was invisible. I guess her tantrum was pretty legendary."

"Now, Brendan Thomas. That will be enough of that," Dermot said firmly from the head of the table. "I'll not have you speaking poorly about Miss Beaumont."

He wasn't sure why his father jumped to Gen's defense but he wouldn't complain about it. At least this way, he wouldn't have to do it.

"Why can't he talk about her?" Erin asked. "Dylan wouldn't even be in trouble with the law if not for her. Isn't that right?"

"Whatever happened to lawyer-client privilege?" he muttered to his brother, across the table.

"Drew didn't say a word about what happened, as much as I nagged him. I heard the whole story out of Charlotte when we went to String Fever for their annual holiday bead fair—where I spent entirely too much money, by the way."

"Thanks," he muttered to Charlotte.

"You should probably know Genevieve is a frequent topic of conversation at String Fever, especially since her ill-fated but gorgeous wedding dress is still on display in the store."

He didn't want to ask—nor did he want to think about her engagement to some jackass who had probably been perfect for her. Except, maybe, for his little habit of impregnating teenagers.

"Everybody was talking about this latest escapade of hers," Charlotte went on. "Word was already out that you had been involved, so people pressed me for details. You'll be happy to know, I glossed over most of the finer points."

"It wasn't *entirely* her fault. I should have minded my own business. Like a few others I could mention in this family," he said pointedly to Charlotte, though he could have been addressing the room as a whole, or at least all those over eighteen.

"I'm still blaming her," Erin said. "I agree with Brendan. She's bad news. She and her mother donated some books to the school library a few years ago and insisted on a full-fledged assembly so they could receive proper recognition from the school for their generosity."

Something told him Laura Beaumont had been the driving force behind that one, though he supposed he could be completely wrong about the situation.

"She's been a really good help so far at A Warrior's Hope," Charlotte said. "In fact, she and Dylan spent all day decorating Christmas trees in the new cabins. You should see them. They're beautiful."

The whole room seemed to descend into silence at that pronouncement and everybody stared at him. A few jaws might have even sagged.

Even Brendan looked amused, and it took a lot to make that happen these days.

"Excuse me," he murmured. "Did you say... Christmas decorating?"

"Yes. They did a really good job, too," Charlotte said.

"Do you even have a Christmas tree at your own cabin?" his thirteen-year-old niece Maggie—named for their mother—asked him with interest.

Dylan felt heat crawl up his cheeks and hoped to hell he wasn't actually blushing.

"Yeah," he growled. "Tucker and I put it up weeks ago. And then we held hands, er, paws and sang Christmas carols all night long."

"Really?" Faith looked wide-eyed at him.

He shook his head at her, feeling kind of bad for being grumpy around her.

"That's what you call sarcasm, honey," Brendan said to his daughter. "Your uncle Dylan is something of an expert at it."

True enough.

"I haven't gotten around to putting a Christmas tree up this year," he answered her more gently. "It's just me and Tucker. There's not much point, especially when I can always enjoy your grandpop's tree when I need one."

Faith seemed to find that a terrible tragedy. Her chin even quivered. "You could always put up a little one. I have one in my room you could borrow, if you want."

He mustered a smile for her, touched to the depths of his hardened, sarcastic, miserable soul. "I appreciate that, honey. I do. I'll tell you what. I'll try to cut down a little one from the forest around my place."

That seemed to satisfy her and he was grateful Brendan didn't bring his kids up to Snowflake Canyon very often for her to check the veracity of that particular claim. He had no intention of cutting down a tree. Decorating six cabins for A Warrior's Hope had rid him of absolutely any desire for a tree of his own. Not that he ever planned to put one up in the first place.

"Genevieve is a beautiful decorator," Charlotte said. "I'm not sure how she pulled it off but she made each one of the cabins magical."

"With Dylan's help, of course." Spencer made sure to emphasize this point, grinning broadly, until Dylan wanted to pound him. If the man didn't seem to fit in so effortlessly with the family and wasn't so obviously crazy about Charlotte, he might have tried, old friend or not.

"Genevieve Beaumont is a nice girl," Dermot insisted. "She always has a kind word for me when she comes into the café. I'll admit, I can't always say the same about her mother, but they're two different people."

He didn't want to talk about Genevieve. He bluntly changed the subject to one he knew would best distract his father. "So, Pop, I bumped into Katherine Thorne the other day."

"Did you?" Dermot seemed inordinately interested in cutting his delicious roast beef with pinpoint precision. Dylan was sure he wasn't the only one of his siblings amused by the color that rose on his father's cheeks. Pop and the elegant city councilwoman must hold the record for world's slowest courtship. It mostly consisted of a lot of hem-hawing around and Dermot pretending he didn't blush every time she walked into the café.

"She and I seem to be on the same schedule for grocery shopping. I see her at the market just about every time I go. If you want me to, I can give you a call next time I'm heading that way and you can meet us there."

Charlotte and Brendan, the only ones really paying attention to the conversation, both snickered, and color rose over Dermot's weathered features. "You all think you're so funny."

"Yes. Yes, we do," Dylan said. Teasing his father about his crush was one of the few things that made him happy these days.

"Well, you're not. Katherine is a lovely woman and I'm happy to count her as a friend. That's all there is to it."

Dylan wanted to say the same about Genevieve but decided the circumstances weren't at all comparable.

CHAPTER EIGHT

AFTER DINNER, he helped clear the table and even managed to make polite conversation with just about everybody while they all worked together to clean the kitchen—all except Pop, who played a game with the grandkids in the great room.

As long as he could remember, the Caine family tradition had held that Pop—and Mom, before cancer took her when he was a teenager—would fix the meal and the kids would clean it up together. All these years later, they still fell into the same habits.

He had never minded much. They would tease and joke and sometimes taunt each other, but the work went fast with seven children.

Growing up in a big family had advantages; he couldn't deny that. He had always known one of his brothers would have his back, whether with playground bullies or on the ball field.

There were also negatives. He couldn't deny that, either. Everybody seemed to think he—or she—had a right to know his business and then offer an opinion on it. Since his injury, that had become more obvious.

As he might have expected, Charlotte managed to corner him just as everybody was wrapping up the dishes.

"I'm so happy you came for Pop's birthday," she said with one of her customary hugs. He loved all his siblings but had a special spot in his heart for her, not only because she was the only girl and they all looked out for her but also because the two of them had been the last Caine kids home while their mother was dying of cancer.

They all shared the grief over Margaret Caine's passing but he and Charlotte had probably felt it most keenly. Unlike their older brothers, they hadn't started moving on with their lives yet or had the distraction of new adventures or challenges.

They had been in this house, forced to try to comfort each other as best they could and to step in where needed to help Pop.

He still had memories of walking downstairs in the middle of the night on more than one occasion and finding Pop sobbing by himself in the dark.

The experience had bound them together as nothing else could.

"I'm not a complete hermit, contrary to popular belief," he said to her now. "I do get out once in a while."

"I've seen you more this last week than I think I have since you've been back in Hope's Crossing."

He grunted and returned their mom's beloved gravy tureen to the top shelf of the cupboard.

"I so wish Aidan could have come for Thanksgiving while Jamie was home on leave. It's been forever since we've all been together."

"Never satisfied, are you?" he teased.

She smiled a little as the group playing a game with Pop in the other room suddenly erupted in laughter.

"You haven't been completely miserable so far working at A Warrior's Hope, have you?"

"Not *completely*."

She rolled her eyes at the heavy emphasis he placed on the word, as if he had been mostly miserable but had somehow endured.

"I'm asking in all seriousness," she said. "I don't want you to hate it. If you don't think you can stand it, I'm sure Spence could work with the court system to find somewhere else for you to fill your community-service hours. The legal system probably doesn't care where you do it, as long as you fill the requirements. You could maybe even do something else at the recreation center without us having to go through the system. Sign out basketballs or something."

He gave her a long look. "I love you, sis. You know I do. But if I live to be two hundred years old, I will never understand you."

She made a face. "Why do you say that?"

"From the minute you and Smoke came up with the crazy idea for A Warrior's Hope, you've been nagging me to help. How many times did you come up to my place to bug me about it?"

"A few," she muttered.

"More than a few, as I recall. I do believe it's come up every time I've seen you in the past six months. You finally got what you wanted, with the help of a little blackmail and one night of stupidity, and now you're trying to weasel out of the deal."

"I am not weaseling out of anything! I want you there. I just…don't want you to feel forced."

Siblings could drive a guy crazy like no one else. He sighed. "I *was* forced. We both know it. I didn't have a choice in the matter. Not really. I can't say I'm thrilled to be volunteering there, but now that I'm into it, I don't want to switch canoes midstream. Change skis halfway down the hill. Whatever metaphor you want to use. I just want to finish my obligation and be done with it so I can go back to my mountain."

"Good. I'm glad you're sticking it out. I'm sorry you've been stuck with Genevieve the first two days. Once the session starts next week, I'll make sure the two of you aren't always assigned the same jobs."

He wanted to tell her not to do that, that he didn't really mind working with Gen, but he had a feeling Charlotte would be quick to misconstrue any such claim.

"Whatever," he said, in what he hoped was a casual tone.

To his relief, one of the twins—Patrick's teenage boys who were almost as tall as Dylan—came in to grab a soda out of the refrigerator and ended the conversation.

Dylan managed to stick it out for another hour, until Pop opened all his presents, before the noise and crowd started to press in on him. He found his coat in his parents' old bedroom and shrugged into it, then went in search of Tucker. Last time he checked, the old dog had been blissfully getting the love from Maggie, Peyton Gregory and Eva, Drew and Erin's daughter.

They were still there, unfortunately, which meant he couldn't quietly slip away.

"Tuck, come on. Home. Sorry, girls."

The dog gave him a disgruntled look but lumbered to his feet and padded over to him.

"You can't be leaving already," Dermot protested. "You haven't had dessert. Erin made a cake and I baked a huckleberry pie just for you."

Since his father didn't even know he was coming, he doubted that, but he didn't want to argue with the man on his birthday.

"I'll take some home, if you don't mind, but I should really head up the canyon before the storm hits."

He had a garage just off the main road where he stored a snowmobile for those times the snow was too deep for his pickup until he plowed, but he would rather not have to use it. Beyond that, the canyon road to his house was twisty and could be tough to navigate in bad conditions, especially when his night vision and nocturnal driving skills weren't the greatest with only one working eyeball and one hand.

"I don't know why you have to live clear up there by yourself, especially in the winter," his father said. "I've all these empty bedrooms, you know. And what's more, I'd be lying if I said I didn't miss that rascal hound of yours."

"I like it up there," he answered quietly. "Even in the winter. When it snows, the silence is absolute."

Dermot looked at him for a long moment then gave a smile tinged with sadness. "I told myself I wouldn't badger you about it. I know you find peace up there and I understand it. But I'm your father. It's my job to worry, especially with winter upon us."

His father would worry in the middle of a blazing summer afternoon. That was just who he was.

"Don't fret about me, Pop. I'm fine. Better every day. Thanks for dinner."

"Stop a minute in the kitchen so I can ready your pie."

He followed his father and leaned against the counter while Dermot set a large piece in one of the café's to-go boxes he always kept at home for the family to package leftovers.

"Thanks," he said when Pop finished, but to his surprise, Dermot slid another piece of the pie in a second box. "I'm sure you won't mind doing a favor for your old man on his birthday."

"What kind of favor?" he asked, wary at the sudden crafty look in his father's eyes.

"Oh, not much. I'd like you to drop a piece of that huckleberry pie to your Christmas-tree-decorating friend Genevieve. Her grandmother's house is right there at the mouth of the canyon, isn't it? It's on your way home. Won't be any trouble at all."

"Pop. Really?"

"I'll have you know, Genevieve loves my pie. She stops into the diner for a slice whenever she's in town from her travels. She even brought that troublemaking fiancé of hers in before she had the good sense to drop him. I never liked him, I can tell you that."

Dermot closed the lid of the box and tucked in the tab closure. "You'll take it for me, won't you? I've a feeling she could use a bit of cheering up. From what I hear, she and her family are on the outs. That can't be easy on a young lady during the holidays."

Had Charlotte been talking to Pop? Or had Dermot picked up some kind of hint while the conversation had revolved around Genevieve that Dylan's feelings for the woman were a big, tangled mess?

He should say no. That would be the wisest course. He could use the weather as an excuse, even though he knew he had a few hours before the storm was supposed to even start.

On the other hand, what would it hurt? He could stop by, say hello, drop off the pie and be on his way in only a few moments.

Besides, after listening to her ramble on about the horrors of her grandmother's house, he was more than a little curious if the place was as bad as she said.

"Yeah. Sure. I can take her a slice of pie."

"While you're at it, you might as well take her some of the mashed potatoes and roast beef, as well. She can warm it for her dinner tomorrow."

SHE HAD TO SAY, she had spent more pleasant Sunday nights.

Removing layer after layer of hideous wallpaper from the dining-room walls was a much more arduous task than she'd expected. In her home-improvement naïveté, she had expected the steamer machine she had rented from the hardware store would make everything sheer away, ripple after ripple of ugliness, but the reality wasn't nearly as cheerful.

After three hours of work, her arms ached, her hair was a frizzy mess and she had only finished one depressingly minuscule section of wall.

"Come...on...and...move!" she muttered, trying to budge the massive buffet where Grandma Pearl had kept her best china. She only needed to push it away from the wall a few feet but even that seemed an impossible undertaking.

She drew in a deep breath and shoved with all her energy. It moved about an inch at the same moment, ironically, that the "Hallelujah Chorus" doorbell rang out through the house.

She froze, muscles twitching. Oh, she hoped that wasn't her parents, stopping in for a pleasant visit. In the mirrored top to the buffet, she caught her reflection. It wasn't pretty. A fine sheen of moisture clung to her skin. The hothouse humidity in here from the steamer had contributed to most of it, along with a considerable amount of perspiration.

Her hair was coming out of the pony holder she had shoved it into and any makeup she had applied earlier that day had long ago dripped away.

Maybe it was the Angel of Hope, the mysterious benefactor in Hope's Crossing who went around doing nice things for people. Paying utility bills, delivering bags of groceries, leaving envelopes of cash for needy families.

Maybe the Angel was dropping off some miraculous gift to help her finish de-wallpapering.

Not likely.

The doorbell rang again. She pushed a bedraggled strand of hair out of her eyes, fiercely tempted to ignore the summons. How could she possibly face anybody in her current situation? She could just imagine her parents' reaction if they unexpectedly came calling on her.

She could hide out in here. On the other hand, every light in the house was on, music was blaring and the curtains were open. Whoever it was could probably hear her and see movement through the windows.

With a sigh, she found the remote to turn down the speakers, wiped her sticky hands off on a rag and headed to the door.

Grandma Pearl didn't have anything as modern as a security peephole, though she did have a chain. Genevieve pulled the door open just wide enough to see who was sending Handel chiming through her house—and just about fell over.

A girl could use a little warning about these things. When she considered all the people she might have expected to see on the other side of the door, Dylan Caine wouldn't have even made the list. Yet there he was, looking completely gorgeous in the light from her porch, dark and forbidding.

He had a couple of boxes of what looked like takeout from his dad's café in his hand, she noticed through her shock as she fumbled with the chain and opened the door wider. For some reason, she thought he looked completely uncomfortable to find himself on her doorstep.

So why was he here?

Though his ranch coat hung on his frame as if he'd lost weight since he bought it, he still had rather delicious muscles. She had noticed that while they were working together at A Warrior's Hope.

She glanced behind her at the dining room and then back at him, making an instant decision she had a feeling she would regret.

"What a coincidence. You're just the guy I need right now."

She grabbed his arm and dragged him across the threshold then closed the door behind him against the December cold that hung heavy with impending snow.

"Am I?" He blinked a little, though she didn't know if he was trying to adjust to the light or her enthusiasm.

Okay, maybe she had been too hasty. She suddenly remembered how awful she must look, bedraggled and damp.

She pushed it away. If she wanted to finish this project, she didn't have room to let vanity stand in the way. "Yes. I desperately need a hand."

He held up both arms, including the empty sleeve. "Yep. I'm your guy, then."

She made a face. "You know I meant it as a figure of speech. What I really need is a strong back. I'm trying to move a piece of furniture that I swear feels like it's bolted down. Can you help me?"

He looked back at the door and then at her. "I guess I can spare a minute." He held out the boxes in his hand. "Where would you like this? I just came from Sunday dinner with my family and my pop wanted me to drop off some leftover roast beef and mashed potatoes for you. Don't ask me why. I have no idea. And pie. Huckleberry. He says it's your favorite."

She gazed at the boxes, her stomach rumbling a little at the realization that she hadn't eaten since a late breakfast.

"How kind," she exclaimed. Her insides completely dissolved into soft, gooey warmth—whatever hadn't already melted from three hours with a wallpaper steamer. "You know, I would marry your father if he were a few years younger."

His mouth quirked just a little. Not quite a smile, but close. "Apparently, he's quite fond of you, too. Who knew? He might even marry you back, if he wasn't already head over heels in love with Katherine Thorne."

"Katherine? Really?" She thought of the elegantly proper city council-woman who used to own Claire McKnight's bead store.

Katherine's granddaughter Taryn had been severely injured in a car accident a few years ago, a passenger in a truck driven by Genevieve's brother, Charlie. Charlie had been drinking when he climbed behind the wheel, and the ripple effect of that one decision had affected countless lives.

Even before the accident, Genevieve had always had the vague feeling Katherine disliked her. Perhaps she was someone else who only saw her as a brainless, snobbish debutante.

"I hadn't heard they were dating," she said now to Dylan.

"Oh, they're not. As friendly as he might be to customers at the café, Pop is actually on the shy side when it comes to women. He might get around to asking her out before they're both in their seventies."

She smiled. These little flashes of Dylan's sense of humor always seemed to take her by surprise.

"If it doesn't work out between them, I'll be waiting to snatch him right up," she said. "I'll just take this in the kitchen for dinner later. Leave your coat on the chair there."

He obeyed with a faintly amused look and followed her into the kitchen. As she placed the takeout containers in the refrigerator, he took a good look around at the harvest-gold, severely outdated appliances, the cheap dark cabinets, the orange-patterned carpeting—ew!—on the floor.

"Didn't I warn you it was hideous?"

"It's not so bad."

She stared at him. "To somebody used to living out of a tent in the desert, maybe."

He again had that faint smile, that tiny easing of his harsh features. She found it amazing how that slight shift in his expression could make him so much more approachable.

"It has four walls and a window, anyway," he answered. "And electricity."

"Don't forget running water. I guess you're right. Why would I need to change a thing?"

This time his smile was almost full-fledged. That smile was a dangerous thing, only because it made her want to wring it out of him, again and again.

"If I had my way, I would like to gut the whole thing and start over. Travertine countertops, stainless-steel appliances, custom cherry cabinetry. Unfortunately, my budget for this entire house project is minuscule to nonexistent. I can afford new paint for some of the rooms but that's about it."

"Don't you have some designer purses or last season's clothes you could sell online?"

As she hadn't expected to be forced to live here for weeks on end, she had left most of her things at her apartment in Paris. She supposed she could have a friend ship them over or liquidate there but she would need them when she was ready to return to her life in Le Marais.

Of course, she did have her little side business nobody knew about, the purses she had started sewing for fun.

She had started making them as a bit of a joke. Her friends in Paris had loved them and on a whim one night she had had a few extras delivered to Maura McKnight's bookstore, just to see if she could sell them.

To her shock, the first order of a half dozen had sold within a week and Maura had written a letter to her mystery supplier, seeking more.

Gen had sent her ten more and they had also sold out. She had decided she should stop there, though Maura had sent multiple letters to the PO Box she had forwarded to her in Paris, requesting more.

She would have to sew all day and all night for weeks and sell everything she made in order to earn enough profit to even afford a square yard of travertine countertop.

"I'm going to have to be content with doing what I can to freshen the place up on a shoestring. I really don't know why I'm bothering. Whoever buys it will probably tear the whole place down to build some mega vacation house anyway."

She looked around at the kitchen, so familiar to her from her childhood, and a little sadness seeped through her. Despite the aesthetic affront, she had many pleasant memories of her grandmother here.

When she was young, she used to stay overnight with Pearl. Her grandmother would make her luscious hot chocolate with whole milk and chocolate chips—oh, the calories!—and they would watch game shows and try to beat each other to the answers.

Pearl had taught her how to sew at this very kitchen table, on her old Singer. She'd made aprons and hot pads and even a few wraparound skirts that had been quite cute.

She pushed away the memories that clung like cobwebs.

"Come on. I'll show you where I need help." She led the way to the dining room next door.

He looked around at the section she had worked on and the curls of wallpaper scrapings that littered the floor. "This looks fun."

"I don't know why Grandma Pearl was compelled to change her wallpaper every other week. And of course, she didn't bother to take off what was underneath—she just slapped up another layer. I swear, every time she changed her hair color, she decided to change the walls, too."

He chuckled a little, and the rough sound sizzled along her nerve endings.

"So where do you want the buffet?"

"I just need to push it a few feet from the wall into the middle of the room so I can work behind it. The two of us should be able to manage it, don't you think?"

He looked a little doubtful and held up his empty sleeve. "Keep in mind, one of us has a little bit of a liability."

She frowned. "Why do you always feel as if you have to point that out?"

"I don't," he said. A little defensively, she thought.

"You've mentioned it twice since you showed up on my doorstep five minutes ago. Do you think I'm going to forget? I know you lost an arm, Dylan. That doesn't mean I think the rest of you is worthless."

As soon as she said the words, she wished she hadn't. His eyes widened and he looked as if she'd just smacked him in the back of the head with the wallpaper steamer. He must think she was an idiot. She really, really hoped he didn't pick up the signs that she had developed a serious crush on him.

"If you take that side, I'll try to move it from here."

He complied. Even with one arm, he had far more strength than she did and was able to push his side several feet to her six inches—and then he moved over and pushed her side, as well.

"That should be far enough. If I have to shove that thing another inch, I'm afraid I'll have a heart attack."

"Or at least break a nail."

She held up her hands. "I've got no nails to break right now, courtesy of all that Christmas decorating we did. I'm going to be in serious need of a manicure if this keeps up."

"Yeah. Same here."

"Thanks. I don't know what I would have done if you hadn't shown up. I probably would have left a buffet-shaped square of wallpaper right there and painted around it. I can't believe how heavy that thing is. It must be solid oak."

"Or maybe your grandma Pearl hid gold bricks in the bottom."

"Wouldn't that be the answer to my prayers? Don't think I haven't gone through every drawer and cupboard in the house looking for old bond notes, hidden cash bundles, gold doubloons. Whatever. So far, no luck."

"I guess that means you're stuck in Hope's Crossing for a while."

She wasn't quite ready to look at the reasons why she didn't find that prospect as depressing now as she might have a week ago.

He looked around. "So what color are you painting the room?"

"I haven't decided yet." She was surprised he asked and had a feeling he was, too. "Hey, I can show you the paint cards and you can help me choose."

"No, really. That's okay—"

She ignored him and grabbed the samples she had picked up from the paint aisle of the hardware store. "I think I'm painting neutral tones through the rest of the house but I wanted something with a little more splash here. I'm thinking a neutral on three of the walls and then something rich on the big one where we moved the buffet."

Though he looked as if he would rather be painting his own fingernails, he dutifully looked at the chips. After a long moment's scrutiny, he pointed to one on the edge of the pile.

"I like this one. Cocoa Heaven. A nice warm brown."

Remarkable! She grinned at him. "You have good taste, Dylan Caine. That's exactly the one I was going to choose. Why did you pick that one?"

He shrugged. "It just reminded me of my dog. He's got a spot on his back exactly that color."

She laughed hard at that; she couldn't help herself. He smiled, too, and the moment seemed to pull and stretch between them. Her heart seemed to give an almost-painful squeeze.

"I should probably go," he said after a pause.

She looked away, flustered at these ridiculous feelings she couldn't seem to control. "Oh. Right. And I've got hours of steaming off wallpaper ahead of me."

He started for the door, stopped for a moment and then turned back around. "Do you need help? I can probably spare an hour or so for you. It might help the work go a little faster with two of us."

She stared at him, shocked by the offer. He looked as if he wasn't quite sure why he had made it—and perhaps was already regretting it—but she didn't care. She was deeply grateful, both at the help and that he seemed to want to spend more time with her, or at least wasn't in a big rush to hurry away.

"I could definitely use a hand."

"Good thing I've only got one, then." He winced. "Sorry. Habit."

Grandma Pearl got a cat from the animal shelter once who hid under the bed and hissed and lashed out a paw, hackles raised, if anybody tried to get close. Her grandmother had explained the cat had been badly abused by a previous owner, and as a result, attacked instinctively before anybody could strike first. Gen wondered if Dylan pointed out his disability in the same sort of protective mechanism.

With love and care, Mr. Fuzzy had eventually learned to trust Grandma Pearl enough that he lost his bristly ways with her and even most of the time with Genevieve. She had to wonder whether Dylan might ever do the same.

"Do you mind if I bring in my dog?" he asked now. "He's out in the truck, since I only thought I was running in for a second."

She wasn't a huge fan of dogs, but what could she say after he'd offered to help her? "Um, sure."

"I'll be back in a second."

She watched him go, pretty certain he wouldn't be lured to her side with a little catnip and a mouse toy.

"You'll have to be on your best behavior, Tuck," Dylan said to his dog as they walked toward Gen's door. "No scratching at fleas, no jumping up on anybody, no leg-humping. I have a feeling Genevieve hasn't had a lot of experience with a couple of mongrels like us."

Tucker gave him a doleful look out of those big droopy hound-dog eyes and then gave the musical *wooo-wooo* bark his breed was famous for, the song

CHRISTMAS IN SNOWFLAKE CANYON

some compared to a choir of angels and others found the most annoying sound in the world.

It was all a matter of perspective.

If he had a single brain cell left in his head, he would just start the truck again, back out of her driveway and head up the canyon. He had no business manufacturing excuses to spend more time with Genevieve Beaumont.

He had no idea why he had. One minute, he had been ready to walk out the door, the next the offer to help had gushed out of him.

Gen made him do the craziest things. Again, no idea why. Bar fights, decorating Christmas trees, stripping wallpaper. What the hell was wrong with him?

He didn't understand any of this—he only knew that she seemed to calm the crazy. He had the strangest feeling of peace when he was with her, as if all the chaos inside him, the anger and bitterness and regret, could finally be still.

She must have been waiting for him to come back. The door opened the moment he rapped on it.

Her eyes grew wary as she looked at the big dog, who reached past her hip. She reached a hand out to offer a tentative pat on Tuck's head. Sensing a sucker, his dog turned those sad, please-love-me eyes in her direction and nudged at her hand as if he hadn't just spent two hours at Pop's getting attention from all the girls.

Gen scratched behind one floppy ear and Tuck's eyes just about rolled back in his head.

"Wow. He's...big. I'm used to smaller dogs. My mom has a bichon frise."

He wasn't quite sure what that was, though an image of a little white ball of fur stuck in his head. His dog was big and brawny, with broad shoulders and that morose face.

"Don't worry. He's a big softy. Aren't you, Tucker?"

At his name, the dog barked a little, nothing too prolonged, as it could be, but Genevieve still looked startled.

"What kind of dog is Tucker?"

"A black-and-tan coonhound. It's quite an honorable breed. George Washington actually had many of them, including the most famous—Drunkard, Taster, Tipler and Tipsy."

"A proud heritage indeed," she said. "Do you, er, hunt raccoons?"

He barely managed to keep from snorting. What kind of good old boy did she think he was? On the other hand, he drove a dilapidated pickup truck and his coat had definitely seen better days.

"No. I actually got him when I was stationed in Georgia. Somebody dropped him and a couple others in his litter by the side of this little back-woods road. I just about hit him one night driving home from visiting a friend but managed to swerve just in time. Instead, I hit a mile marker post and scraped up the fender of a really nice Dodge Ram pickup truck, too. I found homes for the other puppies, but by then Tucker and I were pretty good friends."

He gave the dog an affectionate scratch. Maybe he did have a bit of good old boy in him. His favorite moments were long, lazy summer evenings on the porch of his house watching the shadows stretch over the mountains and the world go dark while Tuck dozed at his feet.

He doubted Genevieve would appreciate knowing Dylan found the same peace with his dog that he did listening to her chatter.

"Does he need anything? Some water or, I don't know, some peanut but-ter on a cracker or something?"

He shook his head. "My nieces and nephews have been giving him treats under the table all evening, none of it good for him. He probably just needs a warm place to take a nap."

As if on cue, the dog headed to a patch of carpet in the living room in front of a heater vent, circled a few times to claim it as his and then stretched out.

Once the dog was settled, Gen turned back to Dylan. "How much ex-perience do you have with a wallpaper steamer?"

"About as much as you've had with black-and-tan coonhounds, I imagine."

She smiled, tucking a stray lock of hair behind her ear. He liked seeing her this way, with her hair a little tousled, her skin flushed, her face fresh and natural.

She would probably look just like this after making love.

Everything inside him seemed to shiver, and he had to take several sharp breaths to regain control.

"I've been thinking about the logistics here," she went on, "and I think it would be best if you direct the steamer while I scrape off the wallpaper."

He could handle that, as long as he could keep these inappropriate sex-ual thoughts at bay.

She frowned. "You're not really dressed for this. It's a messy job. I'm going to be sticky with wallpaper glue and little shreds of paper for weeks."

Pop didn't strictly have a dress code for his Sunday dinners, but he didn't appreciate his family showing up in any old thing, either. Dylan had worn a blue long-sleeved oxford to dinner, with the sleeve pinned up over his stump.

He should have worn the prosthetic arm. As painful as it could be some days, it wasn't quite as unsightly as that empty sleeve.

"It's fine. It will wash."

"Just take off your shirt. I can see you're wearing a T-shirt underneath. You can just work in that and then change back into the other shirt when we're done."

He shifted, wondering what he had gotten himself into. He ought to tell her to forget this whole thing. He hated dressing and undressing with one hand. It was awkward and uncomfortable, especially trying to shrug out of a shirt. He also didn't wear short sleeves much anymore, even in the summertime.

"Sure. Okay," he finally muttered. Feeling stupid, he did his best to unbutton the shirt without looking like a three-year-old learning to undress himself and then pulled it off and hung it over the same chair with his coat.

She was watching him, her eyes wide and her color high. Morbid fascination, he might have thought, except she seemed to be looking more at his chest and his shoulders than the empty spot below his left elbow.

"Where do we start?" he asked.

She cleared her throat and tucked another strand of hair behind her ear. "Um. This is the steamer." She turned it on. Tucker looked up through the doorway at the whining noise then dropped his head again, the lazy old thing.

A hose led from the main machine on the floor to a rectangle panel about the size of a notebook. Tendrils of steam curled out of it.

Gen handed that part to him. "Just hold the plate against the wall to moisten the paper and release the glue, section by section. I'll come along behind you and try to find an edge to lift away with the scraper."

After a few moments, they fell into a comfortable rhythm. Working vertically, he would steam a piece for a moment then she would scrape that while he moved to the next area. By necessity, they had to stay close together, the steam from the machine swirling around them in an oddly intimate way. He was hyperaware of his body—each pulse of blood through his veins, each inhale and exhale.

He was also aware of her, the flex and release of her biceps as she worked, the way she nibbled her lip as she scraped away at a particularly difficult spot, how her T-shirt molded to her chest...

"Oh. I almost forgot," Gen said after a few moments. "I had music going while I worked. I turned it off to answer the door."

She pulled a tiny silver remote out of the pocket of worn jeans and aimed it at a small speaker unit in the corner. Some kind of weird music eased out, lots of accordion and mournful French that sounded like something out of a smoky Paris jazz café.

He raised an eyebrow. "Really?"

Her expression turned rueful. "What can I say? Sometimes I'm in a mood. What would you prefer?"

His music tastes were all over the place but lately he mostly enjoyed classic rock. It might help keep his mind off enjoying a little *ooh là là* with her.

"Got any CCR or Stones?"

"I can make a playlist."

She fiddled with the MP3 player attached to the speakers, and a moment later, Mick and the gang started in on "I Can't Get No Satisfaction."

Perfect.

The work was physically demanding but not disagreeable. He had already found at his house in the canyon that deconstruction—tearing down in order to rebuild—could be oddly satisfying. The experience was the same here.

Together, they made good progress. After maybe half an hour, they finished the second wall. She stopped and shook out her arms.

"Why don't we trade places for a while?" he suggested. "Your arms are probably killing you."

"But I can always switch if one gets tired," she said, her expression solemn.

Something bleak and grim lodged in his chest. "Don't feel sorry for me, Gen," he said quietly. "I feel sorry enough for myself."

He grabbed the scraper away from her and set to work on the section he had last steamed.

After a charged moment, she picked up the steamer. "So I'm thinking about ripping up the carpet next," she said. "I pulled up the tacks in one corner and it looked as if it had hardwood underneath. I have no idea how to refinish floors but I read an article this afternoon online and it didn't sound all that difficult. You have to start with tearing out the carpets, obviously, and then you remove all the tacking strips, which sounds like an awful job. I can't imagine how gross it will be under the carpet. I might have to rent a floor sander but they have those at the home-improvement store."

She started chattering about finishing wood floors, about buying new hardware for the kitchen cabinets, about all the other things she planned to do on the house—many of which she had already told him up at the cabins, but he didn't care. The words surged over and through him, edged with an oddly poignant sweetness that left no room for the bitter.

She knew.

Somehow she knew how much he liked listening to her talk about anything and everything in that throaty, sexy voice.

She couldn't possibly understand why. Even he wasn't sure he comprehended why her conversation filled some gaping chasm inside him, how focusing on the mundane details helped keep all the ugliness at bay.

A fragile sort of tenderness seemed to twist and writhe around them like the steam, easing its way around all that ugliness, scraping him bare just like he peeled away her wall.

He faltered in his steady movements but quickly recovered. He couldn't let himself have feelings for her. Now, *that* was a freaking disaster in the making. He pushed it away and focused instead on the story she was telling him about a trip she took to the wine country of the Loire Valley with some friends.

Before he knew it, she had jabbered her way around the entire room. His arm throbbed from the relentless scraping, but it was a good kind of sore, earned through hard work and effort.

"I guess that's the last of it," she wound down enough to say and turned off the steamer. The music on the media player had stopped, too, without either of them being aware of it.

The room suddenly seemed far too quiet.

"I can't tell you how much I appreciate all your help, Dylan. You've saved me so much time and energy. Thank you."

"You're welcome," he said gruffly, wondering what the hell was wrong with him that he actually felt more centered and calm after an hour of scraping wallpaper layers off a wall with Genevieve Beaumont than he had from sharing dinner with the people he loved most in the world.

"I must have yakked your ears off."

"You didn't. See? Still here." He tugged at an earlobe and she smiled a little.

She tucked that errant hair behind her ear again. Her fingers were long and slender—elegant, even with her battered manicure.

He should leave. Now. The warning bells sounded in his head but he ignored them. Instead, he crossed the small space between them, leaned down and took what he had been thinking about since the moment he walked into her grandmother's ugly house.

CHAPTER NINE

ON THE CRAZY SCALE, kissing Genevieve Beaumont topped out at "Are-you-out-of-your-freaking-mind?"

He knew it intellectually in the tiny sliver of his brain that could still function at that level, but he ignored it. This just felt too right, too perfect. It had been so damn long since he had felt the wonder of a woman's kiss—the soft sweetness of her breath mingling with his, the press of her curves against his chest through thin cotton, the urgent churn of his blood.

Other than a shocked inhale, she didn't react for a few seconds, then he felt the slide of her arms around his neck and she returned his kiss with delicious intensity.

His mouth moved on hers, wondering how he could possibly have forgotten how delicious that surge of blood, that edgy hunger could feel.

She tasted sweet and minty, with just a hint of that vanilla scent that surrounded her. She made a soft, sexy sound in her throat and he deepened the kiss, unable to believe she was here next to him, her mouth warm and enthusiastic against his.

Their mouths fit together perfectly. In his experience, that wasn't always the case. First kisses could be awkward affairs, trying to figure out what to move where, but this... This was better than any of the increasingly heated dreams he'd been having about her since that memorable night at The Speckled Lizard.

She made another sexy sound and drew her hands up around his neck. He had to be closer to her. Without thinking, he went to wrap his arms around her. Both arms.

She faltered a little, just a tiny stiffening, but he felt the sudden tension and ice crackled through him.

He had forgotten. For one brief, amazing moment, he had completely forgotten the vast gulf between them.

He jerked away, his breathing ragged and his heart pulsing in his chest like the first time he'd jumped from a plane in Airborne School.

"You...didn't have to stop."

She sounded breathless, and she looked absolutely delectable—her lips slightly swollen, her cheeks flushed, her eyes dazed. He was almost positive she had been just as into the kiss as he had been.

It was the *almost* there that slayed him.

What if she hadn't been? What if she had only been playing along to protect his feelings, so he didn't feel like an ass for kissing her? They were friends, of a sort. She knew more about him than his family by now.

He knew she had a much softer heart than she let on—maybe she didn't want to hurt his feelings by showing her revulsion.

He grabbed his shirt off the chair in the entryway and shoved his stump through the sleeve, out of sight. He was aghast at his sudden urge to plow his fist through the walls they had just scraped.

He mustered as much calm as he could. "We both know that was a mistake."

"Do we?"

She seemed genuinely confused. How could she act all innocent, as if nothing out of the ordinary had happened, as if the world hadn't suddenly shifted, as if she could see nothing wrong in the kiss?

"For the next few weeks, we're obligated by the court system to work together. How will we do that when things are funky between us?"

"Why would things be funky over a simple kiss?"

It hadn't been simple. To him, the kiss had been magical. Hearts and flowers and choirs of angels singing. Okay, they were naughty angels, yeah, singing about tangled bodies and slick skin and losing himself inside her, but singing nonetheless.

He wasn't about to admit that to her, not when she was acting as if it meant nothing. A simple kiss. Huh.

"Don't worry. It won't happen again. My stump and I won't disgust you anymore."

"Who says you disgust me?"

"Your body language did. Come on, Gen. Don't pretend. I felt how you flinched away when I accidentally touched you."

Her color rose a little higher. "You're imagining things."

"Am I? Go ahead. Touch it." He unpinned his sleeve and shoved the cuff up, extending his arm as far as it would go.

"This is stupid."

She looked at him and at his arm, the puckered edge, the scars. He saw something in her eyes, something deep and troubled. Oddly, it didn't look like disgust. After a pause when she made no move forward, he yanked the sleeve down again and shrugged into his coat.

"Yeah. It is stupid," he said quietly. "So was kissing you. It won't happen again."

She opened her mouth to respond, but he cut her off. "Come on, Tucker."

The dog rose, stretching his hind legs first and then his front before he padded sleepily over to Dylan.

"Wait. You don't have to leave."

He gave her a long, solemn look. "Your wallpaper is down. You should be all ready to paint now."

She chewed her lip. "Dylan—"

"Good night, Gen. See you tomorrow."

After a long pause she sighed, still looking troubled. "Thank you for your help. You saved me a great deal of time and energy."

He nodded, whistled to his dog and headed for the door.

THAT HAD TO rank among the strangest hours of her life.

Gen stood at the window watching Dylan's battered old pickup drive away through the snow that had begun to flutter down, coating the roadway with a thin layer that reflected white in his headlights.

She thought of working beside him as they removed the wallpaper, of that strangely sweet mood, tenderness and affection and that sexual awareness that had swirled around them like the steam.

And then that kiss.

Everything inside her shivered at the memory of his mouth on hers, firm and demanding, of the scent of him, masculine and outdoorsy. In all her twenty-six years, no kiss had ever stirred her like that.

As usual, she had ruined everything, startled by the unexpected feel of his unnaturally smooth arm against her back where she had expected another hand.

He thought she had been repelled. She didn't know how to tell him she hadn't found anything disgusting, only different. If he had given her another minute or two, she would have touched him when he'd demanded it. She hadn't been able to find the nerve, not with him watching her so intently. She had been too busy being overwhelmed with compassion and sorrow for all he had endured.

She closed her eyes, tasting him on her lips again, sweet and sexy. She wanted to savor the moment, especially given his determination that it had been a mistake that wouldn't happen again.

Why would he want to kiss her again? What could she possibly have to interest a man like Dylan? He thought her some kind of empty-headed party girl who only cared about fashion and design.

She sighed and began cleaning up the mess left in the dining room. Shredded paper, sticky with wallpaper paste, covered the floor in piles.

Remodeling a house was sloppy and dirty and hard.

Kind of like her life felt right now.

ONCE AGAIN, Grandma Pearl's annoying Hallelujah doorbell rang just as she was giving her hair a final brush.

Thus far, she hadn't had a single visitor worthy of such a gleeful announcement. She might have been happy to see Dylan the night before but by the time he left, she certainly wasn't singing the man's praises.

Luck still wasn't with her. She opened the door with the security chain in place and saw only a faux-fur coat so authentic-looking she sometimes wondered if it was real.

She wanted to close the door again, lock it tight and sneak out the back. Too bad she instantly saw a few obvious problems with that. For one thing, she wouldn't be able to back out her BMW without smashing her mother's Mercedes SUV in the driveway. For another, eventually Laura would find her, and she was quite sure she wouldn't like dealing with the consequences.

After fumbling with the chain with fingers that felt graceless and awkward, she pulled open the door. "Mother. Here you are again, bright and early."

"I know. Crazy, isn't it? I decided on a whim last night to drive into Denver to finish some last-minute Christmas shopping. When your father and I were in Switzerland in August, I bought a really lovely sweater for my friend Annamaria—you know, that nice tennis pro I've been working with lately. But she told me last month she's expecting a baby. Can you believe that? I certainly can't give her a size-four sweater now, when she won't be able to wear it for a whole year."

"That is a quandary."

"I've shopped in every store in Hope's Crossing without finding anything I think she would like, but I'm sure I'll be able to pick something up in Denver."

"Well, good luck."

Her mother pushed her way into the house and pulled off her leather driving gloves. "I thought perhaps you could come with me, darling. We haven't spent nearly enough time together since you've been home from Paris. Wouldn't it be fun to have lunch at the Brown Palace and walk through our favorite shops?"

Laura gave her a strangely tentative smile. She seemed almost...desperate for Genevieve to go with her.

"Oh, I can't. I have to work at the center today. I wish you had called before driving over here," she said, surprised that she meant the words and that she actually felt a little regret at having to refuse.

Her mother pursed her lips. "Again? Didn't you work several days last week?"

Gen fought back a sigh. Despite having a workaholic husband, Laura seemed to think the rest of the world existed just to fill her own leisure hours. She couldn't always have been this way. The Beaumonts were not wealthy when she was little, only for the past twenty years or so.

"I really am sorry, Mother, but I have to finish a hundred community-service hours by January. I've completed sixteen, which still leaves me eighty-four to go. I'm probably going to have to go every day until Christmas."

"It's ridiculous. That's what it is! I don't understand how your father could let this happen. He said he would fix it. He talked to the judge! I thought everything was settled. You did absolutely nothing wrong. I don't understand how you can let yourself become a virtual slave to that...that wounded-soldier outfit."

"I'm not a slave. And Father did talk to the judge. While he couldn't reduce my time, I did have the option to go somewhere else for the rest of my hours. I chose not to because I have committed to A Warrior's Hope and right now they need me."

She doubted her mother would understand that particular concept.

"You could call in sick. Surely they won't make you come in to work if you're under the weather."

"True, but I'm not under the weather," she pointed out.

"You could tell them you are," her mother persisted. "Everyone deserves a little holiday. I was so looking forward to having a day of shopping, just the two of us. Girls' day in the city. It's just what we both need."

Even if she didn't have to go to the recreation center that day, she couldn't have spared the time to shop with money she didn't have in Denver. Not when she had this horrible house hanging around her neck like a hideous scarf.

"I can't, Mother. They're expecting me today at A Warrior's Hope. We have new guests arriving, which is apparently a stressful time, and I'm in charge of decorating for the welcome reception."

Anticipating the task ahead of her after Charlotte asked her Saturday, Gen had even bought some supplies the day before around town and gathered more from nature. She couldn't wait to see how they turned out. She didn't mind the decorating part of things, but she was more than a little nervous about meeting a roomful of wounded veterans and their families. Would they all be bitter and angry like Dylan? Anxiety fluttered through her.

"Come on, darling. Someone else could do that for you," Laura pressed. "We haven't had a moment together since you arrived. I'm anxious to catch up and find out about all those French men you've been dating."

She didn't have much to tell in that direction. She had dated a few. While she had inevitably been entranced by their charm and wit, she hadn't had a silly girlish crush on any of them. None had made her chest tingle or her stomach twirl with nerves like Dylan Caine did.

She swallowed. "I can't."

Laura heaved a sigh. "I suppose I'll have to spend the day in Denver by myself."

If she didn't know better, Genevieve might think her mother sounded almost...lonely.

On impulse, she stepped forward and kissed her mother's cheek. Laura smelled of Estée Lauder makeup and the Annick Goutal perfume she always wore. "I'll have an afternoon off either Wednesday or Thursday. Perhaps we can go to lunch here in Hope's Crossing. Several new restaurants have opened since I've been back. If that doesn't work out, let's definitely plan on brunch Sunday."

"I have a hair appointment Wednesday and a luncheon party at the country club Thursday. I'll make reservations for Le Passe Montagne for Sunday morning. Charlie is coming home this week after his finals so we can all go together."

"Deal."

Her mother hugged her and then stepped back. She looked around the house, her carefully constructed nose wrinkled with distaste.

"This house. It's terrible. It looks like you're living in a war zone! I don't understand why you can't just sell the place as is. Whoever buys this land will probably tear this horrible house down."

Though she suspected her mother was right, she still felt a pang of regret she didn't quite understand. She hated the house, too, though the funkiness was growing on her. She didn't want to contemplate the idea of someone razing it.

If that was the eventual outcome, she still wanted to pour as much as she could afford, financially and physically, into making the house presentable. The better the house looked, the more she could make in profit from the sale.

Her mother probably couldn't understand that, especially as *she* wasn't the one fighting for a future. Laura had always hated this place, only in part because of the outdated decor that Grandma Pearl refused to change.

Laura and Grandma Pearl hadn't really gotten along. Her grandmother had had little patience for her daughter-in-law's social ambitions, and Laura had had even less for Grandma Pearl's loud, gaudy, sometimes abrasive personality.

"Oh. Look at that," Laura exclaimed. "You've taken down that atrocious wallpaper. That must have been a job by yourself."

She thought about letting the false impression stand but something compelled her to honesty. "I wasn't by myself. I had help. Dylan Caine came over last night and worked with me to strip the walls."

Her stomach tingled again as she remembered that kiss that had happened right about where her mother stood.

Laura frowned. "Which Caine brother is that? There are dozens of them."

"Only six, Mother. He's the youngest son."

Laura looked baffled for a moment, trying to put the pieces together, and then her eyes widened. "Dylan. He's the one who lives up in Snowflake Canyon. The one who lost his arm."

"Yes," she said calmly. "That's the one."

Laura stared at her. "Why would you have him help you? What can he even *do* without an arm?"

Kiss her until she couldn't remember her name, for one thing. He had amazing skills in that direction, but she was quite certain her mother wouldn't appreciate that particular insight.

"Plenty of things. Just about everything." Whether he wanted to believe it or not. "He was amazingly helpful last night. I honestly couldn't have managed without him."

Her mother's frown deepened. "Is there…something going on with you and Dylan Caine your father and I should know about?"

Heaven forbid. Her parents didn't need to know *anything* about whatever might be going on with her and Dylan. Not that there was anything to know.

"Why would you say that?" she countered.

"As I am remembering things now, he's the one who got you into trouble, isn't he? Yes. I remember now. He was in that bar fight with you. And now you tell me he came over on a Sunday night to help you with home renovations. What am I supposed to think?"

How would her family react if she started seeing Dylan? He was so vastly different from Sawyer, her parents' ideal of a potential mate for her. Where Sawyer had been cultured, polite, polished and adroit, Dylan was rough, shaggy. Dangerous.

Her parents would probably totally freak. Her dad would start blustering around about bad boys and silly girls; her mother would shriek and ask what all her friends would think.

Charlie would be cool about it. Since his time in juvenile detention, she sometimes thought her little brother was just about the most grounded person in the family.

Not that it mattered how they might react, since it was the most hypothetical of questions. He had kissed her, yes, but swore it wouldn't happen again.

On that depressing note, she ushered her mother to the door. "You don't need to worry about me and Dylan Caine, Mother. We're friends, that's all. That's why he helped me last night."

Laura didn't look convinced. She opened her mouth to argue, but Genevieve wasn't in the mood to talk about Dylan another minute and especially not with her mother.

"I'm sorry but I've really got to go. I'm already late. Have a great time in Denver. Love you, Mother."

Before Laura could protest or shove one of her black leather boots in the frame, Genevieve managed to close the door and lock it tight.

CHAPTER TEN

THIS WAS BECOMING a habit.

Genevieve adjusted a fold of garland on the seventh Christmas tree she had decorated for A Warrior's Hope then eased back a little to admire the results.

This one—located in the main reception room just off the lobby of the recreation center, with equally stunning views of the mountains—was bigger than those in the cabins. While the tree already had a few basic decorations, they were sparse and lackluster.

Saturday she had bought jute and spray paint at the hardware store and then had stopped into the craft store for a roll of burlap and ribbon.

Just before scraping wallpaper Sunday, she had gathered some bare branches from Grandma Pearl's yard, laid them flat in the garage and spray-painted them with a little silver. Not too much, just a hint.

She had felt more than a little silly spending money she didn't really have, but she was pleased with the results.

As this room with its big river-rock fireplace and wide windows would serve as the main gathering spot for everybody, she had wanted it to be as warm and welcoming as their cabins. The program participants shouldn't want to only spend all their time in their individual spaces.

"Oh, wow. This looks fantastic, Genevieve."

From her perch on top of a ladder, she glanced down to find Dylan's sister watching from the doorway. She looked smart and pretty in tan slacks and a pale blue sweater.

"Do you think so? I was afraid the silver branches were too much."

"Not at all. They're perfect. It sets just the right tone, I think. Not too fancy, with a focus on nature." She moved farther into the room and looked around at the table decorations Gen had thrown together to be reused throughout the week, a mix of flowers donated from the florist in town, the burlap and more of those spray-painted branches.

"All I can say is, it was a lucky thing for A Warrior's Hope that you decided to get into a bar fight at the Lizard."

Gen gave a rueful smile. "I do what I can."

"And we appreciate it." Charlotte gave her a warm look that made Gen glow more than the eight hundred lights on the tree.

"I don't have your aesthetic sense, that's for sure," the other woman continued. "Seriously, have you ever thought about being an interior decorator?"

"Yes, actually." She climbed down from the ladder and was grateful to be on solid ground again. She really didn't like heights. "I graduated from college with a degree in interior design. I'd like to open my own company someday."

"You'll be wonderful at it," Charlotte assured her.

"Thank you."

"I came to tell you they're only fifteen minutes away. Spence just called from the road with a status update."

"Great," she lied, nerves crashing around in her stomach like drunken butterflies. "I had better finish up in here, then, and put away all the supplies."

"I can help you with that."

"You don't have a million other things to do?"

"At this particular moment in time, no. Amazingly enough. Everything is done, as far as I know. Alex and her crew are on the way from Brazen with dinner. We'll have the welcome reception and then dinner, then let everybody settle in after their day of traveling. Tomorrow the fun starts in earnest."

That was a matter of perspective. "Will you be here the whole week?"

"I wish. Unfortunately, I've still got a store to run. Sugar Rush is crazy-busy this time of year, with everybody wanting custom orders at the last minute. I'll be here on and off most of the week. Eden, Chelsea and Mac should have everything under control, with all the other volunteers that come and go. Plus you and Dylan, who will be here full-time."

She hadn't seen the man since he'd left her house the night before after that stunning kiss.

"I guess Dylan went to help with the airport pickups," she said since his sister brought up his name. She tried to inject a casual tone into her voice, but she was afraid she failed when Charlotte flashed her an intent look.

"He wasn't very happy about it, but yes. Spence talked him into going with him."

What would Charlotte say if she knew about that stunning kiss—or that Genevieve fiercely wanted more?

"What would you like me to do during the welcome reception?" she asked, quickly changing the subject.

"Just try to make everyone feel comfortable. That's all. Change can be overwhelming to some of these guys, especially the few we have with head injuries, and the logistics of traveling can be stressful. The first night, we just try to relax and let them settle in, become familiar with the place, that sort of thing."

Those nerves snarled in her stomach again. This part was easy. Hanging a few ornaments, wielding a can of spray paint, arranging some flowers.

Interacting with people who had been through hell was a different situation entirely.

On the other hand, she liked Dylan and had been able to get along fine with him, with only a few faux pas. She would just try to treat the others as she did him.

Except for the serious-crush part. Oh, and the kissing.

THE GUESTS OF A Warrior's Hope arrived at the recreation center in three separate vans. Eden, in her hyperorganized way, had emailed Genevieve— and everyone else, she assumed—a list of everyone attending this eight-day-long camp, as well as photos and a quick biographical sketch and which family members they would be bringing as guests.

The two men using wheelchairs were easy to identify. One was young with blond hair and an open, fresh-faced demeanor. Army Corporal Trey Evans hailed from Alabama, she knew, and had limited use of his legs after a spinal-cord injury. He was also the only warrior attending without any family members.

In quite startling contrast, the other man using a wheelchair must be Army Sergeant Joe Brooks. He was surrounded by family—a wife, Tonya, Gen remembered from the bio, who was just about the most beautiful woman Gen had ever seen in person, and two adorable girls with hair in a flurry of braids, Marisol and Claudia. One of the girls sat on his lap and the other one held her mother's hand as they walked in beside the chair.

She knew two of the men had suffered brain injuries. They were a little harder to pick out, until she remembered one was coming with his parents. Judging by the way an older couple fussed around a tall, good-looking man with a buzz cut, she guessed that was Marine Lance Corporal Robert Augustine and his parents, Robert Sr. and Marie.

She found the other one, Ricardo Torres, and his wife, Elena. When Eden sent his bio picture, Gen had thought he reminded her of one of her friends in Paris. Now she saw the similarity was even more pronounced. That would help her remember his name.

Lieutenant Pam Bryant was quite easy to pick out, as well. She was a pretty, compact woman with severe scarring over one side of her face who walked with a pronounced limp. Beside her was her fiancé, Kevin.

The last group to come in had to be Marine Lance Corporal Jason Reid and his wife, Whitney, who carried a little boy who was probably about three.

They were all talking together and laughing, though a few seemed tired and Jason Reid had a stony expression that discouraged conversation.

What did she have to talk about with any of these people anyway? She knew nothing of what they had endured. Feeling awkward and superfluous, she stood in one corner, trying to gather the courage to mingle.

Eden and Mac moved through the crowd, handing out appetizers, drinks, snacks for the children. Even Dylan was deep in conversation with Pam Bryant.

Etiquette and manners had been drilled into her from the time she used to go to dance class. She knew it was the height of rudeness to stand here in the corner. She had to make some kind of effort. By avoiding interactions, she likely appeared rude and snobbish, exactly how people perceived her.

What was she supposed to say to any of them? The old social nicety of seeking points of commonality seemed ludicrous under these circumstances. What could she and these battle-scarred men—and Lieutenant Bryant— who had seen and done so much, possibly have in common? It seemed ridiculous to even try making faltering conversation.

She stood shifting her weight from foot to foot, gazing out the window to avoid eye contact, wishing she were anywhere else on earth.

Finally, after about ten minutes, one of the men took the matter out of her hands.

"Hey there. What's so interesting out there?"

She turned to find the younger man in the wheelchair had approached without her realizing. Trey Evans, she remembered. Up close, she could see he was about her age, with sun-streaked hair and quite handsome features. Not Dylan-gorgeous but enough to make most women a little flustered.

"It's not a matter of something else being more interesting than present company. I'm just a little...out of my comfort zone."

"Aren't we all, darlin'."

She had to smile at his easy charm and Southern drawl.

"You don't like Colorado?"

"Never been here. All I can say is, you all sure know how to bring it when it comes to mountains and snow."

"We do our best."

He held out a hand. "I'm Trey Evans. You can probably tell I'm not from around here. I'm originally from Wetumpka, Alabama."

She could feel herself relax. He was just a kid who had lost a great deal. She shook his hand. "Hi, Trey. I'm Gen Beaumont. Welcome to Hope's Crossing. I hope you enjoy your stay. I'm actually from here, though I've been living in Paris until recently. Do you know which cabin you're in yet?"

"No idea. Why?"

She felt stupid for asking. "I helped decorate them for the holidays last week. They all have different themes and I have a few of my favorites. I was just curious which one you would be staying in."

"So you're, what, the staff decorator or something?"

She could feel more tension seep away. This wasn't so bad. She could handle small talk. "Something like that. Mostly, I do what they tell me."

Except for the part about relaxing and making everyone feel comfortable. So far, that was a big fail on her part.

"You're the general dogsbody, then."

"I don't have any idea what that means, but, um, sure."

He laughed, taking a sip of the drink he had somehow managed to prop on his lap when he wheeled over. "My grandpap used to call me that when I was a kid and would spend the day at his store being his grunt. Running for change to the bank, sweeping the floors, grabbing him another coffee next door. It means errand boy. Gofer. Whatever you want to call it."

"That would be me." Something in this young man's casual friendliness appealed to her, maybe because it presented such a sharp contrast to Dylan's general surly reticence. "If you want to know the truth, I'm here for court-ordered community service."

He nearly spilled his precariously balanced drink. She saw him catch it just in time, eyes wide, though some dribbled over the lip of the cup onto his slacks. "Community service? Wow. Didn't expect that one. Seriously?"

She scooped up a napkin from a nearby table and handed it to him. "Do I look like the kind of girl who would lie about something as embarrassing as that?"

His long scrutiny wasn't flirtatious, only friendly, edged with a daub of sadness she didn't quite understand given their lighthearted conversation.

"No. But I have to say, you don't look like the kind of girl who would be here on court-ordered community service, either. What did you do? Let me guess." He narrowed his gaze. "Shoplifting."

"I beg your pardon." She sniffed. She had many faults, but she considered herself an honest person in general and disliked deception in others. She'd broken an engagement over it, for heaven's sake.

"No?" He set his drink on a table and wheeled around her adeptly, trying to see her from a different angle. "How about...tax evasion."

"Not even close."

Dylan had moved closer, she saw, and was now in conversation with the Augustines about six feet away. When she glanced over, she found him watching her interaction with Trey out of the corner of his gaze—quite a trick, when one eye was covered by that ever-present black eye patch.

She turned back to Trey, suddenly enjoying herself much more than she expected. "Do you want to hear the ugly truth?"

"Oh, hell yeah. Lay it on me."

She smiled, leaned in close and tried for her best bad-girl voice. "I started a bar fight and ended up busting the nose of the assistant district attorney."

Trey laughed so hard some of the other guests looked over with curious looks—including Dylan, whose expression was far more inscrutable.

"I would have paid good money to see that."

"Sorry to disappoint you, but I don't intend for there to ever be a repeat performance. It was purely a one-off. I learned my lesson. The next time some idiot decides to play every conceivable rendition of 'The Little Drummer Boy' on the jukebox of the worst dive in town, I plan to pay my tab and leave."

He laughed again, so hard that Lieutenant Bryant and her fiancé approached.

"What's so funny over here?" the woman asked.

"This is Gen Beaumont. She was just telling me a story about breaking a woman's nose over Christmas carols."

Lieutenant Bryant grinned. "Wow. Remind me not to sing 'Jingle Bells' around you."

At first, Genevieve was uncomfortable looking at that scarred face that must have once been quite pretty, but after a few moments' conversation, she relaxed, especially when the other woman commented about how much she loved her sweater and asked where she could find one.

Gen launched into a conversation about her favorite of the few shopping spots in town, which drew the attention of Tonya Brooks and Elena Torres. Before she knew it, she was offering to take the women on a shopping expedition into town if it could be arranged.

Perhaps this wasn't such a bad way to spend her community-service hours after all.

CHAPTER ELEVEN

IF HE HADN'T seen it with his own eyes, he wouldn't have believed it.

While he did his best to make conversation, fighting the urge to escape to his canyon retreat with every breath, Genevieve held court in the corner. She seemed to have charmed just about everyone who had come in contact with her. Every time he turned around, the group was laughing. More often than not, Gen was in the middle of it.

He wasn't quite sure what to think about that. He supposed he should have expected it from a socialite like her. When she put her mind to it, she could probably charm whomever she wanted.

He wasn't sure what switch had been flipped after about the first ten minutes of the gathering, when she had stood in the corner looking awkward and immensely uncomfortable, but now she seemed relaxed and outgoing.

The more she relaxed, the more his tension escalated. For a guy who had lived as a virtual hermit for months, all this socializing left him as edgy as his chickens in a windstorm.

He was wondering how much longer he had to stay when his sister came over with a plate of appetizers she handed him.

"I haven't seen you eating anything. You've got to be hungry, aren't you?"

"Not really."

"Eat. You'll feel better."

Apparently she had inherited the need to feed from their father, who was never happy unless he was cooking up something delicious. He knew she wouldn't let up until he took the plate, so he gave in to the inevitable, even though he felt stupid propping the plate in the inside crook of his left elbow. He had worn one of the prosthetics today. While it could be useful for some tasks, holding a small appetizer plate wasn't among them.

"Thanks for helping with all the airport pickups today. Spence said you were a great help with loading all the luggage."

"I don't recall being given much choice in the matter. Spence basically told me to get my ass in the van."

"You could have stayed here and helped Genevieve decorate, since you're so good at it now."

He glowered at her. It was a good thing he loved her. She would be annoying as hell otherwise.

Genevieve's throaty laugh sounded from the corner, easing through him like a sultry jazz saxophone.

He turned, almost against his will, remembering the magic of having her to himself the night before, that voice soothing him.

That kiss that had left him aching and hungry.

"She's turning out to be rather a surprise, isn't she?" Charlotte said, following his gaze.

"Why do you say that?" he said, his voice gruff. He was really, really grateful his sister couldn't read his mind right now.

"You know what Laura Beaumont is like," Charlotte said with a shrug.

"Not really. I haven't lived in Hope's Crossing in years."

"Don't you remember how exacting she used to be when she would come into the restaurant when we were kids? She demanded perfection. I can remember once when I worked at the diner one summer during college, she made me fix the same Cobb salad three times. Each time, something stupid was wrong. The croutons weren't crisp enough, the tomatoes were wilted, the onions tasted off."

She grinned suddenly, looking young and mischievous, a rarity for a girl who had grown up too quickly after their mother's death. "Here's something funny. The fourth time, I just rearranged the very same salad she had just turned up her nose at and took it back to her table, and she declared it perfection, finally."

"Oh, man. I hope Pop didn't catch you doing that."

"No. He would have been livid about not giving the customer what she wanted. I never did figure out how he could always be so tolerant of her fussiness." She paused. "But then, that's Pop for you. He's entirely too patient when it comes to some people."

By the pointed way she said that last part, he was guessing she meant him. True enough. He hadn't made things easy on their father.

"Anyway," Charlotte went on, "during the process of planning her wedding, Gen gained a reputation in town as basically being a carbon copy of her mother. Nothing was ever good enough for her. My friend Claire, who owns the bead store, was charged with hand-beading the bodice of this incredible wedding gown Genevieve ordered from a designer back East. It took months for Genevieve to agree on the pattern and then more months for Claire to get it just right in her eyes. And then, of course, she had to do it all over again after Genevieve's brother and some other teenagers vandalized Claire's store and destroyed it."

He vaguely remembered hearing something about that in connection with a tragedy that had affected the town some years ago during his second-to-last deployment.

"I'll admit, I don't know her well, especially since she's been gone the last few years, but she has always struck me as someone who demands perfection," Charlotte went on. Though she didn't give him that same pointed look, the implication behind her words was obvious.

Perfection didn't come in the form of a broken-down ex-soldier who could barely hold an appetizer plate.

"She's different somehow. Not what I imagined," Charlotte went on. "She's worked really hard since she's been here. She spent all day today decorating this place by herself. She even brought a lot of supplies with her, things she must have prepared ahead of time. I would never have expected that."

He remembered their kiss the night before, her soft, eager response, the silk of her hair sliding through his fingers.

As far as he was concerned, that had been as close to perfection as anything he had known. Hot and sweet at the same time. He had been awake most of the night, staring at the flames in the fireplace and wishing things could be different.

"Can I have everyone's attention?"

Though diminutive, Eden Davis could really project her voice. Everybody looked up, even the kids who were playing in a corner with some toys someone—probably Charlotte—had provided.

"It's been a long day for everyone and I'm sure you would like to relax a little in your cabins for a while before dinner. Your bags should be waiting in your assigned lodging. A staff member will show you the way and help you settle in. The plan is to meet back here at seven for dinner. I promise, you're in for a treat. One of the premier restaurants in this area is providing the meal for you tonight. Brazen is fantastic. It's got phenomenal reviews. I know you'll enjoy it. So we'll see you back here just before seven. Bring an appetite. Could I have all the Hope's Crossing staff up here for a moment?"

Dylan didn't consider himself staff but Charlotte grabbed his elbow and basically dragged him forward. Eden quickly started handing out assignments and instructions.

"Dylan, do you mind helping Trey to his cabin? Genevieve, will you escort Joe and Tonya and their girls?"

Genevieve nodded, though he could tell she was uncomfortable at the prospect. It couldn't be the wheelchair, since she had been completely at ease with Trey. What made her uneasy?

The youngest little Brooks girl beamed up at Genevieve and reached for her hand. After a long pause, she took it, though with obvious wariness. He nearly chuckled. Of course. She wasn't used to kids. In her perfect little society world, she probably hadn't had many interactions with children.

That was one area where he, on the other hand, was completely at ease. Coming from a big family with an overabundance of nieces and nephews had given him plenty of experience with kids.

He almost offered to trade assignments with her and then changed his mind. The corporal didn't need more opportunities to fall head over heels—or wheels, in this case—for Gen.

He approached Trey, who was chatting up Chelsea, the office manager.

"Guess you get to be my tour guide," Trey said.

"Yeah," Dylan said.

"I'll see you later, Chelsea," the kid said.

She waved and Trey started wheeling toward the door that led to the cabins.

"You need help or anything?" Dylan asked.

"Naw. Just hold the door and point me in the right direction."

"Left," he said.

Trey wheeled outside and headed in the direction of the cabins.

"Man, it's gorgeous here," he said. "Only mountains I've seen this big were the Hindu Kush, and they weren't nearly this pretty."

"Except in springtime," he answered.

"No shit."

Trey was silent as they moved toward his cabin, the closest to the recreation center. It was the first one he and Genevieve had decorated together.

"Smoke Gregory said you were a ranger. You lose your hand in Afghanistan?"

He wanted to tell the kid to mind his own damn business, but he didn't have the heart to stomp on all that open friendliness. More power to the guy for not letting bitterness eat away at him.

"Helmand Province. Twelve-year-old insurgent with a suicide pack."

"Oh, man. That's rough. Kandahar for me. Firefight. Got hit by three rounds. My battle rattle stopped most of it but I caught one in my spinal column just below my flak."

Bad business, there. He wondered how Trey was coping, but that wasn't the kind of thing guys asked each other outside group therapy or something.

"Rehab's a bitch, am I right? I do the exercises, but six months later, I don't know how much good it's doing. My left leg still works but it's weak. At least I can walk with crutches when I have to. The other one might as well be fake, all the good it does me. Sometimes I think a fake leg might even be better. I could put weight on it then, you know?"

"Flesh and blood is better than a prosthetic any way you slice it. So to speak," he muttered.

Trey chuckled as he wheeled up the ramp. "I'll take your word on that."

Dylan helped him with the door and made sure all his luggage was inside waiting for him.

"There's food in the lower cupboards. Should be within reach."

"Thanks."

He felt a little bad about leaving the kid here by himself, especially where everybody else had some kind of family or loved one for support.

"Anything else you need before I take off?"

Trey shook his head. "I should be good. Thanks." He paused. "This is a nice thing you're doing here."

"Not me," he said, quick to disabuse him of any idea to the contrary. "Charlotte, the bossy blonde, is my younger sister and Smoke is an old friend. They dragged me along. I'm only here because I'm doing community service."

Trey looked first surprised and then amused. "No kidding? Seems to be an epidemic of that around Hope's Crossing."

"You must mean Genevieve. We were arrested together."

"Same bar fight?"

He relived that fateful punch and almost laughed out loud. The more he came to know Genevieve, the more funny and completely out of character that moment seemed.

"Yeah. And the same crooked defense attorney—who also happens to be my older brother—arranged this plea deal for us both."

"Doesn't matter why you're here, I suppose. It's still a good thing. And I've got to say, Hope's Crossing might turn out to be more interesting than I expected."

"It has its moments," Dylan answered. "See you later."

"'Bye."

Dylan headed out into the afternoon sunlight that reflected diamonds in the snow, his mind still on the conversation.

Trey might be young and fairly wet behind the ears but he was right about one thing. There was more to Hope's Crossing than some pretty storefronts and a gorgeous setting. There was pain and sorrow, humor and grace.

He had spent his time since returning to town hiding away in Snowflake Canyon, content to be alone in the mountains. While he was busy feeling sorry for himself and thinking his world had ended, others in similar circumstances had somehow managed to move forward.

He had to wonder what they had figured out that he hadn't yet.

"I'LL TELL YOU what A Warrior's Hope needs most. A hot tub."

Genevieve issued her heartfelt declaration to Eden Davis, riding alongside her on a big chestnut mare. They were bringing up the rear of the large group heading up a trail to visit what was supposed to be a spectacular iced-over waterfall.

She looked up the trail, overhung with pines on either side that randomly dropped cold little clumps of snow on them.

"I mean, this is beautiful, magical, a winter wonderland. Yadda yadda yadda," she said to Eden. "I just have to think, if I'm aching this much after a morning cross-country skiing and a half hour on horseback, how much worse must some of the guys feel?"

"I know. Believe me, I know." Eden rotated her shoulders, looking cute and still perky, her cheeks rosy beneath a shiny white Stetson she had probably purchased new just for today's outing. "A hot tub is definitely on the list. We can always use the hot tubs inside by the pool when we get back to the recreation center, but I would really like a few outside. After our first session in early fall, I wrote a grant for a couple. We have the funding, but the ground froze before we could run the electricity for the project. That will be first priority when the snow melts, I promise."

That wouldn't help Genevieve. Not when she needed one now—and they still hadn't reached their destination. Then she had the whole ride home to endure.

Every single muscle in her body ached, right down to her fingers from gripping first telemark poles and then the reins—not to mention priming her dining-room walls long into the night.

She wasn't a completely inexperienced rider. Her mother had insisted on lessons even though Gen hated heights and had always been uncomfortable on horseback. Her horse today was quiet and good-tempered, with a soft, easy gait that would have made riding her a joy if Genevieve hadn't already been stiff from her other activities that day and the night before.

She was achy enough that she was almost tempted to drive to her parents' house after her day ended here at the foundation to soak in theirs.

"It's been a fun day, though, hasn't it?"

"Yes. I think everyone enjoyed it so far," she answered. That morning, they had left early to go cross-country skiing on the groomed trail that ran beside the river and up into U.S. Forest Service land.

The guests of A Warrior's Hope seemed to have all enjoyed it, especially when they skied around a bend and spied a huge moose standing in a hot springs across the way, steam rising up around him and moss dripping from his antlers.

They barely returned from that excursion and had time for a quick, deliciously hearty lunch catered by Dermot Caine's café before they loaded everybody up and took off to the Silver Sage Riding Stables in Snowflake Canyon for an afternoon on horseback.

It was really a beautiful area, with towering pines and spruce and steep-sided mountains angling down to a glittery, half-frozen river running through the canyon floor.

"How much longer before the falls?" she asked Eden.

"We're nearly there, I think."

"Yep," answered Jake, their guide from the ranch—who seemed even more taciturn than Dylan, though she wouldn't have believed that possible. "Not far now."

The creek beside the trail seemed to bubble and hiss beneath a layer of ice. They turned a bend in the trail and suddenly the falls were there ahead of them.

Gen gasped. She couldn't help it. It was spectacularly beautiful, a gnarled, twisting column of unearthly blue ice that rose at least a hundred feet into the air.

"Wow," she whispered.

Some of the guests climbed off their horses to stretch and have a better look. She saw Dylan didn't dismount, just walked his horse a little away from the group. Was he worried about the difficulty of climbing off the horse without the use of both hands?

He lived up here somewhere in Snowflake Canyon. Spence had pointed out his driveway on the way.

"Climbers come from miles around to strap on crampons and reach the top," Eden said. "I'm going to do it sometime, I swear."

"You mean you didn't bring climbing gear?" Pam Bryant and her fiancé actually looked disappointed.

"Not this time," Eden said. "We can try to come back before you leave if you want."

"Not me," Gen muttered with a shiver. She couldn't imagine anything worse than climbing up a tower of ice with nothing but frozen air between her and serious injury.

"You're not ready to try your hand?" Trey Evans had maneuvered his placid gelding beside her. He was another who hadn't dismounted.

"I'm perfectly happy to stay on solid ground, thanks very much."

"Yeah, I'm with you." He smiled, looking young and rather sweet in the pale afternoon sunlight. "I've got to say, you folks sure know how to throw a winter around here. This is something to see."

"Are you enjoying yourself?" she asked.

"Sure." He answered perhaps a little too promptly. "It's nice not to be cooped up in a rehab facility all day long. Everybody here is supernice. Oh, and the cabin's great. Did I tell you that? You did a good job with the decorations. Last night, I sat by a fire and enjoyed the lights on the tree. I even listened to Christmas carols and enjoyed the lights on the tree. Not 'Little Drummer Boy,'" he hastened to add.

She gave a rueful smile. "Nobody believes me when I tell them I generally have no problem with that song. I quite enjoy it under the right circumstances. I just wasn't in the mood for it that night."

"I'm just teasing you," he answered. "Not about the cabin. That's still really nice. In fact, I asked Spence and Eden if I could maybe stay here for a couple of extra days after the session ends. I'm moving into a new apartment in San Antonio when I get back, but it won't be available until after the New Year. All my things are in storage, and I'd rather just stay here if I can."

She frowned, saddened to think about him staying here at the recreation center by himself for the holidays after all the others had left. "Don't you have family somewhere to spend Christmas with?"

"No family. Never knew my dad, and my mom died of an overdose when I was little. My grandpop raised me, but he died, too, when I was fourteen. I was in foster care until I graduated from high school and enlisted."

Oh, poor man. As crazy as her family made her, at least she knew they loved her and would be there if she needed them. She would see them on Christmas Eve. They would have a delicious dinner, maybe play games. Sometimes they attended church services in town.

"You should have a great holiday here in Hope's Crossing," she said, trying for cheerfulness even when sadness seemed to seep through her. "On Christmas Eve just after dusk there's a candlelit ski down the mountainside up at the resort. Everybody in town joins in to ski or just to watch the procession. It's really beautiful."

"That sounds nice. I would offer to join in, except I can just picture me skiing into the person in front of me and starting a domino effect down the whole mountainside, candles tumbling everywhere."

She laughed at the picture he painted. The sound made her horse sidestep a little but she brought it back.

"Do that again."

"What? Lose control of my horse?"

"That laugh," Trey said. "You remind me a lot of...a girl I used to know."

"Somebody you cared about," she guessed.

He gazed at the frozen spill of water. "We were supposed to be getting married this month. This week, actually."

She stared at him, shocked, even as a rush of sympathy surged through her. She didn't know what to say, which was stupid since she knew exactly how it felt to go through months of planning to hitch her life to someone and then to have to watch all her expectations implode.

"You remind me a lot of her. Not just your laugh, but other things. She has the same color eyes and her hair was a lot like yours, except shorter. Even her name is similar. Jenna, instead of Genevieve."

"Jenna what?"

"Jenna Baldwin. She was a schoolteacher at an elementary school near the base where I had basic training. We met at a church service and hit it off right away. She was about the prettiest thing I'd ever seen."

Though he smiled as he spoke, she sensed his light expression hid much deeper emotions.

"Since you're here and Jenna isn't, I guess that means no wedding bells."

"Yeah. We broke things off...after."

"After what?"

His mouth tightened. "After I was injured."

She frowned, shocked even though she had half expected the answer. First he had lost so much physically and then emotionally. It seemed the height of unfairness. How could any woman walk away from this kind, friendly young man so callously?

"I'm sorry," she said quietly as a cold wind slithered through the trees, rippling the boughs.

"It's not your fault," he said.

"Well, I hope this Jenna and I are nothing alike, other than our laughs and our similar names," she said tartly.

He looked startled. "Why would you say that?"

For some reason, she was strangely aware of Dylan, who waited nearby on his horse, the reins loosely clasped in his hand, for everybody else to mount up and start down the mountainside.

Though he didn't appear to be paying attention to their conversation, something told her he was listening.

"I hope I wouldn't have destroyed any chance for a future with someone I care about because of something out of his control."

She looked up and met Dylan's gaze. Something glittery and bright sparked in his gaze, but he quickly bent down to say something to his horse, though he didn't move away.

He probably hadn't heard them anyway. And what would it matter if he had?

"Take me, for instance," she went on. "I'm a pretty shallow girl. I've never denied it. I can't say I'm proud of that fact, but I'm not afraid to face reality. I like nice clothes. I love having a facial. I'm careful with my hair and makeup. I like to look good and I work hard to make sure I do."

"And you look real nice."

She made a face. "I wasn't fishing for compliments, but thank you. I just wanted to make the point that as superficial as I might be about some things, I would hope that if I loved a man, I would be more concerned about his character and about the way he treats me than about what the world might see as a few physical imperfections."

The words seemed to spill out from somewhere deep inside her—she wasn't sure where—but as she spoke them, the truth seemed to pound hard against her heart.

Had she changed so very much in such a short time or had that conviction always lived inside her?

What she said to Trey was truth, as well. She had always considered herself superficial. She'd dated Sawyer originally because he was beautiful and because her friends told her they made a perfect couple.

Because all seemed so shiny and bright on the surface, she had overlooked many glaring flaws just beneath it. He was childish when he didn't get his way; he could be petty to anyone who crossed him; he liked to make cutting remarks about just about everyone, even their so-called friends.

She had been so focused on the perfect fairy-tale romance that she had ignored all the signs. As she sat atop a shifting horse while a cold wind knuckled its way under her coat, she wondered, not for the first time, if she would have been able to go through with the wedding, even if she hadn't found out that Sawyer had fathered a child with Sage McKnight.

Perhaps she had only seized on the first major excuse that came along not to marry him. Maybe she finally had reason to fix what her heart had been telling her all along was a mistake.

"For the record, she didn't dump me."

It took a moment for Trey's words to pierce her distraction. "She didn't?" She frowned. "Wait a minute. You dumped *her?*"

"Let's just say I spared her the trouble." He offered a lopsided smile that held no humor. "I knew it was only a matter of time before Jenna figured out she deserved better than a lifetime stuck with a guy who couldn't even walk her down the aisle."

"You hit first." It was Mr. Fuzzy all over again, crouching under the bed and spitting and clawing at anybody who came close. "You didn't want to give her the chance to be the one to break things off."

She wanted to yell at him and ask what the hell was wrong with him. How could he be so selfish that he would push away somebody who cared about him?

"I just spared us both a lot of trouble," he answered. "It would have happened eventually."

"You don't know that."

He looked down at his legs, dangling in the stirrups. "Come on. Look at me. What kind of woman would want to spend the rest of her life dealing with this?"

"You must not have really loved her, then."

Trey narrowed his gaze at her, and she suddenly remembered that for all his good humor, this was a dangerous man trained in combat. "You don't know anything about it." His voice was suddenly as hard as that frozen waterfall. "You have no idea how much I loved her."

"I don't," she said after a moment. "I just know if I had been your fiancée I wouldn't have let you push me out of your life without a fight. I would have stuck to you like gum in hair."

He didn't say anything for a long moment. Genevieve was aware of Eden ushering everybody back to their horses and helping those who needed it to mount again.

"She doesn't know where I am," Trey finally said, his voice so low she almost didn't hear him over the jingling of tack and the heavy breathing of the horses.

"You didn't tell her you were coming to A Warrior's Hope?"

"No. Before that. I broke things off with her six months ago, the night before I was being transferred to a rehab facility in Texas. I made sure nobody told her where I was headed."

"All this time, she hasn't known where you are?"

With Facebook and Twitter and email, she couldn't believe the woman couldn't have found him, but maybe Trey had stayed off the grid. Closed out his email account, stayed off social networks, changed his phone number.

If a person didn't want to be found, she imagined it couldn't be that difficult to make it happen.

"No," he answered. "It was better this way."

Better for him, maybe. Not for the woman he had shoved out of his life like a pair of mangy old sweats. She opened her mouth to tell him so, but Eden's loud call froze her words.

"We should probably start back before those snowflakes get any bigger," the director said. "Everybody ready to go?"

"Yep," Trey said, urging his horse forward and effectively ending their conversation.

CHAPTER TWELVE

I WOULD HOPE that if I loved a man, I would be more concerned about his character and about the way he treats me than about what the world might see as a few physical imperfections.

Genevieve's words seemed to circle around inside his head like Tucker settling onto the rug beside the fire on a wintry night.

He couldn't push them away. They just echoed there, in all their idealistic glory.

It was a nice thing to say in theory, all noble and well-meaning. She probably liked to believe she was above petty, superficial things like physical infirmities. But the first time one of her snooty friends made some kind of crack about pity dates and taking her charity work a step too far, Genevieve would probably shatter like a Christmas ornament caught under a horse's hoof.

On the other hand, she surprised him at every turn. Just when he figured he had her pegged, she did something unexpected, like befriend a young corporal from Alabama.

He needed to stop thinking about her. His task here was to get through the next week or so with a minimum of trouble and then move on with the rest of his life.

"How are you holding up?"

He glanced over as Spencer Gregory moved his horse along the trail beside Dylan's.

"Fine. Better than you. If you looked any more stiff on the back of a horse, we could spray-paint you gold and set you out in front of the library to replace that statue of old Horace Goodwin nobody likes."

Spence only grinned at the insult. "Yeah, riding isn't my best thing. I would blame my old baseball shoulder injury but, well, given the current company, that would just make me sound like an asshole."

Dylan's own laugh surprised him—and Spence, too, apparently, though he quickly hid it. Dylan had missed his friend over the years. They had been close in high school but had gone their separate ways when he had enlisted and Spence had been drafted to play Major League Baseball.

"Don't worry about me," he said now. "I'm doing fine. Haven't been on a horse in more years than I can remember and I'll probably ache in places I can't politely discuss, but so far, so good."

"Great."

Spence was quiet for a long moment as they rode along through the puffy snowflakes that clung to the horses' manes.

It wasn't an uncomfortable moment. In fact, though he would rather be tied to the saddle and dragged behind this horse than admit it, Dylan was actually rather enjoying himself. The steady, calming rhythm of the horses, the scenery, even the cold air blowing in his face—all of it contributed to an unexpected sort of peace.

He couldn't let Spence know that, not unless he wanted to hear a resounding *I told you so.*

He had been pretty damn antagonistic about A Warrior's Hope and the futility of anybody thinking they could help guys who had endured hell with a week spent in the mountains, but he couldn't deny he could feel a little of his own tension trickle away.

It was only the surroundings, he told himself. The sweet citrus scent of the pines, the cold mountain air, the expectant weight of impending snow in the air.

He tried to tell himself he would have had the same reaction working on his property just a mile or so away from this trail, but the argument fell flat.

"I've been looking for a chance to talk to you," Spence said after another moment.

Spence gripped the reins tightly, shoulders tense where Dylan's had begun to relax.

"Oh?" he asked, suddenly wary.

"Charley tells me I don't need to clear anything with the family but, well, you and I have been friends a long time and it feels right to let you be one of the first to know."

"To know what?" He had a strong suspicion he didn't want to hear the answer.

"I've asked your sister to marry me. She said yes."

Spence spoke the words with a sort of stunned disbelief, as if he were still trying to wrap his head around the whole thing. Despite his own squeamishness—he would probably never be crazy about his sister with *anybody,* and thinking about her with a close friend was just too weird——Dylan almost laughed.

This was Smokin' Hot Spence Gregory, who had women throwing themselves at him everywhere he went. He gave every appearance of a man completely flummoxed by love.

He was glad, for both of them. Charlotte had come a long way in her life. She had worked hard to remake herself and she deserved to be happy. When he thought about it, Spence had done the same. He had taken a chain of his own bad decisions and fate's bad breaks and turned them into something good.

"Congratulations," he said.

"I hope you mean that and aren't secretly wishing you could knock out a few of my teeth."

"I'm keeping the teeth-knocking-out in reserve. You know Charlotte has six older brothers. I figure you're either crazy in love or insanely brave to take her on, knowing if things go south you'll have every single one of us to deal with."

Spence was quiet, his features soft. "The first one you said. I love her, more than I ever imagined it was possible to care about somebody else."

Spence Gregory had once had everything a guy could want. He had once been a sports hero with an incredible fortune and a stunning supermodel for a wife. He drove fabulous cars, he had multiple houses, he was on magazine covers and on TV commercials hawking everything from cell-phone providers to sports drinks.

Not once, in all those years, had Dylan been jealous of the man. Right now, though, listening to Spence talk about what he and Charlotte had together, Dylan was aware of a sharp pinch of envy just under his breastbone.

His own life stretched out as cold and empty as that snow-covered mountainside.

"Good," he said gruffly now. "Just make sure that doesn't change."

Spence smiled. "Charlotte is it for me, man. I promise you that."

Behind them, he suddenly heard Genevieve give that delicious, husky laugh at something.

At the sound, that edge of envy turned to a funny little flutter that instantly horrified him.

No. No way. He would never be stupid enough to fall for someone like Genevieve Beaumont——even if he was drawn to her far more than he knew was good for him.

"WILL YOU SLOW DOWN? I need to talk to you."

Back at the recreation center an hour later, Dylan paused on his way to the storage building. He wanted to ignore Genevieve's call but that would be rude and probably wouldn't accomplish anything other than to make her speed up to catch him.

He turned with more than a little wariness and shifted the weight of the mesh bag filled with riding helmets. Her cheeks and nose were rosy from the cold, and she wore a really ridiculous little pink stocking cap with a puff on the top that perfectly matched her designer parka and gloves.

He had been grateful they rode back to the rec center in separate vans, half hoping he could avoid her the rest of the afternoon—or at least that weird little clutch in his stomach whenever he saw her.

"Let me help you with that," she said, reaching for the bulky, awkward bag of helmets.

"I've got it," he said sharply.

At his tone, she backed off, hands in the air. "Sorry. Do it yourself."

"I will," he retorted, feeling about as mature as his nephew Carter right about now.

Without breaking stride, he continued on his way to the equipment storage building, and she walked double time to keep up with his longer legs.

"So I need some advice and I think you just might be the best person to give it to me."

Right now, all he wanted was to be sitting by his fire with his dog at his feet and a stiff drink in his hand—something he suddenly realized he hadn't had much of since he started at A Warrior's Hope.

He hadn't missed it, either, come to think of it.

"You need my advice, hmm. That can't be good."

She made a face as she reached to open the door of the storage building.

Dylan set down the bag of helmets and flipped on the lights, trying to ignore the rows of adaptive equipment that seemed to mock him.

"Where do these go?" she asked.

He had spent entirely too much time in here with Mac helping with inventory and knew more than he wanted about the organization system. "That shelf against the wall."

He carried them over and set the bag on the empty space provided for it.

"This is really quite amazing, isn't it?" Genevieve looked around the space, filled floor to ceiling with equipment. "I mean, A Warrior's Hope just started and they've already got all this...stuff."

"Spence is really good at getting donations and grants. Some of it is donated equipment from people in town but a lot of it was donated by the manufacturers because of his contacts."

"That's really great."

"Yeah. I guess. What did you need to talk to me about?"

She sighed. "I need your advice about Trey."

His arm suddenly ached, and he realized he was trying to clench a fist that didn't exist anymore. He relaxed his arm and walked out of the storage room and back into the soft snowflakes.

"You want advice about Trey from me."

"Yes, from you," she said impatiently, hurrying after him.

"Don't know what I can tell you. You obviously have another conquest there."

She rolled her eyes. "I'm not looking for a conquest. I like him. He's a sweet kid."

That sweet kid had been injured in a vicious firefight in Afghanistan and had probably seen things Genevieve Beaumont couldn't imagine in her darkest nightmares.

"Sure. Okay."

"Here's the thing," she went on. "He has a fiancée. *Had* a fiancée, I should say. He dumped her after he was injured."

He had heard some of their conversation near the frozen waterfall.

I would hope that if I loved a man, I would be more concerned about his character and about the way he treats me than about what the world might see as a few physical imperfections.

He pushed the words away again. "Yeah. That's not a big surprise. A lot of relationships can't survive the kind of life change Evans is dealing with."

"Did you have a girlfriend when you were injured?"

The question took him by surprise. He'd had a couple of girlfriends in the past, but nothing that had ever developed into more than casual. The best that could be said about his dating relationships was that he enjoyed lighthearted variety.

"Nobody serious."

"Well, Trey did, apparently. Her name is Jenna Baldwin and she sounds lovely. I want to find her and I need your help."

He stared at her. "Why the hell would you want to do that? And why would you ever think I'd help you?"

The little yarn puff on the top of her beanie flounced as she gave him a *duh* sort of look—though she probably wouldn't have called it anything as uncouth.

"Because he needs her. It's Christmas and he's all alone. He has no parents, no siblings, no one."

Dylan, by contrast, had too damn many people constantly asking how he was. Every time he turned around, Charlotte or Pop or one of the brothers was in his space, checking on him.

"So?"

"He met her when he was doing his basic training, but I don't know where that was."

He knew. That very day at lunch, he and Trey had talked about Fort Benning, as both had been stationed there around the same time.

"She was a schoolteacher near the base. Before I do an internet search, I just want to make sure I'm in the right region of the country."

"What makes you think she's still in Georgia?"

Her features lit up. "Georgia? Oh, thank you! That helps a *ton*. At least it gives me a place to start."

Crap. He was an army ranger trained to withstand torture. How could he have given that up so easily? Maybe because of those delectable rosy cheeks or the scent of cinnamon and vanilla that seduced his senses—or maybe just the fact that when she talked to him in that husky voice, he could barely manage to string together a coherent thought.

"I don't suppose you're willing to forget I said that, are you?"

She grinned as they walked toward the recreation center again. A few stray snowflakes glimmered on her cheeks and he wanted to lick them off....

"No," she answered. "But I might be willing to forget you're the one who told me."

"She could have moved. She could have married someone else. What makes you think she wants to be found?"

"I don't know. Maybe she doesn't."

"They did break up, after all," he pointed out. "I don't see her here."

She stopped walking. "He dumped her the night before he was leaving for another rehab facility. Get this—he left without giving her a forwarding address. I think that's terrible, don't you?"

He didn't answer but Genevieve apparently didn't need a response.

"I just want to let her know where he is and how he's doing. What she does with that information is her business."

He saw the potential for a whole wall of trouble to come crashing down. If he were Evans and had broken up with a woman for whatever reason, he would be severely pissed if somebody stepped into the middle of things.

"Don't do this, Gen. Just butt out."

"I have to try. What can a phone call hurt?"

"This is none of your business. Let it go."

She frowned. "But you should have seen his face when he talked about her. His eyes went all soft and warm. He said my laugh reminds him of hers. I just feel so terrible when I think about him being all alone on Christmas. Wouldn't it be the most perfect holiday if we could help them find each other again?"

If this Jenna Baldwin was at all like Genevieve, all light and laughter and energy, he could certainly understand how Trey Evans could have been in love with her.

He didn't want to crush her romantic bubble—which, he had to admit, he found more than a little surprising, given her own less-than-ideal relationship history—but he couldn't let her pursue this crazy idea.

"There is no *we* here. I don't want any part of this. This is a huge mistake," he warned. "Mind your business, Gen. Trust me. Don't stick your pretty little nose into matters of someone else's heart. Ask the assistant district attorney how uncomfortable nasal-reconstruction surgery can be."

Uneasiness flickered in her gaze for just a moment, then she shook her head, once more the determined, indulged woman whose parents had likely never denied her anything she wanted. "Oh, stop. You're just trying to scare me."

"With good reason. Is it working?"

"No," she declared, her jaw set. "You didn't see his face. He loves her."

"So what? A man can be crazy in love with a woman, but that doesn't mean they're at all good for each other."

She gazed at him, not breathing, eyes wide, and he was oddly reminded of times when he would be leading a patrol and would become keenly aware of the world around him, all his senses on hyperalert.

Just now he could hear the wind in the treetops and the far-distant laughter of someone on the trail on the other side of the river and the sound of a car with a bad muffler pulling out of the parking lot.

The moment seemed frozen like that eerily blue waterfall, scattered droplets suspended in space and time.

"I know," she finally said, her voice almost hushed. "I know that. I just... I want to make a phone call to tell her where he is. She must be worried about him. I'll just let her know he's safe and sound. If she doesn't want anything to do with him, so be it. It serves him right. I think it's cruel of him to leave like that, just sneak away in the night without giving her the chance to prove her love."

"You're going to be sorry," he warned.

"What else is new?" she muttered. "I'm sorry about a lot of things."

Nothing he could say would change her mind. He suddenly knew it. Gen Beaumont was an unstoppable force when she wanted to be—and apparently, right now she had a goal and wouldn't let anything sway her from it.

"When this comes back to bite you in the ass, just remember I tried to warn you."

She didn't stick her tongue out at him, but he had a feeling it was a close thing. "And when I bring together two people who love each other and help them find their happy-ever-after, you remember that I was absolutely right all along and that I did a wonderful thing, while you stood there with your callous, bitter, shriveled old soul, prophesying doom and gloom."

At her impassioned words, he laughed. He couldn't help himself. The sound was rough and rusty, startling a magpie that must have been overwintering in the tree above Gen's head. As he flew off, a huge clump of snow fell from the branch he vacated and landed right smack-dab on the little puff of her beanie and trickled down her cheek, which only made him laugh harder.

She narrowed her gaze at him, and before he realized what she intended, she scooped up a handful of snow and chucked it at him. By sheer luck, the loose snowball hit him on the cheek just below his eye patch. Ice crystals clung to his skin, so cold it stung, but it was somehow life-affirming, too, in a weird sort of way.

"My shriveled, bitter old soul and I did not appreciate that," he said, wiping it away with the sleeve of his coat.

She was fighting a smile, he could see, even as she pulled off her hat to shake the snow out. She had serious hat hair but he still wanted to run his fingers through it. . . .

"Tough," she retorted. "You deserved it. You probably trained that bird to dump that snow on me, didn't you?"

"Yes. I have a whole battalion of forest creatures waiting to obey my every command."

"Figures."

A little snow clung to the arch of her eyebrow and stuck in her hair and he couldn't resist reaching out, brushing it away.

When he lowered his hand, she swallowed hard, and he could feel his pulse race at the expression in her eyes.

Genevieve Beaumont was staring at him as if he was all she wanted wrapped and waiting under her Christmas tree. He desperately wanted to kiss her. Just toss that hat into the snow, reach out and capture her cold lips with his.

He could warm her. Warm them both. Judging by their kiss the other night, if he touched her again, they would soon be generating enough heat to melt the whole mountainside.

No. He couldn't kiss her. He was no better for Genevieve Beaumont than Trey Evans was for his Jenna.

He shoved his hand in his pocket to keep from reaching for her and stepped away, back to safety.

"That looks like the last of the snow. I'll try to keep my forest minions out of your way."

"Thanks," she mumbled.

He turned abruptly and headed back toward the recreation center. Only when he was almost there did he see his sister standing by the window inside, watching the whole interaction.

CHAPTER THIRTEEN

"WHERE'S MY MOMMY?"

A question designed to spark panic in all but the most calm of hearts. Genevieve looked helplessly down at the little girl beside her, gazing up at her out of big, distressed dark eyes.

"She's still out there on the mountain, Claudia. Remember? We talked about this. She's skiing with your daddy and with your big sister. Your dad has a very cool chair he gets to ski on. You and I are having fun here with our hot chocolate and our coloring."

"I want my mommy."

And Genevieve thought things had been going so well. She was far from an expert on children and could probably count on one hand the in-depth interactions she'd had with any. Volunteering to stay behind with little Claudia Brooks had really been an act of self-protective desperation. When confronted with two things that scared her—the terrifying height of ski lifts or the only-slightly-less-terrifying prospect of a few hours entertaining a very cute little girl—she had picked the one with the least potential to cause death or serious maiming.

It had seemed like the smart choice, but now, a few hours in, she was running out of ways to entertain Claudia, who seemed to be growing increasingly restless.

"They should be back soon," she said, a little desperately. "Should we put our coats on again and take a walk outside so we can look for them?"

They had walked out twice and had watched Joe Brooks in his sit-ski once. Later, they found Tonya and Marisol riding the magic carpet, a beginner conveyor-belt lift that worked much like an airport moving sidewalk only going uphill.

"No outside." Claudia stuck out her bottom lip.

Okay. Genevieve scanned the little corner of the ski lodge they had taken over as their base. Her gaze landed on the almost-new box of crayons. "We could color another picture for Mommy and Daddy."

"No."

She pointed to her tablet computer and its fabulous entertainment offerings. "How about a game? Or we could watch another *Sesame Street?*"

Claudia's cornucopia of colorful barrettes quivered as she shook her head, braids flying. The girl really was adorable, with those huge eyes and dimples and all that beautiful café-au-lait skin, like her mother. Hanging around with her for the past few hours had really been quite entertaining.

There had even been a minute or two—when Claudia had insisted on sitting on Gen's lap while they read a Dr. Seuss book she hastily downloaded on her tablet—that Gen had felt a strange, soft, completely unexpected tenderness tug at her heart at the small, warm weight in her arms.

Claudia had this funny habit of playing with Gen's hair when she sat on her lap, almost as if she didn't know she was doing it, twisting it around and around her finger.

Just now, Gen was running out of options. She picked up Claudia's cute doll, all dressed up in a darling après-ski outfit of her own, and danced her a little in the air, side to side. "We could play with Penelope more. I bet she's getting tired of just hanging around, doing nothing," she tried.

"No."

That bottom lip started to quiver ominously, and panic skittered through Genevieve.

Okay, what would you like to do? she wanted to demand, but she knew that wouldn't accomplish anything except to make them both more frustrated.

Claudia yawned widely and blinked her eyes. Gen wanted to give herself a head slap. Oh. Of course. Little creatures sometimes needed naps. She should have realized.

The crowded, noisy ski lodge didn't seem the ideal place for a snooze, and Gen had no idea how to accomplish that particular feat amid all the bustle.

She finally settled into a comfortable armchair in a fairly secluded corner near the window, providing beautiful views up the slopes, then held her arms out to Claudia. "Why don't you sit right here and I'll tell you a story."

After a pause, Claudia grabbed her doll, ski parka and all, and climbed onto Genevieve's lap and promptly shoved her thumb in her mouth. Wishing for a warm, cuddly blanket, Gen settled for pulling her wool coat over both of them.

"Once upon a time, there was a beautiful princess who lived in a castle set on a huge hill," she began.

Claudia pulled her thumb from her mouth and pointed out the window. "That hill?"

"Why, yes. I believe it was. This princess didn't like snow and she really hated waking up with icicles hanging from her toes. Her days were spent trying on new dresses or brushing her hair or painting her toenails."

Claudia held out her little hand to show the vibrant pink polish there. Though barely three, the girl was definitely a fashionista.

"And painting her fingernails," Genevieve said with a smile. "She thought she was happy with her life. Surely no other princess lived in such a beautiful castle and had such stunning dresses to wear or could paint her toenails such spectacular colors. But one day the princess woke up. After shaking the icicles off her toes, just like usual, she started to try on another new dress and realized she didn't want to wear any of the dresses in her closet. They were beautiful and she still loved the bright colors and the silky feeling when she slid them on her head. But when she was wearing one of the dresses, she couldn't climb a tree or ride her horse or do somersaults down the mountainside, end over end until she reached the bottom."

Claudia smiled a little, though her eyes were half-closed as she listened. Genevieve lowered her voice to a slow, soothing cadence and proceeded to spin a tale about the princess's longing for adventure, for something more, and the silly steps she took to find it.

After a few more moments, she looked down to find Claudia's eyes closed, her chin drooping onto her chest. Gen stopped talking in the middle of telling about the princess trying to fly and just enjoyed the moment.

She had never really envisioned having children. Oh, eventually she supposed it would have been required of her and Sawyer, to carry on the Danforth legacy, but that sort of future had seemed nebulous at best, years in the future.

Now, as she held this darling little girl in her arms, she had a fierce urge for a child of her own. Someone who would love her as she was and wouldn't find her lacking.

Perhaps a little boy with vivid blue eyes.... The thought made her blush and quickly shy away from thoughts of Dylan Caine.

After a few moments, her arms started to ache. She shifted in the chair for a more comfortable position and was relieved when Claudia slept on. She thought about trying to settle the little girl on the adjacent sofa but she was afraid of waking her. This worked for now.

She might have dozed, but she wasn't sure how long. When she woke, her arms were just about numb and Charlotte Caine was coming toward her.

"How's it going in here?" Dylan's sister asked.

Genevieve pressed a finger to her mouth and pointed to the sleeping girl. Charlotte winced. "Sorry. I didn't notice she was asleep," she whispered. "She dozed off a little while ago."

Charlotte took the vacant seat on the sofa. "How did you get roped into babysitting duty?" she whispered.

"Nobody roped anybody into anything. I offered. The truth is, I was kind of glad of the excuse to stay in the warm lodge. I'm not supercrazy about skiing. It's a height thing."

Charlotte snickered softly. "Don't you find that a little ironic, considering your father was one of the original founders of the ski resort?"

Her father had been savvy with investments, saving enough from his fledging law firm to throw wholehearted support behind Harry Lange when he came up with the crazy idea of building the Silver Strike resort, which was now a huge industry that had become the driving force of the Hope's Crossing economy.

She shrugged. "Maybe. I can't help it. I've never really liked skiing. Sawyer used to make me go with him and I was always miserable."

She instantly wished she hadn't said that when Charlotte gave her a surprised, sympathetic look.

"What about you?" she asked quickly. "You're not skiing?"

Charlotte shrugged out of her parka. She wore a turtleneck underneath that revealed a curvy, attractive figure, a far cry from what she used to look like.

"I injured my ankle this summer, and it's still not as strong as I'd like it to be. It's aching a little, so I figured I would take it easy. I went down a few runs but decided that was enough."

As she tossed her parka over the arm of the sofa, the light glimmered off a huge ring on her left hand. Gen had heard whispers that Charlotte and Smokin' Hot Spence Gregory were taking their relationship to the next level. She wouldn't have believed it if she hadn't seen them together the past few days. They were really quite cute together.

For a moment, she was tempted to confide in Charlotte about her thus-far-fruitless effort to find Trey's ex-fiancée. She hesitated, not eager to hear Dylan's sister tell her it was a lousy idea, too.

After a few hours of internet searches the night before, she had found an email address from an obscure school directory at an elementary school near Fort Benning, but she couldn't locate any kind of corresponding phone number. She had sent an email, not sure if it was even the right person or if the account was still open, but she hadn't had a response yet.

Before she could ask the other woman her opinion about the wisdom of continuing the search, Charlotte spoke. "I'm glad I caught you alone for a minute, actually," she said, her voice serious. "I need to ask you something."

Gen's arms tensed around the little girl in her arms. Claudia wriggled a little in her sleep, and Gen realized what she was doing and relaxed.

"Oh?" she asked, trying for studied casualness. She had visions of her asking some kind of embarrassingly awkward question, like *what are you doing, kissing my brother?*

"I was wondering if you have plans tonight," Charlotte asked.

As usual, her plans revolved around Grandma Pearl's house. She had finished painting the dining room the night before and had thought about adding a second coat if it needed it. If not, she would continue with the endless effort of steaming off wallpaper in the other rooms.

Considering her biceps throbbed and her hair felt permanently frizzed from that particular activity, she welcomed any excuse to have a break from it.

"Nothing that can't wait. Why?"

Charlotte fiddled with a loose thread on the wristband of her sweater. "I'm supposed to go to a Christmas party tonight—women only—and was wondering if you might like to come with me. It should be a lot of fun. There's always good food and wonderful company."

After Genevieve had shut Charlotte down the last time she asked her to a social event, she would have thought the other woman wouldn't ask her again.

She didn't want to turn her down again. She had a feeling their fledgling friendship would die a quick, painful death if she did.

"Sure," she said, before she could talk herself out of it. "A Christmas party with girl talk sounds fun, especially if it means I don't have to steam wallpaper off the wall for a few hours."

Charlotte smiled, looking relieved. "Oh, I'm so glad. I was hoping you could make it, even though it's short notice. The party starts at seven. Why don't I pick you up at quarter to, at your grandma Pearl's house?"

"That sounds great. Thanks."

Charlotte smiled again and settled into the sofa, her eyes on little Claudia.

"I've always considered myself a pretty good judge of character. As a result, I'm not often surprised by people. You are turning out to be…different than I expected."

She wasn't quite sure how to respond. "Are you saying there's a chance maybe I'm not the spoiled bitch everybody thought?"

Color climbed Charlotte's cheeks and she gave a shocked little laugh. "I didn't say that."

"You don't have to say it," Gen said. "I know how people see me. That I insist on my own way, that I'm demanding, that I ran roughshod over the town leading up to my grand society wedding that never happened."

Charlotte didn't deny her claim—confirmation in itself. "You have to admit, you were Bridezilla on steroids."

"Or worse," she muttered.

She hated looking back on that time. She couldn't really explain it, to Charlotte or to herself. That time nearly two years ago seemed a lifetime away. When she looked back, that person seemed like someone else entirely.

"In my heart, I think I knew I was making a huge mistake," she finally said. She wasn't sure why she felt compelled to confess this to Charlotte, but somehow the moment seemed right, here in the lodge, with the soft weight of a sleeping child on her lap.

She admired Charlotte. More than that, she *liked* her. By asking to spend time together that evening, Charlotte was offering her a tentative friendship and Gen didn't want to screw it up. She wanted to tell her about how things had been during her engagement, if only to explain that wasn't all she was.

"I tried to convince myself things were fine. As I look back, I think I had to focus on making sure every detail of the wedding was flawless—down to the pattern on the china and the hemline on the flower-girl dresses—so that I didn't have to face the emptiness of our relationship. I guess maybe I thought if we had the ideal fairy-tale wedding, the marriage would have to be perfect, too. Stupid, isn't it?"

Charlotte didn't say anything for a long moment. When she did, her question was startling in its boldness.

"Do you have feelings for my brother?"

Gen inhaled sharply, emotions jumbling through her so quickly she didn't know how to sort them out.

"Sorry. Don't answer that. It's none of my business. Spence told me to stay out of things and here I am barging in anyway. It's just... I saw you yesterday by the river. I saw him laughing. Do you have any idea how long it's been since I've seen him laugh like that?"

"I... No."

"Forever. Oh, he'll smile once in a while, and he does give this terrible, hard laugh I hate. Genuine laughter, though, has been missing since he came back."

Again, she didn't know what to say. Not the most auspicious beginning to a friendship, when she was either spilling her innermost secrets or completely clamming up.

"He almost died, you know," Charlotte said, her mouth tight and her eyes glimmering. "At one point, the military doctors told us to prepare for the worst as the infection ravaged through him. But he was stronger than they gave him credit for. I always knew he was. He came through it, even though they couldn't save his eye."

She had wondered about his vision. He sometimes referred bitterly to not having a hand but she had rarely heard him discuss his eye.

"He's been through so much. Though he doesn't talk about it, I know he carries the weight of terrible things inside him. He lost five good friends in the explosion that injured him and for a while this summer, I was afraid he..." Her voice trailed off and her mouth pressed into a line.

"That he what?"

She didn't answer. "I want so much for him to be able to find joy again. To laugh like he used to. To move forward with his life."

"I want that, too," Gen said.

"I hope you mean that," Charlotte said. For being the sweet owner of a candy store and someone Gen had always considered quiet and unassuming, the other woman's voice was suddenly as sharp as the edge of a newly waxed ski.

"If you hurt him, Gen Beaumont, I swear to you I will find some way to make you pay. I don't know how yet, but I'll figure something out."

The very sincere threat might have made her shudder if she wasn't so touched at the love Charlotte had for her brother.

She wanted to tell the other woman Genevieve didn't think she had anything to worry about. There was little danger of Dylan ever giving her any power to hurt him, not when he kept his feelings so tightly locked up and pushed her away at every opportunity.

"Is that the reason you invited me to the Christmas party tonight?" she asked, more amused than offended. "You want to befriend me so you can keep an eye on me and make sure I'm not going to break your brother's heart?"

Charlotte gave a surprised-sounding laugh. "I wish I were that clever. I'm afraid I had planned to ask you to the party before I saw the two of you together yesterday afternoon."

"Ah. Well, don't worry about Dylan. For one thing, I'm pretty sure he can take care of himself."

"He *thinks* he can, anyway."

She smiled but quickly grew serious, a sudden ache in her chest that had nothing to do with the little weight resting against it. "For another, even if I had feelings for him—which I'm not saying I do—he's made it quite clear he doesn't feel the same. We're friends. That's all."

Charlotte looked as if she wanted to discuss the issue further, but to Gen's relief, Tonya Brooks came in with a tired-looking Marisol. By some rather spooky instinct, Claudia awoke upon her mother's approach, and the moment was gone.

THE FIRST BURST of panic didn't hit until Charlotte parked her little SUV on Main Street.

"Where is this party?" Genevieve asked.

She suddenly didn't want to hear the answer.

"At Dog-Eared Books & Brew," Charlotte said nonchalantly, opening the hatch of her SUV then walking around to lift out a basket of Sugar Rush treats. "Our book club has a big Christmas party every year, and this year we're each supposed to bring someone new."

Dog-Eared Books & Brew. Maura McKnight Lange's store.

Dread lodged in her stomach, hot and greasy. Oh, she was an idiot! Why hadn't she bothered to ask before? She should have figured it out! She had no real explanation for such airheaded negligence, except she had been flattered at the invitation and very much wanted Charlotte to be her friend.

She knew Charlotte was friendly with the McKnights. That was the very reason she had declined her dinner invitation the week before, because she had worried about going to Brazen and having to face the owner, Alex McKnight.

She should have *known,* darn it. Her mind raced as she frantically tried to figure a way out of this without completely alienating Charlotte. Maybe she could feign illness. It wasn't a complete lie—she was feeling fairly nauseous right now and her head was beginning to throb.

She was bound to see Maura Lange there—and perhaps even her daughter, Sage.

She shivered from more than the chill of a December evening. She didn't know how to face them, not after the way she had acted.

The whole thing made her feel so small and stupid and she hated it. Yes, Sage had slept with her fiancé just months before their wedding, knowing perfectly well he was engaged. Yes, she had become pregnant with Sawyer's baby. It still infuriated her, humiliated her.

Deep inside, some terrible, narcissistic part of her couldn't help wondering what Sage had that *she* hadn't.

She couldn't deny Sage was pretty in a granola-eater sort of way. She had dark curly hair, dimples, the pretty green eyes all the McKnights seemed to share. But she wore hideous clothing designed more for comfort than fashion—Birkenstock sandals, leggings, loose T-shirts with funny, tacky little sayings on them. She hardly ever bothered with makeup and she always had her nose in a book. And she was young! Not even twenty when she and Sawyer slept together.

That horrible night when Gen found out Sage was pregnant and that Sawyer was the father, she hadn't doubted the girl's story for a moment, even though her mother tried to convince her Sage and the rest of the McKnights were lying.

Sawyer had never denied sleeping with her, and Sage had been too miserable about the whole thing, acting as if she would have preferred any other man on the planet to be her child's sperm donor.

Genevieve hated thinking of her reaction. She had been angry, yes, but that burning, aching humiliation had been paramount. She had done everything she could to give the man a perfect wedding, to prove she would be the ideal wife for someone with political aspirations beyond Colorado.

Her efforts had been for nothing. Despite doing all she could to show she could make him happy, Sawyer had still preferred a little Hobbit granola-eater who probably didn't even shave her legs—and worse, her very public pregnancy ensured that every single person in town knew it.

How could she go inside that bookstore and be polite to Sage's mother and aunts and grandmother, when she had spent nearly two years being hateful and small to all of them?

"I should have asked where the party was and who might be there," she finally said. The best basis for a friendship was honesty, right? "You know the McKnights won't want me in there."

Charlotte glanced over with a startled look. "Why not?"

"Oh, I don't know," Genevieve said dryly. "We haven't been on the best of terms since Sage McKnight gave birth to my fiancé's child."

Charlotte gave that a dismissive wave of the hand not carrying the basket of goodies, a sort of *oh, that little thing* kind of gesture. "It will be fine. You'll see. Alex and Mary Ella and Maura are wonderful. I promise, everyone will be happy to have you there."

For a moment, she let herself believe in the pretty picture Charlotte painted, but the reality wasn't quite as rosy. Otherwise good people could still hold grudges—and in this case, they had reason to be upset with her.

"Just come for a while," Charlotte said. "If you're having a terrible time, I'll take you home, I promise."

She looked down the sidewalk at the small, puffy flakes under the streetlights. Surely she was tough enough to handle a few raised eyebrows, wasn't she? She liked Charlotte and admired—and envied—the way she had reinvented herself. Gen wanted to be friends with her, for reasons that had nothing to do with the woman's frustrating brother.

If she gave in to her fears and asked Charlotte to take her home, she had a feeling she would be shoving the door closed on any chance of friendship between them.

"You're right. I'm probably overreacting. Let's go."

She held the door open for Charlotte and followed her inside.

The warmth of the store embraced them. Dog-Eared smelled of coffee and ink, quite an appealing combination. She was reminded of a favorite bookshop in Le Marais, a crowded little place on Rue St. Paul.

Charlotte led her through the store to a corner where various plump armchairs had been gathered together to make a private seating area. The chairs were all filled. As she expected, her appearance there was met with a few shocked stares—notably from Ruth Tatum, Claire McKnight's mother, and from Alex McKnight, Maura's younger sister and Sage's aunt.

Maura looked shocked, too, but she hid it quickly and gave a welcoming smile that Genevieve assumed was meant more for Charlotte than her. A quick look around told her Sage wasn't present.

"We're supposed to bring a friend, right?" Charlotte said cheerfully. "Genevieve has been doing such great things at A Warrior's Hope. She's been amazing. After all her hard work, I thought she could probably use a night out."

She hadn't felt this socially awkward ever.

"Come in. Grab a plate of food," Mary Ella Lange, recently married to Harry Lange, insisted to both of them.

"I hadn't heard you were back from your honeymoon," she said politely to Mary Ella.

To her astonishment, her retired high-school English teacher blushed like one of her students. "Yes. We had a wonderful two weeks in Southern France. It was so sunny and beautiful. Harry would have liked to stay longer, but we both wanted to be here to spend Christmas with our family."

She relaxed a little. France, she could discuss. "I love that area. I do hope you spent time in Paris while you were there. You can't visit France without wandering through the Arènes de Lutèce or Le Jardin du Luxembourg."

"We spent a few nights there, but Paris is a bit crowded and noisy for Harry's taste."

She wanted to say something derogatory about Harry's taste if that were truly the case, but she decided that probably wouldn't go over well with his new bride.

"It can be. But it can also be wonderful," she said. She and Mary Ella spent a few more moments discussing favorite spots in France. Evie Thorne chimed in about places she had visited, and after the first few moments, Genevieve could feel the tension in her shoulders begin to relax. Everyone was being surprisingly kind to her.

"I understand William has you fixing up Pearl's house to sell," Katherine Thorne, Evie's mother-in-law, said after a few moments. "How is it going?"

"I'm finding there's a little more to it than I expected." She launched into a description of how many layers of wallpaper she had steamed away, like a time capsule of her grandmother's various tastes and moods at the moment. Katherine even laughed at a few spots and asked her questions about her plans for the house and she relaxed further.

This wasn't so bad, she thought. In fact, she was actually enjoying herself. The rolling music of female conversation reminded her of long afternoons in her favorite café, talking with her Paris friends about anything and everything.

Genevieve was enjoying herself—that was, until she walked over to the refreshment table for more of the fantastic brownies Alex McKnight had brought—she figured she could work it off with painting—and bumped right into Maura Lange, who had just emerged from a back room with a new plate of party food.

The other woman did a bit of a double take before she bustled around the table, making room for the new plate and straightening up the other dishes.

Finally, Genevieve decided to just shoot the elephant in the room.

"How is Sage these days?"

Maura tensed, freezing for a moment before picking up a few stray napkins. "Wonderful," she said shortly. "Why do you ask?"

"Just curious."

Some small, petty part of her wanted to ask if she had slept with anyone else's fiancé lately, but that would just be rude. And beneath her.

"How's the baby?" she asked instead. She hadn't given much thought to the child that came from Sage and Sawyer's one-night affair but after playing with the sweet Claudia all day, little creatures were on her mind.

Maura didn't appear to appreciate the question. "My *son* is now eighteen months," she said, her tone sharp. "His name is Henry and he is very, very loved by his parents and his older sister."

Of course. Maura and her husband, Jack Lange, had adopted Sage's baby as their own. It couldn't have been an easy situation for any of them. She knew Sawyer had signed away any rights. After she stopped taking his phone calls, he had emailed her to tell her so, as if that might make some difference in his own culpability.

Did Sage view the boy as her own or as a younger brother? When she looked at Henry, did she see the smarmy, cheating son of a bitch Gen once thought she would spend the rest of her life with?

For an awkward moment, Genevieve stood at the refreshments table, not knowing quite what to say. Finally, she decided to follow the example of Charlotte, who seemed unfailingly kind.

"I'm glad he could have a good home, with people who love him," she said softly. None of what had happened was the child's fault.

Maura seemed startled by that, enough that she seemed to thaw a little. "We're the blessed ones. He's a complete joy."

She should probably stop there, take her plate of appetizers back to her seat and let the matter drop. But she had come this far. She was actually having a civil conversation with Maura Lange, and neither of them was throwing any food at the other. Yet.

"I believe I owe you and your family an apology," she said quickly, before she could lose her nerve.

"Oh?"

"After… I canceled the wedding, I guess I needed a scapegoat. It was easier to, um, blame your daughter than to admit my own mistakes. I wasn't very subtle about my anger."

"No. You weren't."

At Maura's discouraging expression, Genevieve faltered and would have let things rest there. Her mother would have brazened through the whole thing, acted all these months as if nothing had ever happened between them. That was probably what she *had* done while Gen had run away to Paris, just carried on as normal.

Genevieve wasn't Laura. She never would be, she realized. She needed friendship and respect and suddenly wanted to do whatever necessary to earn it.

"I was wrong and… I'm sorry. Will you please convey my apology to Sage? Contrary to the way I may have acted, I don't believe she was completely responsible for the whole mess. Sawyer certainly played a huge role and… I did, as well."

Well, she had at least succeeded in surprising Maura. The other woman stared at her warily, as if trying to figure out what angle she was playing.

"I was wrong to say what I did about her, publicly and privately. Will you please let her know?"

"I… Yes. Of course. I'll tell her what you said."

"Thank you."

She was about to return to her spot on the edge of the sofa when Maura, in turn, surprised her.

"I couldn't help noticing your bag when you came in."

Heat washed over her. The bag. Oh, no! She had completely forgotten she'd grabbed one of her hand-sewn pieces since the accent color of it so perfectly matched the salmon of her sweater. Maura was bound to recognize it as the same general style of the dozen or so bags she had anonymously shipped to Dog-Eared Books & Brew to sell.

"Did you?" she said, trying for a casual smile. "It's fun, isn't it?"

"Yes. I have one myself that's very similar. May I ask where you found it?"

Again, her mind did a frenzied workout as she tried to come up with an answer that wasn't a complete fabrication. "Paris," she finally said, honestly enough, though she didn't add exactly where: in her apartment, in the tiny spare bedroom/craft room where she hung all the others she had created.

"You don't happen to know where I could find more, would you? I had a few for sale in my store a few months ago and everybody wanted one."

Gen could feel her cheeks turn pink with pleasure and pride. She wanted to tell Maura she had made them but she didn't dare. Not now, when things were still awkward between them.

"I… I don't," she stammered. "I'll keep an eye out and let you know if I see any."

"Yes. Please. I made a nice profit from them and would definitely be open for more."

"Okay."

Flustered and off balance now, she decided she didn't have any appetite. She set her plate back on her chair, grabbed the bag in question and escaped to the restroom.

She fixed her hair quickly and applied a new coat of lipstick. Mostly, she just used the moment to collect her composure again. When she was ready, she left the ladies' room and headed through the shelves toward Charlotte's book-club party.

The sound of someone saying her name halted her footsteps.

"What were you thinking to invite Genevieve Beaumont?"

Gen's stomach contracted suddenly at the condemnation in the voice, which she now recognized as Ruth Tatum, Claire McKnight's mother.

"Everybody agreed to bring someone new, remember? Maura brought her pediatrician. Evie Thorne brought Brodie's new office manager. The whole point was to make the book club more inclusive."

"That was a stupid idea in the first place. Whoever thought of it? Probably Claire."

"Yes, it was my idea, Mother," Claire said. "It's been wonderful to have fresh faces to talk to, new stories to hear. I think we sometimes tend to stick with our own little group and don't always make others feel welcome."

"Why do we need to? Things were fine," Ruth groused. "Anyway, couldn't you find anyone better to bring than Genevieve Beaumont?"

Any warm glow she might have been feeling at trying to make things right with Maura—at holding her own at this party and even trying to form tentative new friendships—seemed to shrivel and die a painful death.

"Stop it, Mom."

"I'm only saying what everyone else is thinking," Ruth Tatum protested. "You all know what Genevieve's like. She's an ice-cold bitch. It's no wonder her fiancé slept around. He was probably desperate for a little warmth."

"That's enough," Claire said sharply, but Genevieve didn't wait to hear more. All the remembered humiliation and hurt of that terrible time after her engagement ended came surging back and she thought she might truly be sick.

Trying not to give in to the further mortification of tears, she pushed around the bookshelf. "That's right," she said bitterly. "I'm the coldest bitch in Hope's Crossing. Sawyer couldn't wait to sleep with anyone who wasn't me."

Why had she even tried to be friends with these small-minded, provincial women who refused to think maybe a person could change?

She wanted to stomp and yell and throw books off the shelves at them. *I never wanted to come to your stupid book-club meeting anyway. You're a bunch of insulated, illiterate rustics who look at Paris and see crowds and noise instead of light and beauty and magic. I feel sorry for all of you.*

Instead, she swallowed down all those words—most of them not even true—and tried for some small semblance of the dignity and strength she wished she had shown after her engagement ended.

"Will you excuse me?" She grabbed her coat, grateful she already had her purse, and drew on the example of her father's pompous haughtiness as she marched toward the door.

She didn't look back, though she heard the shocked, echoing silence that met her pathetically melodramatic exit.

As she might have expected, Charlotte hurried after her, stopping Gen just before she yanked open the door and walked out into the cold.

"I am so sorry, Genevieve. Ruth Tatum is a cranky old biddy. She always has been. If she wasn't Claire's mother, I don't think we could tolerate her."

Apparently old bitches were more bearable than the young ones.

"She only said what everyone else was thinking. I knew this was a mistake before we ever walked in. I should never have come. I should have asked you where we were going. We both know I don't belong here in Hope's Crossing."

"Please. Come back. Everyone will feel so terrible if you leave."

She glanced over at the women in the corner and was rather surprised to see Ruth cornered by Claire and Katherine Thorne, of all people. She couldn't hear what they said, but judging by the way Ruth had her arms folded defensively and the animated expressions of the other two, it looked as if they were scolding her.

Surprising, yes, but not enough to compel her to return to that vipers' den.

"I'm sorry, but... I need to go."

Charlotte looked as if she wanted to argue, but after a long moment, she nodded. "I understand. Let me grab my coat and I'll give you a ride home."

"No. You don't have to leave because of me. It's not far. I don't mind walking."

Charlotte suddenly looked as obstinate as her brother. "Don't be silly. You came here as my guest. I'm not going to let you walk home in the snow."

The random flakes of earlier had turned into a steady snowfall. Already half an inch covered the roadway.

The idea of walking through it didn't appeal to her, especially in her heeled boots.

"Fine," she said. "I'm sure you'll understand if I wait outside."

Charlotte chewed her lip as if she wanted to continue urging Gen to stay at the party. After a pause, she nodded. "I'll be right back."

Genevieve pushed through the doors, into the cold air. The pelting snow was like a wake-up call.

Had she really thought she could make friends here in Hope's Crossing, where everyone would probably always see her as the person she had once been?

More depressed than she had been in a long time, she walked a little distance up the street and suddenly caught a distant chord of music coming from a side street.

Without waiting for Charlotte, she impulsively took a few more steps until she could look down the street and see the lights of The Speckled Lizard.

The site of her downfall.

She glanced back at the bookstore, sending out a different, warmer sort of glow. It was far more appealing, except for the women inside, who were probably chattering like angry magpies about her.

Suddenly, she desperately wanted to be in a place where people didn't care about her history, about her mistakes. Charlotte would understand.

She increased her pace and hurried toward the tavern without looking back.

CHAPTER FOURTEEN

"OH, MAN. Did you see that? Why didn't he just run the reverse?"

"Good question," Dylan muttered to his brother Brendan. An even better question: What the hell was he doing in a crowded bar watching a bowl game with Pop, his brothers and a few friends when he could be sitting by his fire, enjoying the quiet solitude of Snowflake Canyon?

That had been his plan until he made the mistake of stopping at Brendan's to pick up Tucker, who had hung out there that day while Dylan was busy at A Warrior's Hope. Brendan, who rarely asked him for anything, had invited him along to The Speckled Lizard to catch the game.

He hadn't had the heart to say no, not when Brendan seemed in the mood for company—and because he owed him for volunteering, along with Peyton Gregory, for dog-sitting duties so Tuck didn't have to spend the whole day with only the chickens for company.

He hadn't realized the whole family was coming. Pop. Andrew. A few friends. It was a regular party.

"You need another drink?" Pat asked.

He shook his head. "One crappy, watered-down whiskey ought to do it for me. Thanks."

Pat, the bartender, glowered at him. "You said you wanted rocks. I gave you rocks."

"And half the river, too," he muttered.

"Have another drink," Andrew urged. "Or are you afraid you might get wasted and deck somebody again? We're here with the chief of police. He'll keep things cool."

"Don't be so sure." Riley McKnight made a face. "You steal another one of my pretzels and I might throw your ass back in jail."

"Warning duly noted."

"Anybody want to play a little pool during half time?" Brendan asked.

"Sure," Riley said.

Andrew slid off his chair, always up for a challenge. "Yeah, I'm in."

"What about you, son?" Pop asked.

He shook his head, forcing a smile. Billiards used to be one of his favorite things, but he hadn't quite figured out how to manage holding a cue one-handed. He'd seen somebody online who had crafted a wooden cue rest to attach to an amputated arm to help with control and aim. It looked interesting. Maybe he would try to work on that over the Christmas holidays. He had always enjoyed woodworking and had been thinking about trying his hand at it.

"It's been a long day. I should really take off and—"

The door flew open behind Brendan in a swirl of snow and wind, and the rest of the sentence dashed out of his head, lost in the shock of seeing Genevieve Beaumont there.

She looked like an ethereal angel framed in the light of the doorway with that crown of blond hair and her pale wool coat and hat.

"Uh-oh. Here comes trouble," Riley said. "Careful, Dylan. I was only joking about hauling you back to jail. I'd really rather not."

She was upset. He wasn't certain how he knew, but her eyes were shadowed and her mouth trembled a little as she looked around at the mostly male crowd assembled to watch the bowl game.

When her gaze landed on him, her mouth made a little O and a vast relief spread over those lovely features, so unexpected and humbling it made his chest ache.

She headed straight for him. "Dylan! I didn't know you would be here. I can't *begin* to tell you how happy I am to see you."

He was aware of his brothers exchanging glances and didn't miss the mix of curiosity and worry in his pop's eyes. Unfortunately, he could guess what they were all thinking.

He cleared his throat. "What's going on? I thought Charlotte was taking you to her book-club party."

"She did. I left."

Her chin started to wobble again, and he knew she would hate it if she broke down here in the middle of the bar. There was definitely a story here and he wanted to hear it—but not when half his family listened in with avid interest.

"Let's grab a table," he growled.

Ignoring the speculative looks aimed in their direction, he pushed his way through the crowd and found a secluded spot in the corner. Either Pat was overly concerned about the trouble the two of them might cause to-gether, given recent events, or the small bar staff was also curious about what Genevieve Beaumont was doing at a dive like the Lizard on a Wednes-day night. They had barely sat down when Nikki, one of the tavern servers, showed up tableside.

"Can I get you two something?" she asked.

"I really, really want a mojito," Gen said. "But I'd better just have a min-eral water."

"Dylan, anything for you?"

"I'm good."

She rolled her eyes at the paltry order, slapped down a cardboard coaster and napkin and headed toward the bar.

After she left, Gen fidgeted with the coaster and refused to meet Dylan's gaze.

"You going to tell me what happened?" he finally asked.

"I'd rather not," she muttered, focusing on the pool table where it looked as if Andrew was cleaning up, as usual.

"You might as well tell me. I'm trained in interrogation, you know."

She finally did meet his gaze, her delicate eyebrow arched nearly to her hairline. "Well. That explains a lot."

"Such as?"

"You're always trying to make me spill my innermost thoughts. It's a bad habit, soldier."

He wanted to tell her he wasn't a soldier anymore. He wasn't much of anything right now. "My family would tell you I was born naturally nosy. With five older brothers, there were always interesting secrets to discover."

The group around the pool table suddenly exploded in cheers, probably because Brendan had aced a particularly difficult shot to pull ahead of An-drew the pool shark.

Genevieve followed the sound, her eyes wide and envious. "I'm inter-rupting a family thing," she murmured.

"Not at all. Brendan just asked if I wanted to come to the Liz and watch the game for a bit. I don't have great reception at my place when snow gets in the satellite dish, so I decided what the hell."

"You can go back to the game. I'm fine. I don't need a babysitter. I'll just drink my San Pellegrino and go home."

He liked looking at her. Even when she was distressed, she was so lovely it was almost unreal, until a person came to know her. Then he could see the little flaws. A tiny mole on her jawline she concealed with makeup, one ear that was a fraction lower than the other one, a tooth slightly out of alignment when she smiled.

Those little imperfections made her real and endearing. His chest suddenly felt a little tight, clogged by a strange, thick emotion he didn't want to identify.

He had watched her the past week as they worked together at A Warrior's Hope. He didn't think he had been the only one surprised by Genevieve Beaumont. She had been sweet and warm, treating the guests with the perfect mix of lighthearted teasing and respect. The wives all seemed to like her and even the children were drawn to her.

That afternoon he had walked into the lodge and found her sitting on the sofa in earnest conversation with Charlotte and Tonya Brooks, one of the cute little Brooks girls snuggled on her lap, all braids and big eyes and adorable smiles.

His chest had felt the same way then, kind of thick and sluggish.

Maybe he was coming down with something.

Because he had been watching her so intently these past few days, he didn't need her to confirm something had upset her. She wasn't the soft, sweet Gen he was coming to know. There was an edgy brittleness about her, as if she would shatter like an icicle falling off a roof if somebody slammed a door too hard.

"Come on," he pressed. "Tell me what's wrong."

She gave him a haughty look he was coming to realize was simply another defense mechanism. "If this is an example of your interrogation skills, I have to tell you, I'm not impressed. You're not being particularly persuasive. So far, all you've done is order me to talk in that bossy tone. I suppose there's a slim chance you might eventually wear me down but, let's be honest, that could take all night."

He fought a smile he didn't think she would appreciate right now. "How about if I threaten to start another bar fight? Would that do the trick? I'm always looking for an excuse to go after one of my brothers. Annoying bastards, the lot of them."

"I've learned my lesson. If you started throwing punches, I would just sit here primly with my hands folded in my lap, minding my own business."

He snorted. He would believe that when he saw it.

"There's always a chance I might be able to help the situation, but not if you won't tell me what happened."

She opened her mouth to answer, but Nikki returned with her mineral water and a glass of ice and she closed her mouth again. He wanted to growl with frustration.

She drank the water straight from the bottle, ignoring the ice, then wiped at her mouth daintily with the napkin.

"Something happened at the book-club party, obviously."

"Wow. You *are* good," she said dryly.

"Oh, I've got skills you can't begin to guess at," he answered.

"No doubt," she murmured. It was probably just the low lighting in The Speckled Lizard, but for a moment, he was almost positive her gaze flicked to his mouth, sending instant heat curling through him.

He did his best to douse it. "You never know. I might even be able to help with whatever's bothering you."

She fretted with the bottle. "It's nothing. Just… I didn't belong there. I knew it before I walked in. Ruth Tatum even said so. She had some harsh words for Charlotte since she's the one who invited me."

"Seriously? That's why you came in here looking like somebody kicked your dog?"

"I don't have a dog."

"Okay, like somebody kicked *my* dog, then. Do you really care what Ruth Tatum said? She's a cranky bitch and always has been. It's no wonder her husband was going to leave her for a cocktail waitress."

Her finger traced the painted lizard on the coaster. "Funny. That's just what she said about me."

"What?"

"That Sawyer slept around because I'm such a bitch. That he must have been desperate to find a little warmth wherever he could."

"She said that? See? Ruth is not only a bitch but a *crazy* bitch."

Her mouth lifted just a little but quickly sagged at the edges. "She's not wrong. I was terrible during my engagement. Bridezilla on steroids. That's what your sister said."

He frowned, thinking he might need to have a talk with Charlotte if she was calling people names like that. "However you might have acted in the stress of planning a wedding, that's no excuse for what your asshole of a fiancé did to you, humiliating you like that. You said yourself, you're far better off without him."

"I am. I know that. We would have made each other miserable and probably would have divorced within three or four years—if we could have lasted that long. By then we might have had a child or two to add to the mess."

He thought of her that afternoon with the little Brooks girl in her arm, how sweet and patient she had been with her.

"Forget about him. And Ruth Tatum, too. She's not worth wasting a minute on."

She sighed. "Do you want to know what makes me most upset?"

Not really. He just wanted to fix the whole thing and make it all better for her. "What?"

"Before I overheard her, I had been enjoying the party. I was talking to people, listening to their stories, having a good time. But then I heard what Ruth said and nothing else mattered. I let one person's opinion have too much power over me. I've always been that way. I became what my parents wanted of me, what Sawyer wanted. I've never bothered to become who *I* want to be."

"And who would that be?"

"I don't know yet," she said, so softly he had to lean in to hear. "But I think I'm closer to finding out."

He wanted to kiss her, right here in the middle of The Speckled Lizard. And wouldn't that send his family into an uproar?

She winced suddenly. "I should probably text your sister. She was going to give me a ride home, and I sort of ditched her outside the bookstore. What's her number?"

The image of her fleeing into the night like Cinderella would have made him smile if she wasn't so distressed over the whole thing.

"Here. Just use my phone. She's in there, though not under Bossy Little Sister, as she should be."

He pulled his phone out of his pocket and held it out to her. Her hand brushed his as she took it from him. Her fingers were cool from holding the chilled water bottle, and he wanted to fold them in his and tug them against his skin....

He really, really needed to stop thinking like this. They were friends, that was all.

Her thumbs quickly flew over the screen of his phone, then she handed it back to him. He was curious enough to read the message:

Gen here. I'm with Dylan. Don't worry. Sorry I'm a baby. I'll see you tomorrow.

"You still need a ride home. Let me say goodbye to Pop and my brothers, and I'll drop you off on my way up the canyon."

"Why don't any of you Caines think I can walk six blocks by myself?"

"Maybe because it's dark and it's snowing."

"So what? I don't mind walking home. You don't need to leave your game on my account."

"I told you, I was just about to take off before you came in. These long days of recreating are kicking my butt."

She smiled a little, as he intended. Her mood seemed lighter, and he considered that just about his biggest achievement of the day.

"I'll be right back."

She nodded and sipped at her water as he headed for the billiards table.

"I'm taking off," he said.

"With Genevieve Beaumont." Pop's words were a statement, not a question.

He saw Brendan and Andrew exchange looks that made him want to pound both of them.

"I'm only giving her a ride home," he said.

"Good for you," Andrew said. "It's about time you, er, gave somebody a ride."

He was in his brother's face before he even thought it through, ready to go. "You want to say that again?" he snarled.

"That's enough," Dermot said in a long-suffering voice. "Settle down, boys."

Andrew looked startled. "Sorry. I didn't mean anything. I like Genevieve. It took guts to stand up to her father the way she did."

She had guts. She just couldn't seem to see it.

"She needs a lift home. I'm giving her a lift home. That's all."

"Okay, we get it. Go, already."

"I will."

Genevieve joined him at the billiards table with a hesitant smile for his family. He was glad she was oblivious to the currents zinging around.

He wasn't sure what to think when she kissed Dermot on the cheek. "Thank you for the pie the other night," she said. "It was just what I needed."

"Good. When you've got a hankering for another, just let my boy know and I'll be sure to bake one special for you."

"Thank you."

She looked as touched as if Dermot had just offered her keys to a new BMW.

Dermot could see how sweet she was. If his father could be so astute, Dylan had to wonder why everybody else only saw the prickles—including Genevieve herself.

CHAPTER FIFTEEN

THEY WALKED OUTSIDE to more snowfall, big plump flakes that had added at least a few inches to the sidewalk.

"I'm parked the next block over," he said. "Sorry for a bit of a walk."

"I don't mind."

The Christmas lights hanging on just about every downtown business glimmered against the snow, cheery and festive. Hope's Crossing really was a pretty town this time of year. Most times of year, if he were honest. The restaurants and stores still open seemed to be doing a good business. A little foot traffic spilled out onto the sidewalks and everybody seemed to be in a good mood.

It was a far cry from the dust and grit and bleakness of Afghanistan.

With the sidewalks a bit slick, Genevieve slipped her hand into the crook of his arm for support—his good one, as he was always careful to position himself so the left arm was on the other side.

He could feel the heat of her, even through their layers of clothes and outerwear, and he wanted to soak it in.

"Your family is really close, aren't you?" she asked after a moment.

"Yeah. We were always pretty tight-knit, you know? A lot of camping trips, vacations to the coast when Pop could get away from the café. That kind of thing. After our mom died, I think Pop worked extra hard to make sure we didn't drift apart. The older brothers were in college or in the military, but Pop tried to get us all in one place at least a couple times a year. He was an early adopter of technology and even has a private family blog. He used to post at least once a week with information about what everybody was doing. With social media, that's even easier now."

"Your dad is wonderful. You're so lucky. I mean, I know my parents love me and everything, but it's not the same."

He thought about her own family—stiff and pompous William, picky, perfectionist Laura. Compared to what she came from, he *did* feel fortunate. Damn lucky. He had never spent a moment on the earth without knowing he was loved.

"Big families can be good in a lot of ways, but they can be a pain in the ass, too. Everybody thinks he has the right to stick his nose in your life. And try having five older brothers to follow in every sporting activity you ever wanted to participate in. I can't tell you how many times I had to sit and listen to coaches rave about Patrick's three-point percentage or Bren's rushing stats or Jamie's RBIs. It was enough to give a guy a complex."

She smiled a little. "I doubt that. I seem to recall seeing your name on a few awards in the trophy case at school."

That cocky kid who thought the world was his to conquer seemed a lifetime away now.

"Here's my truck," he said. He never bothered to lock the doors, so he reached and opened the passenger side for her. It was a climb up, so he supported her elbow as she stepped in, wishing for the first time since he returned that he had bothered to drive something that wasn't twenty years old, run-down and smelling like dog.

The engine turned over immediately—one of the reasons he still drove this one and not some shiny new thing he'd be afraid to take up the gravel drive to his place.

"I'll just be a second," he said, reaching for the scraper behind the seats. Because the snow was soft, light as cotton puffs, he only needed to brush off what had accumulated on the side and rear windows for visibility. The wipers would take care of the front.

By the time he climbed in, the heater was already blowing out warm air. Yeah, it might not look or smell like much, but he did love this truck. It got the job done.

They encountered little traffic as he pulled out of the parking lot and headed toward the mouth of the canyon and her grandmother's house.

Just about every house was decorated for the holidays. Everybody seemed to be in on the effort to punch up the pretty: little sparkly lights along roof lines or in shrubbery, a big Christmas tree in the window, a family of cheerful snowmen in one yard.

Everything looked magical, especially in the midst of a snowfall that seemed to mute all the colors and merge them together.

They were nearly to her grandmother's house when Genevieve's phone rang. Her ring tone sounded like a jazzy number from *A Charlie Brown Christmas,* which he found inordinately sweet.

She pulled it out of the pocket of her coat and looked at the caller ID.

"Unknown," she said but answered it anyway.

"Hello?" After a moment of silence, she frowned and said the word louder.

"Must have been a wrong number," he said.

"Maybe. I could swear someone was there. Weird."

She shoved the phone back in her pocket as he pulled up in front of her grandmother's house. For some reason, it didn't seem as ugly as he'd first thought. The porch lights were on, and he could see some little twinkly Christmas lights in the front window.

"I finished painting the dining room last night," she said. "Come see."

His fingers tightened on the steering wheel. He wasn't so certain that was a good idea. The more he was with her, the more he was struggling to keep his hands—*hand*—off her. But he knew she would see his refusal as another rejection, on top of an already-painful night.

"For a minute," he finally said. "And then I'd better pick up Tucker. He's been over at Brendan's house all day and is probably ready to go home."

"Why has he been at your brother's place?"

"It's stupid, but when I'm going to be gone all day, I don't like leaving him alone up at the house by himself."

"Will he cause trouble? Chew the cabinets or rip apart all your pillows?"

"Nothing like that. He's a good dog. I just don't like thinking about him being lonely up there by himself."

He also didn't like thinking about her being here in this dark house by herself, alone and unhappy, but, again, didn't think she would appreciate being compared to his dog.

"You're a very sweet man, Dylan Caine," she said.

Any argument he made to that would sound as ridiculous as her statement, so he just glowered at her and climbed out of his pickup to open her door.

GENEVIEVE LED THE way up the snowy sidewalk, aware of Dylan walking beside her with all the enthusiasm of a man heading to a torture chamber in the desert somewhere.

She sighed, wishing she had simply thanked him for the ride and said good-night. She did not understand this man. Sometimes he acted as if he enjoyed her company, savored it, even. The next minute, he would back off so quickly it made her head spin.

Tonight was a prime example. He had been extraordinarily kind to her at The Speckled Lizard, though. She would never forget the vast, aching relief that had swept over her when she walked in and saw him sitting at the bar, big and strong and comforting, as if fate had led her exactly where she needed to be.

He had offered just what she needed—a listening ear, a little wise counsel and a big heaping plate of perspective.

She couldn't believe she had rushed out of the bookstore in such a huff. Dylan was right. Ruth Tatum was a cranky bitch. What did Genevieve care what she thought? The truth was, she really didn't—but she did care what the others thought. Charlotte and Claire McKnight and Maura. She had wanted them to like her, to see that she was trying to change.

Ruth's words had only reinforced how fruitless that effort was. She had a well-earned reputation around town. In Hope's Crossing—like any community, she imagined—becoming something different, something *more,* than what people perceived her to be was a Herculean task.

Her hands trembled with the cold as she tried to unlock the door.

"Need some help?" Dylan asked.

"No. I've got it. It can be sticky." She wiggled the key just right and the door swung open into her house. She flipped on the light and held the door open for him. As he moved inside, she wondered how he had become so dear to her in such a short time.

Until a few weeks ago, she hadn't given the man more than a second's thought. Someone—her father, perhaps—had mentioned the gravity of his injuries in passing during one of their phone calls. She remembered a little pang of sadness for kind Dermot, but that had been about the extent of the attention she paid Dylan in years.

What would her parents think if they knew a gruff wounded army ranger had become her dearest friend in Hope's Crossing?

Forget her parents. What would *Dylan* say if he knew?

"You put up some Christmas decorations. I thought you weren't going to."

"No Christmas tree, you'll notice. My brain hit tree-overload the other day decorating the one at the recreation-center meeting room."

He smiled a little and looked around the living room at the various crèches she had set out—a few above the mantel, a handful more along the big front windowsill, more spilling across the ugly round oak side tables.

"It looks nice."

She had to admit, the Nativity scenes were lovely, especially with the strings of fairy lights she'd scattered around them.

"I suppose I found a little Christmas spirit after all. It seemed a shame not to have anything. I found these in boxes in the crawl space the other night."

"That's a few Nativity sets."

"You don't know the half of them. There's probably a hundred in boxes up there. Grandma Pearl loved them. She collected them from all over, the kitschier the better. I tried to pick the best of the lot to bring down."

She touched a finger to Mary's robe on one of her favorites, a finely wrought porcelain set where the figures each had realistic faces. "From the time I was a little girl, each year she would give me another Nativity set. When I was little, I used to love setting them around in my room. After I turned about twelve, I stopped doing anything with them, but she kept giving them. Every year, without fail. They're probably boxed up somewhere at the house or else Mother threw them out."

She was sorry now that she hadn't truly appreciated the tradition. Living in this house was giving her a new perspective on her grandmother—as well as a deep sorrow that she hadn't made more of an effort to forge a better relationship with Pearl as an adult.

"Come on. Let's go see the dining room," she said, tired of her maudlin mood.

She led the way, flipped on the lights and stood back to enjoy the way the new sage green around three of the walls brightened the room. She also particularly liked the accent wall, which Dylan commented on, too.

"You did paint that wall brown. It's nice. Comforting. Amazing, how a little paint can make such a change."

"Thanks. I agree. It makes me want to hurry and finish the other rooms. I definitely think it will help the house's resale value, even if the prospective buyers end up tearing it down."

He gave her a long look, but she couldn't read the expression in his eye. Not for the first time, she wondered if his thoughts might be easier to read if not for the patch.

"Why are you in such a hurry to leave town?" he asked. "I mean, why couldn't you start an interior-design business here? I would think Hope's Crossing has as much need for your services as anybody in Paris. More, even."

Was his mouth tight like that because he disliked the idea of her leaving? she wondered. Or was he just annoyed at having to bring her home?

"You're right. I'm sure I could stay busy here, especially with all the second homes in town and the new construction. But think about it. How could I even contemplate staying? I told you what happened at the party tonight."

"You really want to build your life around one old crank's opinion?"

"What does it matter to you where I end up starting a business? I would have thought you would be happy to see the last of me. Will you miss me?"

It had been a daring question, only half-teasing. She was tired of not being able to figure out what he was thinking, where she stood with him.

He faced her, a stark expression on his still-handsome features that made her catch her breath.

"Yes," he answered, his voice gruff. "I'll miss you. More than I should."

She swallowed, her face heating. Before she could respond—or even react, beyond initial shock, he quickly changed the subject.

"You could be happy here, Gen. Not everyone is like Ruth. You know that. Anybody who thinks you're spoiled and selfish doesn't know you. You haven't given them the *chance* to know you. You get all stiff and bristly and people mistake that for arrogance and disdain."

Yes, there was truth to that. She had come into town with her defenses raised, in part because of her parents' ultimatum but also because she hated being the subject of whispers and stares, as she had been after her engagement ended.

"Maybe they won't like what they find," she whispered.

"Maybe not," he said, just as quietly. "But you should at least give them a chance to discover the Genevieve that I see."

She gazed at him, standing inside her dining room with the scent of fresh paint swirling around them. He was extraordinarily compelling, even more gorgeous, perhaps, than he would have been without his injuries.

The eye patch, the prosthetic on his arm—she remembered how she had been slightly afraid of those things when she first met him that night at the bar, but now they were badges of honor to her. Signs of his courage and his strength, of the great sacrifices he had made and the challenges he would endure the rest of his life.

Something profound inside her shifted, slid away, revealing absolute, unadorned truth.

She was falling in love with him.

The sweetness of it rushed over her, fierce and strong. Yes. Of course. She should have realized. She was falling in love with Dylan Caine.

The emotions fluttered in her chest, so powerfully real she couldn't believe she had missed them all this time.

She didn't give a thought to how crazy this was or think about the dangers in risking another rejection that night. She only stepped forward, lifted up on her toes and kissed the edge of that unsmiling mouth.

HE FROZE FOR just a moment, and she waited in breathless anticipation, her mouth pressed against his and her blood pulsing loudly in her ears.

Kiss me back. Please kiss me back.

She was terrified he would push her away once more, but then he yanked her hard against his solid strength and returned the kiss with fierce intensity.

His mouth was firm, insistent—hot and delicious with a tiny hint of whiskey, and he kissed her with an edge of desperation.

Oh. My.

She wrapped her arms tightly around him, pressed against him from shoulder to thigh. She wanted him everywhere, the strength of him, the intoxicating taste and scent and feel.

She had never felt anything like this before, this wild, aching rush of heat and need and hunger.

Yes. Only Dylan.

What an amazing difference these fragile, tender feelings made. She almost wanted to cry. It felt so perfect and so right to be here in his arms—as if everything inside her had only been waiting for this man, this moment.

He made a low, incredibly sexy sound in his throat and deepened the kiss. She shivered as a fresh torrent of emotions surged like an avalanche pouring down the mountainside, sweeping away everything in its path—the past, her insecurities. Nothing mattered but Dylan.

She wasn't sure if she was the one who moved first or if he did but somehow they were back in Grandma Pearl's living room with the little strings of fairy lights the only illumination. He was still wearing his coat and she pulled him out of it and then they were on the sofa, body against body, just as she craved.

He was hard everywhere. All this time she had thought him too lean, with the build of a man who had lost weight in recent months and needed a few good meals at his father's café to bulk up again.

He might be lean, but now she realized he was all muscle, unyielding and tough. He kissed her mouth and then trailed kisses to her throat and farther, to the skin bared by the V of her sweater. She arched up, wanting more, wanting everything.

She had always hated Grandma Pearl's sofa but now she was seriously considering a change of mind. The wide cushions she had thought so uncomfortable gave them plenty of room to lie side by side, a distinct advantage so he didn't have to put all his weight on one arm. Instead, he could use that hand to explore, his fingers tangling in her sweater as he bared her skin just a few inches at the waist.

There was no trace of the reluctant Dylan now. He was everywhere, his lips, his tongue, his fingers. He wedged one strong thigh between hers and she arched against him, setting off another wild avalanche of sensations.

She tangled her fingers in his hair, her mouth pressing against everything she could reach. Perfect. The moment was perfect, with the snow fluttering down outside, the lights twinkling, this man she loved in her arms.

And then her phone rang.

She froze as that silly Christmas song rang out from the coat she had thoughtlessly slung over a chair.

"Ignore it," she mumbled, her mouth pressed to the deliciously warm skin along his jawline. "It's nothing."

The sofa didn't offer much room for him to roll away but somehow he managed to put space between them anyway. "It might be."

"I don't care who it is. I don't want you to stop. Kiss me again, Dylan. Please."

The light only filtered across half of his features, the side without the patch, and she saw hunger and need reflected in his gaze, and then to her great relief, he kissed her again, almost as if he couldn't help himself.

After only a moment, though, he jerked away.

"Stop, Gen."

"Why?"

He was only inches away from her, so close she could see each spiky eyelash around that beautiful blue eye.

"I haven't been with a woman in…a long time. I won't want to stop at a few kisses and a little touchy-feely on your grandmother's ugly sofa."

Her insides trembled at the way he was looking at her, as no one else ever had. As if she were everything he had ever wanted.

"Okay," she whispered. She could barely think straight with him looking as if he wanted to eat her alive—yes, please—but she managed to answer with quite remarkable coherence, under the circumstances.

"I've got a bedroom. It has really nice bedding, too. I brought it from Europe."

"Not a good idea."

To her dismay, he sat up on the edge of the sofa, both legs back on the ground.

She deliberately misunderstood him. "Oh, believe me, it was. You should have seen what my grandmother left on the beds. Polyester sheets and those awful bumpy chenille coverlets."

She gave a shiver that wasn't completely feigned. Without his heat against her she was cold, suddenly, even though Grandma Pearl's furnace worked perfectly well.

He studied her, and to her surprise, after a brief hesitation, his mouth quirked up a little on one side. That she could make him smile, even when the air was thick with tension—sexual and otherwise—filled her with effervescent little bubbles of happiness.

"I meant the two of us ripping up those particular sheets together. That's *not* such a great idea."

The finality in his voice was even more chilling than walking barefoot through that snow. There he went, pushing her away again.

"Is this about your hand? Because, I promise, it doesn't matter. When you're kissing me and touching me, I can only think about the parts you're using, not anything that might be missing."

A muscle flexed in his jaw, that heat rekindled in his gaze. She thought for a moment he would kiss her again but then he sighed.

"I'm damaged, Gen. Not just the outside. The whole package."

He rose to his feet, his expression one of regret and sadness and lingering hunger, and reached for the coat she had thrown on the floor.

"You're not damaged to me," she said, climbing to her feet, as well. "I think you're…"

Perfect. Wonderful. The man I love.

"The best person I know," she finally whispered.

It sounded stupid, but she didn't know how else to tell him everything he was coming to mean to her.

"If that's the case, you seriously need to widen your circle of acquaintances."

He reached for her hand and squeezed it gently. "I'm shaking right now because I want you so much, but I'm not going to sleep with you, Gen."

"Why not?"

She wouldn't beg, even though she really, really wanted to.

"Neither one of us is in a good place for this."

"The bedroom is right down the hall," she pointed out.

"You know that's not what I mean." He frowned. "You're vulnerable and upset because of what happened earlier tonight. I get that. But I can't be the man you need. You deserve someone…better. Someone without all the garbage that comes with me."

"I don't want anyone else."

Okay, maybe she *would* beg.

That muscle in his jaw tightened again, and he rubbed at his forehead just above the patch. "You say that now, but if we made love, you would regret it. I would hate that. I'm sorry, Gen. I can't do this. Good night."

Before she could argue, before she could even react, he was out the door.

After the door closed behind him with grim finality, she couldn't seem to move. She sat on the edge of Grandma Pearl's horrid sofa—which she now hated all over again. Her emotions were battered, numb, confused, as if she had just ridden out a tornado.

She loved Dylan Caine, and he had just made it painfully clear he wouldn't let himself feel the same.

Once more, she wasn't enough.

What was she supposed to do now?

She didn't have any idea how she could just go on with her life, when everything had changed so monumentally.

How could she go back to A Warrior's Hope in the morning and face him as if nothing had happened, as if her heart hadn't just been stripped bare and turned inside out?

Even more unsettling, how could she go back to Paris now and throw herself into a new life and new career when everything she had suddenly discovered she wanted was right here?

CHAPTER SIXTEEN

SHE LOOKED HORRIBLE, and this time she couldn't blame the pink tiles in Grandma Pearl's bathroom.

Genevieve gazed into the mirror, gradually reaching the grim realization that no amount of clever makeup magic could fix the effects of a sleepless night. She had tried to go to bed after Dylan left but had ended up climbing back out, throwing on work clothes and stripping wallpaper in the second bedroom until the early hours of the morning.

She did her best, even though she still didn't know how she would possibly face him. With any luck, she could persuade Eden she needed an assignment far, far away from him all day. Perhaps he would decide he'd rather serve jail time after all than be forced to spend more time with her.

So he didn't want her. She could deal with it. Hadn't she been trying to convince herself she was stronger than she'd always given herself credit for?

She sighed and returned her concealer to her makeup bag. After a little more magic, she decided she would do. Though the smudge of shadows remained under her eyes, nobody should be able to see that her heart was broken.

Finally ready, she shrugged into her coat and felt the weight of her phone in the pocket. Suddenly she remembered the call the night before that had ruined everything. She had never bothered to see who was calling.

Probably her mother trying to make plans for another day of shopping, in her oblivious way.

She thought about ignoring it but at the last moment decided to check the caller ID.

She scrolled through the numbers and saw it read Unknown. Whoever it was had left a message, though.

She retrieved the voice mail. As she listened, her eyes grew wider and her heart started to pound. She jotted down the message and let her excitement push away everything else—for now.

NONE OF HER exhilaration had faded by the time she hurried into the recreation center. If anything, the phone call she made after that message had only ratcheted things up a notch. She was giddy with nerves and excitement—okay, and lack of sleep, too.

She suddenly had a little insight into the way the town's Angel of Hope must feel, doing nice things for others. What a baffling concept—that when she was helping someone else, her own troubles and pain seemed more manageable. The sorrow was still there, simmering just under the surface, but she didn't have time to wallow in it. Not when she had a new purpose.

That pesky heartache had a way of pushing itself back into the forefront, though, especially when she walked into the recreation center and immediately spotted Dylan walking in from the other direction.

Fresh hurt and rejection sliced at her, throbbing and raw. She drew in a breath, pushing them down again, and forced a smile.

"You look like you're in a good mood," Dylan said.

"The *best* mood."

He looked a little taken aback. Had he expected her to come in all mopey and morose? If she hadn't had that amazing phone call, she might have been.

"So did you get a ten-million-dollar offer on Pearl's house?"

"No. Something even better."

"Oh?"

She had to tell somebody before she exploded from the excitement, and Dylan was the logical person. He had known her plans from the beginning. If not for his information leak about Fort Benning, she probably would never have been able to find what she needed so quickly.

She gave a quick look around to make sure they wouldn't be overheard, then leaned in close.

"I heard from Jenna Baldwin."

Instead of the reaction she'd hoped for, all she received from him was a blank look.

"You remember. Trey's girlfriend. The schoolteacher from Fort Benning."

"Ah."

"She was so happy I emailed her with my number. You should have *heard* the joy bubbling out of her. She's been trying to find him for months. And get this! She was able to get a last-minute flight and she'll be here tomorrow afternoon!"

He didn't respond for a long moment.

"Oh, Gen. What have you done?" he finally said.

She frowned at the note of dismay in his voice. "What do you mean, what have I done? This is the perfect outcome. She will come out here, he will see how very wrong he was to push her away and they'll live happily ever after."

"You are *completely* delusional."

After he'd put her through the misery of the night before, he actually had the nerve to call her names, to pop the little bubble of happiness that was the only thing keeping her upright and functioning right now?

"And you're the most cynical person I've ever met!" she retorted.

"Yeah, sorry if my life hasn't been all caviar and walks down the Champs-Elysées."

Five minutes ago, she had been so excited, filled with anticipation at doing something right for once. This was supposed to be her own little Christmas gift for a young man who desperately deserved to find some happiness. Now Dylan, Mr. You Don't Need My Garbage, was spitting all over her joy.

"You think my life is so perfect?" She wanted to smack him, but instead she settled for curling her hands into fists and folding them across her chest. "I'm broke. I've got no friends. My own family thinks I'm out of control. I'm serving community-service hours with *you,* for heaven's sake. Yeah, some rosy picture."

"It could be a hell of a lot worse."

"I know that. I'm not a complete idiot. What did I do that was so terrible? I thought I was doing something nice for two people who love each other. I even paid for half her airfare out of my emergency fund since the cost of the last-minute flight was out of a schoolteacher's budget."

"Oh, Gen."

Something warm and soft flitted across his expression but quickly disappeared again, replaced by that stony mask that filled her with self-doubt.

"You're right. It was a stupid idea. The whole thing will explode in my face and be one more screw-up in the loser column, along with maxing out my credit cards and being stupid enough to break the nose of the assistant district attorney."

To her horror, her voice wobbled a little on the last word. She swallowed hard and forced back the angry tears that threatened. Or maybe they weren't angry. Just more of the regular, garden-variety sad kind.

"Don't worry. I'll make sure Trey knows you had nothing to do with it."

"Nothing to do with what?"

She turned around to find the man in question had wheeled up to them without her hearing. Oh, Lord. What was she supposed to do now? She wanted to surprise him. If she told him Jenna was coming the next day, it would ruin everything, but she couldn't think of a way to backtrack.

To her astonishment, Dylan—Mr. Cynical himself—came to her rescue.

"You caught me. The plan is to go out on the snowmobiles this morning. They've got a couple with hand controls and I was trying to arrange things so you could have the most powerful one, since I remembered you were talking about how much you liked to race motorcycles before you were injured."

He had her six. Wasn't that what she'd heard the veterans call it when somebody watched their back? Though he objected to what she wanted to do, he still stepped up to help her out.

Was it any wonder she was crazy in love with him?

"Wow," Trey said, surprise in his voice. "Thanks, man. That's really nice of you."

"Yeah, that's me," Dylan drawled. "I'm nothing if not nice."

He gave Genevieve a hard sort of look. To her relief, Eden and Mack and the others joined them and the moment was gone.

BY THE END of the day, she was exhausted from trying not to burst with nerves.

Every time she came within range of Trey, she had to think of a hundred different distractions to keep from accidentally blurting out the news about Jenna.

Whenever she was near *Dylan* she had to do the same thing—mostly to keep from bursting into tears.

At least she didn't have to add Charlotte into the mix. She hadn't seen Dylan's sister since ditching her at the bookstore the night before. Over lunch, she had heard Spence tell Chelsea that Charlotte had too much work at her candy store and probably wouldn't make it until the dinner meal.

To her relief, Eden must have sensed some of her anxiety. Instead of sending her out while the families went cross-country skiing again, she assigned Gen to work inside the recreation center—away from everyone else, thank heavens. She was to finalize arrangements for the closing reception to be held Sunday night and work her decorating magic on wrapping some farewell gifts the rest of the staff had prepared for the guests and their families.

Everyone was leaving Monday. So much could happen between now and then. She really hoped the outcome of her actions would be a positive one.

She was just tying the ribbon on the last gift—another outfit for cute little Claudia Brooks's doll Penelope—when Spencer Gregory walked into the room off the lobby she had commandeered.

He was so movie-star gorgeous, it always took her by surprise. Smokin' Hot Spence Gregory. During her time working for A Warrior's Hope, she had come to realize he seemed completely unaware of it.

"Here you are. Looks like Eden has you working hard."

She smiled. "She's good at keeping me busy. I'm nearly done. Is everyone back?"

"Not yet. Mac called and said they were heading this way."

"I need to wrap this up—so to speak—and hurry to hide everything."

"We can stow them in my office."

"Okay. I'm almost done here."

"Need help?"

"No. I think I've got it."

He leaned against the table to watch, and she had to wonder again why, as great-looking as he was, he didn't make her stomach jump with nerves like Dylan did.

"So I was just looking through the paper work and realized you and Dylan have made a lot of headway on your community-service hours this week. A few more of these ten-hour days and you'll have finished your obligation to the court and to us."

"I guess that's right."

"I imagine you'll be glad to see the last of this place."

She should be excited to move forward and devote her attention to finishing the work on Grandma Pearl's house. Instead, she found herself unaccountably depressed. She had enjoyed her time here, more than she ever expected.

"It hasn't been bad. Actually, I've really liked working here. Thank you for giving me the chance."

He looked surprised. "You're welcome."

Though she had been in Paris, she knew Spence had come here in the midst of scandal, his name blackened by his wife's untimely death, by his own prescription-drug addiction, by a drug-trafficking scandal that had turned out to be a frame-up.

His life had changed radically since coming back to his hometown.

"Can I just tell you," she said on impulse, "I think it's a wonderful thing you've done here. A Warrior's Hope is a fantastic program. You're changing lives here. This morning I watched Ricardo Torres on the snowmobile with his wife, and they were having a wonderful time together. The first day they arrived, it seemed as if she barely spoke to him. And it was so great yesterday to watch Trey and Joe racing each other down the mountain on their adapted ski seats. Really, the whole program is quite remarkable."

"Thank you, Genevieve. I appreciate you saying that." He gave a rueful smile. "I wish you could convince your family. Your father, especially. Did you know he's trying to pull our conditional use permit?"

She stared. "I'm sure that's not true."

"According to Mayor Beaumont, the Hope's Crossing recreation center should be used only by the residents of Hope's Crossing, not by any Tom, Dick or Harry with a hard-luck story."

Oh, sometimes her father made her *crazy*. "I'm sorry. I'll try to talk to him, but I should warn you, I don't carry a lot of credit with my family right now."

"I'm not too worried about the whole thing, especially since we've got Harry Lange on our side. He and Mary Ella are two of our biggest donors. Your dad might complain about our mission here and make noises about trying to shut us down but I doubt he'll openly defy Harry."

"No. He won't."

He smiled at her, and again she wondered why she didn't feel the same tingle as she did when a certain wounded ranger gifted her with his rare smile.

"So Charlotte told me what happened at the book-club party last night."

She had almost forgotten Ruth Tatum, with everything else on her worry plate right now. Now that he mentioned it again, her face burned with remembered mortification. She avoided his gaze, focusing instead on tying the last bow on the present and arranging a little angel ornament in the folds.

"Not one of my happier moments."

"For the record, Charlotte was very upset about it. She wanted to rush right over to your house to make sure you were all right, but then Dylan called her and yelled at her for letting Ruth mouth off about you like that."

Oh. He did that? The little snowmen on the wrapping present seemed to blur and quiver as her eyes filled. She quickly blinked the tears away, wondering what his sister thought about her running to Dylan from the bookstore—and about Dylan leaping to her defense.

"None of it was Charlotte's fault. I never blamed her."

"She still felt terrible. Everyone did. You shouldn't worry about Ruth Tatum, you know."

She set the present on the pile with the others. "Yes. So everyone tells me."

"Can I share a little wisdom learned from hard experience?"

"I... Of course."

"I know what it is to be the object of people's dislike. Trust me. I've had more than enough experience coping with misconceptions."

She could only imagine how difficult it must have been to live under a cloud someone else had created. He had endured far worse smears to his reputation than a miserable mistake of an engagement.

The difference was, the allegations against him had been false, while she really *had* been a cold bitch.

"When things were at their worst for me, I learned to just keep my head up and do my best to hold on to my pride and my dignity."

"Thank you for the advice. I appreciate it."

"You're welcome. Are you ready to start hiding things away?"

"I guess we need to, unless we want everybody to find their presents early this year."

He picked up an armload and started down the hall. She followed him with her own arms full.

"For the record," she said as they returned for another load, "I'm glad things worked out for you the way they did. You and Charlotte seem very happy together."

His smile was bright, filled with such joy that sharp envy pinched at her. "We are. In fact, we're getting married next summer."

"Congratulations."

She meant the words. She liked and admired Charlotte and could tell she already loved Spence's daughter, Peyton.

For a moment, she was tempted to tell him about Trey's ex-fiancée flying in the next day, but Dylan had filled her with such anxious doubts she decided to keep her mouth shut for now.

CHAPTER SEVENTEEN

BY NOON THE next day, she was a nervous wreck. Throughout the morning, Jenna had been texting her to update her on her travel progress.

In Chicago.
Ready to board connection.
Landed in Denver.
Renting a car.

She had texted back travel instructions and encouraging words, but now that the critical moment was approaching she could hardly breathe around her anxiety.

She should have texted Jenna to board the next plane back to Atlanta and forget the whole thing.

She couldn't bear this suspense. She really hoped Trey would be thrilled to see the woman he loved, would realize his mistake in pushing her away. She tried to focus on their conversation about Jenna that had started the whole thing. He had spoken of her with such tender emotion—and she had seen the loneliness in his eyes as he looked at all these other family units.

That was what she hoped would happen.

At the same time, she was very much afraid he would be furious and find the whole thing a cruel scheme aimed at snarling his life.

"How much longer before the fireworks show?" Dylan asked when they walked inside the recreation center for the lunch catered by one of Brodie Thorne's restaurants.

They hadn't spoken privately since the morning before and simply the sound of his voice filled her with longing. She firmly tamped it down.

"I hope there won't be fireworks, except the romantic kind."

He made a gruff, cynical sound, sending ripples of worry through her all over again.

"It won't be long now. She's about fifteen miles outside of town."

"Funny. For someone trying so hard to earn her cupid wings, you don't sound very excited."

She gave a weak smile, wishing with all her heart she had never sent that email. "Life was much safer when I only cared about myself."

To her astonishment, he reached out and took her fingers in his. "You know anything about physics?"

"Not really. I think I skipped that class for cheerleading practice."

He probably had no idea how much courage his slight smile gave her. "I'm sure you've heard Newton's first law that an object in motion tends to stay in motion."

"I did pick that up somewhere. Again, maybe cheerleading practice. And an object at rest tends to stay at rest, right? In other words, I should have just minded my own business and left well enough alone."

"It's too late for regrets, Gen. You set the boulder tumbling down the hill. Now you just have to wait and see which way it's going to land."

"What if it crashes onto my head?"

He squeezed her fingers, then to her further astonishment, he reached out and tucked a strand of hair behind her ear and gave her a heartbreaking smile. "Then you can fit right in with the rest of us bruised and broken souls."

She didn't know how to convince him she didn't see him as broken. He was a good man. Rough around the edges, maybe, and certainly cynical. But she had watched him this week with the others. Though he claimed in the beginning he wanted nothing to do with A Warrior's Hope, she had seen him exhibit amazing patience to everyone coming through the program. He was playful with the children, kind to the spouses and parents and understanding with the wounded veterans.

She wanted to tell him all the things she had discovered about him but this didn't seem the moment, not when she knew Jenna Baldwin would arrive any moment.

"He's going to hate me, isn't he?"

He sighed. "Maybe. Not much we can do about that now. But even if he's furious, I hope some part of him understands you thought you were doing something in his best interest."

He paused. "It's too late now, anyway."

She followed the direction of his gaze to find a young woman standing in the doorway with a hopeful, nervous expression on her pretty, sweet-natured face.

Dylan squeezed her fingers again. "Guess it's showtime."

In thirty-six hours of fretting, why hadn't she planned ahead enough to arrange a more private reunion between the two of them?

She still could. Trey had gone outside with a couple of others to photograph the bull moose that had lately taken to hanging around the recreation center, browsing on whatever water plants were still alive in the icy river.

She could head Jenna off, move her to a more private setting and then bring Trey in when he returned.

Amazing, how calming a plan could be.

She hurried over to greet the woman. To her surprise, Dylan walked over with her, despite his objections to the whole thing. She wanted to hug him, deeply grateful for his strength and support.

"Hi. You must be Jenna. I'm Genevieve Beaumont. This is Dylan Caine."

Jenna was even prettier up close, delicate and lovely, though her features were strained and she had circles under her eyes that looked as if they had been there for some time.

She twisted her fingers together. "Hello." She smiled nervously, looking fresh and sweet—all the things Genevieve wasn't. Why on earth had Trey ever said she reminded him of this gentle-looking woman? Yes, their hair color was the same and they both had the same blue eyes, but that was the only resemblance.

On impulse, she reached in and hugged the woman. After the past thirty-six hours, she felt as if she knew her well. Gen was certainly invested in the success of this little endeavor, financially and emotionally.

"How was your flight?"

Jenna gave a shaky little laugh. "To be honest, I have no idea. I feel like I've been in a daze since I spoke with you yesterday. Everything has happened so quickly. I... How can I ever thank you?"

Don't thank me yet.

"Don't worry about that."

Jenna craned her neck to look around the room, where Elena and Ricardo and the Augustines were still eating lunch. "Is he here? I don't see him."

Dylan spoke up. "He just stepped out a moment ago. We've had a moose wandering around the grounds for the last few days and several guests went out to take pictures of it down in the river. He should be up any minute now. Can I take your coat? Would you like something to eat or drink?"

Warmth stirred in her chest at this sweet, noncynical side of Dylan he showed so rarely.

"I... Thank you." She handed him her coat. "Some water would be good. I'm afraid I couldn't eat breakfast or lunch. I've been so nervous all day, I haven't been able to swallow anything."

"I'll be right back."

Dylan walked over to the table where the food had been set out buffet-style.

"I'm so anxious, I can hardly breathe."

"Everything will be fine. You'll see." She had nothing to base that particular statement on except hope, which seemed pretty flimsy right now, all things considered.

"What if he doesn't want me here? What if he hasn't reconsidered anything and still won't give me a chance?"

Genevieve shared the very same fear, but she couldn't say that now, in front of this young woman who seemed so pale, fragile as an antique blown-glass ornament.

"Then he will be making a terrible mistake."

Jenna rested a hand on her arm. "Thank you for this, Genevieve. Everything you've done."

She thought about her life merely a month ago in Paris, shopping and decorating her apartment, sewing what she wanted, visiting with friends. All the things she thought were so important. That time seemed a world away—and not merely geographically.

One afternoon when she had nothing else to do, she had wandered into a gallery in the Sixth Arrondissement and had watched an artist create an exquisite papier-mâché sculpture, taking a simple wire-mesh frame and adding strip after strip of adhesive-soaked paper until the result was a thing of substance and beauty.

She wanted to think she was like that sculpture, in the process of adding her own layers upon layers. She was a different person than she had been a month ago. She wouldn't go back. She couldn't.

"You're welcome," she murmured, giving Jenna another hug.

Dylan returned with the water glass. "Why don't we see if we can find a quiet room somewhere for Jenna to wait, away from the crowd?"

"Yes. I think the office next to Spencer's should be available."

Gen started for the door. Before she made it more than a few feet, she heard voices and laughter in the hall and realized they had acted too late. Everyone was returning from outside. She could hear Trey's voice and realized how horribly wrong this could all go, throwing Jenna at him like this, without warning, in front of everyone.

She wanted to stand in front of the woman, to shield her from view and from Trey's wrath.

Pam and her, fiancé, Kevin walked in first, holding hands, as usual. Joe and Tonya came in next, Claudia riding in her favorite place of honor on her father's lap and the quieter Marisol walking beside her mother behind the wheelchair.

Behind them came Trey, wheeling in with his usual cheerful smile.

Gen was aware of Jenna's sharp inhale beside her. Out of the corner of her gaze, she caught the other woman's expression: stark longing and love and sorrow, all jumbled together.

She could certainly relate to that.

He hadn't noticed them yet. "Man, I've never seen a moose that close before. I can't believe the size of that guy. I really thought he was going to come after you."

Tonya snorted. "Are you kidding? He wasn't even close. I was still at least thirty feet away from those big antlers. Anyway, you should see how fast I can move when I have to."

Joe's laugh was warm and infectious. "She's not kidding. Just a few weeks ago, Marisol wandered off for a minute at Walmart. T was a blur racing through those aisles. Found her in the book section, of course. Where else?"

His voice trailed off when he must have realized Trey wasn't listening to him—he was staring at the woman standing numbly beside Genevieve.

He wheeled a few feet in their direction, almost as if he couldn't help himself, then stopped when he was still several yards away.

"Jenna! What is this?"

Genevieve's heart was in her throat. She couldn't read anything on his features—not pleasure or anger or anything. It was like staring at that papier-mâché sculpture.

Jenna gave him a wobbly smile. "Hi, Trey. You look great."

"You look...here."

"Yes." She swallowed. "Merry Christmas."

"*Why* are you here?"

Since he hadn't moved beyond those first few feet, Jenna walked toward him, her hands still twisted together in front of her.

No one else but Dylan knew exactly what was going on, but somehow they must have sensed something significant was happening. Everyone fell silent, even the little ones.

Trey was usually so affable and good-natured. Just now, though, his jaw was tight, his mouth unsmiling. He looked every inch the hardened soldier.

"Why are you here?" he repeated, his voice harsh.

"To see you," she whispered. "To... I don't know, make you see sense."

"Sense." The word came out hard, sharp, like a rock striking a tree trunk.

"Yes." She moved forward and spoke softly. "I missed you, Trey. So much."

For just a moment, he gazed at her with raw yearning before his expression shuttered again.

"How did you find me?" he demanded.

She didn't answer, but her gaze subtly shifted to Genevieve before turning back to Trey. "Does it matter? I had to come. Sunday was supposed to be our wedding day. December twenty-second. I still have all the invitations."

"You should have burned them," he said harshly.

Her chin trembled a little, but she quickly firmed it again, earning even more of Genevieve's respect. She wasn't sure she could face a man who had dumped her, especially in front of nearly a dozen witnesses.

"You can run away all you want, Trey Evans, but it won't change the fact that I still love you, no matter what. I still want to marry you, to start a family with you."

His expression turned even more bleak and wintry, if possible. He shifted to Genevieve.

"You did this, didn't you? This is why you've been so jumpy the last few days. What the hell? You had no right."

"I know." The audacity of her actions was indefensible, and she was suddenly miserable, horrified at what she had set in motion and the additional pain she might have caused the two of them. "It's just...you were all alone. I thought... I wanted to make you happy. A wonderful Christmas gift."

"More like a Christmas nightmare," he growled.

"Why don't we take this somewhere a little more private where we can talk," Dylan suggested.

"Good idea." Spencer Gregory had come into the room in the middle of the drama. He looked baffled but had obviously picked up enough hints to guess at what might be going on—at least enough to give Genevieve a *you're-in-big-trouble* sort of look.

"What's the point? I don't have one damn thing to talk about. I didn't ask for this. Once, Jenna and I were engaged. We broke things off. End of story."

"*You* broke things off and left without even telling me where you were. You didn't even give me a chance to change your mind—you just ran away."

"I didn't run away. I was transferring to the rehab facility in San Antonio. And what would have been the point of dragging things out? You *can't* change my mind."

"Trey—"

"I don't want to marry you. Is that clear enough for you? I'm sorry you came all this way from Georgia, but it was a wasted trip. I don't want to marry you. I don't love you. I don't know if I ever loved you."

Jenna swayed a little, color leaching from her features. "I...see."

Genevieve suddenly remembered the other woman hadn't eaten. She grabbed for her elbow and felt the vibration of her trembling through her sweater and blouse.

Her heart ached at what she had done. Dylan was watching the whole thing with a resigned expression, as if everything had happened just as he'd expected.

She thought of how hard he was pushing her away, just like Trey pushed Jenna away. She wasn't as brave as Jenna. Her feelings were so new, so raw, she hadn't confessed them to Dylan. She probably never would—but she suddenly knew that if she ever did, Dylan would react just as Trey had, lashing out from a place of pain and loss instead of seeing hope and possibilities.

Even as her heart spasmed painfully in her chest, she was furious suddenly, livid with both of them. She had worked too hard for this, spending hours she didn't have on the internet trying to find Jenna and then money she *also* didn't have to fly her here.

It wasn't fair. It wasn't fair and it wasn't right.

"You are a liar, Trey Evans," she burst out, aware of Jenna's trembling fingers in hers. "I heard the yearning in your voice the day you told me about her. How can you deny it? I saw all the emotions in your eyes you now claim you don't feel. You are *lying*. Your feelings haven't changed. You know they haven't. I know they haven't. *Jenna* knows they haven't! I can't believe a man who earned two Purple Hearts in Afghanistan could be such a damn coward."

DYLAN HEARD ALL the assembled veterans give a collective intake of breath. None of them would take one of their own being called a coward sitting down.

He should have pushed to take this somewhere private when he'd had the chance—though how the hell he had let her twist him up in this whole thing was still a mystery.

He stepped up and laid a hand on her arm. "Gen, that's enough."

She whirled on him. "Shut up, Dylan. You're as bad as he is!"

He blinked at that, not sure how this had become about him.

"Come on, everyone," Spence said with sudden firmness. "Let's give them some space to work this out."

In the few minutes it took to usher everyone out, Genevieve marched right up to Trey.

"I'm sure I know what you're thinking," she said when everyone except the four of them had left.

He aimed a stare at her so hard it would cut through concertina wire. "Oh, I doubt that."

"You think she can't want you now. That you're somehow...inadequate."

Dylan froze, wondering just who she was talking to now.

Trey's gaze narrowed. "Look, I appreciate that you thought you had good intentions, but you don't know anything about this."

She darted a quick look at Dylan then jerked her gaze back to Trey. "Maybe not. But I know how lucky the two of you are. Do you have any idea how many women would kill to have the man they love talk about them the way you did when you told me about Jenna? I know you still love her. I heard it in every word you said to me. She must know it, too, or she would never have found the courage to follow you here."

Her voice softened and she touched his arm. "If I were the woman you loved, I would have fought for you, too."

"It's not that easy."

She gave a ragged-sounding laugh. "I'm sure it's not." She paused. "And while I do think you love her, I have to ask myself how you can, when you think so little of her."

"I don't," he protested.

"You think she's weak."

He raked a hand through his hair, genuine confusion on his features. "Where the hell did you get that crazy idea?"

"From you. From your actions. You pushed her away because you must think she's so fragile she can't handle a little imperfection. You seem to think she'll melt with horror if she has to look at some scars."

"I've got more than a few scars! Look at me! I can't walk. Did you happen to notice that little fact? When I realized I wasn't going to miraculously get the strength back, I knew I couldn't go ahead with the wedding. How the hell can I provide for her, can I be any kind of decent father to all the kids she wants? I can't give her what she needs!"

The anguished words resonated inside Dylan. Hell, he had spent the whole summer and fall sitting around at his cabin in Snowflake Canyon, drinking and wallowing in his self-pity, thinking of all he had lost and the options no longer available to him.

Genevieve straightened, fiery, determined…and so lovely she took his breath away.

"Are you really going to throw away something beautiful and good because you're afraid she will reject you later? Jenna loves you. She came all this way to tell you. After she stayed with you those long months in the hospital, don't you think you owe her the courtesy of at least listening to what she has to say?"

Trey said nothing, his hands clenching and unclenching the wheels of his chair. His expression, though, was one of stark longing.

Jenna no longer looked as if she were close to toppling over. Color had returned to her cheeks while Genevieve spoke, and now she stepped forward on Trey's other side.

"Oh, you foolish man. I thought I loved you two years ago when I agreed to marry you. I thought I loved you when you left overseas on another deployment. I thought I would die when they told me you were injured, that you might not survive. This last year, watching your strength and courage as you faced this hardest of challenges has only made me love you more than I ever imagined possible."

She touched his face with a tenderness that made Dylan's chest ache. "Please. Don't push me away again, Trey. I don't think I can bear it."

Trey made a sound, a gasp or a sob, Dylan wasn't sure, but after a long, tense pause, he closed his eyes and pressed his face into her hand.

As Jenna leaned down to kiss him, Dylan grabbed Genevieve by the crook of her elbow and yanked her out of the room.

"Well?" Tonya Brooks seized on Genevieve the moment they joined the others out in the lobby.

She gave a strained smile. "They were kissing when we left, but I think it's too soon to say."

The wives all gave a little cheer. Tonya grinned and hugged Genevieve, and Pam and Elena hugged each other and then Genevieve, too.

Women.

Gen wasn't the only one wiping away tears. Nobody would ever accuse her of being a cold bitch if they could see the soft, happy light in her eyes as she shared in the other women's excitement.

Spence, on the other hand, didn't look nearly as happy at this new development.

"What just happened here?" he demanded, in the same tone of voice he probably used against rookies on the ball field making stupid mistakes.

Guilt flashed in Genevieve's eyes and she nibbled her lips. "Um, a sort of... Christmas miracle, I hope."

"And what part did you play in this *Christmas miracle?*"

She fidgeted. "Um, not much, really. Okay, a little. Trey mentioned his former fiancée to me and the circumstances of their breakup, and I...sort of tracked her down and invited her here."

And helped pay for her airfare, but Dylan decided not to mention that little fact to Spence, who didn't look very happy about what he *did* know.

"We're running a recreational therapy program here, not a matchmaking service."

"I know."

"I hope you haven't seriously compromised the integrity of A Warrior's Hope. We're trying to build a reputation here. What if word gets out that we take personal information our clients offer and interfere in things that are none of our damn business? You completely overstepped."

She looked stricken. "I didn't think. I just wanted to help Trey. He seemed so lonely. Everyone else has a support system but he has...no one."

"This isn't some happy-ever-after fairy tale, where the prince and princess ride off on a white charger to their gleaming castle. These men have been through hell. You have no idea what the climb back is like. As somebody once told me, you can't just step into their lives and think you can sprinkle fairy dust and make everything better."

Dylan gave a little inward wince, remembering he had said those very words to Spence another lifetime ago, it seemed, when Spence had first come up with the idea for A Warrior's Hope.

"You and I both know how important reputation is, Genevieve, and how hard it is to overcome a bad one."

"I'm sorry," she whispered. She looked devastated, and he hated seeing her little moment of triumph—premature though it might be—dissolve into despair.

"She thought she was helping him, Spence," he spoke up.

She sent him a shocked look, as if she'd never expected him to step up and defend her. Spence looked just as surprised.

"No doubt. Her motives aren't in question. It's the outcome I find concerning."

"I know. I'm sorry. I... I didn't think."

Before Spence could respond, Eden came in from outside. "The sleighs just pulled up. Is everybody ready to go for a ride up to see the elk herd?"

The cute little Brooks girls squealed with excitement and hugged each other.

"Elk and moose and a little romantic drama," their mother said. "What else could we possibly need?"

"Our coats are still in there." Quiet Elena pointed to the closed door of the reception room. "Do you think we dare go get them?"

"Why wouldn't you?" Eden, who had just missed the whole thing, asked.

"It's a long story," Spence said. "I'll explain it to you while we load up the sleighs."

Elena tentatively poked her head through the door and then turned back to face the others. "They're not here anymore. They must have gone out the other door."

"Who?" Eden asked.

"Trey and Jenna."

"Oh, that must be the woman I saw him with. I just bumped into them outside, heading toward the cabins. He said he would skip the afternoon activities and see everyone tonight."

A couple of the women giggled, and Tonya gave a throaty, knowing sort of laugh that earned her an affectionate pinch from Joe.

As he watched their interaction and thought about Trey and Jenna and what had just happened, Dylan was aware of a sharp spike of envy—and the niggling fear that he was being an even bigger fool.

CHAPTER EIGHTEEN

ALL AFTERNOON, while they rode on horse-drawn sleighs on a groomed fire road to a high pasture where a large herd of elk grazed, Genevieve fretted.

She hoped she had done the right thing. It looked as if Jenna and Trey would be able to mend their differences, though she certainly knew one kiss didn't necessarily equate to a happy ending.

The lecture from Spence stung, in part because she knew she had earned it. Her impulsive, heedless actions could have damaged two people irreparably—not to mention stained the reputation of A Warrior's Hope.

Dylan seemed to be avoiding her, especially after her outburst that afternoon. He deliberately chose a seat in one of the other sleighs, and when they climbed out to take pictures of the elk from a safe distance, he didn't approach her.

She tried to tell herself his distance didn't hurt but it was a fairly useless lie.

Eden sat next to her on the way back to the recreation center. As soon as the horses headed down the mountainside, bells jingling, she turned to Gen and started interrogating her.

"Okay, I'm getting all kinds of crazy stories about what I missed this afternoon with Trey. Apparently you're the one who knows the whole skinny. What's going on? Who is she?"

"Her name is Jenna Baldwin. She's a schoolteacher in Georgia. They met at church and were engaged until a couple of months ago. Sunday was supposed to be their wedding day."

"No shit?" Eden exclaimed, then winced. "Sorry. I'm trying not to swear. I mean, you're kidding."

"I'm not."

"You said they *were* engaged. What happened?"

"Trey broke things off just before he was transferred to another rehab facility in Texas. I guess he thought Genevieve deserved better than a wounded veteran. She didn't know where he was. He mentioned her to me and I took a little initiative—inappropriately, I realize now—and tracked her down."

"How did you find her?"

Without implicating Dylan, she explained about isolating Jenna's location to Georgia and how she had searched web databases until she found her and then had emailed her.

"It was a thoughtless thing to do. I feel terrible that I've risked the reputation of A Warrior's Hope. It wasn't my intention."

"Wow! That must have taken guts—for you to look for her that way and for this Jenna person to come after him."

"You don't think I overstepped?"

"Well, yeah. But if it works, and you make two people happy, then it was worth it, wasn't it? I mean, what can Spence do? Fire you? Duh. You're a volunteer."

Her surprised laugh turned to stunned disbelief at Eden's next words. "You've done a really great job here, Genevieve," the director said. "Are you sure you wouldn't like to stay on after you finish your hours? We would love to have someone on our volunteer staff with your event-planning skills and your flair for design."

If her circumstances were different, she would jump at the chance, she realized. This past week had been...life-altering.

She was flattered and humbled by the request, even as she knew she had to refuse. "I'm sorry, but I won't be in town much longer. I'm trying to fix up my grandmother's house to sell it. As soon as I do, I'll be heading back to France. I have an apartment there and friends and...well, I'm starting a business."

"I'm sorry to hear that. Happy for you, if this is what you want, I mean, but sorry for us. We'll miss you."

"I'll miss all of you, too," Genevieve said quietly.

"Tell me about your grandmother's house. I'm in the market for something here in town. I've been living in a condo with a short-term lease until I find something I like."

"You don't want this house. It's horrible. Dark, outdated. The location is really good but the house needs so much more work than I'll be able to finish."

"I don't care about the inside, only the bones. I love a challenge. Maybe I could swing by after dinner and take a look. I would love to sneak in and grab something that's not on the market yet."

The faster she sold the house, the less work she would have to finish. She should be thrilled, but she couldn't help a sharp pang at the idea of leaving.

"Sure. Come by tonight. That will be great. You'll have to look past the remodeling projects. I'm afraid it's a bit of a mess."

"My last house in Seattle was definitely a fixer-upper. I can deal with mess."

When they returned to the recreation center, the plan was to split the group into two, one to go ice fishing in the reservoir, the other to skate on the frozen pond in a meadow near the recreation-center parking lot. Eden assigned her to the skating group, much to her relief, so she spent the rest of the afternoon tying laces and handing out hot cocoa.

Dylan went with the ice-fishing group, managing to avoid her for a few more hours without much effort on his part.

Dinner was to be catered by Alex McKnight's restaurant again. She was starving, she realized, as, like Jenna, she had been too nervous that morning to eat much.

When they came in from outside, cheeks rosy, Genevieve found Jenna and Trey in the two-story lobby of the recreation center. He was in his wheelchair and Jenna sat on a chair next to him, though she might as well have been sitting on his lap. They were holding hands, brushing shoulders, touching arms.

Her nerves immediately settled. The two appeared radiant. For all his affable good nature during the past week, she now realized she hadn't seen Trey truly happy until now. All the lonely edges seemed to have been smoothed away.

Jenna rushed to her first and wrapped her arms around Genevieve, promptly bursting into tears. "I can't thank you enough for what you've done. You have no idea."

"Um. You're welcome." She patted the other woman's back, somewhat helpless as Jenna sobbed against her.

"I'm sorry. I'm just so happy."

"Are you?"

"Beyond anything I imagined. I can't believe two days ago I felt as if all the color and joy had been sucked out of my life and now it's all back, brighter than ever."

"I'm glad."

Trey wheeled forward and took her hand. "Thank you," he murmured.

"You're welcome."

"You all might as well be the first to know," he said to the group, strangers brought together by circumstances, who had bonded over the past week. "We're getting married after all, just as soon as we can arrange it."

Marisol clapped her hands, and beside her, Claudia jumped up and down. "Married! I want to see them get married!"

Jenna and Trey exchanged looks. "Well, if we can arrange it on such short notice, we were thinking of trying to make it into the courthouse to find a justice of the peace before we leave town."

Of all the unlikely supporters, given how upset he had been a few hours earlier, Spencer Gregory stepped forward. "Why not get married here? We've already had a few people ask to use the facility for that reason. The reception room where we've been sharing meals would be a beautiful place for a wedding, with the fireplace and the windows overlooking the river and the mountains."

"Yes!" Genevieve exclaimed, her mind already racing with ideas. "We could give you *such* a spectacular wedding. Oh, please. Will you let me do this?"

"You've already done so much," Jenna protested.

"Maybe, but I want to do this, too. You don't know this about me, but I'm kind of an expert at planning weddings. I worked on my own for two years."

They exchanged surprised looks. "I had no idea you were married," Trey said.

"I'm not," she said matter-of-factly. "I dumped the cheating bum a few weeks before the wedding. But trust me, it would have been spectacular."

Jenna smiled, even as she looked a little overwhelmed. "I don't want to be a bother. We can just go to the courthouse."

"No bother. I want to do this for you and Trey."

"You have to let us help," Marie Augustine insisted.

"Yes," agreed Whitney Reid. "I work in a florist shop back home. If I can get my hands on some supplies, I would love to do your bouquet."

"Can I be in your marriage?" Marisol asked shyly.

Jenna was obviously a very good teacher, judging by the patient way she knelt down and spoke with the little girl. "Of course you can be in our wedding, darling, as long as your mom and dad don't mind."

"How soon can we arrange it?" Spence asked Genevieve. "Everybody's supposed to go home Monday afternoon."

"Can I have until Sunday evening? That was supposed to be their wedding day anyway."

Jenna burst into tears again. "That would be so perfect. Oh, thank you."

She noticed Dylan hadn't reacted to the joyful announcement. He had retreated to the windows and was looking out, his features as remote as the snowy landscape.

Oh, she did not want to do this.

Genevieve parked as close as she could to String Fever, in the small public lot a block over. On this, the last Saturday before Christmas, downtown Hope's Crossing was clogged with ski-resort tourists and locals trying to squeeze in a little last-minute shopping.

Everywhere she looked she saw people bustling around with packages, bags of takeout from the restaurants around, even a couple of guys carrying a large wrapped parcel in the shape of a bicycle, probably from Mike's Bikes.

She had too much to do to sit in her car here all morning watching everyone else hurry about, but she couldn't seem to make herself move, could only gaze out at the flakes of snow landing on her windshield.

She didn't want to climb out of the warmth into that cold, especially because she expected she would be in for an even colder reception when she reached her destination, String Fever—Claire McKnight's bead store.

She had been beastly to Claire during her lengthy engagement to Sawyer. That was the bald truth of it. She had been her most exacting, her haughty, patronizing worst. She had hired Claire to hand-bead the bodice of her designer wedding gown and had demanded perfection from the outset.

When her original gown had been vandalized through no fault of Claire's, Genevieve had thrown a spoiled, immature tantrum, quite certain Sawyer wouldn't want to marry her now and everything would be ruined.

The memory of it made her cringe. Claire, and everyone else in town, had been mourning the death of a teenage girl—Maura Lange's youngest daughter—and the severe injuries of Brodie Thorne's daughter Taryn.

In retrospect, Genevieve couldn't believe she had ever been so narcissistic that she had even *cared* about her stupid wedding gown in the midst of such tragedy—especially considering her own younger brother, Charlie, had been driving the vehicle in the accident that had killed Layla and injured Taryn.

Oh, how she wished she could go back and relive that time from the perspective she had now. Of course, if that were possible, she never would have been stupid enough to think she could marry Sawyer Danforth.

A sudden rap on the window startled a squeak out of her. She shifted and saw Dylan standing on the other side of the glass and metal, his gaze concerned.

He looked gorgeous with snow melting in his brown hair. He had trimmed away almost all the shagginess—for the wedding? she wondered. The cut made him look younger, somehow.

He continued watching her with concern and she finally sighed, knowing she was going to have to face him eventually, and hit the power button on the window.

"Everything okay? I saw you pull in. You've been sitting here for a couple of minutes without moving."

In the corner of the lot, she spied his beat-up old pickup truck. She must have been too distracted when she arrived to notice it.

"What are you doing here? Why aren't you with A Warrior's Hope?"

"I had a couple of errands to run, so Eden and Mac agreed to let me have a few hours. I'm heading back there. What about you? Why are you just sitting in your car?"

"Trying to gather my nerve."

"Yeah, the tourist traffic can be a real bear on winter Saturdays in Hope's Crossing."

Despite her angst, she managed a smile at his dry tone. "True. I wish that were all that is worrying me. I have to walk over to the bead store and see if I can ransom my wedding dress."

He leaned back a little on his heels. "Something tells me there's a very interesting story behind that particular statement."

With a sigh, she climbed out of her SUV. She didn't want to tell him, as it didn't show her in a very good light.

"I had this really gorgeous wedding dress created by this up-and-coming designer in New York," she finally said. "I wanted hand-beaded accents on it and I wanted Claire McKnight to do them for me. She did a beautiful job, twice, which is a long story in itself. After things fell apart with Sawyer, I never wanted to see that dress again. I told her so."

"She still has it?"

She nodded. "I owe her the last payment for the work she did. I was terrible to Claire. Rude and condescending. I don't want to face her, especially since I am going there to eat crow."

"How?"

She reached into her purse—another she had sewn—and pulled out the envelope that contained the last of her cash, after helping with Jenna's plane ticket.

"This is most of what I still owe her, short a few hundred dollars. I hope to pay her the rest when I sell the house. I should have paid her a long time ago. I know. You don't have to lecture me."

He raised his eyebrow. "I didn't say a word."

"The truth is, I really didn't want to see the stupid dress again. I guess I was hoping my parents would take care of it while I was in Europe but they can be passive-aggressive about some things. I guess this happened to be one of those times."

"Why do you want the dress now?"

She gazed at the mountains. Why had she never noticed how strong and commanding they looked when they were covered with snow? She had always considered them a prison, keeping her in boring little Hope's Crossing, but that was yet another perspective that had shifted.

"It's a beautiful gown," she answered. "Someone should wear it. I want to give it to Jenna. She deserves something magical when she and Trey get married tomorrow."

For only an instant, she thought she saw something in his eye—a spark, a light, warmth that hadn't been there before—but then it vanished, probably a trick of the shifting clouds.

"Right now I need to go to String Fever and face Claire," she said glumly. "I would rather be scrubbing toilets at The Speckled Lizard."

"That can probably be arranged. Pat would probably love to put you to work."

"Figure of speech. I have to go to the bead store. I just don't want to."

"Want some company?" He looked as shocked by the offer as she was.

"You? Seriously?"

He shrugged and held up a bag in his hand. "I bought the last thing on my list and I've got an hour before I'm supposed to be back at the recreation center. I've got time."

Oh, she was turning into such a baby if one tiny gesture of kindness could make her want to burst into tears. "That would be wonderful. I know I shouldn't be so cowardly."

"You made it this far, didn't you? Now all you've got are a few more steps. Anyway, as far as I'm concerned, there's no shame in being afraid. Only in letting the fear win."

Like you're doing by pushing me away? she wanted to say. But he had offered to help her and she didn't want to start a fight.

After he put his parcels in his truck, they started off in the direction of the bead store, sidestepping slushy spots and piles of snow. Usually when they walked together, Dylan seemed determined that she walk on his right side. This time, she was equally determined not to let him try to protect her. She walked stubbornly as close to the edge of the sidewalk as she could manage, where he would have to be in the gutter if he was going to make a point of it.

He had to get over thinking she would freak out if she touched his residual arm—since she hated the word *stump* she decided that was what she was going to call it.

After a few minutes, she decided to push the issue further. "Would it hurt if I held on to you? I'm nervous about the ice. I love these boots but they're not very practical for a Colorado December."

They were gorgeous, she had to admit. She'd bought them in a fabulous shop in the Sixteenth.

He stopped and held out his right arm. "Come on the other side."

She shook her head. "I prefer this side, as long as it doesn't hurt."

"Gen."

She gave him a firm look and grabbed his elbow. After a long, awkward moment when she thought he might yank away and leave her standing there alone, he gave a little sigh and continued on his way.

As they walked, she was aware of the void just below the spot she held. She looked inside herself for any kind of squeamishness and could find nothing like that. She could find plenty of emotions there, thick and heavy. Admiration for what he had been through, as well as sadness that she wouldn't have many more moments like this with him.

"I think I may have sold the house."

Beneath her fingers, his arm tensed slightly then relaxed. "Really?"

She nodded. "Eden is looking for her own fixer-upper. She came over last night to check out Grandma Pearl's place and says it's just what she wanted. It's in the right location and everything. She even likes the pink tile in the bathroom. Go figure. She wants to figure out her budget but so far the signs look positive."

He cleared his throat. "Great. I guess you can shed the dust of Hope's Crossing earlier than you expected."

"I guess."

She should probably try to sound more enthusiastic about returning to Paris—that was what she'd been saying all along she wanted, right?—but she couldn't quite act that well.

Fearing he would correctly guess the reason she suddenly didn't want to leave, she turned the subject to one she knew would distract him.

"Charlotte told me the other day you had surgery some months ago where they implanted an artificial eye."

She could feel the tension in him again. "Charlotte talks too much."

"Why do you wear the patch if you really don't need it?"

"You don't like the pirate look?"

She wanted to tell him he was perfect to her, just as he was, but she knew he wouldn't believe it. "I just wondered. Does it have anything to do with why you avoid wearing your prosthetic?"

"Which one? I have several. None of them are particularly comfortable. They get in the way and I finally give up in frustration. And no matter how far technology has come, the eye still looks fake. I can't see anything out of it anyway." He paused. "I'm missing a hand and an eye. No prosthetic hand or artificial eye is going to erase that fact. I figure I need to get used to reality, not try to mask it."

"Are you thinking *you* need to face that or everybody else needs to?"

He slanted a look down at her. "Both."

"Can I say something?" she said after a moment.

"Any chance I could stop you?"

She squeezed his arm. "Probably not. I just want to point out that you seem to be the only one focused on what's missing. When I look at you, all I see is a man of strength and courage trying to adjust to tough changes in his life."

He grew silent as they crossed the street and headed for String Fever. Had she overstepped? She really wished she could read him better.

She didn't have time to fret about it for long—she had something else entirely to worry about as they reached the charming little bead store, with its colorful display window and hanging sign.

She used to love coming into String Fever and had even taken a class or two when the store used to be owned by Katherine Thorne. If she were staying in town, she would certainly consider taking another one.

The store seemed to be busy. She spotted a few people who looked familiar at the worktable and Claire and Evie Thorne standing by the cash register, along with a plump but pretty teenage girl she didn't know.

Claire moved away from the counter and headed toward them, trying unsuccessfully to hide the surprise on her soft, pretty features. "Genevieve. And, er, Dylan. Hello. This is an…unexpected pleasure."

She really doubted that. The *pleasure* part, anyway. She tried for a smile. "Hello. I haven't been into String Fever in a while. I like the new paint color."

"Thank you. The walls were looking a little tired. I'm actually glad you stopped by. I owe you an apology."

She hadn't been expecting that. "You…do?"

"The other night. My mother. I'm so sorry. What she said was unconscionably rude. I'm sorry you had to hear that."

Oh. That. "Don't worry about it. It wasn't your fault. If I tried to make amends for everything *my* mother did, it would take me hours just to walk through town."

Claire smiled, and Genevieve suddenly remembered what she *did* have to apologize for.

"Are you two looking for something in particular? We have some nice premade items that make lovely Christmas gifts."

Genevieve turned in the direction Claire indicated, and there, hanging in a glass display case, was her exquisitely designed wedding gown—all that was left of shattered dreams that didn't seem at all important anymore.

She had forgotten how gorgeous it was. Gathered bodice that draped, softly flaring skirt, the Swarovski crystals that gleamed in the light.

Barely realizing what she did, she walked to the case and touched the glass. It was cold against fingers that had been warmed by Dylan's heat.

Jenna would look lovely in it. They were a similar height and measurements, though Gen was a little bigger in the bust. Other than that, she was certain the dress would fit.

She turned and found Dylan at her shoulder, as if he sensed she needed the moral support.

"First, I... You apologized for your mother. I need to apologize for myself."

Claire waited, her expression curious.

"I don't need to tell you how terrible I was during my engagement and how I was even worse after things fell apart. I'm ashamed of my behavior and I'm very sorry for the way I treated you, especially when you were nothing but kind to me through everything."

Dylan reached for her hand and curled his fingers around hers. She couldn't look at him or she knew she would start to cry.

"I don't know what to say," Claire said.

"You don't have to say anything. I don't expect you to forgive me. I was awful to you. I know that."

"You wanted things to be perfect. Most brides do."

"Most brides don't treat everyone in town like their personal slaves."

"It's done. It was two years ago. From everything I've seen and heard since you've been back, you're a different woman than you were then."

She desperately wanted to believe that. She still had a long way to go but she wanted to think she was making progress.

"You said you were here for two reasons," Claire prompted. "What's the second one?"

She reached into her purse. "I would like to take my wedding gown now. This is almost everything I owe you, minus a couple hundred dollars, which I'll pay you as soon as I—"

To her shock, Dylan pulled his wallet out and thrust out a debit card. "She'll pay you the rest now, along with whatever you think is fair in interest and storage fees."

GENEVIEVE AND CLAIRE both stared at him as if he'd suddenly stripped down to his boxers and started belting out "Jingle Bells."

"Dylan!"

He shifted, not sure why he had made the gesture. He only knew it felt right. It had to have taken her buckets of grit to come in here and face her own mistakes. Beyond that, he found it incredibly sweet that she wanted to give a designer dress worth thousands to a woman she had only just met.

Crazy, yeah, but sweet, too.

"Don't worry about it. I would probably just waste it on Johnnie Walker. Let me do something good with my money for a change."

"Fine." She looked stunned, her eyes soft and shiny. "I'll pay *you* back when I sell the house, then."

A weird ball of *something* lodged in his gut at the reminder that she would soon be selling her grandmother's house and heading across the ocean.

"Do you mind if I ask who the bride might be?" Claire asked.

Genevieve smiled. "It's very romantic. Her name is Jenna Baldwin and she's a schoolteacher in Georgia. The groom is Trey Evans. He's one of the guests at A Warrior's Hope. You might have met him at the welcome reception the other night."

"Oh, right. Is he the good-looking guy with the cute Southern accent? As I recall, he's the only one who didn't have anyone with him."

"He does now." Genevieve beamed with pleasure and pride.

"Gen here did a little matchmaking behind the scenes and brought in his ex-fiancée from Georgia to try to patch things up between them."

"He's a really nice young man and he doesn't have any family to help him through the healing process. It seemed ridiculous to me that any man would turn his back on someone who loved him just because of some silly idea that he's not perfect anymore."

She didn't look at Dylan when she spoke but somehow he felt her words tug between them anyway. He didn't miss the glances Claire and Evie ex-

changed, both of them careful to also avoid looking at him, until he felt as
if he were invisible.

"So you're loaning her your wedding gown?" Claire said after an awkward pause. "How kind of you."

Genevieve shook her head. "Not a loan. A gift."

Claire's expression was clearly surprised. He wanted to tell her to get
in line. Gen was full of surprises, when she let down her prickly guard.

"When is the wedding?" Evie asked.

"Tomorrow afternoon," Gen answered. "All the guests are flying home
Monday, and Jenna and Trey wanted them to share in their moment. We've
had to hurry to throw everything together."

"How wonderful." Claire's eyes, predictably, turned soft and dreamy. All
the other women at A Warrior's Hope had the same expression every time
the talk turned to weddings.

"Riley and I had a Christmas wedding, too," she said. "I'm sure everything will be lovely."

"How can we help?" Evie asked.

"You want to help?"

"Yes!" Claire exclaimed. "I can't imagine throwing together a wedding
in such short order. You have to let us pitch in."

"Thank you. I don't know what to say. That's…very kind of you both."

"Everyone will want to help. You know they will. If Alex finds out we
threw a wedding and didn't ask her to take care of the food, she'll never
forgive any of us."

"You know," Evie said thoughtfully, "Mary Ella probably has all the decorations from her own wedding lying around somewhere."

"That's right!" Claire exclaimed. "Do you think the bride would mind
secondhand decorations? They were so elegant—silver, blue, white. Perfect for a wedding during the holidays."

Gen looked as if she wanted to burst into tears. "That would be great!
I was planning something simple, maybe taking some fresh greenery from
the grounds and whatever ribbons and ornaments we could swipe from the
guest cabins. But if Mary Ella wouldn't mind loaning a few things, I'm sure
the bride will be very grateful."

"I'll call her right now," Claire offered.

As she headed into her office, apparently to use the phone, Evie turned
to Gen. "You know, I think we have a necklace-and-earring set that would
go perfectly with that dress. I created it for the school-dance season around
the corner but it always seemed a little old for a teenage girl."

She headed for another jewelry case. When she pulled out a piece, it reflected a swirl of colors.

"Oh. Look at that," Gen exclaimed. "Are those Swarovski crystals like the gown?"

"Yes," Evie said. "The pearls are Swarovski, as well."

"Stunning. Really stunning. I love how light and airy it is, like the gems are suspended there."

"Take it for the bride. It can be a wedding gift from me."

"Thank you. Thank you so much. I know she'll love it."

When Claire returned, she carried a black clothing bag—for the dress, he assumed.

"Mary Ella is *thrilled* to let your bride and groom use their decorations. She and Harry will load everything up tonight in his pickup truck and drop it off at the recreation center. She says for you to use whatever you want and keep the rest in one of the spare rooms at the recreation center. They'll pick it up Sunday night or Monday."

Dylan had a tough time picturing Harry Lange—the wealthiest man in town—delivering wedding decorations for people he didn't know, but apparently marrying Mary Ella McKnight had a mellowing effect, even on the cranky old codger.

"Thank you. I want to give them the most magical wedding they can imagine. This will be wonderful."

"You have to let us help you decorate. Between the Giving Hope gala and all the weddings around here lately, we've become sort of experts at throwing parties."

"Okay. Great." She cleared her throat. "I want to start early in the morning. The earlier the better, no later than eight."

"Perfect. We'll be there. Riley's working tomorrow, so I'll probably have Emma. The older kids will be with their dad. I hope you don't mind. She's a really good baby."

"No. I don't mind."

Claire unlocked the case and pulled out the wedding dress with a sort of reverence he might have found amusing under other circumstances.

"You hold it and I'll zip it in," Claire said.

Genevieve took it. "It really is an exquisite dress. The beading takes it over the top. I knew it would." She touched the edge of the bodice. "You did a really beautiful job, Claire."

"I'm still sorry I didn't get the chance to see you wear it down the aisle,"

Claire said, swooping the last bit of material inside the bag and zipping it tight.

"I'm not," Genevieve declared. "Sawyer Danforth was a womanizing jerk. If I had married him, I don't think I would have liked myself very much. At least not as much as I'm beginning to now."

Claire smiled broadly and hugged Genevieve, dress and all. In that moment, he wanted to kiss Claire Bradford McKnight right on the lips for being the kind, generous person she was—exactly what Gen needed right now.

"So we'll see you tomorrow bright and early," Claire said, waving as they headed out.

The snow had begun to fall in earnest while they were in the store and he imagined Gen was grateful the dress was protected by the zippered bag.

She didn't take either of his arms this time, too busy carrying the dress.

"That wasn't so bad, was it?" he said.

She gave a soft laugh. "Isn't it funny how the things we dread never turn out as poorly as we imagine?"

Sometimes they were worse—far worse—but he didn't want to ruin her little philosophical moment by being such a downer.

"I guess I'd better get up to the recreation center. I told Eden and Mac I'd be back for the afternoon of skiing."

"And I have to find Jenna and have her try this on so I can make any necessary alterations tonight."

"You?"

"You don't have to sound so shocked. Yes, I can sew. It happens to be a necessary skill for an interior designer. Grandma Pearl taught me when I was a girl. She was always patient with me. Even when I had to redo a stitch a half-dozen times, she would never raise her voice or call me stupid."

Who had called her stupid? he wondered. They reached her car before he had a chance to ask.

"Thank you for coming with me. You gave me courage I couldn't find for myself."

He couldn't help himself. He reached out and drew his thumb down her cheek. For just an instant, the wonder of skin on skin overwhelmed him. He suddenly missed his other hand fiercely, deprived forever of the chance to touch her completely.

"You've got more strength than you see, Gen."

She leaned her face into his hand for just an instant—very much like Trey had done with Jenna—then she stepped away.

"I hope I'll have enough," she murmured, rather cryptically, before reaching into the pocket of her coat for her keys.

CHAPTER NINETEEN

GENEVIEVE PLUMPED THE bow on one last silver ribbon and stepped back to admire her handiwork, shaking her fingers out to ease the ache of the repetitive motion.

The room looked like something out of a fairy tale, all silver and blue and magical. After conferring with Jenna and Trey, they had decided to have the ceremony itself in front of the huge wall of windows that overlooked the mountains and river. She had bordered the windows with two of the trees from Mary Ella's wedding decorations, each bare branch covered in yards and yards of twinkly lights. The mantel of the huge river-rock fireplace glowed with evergreens, silver and blue ornaments and elegant silvery branches.

The rows of chairs angled to watch the ceremony had been adorned with elegant silver and blue ribbons entwined with sprigs of evergreens. In one corner, the various colored ornaments on the large Christmas tree she had already decorated once in here had been swapped out with only ornaments matching the rest of the theme—huge blue ornaments as big as bowling balls, silvery icicles, a few crystal snowflakes.

It was truly a winter wonderland.

"Okay, what is missing?" she asked the room in general.

Her large crew consisted of Mary Ella and Maura Lange, Claire McKnight, Alex, Charlotte, Eden, Pam and the wives from the program. Jenna's mother, Patty, who had flown in from Virginia on the last flight into Stapleton the night before, had wanted to help but Genevieve insisted she stay with Jenna to help with her hair and makeup.

Those gathered, though, paused in their various labors to look around.

"I can't see a thing wrong," Mary Ella declared.

"It's going to be exquisite when we're done, Genevieve," Claire said. "I can't believe you put this all together in only two days. It appears as if it was years in the planning."

"I couldn't have done it without all of you—and without Mary Ella's decorations."

"You have such a gift for throwing things together," Tonya Brooks said. "I can't even figure out where to hang my family pictures in our place. Every time we were transferred to a new base, it was the same dilemma."

"I guess we know who to put in charge of the decorations committee for the next Giving Hope gala," Maura said.

She should quickly tell them that by the time the next Giving Hope Day rolled around—held in early June each year—she would be on another continent, probably decorating tiny Parisian apartments. The words clogged in her throat. She only wanted to savor this success, not think about leaving.

The past two hours had been...amazing. The women had rushed in with hugs and energy. They had laughed with her, chattered about everything under the sun and worked hard together to create something beautiful and memorable for a couple most of them didn't even know.

"What's left?"

"Only arranging the table decorations for the luncheon," she said.

The six eight-top tables had been set out on the other side of the fireplace. As she was demonstrating how she wanted the tablecloths she had hastily sewn overnight, a familiar figure came inside the room and stood rather uncomfortably in the doorway.

Genevieve's voice trailed off and she stared. After a frozen moment, she hurried over.

"Mom! What are you doing here?"

Laura looked around at the decorations. "We were supposed to go to brunch this morning, remember? You were going to meet us at Le Passe. Your father and Charlie are still there."

Her stomach dived. "Oh. Oh, my word. I completely forgot. I'm so sorry. I should have called you."

"Yes. You should have."

Between working on the house and filling her community-service hours at A Warrior's Hope—and now organizing a wedding in forty-eight hours—she had barely given her family a thought. "How did you know where to find me?"

"When you didn't answer your cell phone, I was worried about you. I was about to go to Pearl's house to see if you had passed out from the wallpaper-glue fumes or something when Harry and Jackson showed up at the restaurant. When your father asked where their wives were, imagine our surprise when Harry told us Mary Ella and Maura were here helping our daughter decorate for a wedding."

Her mother gave one of her little sniffs that could mean a hundred different things. Disdain. Distaste. Indifference. In this case, she had the sudden, startling insight that her mother's feelings were hurt at being excluded.

Was it possible that Laura felt as isolated and alone as Genevieve did? She saw a flash of something there, just a tiny hint that made her wonder if her mother wore her social position as a shield to keep everyone away.

"Laura. Hello, my dear." Mary Ella stepped up and brushed her cheek against Gen's mother's.

"Mary Ella. How are you?"

"I'm great. Thank you. Look at the fantastic job your daughter has done here. It's all been her. She's incredibly talented. Did you know she sewed the tablecloths herself last night? You must be so proud of her."

"I... Yes. Of course we are. We always have been. I just have one little question. Who is the happy couple, if you don't mind me asking?"

"He's one of the guests at A Warrior's Hope, a young man from Alabama," Genevieve answered. "She is a schoolteacher from Georgia. They're very much in love."

She didn't tell her mother about her role in bringing Trey and Jenna together. Perhaps she would someday—but she did have one confession she couldn't avoid.

"Mother, she's going to wear my wedding gown."

Laura jerked her gaze from the decorations toward Genevieve. "I thought it was still at String Fever."

"No. I have it. Actually, Jenna has it. I gave it to her."

She waited for her mother to make some cutting comment, something about irresponsible, thoughtless benevolence. Instead, Laura surprised her.

"Just as well," she said with an airy wave of her hand. "What else could you have done with it? Sell it, I suppose, but that's about all. It would have been tacky to wear it when you marry someone else."

That question was fairly moot now. How could she ever marry anyone now? No other man could possibly compare to Dylan.

"You're not angry?"

Laura shrugged. "Why should I be angry? It's your dress. You can do as you want with it."

Okay, had she awakened in some alternate universe? First, all the women in Hope's Crossing were being so kind to her, laughing with her, making admiring comments about her flair for decorating. Now her mother was showing remarkable understanding.

Further shocking her, Laura looked around at the little groups of women scattered throughout the room. "Is there anything I can do to help?"

"I'm...sure we could use an extra pair of hands."

Mary Ella stepped forward. "Laura, dear, you have such beautiful handwriting. Why don't you help me make place cards for the tables?"

"I *have* always prided myself on my cursive."

Her mother followed Mary Ella. Genevieve gazed after her for only a second—all the time she could spare.

The alternate-universe theory was seeming more credible by the second.

What were the chances she could stay there?

ALL THE PREDICTIONS came true. It was a truly beautiful ceremony, with a handsome groom and a stunning bride. The love between the fragile-looking Jenna and the damaged soldier was a palpable force that seemed to encircle them, binding them tightly together.

Trey actually stood for the ceremony with the help of his forearm crutches, insisting he wasn't going to take his own wedding sitting down. The sight of him struggling valiantly to his feet before the ceremony even began and standing erect and proud was the first moment Gen cried.

All right. The second. The first had been when Dylan had walked in— without his ever-present eye patch and wearing his prosthetic.

He looked so very different, she couldn't stop stealing glances at him. His left eye drooped slightly more than the right and she could see a network of scars. After all this time of seeing him with the black patch, the absence of it left her disoriented.

He did look gorgeous in a suit and tie. He must have figured out how to tie a Windsor—or found someone to help him. His sister, probably. She was aware of a tiny spasm of pain that he hadn't asked her.

He had given her a brusque nod then slipped into a back row, next to his father and Charlotte and Spence, and then the music started.

Trey had asked Jason Reid to stand up with him, and the sight of two handsome warriors in hastily rented tuxedos—courtesy of Spence, she learned—touched her deeply, especially as she looked around the room at Pam and the others and thought of all they had endured.

While the small string ensemble Spence had also arranged played Pachelbel, the little Brooks girls came in, adorable in matching blue dresses with faux white fur around the wrists and hem. They joyfully skipped up the aisle, scattering glitter and tiny crystals out of winter-white baskets, and then Jenna came in on her mother's arm, glowing with joy and looking absolutely breathtaking in a gown that could have been designed just for her.

When they exchanged vows—Trey in a gruff voice he had to clear a few times to get the words out and Jenna with starry-eyed happiness, Genevieve had to fight back a sob.

Now, the ceremony over, the guests milled around with champagne glasses and small plates of delicious little bites hastily provided by several restaurants in town while the string ensemble played elegant music in the background.

Everything had gone off without a hitch. Maybe she should think about going into the party-planning business instead of interior design. She definitely had a knack.

"Genevieve."

She turned at her father's voice. "Mother. Dad. It's really nice of you to come."

She couldn't have been more shocked when she had seen them walk into the room in time for the ceremony earlier. That alternate-universe theory again...

Her father reached in to brush a kiss on her cheek. "It's the first wedding at the city's new recreation center. It's only right that the mayor and his wife attend."

She tried not to roll her eyes at his pompous tone. As much as she loved him, William could certainly be puffed up in his own importance.

"Mother, thank you for pitching in this morning. We needed every single volunteer to make this happen."

Laura preened a little. "If that's the only chance I have to spend a little time with my only daughter, I'll take what I can find."

She squashed down her twinge of guilt. "Everyone is leaving tomorrow. I only have to help clean up after they go and then my community-service hours are finished. I should be free on Christmas Eve. Are we having dinner, like always?"

Her mother nodded. "Actually, we're doing something different this year. We've invited guests. Larry and Joan Billings. Their sons are spending the holidays with their in-laws this year. Oh, and your father has a young new associate in his law firm and he's all alone this holiday season. We thought the two of you might hit it off."

Perfect. Without asking, her parents had decided to start setting her up with eligible men—and on Christmas Eve, no less. She could imagine few things more miserable. She supposed marrying her off to some up-and-coming associate of her father's was one way for them to make sure she stayed out of trouble and didn't rack up more debt.

She could endure for one night. They would find out soon enough that she was close to selling the house and leaving Hope's Crossing for good.

Out of the corner of her gaze, she spied Dylan speaking with his father. Again, she had that disorienting shift at seeing two blue eyes in that rugged face.

When Harry Lange approached at that moment to greet her father, she seized the diversion as the perfect chance to escape. "Thank you again for coming. Will you excuse me for a moment?"

She walked away, fully aware her parents were watching after her. "Dermot," she said when she reached the pair. "Your tarts are a huge hit. Thank you!"

He gave her an embrace and kissed her cheek. "You're very welcome, my darling. You throw a good party."

"This was a team effort. Everybody pitched in."

"I've heard otherwise. Charlotte was telling me how you were up all night sewing things, making little gewgaws, fixing wedding dresses. Sounds to me like a one-woman show."

"Charlotte exaggerates."

"She has been known to," Dermot said, "but I think in this case she was speaking truth. And you look beautiful doing it. Doesn't she look beautiful, son?"

That muscle she had once pressed her mouth to twitched along Dylan's jawline. "Stunning," he murmured.

"Thank you. Both of you."

She started to ask if they were staying for the dinner being catered by Brazen when Katherine Thorne came over. "Apparently, they're running out of tarts. Alex sent me over to ask if you have more."

To Gen's amusement, color soaked Dermot's cheeks. "Oh, yes. I brought three more trays. I can fetch them."

"Thank you." Katherine smiled, which only made Dermot flush more. "I'll help you."

The two of them walked off, looking completely adorable together.

"Speaking of exaggeration, I thought you were joking about your dad and Katherine."

He looked after his father, his expression slightly amused. "No. Both of

CHRISTMAS IN SNOWFLAKE CANYON

them are obviously interested in the other, but neither will make the first move."

"Maybe they just need a push."

He raised his eyebrows. "Oh, no. Get that thought out of your head right now. One success does not make you the town matchmaker, Gen."

"You have to admit, it was a *spectacular* success."

"Yes. But Pop apparently likes to move at his own pace, which is just about as fast as a snail on sedatives. If you step in, you'll only embarrass him."

She watched Dermot and Katherine for a moment, mostly to get her racing heartbeat under control, then she turned back to Dylan.

"You didn't wear your eye patch."

That muscle flexed again. "Somebody implied I was hiding behind it. I figured maybe it was time."

"You look good. Really good."

He made a face. "It feels strange. Kind of naked after all these months."

She flashed him a look, trying to force her imagination not to go there. Pulling off his jacket, loosening that tie, baring all those muscles...

She cleared her throat. "You'll get used to it, I'm sure. Or if you prefer the eye patch, wear that. It doesn't matter to me."

I love you either way.

"Or anyone else, I'm sure," she quickly added. "Wasn't it great to see Trey standing for the ceremony?"

"Yes. And Jenna's dress was beautiful. I kept picturing you in it, though."

Before she could respond to that, the couple in question approached them, trailing their happiness like Jenna's train.

The bride embraced her, smelling of hair spray and lilies from her exquisite bouquet. "Genevieve. Oh. I don't even know what to say. It was the most beautiful wedding, in front of those big windows with the mountains in the background and that light snowfall."

She smiled and hugged her back. "I can't take credit for the view or the snowfall."

Jenna eased away. She really did look beautiful in that dress. "Everything else is because of you. We can never repay you for the wonderful gift you have given us. Another chance. You've given us a future."

"You had the courage to grab your own future together. I'm so happy for you both."

Trey, still using his forearm crutches, embraced her next. Genevieve kissed his cheek. "I needed a kick in the ass, somebody to show me I was being a stubborn fool. Thank you for giving it to me."

"Anytime." She managed another smile, though it was edged with sadness. Why couldn't Dylan accept he needed her, as Trey had finally opened his heart and his life to Jenna?

"What are your plans now?" Dylan asked.

"I've got a contract to finish up the school year in Georgia," Jenna said. "After that, we're not sure where we'll settle."

"I've decided to go back to school to finish my degree. Mac has convinced me I could work in a program like this one or something similar."

"Oh, wonderful," Genevieve exclaimed. "You would be perfect."

The orchestra set their instruments down and the beginning strains of the romantic pop-ballad recording Jenna had requested for their dance together began playing over the sound system.

"Oh! There it is. Our song. We have to go dance."

He rolled his eyes. "I'll look ridiculous trying to dance. I'm going to topple both of us to the ground."

She gave him a dewy-eyed smile. "Don't you know by now, I'm strong enough to support us both, when I have to?"

Gen watched them go out to the small dance floor she had marked by more of those trees with twinkly lights. The lights dimmed as they walked out while Justin Timberlake and the rest of *NSYNC sang about promising to love forever and battles being won.

Trey used his crutches to go to the middle of the dance floor and then handed them to Jason, something that had obviously been planned ahead of time. He took Jenna in his arms and they held each other, not really moving, mostly swaying in time to the music.

She watched them, the handsome battered warrior and his sweet bride in her beautiful wedding gown. She wasn't the only one crying softly before the song was through.

Dylan handed her a handkerchief. "You did a good thing, Gen."

She wiped her eyes, her heart a heavy ache. When she lowered the handkerchief other couples began to move out to join the newlyweds. Charlotte and Spencer moved past them, Alex McKnight and Sam Delgado. Even Mary Ella and Harry Lange.

He said nothing, just watched as the small dance floor began to fill. Finally she decided this was her only chance and she couldn't let it slip through her fingers. "Dance with me," she said softly.

The moment stretched out, awkward and wooden. She could feel his tension.

"I wasn't a good dancer, even before."

"Do you think I care about that?" *I just want one last chance to be close to you.* She thought the words but couldn't say them.

Finally, when she thought he would leave her standing on the edge of the dance floor, he reached for her hand and they walked out among the twinkly trees.

After some quick mental calculations, she switched the way she would traditionally place her arms and curled her right arm around his neck. After a pause, he put his prosthetic hand around her waist. It wasn't really holding her, just resting on the curve of her hip.

This was another romantic ballad from about a decade ago, obviously also picked by Jenna. She closed her eyes and rested her cheek against his chest, trying to savor every moment. It was magical and she never wanted it to end.

But forever wasn't in the cards for them. As soon as the song was over, he stepped away.

"Thank you for the dance," he said, his voice gruff and stiff, his features once more remote.

She had been wrong about the eye patch. Even when he didn't wear it, his expression wasn't any more clear to her.

"You're welcome," she whispered.

He gave her one last look, then turned around and walked away—not simply from her but from the whole reception, working his way through the dancers and the crowd with single-minded purpose.

A wise woman would simply let him go, since he was so determined to put as much distance between them as he could.

She watched his progress for a moment, aching and miserable and filled with sorrow, then screwed her eyes shut. When had she ever been wise about anything? Why ruin a perfect track record of foolish mistakes?

She drew in her courage and rushed after him.

ALL HE WANTED was to climb back in his truck, drive up to Snowflake Canyon and climb inside the last bottle of Johnnie Walker in the place.

Emotions were a big, messy snarl inside him, like fishing line that had been left in the bottom of the boat over the winter. He didn't want to untangle them right now; he only knew he had to get away.

He didn't want this. These tender, fragile, terrifying feelings.

This was all Jamie's fault. If his brother had never asked to meet him at The Speckled Lizard that night, he never would have stepped in to help Genevieve Beaumont.

He would have been perfectly happy the rest of his life thinking she was a spoiled, snobby bitch instead of the soft, vulnerable, *perfect* woman he had come to know these past few weeks.

A woman who gave away her wedding dress then stayed up all night making alterations so another woman could wear it. Who cried like a baby as she watched a broken soldier dance with his bride. Who looked at him—screwed up, angry, half-missing *him*—as if he was everything to her.

He reached his pickup, telling himself the ache in his chest was only the cold air hitting his lungs.

Just as he opened the door, he heard a swish of fabric, and some sixth sense had him turning around.

Of course. There she was. He should have known she would come after him. She was so damn stubborn when she wanted to be: punching assistant D.A.s and firing her father out of pique and steaming off layer after layer of wallpaper in a dilapidated old house.

She didn't have a coat and her cheeks were pink and he wanted to bundle her up, throw her in the pickup and take her home with him.

"Why are you running so hard from me?" she demanded.

He loosened the stupid tie his father had tied for him as if he were six years old.

"Can't I just be done with the party? I've spent more time surrounded by people these last ten days than I have in my whole life. Is it so hard to believe I might just want to be alone for a while?"

"Not hard at all. I just think it's me you're eager to escape."

He wanted to deny it. It would make things so much easier, all the way around. The last thing he wanted to do was hurt her, but he had to make her face reality somehow.

He rubbed his hand over his face, hating this, hating himself. Even hating *her* a little for forcing him to face all the things he had never, for a moment, thought he wanted—a wife, a family, a future—and the bitter realization that what he wanted was out of reach to him.

"Gen, I can't be the man you need."

She paled a little but lifted her chin. "How can you be so certain?"

"You need someone who wants the same things you do, who is used to the kind of life you've had. Someone polished and cultured. Someone who has no problem listening to that French jazz crap you like and going to museums and escorting you to the opera. That was never me and it sure as hell isn't now."

"A few weeks ago, I would have agreed with you. The man you're describing is exactly the one I've always thought I wanted. Is it so hard to believe I was wrong—about myself and about so many other things?"

"Gen—"

"I love you."

She said the words quickly, as if afraid she would lose her nerve if she didn't rush through them.

He inhaled sharply as some of those emotions seemed to yank free of the snarl.

Love. Of course. *That* was what this was.

He closed his eyes—the real one and the fake one—as the truth soaked through him like somebody had doused him with that bottle of whiskey waiting at home for him.

He loved Genevieve Beaumont. And she apparently felt the same.

He wanted to savor the words as he had that dance, to drink them in, swirl them around inside him and just let them soak through.

He couldn't do that, to either of them.

She must imagine they could have a happy ending like Trey and Jenna.

He wasn't like Trey. Trey had been basically a good soldier who had been injured through no fault of his own. He hadn't been responsible for the deaths of five of his closest friends because of weakness and uncertainty.

What did he have to offer her? A broken-down house in Snowflake Canyon, no career. He did have a great dog, but on the list of things Mayor Beaumont wanted for his daughter, a great black-and-tan coonhound likely wouldn't make the cut.

Nor would a washed-up army ranger with several missing parts.

He drew in a sharp breath. "You don't love me. I'm flattered that you would say so—who wouldn't be?—but you're just caught up in the whole wedding romance thing."

"You really think I'm that shallow?"

A few weeks ago, he would have given an unequivocal yes to that question. Not now. She was so much more.

He couldn't let her love him. Two years from now, what would she want with him when she finally realized he couldn't miraculously regrow an eye and a hand? He wouldn't be able to bear that.

He didn't know what to do, what to say. The only thing that seemed certain to convince her was to strike out where he knew she was most vulnerable.

"What if you're not the kind of woman I want?"

He hated himself more in that moment than he had in all the months since his accident, but he didn't see any other choice but to drive her away irrevocably.

Her features grew even more pale. "Is that so?"

He focused his gaze somewhere over her shoulder, unable to lie straight to her face. "You're incredibly beautiful, and if circumstances were different, I would sleep with you in a second. But you surround yourself with perfection. The way you dress, your makeup, your hair. You can't tolerate anything being out of place. You wrap presents with ribbon ends that have to be exactly equal. Even before I was injured and became very much less than perfect, I wouldn't have been the man for you. Eventually, I probably would have wanted to chew my own arm off to get away from all those expectations."

She stared at him, eyes wide, and he could see her curling into herself, pulling all her protective barriers back in place.

"I...see."

He wanted to call back every word, but all he could picture was a future with her eventually coming to despise him. He wouldn't be able to handle that.

Yeah, it made him the coward she had called Trey a few days ago. He knew that.

Better to be a coward now than completely wrecked later when she finally realized he wasn't enough for her.

"It's cold. You should go back inside."

"I... Yes. I guess you're right."

With each breath, he felt as if knives were carving holes in his chest, but he forced himself to give his best imitation of a casual smile. "It really was a beautiful wedding, Genevieve. Merry Christmas."

"Merry Christmas."

She wouldn't look at him as she turned and fled back to the lights, the music, the fairy-tale ending he could never give her.

CHAPTER TWENTY

"Are you sure you're all right, darling? You hardly touched your dinner, and you've been so pale and quiet all evening."

"I'm fine, Mother." She tried a smile to ease the worry she could see in Laura's features. "I'm only a little tired."

She was working hard to be patient with her parents, trying to remember they had her best interests at heart.

Sometime in the past few days, she had come to the realization that her father had been right to bring her home to Hope's Crossing. She had been aimless in Paris. Oh, she had certainly enjoyed herself but that life had been unsustainable. She had needed to find her purpose—and perhaps the strength inside herself to reach for one.

She could have done without the heartbreak that had come along with it, but blaming her parents for that would be unfair.

"Thank you for dinner. It was delicious. Mrs. Taylor outdid herself."

"Didn't she?" Laura beamed as if *she* had been the one slaving away in the kitchen instead of their longtime housekeeper. "And what did you think of Adam? Isn't he a lovely man?"

"Yes. Lovely." Her father's new associate, Adam Schilling, actually had been quite nice. He was funny and smart and treated her with respect, as if he genuinely cared about her opinion—something of an appealing rarity, in her experience.

She would definitely have been interested in him if circumstances had been different.

Her heart felt achy and sore, as if she had a strange sort of flu. She had cried herself to sleep the past two nights, something she hadn't done once after the end of her engagement.

Having all these tender feelings for a man who didn't want them hurt worse than anything in her life.

Dylan hadn't come to A Warrior's Hope to see their guests on their way the previous day. She had spent the whole night before trying to figure out how she would possibly face him again…and then he hadn't even had the courtesy to make all that effort worthwhile.

No one had explained to her where he was, but she had overheard Charlotte tell Eden he'd phoned her that morning and said he had an appointment he'd forgotten about. He promised he would make up the last of his hours after the holidays.

She knew it was a lie. He wouldn't have forgotten an appointment. He only wanted to avoid the awkwardness of facing her again after that last humiliating scene between them.

She sighed, earning a concerned look from her mother.

"Really, darling," Laura exclaimed. "I think you must be coming down with something. And on Christmas Eve, too! Poor thing. Why don't you stay here tonight instead of going back to your grandmother's house? I can tuck you in, just like old times, and make some of your grandmother's Russian tea you always used to like."

"I'm just tired, I think. A good night's sleep will be just the thing."

"You should definitely stay here, then," William piped up. "You'll sleep better in your own bed than at your grandmother's."

She didn't want to argue with them when so far the evening had been conflict-free. Even so, she had a deep yearning to be alone. Pretending to enjoy herself all evening took emotional energy she just couldn't spare right now.

She had done as they asked by coming to dinner, spending time with them, being polite to their guests. That was all she could handle tonight.

"Thank you, but I would rather go back to Grandma's house. All my things are there—my makeup remover, my moisturizer. I'll be more comfortable there."

Her mother, at least, would certainly understand the importance of good skin care.

"You're coming over tomorrow morning, then, for breakfast and to open presents," Laura insisted.

"Yes. Of course. I'll be here bright and early, I promise."

At that moment, her brother, Charlie, came in from outside, stomping off snow. "It's really coming down. I just scraped your windows, but maybe you ought to stay here."

She rolled her eyes, even as she was immensely touched that her previously troublesome, sullen brother had learned to look outside himself and help others. "Not you, too! Give it a rest, everybody. I'll be fine."

Her words were a lie. She wasn't fine and hadn't been for two days. Though it sounded melodramatic, right now she wasn't sure how she would ever be fine again. How was it possible to ache so deeply for something that had never even had the chance to begin?

With hugs and air-kisses, she said her goodbyes to her family and climbed into her little SUV.

The streets of Hope's Crossing were mostly empty. Just after dark each year, Silver Strike ski resort had a Christmas Eve candlelight ski, when they would turn off the resort lights and the only illumination would be the line of tiny lights held by skiers as they traversed the run. Nearly everyone in town usually attended—her family and her parents' guests had watched, hot cocoa in hand, from the deck of their home not far from the resort and then returned inside for dinner.

By now, all those skiers and the bystanders were back in the warmth of their homes, tucked up together to celebrate the joy of the season together.

Her windshield kept up a steady rhythm to beat away the snow as the Christmas lights of Hope's Crossing glimmered. It really was a pretty little town. She had to keep her eyes on the road because of the inclement conditions, but every once in a while, she caught a vignette inside a frosted window of people gathered around laughing, talking, smiling.

Her feelings for Hope's Crossing had changed, as well. Once she had considered it an insular backwater, filled with small-minded people. Working at A Warrior's Hope and seeing the outpouring of support by people in town toward outsiders they didn't even know had given her new perspective.

She might have reconsidered returning to her flat in Paris, if not for Dylan and her aching heart.

As she pulled into her driveway, she noticed fresh tracks in the snow. It looked as if someone had pulled in and then out again while she had been gone. It must have been some time ago as more snow had filled in the tracks.

Someone had left something on the porch, she could see as she drove into the garage. Curious, she parked her vehicle then walked through the house to the front door to find a shiny red gift bag with a clumsily tied gold bow on the porch.

Odd. Who would be leaving her a gift? Perhaps Charlotte had stopped by, or maybe Eden.

She carried it inside and turned on the lights in Grandma Pearl's living room. She couldn't find a gift label or a card. With a frown, she began to pull away tissue-paper layers. Something solid and dark lay inside, she saw. She reached inside and her hand closed around smooth wood.

A figure.

Three wooden figures, actually.

She pulled them out and caught her breath as her heart started to pound with stunning ferocity.

Three figures: Joseph, Mary, Baby Jesus, each rather roughly carved out of a fine-grained wood, unpainted but stained with a clear finish.

With fingers that trembled suddenly, she set them on the coffee table for a better look. Mary knelt beside the manger, her features in shadow from her head covering. Joseph stood beside her, strong and sturdy, staff in hand, and the tiny Baby Jesus lay in a manger with arms stretched wide.

She looked in the bag again and found nothing to indicate who had left such treasure.

But she knew.

He could have purchased it somewhere, she supposed, or his father or one of his brothers could have made it.

That would have been logical, given his circumstances, but somehow she knew in her heart Dylan had made them himself, to continue the tradition her grandmother had started so long ago.

She pictured him trying with one arm to carve this for her, probably using the prosthetic he hated to hold the wood in place, and she started to sob.

She cried for all he had endured, for her pain the past few days and for the unbearably precious gift he had given her, overwhelming in its magnitude.

When the torrent of tears had slowed to a trickle, she picked up the carving of the baby in the manger. It was raw, primitive, like something out of a folk-art museum, but beautiful in its simplicity, in the young, serene mother, the watchful father, those open arms.

As she looked at it again, the truth washed over her.

He loved her.

Despite what he'd said, all that ridiculous nonsense that had cut so deeply, he loved her. He wouldn't have spent a moment doing this for her otherwise, let alone the hours it must have taken him to painstakingly carve something so lovely.

He loved her and she refused to let him pretend otherwise.

She scooped up all three figures, hugged them close to her heart and hurried back out to her SUV.

DYLAN STIRRED THE fire and watched red-gold embers dance up the chimney.

Christmas Eve, and here he was alone at his cabin in Snowflake Canyon with Tucker, a fire and a book he knew would remain unread.

He had done his best. He had dutifully gone with his family to watch the candlelight ski and then had gone to Pop's place for dinner. He had stayed amid the noise and chaos as long as he could, until his nerves felt as frayed as Tucker's favorite rug and he finally made his excuses.

Then he had made the fatal mistake he had been regretting for the past hour.

He poked at the fire again then tossed in another split log, watching while the flames teased at it for a moment before taking hold.

"I know I'm an idiot, Tuck. You don't have to tell me that."

His dog just looked at him out of those big eyes. Yeah, he had definitely climbed onto the crazy bus. What else would explain the past few days?

The whole thing had started as a whim, just to see if he could still carve. After a frenzied two days with little sleep and countless tries, next thing he knew, he was actually dropping the whole thing off on her porch like the town's do-gooder Angel of Hope.

He couldn't believe he had actually left them, but he had figured, what the hell? What else was he going to do with them?

He supposed on some level, he was trying to atone for his cruel words the other night—which really made no sense at all since he was hoping she wouldn't guess the crappy gift came from him.

Yeah. He was not only riding the crazy bus—at some point in the past few days, he had taken the damn wheel.

He sighed. Nothing for it now but to get through the holidays, wait for her to go back to Paris and then move on with his life.

The snow was still coming down steadily, so he decided to head out to the woodpile to fill up the box on the porch. Few things sucked worse than having to run out in the middle of the night all the way to the woodpile so he could keep the fire going—but even that beat the alternative of waking up to an ice-cold house.

He threw on his boots and his coat but didn't bother with a glove. It wouldn't take him long. In two or three trips to the stack out beyond the house, he could have enough split wood on the porch to last twenty-four hours or more.

"You coming?" he asked Tucker. The dog gave him a "fat chance" sort of look and settled back on his rug in front of the fire.

He was on the second trip to the porch through the snow when he saw a flash of light on the long, winding drive to the main canyon road.

He stopped and stared, the leather wood carrier dangling from his hand.

What the hell? Who would be stupid enough to drive up here in the dark in the middle of a storm?

If it was Charlotte or Pop, he was seriously going to have to start yelling. Couldn't they leave him alone for two damn seconds?

He climbed up to the porch and dumped the wood in the bin then waited while the vehicle drew closer.

He recognized it when it was about twenty yards away, and his pulse started pounding in his ears.

Not Charlotte or Pop.

He shouldn't have bothered with a coat. Despite the cold wind that hurled snow at him, his face and chest felt hot and itchy as he watched Genevieve climb out of her SUV.

She looked like a Christmas angel, with her little cream wool coat, red scarf and a jaunty little matching wool cap.

He drew in a sharp breath, aching with the effort not to run down the steps and yank her into his arms.

"I thought *I* was the crazy one, but you are completely insane," he growled.

"Probably." She stopped at the bottom of the steps.

"No *probably* about it," he snapped. "What were you thinking, driving up here in the middle of a blizzard?"

"This?" She made one of her funny little gestures at the snow steadily piling up. "This is just a few inches."

"You have got to leave now if you want to make it back down and not be stuck up here all night."

She looked up at him for about ten seconds then walked up the steps and into his house without waiting for an invitation, untwisting her scarf as she went.

He followed after her. "Genevieve Beaumont. Get back in that SUV and go home. If you don't, I swear, I'll haul you over my shoulder, toss you in my pickup and take you down myself."

She ignored him, instead looking around his house with interest. She hadn't been here, he realized. He tensed even more, wondering what she saw. Yeah, it was pretty bare-bones but it was comfortable and he liked it.

Tucker the Traitor padded right over to her for a little love, and she knelt down with a slight smile and rubbed just behind his left ear, right where he adored.

"Hey, buddy. How've you been? Hmm?"

"Seriously, Gen," he tried again. "This isn't a joke. The canyon roads can be slick and dangerous even when there's not new snow. If you don't believe me, ask your brother."

Her mouth seemed to tighten a little as she rose to her feet and faced him. "I'm not leaving. At least not until you explain this."

She pulled three wooden figures out of her pocket and set them on the table.

His face turned hot again and he could barely look at them. Crazy bus. Definitely. What the hell had he been thinking? How could he ever have imagined it was a good idea to give them to her?

"Well?" she demanded when he said nothing.

He tried for nonchalance. "I don't know. They look like something a third-grader did in art class."

She crossed her arms across her chest. "They do not. They're beautiful. Absolutely beautiful. I can't believe you did this for me."

Her voice caught a little on the last word and he finally had a clear look at her face.

She had been crying.

He could see the red-rimmed eyes, the traces of tears on her cheeks.

His lungs gave a hard squeeze. Damn it. He hated her tears. Why hadn't he just let this whole thing between them die a natural death?

"You think I did that?" He did the only thing he could think of and tried to brazen through. "You *are* crazy. A one-handed carver. That would be something to see."

He saw just a trace of uncertainty in her gaze as she looked at him and then she gave a slight shake of her head.

"You are *such* a bad liar. I can't believe I didn't see it the other day."

She came closer to him, until they were only a few feet apart. Until the scent of vanilla-drenched cinnamon taunted him, seduced him.

"I don't know what you're talking about."

"Oh, stop. I know you made them. Who else would have given such a gift to me? No one knows about Grandma Pearl and our Nativity tradition except you and my parents, and they would certainly never do something like this."

And there was part of their problem in a nutshell. "No doubt that's true. They would probably give you something that should be in a museum, sculpted out of Italian marble or something."

A small smile lifted the corners of her mouth. "Maybe," she said softly. "That sounds lovely. But it would mean nothing to me. Not compared to this one. I will cherish this gift forever."

Something warm and soft unfurled inside him, pushing away some of his embarrassment. He didn't know what to say, especially not when she moved even closer, just a breath away.

"You lied the other day, too, didn't you?"

"I don't know what you're talking about," he said again, easing away just half a step and hoping she wouldn't notice.

"I was too hurt by everything you said to see clearly but now it all makes perfect sense. You're Mr. Fuzzy."

He blinked. "Excuse me?"

She gave that sweet smile again, looking so stunningly radiant he could hardly breathe.

"Never mind. I'll tell you someday." Before he could react, she reached out between them and grabbed his hand with both of hers. She gazed up at him and the emotion in her eyes sent his pulse racing again.

"I love you, Dylan."

"Gen."

"Let me say this. You said the other day that I need perfection in my life. I suppose there's some truth to that."

He hated thinking about those words he had said to her, the flimsy barriers he had tried to erect.

"But here's the funny thing," she went on. "I once had what some would say was the ideal fiancé—handsome, rich, destined for success—and I was completely miserable, even before he cheated on me."

Her fingers were cool against his, trembling a little, and he wanted to tuck them against his heart and warm them.

"I was miserable because somehow I knew from the beginning that perfect image was all wrong for me. What I needed, you see, was not the perfect man. Just the man who's perfect for *me.* Someone who sees beyond the surface to the person I'm trying to become."

Her fingers trembled a little against his. How much courage must it have taken her to drive up here through the snow, to confront him, to bare her heart like this?

How could he possibly push her away?

He thought of the past two days, how completely wretched he had felt when he drove home from that wedding—more terrible than he ever remembered, even counting the moment he woke up and realized the surgeons had taken his crushed and useless hand.

He had walked into the cabin, grabbed the whiskey bottle and poured three fingers. He planned to get completely hammered so he wouldn't have to think about this ache in his chest, the yawning, endless emptiness that stretched out ahead of him.

He had raised the glass, but before it reached his mouth, an image of her face as he had left her flashed across his mind, devastated and raw, and he couldn't do it.

Instead, he had grabbed Tucker and gone for a long walk in the snow and then had ended up in the run-down barn he used as a workshop. He had seen wood chunks lying there, a leftover piece he had bought to repair a sagging shelf in the bathroom.

He used to spend downtime on deployments playing around, making little toys and knicknacks to pass out to the villagers they sometimes encountered.

The carving tools he used to keep in his pack were still there, untouched since his accident. He rooted through the pile of screwdrivers and wrenches until he found what he needed, and before he knew it, he had carved a simple Baby Jesus.

For hours, he worked on it, trying again and again to make it just right. It hadn't been as hard as he might have expected. He had figured out ways to hold the wood—with his prosthetic or in a vise.

Okay, it had been a hell of a lot harder than it would have been with two hands, but he had managed it anyway.

Maybe that was some kind of metaphor for his life. He would never be able to do things as easily as he once had. He couldn't change that—and pissing and moaning about it sure as hell wasn't helping the situation.

Maybe it was time to just suck it up and deal.

He thought of the sheer grit it must have taken for his Genevieve to drive up here in the middle of a snowstorm and lay her heart bare for him again after he had already flayed it raw.

It would take guts to climb out of the hole he'd been living in these past months and embrace life again. But he was an army ranger, charging headfirst into the toughest of situations. Once a ranger, always a ranger, right?

Was he really going to let some little cream puff in her beret and scarf outdo him in the courage department?

Hell no.

"Gen."

"Admit it. You have feelings for me, don't you?"

He was tired of lying. What was the point, when she saw right through him anyway? "Feelings for you. I guess that's a pretty mild way of saying I'm crazy in love with you. Yeah."

She gazed at him, blue eyes huge and drenched with emotion. "Oh."

She looked so sweet, so beautiful, he had to kiss her. He had been fighting it since the moment she pulled up and he couldn't do it a moment longer.

With her hands still wrapped around him, it was easy to tug her toward him. She landed against his chest with a surprised oomph, which changed to a delicious sigh when he lowered his mouth to hers.

They kissed for a long time, until he was breathless and hungry.

"Please don't push me away again," she murmured, long moments later. "I can't bear if you do."

"I'm not easy to be around, Gen. I'm trying to be better but I don't expect that to miraculously change overnight. I have moods and I get pissed and sometimes I stay awake around the clock to keep the nightmares away."

Those nightmares had been coming with less frequency the past few weeks. He had figured it was because they had been replaced with heated dreams that left him aching and hard.

"If you're looking for easy," she retorted, "I'm not your girl. I'm the coldest bitch in Hope's Crossing. Haven't you heard?"

He had to smile because he just wasn't seeing that. Not anymore.

"We're quite a pair, aren't we?"

"Yes." She smiled and wrapped her arms around his waist, her cheek against his chest. He held her close, his chin resting on her hair, feeling as if this was the safest, most secure place he could ever imagine.

They stayed that way for a long time, until he had to kiss her again. He had a feeling he would never get enough. He leaned his head down but she eased away before he could find that soft, sexy mouth.

"First I want you to admit it."

"Admit what?"

"You were lying. You made those carvings, didn't you?"

He didn't see any point in denying it anymore. "I don't know why I ever gave them to you. I should have just thrown them away. I'll get better with practice, I promise. I'll try again."

"I don't want another one. This will always be my favorite Christmas gift ever. It came from your heart when the words wouldn't."

She got him. He wasn't sure how, but Genevieve Beaumont—rich, pampered, spoiled—understood him like nobody else ever had.

She kissed him once more while the snow fluttered down outside his little cabin and the wind sighed under the eaves. The fire crackled beside them and the dog snuffled in his sleep.

And everything was perfect.

* * * * *